WE BREAK IMMORTALS

THE ADVENT LUMINA CYCLE

VOLUME I

THOMAS HOWARD RILEY

To Allison. To Evan. And to my Mom and Dad.

A book is never *just* a story.
It is a collaboration between the author and your imagination.
So every book is a different book depending on who reads it.
A book changes every time it changes hands.
That is truly extraordinary.

*Editor's note: This author prefers the spelling *grey* for artistic purposes and has advised me to just deal with it

We Break Immortals

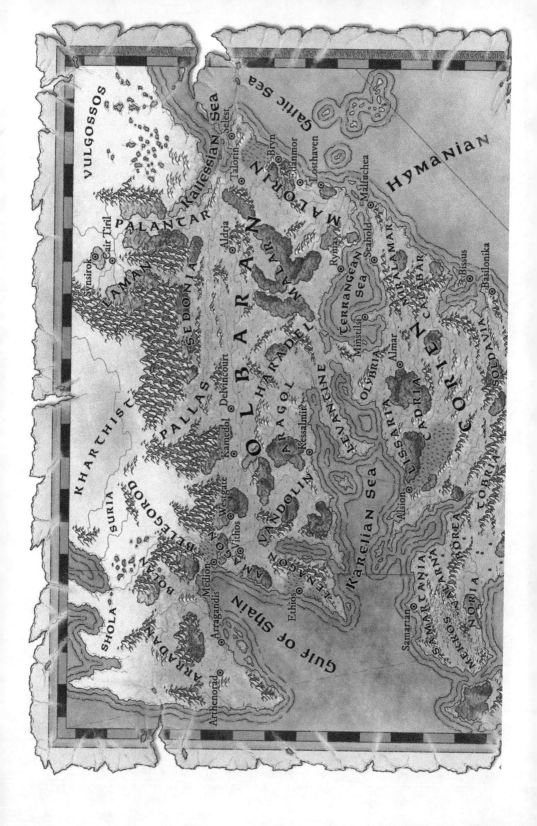

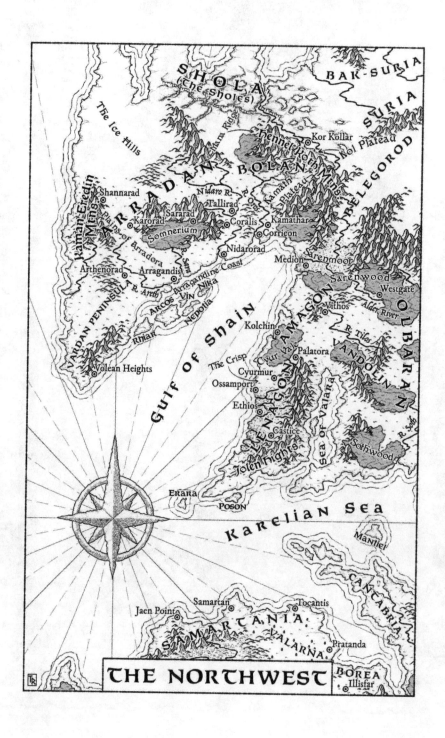

THE NORTHWEST

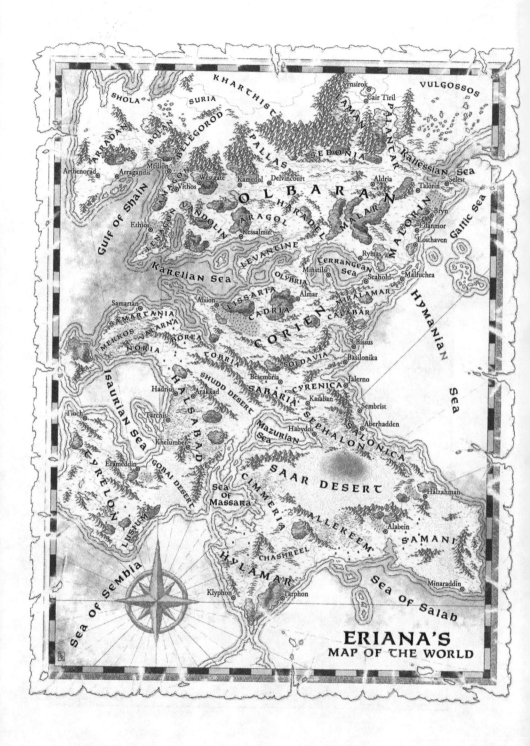

ERIANA'S
MAP OF THE WORLD

CONTENTS

Seb

IT ONLY TOOK SEB one look through the crack of a half-open parlor door at midnight to know that his friend had gone insane.

This young hero, this beautiful sweet boy he had helped raise from barely half past swaddling, grown to a man full and in truth, who held so much promise, had fallen. They had been filling Paladan's head with who knew what for who knew how long. *Never make promises like that to a boy. Never promise them they will be important. They may grow up to believe it.* And now here it was, the fruit of their work. Paladan Algan had surrendered to the sweet seduction of prophecy they had whispered in his ear.

It is high time someone put an end to this charade, Seb thought. He shoved his way past Syman and Laester. The lads tried to bar the door, but Seb's arms were each as thick as any two of theirs, and he brushed them aside as if the door was a broom.

The air struck Seb like a tidal wave of stale sweat and old forgotten exhales stranded in time. The candles and half-dead oil lamps lit the room barely at all. *To think he has been living in this place.*

"Let him in, let him in," Paladan said carelessly over his shoulder, hovering over the far table. He shuffled and reshuffled a half dozen unruly, piss-yellow scrolls stranded atop a haphazard hill of opened books. "He should be here with us."

Seb shook each of his legs and then stood firm. His feet already burned. He had walked a day and a half to come here. He tapped his heel twice on the floor. *Two times for the two halves of the twin god. Give me good luck coming and going.*

"Be here for what, Paladan?" Seb asked carefully. He could feel water begin to bead on his skin. *Moist as the belly of a frog,* he thought. He stopped halfway across the room. He looked at the walls. Pyramids of green jars lived beside towers of ancient leather-bound tomes stacked halfway to the ceiling, and all layered with the melt of scores of candles, one upon another, until the wax was thick enough that it would have piqued the interest of an archeologist. The twin windows on the left and right walls were nearly bricked over with towers of stone tablets unearthed in the distant buried temples of Holy Sephalon.

Seb peered at the books Paladan hovered over, trying to see if he could tell what they were. He only recognized the binding of one. *Of course it is that one. Those fools should never have given him that.* "The ancient story of Caldannon," he whispered. "The god who fell to earth in the wars of a thousand centuries, and somehow saved it with his meaningless, unknowable power to *walk in the light.*"

Paladan ignored him. "I am nearly ready." He stood over it, peering at the words as if they were distant birds he wished to identify. He shuffled more scrolls.

Is he even looking at them? Does he even see them in front of his eyes? "Be here for *what*, Paladan?"

"I am going to stop him," Paladan said. "I am going to stop the *Sanadi*. I am going to kill the invincible man."

"*Sanadi?* That is a word out of a book so old our ancestors ten centuries ago could have looked back another ten and still not have seen when it was written."

"It is what he is."

"There is no such thing."

"You should know better than that, Seb. You of all people know what he has done."

"I never said he wasn't dangerous. I never said I wanted him walking free."

"You taught me to be a man of action, Seb." He turned to face him for the first time.

Seb looked into his eyes, pupils as wide as olives. His sculpted face, which had always made him look the part of the great hero, was now sunken in, pale like sour milk, eyes ringed in violet, and those rings ringed further still in yellow. His black and umber shortcoat and trousers could not hide the fact that his flesh had caved in against his bones, like the juice sucked out of a calpas fruit without peeling the skin.

"You look terrible. Have you been eating enough?" He turned to glare at Syman and Laester. "You need to be sure he eats, you worthless shitsacks. What do you do around here? What are you worth? Less and less."

They both looked at the ground in brief shame, but they quickly glanced up at Paladan and regained their smiles, confident they could ignore even the most obvious of Seb's criticisms.

"We are going to prevail, Seb. I am going to prevail. This is my destiny." Paladan held up a stack of papers within a thin leather folio. "Do you know what this is? It is a *composite*, the Glasseyes call it. This includes detailed copies of the patterns he uses in his magick."

"Where did you get that?"

"One of those Amagon-men stole them for me and brought them here."

"And?"

"And Bann Dester and Zigor are outside in the brush. They are *Stoppers*, Seb. They will prevent his magick from working when he comes here."

"Two men. *Two. Men.* You know what *he* did to all those Glasseyes in Amagon a few years back. And they had *more* than two. They had more than *twenty*."

"I have something they do not."

"What? Tell me. Tell me so that we can end this farce and I can carry you a hundred miles away from this folly.

"I can see through it, Seb. Like the legends say. You know I can. I am a special talent among a forest of special talents. I am the *man of sorrow*, Seb. From the prophecy."

"No, you are not."

"You scoff, but it still fits. I can see what users do without needing the lens to look through. I can see it *with my own eyes*. Read the pages. Every line of it matches me."

"I can look across a field at an army for hours," Seb said. "Does that make me a general? Just because I can see it? Seeing doesn't guarantee much of anything. Come with me. Let us get out of this place and find air fresh, unencumbered by these heavy thoughts. You are not Caldannon. Because *no one* is Caldannon. There *is* no Caldannon. There never was. He is just a story."

"I have the book, Seb."

"What book? The Caldannon book? Why should I care?"

"No, Seb. Not that one."

"What other one?" But he knew the answer before he finished asking the question. He felt the blood abandon his face. He nearly dropped to his knees. He looked down at Paladan's far table and saw the binding. Just beneath the book about Caldannon's journey. "No. Where? Why do you have that? How? What are you doing with it?"

"I do not need even Stoppers at all anymore, because the book taught me that I can walk in the light. If I am in the *light*, I can break his magick. I can do anything."

"*If, Palad. If* you can walk in the light. You cannot do it. Just stop all of this. Stop it. You have read too much, heard too much. You are confused." He reached out a hand.

Paladan allowed the hand to sway right past him, hanging in the air, untouched. "This is the *Advent*, Seb. The *Days of Light* are no longer on the horizon. They are here, now. I am going to stop him. In the light."

"I am ending this," Seb said. "Call everything off. All of you. I am taking you from here before you get yourself killed."

Paladan's face tightened. "You do not understand, Seb. I have *already* called for him to come here."

Seb felt his digestive organs take a sudden drop. He thought they must have hit the floor and left a crater in it. "You. Called. Him."

"I sent the message by runner this morning."

"Why?"

"Because I am not afraid. I am true. I am the one. I have been chosen for this. Me, Seb. Me. I was born to go into the light."

"You do not know how to get into the light. You do not even know if you *can* get into it. None of us has ever seen it. We have only heard the stories."

Paladan smiled. "I am true. I am the one. I know I can do all of this. That book right over there, the *Codex Lumina*, has mantras to open up the real world to the world of light, where all magick comes from. It teaches many tricks of the light. I have seen it. It is real. It is outside of space, Seb. Outside of time. The light is so very bright, but it does not blind."

Seb pounded his fist so hard on a stack of books his bones were ringing. "I cannot believe you just told him where we can be found." *This is madness. I must get you out of here before it is too late.*

But then he heard footsteps outside, on the cobbled path. They approached halfway to the front door and then ceased.

"Could it be someone else?" Syman asked.

"Bann and Zigor must have his streams by now," Paladan said.

"And if they do not?" Seb asked.

"You think he would have let them live if he could?"

As if in answer, Seb heard a heavy boom, deep. It rattled the glass jar pyramids.

Seb froze. Everyone froze. Then something began slamming into the walls and the door. Every other second it boomed against the wall.

Paladan leapt into motion. He began reciting text from one lone page in the *Codex*. He read it over and over, as the walls shook. He had a smile on his face.

Then Seb heard a deeper, denser thud, like the sound of a heavy object slamming against the door.

Paladan jumped back to attention. He flipped the book open to another predetermined page and began reading frantically.

All the while the heavy weight slammed into the door again and again and again.

"Paladan," Seb said. "What have you done?"

"I can fix this," Paladan said. "I can fix it. I can fix it."

Boom. Boom. Boom.

Seb glanced at Syman and Laester. Their faces drained of color to a shade well past ghost. Their hands jittered. Laester wet himself. Neither of them had bothered to draw their swords.

Boom. Boom. Boom.

Paladan read from the book. His voice changed. He no longer had the wide vowels of confidence. He began to furiously glance back and forth among the pages.

"Pala*dan!*" Seb called out.

"I know. I know."

Boom. Boom. Boom.

The door burst inward, snapping free of its hinges.

The bloody broken body of Zigor collapsed atop its splinters, his face and limbs unrecognizable beneath mountains of swollen tissue.

Syman gasped. Dropped his sword. Picked it up again.

Zigor's lifeless body had been the battering ram.

"By the gods," Laester somehow said on his exhale.

"Paladan!" Seb shouted.

"I can do it!" Paladan said. "I swear I can do it!"

The man who Paladan was so sure had to be a Sanadi stepped through the doorway. He surveyed the room and smiled. His eyes were black. If he had any color to them, Seb could not see it. He was dressed in a black cape to match, covering robes of blue and violet, as if the poison flowers of a nightmurder weed had come to life.

Seb looked through the gaping maw of the doorway. He saw Bann's body twisted and broken on the cobblestones outside, soiled and torn beneath the midnight lanterns. "He is not bound!" *He can touch as much of his magick as he wishes.* Seb drew his sword. "Hold, boys!" he cried out. "Hold!"

Syman and Laester raised their swords.

Laester charged first.

An invisible projectile punctured his ribs and blasted out the other side. His arms went limp, sword dropped. His legs tried to keep charging for a step or two after he died, but the ankles went wobbly, the knees buckled, and finally he pitched face forward onto the floor.

"Paladan!" Seb cried.

"Almost there!" Paladan spat through gritted teeth, his face clenched with focus and determination.

But nothing happened.

Syman at least managed to swing his sword.

But he missed.

By a wide margin.

The man with black eyes created another projectile, invisible, unstoppable, lightning-fast.

It struck Syman in the skull, punching a hole the diameter of a fat olive in his head. He spun around in a circle, his body yet unsure if it was dead or not. But then it dropped in turn.

"Paladan!" Seb screamed. His throat shredded itself on the name and he tasted blood.

Paladan flipped to the last of his pages. He desperately read the passage in a chanting half-whisper, trying to open his mind with it.

He read it. He finished it. Nothing happened.

Seb looked over to Paladan with tears in his eyes. He thought of his wife, who had told him not to bother coming over here, and to just let Paladan be, and come home to the children. The last thing he told her was that he had to. And she understood. Seb thought about that and he wept. "Paladan," he whispered.

The man with black eyes created another projectile. It was no different than the first. Or the second. He had not even required a *variety* of his magick to end them all. He did all this without really even trying.

It was hopeless.

Seb raised his sword to swing anyway.

The projectile moved so fast he could not have seen it even if it was visible. It plinked against the blade of his sword, snapping it in half, before boring a hole through his lungs and ripping out the other side, shattering a pyramid of glass bottles behind him.

He fell to the floor facing Paladan. He saw the pain on his face, bending his expression so bitterly into one of sadness.

"No," he heard Paladan say. "It can't be for nothing. It can't. I won't let it. I won't."

Seb tried to breathe but there was no organ left to him that could collect the air. His face felt heavy, so heavy. The room became so dark.

"This can't be for nothing!" Paladan screamed.

Shhhh, Seb thought. *Do not yell, Palad. You are a good boy. You always were. A smile suits you better than a frown.*

Paladan looked into Seb's eyes. "Seb. I'm so sorry, Seb. I thought I was, Seb. I did. I was supposed to be the one. I was supposed to end it."

Shhhh, Seb thought. *No need to worry. Smile, lad. You are a good boy. You always were.*

Paladan shook. His mouth opened to scream but he made no sound. He was trapped within an invisible bubble. But something was happening to him within it. His nose began to bleed, and then his ears, and then his eyes. His skin flattened against his bones. Foam bubbled out his lips. He was being crushed by something Seb could not even see.

Paladan lay down beside Seb. His eyes were frozen open in wonder and terror. Blood leaked from the corner of his mouth, pooling on the floor.

You were a good boy. You always were.

1

Capture

ONE OF THEM WAS going to die.

Aren could feel it.

This was a *capture*.

Down one of these dark corridors, behind a silent door at midnight, waited a madman who could kill with a thought. Any moment now the signal would be given, and in they would go, all together, to get him.

One of us is going to die.

He saw it so clearly, as if this day had already happened, and he was only living the memory of it. He was surrounded by dead men. They moved, they looked around, they drew breath. They did all the things that a man would do, but he could not deny it.

And no matter how hard he tried to stop it, there was a part of him that kept guessing which one it would be. Twig, with his wide eyes, always talking about his mother. Bear, with those strong arms that could wrestle a lion. Bones, with wrinkles around his eyes, but hands steadier with a spear than any he had ever seen. Young man or old, tall or short, strong or weak. It could be anyone.

They were all former soldiers, hardy, tough as steel. Two or three had seen real fighting in the Warhost, survived skirmishes with Kolkothan raiders. That was good. Fighting men do not scare easy. But armor and swords would be of little use here.

Glasseye, he heard them whisper when they thought he could not hear. *It means I have seen the horrors that the magick can wreck upon wood and stone, flesh and blood. They know I have seen it, and they are afraid. I remind them of the terrors that hide in dark rooms, things they would rather pretend don't exist.* His presence meant only one thing—a rogue user did something unspeakable with the magick. That was all he was to them. A Glasseye.

He had learned none of their names either, of course. *Never learn the names,* Sarker had told him. *Then it is too difficult to forget them.* He knew them only by whatever their most visible attribute happened to be. There was Nose, and Chin, and the Twins, and Bear and Twig and Swan and Roundtop and Neck.

Even the youngest of them is older than I am. But I am all they have. I am the Render Tracer. No one else can do this.

None of the men were ever the same from one capture to the next. Who would have ever agreed to a second try? Every time a different location with a new group of faces, a new set of dangers, and a new toss of the dice to see if they would all survive. Aren once heard it said that at least one man died for every seven captures. He didn't doubt it, but he and Sarker had not lost a man for the past twelve.

That means we are overdue.

"Stay focused," he warned them, as he had heard Sarker always say. "You all know the jobs you have to do. Do exactly as I told you and this will all be over in moments." He spoke Sarker's words in Sarker's tone of voice, trying to make himself as convincing as his mentor had been. He had to be. Sarker wouldn't be here to complete this trace with him. He was gone.

These men answer to my commands now. I am all they have to get them through this.

And I will. I will bring this trace to capture. Tonight.

He ran a hand over his forehead, wiping away beading sweat. He had soaked halfway through his tunic already. He scratched at the stubble on his cheeks and chin, unshaven now for days. He looked down at his feet and realized he had worn a hole in the toe of one of his boots. *When did that happen?* He carried nothing but his leather tracer satchel and an unused sword. No plate, no mail. Armor of any kind would be useless in this capture.

He did his best to keep his back straight. His stomach burned, but he would not eat. His mouth screamed for water, but he dared not drink. He tried to wear a mask of calm. He smiled as much as he could without his teeth rattling. He had to keep the others from panic if he could. *Control your breathing. Stand firm. Speak with measured rhythm and tone, as if we are simply masons here to build a wall. That's all it is. Just a wall.*

Already the men were getting jumpy as the reality of what they were about to do was starting to set in.

"That man in there is a monster," Bones said. "The worst of the worst."

"Rapist, I heard," Bear said.

"Murderer," Roundtop said. "Child killer. Madman."

"He deserves to go to the fires for what he did," Aren told them. "Deserves it a hundred times over. And we are the ones who are going to put him there."

"I don't know about this," Nose said, shaking his head. "I don't know if I can do this."

"Maybe we should leave," Roundtop said. "Someone else should do this. Not us. Someone else."

"Listen to me," Aren said. "If Degammon gets away, if he is allowed even one more day—*just one*—he will do it again, to someone else's child. Unless we stop him. Here. Right now. Do you understand?"

They nodded, but they all averted their eyes when he looked at them.

"We should not be here," Neck said. "Not for a sorcerer."

"He is too powerful," Swan said. "Too dangerous."

"You know why I'm here," Aren said. He held up his leather tracer satchel and shook it. "You know what I am."

"Glasseye," Bear said. "You hunt the magick."

Magick.

It sounded so casual, like entertainment, but the *magick* that men like Degammon could employ was a different animal entirely—unthinkably powerful, unimaginably horrifying. They all knew it. Everyone had heard a story. Everyone knew someone who had seen one.

"He can wield powers with his mind," Swan said. "None of us stand a chance."

"Degammon is a *user*," Aren said. "Not a sorcerer. Just a man who uses magick the way you use a sword. He can bleed and he can die. He alters reality with his mind. That's the only difference. But that's why they called me. Breaking men like him is what I do."

Aren glanced at the local magistrate, Benham. He nodded.

It's time.

I have never lost a trace. I do not mean to lose now.

I can do this.

I will.

Degammon is finished.

I will put him in the fires.

I will.

He reached into his tracer satchel and withdrew his primary weapon, the Jecker monocle, a small hazy crystal lens within a bronze frame. Attached to it at one end by a swivel were four different colored lenses—filters—that could be slid over the primary lens. *This is why people call me a Glasseye. With this I can see what no one else can see. I can see the invisible things that monsters do. This is what brought us here. And it will bring us through now.*

He ran his fingers across the Glasseye badge on his chest, circling its iron ring, and touching each of the five prongs projecting out along the upper left quarter, like half an arc of eyelashes. *This is what I am. This is what I do.*

They opened the heavy oak door. Benham darted through, with Aren just behind, followed by a team of Stoppers, and then the rest.

He exchanged glances with the three Stoppers. They all nodded to him. He had worked with two of them before, though he couldn't remember their names. They had proven themselves to be competent, and he had briefed them on the pieces of Degammon's magick they would be looking for. Stoppers did not speak often when preparing for a capture. They required as much of their focus as possible to ensure they were able to do their work.

The Stoppers would come inside the inn with him for the sake of caution. There was no sense giving Degammon the chance to huddle at the far end of the room and possibly stay out of their range. A Stopper had to be close enough to the user to be able to block their magick. If they were even an inch beyond that distance, everyone here would be dead in seconds.

Benham stopped at the end of the hall. He motioned for Aren and the others to wait in the corridor while he cleared the hallways of innocents.

Aren cursed under his breath. *One more delay.* Sarker always said that when a man steels his nerves for the first plunge into action, he is ready, but if he has time to second guess himself, then all the courage he spent so long cultivating will vanish. Aren knew he was right about that. He could feel it happening to himself.

He leaned against the wall, beneath a dusty oil lamp with a half-singed slingspider web around it. "When we go in, make straight for Degammon," he reminded his men. "He needs to use his arms to focus his concentration for his dangerous renders. Your goal will be to prevent him from moving his arms. Above all else, hold his arms. That's it. That is all you have to do. Hold a man's arms for a few seconds. The Stoppers will already have his magick blocked. Stay out of their way. Don't talk to them. Don't touch them. Don't even look at them. Our lives depend on it. They need to be able to concentrate."

"Who are they?" Swan asked. "What are Stoppers??"

Yes, Sarker's voice said in his head. *Get them talking. Keep them focused on the words and their minds will have less room for fear.*

"Stoppers are the ones who make this possible," Aren said.

"They have the magick, too?" Swan asked, leering at them.

"No," Aren said. "They can only touch the *streams* of their magick. These streams are just fibers of altered reality. The building blocks of magick, threads in a tunic, bricks in a wall. Users bind these streams together into a single force that they can render into reality. Everything they do, it all comes from streams, and streams all come from the same place, a place we call the Slipstream. Stoppers just reach into that place and snatch the streams up first, so the user they belong to can't use them. We call it *interdiction*."

"How will they keep us from dying?" Swan asked. "That is all I want to know."

Precedence effect, Aren thought. *The little loophole of magick that makes this all possible, the gap in their armor that we use to our advantage.* "Every user's streams are different, unique. And specific streams can only be pulled and bound *once* at any given time, and if those streams are being held by a Stopper first, no one else can touch them until they let go. But it has limited range, so the Stoppers have to be very close to the user for it to work. That is why they have to go in with us. Understand?"

They all nodded.

Tonight our Stoppers will reach with their minds into the Slipstream, the place where all streams are born, and grab hold of his streams before he can.

"Think of it this way: a Stopper is like someone taking your sword out of your scabbard and just holding it. They may not be *using* it, but as long as they hold your sword, *you* can't use it either. The Stoppers are going to *hold his sword,* so we can bag him. But if he realizes we are here, and runs before we can take him, if he moves *just an inch* outside our Stoppers' range, it will not go well for any of us. That is why we have to be quiet until it is time to take him. This is a dance. Us, the Stoppers. If either of us moves too quickly, this all goes wrong."

"Is this really all it takes to stop one of them?" Bear asked. "A handful of these *Stoppers?*"

"We only have three," Neck said, tugging on his high-collared coat. "I hear Degammon knows how to render a hundred different things with magick. Will three Stoppers be enough? It doesn't feel like enough."

"It will be enough," Aren said. "They don't need to hold *all* of Degammon's streams. They barely need to hold any. My Stoppers only need to pull *one little piece* of each of his *renders* to ruin it. Do you understand? If you take one wheel off a wagon, the whole wagon becomes useless. You don't need to take the entire wagon apart, just one critical piece."

Streams by themselves were just harmless little filaments of altered reality that users could bind together into a *render.* The *render* was what was deadly. And Degammon, like all those abominations, had certain streams that recurred in *most* of his renders, so if a Stopper pulled that specific vital stream, a whole swath of his renders would be denied. *In order to block an archer with a quiver full of arrows, we could take each arrow away from him one by one, but we don't have to. All we have to do is take away the bow, leaving him with a bunch of pointless arrows.*

"I don't know," Swan said. His hands bounced about in his lap like live toads.

"Look at me, all of you. I prepped these Stoppers *myself*. That is what I do. I know where to hit him. Do you think I would be going in there with you if I wasn't sure? Do you?"

Swan shook his head.

"The Stoppers get his *streams*. You get his *arms*. Then we dose him, box him, and roll him off to the fires. That's it. Simple. They are just men. Like you. Like me. Even they have to follow certain rules to do what they do. And I know the tricks to all of those rules. The hard work is already done. What happens in the next few moments should earn you each a bag of silver for just ten seconds of action."

Everyone nodded.

It will be simple.

Please let it be simple.

Benham returned to the end of the hall, motioning that everything was ready.

Finally.

So close now.

Every sound seemed impossibly loud. The floorboards creaked and each time it sounded like a thunderbolt. The metal rings of sword-belts clicked and each time it seemed like the peal of bells. Even his heartbeats seemed like heavy drums pounding in the hallway.

He was painfully aware of one thing. He had never performed a capture *on his own*. Sarker had always been there with him. He had always been the apprentice, assisting the master at his work. And now at the crucial moment of his most dangerous trace, he was the one to oversee the most deadly moment.

I can do this. I can. I know I can. I can do it.

He rounded the corner into a second hallway and stopped behind Benham. *Second door in the second hall of the inn.* Just as the informant told them. The Twins took up positions on either side of the door. Benham stood behind them with the Stoppers. Aren signaled them to take their assigned streams.

There is no sign he expects us.

This is going to work.

Aren nodded to Benham.

The magistrate made a downward chopping motion with his hand. Swan tested the doorknob. Locked. He pulled back, and Bear raised his leg high to his chest, and kicked it through. The wood split around the lock, and the door went swinging inward. Dust sprayed into the air. Bones went through, then Neck, and Bear, then the Stoppers, already holding their streams.

Aren saw only quick flashes of the room between all the moving bodies.

He anticipated the noise of a struggle, but he heard none.

He expected to hear shouts, but he heard none.

He expected to hear curses uttered by a captured user, but he heard none.

Because the room was empty.

Not here! What? Impossible. Aren's heart raced. His stomach fell deep into the earth. His eyes darted everywhere. Each time they moved he forgot every thought he tried to focus on.

He is gone.

Sweat erupted like a thunderstorm from his scalp, running rivers down his forehead. *What do I do? What do I do? What do I do?*

He reached out and took hold of one thought and refused to let it go. *The Stoppers. Are they still ready?* He looked at each of them. Their eyes registered concern but their concentration held.

What next? What next?

Assume your figures are correct, Aren heard Sarker's voice in his head. *What then?*

Possibility of external error.

He turned to Benham. "Are your men certain he didn't leave?"

"My men were watching every exit," Benham said.

"Degammon is supposed to be here," Aren said. "How could he know we were coming?"

"He couldn't. There is no way."

Aren searched the room, eyes racing everywhere. A single lantern lit the chamber, supported by a brass stand. Empty bed. Nothing underneath. Cabinets and mahogany drawers too small to fit a dog. Unwashed clothes covered the chairs, and the bed was a mess of twisted sheets. Tangled in them were a razor, a thimble with a needle forced through one end, a pair of children's shoes, and an old woman's brooch.

He glanced at the Stoppers every few seconds, silent and unmoving, focusing every thought on holding the streams to deny Degammon his magick.

But it would all matter for nothing if he was gone.

A cold silence fell over everyone. No one moved a muscle. Everyone stared. The quiet was paralyzing. Aren felt like his whole body was freezing over.

Think of something.

He reached into his satchel and withdrew the small familiar hexagonal cylinder of polished silver. He focused his eyes on the six-sided crystal lens at one end where four small spheres were fit into tiny grooves. They were unmoving.

Benham leaned over his shoulder.

"Oscillatrix," Aren whispered.

"What is it? What are you doing?"

"This would react if it was close to Degammon's afterglow, his magick residue."

"Is it reacting?" Benham was on the verge of panic. If he lost his calm, the rest of the men were sure to turn around and run.

"Nothing in this room," Aren said. "There are no visible cues, no residual afterglow or vapors, and no reading at all on the Oscillatrix."

He returned the Oscillatrix to its pocket and reached for the Jecker monocle, removing it from its silken pouch, holding it before his eyes. The world became hazy and choppy. But the Jecker monocle was not designed to look at the strata of the physical world.

Afterglow.

The stain of a user. It was almost always invisible, unless viewed through the proper medium.

"What are you doing now?" Benham whispered.

"Looking for sensitized fluorescence," Aren said. "*Every* time a user alters reality he leaves residual afterglow in his wake. *Every* time. Like clouds of patterned color. It floats in the air. It gets on their hands. It gets on their skin. It gets on their clothes. It gets in their hair. It sticks to them like glue. And they take it with them. It will adhere to anything Degammon touched until it fades away. We already know he used in Kirden Village *yesterday*. I already proved it. He may have still had some on him when he came here."

He said it to calm them all. But in his head his thoughts were spiraling. He secretly feared he had misapplied the equations. *Did I do this? Did I fail? Did I let him escape?*

He studied the room through the Jecker monocle. The residual stains were shining bright, silver and green, against the muted, dull background. Little beacons glowed everywhere. He saw a faded glow from the bed and table, and one of the cabinets, the backrest of the chair.

"What is it?" Benham asked. "What do you see?"

Aren attempted the math in his head, battling the fear, wiping stinging sweat from his eyes, trying to ignore that fact that he was running mathematical figures while the most deadly man he had ever hunted could have killed him at any moment. Based on the projected rate of decay, and the degree of fading, he approximated that these had been left only a few hours prior. "He is still close."

"You're sure?" Benham's eyes darted about the room like furious wasps.

"Certain," Aren said. "It matches our composite record of Degammon's renders."

"Could your composite be wrong?"

"We wouldn't have tracked him all this way if it was wrong."

"Where *is* he then?"

"He didn't leave through the door," Aren said. "It's clean." He saw some faded marks on the rug, but he couldn't be sure how old they were. He followed them as best he could. It was difficult to make some of them out, but he managed. They led across the room, terminating at one of the walls. *Why would he stop there?*

Aren looked where Degammon must have looked. A large silken tapestry hung upon wall before him, its fringes tattered and dangling all the way to the floor. The designs were of interlocking squares. *Borean designs. From across the seas.* The quality and artistry of the silk matched nothing else in the room, or in the entire building for that matter.

"Do you see anything?" Benham asked.

"This decoration does not belong." Aren pressed a hand against it. He felt wood beneath the fabric. He tapped it. *Hollow!* He yanked the tapestry aside. Beneath it was a door leading from this room to the next.

"The informant never mentioned interconnected rooms," Benham said. *External error.*

The bolt on this side was unfastened. Upon the door latch was a barely perceptible glow. Degammon had been very careful to touch it with the very tips of his fingers on the far side of the knob. *Subtle.* He knew someone would be looking. Someone else might have missed it. *But not me.*

Benham sent up a flourish of hand signals. His men gathered about the door, ready to break through. He looked to Aren. "Should we wait?"

"There is no time," Aren said. "If he makes it far enough away to get outside the range of precedence effect, he will be able to kill us all. This only works if we are right on top of him. Send them through now. The Stoppers can do their job from in here. Send them now. Go, go, go!"

Benham turned to his men. "Do it."

They broke the door down with a sharp kick. The men flew through the doorway. A table was knocked over. Leather boots pounded the floor like drumbeats. Bear and Twig shouted. They held a single man against the far wall. In the corner a woman lay huddled in her bedclothes, horrified and sobbing, blood on her face, barely visible through pale candlelight.

Aren studied the man they held. His robes were tattered, hanging loose over a sagging, clammy body. He squirmed and tried to flail his arms, shouldering one of the Twins to one knee, but more men rushed to secure him, pinning his arms behind his back. The interdiction held.

Aren smiled.

Then something went wrong.

He heard a grunt and a curse. He whirled around.

He saw one of the Stoppers. *You shouldn't be here*, he thought.

Roundtop was turning to look over his shoulder to see what he had done. He had bumped the Stopper.

Aren stared into the Stopper's eyes, and the expression returned was one of horror. The Stopper's concentration was broken.

No, no, no, no, no, no, no.

The Stopper had lost the stream.

This can't be happening. This is not real. It can't be real.

Aren turned to face Degammon.

His clammy face lit up as he, too, made the realization, feeling into the Slipstream, finding the stream free for the taking.

"No!" Aren shouted, but Degammon had already started binding streams. He didn't rely on arm movement for low magnitude renders, but he did not require anything powerful. Two of the men holding him were knocked to the ground as though fists had hit them—not much force used, but enough to free his arms. The other men panicked, released Degammon, and stumbled over each other to get away.

This cannot be happening.

Aren felt hands pulling on his clothes. He looked down and saw Swan and Roundtop on their knees, tugging at his sleeves and praying to him like penitents. Someone fell on the ground hard behind him. All around him, men were tripping over the chairs, colliding, and scrambling over each other to get out, or hide, or simply give up.

What do I do? What? What am I supposed to do?

Aren couldn't move, couldn't breathe.

Degammon threw up his arms, able to summon his full concentration with their aid. Light bent around him, and Aren's sight narrowed to tunnel vision. Space stretched out and Degammon suddenly seemed far away. Aren staggered, nearly choked. His eyes were swollen. Static clung to him, to his clothes, to everything in the room.

The air abruptly stank like burning fossil oils. *Blank impulses.* They always smelled like that. Degammon's renders were all vectorics—blank forces of altered reality where he controlled the size, mass, velocity, and trajectory.

Such simple things.

So deadly.

An invisible force popped into being at Degammon's hands. Aren couldn't see it, but he could see air distorting around it. It was a massive blank impulse, a wide sphere of invisible air with the weight of a castle inside it.

Aren threw himself to the floor.

Degammon pointed, and it shot outward from his hands. His blank impulse ripped through two of the men, biting an arc the size of a wagon wheel out of Swan's body, and tearing an arm off Twig. It coursed through the wall and part of the ceiling, spraying the room with shattered bits of wood and layering the air with dust. A fine mist of blood sprayed from the two destroyed men, dangling in the air like red fog. It all happened so suddenly that Aren could barely believe that it was real.

Twig lived long enough to utter a piercing scream, and then he was done. Swan was missing a head and arm and most of his body. The rest of his useless limbs fell in a jumble, jiggling and hopping on the floor, inches from Aren's face.

Aren leaned over and vomited. He breathed in some of the blood mist. Vomited again.

What do I do? I don't know what to do.

He closed his eyes.

Don't look at it. Don't look at it.

The noise, the rotten smells, the dust, so thick like smoke. Blood on his fingers, blood in the air.

Aren rose to his knees.

He was too far away to reach Degammon. The arms were already moving again, another render coming.

Concentrate!

His eyes scanned the room.

Something, something, something.

He saw some men back behind Degammon. They were petrified, flattening themselves against the wall, full of fear, frozen.

He recognized Bear and the Twins. "Stop!" he shouted at them.

They heard him. They turned to face him. *They listened before. They trust me. I know they do.*

He screamed at them. "Get his arms! He needs his arms! Get his arms!" Aren waved his hand so hard at Degammon he nearly broke his own wrist.

Bear obeyed instantly. He came up beside Degammon. He slammed his fists down on Degammon's arms. Hard. Pinning them to his waist.

Yes! Aren's heart leapt out of his body and floated in the air above him. His hands balled into celebratory fists without him realizing it until it happened.

It worked. The blow disrupted Degammon's concentration, and whatever streams he had been trying to bind into terrible magick were lost.

Aren turned to the Stopper. He jabbed his finger at him. "Take the stream!"

The Stopper stood like a statue, summoning every ounce of willpower to ignore the chaos around him.

Then he had it. The stream was pulled.

There was no sound to announce it was so. No vision or sensation. But Aren could tell by looking at the relieved smile of the Stopper. Degammon's power was rendered inert, and he flailed uselessly against Bear. More and more men gathered around to subdue him.

It was over.

Aren breathed out like the rattle of an earthquake. His eyes burned and he felt his whole body covered in sweat. His heart beat like the hooves of a racehorse, and blood shot through his veins like liquid fire.

Afterglow danced in the air around him, so fresh it was visible to the naked eye. It whorled in translucent rainbow patterns, a mist of sparkling colors, colliding with each other and with the walls and furniture, clinging even to Aren's shirt wherever it passed over him.

He stood there staring at it for a long moment, just breathing. It was beautiful. It made no sense. How could something this horrible be so beautiful? He took breath after breath, just watching the colors move.

I am alive. He couldn't believe it. Somehow he was alive.

Aren studied the afterglow through the blue filter of the Jecker monocle. The filter muted the vibrant multicolored afterglow into the core color of Degammon's personal resonant pattern. *Brown.* A match to those found at all previous scenes.

Aren returned the Jecker monocle to his satchel, and held his Oscillatrix within each small cloud. "The *rithrin* inside reacts to the frequencies of your afterglow," he explained to Degammon. "I marked down these figures at Kirden. Remember? The place where you took those boys into the granary. Yours are a match."

"I will kill you," Degammon whispered.

I must not show fear.

"You were careless," Aren said. "Not that it mattered in the end. We still would have found you. You just made it easier. Sensitized fluorescence. Everything you touched had your stamp on it. You thought you were getting away, but we were getting closer and closer. Spectral shift—the Render Tracer's best friend. Do you want to know why they call it that, you piece of shit? You affect your own afterglow even *after* you leave it behind. Did you know that? It changes every time you move. Shifting red or blue whether you are moving farther away from what you did, or coming closer. For the last few days your afterglow started blueshifting hard. You were trying to double-back on us. You thought we didn't know."

Degammon hissed at him, and writhed like a worm in the grip of Bear and the Twins.

Aren spoke the words that had been so ingrained in him. "There are only three precepts we go by here. You are not a god. No one is immortal. And no one *ever* gets away."

"Hear that, Degammon?" Benham asked. "You're going to burn."

Degammon looked at him, his eyes milky blue vats of hideous rage.

Aren felt his left eye twitch. He shook his head and rubbed at it, but it continued. He closed it, but when he opened it, he saw a flash of white, like the sun was sitting directly in front of him. For a moment he feared he had gone blind, but the light faded. He began to see the shape of Benham and Degammon and the others, the walls, the furniture. Slowly, like emerging from mist.

I need to get out of here.

He turned to Benham. "I have my samples. He's all yours." He stalked out of the room. His last impression of Degammon was the gurgling rasp as Benham forced a cup of tinwood leaf tea down his throat. Degammon would sleep all the way to the fires.

Aren kept walking until he was sure none of the other men could see him. He leaned against a brick wall and shook like he was submerged in a lake of ice. His eyes turned to water and poured out from behind clenched eyelids. He threw up two more times.

He inhaled for the first time in what felt like years.

Just one more capture.

****

"I am awed by your collection," the visitor said. He was tall and lithe, much to Lord Jacovennes' fancy, and his clothes were of the finest silks, blue and purple. His pupils were so wide Lord Jacovennes could barely see any iris at all, as if he was in an unlit room.

"Thank you," Lord Jacovennes said. "These tapestries were from a little-known kingdom that once existed in the south. They have all been painstakingly restored. And here, these are gilded knives from Adumbar. Look at the craftsmanship."

Sunlight shined through narrow vertical windows of pale rose glass, and delighted the oil paintings and ancient tapestries. Atop each table was a different ancient object, twinkling with the refractions of gemstones in every imaginable color, knives and scepters, decorated with the wealth of lost kings.

"I believe that this was meant to happen," the visitor said. "It had to be you." His eyes came to rest on the hands of Lord Jacovennes—upon one of his finely manicured fingers. A ring of gold hugged tightly to the skin, crowned with an ovular topaz stone, polished and rounded but not cut, so it still retained some of its cloudy yellow texture. "Your ring. I would like to see it."

"Of course," Lord Jacovennes said with pride. He held up his hand. "It came to me at great cost. You are not the only one who noticed its beauty. There was a sweet young Sisterhood collector named Dalain who took quite a close look at it not a fortnight ago."

"I would like to hold it."

"Oh no. It has sentimental value. I never take it off."

"Never?"

"It has not left my finger for a decade. I'm sorry. I'm afraid I will not remove it from my hand."

"Of course. Perhaps you can remove the hand then."

"What? I do not believe I understood you."

The visitor reached out, fingers slipping around the nearest gilded knife of Adumbar.

"What are you doing?" Lord Jacovennes stumbled backward. He turned to run, but the visitor stamped a foot down hard on his trailing robes. Lord Jacovennes was yanked backward by the cape at his neck, and fell to the floor choking. He clutched at his hip. Sharp pain issued down his leg until his toes tingled, going numb.

The visitor loomed over him. "I must save the world." He clutched the hand. He smiled as he began cutting into the wrist.

Lord Jacovennes screamed, agony transforming it into a high-pitched wail, as skin, muscle, and tendons were carved apart. His blood splattered on the white marble tiles. Lord Jacovennes had never known pain like this before, building, unrelenting, endless. He felt like it went on for hours. He gasped gulps of air through tears.

The visitor took the ring off his finger, and tossed the hand back in his lap.

"I did not use magick at all," the visitor said, popping the stone free and discarding the ring. "You are different than the others. They would send the best for a rich man like you. Their best will find nothing." He leaned over Lord Jacovennes. Those eyes were black within black. "You really don't remember me, do you?"

Lord Jacovennes shook his head as he shivered and bled out onto the floor.

The visitor seemed disappointed.

Lord Jacovennes closed his eyes for the last time.

2

A Strong Tree

KNEELING OVER THE BODY of a dead friend is like standing alone at the end of time.

You will always stare into that abyss with no one.

Keluwen gritted her teeth. Her ankles were stiff. Her eyes burned. Her nose drowned in the sulfur smell. Nothing fit right. Her trousers felt too tight, and her tunic too loose. The elbow-length gloves of ocean blue constricted her arms. Her knees ached and her thighs shook, but she would remain crouched here until she had said goodbye to him in her way.

And if any of the others interrupted her, she would hand them back one of their fingers.

She looked at Seb. His face so white, white enough to match his hair. His eyes open like pools of glass. He was so peaceful. Chin tucked into one shoulder, arms outstretched like he was embracing the earth, one leg casually draped over the other. It was as though he merely went to lie down for a while.

Keluwen had seen the murder-dead before. And she had always been surprised how unnatural they looked when they fell—an arm this way, a leg bent wrong, the head askew. She was glad Seb looked like he was comfortable. He deserved that much at least. She would not have to lie to his wife and the children about it. She was glad for that.

He had promised the week before that he was going to have her and Orrinas over for supper sometime soon, to sing and dance with his wife and sweet children, and then eat spiced roast until their bellies were full, sharing stories of all they had seen in their lives over bottles of summerwine.

He had promised.

But he could not have known this was going to happen. He had told her as much the very first time they met, when he found her as a child, sitting all alone on a midnight bench, when she had told him what she had done, and how fate would damn her for it.

That was when he had told her she still had a chance. That was when he had told her nothing was set in stone. *No one can see the future*, he had said. *There is only me and you and what we do.*

No one could see the future. Least of all him. Looking down at him now was the proof. If anyone deserved to be blessed by the gods it was him.

I will see you again, my friend. When never meets forever.

He was wearing the new midnight riding cloak she had given him at the beginning of winter. She remembered how happy he had been when he saw it. He told her it was perfect. *He loved this cloak. He wore it everywhere.* He still wore it even now, though it was well into the end of spring. It made her so happy that she had made him happy. The smile on his face that day could have challenged the sun.

It was one of her favorite memories.

Now that memory was sharing her mind with thoughts of killing.

Seb had worshipped the twin gods of Tobria. She did not know how to honor them on his behalf, so she whispered a prayer to the only god she acknowledged—Belleron, who was the champion of thieves, wanderers, lone wolves, lovers, heroes, self-reliance, redemption, and sacrifice. It was easy to live life according to Belleron. All you had to do was live your own life your own way, as unapologetically as possible.

She stood, shaking her legs back to life, hovered over him for a moment. *I am so sorry this happened. You deserved so much better than this.* She looked at the body of Paladan beside him and pursed her lips. Her mouth twisted into a scowl so full of hatred that her eyes began to water from the rage. *You did this to him. He should never have been here, but he came here for you, fool.* She kicked Paladan's corpse. *You thought you could do this alone. You thought you were special. You fancied yourself a god-slayer. You were wrong. And you did this to him.*

She looked up at the others crammed into the room with her. They were all either looking away from her, or immediately pretended to be. Nils and Cheli knew her best, besides Orrinas. And they eyed the others, wary of how any of them might anger her. Krid Ballar did not know her at all, but he knew better than to tap a woman on the shoulder while she was saying goodbye to a dead friend. Leucas and Hodo knew her well, but were bumbling. They were the ones Nils and Cheli watched the closest.

Keluwen drifted over to Orrinas. He wore his old ivory and grey robes as if they were new and regal, his chin always held high. His hair was red halfway to white, and every year halfway seemed a little bit closer to all he way. Keluwen was fascinated by it. She was at least a decade shy of having a grey hair herself and wondered what such a visible reminder of mortality would feel like. Orrinas seemed to always shrug it off. She doubted she would be able to so easily.

Now that she was standing, the others went back to work. Nils and Cheli were closing and stacking the books into a heavy sack. Krid was similarly bagging dozens of tools and artifacts and jars of substance. She wondered whose priceless library had been sacrificed for Paladan to pursue his fool's errand.

She knew at once which table Paladan had been working at. It had everything on it at once. Every crucial book open, every jar unstopped, everything atop something else.

But there was one conspicuous empty space on that table.

"The book is gone," Cheli said. She threw her black hair over one shoulder with a twist of the waist that only she seemed to have a spine limber enough to perform successfully. Her eyes were little golden gems in a face deep olive and long, high cheeks rosy, especially when she was hard at a task.

She could only mean one book.

"Which book?" Leucas asked, because of course Leucas had to ask.

Hodo smacked him upside the head. "The Codex Lumina."

Leucas rubbed his head. "Ouch. Stop."

Hodo flexed fingers into fists. "We have been on the trail for five months, always in each other's air. I cannot stand your inane questions any longer." He fumed, and then turned away as if embarrassed. He loved Leucas like a brother, and like brothers, they were at each other's throats when you crammed them close enough together.

"We assumed he would take it," Orrinas said.

"You do not seem afraid enough," Krid Ballar said. His hair was grey early, likely on account of him hating anything and everything for little to no reason. He was fond of yelling, and obsessed with the rules, sneering at everything with his glacier blue eyes, bright like little skies in his head.

"Orrinas does not fear anything," Leucas said.

"Neither did Paladan," Keluwen reminded him. "Right up until the end, I presume."

"The others were all killed with tiny blank spheres," Cheli said, her tone scientifically distant. "Just like yours, Kel."

Best choose your words carefully, Cheli girl.

"But not Paladan," Cheli said. "He was killed with a crush bubble."

"Immense pressure," Orrinas said. "Wrapped around him in a sphere. The pressure increasing in increments. Methodically."

"A gruesome end," Krid Ballar said. "Immeasurable pain."

"Used to torture," Cheli said. "It is his signature move; the man with black eyes."

He has killed many of our friends that way. Because we have not stopped him yet.

Keluwen stopped again over Seb's body. She wanted to look away from it. She had said her goodbye to him, and thought all the melancholy thoughts she was willing to allow herself to have. She feared if she looked at him for too long now she would burst into tears. *Not here. Not now. Later. This lot will never have the blessing of my tears. Only Orrinas can have them.*

"What more can he do with the *Codex* that he has not done already?" Hodo asked.

"There is always more," Orrinas said. "But you make a fair point. He has gone from being the most dangerous man in the world to only *a slightly more dangerous version* of the most dangerous man in the world. But the information within that text, if he can decipher it, and interpret it properly, could allow him to do things to the world that none of us could ever imagine. He could upend reality."

"That sounds very bad," Leucas said. Leucas was as short in stature as he was on knowledge of the world. But none of them cared, because he was an expert at what he needed to be good at, which was prepping locations and cleaning afterglow.

Hodo swatted him again. "Speak useful words only, Leucas. Useful."

Leucas rubbed his twice-bruised head. "Stop."

"We need to get that book back from him, whatever the cost," Krid said. "This is bad news."

"Not all bad news," Cheli said.

"No?" Orrinas asked.

"See this here." Cheli hefted a fat leather-bound folio into the air, balanced on the flat of one delicate palm.

"What is that?" Leucas asked.

"Like no book I've ever seen," Hodo added, his round face pinched, making it look even smaller beneath his bald head. His thick arms flexed in agitation.

"This is a *composite*," Cheli said. "A notebook with all the information that a Glasseye has gathered about the powers of a *user*."

Keluwen saw Orrinas smile. *Nothing makes him smile, except for me. What is that composite for?*

Cheli smiled, too. "Lists of renders, individual streams, imprints of the patterns so that Stoppers can memorize them and feel them in the Slipstream so they can block a user from using. No streams means no magick."

"Are they always that big?" Leucas asked. "That must be hundreds of pages."

"I have never seen one even a quarter the size," Cheli said. "Most users are small time. Little to no skill. They run afoul of the authorities early. Most are only a few pages long. The very dangerous ones are those that live long enough to master many different types of renders."

"You mean like Orrinas?" Hodo asked.

"Imagine Orrinas if he was a bad man," Nils said. "Imagine what he could do. That is the only difference between a preserver and a destroyer, what they choose to be. The power is there."

"Is that...?" Hodo began. "Do you mean to say...? Is that...*his* composite?" Cheli smiled.

"How is it possible?" Leucas asked.

"Paladan said he had gotten ahold of something special," Orrinas said.

"But it was not enough," Krid said.

"Because he did not know what to do with it," Orrinas said. "He thought he could do it all himself. We will do better."

"We *must* do better," Keluwen said. She made eyes at Orrinas. *I will not see you done up like them. I will let them all die before I let anyone harm so much as a hair on your head.* She held his gaze to make sure he understood her.

Cheli closed the sack and hoisted it on her shoulders, while Nils and Krid dragged the bodies out. First Syman and Laester, then Zigor and Paladan. And lastly they came for Seb.

Leucas and Hodo stood on either side of her, waiting for her to move before lifting him.

"Seb was a good man," Hodo said.

Keluwen sneered. She raised one foot and drove her heel down onto Hodo's foot. "Good man? Good man? He was a *great* man. You are shit by comparison. You are. I am. We all are. Shit." She punched his shoulders, one and then the other and then kept going, as if she was striking pain-drums to the rhythm of her rage. She could not stop herself.

She felt the patient hands of Orrinas on her shoulders. They slid down her arms to her wrists, his arms covering hers, his body wrapping protectively around hers, until she felt absorbed into him. He held her there for ten seconds, then twenty. Not restraining her, merely enclosing her, cutting her off from the world for just a little while.

Her rage subsided, and his embrace dissolved.

She turned and tried to smile at him, but it came out as a frown. "We could have been here. We should have been here. To stop them from egging Palad on."

"We cannot be everywhere."

"None of us could have known," Cheli said.

"We should have been on his heels," Keluwen said. "Not looking for gems."

Orrinas nodded. "You said you wanted to be a part of this. That means everything."

"We sit idle while he takes more and more girls," Keluwen complained bitterly. "Everywhere he goes, young girls begin to go missing."

"Pulled into his orbit by his luminous charisma," Orrinas said. "Leaving lovers and families behind."

"Then he and his cultists use them up," Krid said. "Sometimes they die quick, and sometimes they die slow. But they always do eventually."

"He doesn't love any of them," Nils said. "At least not as much as he loves the death of them."

"You make it sound like romance gone wrong," Keluwen said. "It is not some tryst. He takes them. He ravages them. Then he destroys them."

"They go willingly," Cheli said. "At least at first."

Keluwen eyed her coolly. "He *takes* them. And all we care about is *rocks*."

Orrinas was firm. "You know why we had to go there. We had to be certain. They are all being stolen. We have to know how close *he* is to know how much time *we* have."

Cheli chimed in, activated by the mere mention of something she was knowledgeable about. "The stone in Kessalmir is gone, and the one in Kamedol has been stolen. The one in Amagon is now unaccounted for."

"Our people are still searching out the rumors of the one in Westgate," Nils said. "But we are not the only ones, apparently. Our agents have been seeing suspicious people poking about. They have seen a Rover trying to talk with the widow."

"If we think she knows where it is, it was only a matter of time before others would wonder the same thing about her," Orrinas said.

"It could just be another suitor," Cheli said. "She goes through men faster than a cup of wine goes through me."

"More like those shitsacks go through her," Keluwen said. "We should just approach her, offer her gold to rummage through her things, find out if she has it, and buy it from her to hide it ourselves, save her from this misery. And us. This will only get worse as more people come to think she has it."

"There is already that Sisterhood Saderan who has been seen in northern Arradan," Krid said. "I hear she asks questions that she should not be able to ask."

"There is another Sister in Amagon as well," Nils said. "And Priests in Medion. Forces are gathering. *He* is not the only one looking."

"We should have taken them all ourselves, chartered a ship and tossed them overboard," Keluwen said. "Let Danab-Dil of the ocean deeps have them."

"They say none are safe in the hands of anyone who knows what they are," Orrinas said.

"Who are *they?*" Keluwen asked bitterly.

"Someone above us. Someone from *Axis Ardent*. That is all we ever know."

"That is all we ever *need* know," Krid added.

He is devout. He truly believes. Keluwen did not exactly *not* believe in the mission of this group that called itself *Axis Ardent*. But she did not worship it the way Krid did. "So if he is going to Westgate, we must be headed there as well."

"Soon," Orrinas said.

"Soon?" Keluwen asked. "Why not now? Why are we not pressing for speed? He thinks he has won now. He will be overconfident. This is our advantage. We must strike him now. He needs to die."

"We are all angry," Nils said.

"I am not *angry*," Keluwen said. "I am *furious*. I want his blood."

"If he has any blood," Cheli said. "He has spent so much time in the source, walking in the light, it may have all turned to tar and black ash in his veins."

"Whatever it is that makes him live and breathe, I want to take that away from him," Keluwen said. "The Priests and the Glasseyes put men like him into fires. I would settle for a knife in the ribs."

"You would never get within a hundred feet of him," Hodo said. "He can break through walls. His bodyguards are terrifying. His magick is too powerful."

"All the magick in the world won't save you from a knife in the back," Keluwen said. "A very smart woman said that to me once. And it has always turned out true."

"Our orders are to go east first, to a band of villages near the border of Amagon," Orrinas said. "Then we shall be along to Westgate."

"We are letting him get away," Keluwen accused.

"We are giving him slack," Orrinas said. "A false head start."

"Our superiors wish to know what he is up to," Krid said. "It is our duty to carry out their instructions."

"And Duran? Where is he? He is supposed to be our eyes out here."

"He will be indisposed," Orrinas said. "For a time at least. If we see him again it will not be for this."

"If?" Keluwen asked. "Where is he?"

"He has been sent to verify something with his own eyes," Orrinas said. "Atop a mountain."

"Have they lost their minds?" Keluwen asked. "They sent Duran up a mountain?"

"His people are mountaineers."

"That is not what I mean and you know it."

"They send us all to where we need to be."

"At a time like this? We need everyone for this. Have they not been paying attention?" Keluwen folded her arms, unfolded them, then folded them again.

"Be careful," Krid warned. "These are our directives and we obey them. You are not one to question the plans of our superiors."

"This is a wasteful mistake," Keluwen said.

"We will follow these commands," Krid said, his voice rising. "You are new to our group. You must learn this very quickly."

Do not dare take that tone with me. Keluwen balled her hands into fists and squeezed until she felt her fingernails bite into her palms through the gloves. "You need to stop talking to me like a child. You are new *to me*. You must learn this very quickly."

"You do not take that tone," he said.

"New," she said. "For a year I have done this work. Just not with you."

"And I have for twenty," Krid said. "And Orrinas for longer."

"And all that time you did not stop him," Keluwen said.

Krid opened his mouth in indignation.

But Orrinas waved him off before Krid started something he knew Keluwen would finish. "We all do our part. Keluwen was a wanderer when she ended up with us."

"Wanderer," Krid said. "A funny name for a thief and a scoundrel. Maybe we should drop you back in the gutter where we found you. Don't you think you belong there? Why are you even here?"

"I know what I was born," Keluwen said. "I know what I had to do to survive. I am here because I want to be more than I am. I want to do something that matters."

"What you want," Krid said, smirking. "Always what you want. That is your problem. It is never about anything else."

"I want this," she said. "You think I want chaos, running through the rain, Render Tracers on my tail. You are wrong. I want to be at peace. I will never have that as long as he is out there. I am ready to give my all for that."

"You are a wanted murderer," Krid said, sucking his teeth awfully. "You will never be anything more."

"There are seven hells, Krid," Keluwen said, eyes narrowing. "Do you want me to show you which one you are going to?"

"Enough," Orrinas said. "Krid is going to go one way, and you will go another, and this will stop. This must stop. We need each other. *All* of each other."

"Fine," Keluwen said. She folded her arms tightly across her chest. She meant to show strength and anger with it, but her thumbnail caught her nipple as she tucked her right hand beneath her left. The pain was instant and annoying. It made her smirk is surprise, which utterly ruined the stern glare she had hoped to see Krid off with.

Damn it.

Orrinas saw what happened and he smiled when none of the others were looking.

"Not funny," she said.

He shrugged. "Humor is subjective."

She narrowed her eyes at him. "It had better not be funny to you either."

"I shall endeavor to find your misfortune tedious then," he said. He cracked the corner of a smile.

She slapped him. "That is for making me smile at a time like this."

"I didn't make you do it."

"Yes you did. You know I cannot hide a smile when I see yours."

"Very unfair of me," he said.

Yes, very unfair of you. But she was relieved to have something happen that was not sorrow or despair.

"When we join together, we give each other strength. You are strong. I know you are. But you can be so much stronger than yourself if you only open yourself up to it. You have to get to a place where you can accept that strength. Will you accept it?"

"I will follow the commands," she said grudgingly.

"I know you will, wife."

"Don't call me that. You know I hate that."

"You might have considered that before marrying me."

"Charity," she said. "You were a sorry sight."

He smiled. He nodded to her, and she walked back across the compound and helped Krid and Nils dig graves. Seb looked so peaceful. *Life is wasted on the living.* Her back went stiff before she even began to sweat. This was not the kind of labor she was used to. *And it had better not ever be something I get used to.*

When the hole was deep enough, three feet, shallow, less than Seb deserved, less than any of them deserved, they stopped. She thought of the letters that would need to be written, explaining that they were all heroes.

Explaining that they were so brave and they went to the end to do what they thought was right. Even Paladan—stupid, stupid fool Paladan. He thought he was going to stop it.

She caught Nils trying to remove Seb's coat to make it easier to lift him.

Keluwen swatted his hand away. "No. He loved this coat. He is going to meet his gods wearing it. Understand?"

Nils backed away, both hands raised apologetically.

Keluwen felt foolish for taking that tone with him. Nils was always kind to her, and obedient, and brave. But saying such an unexpected forever goodbye to Seb was too much for her.

Seb was a heavy man already, but death made everything heavier. It took four of them to slide him into the hole. He landed on his side, his face down in the earth.

Forever goodbye, Seb.

Nils shoveled the dirt atop him. Keluwen tried to help but after only three scoops she had to turn away before the tears tried to come again. She faced the trunk of the tree until her eyes swallowed them back up. A *good tree*, she thought, giving its trunk a shake with both hands. A strong tree. No wind would ever bend or break it. *This is s good tree for Seb*. She was glad for that.

Nils finished covering him, and moved on to the next, and the next. Cheli brought him her own handcloth for him to wipe the sweat from his brow. It was embroidered with the Haradel Cross in the center, from her old family home. He tucked it into his pocket and finished his work.

The sun shined brightly, and the twig birds chirped, and the green jays danced, and children laughed on some road nearby. And while all these things happened around her, underneath an old tree, they buried the bodies of good friends.

The compound itself was a private place, owned by their group. No one had cleaned up these bodies in the days since because no one ever came here uninvited. No one lived close enough to smell the dead. This place was left alone, always. It was where Paladan had held court with his little crew.

Paladan, you damn fool boy.

She turned and went back into the parlor. It was so empty. Not only of things, but of life, of memories. *When you know someone will never again be in a place where you always saw them, do they take those memories with them when they go?* Already she was having difficulty remembering any of the times she laughed within these walls.

She shook her head, and started toward the door. To leave this room. To leave this place. To leave this country and never look back.

I was a wanderer. I am a wanderer still.

She heard the floor creak behind her.

She froze.

She heard the sound of a boot rolling back down from a creaky floorboard. She pretended not to hear it. She mumbled some prayers to herself, to pretend she was unaware of his presence. She heard the boot step a different way, quieter, but she could still hear it.

She reached one hand up to her elbow and hooked a finger in the end of her long glove. *Need to take it off quickly.*

She heard another step.

She pulled the glove slowly down, inch by inch. *Faster, but not so fast that he finds it obvious.* Seb always used to say: *never let them know that you know.* Knowledge was power. Right now it was the difference between life and death.

Another step. So close behind her now.

She slid the glove over her wrist and wriggled her fingers out of it.

She heard the final step at the same time.

She dipped her mind into the Slipstream. She felt her familiar streams reaching out to her. She selected the combination she wished, and bound them together. Her mind centered on a small invisible sphere, imbued with the size, mass, position, direction, and velocity of her choosing.

She spun around, pointing at him with two fingers of her right hand. The sphere rendered into reality. It shot from her fingertips at the same speed she had once seen a sling-ace hurl a stone in competition.

The sphere smacked into the man's forehead, splitting the skin and cracking his skull. He reached up with both hands and felt the spot like he was trying to wash a window. Blood poured out through his fingers. His eyes glossed over and he crumpled on the floor. The way his body landed made it look like he was waiting desperately to relieve his bladder, with one arm pointing away awkwardly.

He was a cutthroat, knife in hand. Not an expensive man to hire. *If he was hired.* He might have been a zealot of some kind, a follower of *his* cult, left behind by the man she was after, the man who thought he was going to be god.

She rifled through his pockets. Nothing to identify him. He was a piss poor assassin. A throwaway man.

She tugged her matching ocean blue glove back on, drawing it up to her elbow. She stepped out of the parlor of the guesthouse. She crossed the cobbles back to where Orrinas was waiting with the others.

They had dragged Bann Dester's body into the grass and set him beneath the gentle oak tree. His grave would be last. The others had all collapsed in exhaustion, but Nils took it all upon himself. He dug the final grave alone without complaint, pausing every few minutes to make sure all the others were all right in the heat, or if he could bring them anything.

We do not deserve you, Nils.

She strode halfway to the tree and stopped. "There was one man in the room," she said.

Orrinas raised an eyebrow. The others were set to a brief frenzy until Orrinas could calm them. He could merely read her expression and know she had already taken care of it. That was why she loved him.

"Will we need to leave sooner than we planned?" he asked.

She shook her head. "A little light cleaning to wash the afterglow off."

He nodded. He snapped his fingers and Leucas led the others back to the parlor to clean it.

She smiled and shrugged.

He just shook his head.

She could tell he wanted to call her wife again, but he didn't. She could see it behind his eyes so green. She loved him for it.

She looked back at the tree where they had put Seb to rest. "We have to catch him this time, Orrinas. We have to stop him."

"I know."

"This cannot keep happening," she said. She felt a tear coming. She leaned her head back and to one side so that it would remain in her eye. "We cannot allow it to keep happening."

He nodded. "We are leaving soon," he said. "Are you ready for what comes next?"

She nodded back at him. *I am ready to have vengeance.*

3

Easy Silver

CORRIN HATED WAITING.

It had been nearly an hour of crouching in darkness, shifting from one leg to another to keep them from going stiff. He felt like his knees would snap if he took a step. The wind was cool off the river, but humid, and uncomfortable for someone with leather and mail over his tunic and trousers.

He hadn't bothered to bring a cloak, and he was glad for it now as he wiped the sweat from his brow. On the other hand, he was ruing the fact that he had neglected to bring a scarf to cover his nose. The river stank like a puking prostitute three weeks from her last bath. He was half-convinced there was a dead body floating in it somewhere nearby. He actually hoped that was the case. He hated to think that this was its natural odor.

With both moons still down, the night was darker than he had anticipated, like trying to stare through a barrel of ale. It was good for him all the same though. It made him less conspicuous.

Silver lining.

Corrin had mastered seven of the arts of not-being-seen, but *being in the dark*, and *dressing entirely in black* were the things he did all the time, so he thought that would not accord him much fanfare in the annals of the school of not-being-seen.

He passed the time thinking about what he would spend his silvers on when this night was over. *Easy silver.* If those fools would hurry a little more he might even spend them *before* the night was over. It would be the fastest silver he had ever made—honestly at any rate. Just for following a few basic instructions.

The first instruction from the purser was to stay out of sight. Corrin kept himself hidden around the corner of an alley, near a lamppost that was missing its oil or its wick. He had a decent vantage of the wharf from here, where the transaction was supposed to take place, and he had arrived well beforehand as per instruction number two from the purser.

Being hired steel was something new to him. Irregular work, but work just the same. The vast majority of his career involved income by way of gambling, stealing, defrauding, and generally finding new and interesting ways of relieving wealthy fools of their coinpurses.

This current work would be less likely to result in the Orange trying to arrest him. *Damnable Orange*. He hated them in their ostentatious orange capes, flaunting their ability to carry blades legally on the streets of Vithos. He could technically be arrested even now for having his longsword with him here.

He was here as a *thug*, as Aren would have called it. Reidos, always the cynic, considered it *a-lot-for-a-little*. Jecks Keberan always called it *darkwork*, work you would rather see done away from the light.

Corrin preferred darkwork to the kind of thing Aren got up to.

Goddamn users.

Aren can keep it. I want nothing to do with wizards.

He was told he would be a precaution, here only as a ward if something went wrong—a disagreement over the terms, or some such. He had been told it was unlikely he would see any action. He knew little else than that.

He knew only that they had hired at least two others at the same tavern, and he had convinced them to hire Reidos as a fourth. Even now Reidos sat on the rooftop above him, an arrow at the ready, steady as a stone. He was silent as a stone as well, save for the occasional piece of loose rock he would drop on Corrin's head to pass the time. *Damn Mahhen*, Corrin thought, though he was quite certain he would have been doing the same. *That farod gets to sit up there and enjoy this game all night at my expense.*

Farod. Corrin's favorite word. It was profanity of course. Corrin would never stoop to having any less than his three favorite words be profane in some way, shape, or form. It was Arradian slang—all the best curse words seemed to come from Arradan. *Farod* was his favorite all the more for how vague and complex its actual definition was. It was...something related to a byproduct of unnatural and ineffective simian intercourse. Even he was not absolutely certain that he could pin down what it meant—after all, he had never actually seen two primates attempting to copulate in the manner so described.

He was not sure where the other two men were hidden. Maybe they never bothered to show up. Corrin and the other two had been given two coppers apiece—four for Corrin, actually, since he had promised to bring a marksman from the Warhost with him. Sure, Reidos had been out of service for years, but Corrin chose not to bother them with such trifles, and besides, Reidos could still shoot the wings off a bat in the dead of night. Or was it an owl? Corrin had used the bat wing line on them for emphasis, but now that he thought about it, an owl would have been much closer to the truth. It didn't matter though. Trifles.

He cracked his knuckles for the thousandth time. It had been at least three hours since his last bottle of wine. The buffoons who had hired him had naturally made the ridiculous request that he not arrive for his function in a state of drunkenness. He had therefore put the cork in it just before dusk. He sucked his teeth, partly out of boredom and partly just in case there were any lingering drops of wine that he had somehow managed not to absorb yet.

He felt another pebble fall on him from above. It thwacked off his head and bounced onto his shoulder. He caught it before it touched the ground. *Damnable Mahhen*. Reidos was a Mahhen, a half-Andristi, but Corrin was convinced there was a third half—jackass.

Another pebble. This one thwapped him on his left ear.

Corrin thumbed the pommel of his longsword, which he lovingly named the *Steel Whore*. He judged the name he had chosen for it as appropriate considering the quantity of steel kisses it handed out to whoever was fool enough to try him.

Corrin did not often name his swords, having the nasty habit of losing them while leaping out of the bedchambers of maidens whose fathers were blessed with exceptional hearing. But this blade was different—it was Sabarian steel, renowned for the hardness and fine edges of any blade forged from it. It was by far the finest blade he had ever held, possessing a dark shadowy hue.

So he named it to honor his favorite profession. His favorite whores were renowned for *their* hardness and fine edges. In the Pleasure Houses of Ethios, where his mother had raised him, the whores were treated like princesses, and rightly so. Some were venerated above actual royalty. When he was a boy they had always been so kind to him. Corrin determined that the least he could do was name a blade for them. It was the finest steel around, save for Saren-steel, but who could afford that anyway? Corrin was determined to go out of his way not to lose this one. It was meant for something legendary.

Another pebble landed on his head. *Something more legendary than this, I am sure*, he promised the sword.

He listened to the air. He heard the wind whistle, the creak of warehouse doors, the ropes tightening to hold the endless line of river-craft in place. A barge bumped against a not-so-distant dock. The wind picked up suddenly, carrying a wave of rank river smell like a fist directly into his face.

The one thing that was conspicuously absent was the sound of footsteps heralding the tardy approach of the parties that were allegedly having the meeting that he was supposed to be watching.

"Ugh," he said.

He had assumed the two who hired him would be here for the exchange, but maybe not. Mayhap they pursed someone else to make the exchange for them. This was just an exchange, after all. Contraband of one sort or another. Corrin was only here in case the deal went badly.

The more time that elapsed—and the more pebbles that made their way off the roof and down onto his head—the more he started to hope that things *would* go badly.

He started going over what he would do with all the silvers he had been promised again, and managed to whittle down the options into his favorite three—drinking, fighting, and fucking, which, if worse came to worst, he could do all of simultaneously.

Then he heard something. A sharp click. Metal on metal, like a sword hilt tapping against a belt buckle. It was across the avenue and further behind him on the more well lit side. He noticed three men there, creeping toward the wharf. At least one was the purser who had handed him his coppers, robed and conspicuous as all the hells combined. The two with him were fighters, both with longswords sheathed.

Corrin turned back toward the wharf and saw four men step out from behind the very last warehouse and amble their way around a few small stacks of boxes until they arrived at the center of the avenue. They were each dressed in old black coats, and they made a ringing jingling sound when they walked.

The purser and the two men in mail made their way to the center of the street as well, stopping some twenty feet away.

Finally, Corrin thought. *Time to make some easy silver.*

He danced himself onto the street and edged his way along the nearside wall. He kept the *Steel Whore* in its sheath. No sense alerting anyone to his presence with such a small but distinct sound as drawing a blade.

He stopped in shadow. Waited. Watched.

The purser entered into whispered negotiation with the four men across from him. The purser raised his hand palm upwards to emphasize some point he had just made. He reached into one of his pockets for something and showed it to the four men.

Corrin tip-toed a little closer.

The one who appeared to be negotiating on the other side was short as a barstool, and bald as wine bottle, wearing an unremarkable shirt and unremarkable trousers. However, he made *very* remarkable frantic gestures with his hands and obscenely demanding expressions with his chubby little face. Corrin could only make out a few words here and there, but he was sure he heard the bald man suspiciously say, "Where is it?"

The three men with him were cloaked in a color best described as I-just-came-from-the-docks-by-a-stinking-river-in-the-middle-of-the-night brown. *Minions. Obviously.*

Corrin did not hear the response from the purser, but the bald man then said, "That was the deal."

Not good. It is never good when someone has to say that part aloud.

The purser waved his hand dismissively.

The bald man whispered something to one of his bodyguards, and raised his hands as he spoke, shaking them in frustration. He reached into his pouch and withdrew an object wrapped in cloth. The bald man turned back and made gestures of acquiescence and compliance and held the object out for the purser to see.

The purser waved one of his bodyguards forward to look at it. He took it in his hands and nodded. Small and rectangular. A book. It had to be a book. He would recognize one of the foul things anywhere. Corrin had been forced to be in the presence of so many damned books by Aren over the years.

The purser suddenly motioned to the shadows where Corrin was standing. Corrin felt his gut tighten up, and a burst of surprise surged through his limbs, as if the purser had just telepathically caught him insulting the little book. His hand took to the hilt of his sword by reflex, but it was not him they were pointing to.

Corrin sighed with relief when a different man stepped out into the light and made his way over to the group. His cloak was as blue as sapphires, and smooth as satin. *Inner Guard?* The Inner Guard of Amagon were well known for being silent as ghosts, showing up to listen like thieves, then disappearing like ghouls back into whatever underground dungeon it was that spawned them. At least Corrin imagined they lived underground. That was the most appropriate place for worms such as them. They were the Lord Protector's spies, listening to anything and everything, and whispering what they heard directly into the Lord Protector's ears.

What would one of their number be doing down at the docks? The only time one of those ghosts spoke up was when they talked to each other. Except the Questioners, of course. Questioners talked plenty when asking questions during the application of thumbscrews. Of all the Inner Guard, they were the ones Corrin liked the least, though that may have just been because he hated thumbscrews.

Corrin looked back at where Reidos was perched atop the building behind him. Still there, crouched low, hidden. Corrin would not have noticed him at all had he not known exactly where to look for the shadowy Mahhen-shape against the night sky.

But when Corrin turned back to the purser, something caught his eye. Two new men were now standing directly across the street. Motionless. Appearing out of nowhere. Just standing there, leaning against the wall, like he was.

What the hell?

He saw two more appear in the shadows on his own side of the street further ahead. Something wasn't right.

He took a step back, and watched as the Inner Guard held out his hand toward the bald man, holding something up for him to see. The bald man squinted, then his face turned suddenly confused, then surprised. He looked up at the Inner Guard. His eyes went wide.

More men started to emerge from the docks, men with cudgels and swords. *Where are they all coming from?* Corrin found it difficult to tell who was working for who at this point, but the majority of the men from the docks appeared to be on the bald man's payroll.

The new men Corrin had noticed near him were also moving toward the meeting.

One of the bald man's bodyguards thumped another, and motioned to the men approaching.

Corrin could see their hands settle on their weapons. He could see their legs tense. He could see them sliding their feet into predetermined stances.

The bald man stepped back. His bodyguards made a ring around him, backing away.

They drew their blades in a flash, and that set off a chain reaction, a syncopated cascade of swords sliding from scabbards—one, two, three, four, ten —as they drew on one another.

Shaot!

That was Corrin's second favorite word, also Arradian slang, referring to the corpulent member of the dark lord of all hells, which had been frequently employed to sodomize the souls of adulterers in Arradian mythology. To Corrin it meant: *Uh oh.*

The street abruptly exploded into melee.

Ah, melee. There you are my old friend.

Corrin had not been given any particular instruction when it came to things going awry. So he was compelled to improvisation.

The purser was already running conspicuously away.

That is the man who pays me. I want my silver.

Corrin had the *Steel Whore* out before he even realized he held it. He looked down at his hand and saw it already there. *Ah, there you are, dear. Ready for a little dancing?*

A handful of the bald man's minions raced to cut off the purser's escape.

Corrin ran full tilt to protect him. He slammed headlong into one of the cudgel-wielders, throwing him flat on his back. The next man nearest him was so stunned by Corrin's appearance that he accidentally dropped his sword. Corrin batted him across the head with the hilt of his own blade, knocking him down. Another man already had the purser by the cuffs, doing what looked very much like the preparation for strangulation.

Well now, that won't do at all.

Corrin cut down hard with his longsword, and took the man's arm off at the elbow with one swing. The man's eyes went wide, but not half as wide as Corrin's. He had never taken a limb off before. He had given his fair share of stabs, some deeper than others. But on none of those occasions had he ever lopped off an entire limb. He was surprised when it actually happened. It was fascinating.

The hand still clutched the purser, but Corrin snatched it and yanked the fingers free.

The purser shrieked.

"Egad," Corrin said in surprise.

He noticed three more men already closing in behind the purser. He had no idea what was going on with the rest. He only had time for what was directly in front of him.

He grabbed the purser by the very cuffs he had just removed the hand from, and swung him around like a sack until he was safely out of the way.

"Reidos! Now might be a good time!"

Before he had even finished speaking, an arrow smacked into the neck of one of the men running at him. Another took a shot to the hip and fell onto his side.

"That's more like it."

The third man reached him. Corrin kept his longsword at a *high guard*, pointing to the stars, ready. The man stabbed left. Corrin parried downward and away, just far enough so that the strike went past his ribs. Corrin turned his parry into a stab, sliding the sweet Sabarian steel down the length of his enemy's sword. The point of his blade slipped into the man's gut and burst out his back.

The man pulled his blade back, trying for a draw cut on Corrin's body as he went. Corrin wasn't too worried about it though. He was in poor position to break Corrin's chain mail that way, and with the rusted piece of garbage the man was trying to pass off as a sword, it ended up not even slicing all the way through the leather vest over it. By the time the man had completed this pointless move, his mind caught up to where his body was, and he crumpled to the ground dead.

Corrin looked up. He saw the bald man's bodyguards hacking at the Inner Guard man, the purser's bodyguards hacking at the men from the docks, and the men from the docks hacking at everyone.

Corrin grabbed the purser and heaved him to his feet. He decided it would be best to get him the hell out of here as quickly as possible, and started looking for a viable route when he heard the sound—like glass shattering *inside* his ear canal while someone simultaneously broke a barstool over his eardrum.

He looked over the purser's shoulder and saw a man *explode*—literally explode. He was there, and then he was a cloud of blood and bits.

That was not real. I did not just see that.

But he did. It was a man, and then it was many pieces of meat and torn fabric falling like hail.

Corrin froze, not afraid, but purely in puzzlement. "What in the hell makes *that* happen?" He found himself staring dumbly at it for what could have been decades.

Everyone was still. The dock men, the purser, the bodyguards. One of them for all intents and purposes *let* Reidos fire an arrow into him.

The wind whistled and no one made a sound.

Then the ground erupted under a purser's bodyguard. The man was lifted off his feet and tumbled headfirst to the ground.

That was when Corrin heard the word.

"*User!*"

Suddenly even the melee seemed calm as a placid mountain lake compared to the mad chaotic scramble of men now hellbent on running away.

Corrin had no magick of his own to stand against that. The most magick he had ever done was pissing into the wind without getting any on himself. He knew one thing for sure about it though. *When a magick user comes to the party, you leave the party.*

Corrin turned to the purser. "Time to go...."

The purser was already running.

"Hey!" Corrin called out, leaping after him.

Men screamed and shouted from behind him.

He looked up at Reidos, and motioned that it would be a good time to leave. By the time he looked back ahead, the purser was already lying face down on the stone, his robes splayed like someone had just dropped a wadded up blanket on a pile of firewood. His belongings were scattered about him.

The man who presumably had just stabbed him to death was already running off down the street, not even stopping to take anything.

He heard Reidos' boots touch down on the street, and then watched as he ran right past the body of the purser. Reidos was always doing stupid things like that. Reidos never thought about money when people were trying to kill him.

Corrin, on the other hand, never stopped thinking about whiskey, and, by extension, that which was required to purchase whiskey. So he planted his feet and skidded to a halt beside the purser, whose namesake had been unceremoniously dumped out on the street, a little pile of silver coins spilling out of it. Corrin gingerly reached into the mass of scattered coins, grabbed up a fistful, and then carried right on running, never looking back.

Easy silver.

****

Sneaking out of the house had been easy, silver moon and all. Hallan's entire family passed into sleep within minutes of the end of Chal's Day feast. They all swallowed plenty of Allon's fresh alderberry cider, and slept sound with bellies full. When Hallan slipped out the back gate he replaced the latch with utmost caution. Even the dogs did not pay him any mind.

Now he lay on the clean emerald grass, inhaling the crisp night air. The wind picked up again. It washed through his hair like the rushing waters of the creek his feet dangled in. The scent of the pines rode high on the wind, and the twisted branches of the collandir evergreens lashed out like the arms of enormous creatures. The water was cool like the breeze and chilled his feet, but he did not mind.

He heard the patting of feet coming up the other side of the hill. Coren was finally there. His comrade leapt over the hilltop and tumbled down.

Hallan stood up and kicked the water from his feet. He slipped on his leather moccasins and shoved his friend, who was late. "The others left without us already. They are at the trees for certain, as long as it was I've waited here."

"The old woman by the mill was still out. I had to go around."

"Always excuses. Anyway Old Lady Weglin is blind. We have to hurry."

Together they sprinted down the hillside, and across the open field toward the familiar clump of trees. They were wheezing by the time they reached the mighty fir where they had played since knee-high to a man. Before Hallan had fully recovered his breath, two small figures hopped from the lower branches.

Murie and Donner each gave him a disapproving look. Hallan just pointed at Coren and shrugged.

Donner was taller and stronger, but Murie could be equally intimidating. Though she was a girl, Murie had proven to be quite adept at adventure. She was nearly three years older than Hallan, and her shoulder-length hair was of shining sienna, but the pale half moon made it look icy blue.

Donner was her brother. He was a giant of a boy, and stood a good six inches taller than even Hallan. Donner's height belied his age, however, for he was the youngest.

Murie waved them on and Hallan and the others followed her lead, scrambling toward the dense forest at the base of Mas Morrin, the solitary mountain whose great grey peak was visible from even the farthest farms of the dale. They finally caught up to her, legs wobbling, their noses running as much as their legs had.

Hallan stepped as quickly and quietly as he could. There was not much time left, but he certainly did not want to risk being seen. He fancied himself a master-spy, and master-spies were not supposed to be caught.

The people of the dale did not come here at night. It was said that strange things happened on the mountain under cover of darkness. Old Myra even told him once that she had seen odd lights during certain phases of the moon. Hallan presumed that they kept Old Myra around just to frighten the children into bed. Only the four of them had ever come out so late.

Hallan held the trees to maintain balance, and trusted little more than luck to keep from tripping over the thick brambles. He saw a dull orange light ahead. Firelight. A warm glow, radiating from a large clearing. He turned to Murie, trying to muster the courage to continue. He crouched behind a small bramble at the base of an old fir. He held the trunk to steady himself, cold sap sticking to his fingers.

He could make out a circle of men shuffling about a bonfire. They were covered from head to toe in thick hooded robes. Some of them made awkward gestures toward the sky. They raised torches in unison and fell in line, marching up the slope of the mountain. Something in the way they moved sent chills into his bones. It was like crippled old Stanwin, or Baby Benn, the manchild, who had never learned to walk properly.

Murie was silent as stone. Coren's breath whistled, and Donner could not stop tapping his dumb, fat knuckles together. Hallan thought for sure the noise would give them away. But it did not.

They made a dash across the clearing to the cover of the trees on the other side. They followed the men up the mountain as closely as their courage would permit. Hallan looked over the edge more than once and felt the dizzying height he had gained over the treetops. He was near the peak now, his boots caked with mud. He and his friends peeked around one final bend.

He saw the men stop around a circle of stones. He abruptly felt like he could not keep his eyes open. He was so tired. The men were moving. What were they doing? Hallan fell down. His eyes closed.

****

Amicien Duran saw the children even as they were congratulating themselves for not being seen. They were not who he sought, but he wanted to be aware of anyone who would share the mountain with him this night.

Duran chose a different path. He climbed the sheer rock face alone. He moved from handhold to handhold with the ease of a master. Where he had been born, this mountain would have been considered no more than a small hill. He ascended to a high perch near the summit, overlooking a wide clearing, marked with a circular arrangement of tall stone blocks positioned around a well.

Duran waited until the robed men came. They formed a circle about the stone slabs, and began to chant, invoking some runic language long since erased from common memory. Mimmions the men were called. Duran was here to watch them. Ordered to do so.

Two of their number stood back from the others, and seemed separate from them somehow, their hooded cloaks fastened with little silver crescents that reflected glittering light from the torches.

Duran wondered who they were. They were not like the others. Their poise was different, severe, demanding. These men handed the leader of the Mimmions a small object, which he placed at the edge of the well.

They then brought forward a bulging burlap sack and overturned it before the Mimmions, dragging a young woman out of it, clutching at her wrists and ankles. A gift for the Mimmions, who were known for their love of human sacrifice.

Duran chewed his lip and squeezed the straps of his rucksack until his knuckles turned white. He felt his blood pumping, his eyes sharpening, his body goading him to action. Demanding action. But he did not move a muscle. He did not dare.

The woman writhed and squirmed and twisted in their grip, but could not break free, a thick wad of cloth choking back her screams. The Mimmions tore her nightdress to pieces. She bucked wildly as they began cutting into her flesh with knives. They carved symbols into her arms, thighs, and belly.

Duran wept for her, but he could not interfere. It was vital that he survived to tell what happened here.

But it hurt him to ignore her pain, and her terror. It took a little piece of him that he would never get back. Someday she could have been a leader, a mother, an adventurer, an artist, or a muse, had her path been only a hairsbreadth different in the loom of the gods.

It was a mercy when they at last finished and tossed her body into the well.

A deep droning chorus from the Mimmions set the air to humming. The well began to glow with a peculiar luminosity that Duran's eyes could not place in any spectrum. Shapes of the light seemed to rise, as if the color itself was being lifted out of the well. How were they doing it? It was not their chanting. That was just for show. Something else was happening.

But before he could even stop his spinning thoughts, Duran saw a blinding light in the night sky. He looked up. He saw a man floating in the air, hovering above the Mimmions. He pointed at the Mimmions, and each time he did, invisible forces issued from his hands. Duran could see the light from the well disturbed by their paths.

Magick.

The man's invisible shapes crashed into the Mimmions, ripping many to pieces, the rest fleeing in panic.

Duran realized the man was standing on a flat plane, an invisible surface that he was controlling. Gods high and low, the confidence to stand in the sky atop a thin square of nothing.

Then the man struck at the well itself, with invisible forces that slammed it into rubble. The shockwave sucked the air out of Duran's lungs. The mountain shook. The light rose up, no longer contained around the mouth of the well, it sprayed out in all directions.

Duran slipped on the sharp rocks. He reached out a hand, grasping for something to hold on to. Then he fell.

4

An Investigation

"YOU LOVE THAT DRUG as much as you hate it," she said, rolling off him.

Aren could not disagree. "Malagayne." He said the name of it as if reminiscing about an old friend. His eyes danced over the imperfections in the ceiling of his bedroom.

Merani reached over and slapped his chest with her slender fingers, one leg laying over his, her fingertips running over the inside of his thighs. "I know what it is called. I have seen grey leaves before. Give me some." She sat up, letting the sheets fall away to reveal her shoulders, breasts, and belly. Her skin was painted gold by the light of the reed candles, her eyes dark and infinite.

He slipped another dried grey leaf into the end of his silver pipe, lit it with a spring-flint, and held it up to her lips. She sipped the cool grey smoke, her eyes closing. Her mouth worked itself into a smile. She exhaled gently, allowing the smoke to hover in a little cloud, infusing the frizzy curls of her bobbed tawny hair. She rolled on top of him, slipping the pipe from his hand. She straddled him, holding it up, examining it, curiosity furrowing her brow.

"Give that back," he said.

She yanked her hands above his reach. "Not so fast." She slid one hand down between her body and his, a mischievous fire in her eyes. She took hold of him and moved her hand back and forth, bringing him to iron all over again, dangling the pipe over his head as she did so.

Aren's eyes rolled back in his head when she lowered herself down. He heard her pry up the spring-flint from the wine-sticky table beside his bed. She lit the pipe, rocking her hips gently against him.

Aren's eyes snapped to the pipe. He felt his neck spasm as he leaned up to make his mouth meet it.

She rocked her hips and held the pipe to his lips. The sensations battled for control of his mind and body. The rocking of her hips easily took possession of his body, squeezing him to stone, making him gently shudder every time she moved.

But as for his mind, the malagayne won. It always won.

She increased her pace, holding the pipe up to her lips and taking three greedy gulps of the sweet smoke. He watched her eyes roll back in her head as she swam into sensation. Her head leaned back and her thighs tightened. Her body flowed like a river around him.

He closed his eyes, swimming in a malagayne haze with her as she melted over him, fingers clawing at his shoulders as she rode, dripping sweat onto his chest. Her pleasure was so profound to feel while floating in the malagayne that he finished this time almost as an afterthought. She remained atop him for a long while after she came, her eyes closed, her body shuddering, her breaths deep and clear.

"Perhaps you should pay *me* this time," Aren mused.

She leaned down and kissed him on the forehead. "You have been holding out on me. I would have discounted for you before had I known how good the leaf is."

"That is likely why it is illegal," he said. "It has been banned in Amagon since before you or I were born."

"All the good things always are. Aren't you a magistrate though? Are you going to arrest yourself?"

Aren laughed. "I'm not that kind of magistrate."

"We are in Vithos. This is the capital city of Amagon. One would think they would mind."

"I know everyone here. And I know who to avoid. They are not nearly as bad here as they are in Medion."

"The City of Towers," she mused. "A place of wonders."

"The Mahhenin people there hate the leaf. It is a sin in their culture. They put more pressure on the magistrates."

"It feels like we live in two kingdoms sometimes. People and Mahhennin."

"Mahhennin are people. Just a different kind. They say Amagon is a nation of teamwork. Born of an alliance between those with Andristi blood and those without."

"I have never had an Andristi between my legs. I am not sure if I could."

He handed her the pipe for a quick sip. "I imagine it would be much the same." He did not mention that one of his best friends was half-Andristi. He was not sure how she would take it.

"This is really quite good," she said. "I feel *elsewhere* better than with any wine or herb. I do not know whether to crawl beneath the covers or run for miles."

"Some people say it is the essence of long dead gods of ages past, rolled crushed and smoked. It can simultaneously energize you and leave you blissfully numb." Easier than looking at the memories of what murderers could do. That much was certain.

Merani kicked the sheets off of them both and bounded to her feet. Her fingers locked around the neck of the last remaining bottle of tart springwine, glass green like the sweet trees of the Sarenwood. She peeled the bottle from the congealed wine coating the table. It came free with a snap. She crossed his room naked, observing his perfectly arranged shelves. She lingered over a tiny vignette replica of Sangbran's life-sized sculpture in distant Qarsus. "What are these little objects suspended in glass? Eleven of them. Isn't that an important number? I always forget."

"That old garbage?"

"It is a pretty display, with eleven people in prayer. Are they meant to be the eleven gods?"

"I do not think they have eleven gods where Sangbran was from. More like seventeen. And I only keep it on the shelf because it was a gift from one of the elders on the Council. I would like to remain in his favor."

"What are the little objects? One of them looks like a sword."

"Sephors," Aren said.

"Where have I heard that word?"

"Artifacts mentioned in the oldest myths of the world. Older than old. They were said to have the power to reshape man, or maybe the world. Tools forged by someone known as the Master before time was recorded. He was said to live in a world of limitless light. They are just stories. Allegories."

"Tools for what?"

He shrugged. "To make people into gods, or gods into bigger gods. No one can keep the story straight about them. That is usually the hallmark of a fraud."

"A long-lived fraud," she observed.

"Just like any of the gods people pray to—Zor, Belleron, Thrax. All fabrications. Dreams in the minds of primitive people long ago that we just cannot seem to kick. I read the Histories, texts written by *actual* scholars, people I trust to pass on the truth. They all agree that gods and Sephors are just make believe. They are not real. Just something controversial for Sangbran to put in his art."

She wrinkled her lip at him. "You have no gods? None? Everyone has gods, from Arradan to Hylamar. Take your pick."

"I take down gods for a living." He took a tiny sip of smoke. "It is hard to believe in a god like Thrax when I keep executing people with powers just like his. Besides, after the things I have seen men do, one thing is clear to me about this world. No god could be this derelict, no demon this cruel."

"By the gods high and low, calm down, calm down. You sure have a hate on for them, for someone so young." She placed it tenderly back onto its shelf. "Pretty all the same." She paused. "I was surprised when it was *you* calling on me with a bag of silver tossers. Your friend is always the one who pays."

"Sarker," Aren said his name. "He is not my friend. He is my mentor."

"A magistrate? Like you?"

"Like me. Yes. Only a hundred times better."

"A hundred times older. That is for certain. Why would they put a boy with an old man to chase those awful people?"

"You think of me as a boy now?"

"You *are* a boy. All men are boys right until the day they become wrinkly old men." She laughed. She scuffed her feet on his Iridian rug, picking up each of his Icarian hero sculptures in turn, inspecting them and then setting them gently back down on their respective shelves.

Aren held up the still smoldering pipe. "He is the reason I have this. It was Sarker who first told me about *burnout*." He rolled over onto his belly and pulled the sheets up over his legs. "Have you ever wondered why so many Glasseyes are young men? Not as young as me, but young. Younger than Sarker by miles and miles."

She shrugged. "I always just assumed you magistrates earned so much salary you could retire on a Lenagon beach with all your silver and gold."

He laughed. "I thought much the same once, but the truth of it is worse. *Users* can be seduced by their own power to commit horrible crimes. I lost count of the victims. Some people can't take it. Most people. Maybe all people. Maybe me someday."

"No wonder." Merani made a sour face. "You hate them. Don't you? Those users. The people with the magick."

"I do."

"But then why are some users left alone? I know of some here in Amagon. Famous people. Celebrities. Why don't you hunt them?"

"Amagon *documents* its users, declares them legal. Most civilized nations do this in some fashion. Users submit their powers for inspection by people like me, so that we can trace them without having to build up evidence first. So that if they slip up, they *know* we will be able to take them down. But the rogues—those who refuse, or hide what they are—they are dangerous. The only way to find them is to study the scenes of their crimes, learn how to stop them from the remains of *what they have already done*. That takes time. A lot of time. And when it comes to one of them, even a day is too long."

She looked at him, suddenly concerned. "I was jesting before, but you really have seen some terrors, haven't you?"

He shrugged a malagayne shrug. "What does it matter? If you want to feel bad for someone, feel bad for the people who became the terrors that I see." He held up the pipe. "That is why this is so valuable to me. It has the power to undo. I use it. Like a tool. Like every tool I use. Like a swordsman uses a whetstone to keep his sword sharp, I use the malagayne for my mind."

The smoke performed its function perfectly—drained his emotions, calmed his nerves, restrained the fires of anger and the oceans of despair. It was his own Glasseye inside his head, relentlessly pursuing the rogue thoughts of his own mind and burning them out.

Seeing what a sword could do to a man was *knowable*. It was *expected*. The sight of it was gruesome, but the sight of it was *anticipated* beforehand. No one could anticipate the kind of horrors that magick could wreak on a human body.

"Give me some more," Merani said.

"Best to use it sparingly."

"The way you do?" She laughed. "You smoke malagayne as much as you talk. And that is quite a lot."

"I thought you liked talking to me."

She smiled. "Do not take offense. It is not a chore. But sometimes I think he hires me more to listen to you talk than to fuck you."

He widened his eyes a bit.

She noticed. "Does it bother you that I don't use the Arradian word for it?"

"No," he said. "We are not *in* Arradan." He gestured at the bare skin between her legs, smooth as silk. "You certainly shave yourself in the *Arradian fashion*."

She smiled and rolled her eyes. "Men of *every* nation like the Arradian fashion."

"Just surprising you would take their style and not their slang."

She bounced her head from side to side. "I have more than my share of *Olbaranian* clientele. Vandolines mostly. They like to *fuck*, not *vanaha*."

"Olbaranians? Here? In Amagon?"

"Sons of the merchants from Westgate. I prefer them young. Like you. You are my only magistrate."

"I feel so special."

She pointed at the malagayne. "You are special it seems."

He shrugged. "I need to keep myself together to do what I do. I am not going to disappoint Sarker. I refuse to quit. I will not be a disgrace to the man who made me who I am."

"You speak of him like a father."

"I have no father."

"You never talk about your family. Are you ever going to tell me about them?"

"No."

She paused and thought to herself for a long time. "You never answered me."

"What?"

"Before. When I asked you where your friend was."

"Sarker."

"Yes. Sarker. Why did he not send me here tonight with a bag of silver?"

"They will not tell me what happened to him."

"Something happened to him?"

Aren shrugged, pulling himself up onto his elbows. "He received a message the day before our last capture. And he left. I haven't seen him since."

"I hope he is well. I liked him. He did not have time for nonsense."

"I wish he had been there," Aren said. "It was my fault, what happened to them. Two men dead. Because of my mistake."

"Mistakes are for learning," she said. "For next time."

"Small consolation to whatever families Twig and Swan may have had."

"How do you even know they had families?"

"I suppose I don't. I left Palatora before I would have found out." But that did not stop his mind from creating families for them: wives and children left penniless, sick brothers or sisters counting on them to return that night, a lover waiting on a street corner for a brave man that would never arrive.

He did not mention that the real reason he had not been present to find out was because he had been buying a large stock of malagayne the morning after he oversaw the capture of Degammon. *Priorities.*

She smiled. "You should stop worrying about what you do not know."

"My entire job is worrying about things I do not know. The malagayne helps."

"Well I won't tell on a magistrate. You pay too well." She winked at him. "And you are not awful looking either."

He laughed. "Your discretion is equal to your beauty."

Merani completed her circuit of his room, having gazed at every object on every shelf. "Your home looks only half lived in."

"It is barely a quarter lived in."

"You are often gone, aren't you?"

He smiled. "Are you suddenly realizing that you miss me when I am away?" He threw a pillow across the room at her.

She batted it away and half-smiled. "More like I miss your silver."

She climbed atop him and rubbed his shoulders until he could barely keep his eyes open. Then she rolled him over and slid her body against his and around his and all through his. Her breath was in his ear, and her body slick against him, and his mind evaporated into a hazy steam of disintegrating thoughts and febrile sensations.

He let her nod off beside him afterwards.

Sleep was elusive. He lay awake. In his bed. The bed he had not slept in for months. In the apartments he had not seen for weeks. Beside the beautiful prostitute who was only there to listen to him because she was paid to be in his room.

My room. He had been so long away from it that he hardly recognized it now. He let his eyes pass over the half-empty dressers, and the cabinets full of keepsakes from his travels—tiny figurines from Dryden, brass censers from traders in Ossamport, small silken tapestries from Kolchin, and delicate carvings from the woodworkers in Westgate. All the proper things a man of means was supposed to have.

He gazed at his carpets, and noticed how clean they were. He had never really had any time to spill anything on them. The room did not even smell familiar. It felt like just another strange room at some faraway inn, with only a hint of a feeling to remind him that it was his own.

Always on the road. Always a strange bed. Always surrounded by strange people who he saw just rarely enough to never quite become friends with.

He lit the pipe again and inhaled.

The sheets of his bed were silken and cool, and he stretched out on them, rolled over, and blinked his eyes.

In the span of that blink, he dreamed he was celebrating the founding of Amagon. The banners flew all around in a glistening rainbow of golds and reds and blues. The soldiers of three armies stood in perfect formation, their freshly polished armor shining in the midday sun. Knights of the Seven Cities were all around him, and Rogar's lords from Olbaran, and every Mahhen clan-warden. A great cheer rose in the coastal morning air. The shovels rose and fell with a rhythm all their own. Around a tiny coastal inlet called Medion would rise a city, and at last the wandering Mahhennin would have a home to share with the men of the west.

The rhythmic pounding grew louder. It became the sound of a fist pounding on an old oak door.

That was when the blink ended. Aren stared around at the darkness of his bedchamber. He sat up in his unfamiliar bed, and squinted at his unfamiliar door. Someone was beating it like a drum.

He lifted himself with difficulty. It was still dark outside. He slammed his knee into a table as he attempted to navigate his bedchamber. He lit a small reed candle, and pulled an unused shirt over his head.

The pounding persisted.

"Right. I hear you." He twisted the lock and yanked the door open. "What is it?"

His half-closed eyes fell upon a short, stocky man. He was dressed in a crimson tunic slightly too long for his small body. "You are Aren, Magistrate of Amagon. I serve the Lord Protector as you do."

"You are Aldarion's man? What do you want with me?"

"The Lord Protector asked me to make all haste in finding you."

"This had better be important." He doubted anyone would have woken Sarker in the middle of the night, but then again, he doubted Sarker would have complained about it if they had.

"Murder," the man said.

"Murder?" Aren raised an eyebrow. "Do they suspect the magick? They must. They wouldn't have called on me if they didn't."

The small man shrugged and waited outside the door.

Merani had already let herself out during the night, taking the little pouch of silver tossers with her, but she did leave behind one double-silver on the table in return. A little refund for the malagayne, or the climax, or both. He tried to pick it up, but it had long since dried into the spilled wine on the tabletop, and was now frozen in time, hard as stone. He chuckled. *Of course.*

He donned his cloak of midnight blue, joining it with the silver pin in the shape of the crescent moon, the symbol of Amagon's magistrates. Upon his breast he affixed his Render Tracer badge, the symbol that marked him as a Glasseye—a perfect circle, with five prongs evenly spaced on one upper quadrant. The all-seeing eye. The symbol users feared more than any other. He dipped his feet into his shiny black boots, strapped his sword about his waist, and shuffled quickly down the hall and out into the night.

One of the moons is out at least. Aren did not like the idea of stumbling through pitch darkness. Anularia, the blue moon, was riding low in the horizon, giving off radiant but lazy beams of deep azure. Silistin, the white moon, was the twin sister of Anularia, but she was absent from the sky this night. Aren loved the nights when both sisters crossed the heavens together, dancing a delicate nocturnal ballet, but tonight one moon would have to do.

"Almost there," the little man called. He led Aren toward a square structure with yellowed walls and rotten eaves. It was a tiny shop, just a stone's throw from where the Lord Protector lived.

He stepped through the open doorway. Shelves of old scrolls, faded books, and fraying maps lined the walls. *How did I never realize this place was here?* He wondered if any of the Histories he was missing from his collection were on these shelves. *Calm yourself, magistrate. Best let the body be cold before we start looting his possessions.* Off to one side sat a small table with a stoneware plate of festering meat and crumbling cinnamon pastries, a bottle of winterwine on its side. Of all the nine wines, Aren could think of none worse to go with this warm weather than winterwine.

One of the Orange stood off to the side of the stairwell, holding a torch. The man barely looked at him. *He knows that I am a Glasseye.* Even the official law enforcers of Amagon, named for their orange capes and sashes, knew to keep a healthy distance from wherever one of his kind was going.

"Don't worry," one of the Orange said. "They already took care of the books."

"Books?" Aren asked.

"He had two texts that had been *indexed*," another said.

"No sense leaving them where one of *those things* could find them," the first said.

He means users, sorcerers. Books about science then. The kind that teach the fundamental laws, the kind where a single page of knowledge could make a user exponentially more dangerous. "But they weren't taken?"

The second one shook his head. "We found them. Shelves weren't touched. *Formulas of Physic* by Caspar Sharnunna, and *Universal Laws* by Belieadas Krim. Inner Guard agents were here already. They took them. They are safe."

Aren nodded. What was a little no-name scholar doing with texts like that? And how could they have escaped the notice of a user? Unless that user knew those formulas already. He shuddered. *Or the user was in too much of a hurry.* Aren preferred the second option.

Aren reached the bottom and was led across a small room with an earthen floor, soft and wet. He slipped on mud and nearly lost his footing. It was as though a tub of water had been overturned, and the mud was churned and soft. He felt his boots sink to the ankles into it with every step.

He saw the Lord Protector's personal investigators. He noticed immediately that there were no Sweepers with them. He grimaced at the thought. It could take hours for a single man to plot the peak points of a user's resonance.

He feigned being happily awake. *A true Render Tracer does not display the weakness of his own body. He has to appear more than a man.*

The men merely nodded to him. None ventured to speak. Aren had become accustomed to the reaction. He was a boy to everyone who saw him. A child, a messenger, a scribe of someone truly important. So often did it occur that he was able to mask his annoyance out of reflex. "What condition is the subject in?"

"You are...Aren?" one asked.

"I am," Aren said in his deepest voice.

"You are not the usual agent," said the tallest, who had a badger's eyebrows and a slender eel of a face.

They would never have questioned Sarker with such a disrespectful tone. "I am usually on dispatch to the south country with Toran Sarker. I was under the impression that I was called for personally." He knew it would be helpful to invoke Sarker's name, and he noticed the effect immediately.

"You were," the man agreed, flustered. "We usually work with other Tracers. We did not understand why they called you. I am Lausser." He took the torch from the Orange and held it over the body.

The limbs were positioned at impossible angles. Blood and bile pooled all over, mixing with the mud. The scalp was cleaved open, and it appeared that every joint had been twisted or snapped. The head no longer possessed its eyes, and a toothless jaw dangled askew from the face.

He stopped and took a deep breath as Sarker had taught him. *Concentrate. Evidence.* He noted that all the fingers of the left hand were gone. "Missing digits," he said.

"His name was Baldamar," Lausser said. "His brother came to check on him after he didn't come home this past night. Some of the Orange even knew him. Said he does personal favors for the Lord Protector himself. Called him one of the friendliest old men in the world."

"The Orange said he was visited frequently by a niece named Dalain," one of the others said. "But that she stopped coming to see him weeks ago. We thought it might have been something scandalous. Her father a user maybe, come for revenge."

Aren nodded. *Conjecture. Pure and simple.* "And the water on the ground here?"

Lausser shrugged. "No leaks, no ground water, and no basins large enough for this quantity. It must have been brought by the magick."

Aren shook his head. "Wrong. If the water had been brought here from another location, there would be a visible mist trail from something so recent. Reduction in pressure could also cause a vacuum that could be used to strip moisture from a well or basin, but such a quantity to create this much would have left dew on the walls and ceiling and furniture. And there is not enough natural humidity in the air for a thermalist user to reduce temperature to squeeze all the moisture from it. It could have been ice that melted, but the resulting water would tend to make crackling sounds when mixed with dirt or soil. If an Elemental created the water, it would have had a silver shine to it. The water must have some kind of natural origin."

He peered up and down the length of the room, employing the Jecker monocle and each of the four filters and still saw nothing. He returned the eyepiece to its pouch. He studied the Oscillatrix, but it registered nothing. "There is no indication that the magick was involved in this crime. I'll prepare the usual briefing for you, but there is no further need for me in the investigation." He rolled his eyes, thinking of the pile of documentation he would be required to undertake.

"You are finished?" interjected the squat little man, reappearing.

Aren jerked his back straight, taken completely off balance by the sudden materialization.

"You have been called to Cayman's Tower."

"Now?" Aren asked. "To see the Protector? What about my investigation? I have a mountain of briefing papers to complete."

"That will be unnecessary. Lausser can handle the investigation himself. You have already ruled out the magick, have you not?"

"How do you know that?"

"Come now. This is an emergency meeting."

Aren staggered up the stairs and to the Lord Protector's home across the street. The little man watched him go alone.

If it was an emergency then why did you waste my time in that basement?

He rubbed his eyes. He thought he might fall asleep if he stood in one place for too long. He fought the urge to run home for a pinch of malagayne, and ascended the steps to the gate. The steel bars rose twelve feet high, spikes rimming the top. "Hail, Cidric." Aren thumped the gate with his fist. "What is this? What's going on?"

Cidric smiled. "Hail, Aren." He wore no coat over his bright orange satin shirt, but seemed to be sweating nonetheless. "My boy, you look younger every time I see you."

I wish you would stop pointing that out. "I am siphoning off Sarker's life essence."

"Hah hah. I have not seen him of late."

"No? I thought they called him back here weeks ago?"

Cidric shook his head. "Not that I know. But then there is little left that I know anymore. Not after tonight."

"What does that mean?"

He gestured for Aren to come closer. "Strange men in here tonight. Been some murders out in the villas. Some are saying it is the cult of the black coats again. Rich men and poor men murdering for the cause of their master. And ebon-shrouds on the frontiers."

"Rumors of the black coats coming back roll in every season. But ebon-shrouds?"

"Deadly as nightshade they are," Cidric said. "Sword masters. It is said that they can kill with a whisper, and they only look at you if you are about to die."

"Many things are said about them."

"And if even half are true, I would run from one faster than all my Lord's executioners."

Aren rolled his eyes. "The fear of them is likely greater than the danger."

"The fear is more than enough for me," Cidric shuddered. "Even a Sarenwalker would walk the other way if an ebon-shroud came along."

Aren laughed. "Doubtful. Ebon-shrouds never live long enough to get very far from their temples in the south."

"Ah yes, I always forget you know all the Histories. You can tell the stories better than I can, my boy." The gate whined as he pulled it open. "Stay away from the dark. The Orange are jumpy. The urns are lit. Walk in the path of the light."

Aren crossed the lawn to the tower—tall, square, and domed, rising fifty feet into the air. Atop it rose a single flag, red-orange like the setting sun, with the golden Moon of Amagon in the center. It was lit even at night by mighty urns spouting flame at the apex.

The lawn was crawling with the Orange, and Inner Guard agents, and even some Stoppers Aren recognized. *What happened while I slept?* He stalked through them without a word and leapt through the open door.

The bright light slapped him in the face. He never had gotten used to that. The interior was always lit up like daylight. The hazy glass light-bowls dangling from chains high above were so overloaded with *melenkeur* stones that he had to shade his eyes.

Melenkeur was a soft, easily pliable mineral found in distant mines, and it glowed for months on end, lighting the rooms of the wealthy, fought over as often as gold. A brick or two of it was enough to light a large room. The Lord

Protector used so many that Aren thought he might be competing with the sun.

Not a soul appeared to greet him. The wide staircase empty. The halls empty. The balcony empty. It was unusual to see less than twenty people moving about in this place.

Aren didn't bother waiting. He went straight for the art. It was rare enough that he was allowed in here. He intended to make the most of it.

Upon the wall at the top of the stairs hung a painting by Loyol, *The Founding,* referring to the founding of Medion by half-Andristi clans who had fled their old homes in the east. They were named Mahhennin, *west-movers,* and settled in Amagon many centuries ago, after being thrown out of first Laman and later Arradan. The painting showed Weirmaheir, lord of the Mahhennin, planting the first spade into the earth five hundred years ago where the magnificent Tower of Medion now stood.

Just like my dream.

Aren gazed upward at the great tower dome from the inside. Its true beauty was its interior, circled by frescoes from Loyol and Marbothan; *Haliban,* golden spear held aloft in victory over Gotha, and *The Finding of the Lady,* featuring the famed Lady of Saren.

At the top of the stairs hung a duplicate of Bordican's famous painting, *Along the Vassian Way.* Travelers on the famous road in old Arradan, guided by a goddess armed with sword and wand.

He moved along the wall from painting to painting, each one a scene from history. They were the things that filled his dreams.

He suddenly felt someone's eyes on him. He looked up.

It was Margol, the Lord Protector's adjutant and bodyguard. His brown hair greyed near his ears, close-cropped and pulled straight back. His face was tanned and pitted, scars and grooves. His lips were thick, and pressed together on his face in a way that made him look like he was pursing them when he wasn't, the same way his eyes made it appear he was staring at prey when he was only looking at you.

"Aren. Should have known I would find you here. Eyes always on the past."

"This is one of Loyol's most famous paintings—*Sanctuary.* It is his depiction of Shaezrod Spur, the high tower in Arradan where the seven Patriarchs of the empire used the magick to save the world from Devron, the mad emperor. When they taught me to be a Render Tracer, *Devron's Folly* was one of the first stories they told from the Histories. Drunk on his own magick, Devron lost control of his power, and unleashed enough force to destroy the world. Shaezrod Spur was a safe haven."

"Sounds to me like they could have used a few Glasseyes. Put Devron down before he could do all that damage. Good thing we have one here tonight then." He nodded to Aren. "Come with me."

Aren followed at his heels, down the long corridor from the tower to the Protector's private rooms. Margol gave two raps on the door, opened it in one fluid motion, and with a glance, indicated that Aren should enter alone. The door closed behind him.

Aren stepped across the thick plush carpet. Burning sage laced the air. An immense glass bowl full of glowing melenkeur dangled from a chain high above, lighting the room like the sun.

There were others already here, clustered around Lord Protector Aldarion's desk. Donnovar was there, and Terrol as well. *Not good.*

"It is good to see you, Aren," Aldarion said. His brow furrowed, and his eyes spoke of sleepless nights. Upon his violet silk shirt he wore a brooch of bright gold with the crescent Moon of Saren worked in emeralds.

He was always a man to get to the point immediately. "Aren, someone tried to kill me tonight."

****

"Beautiful," her lover whispered. "So beautiful."

Lesca let him run his fingers through the thick curls of her hair. His touch was so warm, so inviting. His fingertips felt like fire and ice on her skin. They pulled gently on her hair. She leaned back and let a brief moan escape her lips. He leaned over her, pressing his lips softly and sweetly to her shoulder, her neck, behind her ear. She felt his breath warm like the smoldering coals in the corner of the room.

"I love your eyes," Lesca told him. "I love the way they *see*. So dark. Like looking into the moonless sky at night."

He stood behind her and she felt him run his hands up over her shoulders, and down her chest, pulling open her gown. She looked down at herself as he exposed her skin, and trembled. He leaned over her, running his fingers along the contours of her body, down her back, around her sides, brushing softly against her breasts. Her back arched involuntarily as she watched his hands move in a delirium of anticipation, wanting them to go further.

His hands trailed down over her hips, across her thighs, and up between her legs. Lesca released a gasp, and shivered with sudden delight as his fingers pressed against her. She spread her legs wide and raised a hand to her neck, touching the golden necklace that hung about it, the prize of her family, feeling a tinge of melancholy that it would soon be sold away. She ran her fingers across the winking gem in the center, red like the curls of her hair.

He put his hands gently on her shoulders and squeezed, tenderly massaging her. His voice was low, almost a whisper. "I love your necklace." His hands pressed harder upon her neck, rubbed harder, and pressed harder. It felt so good. Lesca let her eyes drift shut. He rubbed harder still, and then pressed harder, and it was wonderful, and he rubbed harder and pressed harder, and then it started to hurt and she said, "stop," and she raised a hand to her neck and her eyes flashed open, and he did not stop and she cried out.

His hand clamped tightly to her jaw.

His arms twisted so violently that her neck snapped. Her body fell limp to the floor. She could not draw a breath, nor feel her arms or legs, but for a moment her eyes saw and her ears heard.

He ripped the necklace free, breaking the golden chains. He gazed at the gemstone. "Beautiful," she heard him say. "So beautiful."

5

You Leave In The Morning

THIS CHANGES EVERYTHING, Aren thought. *This could be what I have been waiting for.*

He silently fumed at his delay. *I should have been here from the start. They would have made sure Sarker was here before they began.* He quickly surveyed the assemblage, trying to read what he could from their body language.

Evidence.

The ones he did not know were all military men, officers from the Warhost and the Orange. He was surprised he did not see any members of the Council present. It was unusual, even if they were going to war. Which they could not have been.

He knew Terrol well enough, the way the nerves of your skin know a splinter—by how cruelly annoying it is. Terrol stooped slightly, as though only a part of him had come to the meeting, the rest of him out spying on someone. He wore the blue of the Inner Guard, his shirts and cape all soft silks shifting like ocean currents. Every ornament available to a man of his rank was polished and visible—the silver triple nails of a Questioner, the hovering eagle of the Guard, the obsidian hound of a Listener, and the silver circle of the Inner Guard upon the pin which held his silk cloak. Aren was wary of any man who openly admitted being a Listener or a Questioner, let alone both.

Donnovar he knew better, and no memory without a smile. But here he was tense, his posture stiff. He wore the same tunic and leggings he would have ridden into a battle with. Though he was a captain of the Outer Guard, Aren had rarely seen him wear any marks of his rank. This audience was no different. Donnovar could easily have been mistaken for a man pulled right off the street. His hair stood sharp, brown, and short like the military men of the

Warhost, and his eyes were wide and round. His broad chest leaned forward, thick arms resting on the back of Aldarion's chair.

"How?" Aren asked. "I have heard absurd rumors of ebon-shrouds wandering the frontier. Is that what this is about?"

"There have been sightings," Aldarion said. "Too many to be simple fantasy."

"That is not what this is about," Terrol said. "It is the Councils. They are a breeding ground for treason. They have opened the door to this."

Inner Guard were the eyes of the Protector's rule. Nothing ever seemed to sneak up on Terrol. His ears seemed to be in the walls of every back corridor in the city. *Yet he missed this.*

"We have not seen such fear since the *Kinraigan incident*," Donnovar said.

"I would caution against any casual reference to that name," Terrol warned. "The man who owns that name is *still out there*. As is his cult. Rumor says it is growing again after all these years. There have been villages laid waste."

Kinraigan. Aren was all too familiar with that name. The greatest and most terrible user his mentor had ever faced. Kinraigan had done unspeakable damage, relegating even someone as evil as Degammon to a mere footnote in the list of all hells. When he finally fled, Sarker had pursued him, but returned empty-handed. It was the greatest manhunt in the history of Amagon, and yet Kinraigan simply disappeared.

"He was a madman," Donnovar agreed. "As insane as he was powerful. He escaped all attempts to apprehend him. Foiling every Render Tracer sent against him. Killing most who tried."

Terrol smirked at Aren. "*Your* mentor's greatest failure."

"His *only* failure," Donnovar corrected.

"Call it what you will," Terrol said dismissively. "The fact remains that he eluded the great Toran Sarker. The most dangerous man to set foot in Amagon was allowed to escape."

Aren stared hard at him, never letting his eyes waver or wander. *If I have to suffer the indignity of your contempt, I will face it head on, like Sarker taught me.* "Sarker is a Render Tracer," Aren said. "Don't you dare mock him."

"Who do you think *you* are, boy?" Terrol asked. "Sarker's pet Glasseye?"

"Now *senior* Render Tracer," the Lord Protector said.

Terrol laughed again. "This?" He gestured at Aren, as if appraising a worthless toy. "A boy? A thief chaser? Do you wish Amagon's leadership to be mocked from Medion to Palatora? This duty should be given to a *man*."

Aren bit his lip. *You would never speak this way to Sarker.* "I trace more than thieves." Aren thought he was going to say something more profound, to put Terrol in his place, but that was all that came out.

"Why don't you go trace me a goblet of springwine?" Terrol suggested.

"Go and get it yourself," Aren said.

"So sensitive," Terrol said. "Why don't you run off to your mother's skirts, boy? Leave this business to men. Oh, yes. Of course. That would require your mother to be alive, wouldn't it, Glasseye?"

"Enough!" Donnovar shouted.

Terrol straightened, his eyes momentarily widening with fear. *Old habits die hard*, Aren thought, *and a fear of Donnovar dies even harder.* Aren was glad to have the Captain in his corner.

Donnovar glanced at Aldarion. "Aren, what would you say if I told you that someone was smuggling mercenaries from the east into Laman, and then bringing them to Amagon?"

Aren blinked at him. "Is this a real question? That doesn't make sense at all."

"Explain why."

"The only kingdoms which border the far side of Laman are Palantar and Vulgossos. Neither of them are on very good terms with the Lamani throne, and neither are known for even having mercenaries. And the only way *out* of Laman on the nearside is through Farguard Gap. No one gets through Farguard Gap without permission. And why would *anyone* hire mercenaries from so far away? Laman? That's a thousand miles from here. There are companies of Vandolines waiting just across the gulf. Dolar-swords from the Levantine, alpine fighters from the Mekkosi mountain wars, Samartanian second-princes, Olybrian free companies. There are literally a hundred better choices. Seven hells and more, if you gave me fifty silver tossers I could ride down to Ossamport and hire a hundred pennyswords and have them here within a fortnight."

Donnovar glanced at Terrol and Aldarion. "I told you," he said. "He knows this kind of thing backwards and forwards. He is perfect for this."

"Perfect for what?" Aren asked.

Aldarion smiled. "There is a connection between the Kingdom of Laman and the conspirators who tried have me killed. I am sending a group east to find the source of our problems."

"No official from Amagon has been to Laman in a hundred years," Aren said. *I think I might be salivating.*

"Today is a day of firsts," Aldarion said. "I have placed all meetings of the Councils under suspension, and they will remain that way until we know what is going on." He glanced at Terrol and Donnovar and the others. "You are dismissed."

They cleared the room. Aren made to move after them, but Aldarion stopped him.

"Not you, Aren. I want to discuss the mission I have for you." He reached across his desk for a blue bottle. "Have a cup of summerwine."

Aren waived him off. "My stomach is unsettled." He could not handle such a robust flavor in the middle of the night. He was barely able to keep down the ocean of springwine he had guzzled in bed with Merani only hours before.

"Was that even true?" Aren asked. "The mercenaries?"

"No. It was a test. Donnovar knew you would be able to see through it. Terrol was skeptical."

"Terrol has never liked me."

"He doesn't know you."

"I don't want him to know me."

"It is his duty to be suspicious."

"Is it his duty to be an asshole?"

"Forget about Terrol for a moment." The Lord Protector gestured across the room.

Aren heard the door open behind him. He turned to see a small, pale woman of indeterminate age wearing hooded robes of blue and grey like the colors of evening clouds. The hood was drawn over her head, and it bobbed as she stepped across the room on tiny sandals. She had the look of a sprite—pointy eyes, pointy nose, and pointy smile.

"Welcome, Tanashri," Aldarion said warmly. "You are just in time."

"I pride myself on timeliness," she said. "It is the way of the Sisterhood."

"The Sisterhood?" Aren asked. "What is one of them doing here? They are users." Aren felt himself waver under her gaze. He tried to study her, but his eyes shifted themselves away whenever he tried to look too long at her. He did not like her at all. He was distrustful of anyone so...pointy.

"You are familiar with them?" Aldarion asked.

"I've read about them in the Histories," Aren said. "Based in Noria across the sea. A small enclave. They are named the Order of Clymane Lunanok, only no one ever calls them that. They train women exclusively to use magick, in response to the Ministry long ago excluding women from its ranks. They are big fish in a small pond in Noria and dominate the politics there. They have a preferred advisory status in the Kingdom of Bolan, much in the way the Ministry does in Olbaran. Other than that, no official presence in any other nation. They have little influence out in the world. I am honestly surprised you let one in here."

"Tanashri has reached the rank of *Saderan* among their number," Aldarion said. "A Sister free to roam the world with the authority of their High Maja."

"I am aware of the position," Aren said.

"It's similar to your rank of magistrate. The two of you have much in common."

"We have *the magick* in common," Aren said.

"Precisely," Aldarion said. "You have always been very quick. This killer is no ordinary man. He has special talents which keep him one step ahead of my men, even my Sarenwalkers."

Aren suddenly knew why he was here. "He has the magick. The assassin used magick." His eyes went wide.

"This man used the magick *during* his escape," Aldarion said. "He has fled. We think on the way to Westgate in Olbaran, and from there to Laman. You can trace him. You are one of the best."

Aren suddenly did not know what to do with his hands, alternating resting them on his hips, waist, or belt. *A mission for the Lord Protector himself.* He could think of no other trace of such importance in the history of Amagon. *This is the chance of a lifetime.* But there was a nagging thought keeping his feet fixed firmly on the ground.

"The user is in the rough," Aren said. "Loose in the wide open. You want me to try to *ride rough* after him? That is not my forte."

Aldarion cleared his throat, and sipped from the cup on his desk. "I was told you are the best. You were the youngest successful apprentice in history, your record is exemplary, and most important of all, you have never lost a trace."

"A trace across open country is nearly impossible." *Sarker could tell you that.*

"I have faith in your abilities," Aldarion said. "You are indeed your master's student."

"I can't promise anything. How cold is the scene? What state was the afterglow in?"

"The Sweepers have already made a full report," Aldarion said. "You will receive the only copies of their findings. I trust in your skill."

"They have obtained significant samples of sensitized fluorescence," Tanashri said. "Two samples from a recent scene were sealed in glass jars."

Oh thank the many, many gods. Two separate samples of sensitized fluorescence means I can run the spectral shift algorithms to calculate direction and location. "How quickly were they sealed? How high in magnitude were they? I need to know how long before they fade out to know how much time we have."

"Everything will be included in the report," Aldarion said. "It is important that your pursuit begin immediately. The user did more than just try to kill me, Aren. He took three girls with him."

"Girls?" Aren felt his stomach knot. "Who are they? Where did they come from?"

"Never mind that. The details are unimportant. Aren, we do not expect them all to survive the journey to Laman with this user. You need to find them first if you can."

Aren hardened his expression. "I will."

"I knew this knowledge would make you focus your attention as best you can."

"Where does Laman fit into this?" Aren asked. "How do they know he is going that direction?"

"Did my man show you the dead body before bringing you here?"

Aren nodded. "I saw him. He was killed conventionally."

"A map was stolen from the premises," Aldarion said. "A map of Laman."

"The assassin killed him for a map?"

"A very specific one. That, combined with information Terrol has uncovered, confirms it. Because we know where he is going, we have an advantage. Even better, he is not aware that we know."

"I'll catch him. I promise."

"This is a very dangerous user. An entire village on the frontier we share with the Kingdom of Olbaran was massacred. This is no ordinary person."

Aren was already watching imaginary evidence dancing in his mind, wondering what hint and trick he would find to unspool the mystery of the assassin.

Then the door opened again.

A man stepped through and hovered at the far end of the room. His shoulders stooped, though he was very tall. His joints were bent as if incredibly rheumatic. He wore shirts of many shades of grey, with a faded black cloak over them. He had eyes of indiscernible color sunken deep within his bony face. He looked like a beggar or a woodsman freshly returned from a long ranging.

"This is Raviel," Aldarion said.

"Why is he here?" Aren asked.

"Aren," Aldarion said. "You must understand..."

Aren pointed at Raviel. "I don't know who this is. Who is this? Why is this person standing here?"

"Raviel is bringing a wealth of history to this," Aldarion said.

"Why is he here? Why is the Saderan here? I don't know these people. I can't trust people I don't know, and I can't work with people I don't trust."

"Aren, there is an explanation..."

"Damn it all, you know who the best Glasseye in all of Amagon is. Where is he? Why am I not standing next to Toran Sarker?"

Aldarion paused a long time. He glanced at Tanashri, and then back to Aren. He let out long breath. "Aren, Sarker is dead."

Aren tipped over backward, crashed through the floor, and fell into the earth, to its very center and back to standing again. Tremors gripped his hands. He shook his head, refusing the very idea of it. "Dead, no, no. Dead. No, not dead. He is not dead. That is wrong. He is not dead. That can't be. How can that be?"

"Donnovar's people tracked him to a border town. He had been meeting with a group of people there. We are not sure who. But when he was making his return, he was killed."

Aren nodded his head, staring at the desk, the carpets, the tapestries, anywhere but another person's eyes. "Magick?"

"We can't say for sure. But it appears likely."

"Same user? The same one?"

Aldarion nodded. "We think so."

"He's gone," Aren whispered. It didn't make sense. Sarker was like an old coat, a nagging cough, the sky itself. It was something that you grew accustomed to always being there, and to one day have it not was more than Aren could fathom.

"Raviel is being sent with you in his stead," the Lord Protector said. "He is a Glasseye."

Aren looked him over with revulsion. "He is an outlander. He is not even from here. Where is he from?"

"He has been spoken of highly by the court of the Kingdom of Lenagon. And Tanashri is an expert in captures. They will aid you on the trace. I have faith in you. Understand?"

"Yes."

"This man you seek is of special interest to the Sisterhood," Tanashri said. "I will assist you in taking him into custody, then he will be brought before the High Maja and put into the fires. This arrangement will benefit all."

"You will find Stoppers in Westgate," Aldarion said. "There is a secret station of the Outer Guard located there. You will brief them on their functions. Tanashri will be there to oversee the capture."

"As you wish," Aren said.

"There is more. You will all ultimately answer to *Raviel*."

Aren flinched. "The outlander?"

Aldarion nodded. "He is a skilled Tracer, and is familiar with the back roads of Olbaran."

Raviel bore a half-concealed grin.

Aren noticed, and his eyes glazed over with suspicion. *They are trying to replace Sarker with this half-drawn caricature. I do not need his help.* He wished he could tell them to send the Lenagon-man away.

"You will ride out tomorrow. Donnovar will lead a full battalion of the Outer Guard to Laman under the guise of a diplomatic mission. Your status will be that of a military ambassador. It will prevent unwanted questions. Having you among them will have a benefit of masking your pursuit from the assassin. Glasseyes from our Render Tracer corps normally pursue alone or in small teams. No one will suspect you would be attached to such a large group, and Donnovar assures me his men will be able to move as fast as any Rough Rider Pursuit Squadron."

"A full battalion? Moving that many men through Olbaran would be difficult to keep secret."

"Arrangements have been made. Raviel has the necessary passes, and you will have a path to follow that will keep you away from the lands of certain lords, and away from the cities beyond Westgate. This mission must be accomplished secretly. We do not want Olbaran aware that one of our Glasseyes is operating within their boundaries. They would try to arrest you. Once you are past Westgate, you will take only backways and lonely roads. Terrol is going with you to make sure our cover holds."

"Why him? This is a mission for the *Outer* Guard. He belongs *inside* Amagon."

"I know he is not the most personable officer, but he is the best at what he does. I am sending Margol as well."

"Your bodyguard? You need him now more than ever."

"His mission is to protect Donnovar. This expedition is a matter of priority, and it requires every possible precaution. Its success will protect my person better than a bodyguard."

Aren was stunned into silence. *I am more than a magistrate now. I will have authority beyond any Glasseye. I have the freedom to make decisions, and I have a voice in every discussion. I am no longer Toran Sarker's apprentice. I am his equal. I am Aren of Amagon, and I can make my own name remembered.* The prestige of this expedition would quiet even the loudest of his detractors. They would be forced to respect him. Finally.

He forced himself to speak. "Of course I will go."

"You will choose some trusted men to accompany you. Your close council and the like. Tell them no more than is necessary, and say nothing of our meeting. You understand your duty, I gather?"

"Of course."

"Rest up. Sunrise is not far off. You leave in the morning. You are dismissed."

＊＊＊＊＊＊＊＊＊＊

Hallan awoke on his back in tangled weeds on the shore of an unfamiliar river. His fingers trembled and his legs stiffened painfully when he attempted to move. He did not know how he came to be here.

He thought the woman seated upright beside him was his mother. But when he rubbed his eyes he saw she was someone else, a young lady, unwashed hair, a birthmark like a half moon under her ear. She wore a wrinkled summer dress, turned brown from the mud, and stiff from use.

He propped himself up on his elbows and lay still. She noticed him, and held a finger over her lips. "You have to be quiet," she said. "He likes it when we are quiet." She never once looked up at him after that. She went back to braiding rushes into little shapes and designs.

"Who does?"

"The man."

He looked all around. "Where are we?"

"On the way to Westgate."

"I have a friend. His brother lives there," Hallan said.

"Keep your voice down. He likes it when we are quiet."

"Where is my mother?"

She shrugged. "He took you from a mountain. He says he stopped what they were doing, so that some lord would not get it. But it went to you instead. He said he is keeping you for himself. To study you. To find out how they did it. So he can do it himself, the same way they did it to you. For his ordeal. He says the thing he does is dangerous. He says he can use you to keep him from dying when the time comes."

"What does that mean?" he asked.

She shrugged.

"Does he talk to you a lot?" he asked.

"Sometimes. When he is finished. He talks a lot then. But who knows what it means. "

"I don't remember the mountain. Where is my family? Where are my friends?"

She shrugged again. "He says the lord should not have betrayed him. So he stole what the lord wanted."

"What lord? I have never seen a lord."

"That is just what Mayvene told me."

"Who is Mayvene?"

"The oldest." She paused and thought. "And the newest. She has long legs. We think she is the one who is going to run away next."

"Are there any boys here?" he asked.

"No. Just girls. He doesn't like boys. But you are special."

He felt something in his pocket. He pulled it out and raised it to his eyes. The object was small and rounded, black stone. It was a sculpted figurine, jet black, polished to a shine, as smooth as glass. A man with no head and no legs, a fat belly and arms, with odd shapes instead of hands.

She glanced at it. "Where did you get that?"

He shrugged.

"Don't let him see it. He doesn't like us to have things."

"I want to go home."

"There won't be one."

"My friend Murie is a girl. Is she here?"

The girl thought for a moment, then shook her head. "No. No new girls. Just you."

"What happens when people try to leave?"

"One got away once, I think."

"When do we meet Mayvene?" Hallan asked.

"Tonight. Then we walk a long way. If you are nice, Mayvene might carry you some of the way."

"I will be nice," Hallan said.

"Shhhh. He likes it when we are quiet."

6

My Kind

"THEY ARE BURNING AGAIN." Keluwen sniffed the air. The sun was high, the heat clinging to her like a blanket. She could not tell which way the smoke was coming from. The valley was a vast green sea, the villages hidden by thick knots of trees. The frontier between Amagon and Olbaran was like this for a hundred miles in any direction. Green grass, old trees, and villages tucked between like clusters of mushrooms.

"They caught another one," Cheli said.

"Another one of *my* kind," Keluwen said. She squeezed the grass between her fingers, feeling it through her gloves. She wished they had not chosen to meet up with the rest of their crew here. *Why couldn't it have been in a city? I like cities.* She hated wide open spaces enough as it was. It was tenfold worse among the old frontier villages. She had learned from the third time she had been hunted that men with hoes and rakes were just as bad as men with swords and spears. The look of terror and rage in their eyes was the same. The relieved laughter when they watched the flesh burn was the same. *They all hate my kind.*

Never trust one of us, Seb had told her. *We will only let you down.* Only he never let her down. Not once. The greatest friend in the world right until the end. Right up until she let *him* down.

Cheli made a face at her. "Orrinas is user, and Krid, and Vessander, and Zalash. You are not the only one, Kel."

"Here, yes. In this group. But in the world we are practically alone."

"True."

"It is the worst in little villages like this. Remote. Traditional. Superstitious. They think everyone special is a demon."

"They are not going to bother Orrinas or the others while they are over there," Cheli said. "No one knows who they are. They will be all right."

"I know that. Orrinas can protect himself. They all can. But no one protects the little children. They do not know any better. They are not clever. They cannot make anything strong. They cannot fight. So they are caught. And they are burned."

"That is not always the way it goes."

"Should I tell you about all the times I have been hunted by Glasseyes? Cheli girl? Hmm? Why do you think we have to hide out here and watch to be sure our *talented* friends are not pursued when they stroll out of the village they are lodging in? Why do we need this escape contingency? Because normals can turn on our kind in the blink of an eye. Even someone who has loved you your whole life up to then."

She held up her hand. "I am sorry, Kel. I do not mean to downplay. You are right of course. There should be a better way."

"They hate us," Keluwen said, turning back to look over the vacant hills. "Normals. I think deep down even *you* hate us, Cheli."

Cheli frowned. "You put words in others' mouths and thoughts in others' heads far too often."

"I know. I can't help it."

Cheli turned to look at her. "Leucas is in awe of you. And Hodo adores you. And whenever I stop being mad at you, I love you as well."

Keluwen cracked a smile. "I love you, too, Cheli girl. I'm sorry that I'm the way I am."

Cheli narrowed her eyes. "I forgive you. But I'm still mad at you."

Keluwen did not look at her. She smiled to herself. She had omitted one little detail from Cheli. *Even I hate my kind. I shouldn't, but I do.* She hated wizards and sorcerers. She hated all users. She hated the magick she used. She hated it for existing. If there was no magick, then she would never have been able to be born with it. She would never have been anything but normal. She would never have needed to run. Have been hunted. Have done what she did. "I wonder what this one did. Stole a loaf a bread? A handful of copper tossers? Knock down a bully from a wealthy family?"

"It must be something worse than that," Cheli said. "Murder. Or rape. Violence of some kind."

"You claim to be worldly, but you know little and less of what goes on. Safe in your little enclaves, reading your old books, all of you. Even crusty old Krid spends too much time in hiding. You come out into the real world for little dalliances, to listen to secrets one day and whisper them again another. You never see what is before your eyes. They burn us for next to nothing."

"You are assuming."

"I have seen it. For every one that deserved a fire, there were ten more who didn't."

"Subjective," Cheli said.

"You have never left the northlands, Cheli girl," Keluwen said. "In Cadria the Priests come for the girls like monsters." She released a cynical chuckle. "At least they have balance. They love the boys, to make more like themselves. Axis Ardent should love them. The Ministry's hatred is so well organized."

"We hate the Priests and you know it well," Cheli said.

"It is worse in the south," Keluwen said. "I have heard when the Priests go on crusade in Mekrash Valley they even burn the infants, boys or girls if they catch them, everyone. What some call justice, others call atrocity."

"What do you want me to do about it, Kel?" Cheli asked.

Nothing. No one can do anything. This is the way the world is. "I do not like the fires," Keluwen said, taking a swig of water from her leather bladder.

"They are going to burn *him* though," Cheli said. "You want that, don't you?"

"We all make exceptions, don't we? Some more than others." She licked the last drops of summerwine from the bottle she had opened only that morning. "Ones like him are the reason they burn all the rest. If anyone deserves to burn it is him. They ruin it for everyone else."

"Are you two going to argue all day?" Nils asked, sitting down behind them. He handed a bowl a sweetmeal to Cheli.

"Thank you, Nils," Cheli said, genuinely and urgently.

"None for me, Nils?" Keluwen asked.

He shrugged. "I didn't know you wanted any."

Yet you somehow knew Cheli wanted some. I am onto you, sly devil. "It is fine. My appetite is waning."

"Here, let me watch through the scope so you can eat," Nils offered.

"Are you certain?" Cheli asked. "It is not your shift."

He waved it over. "I do it gladly," he said. He reached into his coat and casually brought out Cheli's handcloth to wipe his brow.

He still has it. And she has not asked for it back.

Cheli plopped the scope down in his hands, and then turned her face hard into the sun to hide her blush.

You little shits are too sweet by half.

Nils watched the valley below, and Cheli ate, and Keluwen ruminated. It did not take long for Cheli's bowl to be empty, or for Keluwen's mind to be raging against boredom. It was sweet deliverance from Belleron when they spotted Orrinas returning.

"Here they are," Cheli said, peeking over the hill. "Orrinas is bringing them now."

Keluwen turned around and scooted down the hill on her rear until she reached the camp. She ignored Leucas and Hodo and Nils. She tried to ignore Krid Ballar, too, but his constant scowl made her remember how much she disliked him every few seconds. She feasted on Lissarian spiced breads, submerged in olive oil, and gnawed on a stick of dried beef while she waited.

When Orrinas came over the hill, she pretended not to see him. She was not sure why she did that.

He smiled regardless, leading the other half of their crew behind him. She barely knew anything about these three men. She never trusted strangers, but Orrinas told her he had confidence in each of them, and she trusted Orrinas more than all the rest of the world combined.

"Glad greetings," Leucas said. "Our brothers have returned."

Keluwen had never met Bonsinar or Zalash before. They were southerners, with heavy accents. Bonsinar preferred unhelpful smirks and an old wool coat, dyed green, long since faded to olive. Zalash was in danger of going cross-eyed from the frequency with which he looked down his nose at everyone else. He wore triple layer silks, crawling with golden vines, to make sure everyone remembered exactly how far beneath him they were. She never bothered to ask where they hailed from. She didn't care.

She *had* spoken to Vessander once or twice. His accent was cleaner, and his demeanor brighter. He wore an olive velvet vest over a cream colored tunic, sleeves rolled up to his elbows the way the corners of his mouth rolled up into autonomous smiles. Samartanians were perpetually cheerful. But she would have been fine with it even if he wasn't.

These people are not here to be friends.

And I am not here to make any.

They are here to help us stop him.

All three were users.

My kind.

Introductions were made, and pleasantries exchanged. Keluwen stayed out of it.

"Our friends have news," Orrinas told the others.

Keluwen listened while facing the other way, as if merely an eavesdropper.

"He is still in Westgate," Orrinas went on. "This is good news for us. A chance."

"Why?" Cheli asked. "Why is he still there?"

"We do not know," Bonsinar said.

Bonsinar was a purveyor of *blank impulses*, like Keluwen. A *puncher*. The most common renders that users could learn and use were simple shapes—spheres, circles, squares, lines—imbued with a size, strength, and duration if they were intended to be stationary, *or* with a size, mass, velocity, and direction if they were intended to be a projectile. Most of her kind could use them, she knew. Even if they had mastered the bending of other physical laws, they often possessed an arsenal of blank impulses and blank shields as well.

Bonsinar was far stronger than she, far more experienced, less wasteful with his energy. *But I have precision. I waste more, but aim better. I can imbue direction streams and hit a silver tosser on the ground at a hundred paces with just my peripheral vision. Let him try to make anything that can do that.*

"The man with black eyes always hits and moves on," Nils said. "He never stops. Never stays in the same city for more that a day or two."

"He has this time though," Zalash said.

Zalash was a *massman*. He could increase or reduce the mass of any object, the degree of change based on which streams he could command. Orrinas said Zalash had many degrees of change he could render. Some like him could only alter the equivalent of a few pounds either way. But he had mastered the streams of hundreds of different mass changes, all the way up to thousands of pounds. Perhaps tens of thousands. With that many different streams of mass change in his repertoire, the only thing restricting him was his own body and how much energy he could put into the change before he ran out and had to eat and sleep. He was very good, and he knew it, and by the look of things, he wanted to make sure everyone else knew it, too.

"What has changed?" Keluwen asked. "Something must be different."

"Maybe he knows the southlander is coming for him?" Leucas suggested, between bites of mutton sandwich.

Hodo Grubb nodded. "The southlander has not exactly been keeping his movements hidden."

"I don't like it," Krid said, scratching his unshaven face. "He knows something."

Krid was as suspicious as he was strong, neither of which were half as much as he was an asshole. He could form blank impulses, but Orrinas told her they were nothing memorable. He was a specialist in another area. He was a *frictioneer*. He could alter the effects of friction between two objects. His powers were what they called the *passive* variety. He could only increase or decrease *previously existing* friction. Orrinas had told her that some frictioneers with *active* streams could create friction between two objects that were not even in contact. But this was good enough. Everyone had to touch something sometime, and when they did, Krid could make them pay for it.

"Maybe he is having trouble finding what he is looking for there," Cheli said.

"He has been preparing for this for a decade," Krid said. "You truly believe he has not figured everything out in advance? He has scooped up every stone in a matter of weeks. That means he has known where they were for a long time. He was waiting until he could take them all at once. So as not to tip his hand."

"He knew we would have moved them," Nils said.

"Is he really that good?" Leucas asked.

"I am telling you, he planned this all in advance," Krid said.

"Plans rarely last the time it takes to write them down," Cheli said.

Krid grimaced at her.

"Our informant in Westgate says she knows for certain that he is still there. Visiting the widow. Living with her."

"He is with the widow?" Cheli asked, holding a hand to her mouth.

"Proof positive that he knows," Vessander said. "And that time is running out."

Vessander was a *darknician*. He could change the way light behaved over a certain distance, reducing the reflection of light to zero within that zone. She was not certain what his maximum dimensions were, but Orrinas said they would be sufficient for whatever work needed to be done. Of all of them, he was the only one who had no blank impulses of his own.

"The informant says the Rover is still there as well," Bonsinar said. "But is unable to tell if he is after the same thing, or just what is left of her fortune. He is keeping a close eye on her though. We will hopefully know more soon."

"So all we know is that he suspects it is there," Nils said.

"His whole life has been this pursuit," Orrinas said. "Let each of us remember this when we think about how far we think we are ahead of him."

Sweet Orrinas. Her husband. Her very old man, caution burned into him with age. He was what they called a *heater*. He could increase the amount of heat in a system by pulling in altered reality. He could decrease it as well, but less efficiently. He was the most experienced of them all. She knew this without ever having to know anything about the others. He possessed so many learned streams that he could raise temperature incrementally a few degrees at a time from the point where he could freeze water all the way to the point where he could make steel turn white hot and begin to liquify. No other she had ever met had such precise control, and such strength.

She smiled.

My kind.

"What about the elder?" Cheli asked. "He must know something about this."

"I have asked Romi and her brothers to seek him out," Orrinas said. "But it has been difficult. Lawlessness has increased in the slum he inhabits. They will get to him by the time we arrive, I am certain."

"The old man's words must be taken with a grain of salt," Zalash said. "He speaks in poetry and riddles."

"All that matters is that he is there," Keluwen said, still not turning to face any of them. "That means we can catch up to him."

"And do what?" Bonsinar asked.

Cheli fished a hand into Orrinas' rucksack without permission and lifted the leather-bound folio. "We have this"

"Which is *what* exactly?" Zalash asked.

"His composite," Cheli said. "Straight from Amagon."

Zalash's mouth fell open. "Where did you get this?"

"The one silver lining of Paladan's misadventure," Keluwen said. "He persuaded someone to steal this from their sealed archives and bring it to him."

Bonsinar stared at it as if he was watching the grass turn into gold. "How long?"

"It has been sitting there collecting dust for *three years*," Orrinas said.

"And now it is ours," Krid said. "Every stream from every render from every scene where he has ever opened the door to the Slipstream. All marked, imprinted, analyzed."

"How do we know it is everything he can do?" Vessander asked. "He could have held something back."

"How often do you hold something back, Vessander?" Keluwen asked. "Users like us do not know how to hold anything back. We use magick, and we cannot stop ourselves. How careful do you think he would be to hold something back any of the half-dozen times they had him surrounded?"

"Each time they faced him they knew more of his streams," Orrinas said. "Forcing him to use novel renders each time. The reports indicate he was running out of new streams by the end. If they had but a little more advantage, they would have had him that time."

"And now the fruits of their blood and toil is a gift to us," Cheli said. "We will begin from a place ten moves ahead of him."

"You will each be given a set of *imprints*," Orrinas said. "Nils and Hodo will go over them with you. Memorize your list of streams well. It will be up to each of us who can touch the Slipstream to hold his streams, even while we use our own. Bandi has Stoppers, but not enough. We will have to do double work. It will be the only way we can defeat him. We have no access to tinwood leaf resin, and he always has a bodyguard of his cultists around him when he moves in cities to screen him from surprise with conventional weapons."

"How exactly will we spring this trap?" Keluwen asked. "I know we have the *composite*, but how will we get him to come to a place of our choosing?"

She could feel Orrinas glaring at her. "We must put our plan in place. If we can arrive in time, we will need a *lure*."

"Bait, you mean," Keluwen said.

Krid shrugged. "We know what that scum likes."

"Always happy to make a sacrificial lamb of one of the normals, eh Krid?" *It makes it easier to hate my own kind because you are among them, Krid.*

"We have no leverage," Zalash said. "He is there seeking what he needs. He follows his own goals without emotion, and then he disappears into the night. No one can track him."

"We have to think of something," Keluwen said.

"We do," Zalash said. "I recall hearing things did not work out so well the last time Orrinas let you come along on a hunt, Keluwen." He pronounced her name Kel-U-wen.

She hated the way he said her name more than she hated standing shoeless on burning coals. She hated it all the more because she knew he was doing it on purpose. "Say my name, Zalash. Say KEL-uwen."

"You nearly cost us—" Zalash said.

"But we caught Shadro Herrick," Cheli said. "We stopped him before he ever became luminous. And we couldn't have done it without Kel."

Thank you, Cheli girl. I shouldn't have argued with you.

"But we know his proclivities," Vessander said cheerfully. "Our only chance is to distract him from his goal by giving him something else he *wants*."

"You mean giving him a *little girl*," Keluwen said, turning around to face them. "Isn't that what you mean, Vessander?"

"For the good of the many," Bonsinar said.

"You are fucking disgusting," Keluwen said. "*We* are fucking disgusting." *Because I am going to sit by and let you do this.*

Zalash turned to Orrinas. "Are you certain she is up to this?"

"Fuck you," Keluwen said. "I am up to anything."

Zalash ignored her. "Is she, Orrinas? If there is but a hint she will not have the proper discipline, we must remove her from this group now."

To all the hells with him. He wants tact. He wants dignity to these proceedings. I gave up on dignity a long time ago. "Go ahead. Remove me. See how well you do without."

"She is headstrong, Zalash," Orrinas said. "And she is powerful. Precise. Devious."

"She is rash," Zalash said. "Overconfident. Indecisive. Deceitful."

Fuck you, too, Zalash. You were no prince where you came from either.

"She is going," Orrinas said. "We need her. We need everyone. I feel we need more than *Axis Ardent* has given to us."

There we go with the powers above again. Who is making these calls? Who decides whether the most dangerous man in the world can be defeated by three users? Or five? But not seven, or ten? "Just get me to Westgate," she said. "I will make sure he never draws another breath."

Zalash did not seem convinced. Bonsinar seemed on the fence. Vessander looked like he was leaning toward her side of the argument.

But none of them mattered. Orrinas ran this cadre. It was his decision. *And he would not dare cut his wife out of this.*

"We already have an ally leading a force after our quarry," Orrinas said. "The southlander."

"A *force?*" Keluwen asked. "The southerner is leading a force after *him?*"

"Something very conspicuous," Orrinas said. "All *his* attention will be on it."

"Directing his eyes away from us," Krid said.

"We must hire a longrunner," Orrinas said. "To deliver our instructions to Westgate."

"Why not ask Duran?" Keluwen asked. "He is always in that area."

"He is already in Westgate," Orrinas said. "But not to meet with us."

"What? Why? Since when? If not to help us, then what is the point?"

"I received a new message," Orrinas said. "He came down from the mountain. He has gone to Westgate. He is there now, looking for someone else, a missing child."

Keluwen spit up the water she had been trying to sip, and nearly choked to death with laughter. "You have got to be kidding me. Now? Of all times? That is what they are wasting our time with? In the midst of all this? Do they not know what is happening here? We are close, Orrinas. We could catch him this time. We could really, truly end it. And they are going to play these games?"

"What did I say about respect?" Krid asked. "We serve *Axis Ardent. Axis Ardent* tells us what to do. Our organization has never steered us wrong."

"Mayhap they could have sent a letter to Palad sooner then," Keluwen said bitterly. "Or were they sleeping in that day?"

"I am warning you," Krid said.

"Oh, gum your own asshole, Krid," she said. "I am sick well nigh unto death of the sound your mouth makes."

He lurched to his feet, the tin plate of half-eaten lamb and beans tumbling into the noonday grass. His eyes poked out of his head like knives. "You wretched, little—"

"Say it," Keluwen goaded him, she slid one of her sapphire gloves down from the elbow to the wrist. "Go on. Be honest with me."

Krid froze. He watched her gloves closely. He shook with rage, his hands in fists, the tendons around his knuckles tight as cords.

But Cheli stepped between them. "This is infantile," she said to Krid. Then she turned to face Keluwen. "Of *both* of you."

Keluwen took a step back.

Krid turned and walked away, mumbling to himself.

"We serve Axis Ardent," Orrinas said. "We do not know why, and we do not have to know why. And we must not lament it. Any more than we would lament the sky turning dark when the sun has set. It is simply something that happens, and we must endeavor to work around it."

Keluwen spat in the grass, but managed to get most of it on her own boots. *Shit.* "I doubt this is more important than destroying a *luminous immortal.*"

"It does not matter," Orrinas said. "Duran will not be able to help us, and the sun sets in the west. Neither of these things you can change."

"Give me half a chance," she said.

He smiled. "Now put your mind to work. We need a plan. And if you want one without bait, then you must think of an alternative."

"I already have," she said. "But you are not going to like it."

7

Trace

HORSESHIT; WHEN THERE WAS enough of it, it became more than a smell. And right now it threatened to take over Aren's whole life.

The heat made it worse. The dust made it worse still. The way the saddle bent his legs made it abysmal. He found that the joy of the trace was tempered by how awful it was to ride rough.

"How long has it been since you had to ride on a horse?" Corrin asked.

"A long time," Aren said, holding the reins for dear life. "Maybe not since I was a scribe for the Warhost, and I was not very good at it then." He wiped the sweat from his eyes, and brushed some of the dust away from his riding cloak. A pouch of malagayne sat lightly on his hip, tethered to his belt. Beside it was strapped the sword he never used. His tracer satchel was secured tightly to the saddle behind him. "Whenever it was, it was too long ago. Perhaps about the time you forgot that clothing was made in varieties of color other than black. Don't you know it's summertime?"

"It couldn't have been that long ago," Corrin said, putting one hand above his eyes to block the sunlight and slapping his saddle with the other. As usual, he wore black wool trousers, black leather riding boots, a soft black wool shirt under a black tunic beneath a coat of black iron mail slit to the waist, with a boiled black leather vest over both of those, and a black wool cloak draped over his shoulders.

As Aren swayed along with the column of cavalry, grinding their way along the old dusty road, rolling past the emerald trees of the fringe of the Sarenwood, he silently wondered how many black sheep had been bereft of their warmth for this one man's wardrobe. "It has only been two days and I'm already sore from the saddle."

Corrin smirked. "I believe that this is evidence that you have been a magistrate for too long. Traveling everywhere by coach makes a man soft. Even a Glasseye."

"It's part of the job. Pleasant rides on cushioned seats."

"Do they let you wear slippers and bedclothes too? I thought you were a Render Tracer, not a princess from Hylamar."

"If you ever found a steady profession, you might get to enjoy better treatment, too."

"I already have a profession," Corrin announced. "Drinking ale, bedding women, and cutting people with swords. The perks suit me just fine. Just because my best friend suits up as a lackey for the Lord Protector doesn't mean I have to do the same."

Aren laughed. "So instead you are the lackey of the lackey. You certainly jumped on that purse full of silvers I dropped in your lap quick enough."

"At least I don't have to pay my friends to spend time with me," Corrin said. "What do you think, Reidos?"

Reidos turned to him and yawned. His auburn hair was draped low across his face this morning. "I think you both have selected appropriate professions."

Behind Reidos, Inrianne rode her own small pony, which was a dwarf among the strong war-horses of the Outer Guard. She came with Tanashri, but did not seem to be a Sister herself. Aren was uncertain of the particulars of their relationship. She had a thick golden mane of hair, and slender eyes. She wore a bright white sheer gown beneath robes that she always seemed to allow to fall off her shoulders and open over her chest.

"I suppose being an expert marksman doesn't automatically give you the innate and deeply spiritual understanding needed to decide a profession," Corrin said. "Even if you are eighty years old."

"Forty," Reidos corrected him. "And I look better than you did at seventeen."

"Damn Andristi," Corrin said. "Get a little bit of their blood in your ancestry and you live an extra century."

"What is this about Andristi blood?" Inrianne asked.

"The Andristi age more slowly than other people," Aren told her. "They hit an age plateau when they mature, and remain the same for decades before aging begins. Reidos is half Andristi. With half the blood comes half the reward. His mother was from one of the Andristi clans descended from the Mahhennin, Weirmaheir's people, who rallied to his banner during the Great War against the Tyrant Kradishah and the tree-burners."

"Reidos is more than twice our age," Corrin said. "That's why he's here. We need the wisdom of the elderly."

"And why then are you here?" Inrianne asked coolly.

Corrin smiled broadly. "Because I happen to be a warrior of great magnificence, and Aren knows I can outwit, outfight, or outrun anyone."

Reidos raised his eyebrows to that.

"*Almost* anyone," Corrin corrected himself.

"I think it had more to do with it being short notice, and you being the only pennysword in Amagon who spends every night at the same tavern, and who could blow through their last purse of silver in a fortnight," Reidos said.

"You were there, too," Corrin said.

"Never said I wasn't. I'm in for the pennies, not the braggadocio."

"That makes about as much sense as *not* bringing a keg of whiskey on this journey," Corrin said, pointing to the massive wagons stacked with barrels of ale. "What am I supposed to drink on this trip? Ale? Just ale? Ale is not legendary enough for a man of my stature."

"So you are friends?" Inrianne asked uncertainly. "Because it seems like you all hate each other."

Reidos laughed. "That is the secret of true friendship; to always be one step away from being sick to death of each other."

Corrin looked on ahead at the column of horses. "Friend means after you call them names and kick shit in their eyes, you turn around and walk through fire for them. You brave the storm for them. You walk the wind for them. You cross the world and shake the heavens for them. You meet their enemies as if they were your own, steel in your hand. You love them to hell and back."

Aren smiled. *Hard edges but soft as shit.*

Reidos threw a pebble at Corrin. It struck him in the left ear.

Corrin winced and cupped a hand over it. "Is that from the roof? Have you been holding that and waiting all this time? You piece of shit farod. I am going drown you in ale in your sleep."

"One man's threat is another man's good time." Reidos chuckled.

"Aren obviously met you in a tavern, Corrin," Inrianne said. "But how did he meet you, Reidos?"

"In the Warhost of Amagon," Reidos said. "I was a shooter in the archery corps. Aren secretaried for the quartermaster when he was a boy."

"You should show her *your* medals," Corrin laughed. "They always make a lady's eyes twinkle."

"Marksmanship," Aren said. "Reidos could hit anything. He might as well have been born in the Sarenwood."

"Speaking of the Sarenwood, it looks like we have some actual Sarenwalkers with us," Reidos changed the subject.

"Five of them," Corrin said. "Do they always send that many?"

"I don't know for sure," Reidos said.

"Not you, halfwit," Corrin said. "The one who knows everything. Aren, what say you?"

"It's not unheard of for an officer of Donnovar's rank to have them in his personal retinue," Aren said.

"Five," Corrin said. "A party of Sarenwalkers of that size is the same as having another hundred soldiers."

The Sarenwalkers wore brilliant emerald cloaks pinned with the Moon of Saren in silver with traces of Tobrian jade and glittering aquamarine. Underneath they were dressed alike in long-sleeved linen shirts and trousers of varying shades of brown. They had tied their bows and quivers to their saddle rigging. Their fighting staffs were strapped to their backs and poked up above their heads like banner poles without the banners.

"The Sarenwood produces the best trackers in Amagon," Reidos told Inrianne. "They say a Sarenwalker can follow the path of the wind."

"They are also the best trained fighters in the west," Corrin said.

"They do not carry swords," Inrianne observed. "Or wear armor."

"Sarenwalkers hardly ever carry swords," Reidos said. "They usually prefer quarterstaffs, and they are famous for their use of *somashalk* hand-axes." He pointed at one of them, its handle the length of a man's arm from wrist to shoulder, with a polished axe head the size of a flat hand.

"One of *these* Sarenwalkers has a sword," Corrin said. "Look right there."

"I see it," Aren said, noticing a faint shimmer of blue from its hilt. "Look at the blue tint. That means it was folded with Saren-steel."

"A rare weapon," Reidos said. "Saren-steel won't chip or rust."

"And the edges can be sharpened beyond any ordinary blade," Corrin drawled, salivating. "I would kill for a blade like that. I mean literally. I am considering it."

Behind them rode the regulars of the Outer Guard. They wore thick steel cuirasses over coats of mail, and their helmets had narrow tops terminating in sharp points. They all wore sashes of the patriotic golden-orange of Amagon, which twined around their necks like brightly colored serpents. One and all rode upon massive warhorses, animals that could have trampled a giant. Their guttural snorts and shrill whinnies were enough to make Aren flinch. And their shitpiles were enough to make him throw up in his mouth a little every quarter mile or so.

"They polish their armor too much," Corrin complained. "It keeps shining the sun in my eyes."

"He still whines like a baby," Reidos observed.

"We should have brought his mother," Aren said.

"Well, we may not have a mother, but we definitely have a Sister," Reidos said.

"They are not known for their charm." Aren glanced at Tanashri. She seemed so tiny next to the men of the Outer Guard. He had to look at her twice to be sure she was the same person he had spoken with in Aldarion's chamber. For some reason he remembered her being much taller and more intimidating. Her pale face hovered beneath the cowl of her blue-grey robe, and her chin stood out sharply, not large or long, just pointy. Her eyes scanned everything with her usual Sisterhood indifference.

Beside her Aren saw Terrol perched on his horse like some vile crossbreed of a bluejay and a vulture. He stared at everything around him, as if even nature itself was suspect. He stared at Aren frequently, eyes accusing him of being terrible at his job, sneer declaring him unfit for the task, posture announcing him inferior.

Donnovar, on the other hand, sat like a titan atop his horse. He wore a cuirass of red steel, well polished, with matching bracers and faulds. Aren had worked with him on a trace or two, and had grown to enjoy his company in the taverns after long meetings with the Lord Protector. Donnovar had always treated Sarker like a brother and Aren like a nephew. His officers rode always close to him, Sebel, the lieutenant; Balthoren, the battalion crossbow specialist; and Retheld, the axeman.

"Look at that Donnovar fellow," Corrin said. "Now *that* is a true war captain."

"As compared to what?" Reidos asked.

"To Aren for one thing," Corrin said. "And then you. Then everyone else. But definitely not me."

"You really think you would make a better war captain than that?" Reidos asked, chuckling. "You would lead an army of none, if you ever sobered up enough to make it out your front door."

Corrin pinched his lips and squinted at him. "I am here, aren't I?"

Reidos pointed. "Look at that, would you? The greatsword strapped to his back is only a head shorter than the tiny Saderan riding beside him."

Aren recognized the polished red steel of the hilt and the tiny sapphire upon the crossguard. "*Braxis*, the sword is named. A gift from one of the Lord Protector's predecessors, Trier. Forged by Allyn Moros, the most skilled swordsmith in Medion."

Corrin regarded him suspiciously. "You seem to know an awful lot about another man's weapon."

Aren smiled. "It's Bravonian steel, Corrin."

"A Bravonian steel blade," Corrin drooled. "I knew there was a reason I was friends with you. Blue steel and green steel on the same trip. They had better sleep with those blades if they want to keep them."

"You couldn't even lift something like that," Reidos said. "And Donnovar's armor is battle worn. He doesn't strike me as someone who would shrink from a fight with the likes of you."

"The Sarenmoor," Aren said. "Dirty fighting there."

"But Donnovar still polishes the plates well," Reidos said. "Dents and all."

"He doesn't do that for show," Aren said. "He doesn't care how shiny he looks for the Council. He does it because he thinks it is the proper way for a commander to appear before his men."

"He looks regal," Inrianne said. "Like a king."

"Donnovar has the unwavering respect of these men," Aren said. "This same battalion has followed him on countless expeditions. They would ride with him to the ends of the earth. So would I."

"You idolize him," Inrianne said.

"You have a lot to say for someone I do not know," Aren said.

She recoiled. "Your friend has a rude streak, Reidos."

I know all I need to know about you, Inrianne. He thought about why she was here, why Tanashri was so interested in her. She was a user of *magick*. He had needed thorough convincing that she was documented, and had no warrants out for her capture, and he forced Tanashri to supply her documentation papers before agreeing to it. *I will not travel with a rogue user.*

"Remember that farmer from Palatora?" Reidos asked, always quick to change the subject to avoid an argument. "We followed him for days. Turned out to be a swordmaster from the Lenagon School."

"That was years ago," Aren said.

"Corrin cuffed his ears. Remember? He didn't have his sword ready though."

"Are you telling that story again?" Corrin asked, rolling his eyes.

"He knocked you upside the head so hard you flopped like a sack," Reidos said. "You thought he was just a farmer."

"Why must you dwell on the stories that make me look like an idiot?" Corrin asked. "How was I supposed to know he had trained a hundred fighters right out of his barn?"

"I can't help it," Reidos said. "I don't think there are any stories that make you look good."

"Ugh!" Corrin said. "You do this every time I see you."

"Do what?" Reidos threw up his hands innocently. He laughed uncontrollably.

"Might I remind you that I was the one who saved your ass from that woodsman who liked to burn Mahhennin alive inside wicker baskets?" Corrin asked. "I don't hear thanks very often for *that* one."

"I would have escaped sooner or later," Reidos said.

"I should have let you die," Corrin complained. "It would have put a stop to your ridiculous jokes, like the one about the man from Noria."

"What's wrong with my jokes?" Reidos asked.

"You have too many," Corrin said. "You always mix up the punch lines."

"I do no such thing," Reidos said.

"You do too," Corrin said. "I quote, *There once was a man from Noria, and that's how the barbarian cut the cheese.*"

"That's not how it goes," Reidos said.

"The women always loved your jokes," Aren added. "They thought you were *so* clever."

"That speaks more for the caliber of the women than of the jokes," Corrin said.

Aren noticed Inrianne sneering again, this time at Corrin.

"We should see Westgate soon," Reidos changed the subject once again.

Corrin smirked. "Plenty of taverns in Westgate, and a few noteworthy brothels."

"What is so important about Westgate?" Inrianne asked.

"Westgate in one of the great cities of Olbaran," Aren said. "The junction point of all the roads coming west from Delvincourt, and north from Kessalmir."

"Are we boarding at a reputable inn at least?" Corrin asked.

Aren shook his head. "We'll be at the *way-station.*"

"Ugh," Corrin said. "Foul. Those things are ancient."

"They keep them up," Aren said. "The way-station in Westgate is the first and the largest of its kind. A massive warehouse full of bunks, stables, cookfires."

"Way-stations in Olbaran are free to all travelers for rest on long journeys," Reidos said. "I have slept in one that was no more than a shack on the side of a valley road."

"This one will be bigger," Aren promised.

"How old is this way-station?" Inrianne asked.

"Centuries older than any of us," Aren said.

"Any of us except Reidos," Corrin corrected. "He is ten thousand years older than sand."

Reidos made the sign of the witch at him and laughed.

Corrin gave him the Bravonian finger in response.

Inrianne rolled her eyes.

Aren stared off into the distance, abruptly remembering what he was doing out here, like a bolt out of the blue, how serious it was, how time was running out before he even took his first step on this journey. Somewhere ahead in the distance was a user that he was going to kill.

They are only men, Sarker had always said. *There are rules for what they do as surely as for anyone else. When a cook prepares a meal with fewer ingredients, the result is ruined. If he tries to mix them without a pot, the food falls to the floor. When he forgets to apply heat to bread, it remains a glob of dough. If he stirs without a ladle, he will burn his fingers. And without water, stew is just a pile of vegetables.*

But Sarker is dead now. Aren jammed his finger against his forehead until the pain dissuaded that particular memory from lounging around in his head.

I have more important things to do than grieve.

He noticed Corrin looking at him. "What?"

"Aren't you going to stare at your empty jar collection again?" Corrin asked. "The sun has moved a quarter of a degree since last time."

"They are jars of *evidence*," Aren said. "And they only look empty until they are viewed through a Jecker monocle." He pulled the slender twin jars out of his tracer satchel. They each held pieces of debris from an explosion caused by one of the assassin's renders. He eyed them both through the blue filter and isolated the afterglow core colors. He calculated the amount of redshift. *Still slowing down. Good. They must be hanging around Westgate. We may be able to close the gap sooner than we thought.*

"I am just surprised that they finally found something for you to do that would get your head out of your books for five minutes," Corrin said. He gestured at Aren's carry-bag. "Though I see you brought a small library with you."

"Just a few of my favorite Histories, a Mythology, and the Jebbel Dedder Manual. Don't you have a sword to sharpen?"

"If I liked swords half as much as you like books, we would all be in a lot of trouble."

"You should talk to Balthoren," Aren said. "He has as many crossbows as you have knives."

"Never trust a man who won't pull his own string," Corrin said. "Besides, it would offend Reidos. He is a man of the bow, and his old age makes him sensitive. But here we are at least. It is good to have us all back together again. Even if it is for something as boring as work."

Aren laughed. "This *boring work* is exactly what I have been waiting for."

"What? Having a sore ass and a nose full of horseshit?"

"After years of hunting through back alleys and hostelries for petty little men, I have a chance to be something big."

"I thought you hunted murderers, *Lord Glasseye*," Corrin said. "Is that not enough adventure for you?"

"I stop rogue users. I catch them and send them to the fires. That is what all the Render Tracers do. *This* is different. If this goes the right way, my name will be more than a mere scribble in the chancellor's list of Glasseyes. This journey we are on right now is something that will be *remembered* in Amagon. That is what I am talking about, Corrin. This journey is for the Lord Protector himself. This is the next step for me."

"Is this really so important?" Corrin asked.

"Even if there was no user to trace, and no victim to save, just going to Laman at all is an honor. I have dreamed of making the journey there since I was knee-high to a man."

"Ugh," Corrin said. "No need to remind me about you and the Andristi. You never could shut up about the damned *long-lifers*."

"The mystique of the ancient kingdom of Laman has lured the hearts of better people than me. Even Loyol himself, the greatest artist in the history of Amagon, made a pilgrimage. He lived there for years before returning to Amagon."

"Oh, well, if there is art *and* history involved, best everyone just get the hell out of your way then, I suppose."

"The Andristi were born of the heroes of long forgotten times, when the northlands were warm and..."

"Let me stop you there," Corrin said. "Before you declare your intentions to marry Laman and take it to bed and fuck it senseless."

Aren laughed. "You brought it up."

"And I regret it every second," Corrin said.

Corrin spent the rest of the day mocking most everything. Inrianne spent the same time hating everything he said. Reidos, oblivious to either of them, shared endless stories and jokes with the Outer Guard to pass the time—of journeys and adventures; of gambling and of fighting over women and of tricking young nobles out of a few of their coins; of duels and chases and escapes. Reidos loved to tell the tales, and would repeat them over and over to any and all newcomers to the conversation, no matter how many times he had already just told them.

Aren tried to laugh with the others to pass the time. There was a lot of time to be passed when riding rough. Boredom, complacency—those were the enemies out here.

He glanced at the mysterious Glasseye, Raviel, riding ahead of everyone. He spoke hardly at all, and usually only to Tanashri. Aren's suspicion of him grew every hour. *I am supposed to defer to you about this trace, but there is not a chance in any hell that I will work with you, outlander. You are no Toran Sarker.*

The grassy hills stretched on for the rest of the day before they finally came to the village of Roare, which sat right up against the thick trunks of the Saren trees. It was a welcome sight to Aren. He was looking forward to feasting upon fresh breads and meats.

The villagers were overjoyed to have anyone as a visitor, and seemed quite at ease catering to the needs of the camp. They roasted delicious meats, the air swelling with the smells of spiced sausages and sage. The entire battalion eagerly wolfed down the food as soon as it was set before them. And after supper was over they served sweetrolls covered in custard and wild berries. Some of the men brought out curious flutes, and played brisk tempos while the unmarried girls danced about the fires. Mead was poured for any man who asked, and the soldiers wandered off to camp with full stomachs and free bottles from the abundant stock of summerwine.

Aren was careful to step around the charred black circle beside the old abandoned stable, cleared of grass from fire after fire. This was where they brought the rogue users from up and down this valley for burning. He almost felt like he could still smell it in the air, burnt flesh and screams, relief and catharsis, terror mixed with justice. He tried not to look at anyone when he walked by it, but some forced eye contact, nodding to him and bowing to his satchel.

He walked toward Donnovar, but the Captain was hemmed in between Raviel and Terrol, and so he waved Aren off with a shrug. Aren pretended to smile, but sneered once he turned away and walked on.

He nearly stumbled into the five Sarenwalkers, all kneeling in prayer. Each had taken one knee, head bent down, eyes closed. They held their *somashalks* flat on the ground in front of them. Save for the one with the Saren-sword. He held it blade-down in the dirt, his forehead touching the hilt. Together they recited the Sarenwalker mantra over and over. "*I am Sarenwalker. I am thought made action. I fear neither death nor pain. I possess no emotion, only perfection. I am Sarenwalker.*"

Aren watched them for a long while. By the time he remembered he had stew to finish eating he could not be certain if he stood there for seconds or hours.

He glanced up and realized Margol was standing next to him. He very nearly gasped, but managed to keep his mouth closed. *I should not startle this easily. What is wrong with me?*

Margol seemed to have aged since the journey began, short hair going from grey to white above his ears. But his expression was warm. Odd thing for him. He was usually the stoic type, with a lack of expression to challenge a Sarenwalker's. When he smiled it was like looking at a different person. If Aren hadn't known him better he would have thought the pleasantness suspicious.

"You are keeping up your trace?" Margol asked. "I hope the journey is not too much distraction."

Small talk was also odd for him. Aren still wasn't sure why Margol was ordered to come here in the first place. What could he do that Donnovar, Terrol, a Saderan, and five hundred soldiers could not? "I am not sure if I should resent the implication that I cannot do my job. Terrol alone is enough to remind me that I am underestimated."

Margol huffed a laugh. "The Lord Protector knows you can do this. That is why Aldarion sent you. Those missing girls are counting on you. He knows you won't let them down."

Aren's thoughts flattened. His frustration and suspicion drained away. The thought of anyone trapped with a rogue user was enough to make him sick with rage. He did not have time to think about Terrol or Margol or Sarker or any of it when that thought crept into his mind. "I can focus. Even out here."

"Good." He paused, looking across the village. He spat. Chewed his lip. "Keep your distance from Raviel."

The words caught Aren off guard. He glanced at the side of Margol's face. "Why?"

"He cannot be trusted."

"Why did Aldarion send him with me then?"

Margol thought to himself for a moment. "There were political reasons at play. But I don't trust him. Neither does the Lord Protector. Keep clear of him. Nothing good could come from him talking to you. It would only upset you, distract you."

As if I don't already know that. This only reinforced Aren's urgent desire to never speak with Raviel. Outlander. Lenagon-man. Replacement. Unfit to wipe the shit from Sarker's shoes. "He won't have one word from me. He won't keep me from running this trace."

Margol turned to face him and smiled. "I know, lad. You just do what you do. And don't worry about Terrol. He never thinks anyone can do anything as good as he can."

Aren nodded. Margol left him, and he moved on toward his tent, his stew now hopelessly cold.

He found tiny Tanashri tending the fire outside his row of tents. He sat down across the coals from her, setting his bowl beside the flames, hoping to warm it some.

Tanashri ate her own stew as if thinking the food into her head. He was not sure if he ever saw her chew. Her Saderan-grey eyes were like mirrors. Her robes looked orange in the firelight. Aren reached into his satchel and removed the *composite* of the wizard he was here to trace. *All right, user. Let us have another look at you.* He flipped the pages in the light from the fire. He had looked over it three times already, but could not stand to let an unsolved puzzle lie.

"You will burn the words off the parchment with your eyes if you read that many more times," Tanashri said.

Aren glanced up at her. She scooted her way around, until she sat beside him, their legs nearly touching.

"Are you here to pretend that we know each other?" he asked.

"You cannot run a trace alone."

"Watch me."

"You have not spoken with Raviel once. If you intend to do this yourself, you must practice. You must prepare."

"Why do you care how I do my job?"

"Because my success depends on your success. We will be conducting this capture together. I must be certain you know how."

"Why would they have chosen me to go if I didn't know how?"

"Tell me your interpretation of the evidence. What does it tell you?"

He eyed her coolly. "The *prismatic dispersion* from the imprints using the white filter indicates low energy output. They point to a user with a modest core limit of natural energy."

"But?"

"But these results do not seem compatible with the other evidence. The residuals at the scene were subtle, indicative of both skill and experience."

"What else?"

"The *resonance spectrum* signifies a great quantity of different renders were employed, but the number of renders in a user's repertoire usually increases *linearly* with their core strength."

"Strength and experience usually coincide."

"The *primary values* of the user's power output at the scene were modest."

"Low amplitude and frequency. More evidence of low strength. What else?"

"Look at the rose filter imprint. It shows the *glow curve*, plotting the way in which the streams were bound into the final results. See here, here, and here. It is shallow all the way across, which again points to *experience*. The curve is usually steep for a user with low magnitude renders."

She nodded. "The more shallow the curve, the more congruous the altered reality of the render is with the reality around it, meaning the lesser likelihood that the render will have unwanted side effects. Good. Continue."

"This is no common user. Very experienced, but weak. I think it means he has been trained by someone more experienced, learning faster than the average. That is the only way to have the skill without the power."

She held out one tiny hand.

He paused. "I don't like people looking over my shoulder."

She kept her hand out, never breaking eye contact. "I will stand beside you instead. Is that satisfactory?"

He looked at her a long while, mouth flat, brow hardened. But her patient resolve made him crack a smile.

He handed it to her, and the she began reading it aloud to him, the way Sarker used to do. "Mechanist user type," she said. "Mostly vectoric renders. Low end of the resonance spectrum."

"Likely his skills are primarily passive," Aren said.

"Core residuals tend to leave pale afterglow. Like the color of peaches."

"That's peculiar. Rare color. Should make it a lot easier to find him."

"Why?"

"The *core color* is a byproduct of the key each user applies to bridge the gap between reality and possibility. The *blue* filter on the Jecker monocle filters out the natural colors of a render's afterglow, and leaves only the aural resonance of the key pattern itself."

She nodded. "Core color is like eye color—it never changes no matter how powerful the user, or how varied his skills. And orange is very rare."

"It is like a person with golden eyes—not unheard of, but certainly something one would not forget."

She shuffled through the imprints. "Anything else?"

"One other thing gnaws at me—the degree to which the user went to hide his structures. The renders were covered with a backward mask of layered waveform compression, a masking technique that is extraordinarily difficult to produce."

"Why is that strange?" She handed it back to him.

"No one ever uses masking," Aren said. "It's too concentration-consuming. Users like to use in a hurry. The good ones tend to be obsessed with efficiency. Anything that slows them down is usually left out. But this user puts it in *every single render*. Every time. If I didn't have those two jars of sensitized material I would not have believed this was a real composite." He closed the folio sourly and replaced it in his satchel.

"Those traces were very lucky indeed. Out here in the wilds it is likely that any trace will be the dimmest of embers."

"I hate rough riding almost as much as I hate cold scenes. But that other tracer, Raviel, the outlander, he is vying to be counted among them."

She stood and brushed her robes flat. "Out here we are all outlanders."

Aren looked at her coolly. "Where did Sarker go? Before he died. You know, don't you? He was gone for weeks."

"We all have our responsibilities," she said.

"What does that mean? He never left in the middle of a trace in all the time I knew him."

"You have only known him for a year."

"A year and a half."

She flattened her tiny mouth. "A man that old would have lived a lifetime already before you were ever born. A lifetime is a long while to accumulate secrets."

"Fine. If you won't answer a simple question, so be it."

She paused. "Aren, there is something they did not tell you."

"A rogue user is a rogue user."

She shook her head. "The Outer Guard battalion was not sent solely as a cover for our trace. Not everyone on this expedition is seeking the same thing. There is something the Lord Protector wants in Laman."

"Why are you telling me this?"

"Because I do not like that they seem to have intentionally hid it from you."

"You don't even know me. Why would you care what they tell me?" He didn't like it. It felt like manipulation. "So, in this story, you are the hero, turning me against my own people, and I am supposed to believe it without any explanation or any proof?"

She flattened her mouth. "This was a mistake."

"Yes. Yes, it was. I have enough on my mind with this trace. If you think you can take me out of my game for some benefit to you, you are sadly mistaken. I am going to catch this user. You may be coming along, but *I* will catch him. You are not going to steal this from me."

"I do not know the answer to your question about Sarker. Not in the way you hope, anyway. But I wanted to warn you to be careful who you trust."

"Thank you for nothing, I suppose."

She nodded. "I will leave you be. There are many long days ahead."

He gave a slight bow from his seat, as fake as he could make it. She left. He took his satchel and meandered until he found another fire where Reidos and Inrianne were speaking quietly alone.

Aren sat on a fat tree stump beside Reidos as he slurped his stew, now halfway cold again.

"Come into the light," Reidos suggested. "Any closer to your trace?"

Aren leaned forward. "Always closer."

"Weather should be even better once we turn north," Reidos said. "I could go for a mountain breeze right now. And a long bath. If we were going to any other place I would have expected you to turn around by now. But I know you. You would never pass up an opportunity to go to Laman. You would sell your soul and half of mine to see their ancient cities."

"You know me well."

"Well enough to know something is bothering you."

"That obvious, eh? I am wondering how I am going to run this trace with so may people trying to undermine me. The Sister. Terrol looking over my shoulder. And that outlander, Raviel."

"Isn't he supposed to be one of you? A Render Tracer?"

"That is what they say."

"Shouldn't you be comparing notes with him? Shuffling papers? Looking at evidence of one thing or another?"

"That would be the usual way. But he has not spoken to me once."

"Have you tried speaking to him?"

Aren sneered at the very concept. "No. Why would I? I don't need him to run this trace. I can do this without him."

"Do you wonder if he is thinking the same thing about you?"

"Shaot. Whose side are you on?"

"I thought we all were on the same one."

"I have a feeling that he knows more about what's going on than he lets on."

"What is he doing to undermine you exactly?"

"Well, nothing specifically. But he shouldn't be here. Just being here undermines me. It makes me look like I can't do it myself."

"That sounds like pride talking."

"I should have expected that response from you."

"Maybe you should have asked Corrin then."

Aren chuckled. "He would just tell me to solve my problem by stabbing everyone."

"Not ideal."

"Especially not with Donnovar recognizing the authority of the outlander. How are the soldiers holding up?"

Reidos chuckled. "Many of the men are not happy to be in Olbaran at all. Most of them have never made journey here, and all talk of how barbaric Olbaran is. They like the prospects of Laman even less. All they do is repeat exaggerated tales of Andristi savagery. If only they knew I was an old grumpy half-breed." He laughed. "They seem to think we're going into a land of cannibals. I told them the Andristi culture is the wealthiest, most civilized in all the world, but you know how superstitious those Kolcha folk can be."

Corrin stomped up to the fire. "Let's just kill something and get it over with," he said. He hugged a bundle of logs in his arms. "Found some more wood," he announced. "Those coals are old and about to die. Just like Reidos." He laughed to himself. He dropped the wood atop the embers, kicked some kindling underneath, and began searching his pockets for a flint to strike a new flame.

Before he could manage to find one, Inrianne leaned casually past him, and extended her forefinger. A tiny flame appeared from her fingertip, and fluttered like candlelight.

Corrin jumped back, a look of shock exploding onto his face. "Seven hells," he said. "Warn me when you're going to do something weird like that."

Inrianne sneered at him, but kept her gaze affixed to her flame. She held it near the wood. It seemed to flutter every five seconds.

"Looping," Aren said.

"What was that?" Corrin blinked at him.

"It's a user technique," Aren said, ignoring the fact that Inrianne flinched at the word *user*. "So they can render something, and then set it to repeat at a certain interval. It helps keep their core strength free for other actions. It takes more energy to make a fire that sustains for a long time. By looping, the incidence of the fire repeats itself. See the flickers?" He pointed at her finger. "For just a moment the fire seems to die out because the loop takes time to restart. Half a second."

Corrin looked at him blankly. "You read too much. A spring-flint or a fire-stick would have been faster."

Inrianne smiled, and the tiny candle-like flame suddenly squirted like liquid fire into the fresh logs, setting them alight. Inrianne pulled her hand back, and the spark extinguished itself on her finger, leaving a little puff of sparkling orange haze dangling in the air.

Afterglow.

Corrin hopped in his boots. "Shaot! What did I just say? Don't do that."

"Stop being scared of a little fire," Reidos said.

"I'm not afraid of fire, *ass*. This magick thing though...strange." He nodded his head as though he had just spoken a magnificent scientific fact.

"You're an Elemental, aren't you?" Aren asked.

Inrianne froze. "Stay away from me," she said. She stared at him for a long moment, and then stood and left.

Corrin threw his arms up in resignation, and retreated to his sleeping sack.

Reidos smiled. "Remember the lady from Ethios? The one who could tie a sailor's knot with her teeth?"

"Those were good times," Aren said.

"Good times, indeed."

Aren nodded to him. He returned to his tent and fell atop his sleeping roll. He gently touched the pouch at his belt. He had crammed every bit of malagayne he had into it—the small sacks of powder and fistfuls of leaves. It sat like a fluffed pillow at his waist. He kept it there even when he slept.

He dabbed a finger in the interior pocket, brimming with powder. He held it to his nose and sniffed. Instant respite. Instant relaxation. Instant rapture. Desire thrown down a well. Head sitting easy on his shoulders. He thought he saw Raviel wandering through the camp before he fell asleep, though he couldn't be sure if it was real or just a dream.

8

Missing

AREN GLARED AT THE four walls of a vacant upstairs room in a hidden apartment in the city of Westgate. It was so quiet he could hear his own heartbeat. There should have been two dozen people crammed into these tiny rooms. But there was no one. No one at all.

"Where are my Stoppers, Fainen?" he asked.

The Sarenwalker blinked at him. "Is this question rhetorical?" He kept the hood of his emerald green cloak down, showing reddish-brown hair short upon his head, standing upright, and dancing like ruby glass. His eyes were the greenest of greens—the color of the Sarenwood.

Aren nodded. "You are sure this is the right place?" He heard nothing but a faint buzz of chaotic dialogue filtering through shuttered windows from the streets outside. The door had been unlocked. The room seemed untouched.

"Yes." Fainen pointed to a window with an open shutter with his glistening blue Saren-sword. *Glimmer*, it was named. An ancient blade handed down for generations. "That fountain is the landmark. These papers are theirs."

Aren smirked at his bodyguard-of-the-day. But the Sarenwalker was right. This had to be the staging house, nestled between a cobbler and a carpenter in the upper rooms of a popular hat-maker.

Aren kept hoping there was a way for it to not be true. The strap of his tracer satchel dug into his shoulder like a knife. His mind would not focus on details. He was too busy trying to figure out what to do. These Stoppers had been sent here in advance. There would be no time to stop and wait for any replacements. They were the only Amagonian Stoppers for a hundred miles.

But where were they?

Aren clenched his teeth. "This is a problem. The worst kind. They were supposed to be here. They should be waiting for us. For me. We need them. The capture does not work without them."

Stoppers were the foundation of a capture, much like the sturdy bases of the fruit pyramids on the carts of the peddlers outside. Without Stoppers, there would be no interdiction. Without interdiction there would be no capture. *Not without relying solely on the Sister anyway.*

He thought of tiny Tanashri, and hoped her skills were larger than her body was. *I will need to pore over the schematics with her and pray that she has the skill to find every stream, and the concentration to hold them all long enough.*

Now the Saderan was no longer merely a supplemental component to the most integral part of the capture, she was elevated to its centerpiece, and having only one user to act as a surrogate Stopper would make for a dangerous situation.

He closed his eyes and saw a flash of memory from Degammon's capture. He involuntarily set his hand atop the pouch of malagayne, fingernails scratching its surface. His mouth tightened in silence, but within his head frantic alarms were raging. The pyramid of fruit tumbled down without its base and left only shattered bits.

Aren had begun the morning giddy. Over the prior seven days they had caught up significantly. The sealed sensitized debris pair had faded out only two days before, but when last he checked, the assassin was still in Westgate. He had been anticipating hunting him to capture right here in this city, without needing to worry about going to Laman at all.

Now he was sullen.

He attended the walls, the tables and chairs, the areas beneath rugs. He used the Jecker monocle. Nothing. He shoveled with his hands like a delirious archaeologist through thick piles of parchment—letters and notes and requisitions and journals. Nothing made any reference or even hinted at the faintest possibility of an explanation. He found the original message notifying the staging-captain of the impending arrival of the Stoppers. The Stoppers who were now missing. Along with the staging-captain. Along with everyone.

"I need you to go to Donnovar," he told Fainen.

"I am ordered to ward you," Fainen said.

"Am I one of the leaders of this expedition?" Aren asked.

"Yes. A technicality."

"Of the same authority as Donnovar?"

"Yes."

"Then my command should have weight equal to his."

Fainen thought for a moment. "In this circumstance you would be correct."

"Then go. The Captain needs to be made aware of this at once. I need to start looking for answers."

The Sarenwalker gave him a curious look, but he obeyed and disappeared out into the streets.

I can't go back to the way-station empty-handed. He could not face Donnovar and Terrol with this news without even the slightest of answers. He needed to find out what happened to the Stoppers. Some hint, some clue, *something.* Some answer for when they asked him what could have happened. Saying *I don't know* in that instance was unthinkably humiliating.

Aren lurched down the stairs and out into the sunlight. He looked up and down the avenues, so full of merchants and servants and peddlers and panhandlers and thieves and rogues and artists and craftsmen. Someone must have seen *something.* He needed only to root out the trace of memory as he did a trace of sensitized fluorescence.

He checked the shops on either side, operated by shrewd and tightlipped proprietors who claimed to know nothing. He stopped people randomly in the street, trying not to give off the look of a Glasseye. Some shrugged themselves away in annoyance. Others waved him off, too busy to care. Those who did speak offered little, none of them too familiar with those who kept their home above the hat-maker, some who had never seen them, and others who never knew anyone lived there at all.

Someone must know something.

He stepped through the door of a tavern across the avenue, nestled between four-story tenements, and found a nervous bartender hidden among stands of mugs and fine glasses hanging upside down from trellises overhead. He had a mustache like a zebra stripe and an unfavorable odor, and he had never seen anything unusual across the street, nor would he be one for gossiping if he had.

So Aren ordered himself a mug of ale and sat himself at the end of the bar beside two gruff Polonian pole-men from the docks where the river barges were unloaded. They were grizzly and bristled like wildlife snatched from the woods and dropped into civilization. They laughed constantly and awfully, and seemed to have no locks to hold back their tongues.

"If you are looking to know what goes on around here go see sweet Joli," one said, chuckling. "She works for old tavern master Holliver Ward in his place. *Home of the Moon*, it's called. Its doors are open wide all night, just like Joli's legs, hah." He laughed to himself and clapped his hands.

His friend swatted him on the shoulder. "None of that. Joli is but a sweet girl."

"Aye, she is," he agreed. "And twice so when she's on her back. *Home of the Moon* is just next door to where that poor lady got herself murdered."

"Murdered?" Aren asked. "When?"

"Last night," he said. "Or was it night before? Maybe last week. Stabbed, I heard."

"Nah, strangled," the other argued. "You are thinking of that string of cult murders. Bloody signs and sigils, bodies half-skinned."

"Where is this *Home of the Moon*?" Aren asked.

They gave him directions. Aren tossed a few copper bits on the bar for their next pints, and was on his way out the back door before they stopped clinking. He strode into the alley, scanning it from end to end with the Jecker monocle. Nothing.

He saw a small boy running around aimlessly, like a butterfly caught in a strong breeze. A dog growled at a thick, truculent rat, as they prepared to do battle over a cat carcass. A gate swung open, and a man tossed shit from a rusted iron bucket, and it splashed unctuously right up to someone else's front door across the way.

Aren at last found a door with one hinge iron and the other copper with a worn tin crescent, enameled white. He pulled it open, and was met by the soft thumping of a dull muted drum, balanced with low droning notes from a bowed zala and lazily plucked melodies from a dromba.

Two elevated galleries ran along either side, supported by posts covered with moons and winking stars enameled in a reflective substance. There were many dark corners and tables and cushioned booths scattered with crisscrossed shadows, where the light of the bronze chandeliers did not reach. There were only a handful of people inside.

Aren chose the nearest to him, a man with a shiny bald head at the top, but above his ears ran a charcoal grey ring of long flowing hair, and his eyes were spaced close together and seemed to be two different shapes.

"I am looking for Joli," Aren said.

The man looked up, which made his eyes look even more different from one another. "Sweet Joli." He pointed with one crooked finger at a girl with hair as soft and shiny as satin, the shade of rose petals at dusk.

"You are the second one to call her sweet today," Aren said.

His eyes wandered up and down the contours of her hips and thighs. Her hair brushed like silk against the nape of her neck. Her dress was hair-thin black fabric slit down the back nearly to her waist, the front supported by barely a string that wound up about her neck.

"Especially when she be..." The old man started.

"On her back, yes, I have heard this," Aren said impatiently, though he felt a tightening up in his muscles and a sudden quickness to his pulse. He remembered his last night with Merani, and wondered how Joli might play all tangled up in his sheets. He silently agreed that she would certainly be sweet on her back, or her front or her side or upside down for that matter, if she were willing.

"Joli?" Aren asked.

She turned to him, wiping dry a cup, and setting it upside down upon a dark cherry counter. She smiled with lips as pale as rosewater, and winked one aqueous eye at him.

He stood gawking for what seemed a long time. "I heard a woman died here," he finally said.

Her smile vanished, and she looked him up and down, lingering at his tracer satchel. But then a sly little smirk developed, and her eyes narrowed. "Are you another one of those ghost hunters?" she asked, her tone playful and derisive all at once. "Another Glasseye?"

"Something of that nature," he said, trying to regain some composure.

"Well, I told the others all I know. I didn't know Lesca very well, just gossip. She came in here sometimes, but *Home of the Moon* is expensive for her sort."

"Sort?" Aren raised an eyebrow.

"She was married to a man with money, but he died, and she married another man who took half of it and then left after a month. She married again, but he was a gambler and lost more to the dice. Then her brother came to help her settle the debts, but he just took what he could grab and ran. She has been selling off the last of her mother's jewelry. She cries when she parts with them, but they are all she has left. No one else has any interest in taking a thrice cursed woman to wife after all that, and she couldn't even make a decent washerwoman. There have been a few suitors here and there, and there was a little woman who came to see her months ago. Dalain, I think. I thought she was her cousin. Perhaps not. I just assumed. She knew a lot about her. I think I heard her say she was going to come into some money very soon though, but I'm not sure how. Do you want a bit to drink?"

"No, thank you," he stammered. "I have work yet to be done today."

"I think you work too hard," she said, running a finger playfully down his sleeve and brushing her hand softly across the buckle of his belt. "Drinks are more fun."

Sweet Joli. "There was some trouble. One street over. Men going missing."

She bit her lip and her eyes glanced up to the bronze chandelier. "Holliver knows better than me. He is in the kitchen. I'll fetch him if he isn't too busy."

When Holliver Ward came out, he looked exactly as tall and as stocky as Aren had imagined, with peppered grey hair trimmed short like a crescent moon hanging on his forehead. He was wiping his hands with a wrinkled cloth and squinting. "What's your business? You another from the Home Guard? I already spoke with all them."

"I merely need to...clarify the facts," Aren said.

"I was always worried about those lads," he said. "They always had their nerves all on edge, but even more so the last few days. They had some people come stay with them, some cousins or friends or some such."

The Stoppers. So they made it safely here at least. "What happened?"

"The way I heard, was that one day one of their friends went out in the day and just never came home. They went out and looked for him, even asked me if he had been here, but of course he hadn't. He might have run off with some girl, I said, or he might have ended up face down in the river, but who can say? Things quieted down after that for a day or two, but then they came around again. Another of those boys never made it home. They all went out searching that very night, but then two more never returned from the searching. Three of them took their horses and ran off, maybe to go looking, or maybe to get a message to wherever those boys came from. They left and never came back."

"What about the one with dark hair?" Joli prompted.

"Oh yes," Holliver said. "He would sulk in here every night, mumbling to himself and jumping every time the door would open or a plate was set down too hard. He said a lot of things that didn't make much sense to me, but from what I gathered, they would wake up in their rooms, and some of their friends just wouldn't be there anymore, like they just left in the middle of the night. He just mumbled to himself about black eyes at night, and told me he wouldn't go back there. He would sleep in my back room sometimes. I remember clear as day the last time he came in. He sat himself right down, and when I went to give him his wine, he just said, *they're all gone.* I'm certain he meant those boys, his friends. And after that, he was gone too. I never saw him again."

Aren nodded, tendrils of fear creeping up his spine. "Could you show me where Lesca died?" He knew he would be taking a risk. If the Home Guard were still there they could arrest him if they learned what he was.

Joli shrugged and led him out into a back alley. She pointed to a small wall with a rusted iron gate. "Walk lightly until you find her gate. They toss slops out there."

Aren thanked her, and crossed to Lesca's home. The sun was already past its apex.

He went cautiously through the open gate and across a garden of tiny flowers and subtle vines and a little water dish that twig birds gathered around to drink and bath in. Bells dangled from rusted chains above the door.

He searched long with the Jecker monocle and the Oscillatrix, but found nothing. No renders had been used on the victim. She died of a natural murder.

He returned nonplussed to the rear door of the *Home of the Moon*. His eyes were slow to adjust back to the faint candlelight, and he barely saw the steps his own feet were taking. He realized suddenly and urgently that he wanted to smoke malagayne. His face tightened in pain, bending his mouth to an agonizing smile. His skin felt cold, muscles like crisped meat, bones like brittle stone cracking under the weight of ages.

"Are you well?" Joli asked. "You look as if you have a fever. You should sit down."

She guided him to a soft cushioned chair, and disappeared to fetch some water. He dipped into his pouch and scooped malagayne powder up his nose, inhaling like wind sucking snow from a frigid mountain peak. The droning music carried on, and his eyelids suddenly felt very heavy.

"Troubled?" asked a man lounging upon two cushioned chairs pushed together. "You look as pale as a ghost." He leaned back in repose, one booted foot draped unceremoniously across his table beside a plate of half-eaten biscuits flooded with butter. The boots were fine leather, and were certainly more expensive than Aren's entire wardrobe. He wore tailored black wool trousers, held up by a belt featuring an enormous silver buckle with engravings on its surface. He wore a soft burgundy velvet vest over an ivory linen shirt.

His head was as shiny bald as a piece of polished brass, and as brown as saddle leather. His eyes were pale milky green and serpentine. His brow was wide and gently curving, making his eyes appear slightly sad. All the parts of his face came together perfectly, as if it had been planned and assembled by an engineer, so that none stood out more than any other.

"I...it may have been something I ate," Aren said.

"In that case, I would recommend you avoid the shellfish. I take it you are not one of the Olbaranian Home Guard Glasseyes."

Aren kept silent.

"My name is Redevir," the man said. "I am not of the Home Guard either." He extended his hand with a wink and a flash of a smile.

"Aren. Aren of Amagon."

"Ah, well, an Amagon-man, eh? You must have urgent business to abandon all those lovely beaches in the height of summer."

"I am on a diplomatic mission," Aren said. "We are crossing Olbaran."

"Olbaran takes up too much space. One must cross it to get to virtually everywhere else on this earth." Redevir sat up. He leaned forward, planting his hands on his knees. "A curious man might wonder what you sought in the murder chamber of a freshly dead widow."

Aren chuckled awkwardly, looking around for Joli and the promised water.

Redevir studied him. "What is it that troubles you?"

"I found something not as it was expected to be."

"Tsk. I hate when that happens. The disappointment is doubled when the expectations have already been set high, just as my expectation of Joli's prowess in the bedchamber has been raised to an unfortunate height by many of the locals. I fear now that no matter what happens I may be doomed to disappointment."

Joli returned just then with a small cup of fresh water. Aren took it carefully.

Redevir became suddenly serious. "This expectation of yours that was... diminished, had it to do with the woman that once lived next door?"

"No," Aren said. "I thought that it might, but it doesn't seem to."

"I hoped you might have known her. I was supposed to...discuss something with her. The day she died. We had been in correspondence, you see."

Aren squinted at him.

"Never mind," Redevir shrugged. "It's moot now."

"I was supposed to meet some people. But they were gone without a trace. It looks like something very bad happened to them."

"That is indeed troubling." Redevir tapped a dull staccato rhythm on his chin, pondering. "It seems that we both have arrived to find things not as they were supposed to be here in Westgate. It is a shame for the both of us. I recall reading recently that there was once a great Arradian emperor who suffered a similar disappointment."

"You probably mean Chythoman II," Aren said, looking up with sudden interest. "He was marching his last army in a desperate hope of joining reinforcements from his western provinces to defeat a rebellion among his own ministers. His last chance was to race to meet them at a place called the Well of Wings before his enemies caught up to him."

"You know the story?" Redevir asked.

Aren nodded. "One of his loyalist ministers died on the way, another general was confused by heavy rains and ended up waiting in the wrong place, and the third defected to join the emperor's enemies. Chythoman was in such despair that he threw himself on his own sword, and as he bled to death, he commanded his eunuchs to slay his wife and children rather than let them fall into the hands of his enemies."

"A sad story indeed," Redevir said. "I had not heard details."

"The Histories written by Jordanus were very vivid, describing down to the moment where his eunuchs made council to decide the method of slaying the royal family with the most dignity."

"Have you ever heard of the white-faces of Abernaith?" Redevir asked.

"Yes," Aren said. "From Tolobria."

His eyes widened. "Well, you have earned my respect. I was not expecting you to know about them. I was going to use them to start a poor joke at your expense. Or rather, at the expense of your illness. I recommend another sip or two of that water."

Aren took another drink. "I think they were priests who put on the faces of the dead to chase away evil spirits."

"Correct. It was said that only the dead could harm those spirits. They overcame their demons by using the *fear* the spirits felt for the dead. You seem to know a great deal of these Histories for one so young."

"They are a pastime. I'm no scholar."

"Well, you certainly could fool a common crow like myself," Redevir said. "You instantly knew two stories I tossed out at random. Not even the scholars in Kamedol had heard of the white-faces."

Aren sipped at his water. He forced a swallow, stood, summoned his balance and took another sip, bracing himself with a hand on one of the posts.

Redevir's eyes suddenly stared wide. "Look there." He nodded urgently to the front window.

Aren saw men in blue garb outside, some with cloaks and some without, some with rough unwashed tunics, and others that were deep azure. They milled about, some entering doorways across the street, and others speaking hurriedly with people outside. "Home Guard," he said. "Common men, volunteers to the militias. They police Talvor's cities."

"I have seen them about. Poor men given free swords and a title. A terrifying combination."

He noticed at least one who must have been an officer. He was questioning an old man across the street. The man held a hand up to his eye and began peering back and forth in some pantomime of a Glasseye. Then he pointed at the door to the *Home of the Moon*.

Shaot, one of their informants must have seen me.

Aren raced for the rear door. He heard the Home Guard coming in through the front door as he was slipping out the back. Redevir's boots echoed in the hallway behind him. He did not question Redevir's company. He didn't have time to. His only thought was to avoid being found. If caught, he could be detained by these fools for weeks, and even if his tracer tools were not destroyed by careless hands, the entire mission would be fatally set back, an utter failure.

He scurried toward Lesca's walled patio, slid through the open gate, and crouched behind the wall. Redevir fell in beside him with the ease and grace of a tumbler. Aren heard the boots coming, and held his index finger to his lips. Redevir sat patiently, with an expression of raw childish excitement, as if it was all just a game.

The boots clattered, words and signals were exchanged, and then the boots went on away. The air was still again. Aren took a deep breath and whistled the exhale.

"Someday you must tell me what that was all about," Redevir said, smiling.

Aren peered over the wall. He kicked the bricks. "The Home Guard are out now. The path back to the way-station must be crawling with them. And here the sun is already falling. I have to get back." He was already imagining how humiliating it would be if the Home Guard apprehended him—the disappointment on Donnovar's face, the smiling nod of Terrol, being proven right that Aren was no good at his work, the smug satisfaction of the outlander, Raviel.

"Might I suggest an alternative route?" Redevir asked.

"You know one?" *Anything to get me out of this.*

"I do indeed," Redevir said. "I have been learning my way around Westgate these past few weeks."

"Which way?" Aren asked.

"Through the old slums."

"The slums?" Aren asked. "Is it safe?"

"Safe enough. The Hezzam migrants are always delighted to see me. They have carts on every street. Fried meats. Fresh calpas fruit. Come along. I will get you back to your way-station in no time. I have an errand in that area. A little stop along the way. You don't mind, do you?"

"What kind of errand?" Aren asked.

"To pay a visit to someone. I made an arrangement with an elder there. I intend to barter for something he has obtained for me. A book, called *Mercury Woods.*"

"Eastern philosophy," Aren said. "I know it. Andristi Mysticism. It was adapted by Curwen. He spoke to the heads of religious and military orders in Laman."

"It isn't Curwen's text itself," Redevir said. "There are copies of it residing in many of the great Libraries. I needed *this* specific version, the Banwick translation. It has notes added by Banwick at the end of every chapter. I need the notes."

"Can't you take your own notes?" Aren asked.

"These notes contain something very important," Redevir said. "References. Clues. I need them." He shrugged. "And the man I am going to see knows quite a bit about what happens in this city. Perhaps he might be able to help you find the answers you're looking for."

"A man in the slums?" Aren gave a dubious look.

"Best we get going," Redevir said. "It is nearing sunset."

Redevir navigated them past a team repairing a section of the cobbled streets, another tending to a clogged sewage drain, and still another fitting a new wheel to a carriage full of chests containing the month's taxes, guarded by a dozen private soldiers armed with swords and spears, lest anyone get any ideas.

The chatter of thousands strutting up and down the streets blended seamlessly with the barking of dogs and the creaking of wagon wheels and the chopping of wood and the strikes of hammers on anvils like bells chiming. Aren was glad to be back on paved roads. He hated being in the rough. He wanted walls and narrow streets and bustling neighborhoods.

Redevir kept an even pace and it wasn't long before they were submerged in an ocean of rough sweat and musk in the middle markets. Buyers clapped for attention from whistling merchants, peddling rare southern fruits and reams of Tobrian wool to stave off the chill of the approaching autumn.

It was a meeting place for Halsabadi master-sellers and dealers of precious metals from Tioch, goldsmiths from Liturna and Alsion, sculptors from the ancient holy lands around the Mazurian Sea, and even grizzly Bolanese whalers from the ice fields of the northmost straights. Huge caravans sometimes arrived even from secluded Shezail Valley.

"Keep you eyes peeled for thieves," Redevir said. "They have so many pickpockets, they pick each other."

Redevir managed to find a narrow alley that offered escape. It spit them out among the warehouses of the many merchant princes, where Aren was swarmed by a host of flies and the stench of dung from the stalls for the wagon teams.

They cut through an old courtyard, ringed with small shops, people gathered in small clusters of conversations throughout. It seemed like a welcome respite after the tumultuous markets. But that was before they saw the Priest.

Aren had known they held sway here, advising lords and even the High King of Olbaram himself. But it was another thing to see them. The Priest dressed in the traditional shiny brown leather longcoat, slit up the front and back to the waist, buttoned up the left side of his torso, hands clasped behind his back. His eyes were green and severe and impossible.

He directed six Home Guard soldiers to drag a shrieking man from his shop.

"Please," the man pleaded with them. "A mistake. Just a mistake."

Aren took Redevir's elbow and dragged him along, not wanted to stop anywhere near them.

Two more of the Home Guard carried out armloads of old books, dumping them in a pile in the street, while a third doused them in oil and set them to flame. The Priest stared at the fire, while the man was dragged away, his cries dwindling.

"What was that about?" Redevir asked.

"Those books must be in the Ministry index. Forbidden texts. Dangerous knowledge for users."

"I have never seen that done publicly," he said.

"Nor me. Best keep moving on." *Before one of them notices my satchel.*

He rounded a bend on Redevir's heels, hoping to find another quiet street, but instead found himself spilling into a courtyard brimming with jostling people. They were all shouting and shoving and waving handfuls of coins in the air. Old sweat and stale breaths slapped him in the face.

At the center, a handful of the private bodyguards formed a circle around a massive man, wrapped in an old cloak the size of a small tent. He stood ten feet tall. The huge head was shaved, save for a long strand of black hair from a topknot at its pinnacle. A scar squirmed its way down his forehead and across one cheek.

The enormous man shrugged his cloak to the ground, exposing a colossal body, thick with muscle. The skin was deep crimson, streaked with white, and it creased as he flexed his titanic arms. The giant wore no shirt or boots, and his enormous black trousers looked like they had been sewn for a mammoth. The sight of him aroused a hail of cries, as terror-stricken people pushed against the crowd to escape, while others moved in for a closer look.

The giant brandished an immense battle-axe, double-edged, polished, with gold filigree. It should have taken three men to wield. Massive hands gripped it, crimson knuckles turning white as he waved the weapon about. He lashed out with it, swung it about his head, and tossed it back and forth in his hands like a juggler.

"Well, we cannot go this way," Redevir said.

"But he is only a performer, isn't he?" Aren asked.

"Performance and murder are likely synonymous to Redscar," Redevir warned.

"How do you know its name?" Aren asked suspiciously.

"You meet a variety of people in my line of work," Redevir said.

"I hesitate to call that thing *people*," Aren said.

"I chanced across him before. In the deep south. His *performances* tend to leave corpses in their wake. Ask any pit fighter who has ever survived a Besembrian Bloodhouse or the sandpits of Rhodas. He has never been north of Olybria before. I don't know who his handlers are now, but this does not seem the proper venue for someone like him. We have to try to edge around the crowd. This way."

Aren followed him. Above the bobbing heads, he caught glimpses of the red titan flailing his arms and his axe. Shrieks erupted from the crowd, but he wasn't sure if they were cheers or cries of fear.

Aren put a hand on his pouch of malagayne. He desperately needed a sniff. His body ached for it. His mind screamed for it. Just one. He could get by on just one, but he had no chance to take it. He could do nothing but walk in silence until the craving subsided.

It was a blessing when they reached narrow avenues lined with small homes and shops and temples and shrines of gods great and small, rising three stories high in some places, and not even waist height in others. Awnings the texture of bat wings protruded above every window, making the streets into endless tunnels, where sour soups and sweet teas suffused the air. Clouds of incense and sizzling spices made his stomach grumble.

Somewhere along the way the sun dropped below the horizon. Aren swatted at flies and Redevir stalked furiously, barely looking forward long enough to guide his feet.

A slender scaled-cat perched atop a pile of calpas fruit in a cart across the street. It shifted its balance, and toppled the painstakingly constructed fruit pyramid to the ground, dashing half of the fruit to bits. It hissed and scurried away, leaving the mess of pink pulp and split yellow rinds, eagerly dragged away by fruit rats.

"Are we close, Redevir?" Aren asked. "I really should be going back."

Redevir chose a house across from the cart, seemingly at random. The door was open and the way unbarred. "This is it."

9

Cursed

CORRIN WAS SO SOBER that he felt ill. He had not had a stiff drink since Roare, and even that had been lukewarm sharpwine. Warm sharpwine was like warm milk—filling, but absurdly unsatisfying. It simply would not do to miss what was likely the last opportunity he would have to get a good cool sip of chilled ale for the next few hundred miles.

He set about immediately to find a Westgate tavern that would suit him properly, though he wasn't sure if that meant he should be looking for one clean and polished, or one in sagging disrepair.

Of course Reidos came with him, and he made the unfortunate decision to invite Inrianne along, ice-cold like pale milk both inside and out. She was likely warm in a few places, he conceded; the tits and the midnight lips, just the right ones to drive Reidos to the insane distraction necessary for him to put up with her indefatigable sourness.

Oh, a warm place would certainly do Reidos some good at his age—he was almost an antiquity, after all. But it should have been someone else—literally anyone but her, in Corrin's opinion. But the madness did as the madness would.

Corrin had always taken careful precautions to avoid such madness himself, mostly by never learning a name, taking women from behind as often as possible, and both coming and going from beds drunk and at night in order to prevent them from remembering how to find him, and vice versa. He always sought out the most flirtatious, the most gaudy, the most garrulous, fiery, impetuous, ravenous, improper, and untenable ladies he could find. The ones who would give him only lust and laughter and release, and nothing more.

He found a decently dressed man in the markets who recommended the taverns on a hill along the Causeway Road.

Corrin took his steps leisurely, smiling to the prettiest girls, and winking at those less pretty. He crossed numerous alleys, two wide thoroughfares, and passed a number of dice-dens that he dared not venture into for risk of forgetting his mission in favor of gambling.

He navigated the throng of buyers and sellers, of peasants, merchants, and craftsmen, his eyes constantly alert for pickpockets. He stepped through clouds of sweet incense, cinnamon and lavender and myrrh—brought from the four corners of the world.

Looking between two carts of worn ceramics, he watched a boy no older than seven years of age snatch a woman's brooch of bright opals right from her robes, and dart away unnoticed. He admired the lad. Skill and bravery.

He found the Causeway Road, but quickly became lost among steaming fish-friers, and winesinks, and abandoned hostelries—and a few that should have been abandoned, but were for some reason still occupied despite numerous and obvious structural defects.

Reidos was no help, absorbed in his relentless cooing with that ridiculous woman, and as the sun began to set lazily in the west, Corrin discovered that he was hopelessly lost.

He found the least contemptible Cantabrian crab merchant in the vicinity and was able to procure directions. Apparently, there was an Upper Causeway Road, a Lower Causeway Road, and an Old Causeway Road. He was informed that the lowest rents were to be found on Upper Causeway Road, and the best brothels on the Lower Causeway Road, but that the magisterial abodes he sought were in fact to be found on the Old Causeway Road. And, unfortunately, none of the three streets were connected to one another. He was not able to resolve Corrin's question of whether there had ever been an actual Causeway to justify naming no less than three streets for it.

Corrin spent the next hour pretending that he was not lost. By the time the sun had set, however, Reidos was beginning to notice. Corrin stopped to purchase a small calpas fruit from one of the nearby carts, hoping to also buy himself some time to think of a good excuse for why he did not seem to know where he was going.

He was halfway to inventing a decent one, when his ears caught a familiar sound. He heard the clear and distinct voice of an Amagon-man.

I have heard that voice before.

It was *Terrol*. Aren's least favorite Listener. His voice was all too easy to distinguish. *Inner Guard ghosts make me sick.*

Corrin leaned against a wall, and peered around the corner into the alley beyond.

There he was. A Whisperer doing what they do best—whispering. The man he was speaking to was clad in the traditional jumpsuit and heavy black turban of the Hezzam, but he sounded suspiciously like any other Amagon-man.

"You know what you will have to do," Terrol said. "I think he is getting too close."

The man nodded. "Do you think he suspects?" He spoke perfect Westrin.

Terrol glanced around anxiously. "I would not have desired a confrontation so soon, but he may soon find out too much." He ran his hands inside his cloak. "They have been pushing me so hard to make the move as soon as possible. I don't know why. Too many things are happening in this city."

"What then?" the Hezzam asked. "Proceed as planned?"

"Yes," Terrol said. "I loathe this environment. Too many variables." He looked around and sniffed, as though he could smell those same variables. "But it has to be in a city. We will not have any way to sneak you into the camp with Donnovar's men watching."

"If we can find him, we can do it tonight. If not, then not."

"Now go," Terrol hissed suddenly, looking suspiciously over his shoulder. "We must not be seen together." At that, he lifted his hood and began to trot down the street.

Treachery among the ranks. What a farod. He wondered who Terrol had meant. Aren? Donnovar? *I have to remember to tell Aren about this.*

His eyes narrowed, looking across the square, past dark corners and dry fountains and abandoned storefronts. He saw what appeared to be a decent taproom in a secluded courtyard behind the back alley of an unpopular market square. He grabbed Reidos by the elbow and pointed. "That looks like an affordable tavern right over there."

They trotted over to it.

It was appropriately named the *Red God*, its beams and floors all of bright redwood from the Kolcha Belt. The stools were too tall, the tables were water warped, and there was a general scent of rotten laziness in its air.

But the woman who poured his eveningwine was such a vivacious combination of smiles and curves that he reckoned it cancelled out the rest. He could endure almost any smell to work himself under the skirts of that golden bouncing temptress. He found his mouth watering more at the thought of tasting the skin of her neck than at the thought of the spiced roast he had demanded they serve him at half price.

His little golden temptress had agreed with a wink and a strategically placed hand on his thigh. He had already imagined fucking her forty-seven different times. That made it forty-eight. He began stretching in preparation for the acrobatics he intended to visit upon her even before he took his first bite.

The food was brought out by a fat man with wet boots that made sucking sounds as he walked, which only furthered Corrin's mind in the direction of the blond territory his armies were fully prepared to invade.

Reidos was being quiet for once, and so Corrin sat in silence, listening to his own chewing and sharing the occasional mischievous glances with the little golden lovely.

He became abruptly aware of a splinter sticking out of one of the beams. Just between his table and the door to the lavatory. It looked like it was waiting for him to catch his cloak on it. *What are you doing there, splinter? Who put you up to this? It was Reidos, wasn't it? Damnable Mahhen.*

He realized he had been staring at it. He pretended to be scanning the room so as to look modestly less insane. About this time he became aware that the golden lovely had not been back for a while, nor the man with the squishy boots. A moment later he realized that the room was empty, and may have always been empty. And now Reidos and Inrianne both had empty wine cups to match.

He pushed his chair back from the table, the legs grinding across the floor with a whistle and a whine. He almost didn't hear the back door creak open. But he definitely heard it click shut.

Is that them? Did this splinter make me miss them leaving out that door?

It was not the golden lovely. It was not the fat man with squishy boots.

It was a young girl carrying a child half her size. A boy.

Corrin blinked. There was something odd about her. More odd than a warrior, a Mahhen, and a woman in a gown sitting in the belly of a god.

She was covered in blood. None of it hers, by the look of it. Her legs wobbled with exhaustion and her eyes flared with fear. Her hair was a spectacular disaster, like an ambitious sculpture worked halfway then abandoned, a mottled mess of crimson strands. She had cuts on her hands and a deep one in her cheek. She has been aggressively crying well before she arrived.

The boy was mute, but didn't seem harmed. His hair was short and black, thin as strands of silk, but dirty.

Corrin looked at his warm meal, then back at her. He scooted his chair back an inch. The leg whistled across the floor.

The woman shrieked. Her eyes darted around, as if she had screamed by accident.

"She is terrified," Inrianne said. "Look at her."

"I am looking at her," Corrin said. "What am I supposed to do about it exactly?"

"Don't just stand there," Inrianne said. "Help her."

"Help her? The way I usually help people is by cutting someone or something with a sword. One look tells me I will likely need and axe to chop apart this girl's problems."

Inrianne urged him forward with a withering glare.

"My name is Corrin the Magnificent," Corrin told the girl. "You appear to be in trouble."

She shivered. "Please help."

"Show me the nature of your trouble and I shall chop it to bits."

"Please. I have to go. They are coming. He won't stop."

"Who's coming?" Reidos asked.

"I have to get away," she said. "He should have let them give up by now."

"I feel like this is the kind of trouble Aren said we were supposed to avoid," Corrin said. This girl was running from shadows, perhaps even her own. Corrin doubted he could cut her free of her shadow, no matter how well he sharpened his blade.

"By the gods high and low," Inrianne said impatiently. "She is afraid. She has been hurt. We need to help her."

"Fine," Corrin said. "Come with us. This Mahhen and woman can help you while I supervise."

Inrianne sneered at him.

The girl took a pair of hesitant steps.

This could have gone worse, Corrin thought.

But just then he heard the sound of little bells jingling. "Where is that? What is that? Why do I hear jinglebells?"

When the girl heard it she winced and began to cry.

Corrin saw movement behind her, men dressed in black filtering in through a doorway from a back room, spilling around the support beams, kicking chairs aside as they went. He was sure one of them had teeth, and one had a mustache, one had a limp, and two had hair down past their shoulders. One wore a fine coat, one wore bells on his shoes, one wore an old blanket, and two wore long black coats faded well on the way to grey. One looked like he was fresh from a bath, one looked like he hadn't bathed in a while, one looked like he hadn't bathed at all ever, and two smelled like they didn't even know what a bath was.

Then there was a sixth one. He was bald and he was bald and he was bald, and for some reason Corrin could not discern any memorable details about him otherwise.

"You shouldn't be out here," Mustache said.

"Get back in there," Limp said.

"No, please," she said. "Please. I don't want to anymore."

Mustache held out his hand. "Come."

"Sounds to me like she politely declined," Corrin said.

"Who the fuck are you?" Limp asked.

"I am the one who is going to cut you, judging by your tone," Corrin said. He really did not like the fact that they were all dressed in black. *That is my color.*

"I'll remember you said that when we are dancing in your blood," Limp said.

"You don't look like you do much dancing." Corrin said, gesturing at his warped leg.

The men glanced at one another.

Corrin looked up at the ceiling and sighed. "This is already taking too long." He drew his Sabarian steel longsword. "You all look lonely. This is the *Steel Whore.* If it's a little kiss you want, she would be happy to give it. The price is just a tiny smidgen of your blood."

Limp looked at Mustache.

"Are you ready to dance, or aren't you?" Corrin asked.

Mustache turned to the others. "Get her."

They started forward.

"Finally," Corrin said, relieved.

Teeth had a sword. He drew it. It was not well cared for. Corrin could see spots of rust.

You don't deserve to hold that.

Teeth tried for an upward swing from left to right. Corrin leaned back, waited for the blade to pass his body, then danced forward five inches, leaned out on his leading knee, and stretched his arm until his blade slid into Teeth's neck. An inch was all he needed.

Just a touch is all it takes. No need to run a man all the way through when a little poke at a good bloodspot did the trick.

Teeth fell down, his neck open like a raingutter emptying over stones.

Corrin shoved his table at the others, forcing them to back up and diverge around it.

The bald man responded by raising his hands.

The air felt odd, wavy. Corrin's flesh tickled.

User.

So there is something memorable about him after all.

Bald instantly became the greatest threat.

Corrin scooped up a full glass of something off the table and hurled it. It smashed into the user's face. He recoiled, shrieking, banging his head against a support beam.

Concentrate on that, farod.

Corrin piggybacked off that attack with a swing from his sword. The very tip of the *Steel Whore* scraped its way through the skin of the user's arm, down to the webbing of his fingers, before embedding itself in the edge of the beam, momentarily sticking.

The user shrieked and backed away, cradling his hand like a prize rooster. He turned and ran. And ran. And ran. Right out the back door.

Users, Corrin thought. He twisted his blade free of the post.

He noticed two of the others were trying to rush the girl. Their smells preceded them both by at least ten miles.

Corrin double-stepped to the right and kicked one of the chairs, sliding it into their path. The first man danced sideways around it. The second looked like he couldn't make up his mind whether to kick it or step on it and only managed to fall over it, tipping nose-first into the floor.

Corrin backed the girl away.

Limp came left. The man of great smells came right. They both had swords, rather nice ones. *Not as nice as mine though.*

Their arms danced, tensing and releasing. *They both want to attack at once. But neither can decide who is brave enough to commit first.*

So Corrin decided for them.

He turned and charged the more unctuous of the two, swinging two-handed cuts at the neck—right, left, right, left, right, left. Then he switched to one side—left, left, left, left. The interruption of the pattern took the man off guard and he faltered. Corrin bound up his sword and leaned into him, shouldering him into one of the vertical beams.

Corrin heard Limp sliding his way across the room behind him. But the smelly man held strong in the bind.

Must go faster.

Corrin leaned all his weight on the stinking man, forcing his blade flat up against his body. He pulled his left hand back as fast as he could. He slipped his Cambrian dirk free of his belt loop and smacked it down on top of one smelly hand. The sword it had been holding dropped conclusively to the floor, and he screamed a smelly scream.

Corrin punched with his crossguard, cracking him in the nose, spraying blood down his chin. Corrin twisted and turned. He rolled the smelly man over and threw him into Limp. They both collapsed, one atop the other.

Corrin slid his longsword through the back of one and the front of the other, uniting them in a sweet embrace. He drew back and wiped the blood on their cloaks.

He looked up. Mustache was looking at him.

"Oh, that's right," Corrin said. "You were there, too."

Mustache had the bells on his shoes. He jingled his way forward, a pair of shortswords in his hands.

"Two swords," Corrin said. "Twice the price." He held up his weapon. "She is waiting."

But before he was able to manage anything remotely magnificent, the other odious man rose behind him and wrapped his arms up in a bear hug. *Shaot. Forgot about you.* Corrin dropped his sword. Mustache jingled closer.

Not good. Not good.

But then Corrin heard a *plunk*. The arms holding him went limp. His back felt wet. He glanced over his shoulder at the man holding him. Sticking out of his neck was what appeared to be a knife that looked *very* similar to the one Corrin had told Reidos hundreds of time to never use as a throwing weapon because the weight was wrong and it would be prone to missing its intended target.

Corrin shrugged out of the corpse's grasp, letting him fall. He pursed his lips and squinted at Reidos.

Reidos shrugged.

Mustache darted out the back door, his jinglebells telling the tale of his flight.

"You see what you did there?" Corrin chastised. "You frightened the other one off before I was finished."

"You are welcome," Reidos said.

"For fouling up my grand finale?"

"You are a madman, Corrin," Inrianne said.

Corrin bowed. "Compliments are always welcome."

Corrin heard a rustling beside him. He turned. The girl was still there. The boy was still in her arms.

"Ah, there we were," Corrin said. "Now I remember. We were supposed to do something with you."

"Help her," Inrianne said. "We are supposed to help her."

"Right," Corrin said. "Well, we ought to get out of here. Someone might find this mess and try to blame me for it."

"You made the mess," Inrianne said.

"Don't bother me with trifles," Corrin said. "I was *barely* involved."

"Donnovar," Reidos said. "We should take her to Donnovar. He will know what to do."

Corrin glanced back at the door his golden lovely had disappeared through and he grimaced until he was grinding his teeth. *She won't be coming back any time soon. Not without a legion of the Home Guard anyway.* He spat on the redwood floor.

This Red God is cursed, he decided.

The walk was a long one. The woman would not allow herself to be touched, even to wipe some of the blood from her face. She would flinch and groan at every sound. She had battle-terror as bad as a green boy-soldier in a slaughterfield on the Sarenmoor. Walking through the streets with her did well to earn long, concerned stares.

Her eyes could not sit still, watching the streets, the rooftops, and the alleyways, flickering nervously over every door and window. The boy never moved, like a doll in her arms.

When they finally arrived at the entrance to the way-station, he saw Donnovar immediately. It was hard not to when he stood head and shoulders taller than everyone around him. Margol the bodyguard and Balthoren the crossbowman were like children beside him. He was thick enough with muscle to make even the Sarenwalkers look like fragile porcelain dolls.

"Captain," Corrin called out.

Donnovar's eyes glanced upward from the maps he had been discussing with his lieutenants, and widened a bit when he saw them.

"What is this?" Donnovar asked.

"We chanced across this woman," Corrin said. He paused. "While just a little bit, marginally, tangentially involved in a little baby of a sword fight."

Donnovar could have cut stone with his stare. "Sword fight?"

"A little bitty nothing," Corrin assured him. "Not something to worry about." He thought it best not to mention the men he had killed. That was liable to set him to a frenzy.

Balthoren unslung one of his crossbows. "I could go have a look."

Donnovar waved him off. He stared at Corrin. "We are not supposed to be causing trouble here. I am certain Aren mentioned to you the importance of our profile remaining low."

"Oh yes, very low. The lowest. Honestly, the Home Guard here may give me an award of some kind. You see, these surprisingly memorable fellows were holding this fair lady as hostage."

"You expect me to believe you lot rescued a woman being held captive?"

"Yes."

"Where?"

"In a...tavern. I can see how this might look bad. Allow me to explain."

Donnovar held up one titanic fist in front of Corrin's face. He methodically unfurled his index finger until it was pointing at Corrin's forehead. "I think it would be best for all if you ceased explaining everything for however long forever is."

Corrin nodded, pursing his lips in agreement, as if they had come to that decision together.

Donnovar turned to the girl. "Is this true? Were you captive?"

Her eyes snapped up to meet his. She looked at him as though his words were the subtle promises of her long lost love. "Yes."

"Your name?"

She smiled and tears suddenly spilled down her face. She sobbed like a lovesick young girl who had been in her cups for a fortnight. "Mayvene," she said. "My name is Mayvene."

Donnovar wagged a finger at his men. "Clean her face. She is covered in blood."

Balthoren held out a cloth to her.

"No," she pleaded. "Please don't touch me."

"What would you have us do then?" Donnovar asked.

"I don't know," she said. "I...I don't know. He won't leave me alone. He won't ever leave me alone." She closed her eyes and shook her head hopelessly.

"We could escort you somewhere safe," Donnovar offered. "My Sarenwalkers could protect you. No one would lay a hand on you in their presence."

Mayvene shuddered. "They can't protect me. You can't protect me. None of you can."

Donnovar looked at her, perplexed. "We are five hundred soldiers."

"It doesn't matter," she said.

"What *can* we do then? Other than leave you standing here on the street alone?"

"I have to go," she said. "I should go. I have to go. I need to go. I won't go back. I need to go far."

"The boy," Donnovar said. "Is he your blood?"

"No."

"Is he kith to you?"

"I do not know him at all," she said. "But I couldn't leave him."

"Leave him with us," Donnovar said. "My men are soldiers with soldiers' duties. But we can ensure he is cared for. We fear nothing."

She looked at the soldiers and Sarenwalkers warily. "You? You could look after him?"

"I will look after him myself, Captain," a man said.

Donnovar turned to face him. "Which of you spoke?"

"I did," one of the cook's attendants said. "I am named Duran. Amicien Duran. I will care for the boy. He could ride with the wagons, my Captain. It would be no trouble to me."

Corrin looked at Duran. He had deep-set eyes. His chin formed a sharp tip on the end of a round face. He wore a short mud-colored jerkin over a worn grey shirt.

Donnovar looked back and forth between them. He waved his hand, and two of his Sarenwalkers lifted the boy gently out of her hands and brought him to Duran.

He then turned back to Mayvene. The girl was still shaking, but at least her tears had stopped. "What is his name?"

"Hallan," she whimpered. "He told me his name was Hallan on the first day that I met him. He doesn't talk anymore, not even to me. He did once, but not anymore." Mayvene grinned wide. She nodded over and over. She shrank back, clasping her arms over her chest. She turned and bolted across the courtyard, never slowing, never even looking back.

"Wait!" Donnovar called, but she did not stop.

"Shall I return her?" a Sarenwalker asked.

Donnovar shook his head. "Let her go. Just let her go."

Corrin deemed it best not to speak.

Donnovar turned to him and stared, his hands on his hips, chewing his lip as if it were a piece of gristle. He half-laughed, stopped, did it again, then shook his head from side to side in resignation. "Did you happen to see Aren out on the streets?"

"No," Corrin said. "Is he missing? Have you checked all the libraries? Are there any ancient shrines nearby? Old paintings? Stacks of papers?"

"If you see Aren out on the streets, be sure to tell him we need to talk." Donnovar eyed him coolly. "And see that you avoid any additional mishaps. If any more women need help, call for the Home Guard."

"Of course," Corrin said.

The Captain turned back to his officers.

"You neglected to mention the men we killed," Reidos said.

"Trifles." Corrin patted himself down, touching the hilt of each of his weapons one by one. But when he came to the second loop on his left side he found it vacant. "Shaot."

"What now?" Reidos asked.

"You are going to get mad."

Reidos folded his arms and tapped his foot. "Speak."

"I may have left my Cambrian dirk back at the *Red God*."

Reidos rolled his eyes. "We are not going."

"I am not leaving it behind. It cost ten silver tossers."

"That place will be crawling with Home Guard soldiers looking for a couple of murderers who look exactly like us. Because they *are* us."

"Love will find a way." He snatched Reidos by the shoulder. "You too, Mahhen. I will require someone to talk to while I walk."

Back into the winding streets he went.

When he came within distant view of the *Red God* again, he made the sign of the witch at it. *How dare you steal from me?* It was like an awkward reunion with an old acquaintance he had been hoping to avoid. *Good to see you again, sir. No. No time for a drink. I have business to attend to.*

"Well? Aren't you going to go in and get your knife?" Reidos looked over his shoulder, expecting Home Guard volunteers to materialize at any moment.

"First of all, it is not a knife, it is a Cambrian dirk, you swine. And secondly, something is different." He noticed a dull azure glow, a winking haze, coming from the door. He walked up to it, and pulled on the handle. The door slid open and a cloud of strange vapor hovered beyond it, floating in the air like liquid color. It hugged the ground like water, evaporating at the fringes.

He staggered backward. He stumbled over a potted plant and banged his hip into an iron table.

"Afterglow," Reidos said. "The telltale of a user."

Corrin blinked through the glow, straining to peer into the pulsing light. At every glance it was different. It would be a hissing cloud, or a vibrating wave, or distinct and completely individual particles, or a solid wall of color.

His eyes slowly adjusted, and he began to make out the shape of something, a cross shape upon the opposite wall. It was a man, or what had been a man once, hung like a tapestry, arms outstretched upon the wall like a sacrifice to some long extinct Adumbari god.

"When did that happen?" Corrin asked.

"We must bring Aren," Reidos said.

Corrin looked at the *Red God*. He thought of the girl with golden hair, now long gone. "This place is cursed."

10

Questions

IT COULD HAVE BEEN the home of the elder, or someone could have stolen one random item from each merchant cart in the old market and then decorated a room with the results.

Small ivory statuettes and incense basins were left carelessly overturned. An unlit fireplace overflowed with ashes, long burned out. Large pots in the corners held sinister plants, full of slender, creeping leaves. A bronze urn sat on the floor, placed casually beside an iron cooking pot, still half full of partially congealed spiced stew, from which a small cat eagerly lapped. Vases stood in every conceivable location, each containing a different treasure: reeds of watershiver plants, rolled scrolls tied with hemp, sets of silver utensils, alchemical instruments, and a bright yellow rose.

A wiry old man appeared in the hallway opposite them. His face was drooped and shrunken with age, the skin of his forehead tightly wrinkled like a desiccated fruit. A wispy white beard brushed against his chest. He wore an ancient aba robe, faded by decades of wearing, pale blue, as thin as a single hair.

At the far end of the corridor was a musty stair descending into darkness. Aren and Redevir followed him down until they were at least two stories underground. They were guided into a room, which amounted to little more than an alcove. Gnarled reed candles perched in every corner.

The elder beckoned them both to sit in miniature wooden chairs. They creaked under the weight. The man seated himself on an ancient rug, frayed at the edges, the design of interlocking swirling circles, like the sand-patterns of Minaraddin. He lit a small censer beside him, and the smoke of myrrh slithered out like snakes.

The elder's voice was high pitched and sonorous, like an Olybrian pheasant. "Have you brought me a boy?"

"He is not for you," Redevir said. "I have something else to gift you...if you obtained what I desire."

The elder held up a small tome with his tiny arm. Its meager weight looked like it might snap his wrist. Faded blue cloth cover, scratched and rough around the edges, and in the center, in faded script, was the title, *Mercury Woods*. "Seek for the words of poets where none should be."

Redevir gently removed the book from the old man's hand, and in its place he deposited a scroll of worn parchment from his own carry-bag.

The elder nodded approvingly.

"My search has been difficult," Redevir said.

"Worthy quests bring competition," the old man said.

"I went to find a rose, and found that it had already wilted."

"Not even a sack full of gold can stop a dark winter."

"Dark winter does not often come in the height of summer."

"He is unseasonable," the old man agreed. "Time must be running out for him to come so early. Perhaps there is a dog at his heels."

Redevir smiled briefly. Then his questions become suddenly direct. "Is the fourth found?"

"Many things are found every day."

"And the fifth?"

"Many things, but not that one."

"Good," Redevir said. "There is still time for me to make the journey east."

"That's it?" Aren asked. "Just those questions?"

"They were just affirmation of what I presumed to be true. The answers I need will be in this book." He motioned to the elder. "Your turn. Go on, ask away. He loves to talk."

Aren looked the old man up and down. "Are you sure? This feels silly."

"Go on," Redevir said. "You might be surprised."

Aren wrinkled his lip. *A test question then. To see what I am in for.* "We saw a giant on our way here."

"Redscar. A titan of Chashreel. His real name is Rashkhadhavazar. But no one calls him by that name anymore. Not even the people of Chashreel. He was renamed by promoters of bloodsport in Mekrash Valley. They all spoke the same tongue as you, boy."

"You know him?"

"No. But I know he is here."

"How do you know his name? Who told you who he was?"

"Who told you that the sky was blue?"

"Cute. Real cute. Fine. How did he come to be here?"

"A contract was written between two men to perform feats of strength for the *twenty days of delight* after Chal's Day."

He does not pause in his responses. He exhibited none of the common tells of deception—dancing eyes, sweat response, abundant hand movements. So *he seems to know what he is talking about. He has ears to the ground here.*

"Why don't you ask me what you truly want to ask me, boy?"

"To the point. Fine. There were men of Amagon here. My people. They have disappeared."

"They were hunted. Like animals in the streets. They became prey."

"Hunted? Who hunted them?"

"It means he is not invincible yet."

"Who? The High King of Olbaran? What does that mean?"

"One who is invincible is threatened by nothing. All fear is gone. This was done by one who still thinks about fear."

"Are the rest of us in danger now?" Aren asked.

"There is always danger, even when the sun shines and the children play."

Interesting. All right then. Let us see what kind of insights you have about something you know nothing about. "I am traveling with a man named Raviel. Can he be trusted?"

"Can a dog be trusted to be a dog? Or a snake a snake? Or a fool a fool? An animal may eat from your hand, or it may bite, or it may leave you alone. Any one man may have many motives. Even a friend can set himself against you."

"That was not an answer."

"You asked no question," the old man said. "You sought validation for a choice you have already made."

"I was sent on a trace. To hunt someone dangerous. A murderer. An assassin. A user."

"He made the first move," the elder said. "Everything else that comes is because of that."

"Who made the first move? The assassin?"

The elder would not answer.

Aren folded his arms, annoyed. "Fine. Answer me this. Can I catch the assassin?"

"No."

"What do you mean, *no?*" *As if this one little old man could know the future.* Yet Aren still felt it sting that these shallow, brittle prognostications would label him a failure.

"One cannot be an assassin if one does not seek to assassinate. You are trying to stop someone who never existed. You are trying to prevent something that will never happen. If that is so, perhaps you might ask yourself what you are *really* doing here."

"Why else would I be here?"

"They have many plans."

"Who does?"

"One is the victor in this first game."

"But there are more games to be played?"

The old man smiled. "You are quick to learn the truth. That is the first step on the path to wisdom. The second game has already begun. You have been one of the pieces, but now you will be one of the players."

"What do you mean *I'm* one of the players? Who do you think I am?"

"I have seen many things. I have seen a throne rot from within, and friends make war upon one another. I have seen evil hide and walk in plain sight. I have seen empires fall and families die. I have seen mountains crumble and the earth sink beneath the waves. I have seen three sisters play a game of dice with god, and I have seen love suffer at the hands of fate. I have seen the Advent. I have seen the Days of Light upon the earth."

"I don't believe in any gods," Aren said. "And I don't believe in you either."

"There is a legend, one that is very old, when the hero Caldannon wrestled the Three Terrors in a battle that broke the world, and though he could not destroy them, he locked them deep within the earth eternally. A legend where the gods fell to the earth and perished in a war of centuries, leaving this world behind forever. The last of them prophesied that when again a man came to the world like a *Sanadi* of old, only one could defeat him, a champion who would come and face down that power. It is spoken of in the History of Jordanus. The Days of Light will begin with those who cannot do, but *see*. Jordanus says that *he of sorrow* is the hero who will end this terror. He is the *man of sorrow*. The *sorrowful man*. When that time comes, only he will prevail."

Sanadi. Aren had heard the term. Legendary people of unimaginable power, more gods than men really. It was said that the magick they were capable of wielding could shape the world itself to their designs. "If you are trying to frighten me..."

The elder reached forward, gripped Aren's wrist with one icy claw of a hand.

Aren felt a sudden surge of pain wash through his body, like icicles in his veins. "Stop. Let me go."

"I have seen them come who can see through the world. Those who can go where no others can go. The light made flesh, the Advent Lumina. There will be one above them. There will be others like him, but only one can be him.

The man of sorrow must come. The sorrowful man. Caldannon could only win because he could see what no one else could see."

"I can already see everything I need to see. I am a Glasseye." Aren pulled back and tried to wrench his hand away, but the old man squeezed his wrist even tighter.

"The *Days of Light* are coming," he hissed. "Soon they will outshine the sun. Just wait. You will see. You will *see*."

Aren recoiled, cupping one hand about his wrist, his curiosity wiped away by sudden fear. "How could you know anything about me? You do not even know who I am."

"I know *what* you are."

"I am a Render Tracer."

"You are the s—" the old man began.

Aren cut him off. "The *sorrowful man*? Save your breath. I don't buy into any of what you are selling."

"Aren—" Redevir reached for his elbow.

Aren yanked it away. "No, Redevir. He is trying to get me to do something, or say something, or buy something from his cousin. And I am not interested."

"He knew about your people," Redevir said.

"*Word on the street* is not some mystical feat," Aren said. "People talk, others listen. But if you expect me to believe this little old man can see the future, you are dead wrong."

Redevir shrugged.

The elder offered them the utmost courtesy when showing them out, but as Aren was returning to the streets, the old man spoke. "Cruel secrets burden the man with leaves that never leave him."

Aren cringed. *The malagayne. He knows.*

"What did that last bit mean?" Redevir asked.

Aren willed his smile to return to cover his fear. "I didn't understand half of the things he said."

Redevir chuckled.

Aren sighed with relief. "I have learned nothing at all. I could not mention one word of this to Donnovar without sounding like a raving madman."

Redevir shrugged. "Apologies. I thought his words might have been as illuminating for you as they always have been for me. I was surprised how long he went on."

"How did you even know about him? The elder."

Redevir let out a long breath. "That is a long story. Too long for tonight."

Aren decided he did not mind not knowing.

They moved out into the night. Escape had never smelled more pungent, nor looked more treacherous. The streets were empty and silent, save for the piping and hissing of unseen subterranean gases from long abandoned sewers. What they lacked in action, they made up for in stench. He had never thought someone would find it necessary to saute raw garbage in liquid shit, but if someone ever did, he would at least know what to expect.

Aren kept the conversation short. He listened to the streets. He knew better than to feel safe here. He knew what lurked in every city after dark, because he walked cities at night, hunting. He knew the robbers would become more brazen. He studied the sounds of his footfalls in the hopes of discerning any kind of pursuit. He knew he would hear it soon. Survival was the way of these places when the sun fell. It turned into a maze of predators, feeding on the weak.

"Want to hear a story?" Aren asked.

"Are you sure this is a good time to tell a story?"

"It's about the Hezzam," Aren said. "From the legends of Shezail Valley."

"I'm game," Redevir said.

"In the tale of Zhakris, Ildrun the Sorcerer had engaged in an affair with the Emperor's daughter."

"Sounds dangerous," Redevir said.

"The emperor called for Ildrun's head. He sent his most trusted assassins."

"Hezzam assassins?" Redevir asked.

Aren nodded. "They followed Ildrun to the metropolis of Halzahman. In the legend the Hezzam were driven away when Ildrun invoked the name of a Ghomras, enormous worms that snake silently under the sands of the Samani deserts."

"Giant worms?"

"They were said to swim through the dunes as though the sands were made of water," Aren said. "The legends claim that the Ghomrai were mastered by powerful sorcerers, and that they would rise to defend their masters if called upon, no matter how far from their homes."

"It sounds far-fetched," Redevir said.

"But the Hezzam are a singularly superstitious people," Aren said. "And would fear such words far more than they would fear a hundred armored knights."

It was then that Aren heard several quiet steps echoing behind his own. They grew in number, and in volume. Aren waited until they were close, so that he would be able to see them clearly, and they him. He stopped in his tracks and whirled on his heels to face them.

Hezzam. A dozen. More than he thought there would be. They fanned out in a tight arc, stopping ten paces away. Dark robes covered them from head to foot, and strapped sandals grasped their feet like insects strangling their prey. Only the eyes were visible between thick veils and heavy turbans, giving off stares as sharp as the steel in their hands. Their long, curved daggers tapered to fine piercing points.

Aren kept his gaze straight ahead, and his blade only half drawn.

The one in the center stepped forward. He must have been the leader. He was the one Aren would target. When they took another step, Aren drew his own sword to its full length and reared back, throwing his arm high over his head, pointing the blade to the stars.

The Hezzam jerked backward, stunned by the surprise of motion. They tried to recover, but Aren called out a name into the air. "Za'ruk Sakkis!" It was the name of a Ghomras.

The Hezzam knew instantly what Aren had done, and there was not one among them who didn't take a step back. They all knew, as he did, that Za'ruk was the surname of a Ghomras, and Sakkis was a very well known worm of legend. They would have heard its name since childhood.

Several heartbeats passed, silence blanketing the street.

Aren waited until their uncertainty was at its peak, as they looked to each other to see if they could decide what to do next. It was then that he brought the tip of his blade down to point at their feet of their leader—the motion that would signal his enemies to the Ghomras. Every single one of the Hezzam bolted instantaneously, scampering away down street, disappearing in shadows.

Aren smiled, sheathing his sword. "Believe in the story now?"

"You had no doubt, did you?" Redevir asked.

"The Hezzam are a mysterious people," Aren said. "But all through the Histories their superstition is very predictable. That is the practical use of myths and religions. Fear. Fear that can be used to control people. It is the same reason I don't believe a word your elder said to me about legends or prophecies or destiny."

"Fair enough," Redevir chuckled. "I suppose they will spread the word of this among their kinsmen. I wouldn't be surprised if there is talk tomorrow of wizards roaming the streets at night." He paused. "Did the worm really come after Ildrun's enemies?"

"The tale doesn't say," Aren said. "Nothing will chase after these ones, though. I'm no sorcerer." He paused. He smiled at Redevir. "I did not use the Ghomrai themselves, but rather the fear they felt for the Ghomrai."

Redevir gave a slight bow. "Like the white-faces. Very clever. I am impressed. Well done."

"Now get me back to the way-station, if you would. I need to speak with my people."

But as Aren turned around, there was suddenly a man standing before him. Aren's shoulder brushed against him as he turned, and the shock nearly jolted him from his feet.

This was no Hezzam robber. This man stood tall, even taller than Aren, with hair black like shadows, with flowing robes and midnight cloak. His eyes *stared* in a way that no one should ever look at anything.

Aren felt his courage melt away. He forgot Redevir entirely. He just stood there stuttering apologies, before finally backing away. The unseeable face seemed to either smile or smirk. Aren could not tell for certain.

"It is finally you," he said. His voice grated in Aren's ears like a pitchfork scratching across slate. The pale beam of a street lantern illuminated half his face.

"Me?" Aren did not recognize him at all, though the man acted as though they had met before.

"The next one. The last one."

"The next what?"

"You know what I am becoming."

"Who are you?"

"They think prophecies can defeat me. Do you believe enough? They all think they can make them come true if they believe enough. But they are wrong. You won't be the first *chosen one* to give up and join me."

Aren took a step back. *He is a madman. He could be dangerous.* He kept glancing at his hands for sign of a knife. "What do you want with me?"

"To change you," the man said earnestly. "To make you right again. To make you walk the right path. To make you perfect. Your path is wrong. It must be changed. You are wasted here. I choose you. The way you once chose me. You should be a part of this. *This* should be your destiny, not the promises of fools."

"I have never seen you before in my life. I have never spoken to you. We have never met. You mistake me for someone else."

"No," he said. "It is you. You are the same."

Aren felt his stomach sinking into his bowels. He felt like he wanted to listen to everything the man said, to follow his path, his words chiming inside his head. *Something is wrong. I don't feel well.*

"Imagine a world without pain. Without suffering. Without fear. What could the world become when it is free of all these horrors? Caldannon tried and failed. They say the *Three Terrors* are monsters, beasts that cannot be slain. But they are not truly animals. They are pride, wrath, sorrow—the children of desire. Caldannon could not tame them because he did not recognize them for what they were. *I will.*"

Aren froze. *There is no way he could have known what the elder said.* He couldn't. It wasn't possible.

"They all die, you know. They always do. Those who sow pain and terror will perish. Their friends will wither away and their towers will crumble. It was never meant for them. They stole it through fraud. They rule it through brutality and fear. All lords and kings are complicit. There is only one *true* crown fit for an immortal. I must have it, and you will be the one to give it to me. You swore it. It is the only way to save them all."

"I. Don't. Know you," Aren said.

"You are not yet free. They still hold you back. I have more work to do to make you what you need to be." The man took a step back, and smiled. He turned and walked away. He rounded a corner and it was as if he had never even been there.

Aren stood frozen. The man was gone, but the words remained in his memory, as permanent as stone, as cryptic as the words of the elder. It felt like he had been threatened, and yet somehow also invited to a party. He glanced right and left, shook his head, and let out a long breath.

Then Redevir put a hand to his shoulder. Aren turned, and was surprised to see him, though he knew he had been there the whole time.

"Aren," Redevir said, giving him a shake. "That was quite a riddle of a man, was it not?"

Aren stared down the dark street. "I...I do not know what to think about that."

"Was he telling the truth?" Redevir asked. "Do you know him?"

"No. Not at all. Not even a little."

"He certainly seemed to know you," Redevir said. "He acted like you were old friends."

"He was crazy," Aren said. "Some transient pauper. A lunatic."

"A curious fellow no matter how the calpas is sliced," Redevir said.

Aren shook the feeling back into his hands and feet. He slipped the Jecker monocle from its pouch. Fumbled with it. Nearly dropped it. He held the lens to his eyes. He saw nothing but night air through the thin crystal disc. He scanned the street, and the air above it. He furiously slid the filters over the lens.

Nothing. No afterglow, no residuals, nothing. He is not the assassin. He is not the one who has the girls. There was no link to his trace. He let his arm sway to his side, and tapped the lens against his belt. "What is going on here, Redevir?"

Redevir held up both hands, and offered an innocent look. "I thought you were the investigator. What are the Three Terrors anyway? He said something about them. The elder just mentioned the very same thing."

"What Caldannon feared," Aren said. "In the ancient Caldannon myth, the three most terrible of his enemies were ancient creatures from beyond time, called the Three Terrors, who were prophesied to come to destroy the world thrice over. Bol-Demar, *Duramathios*, the Eater of Worlds, would swallow everything alive; Shaab-Gulod, *Kallathadios*, the Enemy from Hell, would burn every memory of man from the face of the earth; and Danab-Dil, *Chythokosholos*, the Horror of the Depths, would drown the earth beneath the waves. One of Caldannon's sworn battle-brothers, Gallanor, was the one who brought the three terrors into the world, thinking he could control them, but his hubris was nearly the end of the world. Caldannon and his *People of the Bright* fought against them. Fought them but could not *defeat* them. As the world was breaking, Caldannon sacrificed himself to drag the three terrors to the center of the earth, where he holds them eternal in his embrace, keeping them far away from all of us."

"Charming," Redevir said. "He must think quite highly of himself to claim them as company. But the elder said Jordanus wrote about it. I thought he was a historian. Why would he be spreading prophecies? I thought the Histories avoided fable."

"They are just a part of the Caldannon myth," Aren said. "A tale just like Zhakris and the Ghomras. The Abbadi were fond of apocalyptic myths. It might have been a result of the centuries of wars they fought against Adumbar. Caldannon is just the most famous of the tales. That man was just trying to frighten us, the same way we frightened the Hezzam."

"You know an awful lot about ancient prophecies for a man who claims to loathe ancient prophecies."

Aren shrugged. "I read the Histories. Mythologies are a part of history. I don't have to believe them. There is a difference in describing mythology for posterity and actually proselytizing it. The Caldannon version of the myth came from the Vardan traditions of the Empire of Arradan. That is Jordanus' specialty. That is why the Three Terrors all have Vardan names. So when Jordanus is talking about *he of sorrow* he is just reporting what the story said, not lending weight to it. Besides, Jordanus was notorious for making mistakes. He is the last historian I would want to base the accuracy of my prophecy on."

Redevir then fulfilled his promise and led Aren back to the way-station. Aren could see it looming just over a row of rooftops.

He imagined how good it would feel to slough off his clothes and equipment and collapse into a sleeping cot for the night.

But then he heard someone calling his name.

He thought at first that it must have been Terrol, come to find him and snicker at his pathetic inability to find out what happened to their missing men. But it was not his voice.

Aren spun around. *Who else could know me here?*

His eyes settled on a disgruntled man dressed all in black.

It was Corrin. And Reidos with him.

"What in all hells are you doing here, Corrin?"

"You know him?" Redevir asked.

"Unfortunately."

"Rude," Corrin said. "Who is this?"

"Someone I just met," Aren said. "What do you want?"

"Well, I *wanted* a drink. That was where this whole mess began."

"Speak plainly."

"Well, magick was magicked," Corrin said. "And, as I recall, you are the one who likes to look directly at that sort of thing."

Aren narrowed his eyes. "Show me."

****

The man with black eyes followed the elder to the incense hall. He entered, and navigated his way among the other penitents who prayed upon the floor and leaned against the walls. Most did not notice his passage, the rest did not care. They minded their own business here, content to sit in their own trances, following whatever sundry spiritual journeys their potent hallucinogens provided.

He entered the alcove reserved for the elder in the far corner. He parted the veil, and then pulled it shut behind him, sealing himself inside. The elder sat unmoving on a stained and dusty pillow. His incense was raging, sending its furious plumes of smoke up from a tarnished brass censer.

He circled the elder until he stood directly behind him.

"You should not have given it to him," the man said.

The elder said nothing.

"You should not have made promises about what is to come. I have already changed everything."

The elder said nothing.

"You have only written yourself into my story as another obstacle. They say the Advent is describing a clock counting down time. They are wrong. *I am the*

Advent. I am what is coming. Mine is a story of salvation for this world, and you have set yourself apart from that. I will not weep for you. Overcoming such an obstruction is worth celebrating."

The elder said nothing.

The man raised an eyebrow with a sudden realization. "You knew this was going to happen, didn't you?"

The elder said nothing.

It was easy to snap the elder's neck. It was brittle and frail. The man left the other penitents where they lay, and stepped back out into the streets.

11

Where The Body Was

THERE WAS NO BODY.

The back street was empty and quiet. Aren stood in darkness beneath a chestnut tree outside the back door of the *Red God*. The nearest street lamp was one row over, the light leaking through the space between two red brick warehouses.

He peered through the open door at the wall within. The nails were still there, lit by oil lamps. And the blood. Urine on the floor underneath, still drying. So Corrin had not imagined it. There had been a man crucified against the wall. "Someone definitely cleaned this place," Aren said. "There is talcum residue. Lye as well. Water on the walls and floor here. And some kind of smoke. Not sandalwood. Something else."

"Shaot," Corrin said. "Where is it?"

"You mean, where are *they?*" Reidos peered down the back hallway and between the tables and chairs. "We killed four men in there."

"*I* killed *three* men," Corrin said. "*You* killed maybe half of one. Let us not begin this by misrepresenting my exploits."

"This makes no sense," Reidos said. "Why would the Olbaranian Home Guard come in and clear out the bodies and just leave?"

"They wouldn't," Aren said. "Especially if there was a user here. There should be Glasseyes and Sweepers combing this place for traces."

"Unless they never knew anything happened," Reidos said.

Aren nodded.

Corrin glanced over his shoulder. "Seems quite a bit like *no one* knew anything happened here. Where is the bartender? Where is the serving girl? Why are there no people walking up and down the alley? Why are there no people stumbling in? Why isn't some old woman looking out her second floor window at what all the commotion was? I feel like there is always one of those whenever I happen to be climbing out of the bedroom window of a magistrate's marriageable daughter. Murder and magick seems at least half as interesting as that."

"He is right," Redevir said. "I have been in Westgate for weeks and I have never seen a street so empty."

"They can't all be afraid of me," Corrin said. "They don't even know who I am. Although Reidos will tell you I clipped that user's wings before he ran."

"User?" Aren asked. "You *saw* the user? The one that did this?"

"Well, I saw him, I sliced him before he could magickally magick his magick at me, and then he ran away. Got my blade wedged into the beam there. That shit farod is lucky this is Sabarian steel or it might have damaged the blade."

"So you did not see him do *this*?" Aren asked.

"Oh, no. The body, the nails, this part happened while we were away. We chanced across it on the way back. It must have been the same fellow though, right? How many users can there be who come to this one cursed tavern on the same day?"

"I am about to find out," Aren said. He took one step inside. The smell of almonds immediately registered with his nose. *Almonds. Pressure renders leave the smell of almonds in the air.*

"This is the magick?" Redevir asked. "It looks suspiciously like plain vacant air. Hmm, smells nice, actually."

"You have to look at it the right way," Aren said, withdrawing the Jecker monocle. "The afterglow fades over time, but it can be seen longer with this."
Evidence.

He scanned the hallway through the lens, saw afterglow dancing a fourth-dimensional waltz in the air. *A fresh scene. No more than a few hours old at most.*

He could not flip through the filters fast enough—white, rose, green, and blue—each time the world transforming into a stranger version of itself.

He could see how the user had killed, how he had lifted the corpse, how he had severed the hands cleanly, how he had suspended the body. Each new world told him more of the story of what had happened, like the unfolding of a tale from the Histories. The spectral lines, the warping, the time-arching, the patterns, the colors—each was its own chapter in the thin volume of a murder.

The blue filter plunged the world into an ocean of sapphire light, and all but the core color of the afterglow became cold and dark as if submerged in murky water. "Pale orange," he said. "And they've been masked. He uses waveform compression masking every time, on every single render. The concentration wasted on all this unnecessary masking is astonishing. This user is *obsessed* with it. It is like he can't bring himself to render without a stream of waveform compression to muddy the pattern of his bind structure." He double-checked the redshift. Very faint, but it was there. Whoever had done this was moving away.

Everything seemed closer through the green filter, lamplight became moonlight, and everything was bathed in the cool green darkness, the *spectral lines* shining in arcs like the glint of light on a knife. They looked like the wake of a ship in the air, frozen in time, showing the size, position, and path of travel of every shape and force rendered. They were ghostly silvery white outlines hanging in the air. He could walk around and in between them. He saw arcs of resistance where the elbows and wrists would have been, rings about the waist and ankles, slender and delicate lines hovering quietly about the face and torso that had sliced him open, torn flesh, bled him out, eviscerated him.

The white filter showed a world hidden by clouds, with sparkling afterglow shining like rainbows. It diminished the residual glow, making the colors hazy and smoky, but removed the uncomfortable time-arching. Aren analyzed the warping. *High prismatic dispersion. He has used these renders before, often enough to be exceptionally comfortable using them like this.* "This user has a great level of control. Disciplined, pragmatic, intentional in every act." There would be no simple mistakes from such a user.

What else? Sarker's voice asked in his head.

Aren switched filters again.

The rose filter turned the brightest light into a faint sunset, everything hazy, crimson, and distant. It warmed the colors and made them run together, and where they merged, the glow curve resonated richly with so many interconnected streams. "It almost seems as though the user had used more renders than was necessary to create his results. No, not *almost.* I am certain of it."

A user of this skill level would not make such an error. The additional streams were bound together on purpose. "The renders holding him in place were set at levels thousands of times stronger than would have been needed to subdue one man. This user wasted his energy *on purpose.* This makes no sense."

Aren removed the Oscillatrix from his pocket. He adjusted the dial on the cylinder, and held it up over his head. The spheres were shifting and cycling through different levels, disturbing any attempt at accurate reading.

Wave pockets. That was the only explanation. There must have been many of them. "There are wave-pockets in the air," he said. "They are floating fairly high, but they are not very old."

Corrin looked up in the air. "I don't see a damn thing, and what is a wave-pocket anyway?" He glanced over his shoulder uncomfortably.

"They occur when someone is funneling a lot of power very quickly into their renders," Aren said. "Leftover altered reality. Waste streams. Stuck half-in and half-out of reality. They happen when a user is binding too fast to manage it all."

"Are wave-pockets dangerous?" Corrin asked, tickling the hilt of his sword as if he expected the wave pockets to attack him.

"They can be if they're punctured," Aren said. "A lot of leftover energy in them. But we don't have anything to worry about. They are only half-real. Wave pockets pass right through brick walls, even right through you, but not through a user's shield wall. They don't react to real physical objects unless they rupture, only other altered reality. A user would have to hit them with magick to rip them open, but to do that a user would have to know they were there. They can't even be seen with a Jecker monocle. The only way we know they exist is by their effects on other residuals."

He tapped the Jecker monocle on his thigh and bit his lip.

"This is so similar to the Lord Protector's assassin. But it is so much more power than the user described by the composite they gave me. These primary values are through the roof. It is like it was the same man, but *not* the same man."

"Could it be the same man trying harder?" Reidos asked. "Using more power?"

"It doesn't work that way," Aren said, trying to get a better angle with the monocle. "He can't reduce his own *natural power level.* Just like if you punch Corrin when he is being an asshole, you don't *have* to use *all* of your strength in each punch, but you can never use *more* strength than you have, and you can never *have* less strength than you do."

"Unless I *make* myself stronger," Reidos said. "If I *really* want to punch him."

"But to do that you have to train yourself, exercise your body to make it stronger over time. A user can increase their natural power *over time* with constant use and training, but we are talking months or years here, not days. And once a user reaches a higher energy level, they can't be less strong than they are. A user can't lower his oscillation on command."

"You can tell all that?" Reidos asked. "Just from looking at the air? Amazing."

"The things I can see with these tools can tell me much more than just your eyes alone. The user's *primary values* that I can read in their afterglow would be like you leaving a stamp on Corrin every time you punch him that would tell us exactly how strong your punch *could have been* if you had used *all* your strength in it at that moment in time."

"I do not like where this analogy is going," Corrin said, arms folded.

"So a user leaves a mark every time he...renders, and it says how strong he is at that moment," Redevir said.

"Yes," Aren said. "It doesn't mean he can render *indefinitely*. Just like Reidos here can only punch Corrin a certain number of times before he needs to rest and eat to replenish himself before he can resume punching Corrin."

"Enough already!" Corrin said.

"And the number of punches before needing rest depends on the amount of force and concentration put behind each one," Aren said.

"That does it," Corrin said. "I'm leaving."

"The difference for users is that if they go past their core limit and use up all their strength, they don't just get tired," Aren said. "They might suffer mental deficiencies, or become comatose for days, or just drop dead on the spot."

"Forgive my inexperience here," Redevir said. "But what is the magick really? You talk about strength and power. What *is* it? What are users actually doing? What do you see when you look at it? What do you write down about it?"

"The *Introduction-Of-Change* key is the user's starting point," Aren said. "The key that unlocks the Slipstream, to bridge the gap between reality and possibility. Every user has a unique *Introduction-of-Change* key pattern, like a fingerprint. It's one of the ways I track them."

"Slipstream?" Redevir asked. "What is that?"

"That is just what Jebbel Dedder called the source," Aren said. "An infinite white light where all streams are born. Streams are replacements of everything around us—time, space, matter, energy, and motion. A stream is a filament of altered reality, matter or energy, size or shape, direction or magnitude. A user can manipulate streams and bind them together into a structure from the natural chaos to achieve a very specific, very un-chaotic result."

"So streams are the pieces," Redevir said.

"A stream could be the spark for a fire," Aren said. "Or the direction of force, or the velocity, or the power behind the motion or stress, a change of temperature, friction, or acceleration, or the temporal duration of a render. Each render has an *ingredient list* of streams. I have to record every ingredient list to spot recurring streams. It is how I plan an interdiction."

"Forgive my weird desire to live," Corrin said. "But shouldn't we get out of here? What if this user comes back?"

"He is not coming back," Aren said. "At least not now. His core colors have been steadily redshifting. He is moving away from us. This is what I do at scenes back in Amagon all the time. Users want to get away from Glasseyes. They do not come toward them."

He removed a small flat panel the size of the palm of his hand from his satchel, and pulled off its leather cover. He placed a piece of parchment of equal size upon it. He then placed the tablet with the parchment atop it in the precise spot he knew the user had stood.

"This is an Imprinter," he said. "Composed of certain materials that are very sensitive to afterglow. When it is near enough, it can capture the patterns of afterglow onto paper. Then I can compare it more closely to another imprint from the other scene, or show it to a Stopper to teach them the user's streams." Aren drew out a small flash-flare, held it at head height, directly above the Imprinter, with the Jecker monocle in between. "Shield your eyes," he said. He struck the tip with his thumb. The light was furious and blinding. It crackled, and shined like the sun through his eyelids. He took one deep breath, and the light faded away to nothing. He tossed the spent flash-flare aside. He took the parchment from the imprinter, and stared at it for a moment.

"Was it the same man?" Corrin asked.

Aren withdrew the pages of the composite from Vithos. He stared at the two side by side, but no matter how closely he looked, he could not find any similarities. "No. The *Introduction-of-Change* doesn't match the composite. The pattern from Vithos is very precise. This one couldn't have been attempted by the same man. It's just not possible. This is the scene of a different user."

He moved around to other locations in the room, taking imprints through the Jecker monocle while alternating the filters. "Well this is odd," he said. He tried to crawl under the afterglow, looking up at it from underneath.

Corrin rolled his eyes. "What a tease you are. Well, go on. I'm quite certain you are just dying to tell us all forwards and backwards and upside down just precisely *how* odd it is."

"Most users learn only a certain number of streams of magnitude to put into the renders—their version of *strong, stronger,* and *strongest,* unique to them. Exactly *how strong* each of those are can vary wildly from user to user. But the less options you have the more opportunity there is for you to waste your energy. If you only have three different streams of magnitude, and your three are strong enough to push a marble, a crabatz ball, or a boulder, what do you do if you need to move an object only one ounce heavier than a crabatz ball?"

"You would have to use the stream with the strength to move a boulder," Redevir said.

"I am quite ready to move that boulder on top of you, Aren," Corrin said. "I'm thirsty. Let us do this faster."

"The problem there is you will be wasting a huge amount of your own energy. The greater magnitude a user renders, the more of their strength is used up, the sooner they will reach their core limit. Users like efficiency. The more experience they get, the more likely they are to have five different variations of strength streams, or size streams, or what have you. Some have twenty. Rare ones have hundreds."

"What does any of that have to do with why I do not have whiskey in my mouth *right now?*" Corrin asked. "Tedious. This is tedious."

Aren set the imprinter once more. "A user binding a force that could throw Corrin into the air would not have the right streams to tailor it to Corrin's specific weight. He would use his version of *strong, stronger,* or *strongest.* The fewer options they have to choose from, the more likely they will waste their energy. If his version of *strong* is not enough to lift Corrin, then nothing happens, energy wasted. If his *strongest* is double Corrin's weight, he will throw Corrin, but will waste half the energy to do it."

"I should never have agreed to be friends with you," Corrin complained.

"Experienced users do whatever they can to prevent waste," Aren said. He pointed at the wall. "This user likely had a hundred different degrees of *strong.* He had the control, the focus, and the confidence to do all of this without even a pinch of wasted energy. But he wasted it *anyway.*"

"Seems silly to do that," Redevir agreed.

"That is what bothers me," Aren said. "A user attacking an ordinary person is like a grown man fighting a small child. It would be a hopeless contest for the one without the magick. Why would someone ever use more force than they needed to?"

"Maybe to scare him," Reidos said. "Terrorize him. Like an interrogation."

"But the man nailed to the wall was dead almost immediately after this attack began. I cannot think of any reason to induce fear into someone who is already dead."

"That means the user was a madman," Corrin said. "Right? Like the madmen you hunt in Amagon."

"Well, it certainly frightened me," Reidos said.

What does it mean? The words of Sarker were in his head. *What else? What are you forgetting?*

Aren probed deeper into the room, the others crawling under where he told them the afterglow was. He had to slap Corrin's hand away from an abandoned bottle of wine more than once. He moved the Oscillatrix around the room, behind tables, around pillars and beams and toward the back rooms where Corrin had said the girl first appeared.

Something caught his attention. The little spheres on the top on the Oscillatrix jumped in their grooves to their maximum marks. "Some interesting readings here."

"Now what?" Corrin asked.

"The energy level needed to confuse an Oscillatrix like this would be massive," Aren said. "It would have to be someone using active magick right on top of it."

"How much magick?" Reidos asked.

"Enough to level this building," Aren said. "And five city blocks besides."

Corrin folded his arms. "So you are saying that your little instruments are telling you that someone is using magick right now, right here, and vaporizing all of us, and we just...don't notice?"

"I said it was interesting."

"You seem to use the word *interesting* the way most people use the word *insane*," Corrin said.

"I have no way to account for it. It's not related to the man nailed to the wall. There isn't even any afterglow. It's like the Oscillatrix is picking up the shadow of magick that *could have happened* but didn't."

"You just get weirder and weirder," Corrin said. "I am bored with this whole affair. I am now undrunk, unfed, unfucked, *and* unrested. Time to go."

"What about the girl?" Aren asked. "You said there was a girl."

"Yes," Corrin said. "More of a woman. At least as old as me, but definitely one thousand years younger than Reidos. What was here name? Mayqueen? Maileen?"

"Mayvene," Reidos said. "She was carrying this little boy. It seemed very much like the men we killed were keeping her here. Likely one of the rent-rooms upstairs."

"The man I am looking for took some girls with him," Aren said. "Not sure how many. At least three. But I don't understand why he would be with a group of cutthroats. And whoever nailed the man to the wall—no offense, Corrin—is not the kind of user who would *run away* from *any* sword-fighter."

Corrin folded his arms. "I *am* taking offense to that and you can't stop me."

"Wait," Aren said. "The user you hit. Was he *rendering*?"

"I told you he was magicking," Corrin said. "He was trying to magick at me. He made little silver sparklies."

"Where?"

Corrin pointed to the beam he stood beside.

Aren turned to it with the Jecker monocle in hand. He scanned the area. "They cleaned the area where the man was on the wall. But they did not clean over here." He saw little patches of hovering swirling silver blotches in the air gleaming at him. *Vectorics. He was trying to punch a sphere through Corrin right here.* "I don't think you realize how close you were to being murder-dead, Corrin."

"Same as always," Corrin said. "And Reidos is closer to *old-age-dead* on any given day than I ever am at the end of a sword. Or a weird user's finger."

Aren checked the little clouds with his Oscillatrix. The primary values were a match to the composite of the assassin. He clicked the blue filter into place. No redshift or blueshift. *He is static at his current location.* Core color pale orange. *Hard to find a match better than that.* But Aren had to be sure. He took an imprint through the blue filter to be certain the *Introduction-Of-Change* key was the same as the composite from Amagon. It was. "This was him. He was right here. You were looking in the eyes of the assassin, Corrin. What happened to that girl? Mayvene? Where did she go?"

"She ran away. After we brought her to Donnovar she dropped the boy on one of the cooks and ran."

"Shaot. I wish I could have talked to her. She could be one of the girls he abducted from Vithos."

"Well," Corrin said. "Safer in the wind than with that lot."

Aren nodded. "I wish there was some sensitized material. Something I could take with me to triangulate his position." The blotches had not come into contact with any surface. He tried to waft the air with his hands, but it only made them swirl in place, too faded to adhere to anything he waved through it. "Afterglow can tell me a lot of information, but I can't take it with me from this scene. Shaot."

"We should leave regardless," Reidos said. "We have been here too long. I hear voices one street over. I think the Captain would have all our hides if we got ourselves caught by the Home Guard."

"Agreed," Aren said. "Let's go." He started for the door, but paused. "Wait."

"What?" Corrin asked.

"You said you clipped him with your sword."

"I certainly did. And what a clip it was. One for the storybooks."

"Let me see your sword."

Corrin pulled back reflexively. "Never ask to see another man's sword. Foul."

"Just draw it."

Corrin drew it.

Aren leaned in close, monocle in hand. Nothing. Clean as running water.

"I wiped it down," Corrin said. "Never leave a blade dirty. Ever. Blood should only be on a blade when it is fresh and hot. After that you had better clean it good and pure. Jecks Keberan always said a dirty blade was the sign of a dull mind."

Nothing. He had nothing. But then he recalled something Corrin had said. "You got your sword stuck in a post?"

"That one," Corrin said. "Right there."

Aren flew to it. He had the monocle so close to his eyes it pressed on his skin. He found a little groove in the wood, where Corrin's sword had cleaved and stuck. Stuck *after* it had swung through a cloud of freshly forming afterglow.

There it was. A tiny shine inside the groove. Aren fumbled in the Tracer satchel and drew out his plying tool and his scraper. He detached two thick splinters of wood from within, and painstakingly dropped them into empty vials, and plugged them with corks. "Corrin, you are a magnificent bastard, and maybe an accidental genius."

"Hah!" Corrin said. "I knew it. You see, Reidos? From the lips of a scholar."

Reidos shook his head. "Look what you've done now, Aren."

Aren was too busy smiling to respond. *I have him. Right here. In Westgate. I can capture him. Today.* He stomped out of the *Red God* and began his pursuit, barely caring if the others caught up to him or not.

To his surprise, Redevir was still there, standing confidently with his arms folded across his chest, and a wide grin on his face. "Were the results of your inquiries to your satisfaction?"

"Yes. I am on the hunt." He held the two vials with one hand, separating them by just a few inches. He looked at them in the Jecker monocle. He started walking. He turned left through an alley, and right in a walkspace separating two butcheries, and belched himself out onto a major thoroughfare.

"Where are you going?" Redevir asked.

"I need to move. Since the user that left this is not moving, I need to move *this* relative to his position to see which way the color shifts. If I am careful, I can follow it right to him." He moved down the street. The shift changed. More blue on the left than the right. Aren turned left.

His hip caught on a street cart heaped with trays of fried spiced lamb and Olybrian cheese. The owner shouted angrily at him in the Halsabadi tongue. Aren held up his hands and very nearly dropped both vials, barely catching them at the last moment. *Shaot.* He closed his eyes and shook his head.

"You get a bit in your own head sometimes, don't you?" Redevir asked.

"And how," Corrin said, jogging to catch up. "He gets so deep into trying to solve riddles he forgets how to walk properly."

"Perhaps I could be of assistance," Redevir said. "I have been in Westgate for a little while. I managed to bring you safely around the Home Guard. Perhaps I could help guide you where you need to go once more."

"I don't know," Aren said.

"At the very least I could make sure you do not run into a dead end, or a canal. I do not suppose those little pieces of wood are going to give fair warning whether their will be a bridge over the river where you need to go."

"True," Aren said.

"Which way do you need to go?" Redevir asked.

Aren looked at the vials through the monocle. He pointed east. "That way."

"Good," Redevir said. "That street runs into a wall at the Gardens of Aranax. This street and the ten streets on either side. I will have to take you up to the New Causeway Road to get around it."

"Not that again," Corrin said. "Goddamn causeways."

Aren followed Redevir, the others trailing behind with degrees of proximity directly proportional to how much they gave a shit about Aren's trace. That meant Corrin was by far the furthest behind.

Every time they passed some landmark, or skirted some impassable district, Aren would consult the vials, determine the direction and let Redevir dictate the path. The method was sound. But it was not without its hiccups.

They turned one corner, and Redevir stopped in his tracks. Aren peered past him, staring into the crowd down the narrow street. A dark shape ambled casually toward them, moving between carts of iron necklaces and knitted scarves.

Ebon-shroud.

Wrapped in a hooded cloak, he drifted towards them, his face wholly hidden from view. Every movement it made was fluid and somehow terrifying. The dark cloak was unmistakable, a color deeper and more futile than black. The objects and people it passed seemed to vanish, not simply out of sight, but as if they ceased to exist at all behind it. And yet no one disturbed the man in his hideous cloak. No one seemed to notice him at all.

"I heard rumors some of them had been seen in Amagon," Aren said. "What are they doing in Westgate? How could one of them even be allowed here?" He shuddered. No one crossed an ebon-shroud. One of the emperors of Halsabad had even let them come and go as they pleased through his palace and even his treasury, for fear of offending them.

Redevir gently urged Aren back with his hand. "Go," he hissed.

"What is it?" Corrin demanded, peering over his shoulder.

"An ebon-shroud in the city," Redevir whispered.

"Swordsmen," Aren said. "Religious zealots who live and train their whole lives in temples deep underground in places so far away you have never heard of them."

"Men I would not trifle with," Reidos said. "Like Sarenwalkers from the deepest hell. What do we do?"

"Let it pass," Redevir advised. "Whenever one crosses your path, you change your path."

"They are addicted to death," Aren whispered. "They see every combat as a prayer for their own death, to end their suffering, and can only allow themselves to die when someone bests them. When their training is complete they set out into the world to find their savior who will lead them to death. It is a different path for each of them."

"What kind of savior would an ebon-shroud believe in?" Corrin asked.

Aren shook his head. "I don't exactly know. Something awful. Death maybe."

"Well," Corrin said. "As a representative of living people, I would think that one of those fellows may run afoul of my beliefs. Why don't you walk us into a bear trap while you are at it, Redevir?"

"I will take us around," Redevir said.

They skirted the markets, and bypassed the old slums. They crossed a noisome tannery district, a place of odors more foul than a bog laden with corpses, where the urge to vomit was only tempered by the urge to weep.

They ended up in the crumbling old tenements that had been the jewel of King Ledo II's building projects from eighty years ago. They had once been grand four-story squat towers of stone and Arradian concrete, with transparent glass in their windows. Now they were in disrepair, and their rooms were no longer sought after by elites, but rather rented for silver bits night by night.

Fewer and fewer people walked the streets, but more and more seemed to watch suspiciously from windows.

Aren kept his eyes on the vials. The shift was nearly as red as it could get. Aren pulled up short, and gestured for the others to wait behind him. He gave one vial to Reidos and one to Corrin and had each of them hold one up ten feet apart and slowly walk toward him, and then away from him. Aren judged the variance of the shift for each and ran them through his algorithms. At last he triangulated the source user who had made the sensitized material.

He looked up at a tenement across the avenue, two buildings over, second level. "There. He is right there."

"What do we do now?" Corrin asked.

Aren licked his lips. A smile spread until it was his whole face. His sore legs and stiff back, aching from a day of desperate hiking through an unfamiliar city, loosened until fresh as if he had just emerged from a hot bath. Pain dissolved into rapture.

Now, when Terrol tried to back him down with accusations about the Stoppers, Aren would have the perfect response. *No Stoppers. But I found the user. In a place where we can take him by surprise. I win. I did this. Not Raviel. Not Terrol. Not Tanashri. Me. Aren of Amagon. I am the Render Tracer. I put rogues in the fires. I will.*

"Now we go back to Donnovar," Aren said. "It is time for a capture."

12

I Promise You

KELUWEN WAS RIGHT. Orrinas hated her idea.

He hated it when she told him that she would be the lure. *I have always looked younger than my years.* It would not be so difficult for her to pass herself off as a girl of fourteen summers. "It is all in the posture," she told him. "And the expressions you make."

He hated it when she showed him what she would be wearing—a tight-fitting bodice, skirts that left little to the imagination, corseted, leaving her shoulders bare, and her chest exposing cleavage down five inches below what would be considered scandalous in one of the Pleasure Houses of Ethios.

She had never thought of herself as robust in that attribute, but it did not take a girl more than a time or two to realize that it almost never ever mattered. If you showed enough of them, no matter their size, or shape, or orientation, a man's eyes would fall into them like stones into a well, and remain there as if held down by glue.

"I need him to barely glance at my face," she told Orrinas. And he knew it was true. But that did not mean that he liked it.

"It should not need to be said that I do not like having you in that room," he told her.

"We are not going to give him one more life," Keluwen said. "I can take care of myself and you know I can." She tugged on the ends of her elbow-length gloves for emphasis. She was pleased that they merely appeared to be part of her ensemble.

"I do."

"Then cease babying me in front of the others. I can shield myself as well as I can cover the door."

"We hope," he said. "Romi and her brothers will be in the closet and in the lavatory, ready to come out with their crossbows, but that will take time."

"He will be disoriented," she said. "When we spring this trap he will be in a stupor from his blood being hot for what he assumes he will be having."

"That is an assumption. A rather large one."

"I know men," she said. "Weak, strong, kind, petty, cruel—they all lose themselves when the blood rises between their legs. Even you."

He looked away briefly, then at his feet, and then over her head.

Glad to know I can still make even the great Orrinas uncomfortable.

"Is everything ready?" Nils asked, leaning his head through the doorway, pretending that he had not been listening to their every word.

Keluwen looked at Orrinas, made deliberate eye contact. "Yes. Ready." She flashed a victorious smirk at him.

"Let me know if you need anything," Nils said. "Water, towel, food. Say the word."

"Thank you, Nils. I am fine."

"We are still waiting on Bonsinar," Cheli called out from down the hallway.

"Where the hell is he?" Keluwen asked.

Nils shrugged. "I have not seen him since this morning. He went to a cafe for omelets and morningwine."

"Where?"

"He didn't say."

"And you didn't ask," Keluwen said.

"He knows his bearings," Nils said. "What was I supposed to do, stand in his way? Half of us were out on the streets today. Everyone came back."

"Send someone to find him," Orrinas said. "Before it is too late."

"It already is too late," Keluwen said. "He drank himself to forgetfulness."

"It seems odd," Orrinas said.

Keluwen waved off his concern. "I will bend him over and take a switch to him when he crawls back here. After the deeds of real heroes are long done."

"We will not have anyone to watch the windows," Orrinas warned.

"I will watch them myself," Keluwen said. "I will be right there."

He looked at her skeptically. "You may have one or two other things on your mind. Tunnel vision is not merely an artifact of the magick. Any stressful situation can bring it on."

"I can handle this." She brushed her fingers playfully, seductively through her hair, frizzing the bob out below her ears, and opening her eyes wide as a doe. "Do I look convincing?"

Orrinas flattened his mouth.

She smiled.

He grimaced.

She kept smiling.

The corner of his mouth raised.

She widened her eyes.

He finally smiled.

"There it is," she said.

"Not much cause for smiling just yet."

"We are together, what other cause need there be?"

"Go get yourself into position or I will call you my wife again."

"You had better not," she warned, smiling.

Keluwen turned away from him. She stepped out of the room and strode down the hall toward the farthest of the third-story apartments, the place where they would finish this once and for all.

As soon as she was facing away from him, her smile disintegrated. Her face dropped into an expressionless mask. Her mind raced. Orrinas' face was all that had been keeping her thoughts at bay. Now that she was not looking at him, they began to gnaw at her bones.

It had been a long time since she had felt this particular feeling. *Terror.* Fear was fear and came with the territory. But this was something else, and she knew it. She thought of Seb and Palad and the boys all in pools of blood and shivered.

The rooms smelled of wet clay, half-dry urine, and old chimneys. But this building had not been chosen for its olfactory appeal. It was selected for its location, being in a district of Westgate that was both cheap enough to rent out much of the second, third, and fourth stories of a tenement this size, and also odious enough that the local Home Guard would be disinclined to respond with any semblance of alacrity to strange people, or unexplained disturbances.

This particular building had been chosen for the flat roof it boasted, as well as those of the neighboring tenements across the avenue. This suite within it was chosen because one of the bedrooms was a corner room, with windows on the north and east side, both of glass, still surviving the time when this place had been wealthy enough to boast glass in its windows. Unshuttered, they gave ample view of the approaches from every direction to the intersection below.

The closer she came to the room, the more her boots scraped on the sheen of sand on the floor. *Nils is not finished sweeping yet.*

They had been wheeling sand from the golden riverbanks, and carrying it, bucket by bucket, up the stairs to spread on the floor of this corner bedroom. Krid could not muster sufficient concentration to fix someone's boots to a smooth surface with friction. He needed it to be rough, with depth to arrest motion. Dirt, mud, water, honey. Sand was what they had, so sand it was.

Krid told them it needed to be at least a half-inch deep for him to work with, and it needed to cover every inch of the floor, so they would be covered no matter where he, or any of his followers opted to stand once they arrived. It could not be too deep, however, or it would be noticed how unusual it was too quickly, before the trap could spring.

Night fell as she watched Nils finish with the floors. Then she stepped carefully into the room. The doorway opened into one corner, near the two windows. The room extended deep along the eastern side. At the far end was a large closet, vacant of clothes, soon to be full of Romi's brothers, their crossbows loaded and ready. Romi herself would hide in the lavatory further back, her knives ready to hamstring any takers, and gut them once they hit the floor.

Keluwen liked Romi. Tall, large of face, wide of smile, with the legs of a stone-pusher, and the arms of an acrobat. Even if she was not a user herself, she was exactly who Keluwen trusted to watch her back.

My kind.

"It is almost time," Hodo called from his perch in the stairwell. "Joli said ten minutes from the lighting of the lanterns."

Keluwen leaned out a window. She watched as one by one, the lamplighters lit the oil lamps atop the ten foot black iron posts. They used long poles, some with oil spigots and some with wicks at the end, and the street turned from sea-bottom blue to mustard yellow. She turned back inside. "Is everyone ready?"

Nils lit the oil lamps in the room. Keluwen watched a flicker take to each, each one making her feel more and more exposed. She laughed in her own head. *To think, I am more uncomfortable than Orrinas was.* She decided she would not mention that part to him.

The three brothers nodded to her, and pulled the twin doors to the closet closed on themselves. Romi winked from the lavatory and pulled the door until it was just shy of the latch clicking. Keluwen looked up at the ceiling. They had cut a hole two feet by two out of it, and then nailed a tapestry over it to mask its existence. With the upper floor unlit, Krid Ballar and Vessander would be able to just barely see through the tapestry to know when all were in play. That was all they needed to do their work. Line of sight was critical to anyone hoping to render magick.

Krid would render friction, locking their feet in place. Then Vessander would shroud the entire room in impenetrable darkness, such that even if they were to try to light their own torches within his gloom, they would not be able to see those either. He would render light incapable of reflecting off of anything within the bounds of his field.

Unable to see, they would not be able to strike out with any accuracy.

The close proximity would also allow them to save much needed energy. Magick was always easier on the body when rendered close by than at a distance. Even Keluwen's tiny blank impulses were so much lighter a drain on her strength when she made them close to hand and shot them out like a projectile, than if she created them fifty, twenty, or even ten feet away from her fingers. *That is why users always throw blank impulses rather than imagine them coming from out of nowhere. Why gamble on one from an odd starting point, when you could have ten or twenty sure things?* She tugged on the fringes of her gloves.

Zalash stepped up to the doorway. He leaned his head in and thumped the doorjamb twice with his palm. He would station himself in a room down the hall. Once the trap was sprung, he would complete it. He would race down the hall to this doorway and then create a mass-altering field, large enough to include anyone standing within it, and raise the mass of their target and any bodyguards he brought with him until they were each ten thousand pounds. They would be pushed to the ground by their own weight. And if that did not kill them all outright, Romi and her brothers would enter the fray, loosing bolts from the crossbows and slices from the knives, while Keluwen sent blank impulses into the gloom.

All the while Orrinas would be across the hall, undisturbed, with renowned conductor of Stoppers, Bandi Coheed, and the Stoppers that Axis Ardent had provided. Seven of them. Each with the talent to hold dozens of streams at once. And Orrinas, the master, would hold a hundred more all by himself. She licked her lips when she thought of Orrinas. *God damn the whole world, he is so fucking good,* she thought. *And he is mine.*

Nils would be on the roof to keep lookout, in case more bodyguards stationed themselves outside. If so, he would signal Leucas and Hodo who were ready with arrows strung. They were both piss poor marksmen, but they would be enough to hold off anyone for the little while it took to finish this.

Cheli arrived with a cup of water. She handed it to Keluwen. *Thank every god for you, Cheli girl.* She had not realized how parched her throat had become. It was getting close now. She danced from one foot to the other. She began to sweat in anticipation. She raised her arms and locked her fingers atop her head, leaning toward the window, hoping for a breeze.

Cheli popped back in not two minutes later. "They are coming up the street," she said. She bit her lip. "There are nine of them."

"Nine?" Keluwen felt her legs begin to shake. *Damn it.* "Joli was supposed to get him to come alone."

"All she could do was hint that she knew where young girls of his preference might be. It took a lot of doing, Kel. It is not easy to hint at something that specific out of the blue while making it look like it was not out of the blue."

"I know." She gritted her teeth.

"She had to keep mentioning it in general ways, to multiple patrons, before slowly getting more specific. We are lucky he did not leave before she could accomplish it."

"I said, I know." She sat down in a rotten wood chair in the corner.

Cheli ducked her head out, but then ducked it back in again. "Just...try to look irresistible."

Keluwen looked down at herself, corset too low, skirts too high, nothing but pale legs and perilous cleavage. She held up her hands as if to say *isn't this enough?*

Cheli smiled. She ducked back out. Then she ducked right back in again. "But don't look too good to be true."

"Enough, Cheli. Go away now."

Her eyes widened. "Right. Sorry." She ducked out the door and drifted down the hallway.

The reality of what was about to happen finally began to hit her. It was like a slap in the mouth. Her face grew hot, but her legs grew cold. Her stomach transformed into a pit, bottomless, yet she had no appetite at all. She suddenly felt like she had to piss, though she had only just done so. She began to pace in short strides, back and forth, scraping her boots in the sand. *Why did I volunteer for this?*

Because I want to be the one who does it. Who ends it. Once and for all. Here. Tonight. Two decades of horrors, and untold centuries more yet to come, would be brought to a close in this room.

She heard the door at the bottom of the stairs creak open. She heard boots thumping the stairs. When they creaked, every wall seemed to creak with them. *Are you sure it is only nine?* It sounded like fifty.

Then they were at the top of the stairs. They were coming down the hall. There was no way out of this now. None. The only ways out of this room were the door they were coming in, and the glass window leading to a twenty-foot drop onto cold stone.

It struck her then, in a way that she had not felt it before. The fear. She had not felt anything close to this sensation since the very day she broke free from the slowdeath chamber of Second Thrifty's pain barons, and left her secondparents behind for good.

Since that day, every single day from then to now, she had never felt cornered. She had made sure of it. Every decision she had made was carefully calculated to prevent her from ever again feeling trapped.

Every decision until today.

She realized it now with painful clarity that she was sacrificing that streak to make this happen.

She looked down at herself once more, at the clothes of a whore on her body. *Those girls make themselves trapped every time the let a man on top of them.* Never knowing if the hundredth time they did would be as innocuous as the previous ninety-nine, or if it would be with someone who would strangle them silently until blue.

He will not do this to any more of them.

It ends today.

She turned to look over her shoulder down the shallow hall to the lavatory. She nodded to Romi through the sliver of a crack in the door. She tapped her finger three times on the shutters of the closet behind her chair to let the three brothers know it was time.

She heard Joli's voice in the hall. "She is in there. She is smart but she is young. If you left ten double silvers for the lot of you, she would likely not realize she was being underpaid."

Her heart jumped into her throat. She worried she might choke.

The first glimpse she had was of the toe of an old black boot, the sole loose at the edge, flapping like a duckbill. Her stomach dropped so far she thought she might have shit it out onto the chair. Blood surged to her arms and legs until she could not be sure she had a body any longer to hold them all together.

The face of the first man leaned in, scanning all around, floors, ceiling, everything. He had the nose of a rat and the chin of a rat and the eyes of a rat, but he had the smile of a snake. He saw everything in the room and then he saw her. His eyes widened. He stepped in, his boots gently crunching in the sand. He heard it, and glanced down, but he had already seen Keluwen.

Yes. Me. Me. Look at the pale skin. Look at my legs. Look at my arms. Look at my bare shoulders and the nape of my neck. Look at every inch of me but don't look down.

He walked halfway across the room, wearing an old cloak over a butcher's apron, sword on his hip.

Then came two more. They were much less careful. They followed the footsteps of the first. They could have been twins had their noses not been so diametrically opposed. One was upturned like a pig snout, the other drooped like a crane. The pig licked his lips. The crane glanced away, uncomfortable.

Then came the rest. Five men in a ring about a sixth. *It's him.*

She saw his head bobbing here and there between them as they walked into the room, and as they spread out, his face showed itself to her.

His eyes were black. Pupils swollen as if the lamplight was pure darkness. His face was a glacier, snow white and beautiful, but underneath the skin it was grinding and scarring the earth. His smile made her feel ill. It was so... peaceful. His posture relaxed. His expression serene. It terrified her more than anything else about him.

Here stood this creature who slaughtered innocents, who razed villages and burned families and murdered her best friend, and he was happy, sublime. It was something else wearing a man's skin. It horrified her.

He crossed the room. He noticed the sand. He began to look down.

No! No! Here! Here!

She raised her arms over her head, stretching her torso, lifting her breasts up out of the corset until her nipples just barely crested, like half moons rising on a lace horizon. *Look at my body. So smooth for you to touch. Look at my skin. So soft for you to put your hands on.* She ran her fingers through her hair, bouncing it playfully. *Look at my hair, fine enough to run your fingers through, but thick enough to grab hold of when you take me.* She spread her legs a fraction of an inch, hinting. *Look at my thighs, pointing the way.*

It worked. He forgot what he had been glancing at. He looked at her. They all looked at her, their eyes locked in orbit. And when he stepped toward her, they all did. Closer and closer.

Five were in the sand. And then six.

Her heart was already racing as fast as she thought it could go, but this made it run faster. She began to sweat even harder in the cool night air. He was leaning down. Looking into her. Eyes all over her. Rubbing her flesh like tongues. Making her shiver. Making her reluctance disintegrate. Making her arms go cold and her legs flush warm.

Seven.

He hovered over her. His posture was a perfection of confidence. She had to resist the reflexive urge to reach out and put a hand on him. He was not touching her, but it felt somehow like he already had. That his fingers had already run themselves over her shoulders, and down her sides, and under her arms, and across her belly, tearing the corset off her, and plunging between her legs.

What the fuck is happening to me?

One of his hands touched her thigh and she thought she had been stabbed with a knife. She hopped involuntarily. He leaned down until his face was an inch from hers, slightly askew, so that his lips were talking past hers. "Don't you want to change?" he asked.

"Yes." Her eyes closed. Her back arched. She felt her body rising up, her mouth trying to find his. She had to force herself back down. She did not know what to do. His power was overflowing his physical body. He was not a normal man.

Is this what it means to be luminous?

His hand slid between her legs and warmth overflowed her and she gasped. She kept her arms above her head, her hands tangled in her hair, trying to hold her mind together. She opened her eyes and forced them to look past him.

Eight. Eight on the sand.

She had to remind herself that she did not want this. That this was not why she was here. She forced the thought into her head and kept it there by force.

The last of them stepped in the sand. Nine.

Keluwen gave the signal. She forced the words out her mouth. "I'm glad you came."

He pulled back and looked into her and through her and around her and back and forth all over her with the black shadows of his eyes.

He felt it. He felt the ripples in the Slipstream a fraction of a second before they became reality. But he was caught up in her and too slow to respond. He released her and stood up straight, backing up into the middle of his men. But that was as far as he got. His men tried to draw weapons, but mostly failed.

Krid rendered friction into the sand. Their feet were locked up in it, unable to move.

One of the men noticed that he could not shift his feet any longer. "Hey!" he shouted. He backhanded a slap across the shoulder of one of the others. They began to struggle.

The Stoppers had pulled his streams. She could tell by the look on his face. How his smile turned sour. The first streams he reached for were not there for him to pull. Without the streams there would be nothing to bind, no way for him to render anything into reality.

He reached for a second group of streams. And a third. And a fourth. None were there. Fifth, sixth, seventh, twentieth. Everything he had ever used at any of the scenes where he faced off against the Glasseyes in Amagon that had been in that composite was gone, lost to him. Hundreds upon hundreds of renders. And all of them his most powerful. When fighting those Glasseyes, he would have been forced to use his most powerful renders to escape. He had nothing in reserve.

Interdiction.

His face turned bitter. He glanced at each of the walls, and then at her. His jaw reached out in rage like a snake trying to swallow a rat.

And then the room went black.

Vessander rendered darkness in a cube, filling the room from floor to ceiling, from the doorway right up to just before where Keluwen stood. One moment she had been looking into his eyes, and the next she was gazing at a wall of black. She heard the men shouting. She wondered if he was still facing her, trying to see her through the cube of impenetrable gloom.

Romi burst into the room. The closet opened and her brothers raised their crossbows aiming into the black.

Keluwen remembered herself. She looked around the sides of the cube, checking the window and the door, ready to *punch* anyone with a blank impulse if they came through.

Then Zalash rendered mass over the same cube area that the men were standing in, driving the mass of each man and each object up to ten times where they began, then twenty. Knives broke themselves off of belts. The men were pressed down into themselves. Unable to lift their heels or turn their feet, they would be forced to squat over their ankles, until their ankles broke.

One man among them tried to throw a knife, but even though he weighed over a ton, his strength was the same as it was normally. He could only have barely moved his arm. And the knife, once less than a pound, was now a twenty-pound weight. It barely made it out of the cube, thudding to the ground at Keluwen's feet. As soon as it was out of the mass field, it regained its original weight. She leaned down and picked it up. It still had dried blood on it from whoever he had last used it on.

She listened with delight as the men groaned and wept as their own bodies crushed themselves. Zalash pushed their mass higher and higher. And their all-powerful master could do nothing for them. His powers were gone. Hundreds of his renders were tied up in the streams that Orrinas and Bandi's Stoppers held.

A few more seconds and they would have no need for the crossbows and the blank impulses.

But then she felt a strange wind gust against her face. It swished through her hair. *What is that?* She glanced at the window. It was still closed, sealed with glass. *How is there a breeze?*

The sounds of the groaning men all abruptly ceased.

The room turned instantly silent.

Shit.

"How is the mass field?!" she screamed.

"Holding!" Zalash said, and meant it. She trusted him as much as she hated him.

She raised both hands and pointed.

She still had her gloves on.

Shit.

She grabbed the middle finger of each in her teeth and slid her bare hands free. She spat them onto the floor and pointed double fingers into the black. She rendered two blank impulses to where she had least seen men, dipped low to account for where they must have been crushed. She released them and they raced through the air.

Romi's brothers pulled their triggers. Three crossbows fired bolts.

She heard the crack and snap as he spheres punched into the far walls, and the click and the thud and the bolts bounced off the floor inside the mass field. Even slowed by the mass field they should have hit something.

They all stood silent.

Nothing. No sound at all. No sound of men moving. No sound of men dying.

Nothing.

The silence was so shocking that the brothers never bothered to reload their crossbows.

What the fuck is going on?

"Orrinas!" she called out.

"What?" Vessander answered instead, hovering over the hole in the ceiling.

"Drop the darkness," she told him. "Something's wrong."

Vessander released the darkness. The cube vanished.

The sudden presence of images before her eyes nearly knocked Keluwen off her feet. The light from the oil lamps, and even the street lamps outside the window, were for an instant as bright as suns.

The shock was worse when she could see them.

The men were all dead. All slumped over and sprawled in the sand from where they had tipped over while squatting. Blood soaked into the sand, dyeing it cherry red.

Romi and her brothers were still and slack-jawed as she.

"What happened to them?" Romi asked.

There were no arrows. No swords. None of them had drawn their weapons, save for the one knife that had been thrown. They all simply oozed blood from single wounds. Not even the bolts of the crossbows had hit anyone.

The wind. Someone had used blank impulses. Keluwen's mind raced, trying to place one of her companions into a scenario in which they would have come in and done this to the surprise of everyone.

But there was no such scenario.

They had to have killed each other somehow.

"Eight," Romi said.

"What?" Keluwen asked.

"I only see eight bodies."

Keluwen felt her insides dissolve. *No!*

He was gone. The man with black eyes was gone.

"What is going on?" Vessander called from the hole in the ceiling.

"He is gone," Keluwen said.

"Impossible," Krid said. "Friction is still rendered."

He was right. She could see the soles of the feet of each man still stuck in place, with altered friction locking their feet in the sand.

Then she saw it.

In the center of the sand, in the middle of them all, between the bodies, a pair of shoes.

She stared at them in horror. The shoes were locked in place in the sand. He had not broken free. He had simply stepped out of his shoes.

Keluwen panicked. Her eyes darted from door to window and back.

Nothing.

Bandi appeared in the doorway.

"Did he?" Keluwen asked.

Bandi's head shook. "Roof clear. Stairwell clear."

The glass was still on the windows.

It's like he never left this room.

Keluwen's eyes tilted upward.

Oh shit.

He was on the ceiling, holding himself flat to it, as if it was a mattress he was resting peacefully on.

How did he...?

He was still in the mass field. His body still weighed thousands of pounds. How could he still have renders strong enough?

The composite from Amagon was incomplete. He had still *more* streams.

He rendered a hundred blank impulses, each a slightly different size of marble, and each with a slightly different direction and a tiny variance in velocity. He avoided precedence effect with a precision that dwarfed even Orrinas. It was as breathtaking as it was horrifying. Keluwen could feel them rippling through the Slipstream as they came into being. Hundreds *in addition to* the ones Orrinas and the Stoppers *already* held.

"Down!" Keluwen screamed.

She turned and dived into the closet, smacking her left shoulder on the half-open door. She landed on her stomach. The wind gusted out of her and she rolled.

The blank impulses released like a flight of arrows, flying in all directions. They peppered the walls, and shredded the floor. They burst through the ceiling and riddled the doors with holes.

Romi was ripped apart, hit by so many that the accumulation of holes ripping through her body severed both her arms and one of her legs below the knee.

All three of her brothers were shot through a dozen times. They collapsed backwards on top of Keluwen, pressing her down into the floor. She tried to roll over. Struggled to turn her head.

She saw the man with black eyes float gently to the ground. He rendered a blank spherical shield around himself. It was strong, with him tethered in the center of it, so as it floated, he floated in the air with it. Keluwen could not see it. But she could see air interacting with it, and she could feel its presence, shape and strength rippling to her as she touched the Slipstream.

Bandi raced into the room with two local mercenaries, each armed with double-fire crossbows. They tried to spread out behind him. They had no idea the shield was there. They fired bolts at him. All glanced off the shield.

Then he swapped out one stream in the *ingredient list* of his shield. He removed the stream of *size* that made it just barely bigger than he, and in its place he imparted its size with a diameter as wide as the room. The sphere instantly expanded, crushing a bowl shape into the floor and ceiling and two of the walls. Bandi and one mercenary were crushed up against the wall, mashed into the wood and stone, their bones pulverized. The other mercenary was bounced backward by the expanded sphere, smashing out the window and plummeting to the street, a rain of glass atop him.

The man with black eyes shrank his sphere once more, rotating to face the door.

Keluwen wriggled free of the bodies. She had blood all over her hands, all over the left side of her body. None of it hers.

Belleron, give me strength and speed and luck all three.

She ran for the shattered window.

He turned his head.

She leapt headfirst out the window.

His eyes never quite passed over her.

She fell through the air. She closed her eyes.

She focused every ounce of concentration she yet had.

She rendered a flat horizontal plane in midair, just above the ground. She imbued it with streams of *size*. Like a mattress. *Position.* Directly in her path. *Duration.* Five seconds. *Strength.* Double what would be needed to keep her from breaking through it. And lastly, a stream of *elasticity*. She knew the right amount. It was the same render she had used to jump out the high window of her thirdparents' towerhouse.

She knew it was there, but seeing the ground still rushing up to meet here was like a kick in the gut.

She landed on her plane. She rebounded. She landed on it again. Bounced. It bowed inward under her weight, flexing three times before it straightened out.

Thank you, Belleron.

Then its duration ended. The flat plane winked out of existence. Keluwen dropped in a brief three-foot free fall flat on her back. She knocked the wind out of herself all over again.

Hodo and Leucas were already racing out from the ground floor door, wearing coveralls and masks. They grabbed her and yanked her to her feet and half-carried her around the corner, into a dark doorway, across an unlit room, down a flight of stairs, into a tunnel, out the other side, into another door.

There they set her down near a washbasin, already filled with water. There was a supply of talcum powder, and sandalwood for burning. Fresh clothes, granulum crystal soaps, and fine sand of obsidian.

This was one of the escape rooms, meant to be used by her and the others to clean off the stains of residual afterglow of magick to escape any possibility of pursuit by Olbaran's Glasseyes. Now she had something more urgent. To clean herself of *fully visible* aural afterglow that the luminous immortal's followers could see plainly with their own eyes.

Leucas and Hodo were already ripping her skirts away and cutting her out of the corset. They moved with the speed and precision of surgeons, lifting her naked into the washbasin. They scrubbed her with coarse brushes dipped in ranum crystal powder.

Keluwen usually hated this part. The tedium of it was so relentless that most times she thought she would drown in it.

Not this time.

She needed every second of it to calm her heart, to cut herself free of nagging fear, and to scrape off the disgust she felt in her bones for how she had very nearly failed to hold onto herself when he touched her. She washed her skin until it very nearly bled. She washed it as hard as she wanted to wash out the memory of how she had very nearly let the luminous immortal have her willingly.

I hate you, you piece of shit. I hate everything about you. You will never, ever touch me again. She couldn't let him. He had very nearly taken her for his own. Without force. Without coercion. *It is not possible*, she told herself. Over and over. He must have taken control of her, manipulated her mind somehow.

There is no way I could melt under a man's touch that way. Like I was falling out of my own body. It was like Belleron himself had descended from everwonder upon her. *No one can do that. It doesn't work that way.*

Leucas and Hodo confiscated the brush from her and helped her climb out onto a pile of towels. She rubbed herself dry while Hodo tossed cupfuls of talcum powder over her. Leucas lit the sandalwood and wafted it toward her. She rolled herself off the towels and pulled on a fresh pair of hose and a blue tunic with long sleeves. Lastly, a brand new pair of gloves, which she pulled up to her elbows.

Leucas and Hodo shook themselves free of the coveralls and the sensitized fluorescence staining them, and dropped the masks atop them. They moved to the door, and held it open for her.

"You still have blood on your face," Leucas told her.

"That is the thing I am worried least about," she said.

They moved down an alley and through a series of abandoned warehouses to a safe house, where they forced her to sit still on an old stool. There, while she waited for Orrinas and the others, Keluwen proceeded to tap her heel so hard on the floor she nearly dug a basement.

One by one they trickled in.

First Cheli. Then Vessander and Krid. Then Zalash and a handful of the Stoppers.

Finally Nils and Orrinas.

She nearly wept when she finally saw him, the relief washing over her like a wave, more powerful than any other emotion she had ever felt. She held her tears. *Stay where you are, tears. You are for Orrinas and no one else.*

She saw the relief on his face was palpable as well, but there was something else. Something dark.

"What happened. Orrinas?" Krid asked. He slammed his fist on the wall. "Did he turn Bonsinar? Did he make him into one of his cultists? Did Bonsinar give us away?"

Orrinas shook his head. "He did not turn Bonsinar to his cause. The man with black eyes did this on his own."

"We had him," Zalash said. "How could he have done this?"

"He had *hundreds* more renders," Keluwen said. "Hundreds. How?"

"No one could have held back that many of his renders from dozens of scenes and four confrontations with Glasseyes," Vessander agreed.

"Or learn and memorize one hundred new ones well enough to summon them all at once, while also knowing which of those most like them were held by us," Orrinas said. "Yes, I know."

"What *is* he?" Vessander asked. "This is madness."

"I have never seen anything like that," Zalash agreed. "It was like we were normals. There was nothing we did that he did not find an immediate path around. He levitated himself while still *within* my mass field."

"We will only have one more chance at this," Cheli said. "Our friend knows the man with black eyes will go to Cair Tiril. We have to follow."

"And do what?" Vessander asked. "Fail again? We have been beaten."

"I have worse news," Orrinas said.

"What in all fucking hells could be worse than what just happened?" Krid Ballar asked.

"I was late coming here because I found Loga waiting for me at the cleaning station," Orrinas said.

"Loga?" Krid asked. "What was he even doing there? He was not supposed to be a part of this."

"He brought ill news," Orrinas said. "The elder is dead."

Everyone gasped. Everyone but Keluwen.

"What?" Nils asked. "What happened?"

"Murdered," Orrinas said. "We do not know by whom."

"Magick?" Vessander asked.

"No. Broken neck."

"Wait, what was Loga doing at a *cleaning station?*" Hodo asked. "We are not supposed to go to one unless we touch *afterglow.*"

"Because he *did* touch afterglow," Orrinas said.

"Where?" Leucas asked. "Here?"

"Across the city," Orrinas said. "Near sundown."

"That is all but a few hours ago," Nils said.

Orrinas nodded. "He found Bonsinar's body."

Everyone gasped again. Even Keluwen this time.

"By the gods high and low," Hodo said.

"Found him nailed to a wall, he told me," Orrinas said. "Missing his hands. At a place called the *Red God.*"

"Who? How?"

"Who do you think?" Orrinas asked.

"It can't be," Nils said. "He would have had to have just done it, then wash himself of his afterglow, and then calmly sit down at a tavern for hours while Joli tried to convince him to come. That is insane."

"Where is Joli?" Keluwen asked.

"I don't know," Orrinas said. "Holliver told Loga she finished her shift. He doesn't know where she went after she brought him to us."

"What are we going to do?" Leucas asked. "How do we contend with this?"

"Loga has a man among the Westgate Glasseyes," Orrinas said. "He is bringing them to the scene. They will record every single stream he used against us tonight, and Loga will bring it to us. We will add it to what we *already* have. Then we will face him again. That is how the Glasseyes do it. It works for them every time. Eventually."

"How many more *eventuallys* can we stand?" Keluwen asked.

Orrinas closed his eyes, and turned his head down as if in prayer. "None like this. We will be even better prepared next time. We have to be."

"If he took Bonsinar before even coming here, then he must have known we were here already," Krid said. "To hunt one of us in broad daylight? He knew."

"That reminds me of one other thing Loga told me," Orrinas said. "One of his locals saw our quarry on the streets earlier this evening, at the end of dusk. Speaking with one of the Amagon-men."

"Amagon-men?" Cheli asked. "The ones staying at the way-station? The soldiers?"

"It was not one of the soldiers he was seen speaking to," Orrinas said. "It was their Glasseye."

"Glasseye?!" Keluwen threw herself up out of her chair.

"This same Glasseye spent the better part of the morning questioning Joli at the *Home of the Moon*," Orrinas said.

"He gave us away?" she asked.

"It looks that way," Orrinas said.

"That scum," she hissed.

"But I thought we already had our people in with the Amagon-men," Nils said.

"They sent one of their own," Orrinas said. "In addition to the one we expected."

"*His* hands are all over this," Keluwen said. "Of course he would have infiltrated them. He turns men to his side all over. His light is hypnotic. He makes his enemies want to be his allies." *And now I understand it.*

"We do not know of a certainty though," Nils said. "Do we?"

Orrinas looked away. "There was *also* a man seen at the place where Bonsinar's body was found. There was *also* a man seen leaving the home of the elder in the Hezzam district just this afternoon, just before he died. These men are the *same person*. You will never guess who."

"The Amagon-man," Keluwen said, her eyes sharpening to needles.

"The Amagon-man," Orrinas said, nodding.

"Who is he?" Nils asked. "This Glasseye?"

"His name is Aren," Orrinas said. "Aren of Amagon."

I will have you, Aren of Amagon. I will find you and I will kill you. I promise you that.

She thought of Bandi and Romi and her three brothers, and Seb and Palad and all the rest.

I will look into your eyes when you die, Aren of Amagon. I promise you that.

13

A Man In A Room With A Dead Woman

THE STAIRS CREAKED AND groaned beneath his feet. The edges had worn down to more of a slope than a flat plank, and Aren found it impossible to mask his ascent.

They moved toward the second level of the tenement, two of the Sarenwalkers in the lead, Hayles and Fainen. Then came two veteran Outer Guard men, Retheld with a heavy axe, and Balthoren with his abundance of crossbows. Then came Donnovar himself, with Margol, Terrol, Aren, and Tanashri. Two more Sarenwalkers, Tamlin and Doles, brought up the rear.

Aren checked for afterglow, but detected nothing anywhere. The fluorescence on the splinters had gone cold halfway back to get Donnovar. But Aren was convinced he would be there. *He is still in there. He has to be.*

They crept softly toward the door. The Saderan closed her eyes and did as they had practiced every day since departing Vithos. She pulled in every crucial stream Aren had identified from the assassin's composite.

Donnovar glanced to Aren and then Tanashri.

Aren nodded. "She is ready."

The Captain unsheathed his greatsword. Fainen drew *Glimmer*, its Sarensteel a shimmering blue. The other Sarenwalkers readied their *somashalks*.

Donnovar waved his hand. Tamlin heaved a heavy log into the door. The frame splintered, and two Sarenwalkers flew inside

Aren saw a single man sitting atop a lone bed, only illuminated by a reed candle on a side table and silver moonlight through the cracks in the window shutters. The man hopped to his feet, eyes wide. He turned to run for the window, But Hayles caught him by his cuff and dragged him backwards into the middle of the room. They forced him to his knees and held him. Hayles pinched his jaw, forcing his mouth open. Aren rushed in. He had a flask of tinwood leaf tea ready, and poured it all down his throat.

The man shrieked, but then was still. He became quickly docile, confused, friendly. He looked around the room as if he had never seen it. Within a few minutes he gazed at it as if he had never even heard of the concept of a room before.

The man wore only a nightshirt. It was soiled and stank, as if he had been wearing it beneath his clothes for days of labor. His trousers and coat were found inside out on the floor, pockets empty. A rucksack was discovered under the bed and overturned. A pair of clean boots, three knives, and a skullcap shared space with a handful of acorns, a tin of meal, and an old wool scarf.

His face was an eggplant, head narrow and jowls wide. His lips could have fit two of anyone else's end to end. He was unshaven, bristly, skin savaged by the sun, wrinkled at his forehead and his curly hair infinitely damp.

The walls were chipped and cracked, and the wind whistled at the shutters. The sheets were disheveled and a bottle of Haradel cinnamon brandy sat half-empty on a bedside table. Another bottle lay on its side on the floor, rolling back and forth.

The Sarenwalkers spread throughout the room. They found the body of a dead girl beneath a wobbly table, a moldy cheese of a rug draped over her. She had auburn hair and pale skin and a birthmark under her ear. Aren frowned and closed his eyes, shaking his head. *We weren't fast enough. We should have been faster. I should have been faster.*

"This is him?" Donnovar asked.

Aren held the Jecker monocle to his eyes, peering up and down at the man. *Evidence.*

He found what he had been expecting without pause. *Afterglow.* He stared hard at the twinkling colors, which radiated simultaneously as waves and particles. "Sensitized fluorescence all over the shirt. At the hands. A few smudges on the face. Some on the bottle. Silvery and clear as crystal. Vectoric afterglow if I have ever seen it."

Aren switched the blue filter in place. Everything else around him disappeared, lost in the sapphire shadows. Everything but the afterglow. The cores gleamed pale orange.

"It's a match," Aren said. "This afterglow was left by the same user as the one who tried to kill the Lord Protector."

"So we have him then." Donnovar smiled.

Aren nodded toward the poor girl under the table. "I think it has to be him. Everything fits."

"Well done, Aren," Donnovar said. "By the gods high and low, after the terrible day we have been faced with, to come out of it like this, and all thanks to you and your crew."

Aren smiled. He couldn't believe it had been so easy. He reached out to hold on to the wall to keep himself from floating away. *I did it. I solved it. I completed the trace. They are going to talk about this for years to come.*

"We still need to question him," Terrol said.

Aren bit his lip to keep from saying something regretful. *I know that. Everyone knows that.* There was no reason to say it aloud other than to try to make rainclouds over Aren's success. *Fuck you, Terrol. You can't step on me this time. Or ever again.*

"It may be a while before he is ready," Aren said. "I have alumide salts I can give him to counteract the tinwood leaf, but with this fresh a dose in his system it will take at least half a day to before he will be able to form cohesive thoughts or answer questions."

"This is good work, Aren," Donnovar said. "Damn good work."

"He has been here twelve days," Terrol said. "According to the landlord, he came in with a group of mummers from Vithos, parted ways and went to work for a warehouser for night duty."

"Cover of darkness to commit his crimes," Donnovar said. "It fits. That is how he snuck out of Vithos and fled Amagon." He clapped Margol on the shoulder. "We caught him."

"Yes," Margol said. "Praise to the gods." He smiled again, but his enthusiasm was subdued, at least as far as bringing to justice the man who tried to kill his master was concerned. "And you did it without Raviel, Aren. You did the right thing."

Terrol seemed to notice as well, and cocked his head to one side, watching Margol. At least until he glanced at Aren and realized Aren was watching *him* watch Margol. Terrol turned away and said nothing.

Aren started for the door. *Just need to slip out for a little malagayne.* But as he tried to slide through the doorway, someone else very nearly flattened him coming in the other way.

It was Raviel.

"What goes on here?" Raviel demanded, his voice like a loaf of bread twisting apart. His face seemed to have aged a decade and his old coat seemed to have aged a century. "Your lieutenant told me you were conducting an operation here."

"Aren has caught us the assassin," Donnovar said.

Raviel swiveled his gaze to Aren and sneered. "Oh he did, did he?" It was the first time since the journey began that Raviel had said one word to him.

Aren clenched his teeth and narrowed his eyes. "I did. We caught him. Tonight. Without *you*."

Raviel looked at the dead man on the bed.

Yes, see my victory, farod.

But Raviel did not even pause to look at the dead man. His eyes passed over it like they did every crack in the wall, every crease of the sheets.

Do you not even care what we have done here?

"So that is your story?" Raviel asked Aren.

"My *story*? It is *what happened*."

Raviel narrowed his eyes. "Of course it is."

Aren turned on him. "You have been trying to undermine me since the beginning. It makes me wonder what you are even doing here? I wonder if you wanted to catch this man at all."

"Undermine you? Well, clearly I cannot do that. You have completed the trace. You should be so very proud of yourself."

"Let us calm down," Tanashri suggested. "Take this elsewhere."

"He can take himself off a bridge into the river," Aren said. *That's right. I won. I came out on top and you can't stand it, you old wretch. You are no Toran Sarker.* He smiled, satisfied. *Finally I get to say what I have wanted to say since we left Vithos.*

Raviel stared into his eyes for a long time.

Aren never flinched.

Raviel leaned in close, so close no one else could hear his whisper. "Don't think I don't know why he chose you," Raviel said. "You can say the words and *celebrate* all you like, but do not for one moment think that I don't know."

What in seven hells does that mean? "Where were you? Donnovar told me you disappeared. You were gone all day. Without telling anyone. What were you doing?"

Raviel studied him coldly. "You mean while you were investigating the scene of a murder without telling anyone?"

Aren glanced nervously at Donnovar. "That had nothing to do with our user. And if I hadn't been there we never would have found this place."

"How very convenient," Raviel said. "I was seeking out what happened to the Stoppers. The ones you were supposed to come back with this morning."

"I found out what happened to them," Aren said. "I investigated."

"Without telling anyone," Raviel said.

"I was performing my official duties," Aren said, face reddening.

"And what part of your official duties involved hiding your actions from us?" Raviel asked. "You went out into the streets alone. What part of your official duties involved wandering into the slums?"

Shaot. He knows about the elder. Aren straightened his back. turned his chin up. "I was doing what needed to be done, to find out what happened to our Stoppers, to find our trace, to bring us to this capture."

"Enough of this arguing," Tanashri said. "We need to be back to the way-station."

"Not until he tells me what he was doing there," Raviel said.

"How do you know anything about where I was?" Aren asked.

Raviel smiled. "There was a man asking about us in the markets all evening. He seemed most interested in the particulars of our company. He inquired about our troop strength and markings and intent. This spy had specific knowledge about us. Knowledge he received from *you.*"

Aren took a step back. Fear surged up and down his limbs. "What are you talking about?" He was unable to keep the fear from making his voice waver. He knew Donnovar was looking at him. Terrol, Margol, and Tanashri, too. He began to feel like he was shrinking.

Raviel leaned over his shoulder to one of Donnovar's men. "Bring him up."

Aren looked at Donnovar. The Captain chewed his lip, brow narrow. He was not happy about Raviel giving orders to his men, but something made him hold back.

The command was echoed down the stairs, and out into the street below.

"So you took an Olbaranian into your custody?" Terrol asked. "Without consulting us?"

My sentiments exactly.

Raviel growled. "He was observed entering a certain neighborhood. I found him with a woman dead at a location I had reason to believe was relevant to our trace."

"When did this happen?" Terrol asked.

"Tonight," Raviel said. "Under an hour ago."

Terrol pointed at the user trussed up on the bed. "This appears *more* relevant."

Raviel glared at him, and then at Aren. His stare was hideous and terrifying. "You may ask the man yourself. He has many interesting things to say about you, Aren."

Two of the Outer Guard marched a bound man into the room, ankles roped together, hands behind his back. He wore black trousers, and a burgundy vest over an ivory shirt.

Oh shaot.

It was Redevir.

He wore a leather band about his head in the style of the old revelers of Signal Mountain. *He's a Rover then*, Aren thought. *Only the wanderers from Signal Mountain would wear a strap like that.*

"What is this?" Redevir demanded. "Where are you fools taking me?" He went quiet and his eyes blinked wide when they passed over Aren. He looked back and forth between Aren and Raviel, as if the world had suddenly turned upside down. He looked at the man trussed up and dosed on the bed. "I see you found your man, Aren."

Everyone turned to look at Aren.

Donnovar narrowed his eyes. "Aren, do you *know* this man?"

Aren sighed. "This is just Redevir. I met him earlier. He helped us navigate the city. He truly aided me in finding this room. That is all. There was no secret. And I told him little enough of who we are."

Tanashri was appalled. "You discussed our purpose with a random stranger in a foreign city? What were you thinking?"

"I...it wasn't like that. This is getting twisted around."

"A *murderer*, Aren?" Donnovar raised an eyebrow.

"I am quite innocent," Redevir said.

"Tell them about the dead woman," Raviel said.

"A setup," Redevir said. "She was already in that state when I found her. I swear it."

"A murder an hour ago has nothing to do with us," Aren said. "The user has been right here. I pinpointed him, and went straight back to the way-station to organize this capture. The user was here in this room the entire time. And I doubt he knows the same Rover I chanced across today."

"We will see then, won't we?" Raviel said. "Wake him up. Give him the alumide salts. Wake him. We will ask him exactly who he is."

"We *know* who he is," Aren said, sneering. *You farod.*

"Of course you do," Raviel mocked.

"Fine." Aren turned to administer the salts. But he caught a brief hint of motion in his periphery. He saw Balthoren raising his crossbow.

Aren spun around to look at what danger Balthoren was aiming at. But he saw nothing. *What?*

Balthoren took careful aim.

Donnovar noticed, and Margol. Fainen reached toward him.

"What are you doing?" Terrol asked.

Aren saw where the tip of the bolt was aiming. *The user.* He reached out a hand. "Wait!"

Balthoren pulled the trigger.

Aren heard the click and twang, and the bolt slammed into the user's chest, between the ribs, into the heart. He flopped over backwards onto the bed, bubbling blood onto the sheets.

Terrol ducked back. Tanashri blended into the wall. The Sarenwalkers collapsed around Donnovar to protect him.

Balthoren unshouldered another crossbow.

Aren dropped to his hands and knees and scrambled to the foot of the bed. He looked up. Balthoren hovered just above him.

Retheld reached out and put a hand on Balthoren's shoulder, holding his axe against his chest with the other. Balthoren cracked him across the face with the crossbow, staggering him. He aimed it at where Donnovar and Raviel stood.

Aren looked up at the crossbow above him. *Shaot. What do I do?* He took the strap of his tracer satchel in both hands and swung upward. Its weight slammed the crossbow up. It threw off Balthoren's aim, and the bolt flew wide.

Balthoren growled, reached down for Aren.

But Donnovar broke out of the circle of his bodyguards, swatting Balthoren's hand aside. He slammed into Balthoren, shouldered him back. Donnovar snatched a fistful of tunic with one hand and clamped down on the belt with the other. He lifted Balthoren off his feet, and threw him across the room. Balthoren hit the wall and flopped awkwardly on the floor, but he regained his feet in a heartbeat.

Balthoren reared back and hurled the spent crossbow. One of the Sarenwalkers brought down a hammer fist onto it in mid-flight, deflecting it down at the last moment.

Balthoren raised a loaded handbow. Fainen instantly placed himself between it and Donnovar. But Retheld recovered and swung his axe down, clipping the handbow, just as the trigger was pulled, and the bolt embedded itself in the wall behind him.

Balthoren scrambled away. He jumped headfirst through the window, splintering the shutters.

Retheld and Fainen ran to the window and peered out, but they could not see where he had gone.

Raviel stared at the open window, his hands balled into fists at his sides. He growled and tore out of the room and down the stairs.

Donnovar turned to his Sarenwalkers, Tamlin and Doles. "Go with him," he commanded. "Watch Raviel's back in case he catches up with Balthoren."

Aren looked at his hands and saw them shaking. His skin felt thick, and everything seemed far away, as if he was not even there, but watching through someone else's eyes. He felt the weight of the malagayne in his pouch. He thought he could hear it calling his name faintly over the stamping of armored feet. His hands moved toward it without conscious thought. He had to forcibly stop himself in the act.

He blinked and his eyes strained. They fogged over again, and he squinted and rubbed at them. He opened them and the world was lost in a white mist. He saw sharp silver lines in the air, and shimmering clouds. He slammed his eyes shut. He counted down from ten and then he opened them. The room was just a room again.

He looked up. Hayles the Sarenwalker hovered near him. He held out the tracer satchel by its strap, waiting patiently for Aren to take it.

Aren nodded thanks, and took it.

Donnovar gave out orders to his men. They secured the building, and Retheld was posted at the door, axe at the ready.

"What just happened here?" Tanashri asked.

Terrol turned to Donnovar. "How long has Balthoren been attached to your command?"

"Years," Donnovar said. "He has been one of my officers for years. One of my best men. I cannot imagine what came over him."

"He has turned on us," Hayles said. "He raised arms against his Captain." His eyes burned with a subdued rage.

"Get back to the way-station," Donnovar said. "Let everyone know Balthoren has turned. From this moment forward he is an enemy."

Aren nodded to the Sarenwalker as he went. Hayles gave a barely perceptible nod, his face a sculpture of stoic murderous perfection.

"Why did he kill the assassin?" Aren asked. "He was going to be executed anyway."

"Paid off by the conspirators among the Amagon Council?" Tanashri suggested.

"But why?" Aren asked. "Why did he give up his life to kill one man that we already captured?" He turned and looked at the body. Mouth dangling open, eyes wide and sad, blood and shit on the sheets, mouth frozen in a scream behind the gag. He looked away and shook his head.

Donnovar looked afraid for the first time Aren could remember. He let out a long breath. "I have never seen anything like that. It was like he was someone else, out of his mind."

"What do we do?" Aren asked. "What happens if we can't find him? What if the Home Guard pick him up? Could he do anything to us?"

"We have passes," Donnovar said. "We can disavow him if we have to."

"Raviel certainly tore out of here at a good clip after him," Terrol said. He meant it to be more suspicious than Donnovar took it.

"But then who is this?" Donnovar asked. "Who is this Rover?"

"I am a treasure hunter," Redevir said. "An archeologist. I have traveled far to come to Westgate. I had a meeting with a woman named Lesca. I sought her out to make a trade. Aren could tell you, if he chose to. We searched her domicile together."

That is why Redevir had been so interested in whether I had found evidence of magick in her room.

Donnovar glanced at Aren. Aren nodded.

"Trade?" Donnovar asked.

"She possessed an heirloom that I wished to purchase," Redevir said. "I brought gold. Of course she...no longer had it by the time I arrived. Whoever killed her, took it with them. It was part of a set of five stones. Have you heard of the Sephors?"

The Sephors, Aren thought. *He actually believes they are real.* "I have."

"What are they?" Donnovar asked.

"Priceless artifacts," Redevir said. "They are my life's work. These five stones are said to be related to the Sephors. I have been searching for them for a long time, unearthing their whereabouts. I have been racing to collect them, but they are all missing from the places that I expect them to be. Now I know why. If people are willing to kill a woman just for speaking with me about them, then they would certainly be willing to kill one who was going to sell one to me."

"So she was the woman who was just murdered?" Donnovar asked.

"Not tonight," Redevir said, embarrassed. "Tonight it was a different woman. Though when I got there she was already dead as well."

"Wait," Donnovar said. "Another woman? Death seems to follow you like a shadow, Rover."

"It's certainly starting to look that way," Redevir agreed. He nodded to the table with the girl's body beneath it. "Though no more so than you, it seems."

"Who was she?" Aren asked.

"You might remember her. Sweet Joli."

Aren's eyes went wide.

"And what were you visiting *her* for?" Donnovar asked.

"I sought a much baser reward from her," Redevir admitted. "At least that is why I thought I was there. The room did not belong to her. I do not know why she invited me there. I would have loved to find out."

"Why would they kill her?" Aren asked.

"Because she talked to me?" Redevir guessed. "Or maybe they were looking for me and arrived early. I have no idea, truly. I did not see anyone else nearby, except for a man with bells on his shoes. He whistled when he walked."

Or maybe it was because she talked to me, Aren thought, horrified. He glanced at the body in the corner within its frayed blanket sarcophagus. He rested his hand on his pouch of malagayne. "We didn't capture the user fast enough."

"You were inquiring into our business, Rover," Donnovar said. "What reason would you have to do that?"

"It was only casual curiosity. I wanted to know where Aren came from. Then I became more curious when someone mentioned that *Raviel* was leading you."

Aren was taken aback. "You...*know him?*"

"I know *of* him," Redevir said. "And now that I have met him, I am glad I never have before. He visited one of my contacts before I came north. He was looking for something. Something that draws the most *interesting* competition. He was particularly interested in old tales of the Andristi."

Margol shifted in his footing. Aren noticed it. Something in Redevir's words was disturbing him.

"Tales? Legends?" Aren asked.

"I assumed he was searching for something that is rumored to reside there. I guessed you to be his escort."

"Raviel is assisting us in an investigation," Donnovar corrected.

"Of course," Redevir said. "My mistake. I was only speculating. It seems only a bit odd that you are heading in that direction, to the same location of his inquiries. Quite by coincidence, I happen to interested in heading there myself."

"Really?" Aren asked.

"Indeed," Redevir said. "It seems I'm fighting a losing battle in Olbaran, running a losing race, riding a...well, you get the idea. I find it necessary to diverge from my prior goals, especially considering the circumstances."

"Would you be willing to join us as we travel east?" Aren asked. *He knows who Raviel is. I need to find out why the Lord Protector would ever trust him.*

"I am not sure that is a good idea," Donnovar began. "We don't even know this man. What kind of man is a Rover?"

"He could be of assistance to us," Aren said. *To me. I need to know what is happening.* "For information. He knows about Raviel. He can be an advisor. That is why Tanashri is with us. If we are placing trust in a Sister, why not a Rover?" He turned to glance at Tanashri. "No offense."

The Saderan said nothing, but nodded to him with her pointy chin.

"I agree with Aren," Terrol said.

Is that so? Aren thought.

"If this Rover will permit me to question him about what he knows of our Lenagon-man," Terrol added. "I would like to hear this...information as well."

"Interrogation, is it?" Redevir asked.

"Just a chat," Terrol said.

"I have no problem with that," Redevir said. "I like chats."

Is that really all it takes to pacify Terrol all of a sudden? A little bit of information about Raviel? I thought they were both...

They were not allies either. Terrol seemed to distrust Raviel as much as Aren did. He realized there may have been more secrets floating around the Lenagon-man than he thought.

"All right," Donnovar said, shaking his head. "He will not cause too much trouble among five-hundred Outer Guard." He looked at Redevir. "But you will provide your own horse, and some of your own coin will go to provisions for yourself for the duration. We are the Outer Guard, not a charity."

"Well," Redevir said. "Such a twist of fate. The inexorable pull of destiny. The whole universe must want me to go to Laman. I dare not go against that."

Fainen set himself to untying Redevir's bonds, and returning his possessions and gold that Raviel had ordered confiscated. He excused himself to return to the inn he was staying at, to collect his things before joining the Outer Guard on the road east.

Aren sighed. It was ended. It was done. And although there were now a few little details that soured the taste of victory, it was still a victory. The mission was concluded. *I have never lost a trace.*

Donnovar abruptly clapped him on the shoulders.

"I did not mean to overstep," Aren said. "I thought he could help."

"It is nothing to be concerned about," Donnovar said. "Many of the men have guests among the camp followers and attendants. What is one more? Besides, if Terrol agrees to it, then the hardest one to convince is already game."

"Raviel will likely be furious that we are allowing him to travel freely with us."

"Raviel is irascible. Don't let it weigh on you. He is like that with everyone. I do not think he knows any other way."

Aren smiled and started for the door, but Donnovar stopped him with a firm hand on his shoulder. Aren winced, expecting a rebuke for acting out on his own, or for arguing with Raviel in front of everyone, for getting himself lost in the city all day, for inviting Redevir to accompany him, or for all of those.

But Donnovar only smiled. "You did well tonight, Aren."

Aren felt his eyes open wide like full moons. "I did?"

"You took charge of the situation. Better perhaps than even I could have. Those missing Stoppers would have staggered the most veteran Render Tracer. But it did not even slow you down. You took a hit and got right back on your feet. I have known you a long time, since you were but a boy, following Sarker about. It has been a great thing to work with you, to see you grow."

"I couldn't tell you how it came together. Every time I feel like the memories vanish."

"That is the way of *any* battle. For a general it is a *whole*, but for a man on the field it is only a series of moments—one enemy to the next, one swing of the sword to the next, or, in this case, one word to the next. When you look at your papers you are a general, but when you are on the streets, you become the soldier."

Aren nodded agreement.

"Battle is chaos," Donnovar said. "Capture is chaos. The key is being able to keep your wits about you when you are in the thick of it. And you did that. That is what I demand of my men. That is what I respect. You must be able to ignore the chaos. You handled it as good as any."

"Thank you."

"Sometimes things are difficult to say," Donnovar said, then paused as if searching a quiet battlefield for the words he wished to use. "When I met you, you were a boy. But you are not that any longer. I see now you are a man in truth. Today I am...proud...of you."

Aren was silent. He looked at the Captain dumbly, unable to formulate a coherent reply.

"I did not mean to put you on the spot," Donnovar said. "Such things are difficult to speak of among men, and seem silly even though they are known to be true."

"Of course," Aren said. "And thank you. For what you said, I mean. You honor me by saying it."

"Get yourself back to the way-station and salvage what little sleep is left for you tonight."

"I will," Aren said. He felt odd, embarrassed. "Thank you, Captain."

Aren turned. Three more hours for sleep, maybe four. He doubted he would be able to get three minutes the way his mind was racing. A little malagayne would be in order. He started for the door, but stopped. He took one last look at the dead user on the bed.

He slipped over when no one was looking. He took out his utility knife and cut a piece of the user's old shirt where he had seen the sensitized fluorescence.

A little memento.

He dropped it into one of his clean glass jars. He held the Jecker monocle up and smiled. It was still set with the blue filter, but that was fine. He wanted one last glimpse of it. He looked through it, seeing the greenish silvery glow on the fabric. He started for the door once more.

But then he stopped, still looking through the monocle. He took another step. Then two more. Further from the user. Out into the hall.

The sensitized cloth wasn't redshifting.

He looked over his shoulder at the dead user.

The shift doesn't care about alive or dead. It should still be shifting.

He took it down the hall, and down the stairs, and down the street. Further and further he went. He stared at it through the blue filter all the while.

His heart raced. His stomach burned.

The core color wasn't redshifting at all.

It was blueshifting.

There should only have been a blueshift when the fluorescence came *closer* to its creator.

And he was walking *away* from the dead man.

Impossible.

14

The Long Ride

"WHY CAN'T YOU JUST relax?" Corrin asked.

Aren put the little jar back in his tracer satchel. He dropped the Jecker monocle into its silk pouch, and secured it as well. He flipped the lid closed, locked it and fastened the buckles. "I just wanted to see."

The fabric from the man's shirt had ceased to fluoresce weeks ago, hundreds of miles ago, forever ago. But he kept looking at it fifty times a day, needing it to redshift, needing it to belong to the man they had captured in Westgate. He needed it to be over. He needed to not be going mad.

His life these past weeks had felt frozen in time, always in the saddle, always green grass beneath him, no matter which province of Olbaran they passed through. To his left was always the same view of the endless undulations of the great grey peaks of the Kaman-Than, the tallest mountains of the north continent. He wondered if they would ever end, even though he knew they did, he had seen the maps. They rose like sentinels, ever keeping out the savage nations of Kharthist, the ancient home of Kradishah's legions, whose invasions had ravaged every nation from Arradan to Laman.

"Settle down," Corrin suggested. "It's over. You are a great success. Your destiny is fulfilled. Stop being unsatisfied for one damn minute and enjoy the fact that you are going to Laman free of expense, with nothing to do but enjoy it once you get there. It is what you always wanted."

"It is. It couldn't be more perfect." The air was always cold in the northeast of Olbaran. Every text always said so. And they were right. Here it was the beginning of summer and he was hugging his riding cloak close. Laman was said to be kinder of weather, the high mountains hemming in its western and southern borders, protecting it from the endless westerlies.

Corrin clapped his hands. "Think of all the brandy. Sweet Andristi brandy. The finest variety." He thought for a moment. "I suppose over there they just call it ordinary brandy."

"I just can't help but wonder if I was wrong about something."

"You are liable to turn into Terrol if you keep this up. He was agonizing over something so badly that he is having us followed by a clutch of farods. Or is it a gaggle of farods? I can never remember. Do you want to end up *that* paranoid?"

"Wait. What?"

"Oh, did I forget to mention that? Terrol is having some farods follow us."

"*What* is following us?"

"Well...where to begin? When a male ape of a certain size is in the act of defecating and has a female ape at a certain angle with respect to his..."

"Not the *word* farod," Aren said. "Who are the *people* that you keep *referring to* as farods?"

"I overheard him that night in Westgate. He was out on the streets. I saw him the same night we ran into those vestiguals at the *Red God*."

"Residuals," Aren corrected.

"Vestiguals—like I said. You may want to keep you voice down while we gossip about Terrol. Men who wear the Listener badge tend to have very good hearing. It is one of life's great coincidences."

"Who was he talking to?"

"Someone dressed in a Hezzam disguise."

"Are you certain it was *Terrol?*"

"I saw him at ten paces. I am not mistaken. White skin, crooked nose, smells of milk and worms. Are you sure I never mentioned this?"

Aren shook his head. "Did he say why?"

"He said someone was getting too close, that they might find out too much. I do not recall the rest. But he definitely mentioned sending someone after one of us."

"And you just now brought this to my attention? After all this time? I want my silver back."

Corrin gave him a look. "I am not paid for my memory. I am paid to cut things. And would you rather I never mentioned that there is a traitor in your midst?"

"Balthoren was the traitor. Terrol is just an asshole."

"But you hate Terrol."

"Well, just because I hate him does not make him a traitor."

"He is up to something," Corrin said. "I should call out thrice to the gibbous moon and summon Shaab-Gulod to squash him."

"Shaab-Gulod isn't real. It would not be likely to squash much of anything, particularly if someone as insignificant as you called on it."

"If that Caldannon fellow could do it, then so can Corrin the Magnificent. You obviously are not sophisticated enough to recognize my legendary nature."

"If there was a Shaab-Gulod, he would eat you with his mouth of fire and shit you out his steaming ass."

"Bah," Corrin said. "You will read about me in one of your useless books someday, if you live through the attack of Terrol's secret flock of assassins. I should probably kill him as quickly as possible."

"You are not killing an officer of Amagon. You are, as of this minute, not even *talking* about killing one. Understand?"

"Bossy of a sudden, are you, *Lord Aren?*"

Aren made the sign of the witch at him.

"How dare you hex me?" Corrin accused, offended. "You'll pay for that."

"I'm sure," Aren said.

Aren felt as though he had lost the ability to notice the passage of time. Every day he worried about what happened in Westgate. Every day he wondered if the shift he saw on the material was really what he saw. Every day he wondered if there were more girls out there.

He tried to question the boy, Hallan, to find out where he had been, who he had seen. But he did not speak. Not to Terrol, not to Tanashri, not even to Duran, who fed him every meal and cared for him each day.

Donnovar was convinced it was all tied up in a neat little bow. And the others all kept quiet about it. *Am I the only one who thinks something else is going on here?*

He shook his head, and gave a little heel squeeze to his mount until she caught up alongside Redevir. The Rover's leather strap was tight around his shaven head, and a brown leather coat covered his fine linen shirt, and vest of burgundy velvet. His boots always seemed to have the shine of new leather, fitted tightly with silver buckles, swaying as his horse ambled along beside the silver column of the Outer Guard.

He caught the Rover reading a little poem to himself out of *Mercury Woods*. "*A bridge from father to son, though he was not the only one. From the shrine of the nameless end, hurt that the son of his son would mend, on the road of the king of the hall, who stood like the trees only not so tall. Endless be the shining green of the twins, for he who has eyes to see is not always he who wins.*"

"Charming," Aren said.

"Aren, I was wondering when you were going to find the time."

"How are your daily *chats* with Terrol?"

"That man is even more charming than he appears."

"Are they always about Raviel?"

"Mostly. His interests varied remarkably." Redevir paused. "I am curious. Why do you always refer to each other as Amagon-men or Lenagon-men? No other nation of people on this earth refer to each other in this way. And you lot do not call each other Amagon-men, but Raviel does, so I presume people from the Kingdom of Lenagon do not call each other Lenagon-men, only you people do that. Why?"

Aren laughed. "We are sibling nations. Created at the same time from the carcass of the same dying empire. But with two different origins. Amagon was founded by westermen and Mahhennin together. Lenagon was founded by westermen alone. Like any siblings, there is somewhat of a rivalry."

"It certainly seems to make it easier for you all to hate each other."

"Hate doesn't need a border. I hate Terrol just as much as Raviel. And I hate rogue users no matter where they come from."

Redevir laughed. "Fair enough."

"Well, what do *you* think Raviel is doing here?"

"I thought he was leading you all somewhere."

"I know nothing about him," Aren said. "He *is* taking us to Laman, but I do not know *why* he was given that power. My people tell me not to trust him, but they are the reason he is here. He is supposed to be a Glasseye, like me. But I don't know why he is still even with us if he was only here to help catch the assassin we already caught."

"That is a riddle."

"I solve riddles every day. But I can't crack this one."

"Perhaps he is a treasure seeker." Redevir laughed.

"Like you?"

"Only because he is going the same way I am. And because he spends almost as much time at libraries as I do. I have seen him before in the south, in Ethios and Alsion both. He floated in some of the same circles as I."

"There is something about him. I can't put my finger on it."

"I used to think he was working with the Ministry."

"Used to think?"

"Rumor has it that he used to frequent the monasteries around Talathat, and even one of the cathedrals. Big library there. But eventually he cut off his trips to the Priests. It must have been something irreconcilable, otherwise the Ministry wouldn't have handed down the order of Halospex."

"Raviel was ringed? Halospex is a serious punishment. They reserve it for the most heinous of sinners."

"I haven't heard much about him in years. No one seems to know what he has been up to. And no one knows why he was ringed. But I do know one thing for certain; he is not from Lenagon. He may have wormed his way in there, but as far as I know he had never been north of Olybria until a year ago."

"I was hoping for more."

"So was your friend, Terrol."

"He is not my friend. I don't think he is anyone's friend."

"Well, he left very disappointed."

"It should have been me and Sarker. Not some outlander."

"Sarker. Is that the old man I hear you talk about all the time?"

Aren nodded. "My mentor. He died. Just before this trace began."

"You cared for him. I can see it."

"He was the one who made me what I am. This is what I wanted to be, and he was the one who lifted me up to it. I owe him everything."

"I am sure he would be proud of the work you have done. Everyone here tells me that you are the youngest of your kind."

"In Amagon, yes."

"I have a question. Are you as good with the Histories as you are with tracing?"

"I know them inside and out," Aren said. "I prefer Pellagien's books, but Durnan's were also quite good. Faber of Idessa wrote the best history of Samani, and Julian of Nissus was the most prolific with his eighteen-volume history of Arradan, Halsabad, and Tyrelon. Torquin followed the cultural collapse of holy Sephalon, and Carle of Icaria presented the entire history of the northlands in a single volume. And you know Borgas, who wrote of everyone and everything."

Redevir laughed. Then he looked at Aren. Then he laughed some more.

"What?"

"I definitely did not ask you for all that."

"Apologies. Once I get going...I have been told I don't know when to stop."

"Never apologize for that. That is actually exactly what I was hoping for. I never took to the Histories. And I regret it every day. They hold a great many secrets. I wish I spent more time with them. A challenge: tell me the most confounding thing you have ever found in one of them."

"That is an easy one for me. It would be Gorman's *History of Mekkos*. The one where he forgot to distinguish between the *seventeen* kings with the name Aggele, and for three hundred pages no one can tell which was riding into a battle, which was the hideous old man, or which was still a baby suckling at a wet-nurse's breast, or if all three were the same."

Redevir laughed. He slapped his saddle. "I knew I was right about you."

"You said you were thinking of going to Laman already before we met. Is it really because of the Sephors? Or was that some lark?"

"Oh, it is real. It is me. I declare it without shame. There is no treasure seeker alive who doesn't think about them. Most go around pretending they don't, for the sake of their reputations. I *believe* in them. And I am more than happy to sacrifice something as mundane as a reputation to go after what I believe."

"They are the symbol of the unattainable goal. The graveyards of archeologists are full of men who spent their whole lives never finding one. Even Jordanus refused to write about them, and he wrote that dogshit about *he of sorrow*."

"They are the *perfect* goal. They are the *oldest* things in the world, they have *never* been found, and the most frugal man would give his entire fortune just to see them."

"You are aware that they are only a myth, aren't you?"

"Of course they are," Redevir said. "Everything is a myth until it is discovered. You think they don't exist because no one has ever found them. No one caught your man in Westgate until you did. You hunt users. I hunt treasures. We each have our games."

"A rare commodity is a highly prized one."

"I have a dread of mediocrity," Redevir said. "I will never be a prince or a king, so I have found my own way to put my name in the Histories. Time is the enemy I do battle with. Time is powerful. Time washes away small things, ordinary things. Only the most well known names remain when the wash of time cleans the canvas. The more lips that speak your name, the more powerful your name becomes, and it must be powerful indeed to resist the relentless tide of time. The Sephors are the greatest discovery. He who finds them will be remembered forever. His name will be invincible to the onslaught of time. That is immortality."

"It must be some life to live. Searching all over the world."

"Trust me, most of the *search* is in the reading. I spend a great deal of time standing still. You must be still to think clearly. You are taking a second look at the knowledge of the world, hoping to bring forth something new from it. Movement comes only at the end, when your feet must catch up to where your mind has already been." He tugged at his shirtsleeve. "Though it does reward those who do it well."

Aren laughed. "So you are off to Laman to find a Sephor."

"A possibility. Just hints and rumors really. With a bit of patience, and a pinch of perseverance, I think that I can find at least one." Redevir paused for a moment. "Aren, you know about the Histories. I have a question for you."

"Of course."

"Have you ever heard the phrase, *the mercury of this world is the foundation of the emerald womb*, in your reading?"

"It sounds like Pellagien the Historian," Aren said. "He was always very poetic. He wrote some of the more colorful passages in the Histories, and he is often quoted as a result. Mercury is a metaphor, a reference to the Andristi culture, the fluidity of their language, their calm and poise, and their willingness to sacrifice all for their kinsmen."

"Interesting. What about the emerald womb? What does that mean?"

"It's a symbol for the birthplace of Andristi culture, the woods of Synsiros, where the clans first united under Ismorien."

"Ismorien?"

"The first *Great King* of Laman."

"I thought the *White City* of Cair Tiril was the home of the Great Kings."

"It is now, but it was once Synsirok, the *City in the Trees*. Named for their greatest mythical hero, Syn. Why do you ask, by the way?"

"I've found plenty of clues to my search, hints goading me to the east. It is one thing to know the path you must take, but without a place to start, you can never begin."

"What do you mean?"

"I mean that you just helped me find the starting place for my search. My hunt begins in Synsirok."

"I don't understand. What does Pellagien have to do with your quest?"

Redevir tapped his chin with his index finger. "Not Pellagien, but someone he was quoting, an old philosopher named Curwen."

"The mystic? Curwen of Finneron?"

"That's him, but I think he knew a little bit more than how to philosophize. There was more to his passage. Pellagien left it out of his History. He thought it was meaningless fable."

"What is the rest of the passage?"

"He said that *the emerald womb was calm and clear, and its purity and perfection was like unto a mercuric Sephor.*"

"It actually says that?"

"The *complete* quote was included by Banwick in the notes of his translation." Redevir held up the copy of *Mercury Woods* and tapped it on his head. "That is why I wanted this copy so badly that I was willing to trade a two-thousand-year-old laminated scroll for it."

"So you think the lines refer to an actual resting place for one of them?"

"Not just any Sephor. The mercurial Sephor, the *Dagger*. Synsirok. I knew it had to be in Laman, and you just confirmed it for me."

"I told you what the line meant," Aren said cautiously. "I never said it would lead you to anything real."

"Of course. Thank you for humoring an old Rover's curiosity."

"I don't know where Donnovar's mission will take us, but I doubt that we will come to Synsirok, as much as I would like to see it."

"Well, when the time comes, I shall go my way, and you can go yours. That is the way of things."

"That it is."

Aren pretended otherwise, but he found it invigorating to finally find someone who put as much stock in the Histories as he did. Even in Amagon, where literacy was a much more common condition than most lands, there were not many that would care enough to read more than the Council's edicts, or a merchant's cargo manifest.

But even this new excitement could not overcome one thing. The only thing; that the world was dull monotony without a trace in front of him. One day became many days. And many days became all days. Every one the same. Every one vacant. Every one missing something vital to set it apart. Every one missing a *trace*.

Days of riding. How many days? He couldn't remember. Reidos spoke and Aren heard him, but could not truly listen. Redevir told him stories of the Sephors, but he forgot them all. He couldn't keep them from spilling out of his head, leaving him with only vague impressions, as if every yesterday was a dream.

It was nearing sunset when Aren saw the opening in the sheer cliff face and knew that this day at least would be different. They had made it to the pass. It was hidden behind thickly overgrown thornbrush, and although there were no trees to hide it, it was nearly invisible within the folds of grey rock. There was only one safe way through the labyrinth of winding crags and steep cliffs shielding Laman from Olbaran, and this was it.

Farguard Gap.

It cut through the thick mountains like the slice of a knife, and led right into the Lamani heartlands. The first half was rocky and desolate, climbing ever higher, the walls of speckled granite providing shelter from the chill westerly winds.

They reached the midpoint after a day and a night, and they were greeted with the sight of Laman as the sun began to rise, the ground dropping away sharply to reveal a view of the wide forests below. The canopy stretched on to the horizon, and the path dropped them down into the trees, submerging them in darkness.

Tallithlos was a thick and murky forest, with only one passable route. The rise fell immediately into a steep downslope to the valley floor, and soon he was enveloped by low hanging branches and thickets of thornbrush. Sunlight filtered through the leaves and needles as a patchwork of glittering gold rays through the haze, almost like starlight.

At midday, Hayles the Sarenwalker returned from his scouting. "Andristi kill teams," he said. "Dozens. Twenty or thirty men at each." The senior Sarenwalker's hair was greying. His cheeks were rounded, but his chin, nose, and brow were sharp lines. He maintained a perfect posture at all times, no matter the strain on his body, and he looked at Donnovar with unblinking eyes, as steady as two brilliant green stones.

"That seems more than is usual to guard the Gap," Donnovar said.

"They kept a tight guard. I found it difficult to move among them without being seen."

"We follow the thoroughfare and ride to them head-on," Donnovar said. "We will not attempt to evade them. We hold passes bearing their king's seal."

Hayles bowed and held it three full seconds, as if he was bowing before a god.

Donnovar nodded to Aren. "Do not wander into the darkness away from the road. Stay in the light." He then waved his men forward, riding out front, only the two Sarenwalkers before him.

Hayles and Fainen kept their heads cocked to one side, riding well ahead, listening for the slightest sound of men waiting in ambush. It was not long before they slowed their pace, making silent gestures to the other Sarenwalkers. One leaned in to whisper to Donnovar, who reined in his steed a bit, slowing the entire battalion.

An arrow sprang from somewhere within the tree line. It studded into the earth just ahead of Fainen's horse. Donnovar gave a quick signal to his sergeants, forbidding the raising of arms. They echoed his command down the length of the column.

The Andristi poured out of the woods on either side like rushing ants. Their bows were small, arrows strung, but no pull yet on their bowstrings. They stood like statues, with their cloaks hanging silent, eyes as sharp as knife thrusts.

Lamani Greycloaks.

Hayles and Fainen stared on ahead, as if the arrows trained on them were no more than bits of straw in the hands of children.

"Hail," Donnovar said. "Who is your commander?"

A young man—or at least with the look of youth, for who could tell with the Andristi—stepped from behind two of his fellow archers. "I am Hilder. I speak the Westrin tongue. You are trespassers here." His eyes were grey slits below his shallow brow, and his narrow chin and small mouth gave him the look of a doll.

"We are on an errand for the Lord Protector of Amagon," Donnovar said. "We are expected by the Great King."

"We hold here writs of passage bearing is seal," Raviel said, his voice like rocks scraping against mud. "See them here." He pulled the documents from his saddlebag.

Hilder stepped forward cautiously. His boots made no sound.

How had Hayles and Fainen heard these men?

Hilder looked over the documents carefully. He returned them and withdrew a step. "You are guests of the Great King. You shall not be harmed. But you choose a dangerous time to be in these woods. We have been ordered to turn back any wanderer who crosses the Gap, and kill anyone who tries to sneak past."

"An extreme response," Donnovar said. "Even for Farguard Gap."

Hilder nodded. "Warbands from Vulgossos crossed our borders, ranging as far south as these woods. Some are close to this place."

"Vuls?" Donnovar asked. "This seems a very far place from their borders to range unopposed. How did they make it past your armies, your cities?"

Hilder frowned. "Very unexpected. It is the end of their campaigning season. Yet they are suddenly everywhere. From the woods of Synsiros all the way to Talithlin. We are uncertain how they penetrated so deeply before being seen. Dark magick is being blamed. There are rumors of strange beasts with them. War animals of some sort. Superstitious men call them Shillilim."

"*With the Vuls?*" Aren asked. *Shillilim* was the Sinjan Andristi word for *Ghiroergans*, amphibious fish trolls of the Vulgos wastes. They were supposed to be untamable wild beasts.

"I do not like the sound of that," Corrin said. "Well, clearly time to turn back and..."

"We will not turn back, despite these dangers," Donnovar said.

"Shaot," Corrin said.

"I will take you to the White City," Hilder said. "You must be brought to Great Santhalian."

15

High Above

KELUWEN HAD NEVER DONE anything like this before. Orrinas said he had done it more than once, but he had never brought up such a thing to her.

She looked up at the wall of ancient pines. Wind whistled through the needles, and set every branch to shivering. *Are we going to be that high? No. Higher.* She felt her lunch rise a quarter of the way back up. She tilted her neck forward and fixed her eyes firmly on solid ground.

"Everyone be ready," Orrinas said. "We travel in twenty minutes."

Keluwen checked and then rechecked her rucksack. She was sure she would be ready by then, but every minute that slipped away she felt further from ready. After stowing her gear this way every morning for hundreds of miles as she hiked her way across the hills and wildernesses of Olbaran, one would have thought she would be able to do it in her sleep. But knowing what she was about to do made her feel like she had never done it before.

She glanced at each of the others to see who was handling the preparations better than her, and worse than her.

Cheli was terrified but hiding it well. Nils had given himself wholly over to Orrinas, and he trusted if Orrinas said it was possible, that it would be. Hodo Grubb was singing his Norian mantras to bring himself peace. Leucas Brej was pacing and talking either to himself or to a god. Zalash lived in confidence, his nose upturned. Vessander wore a smile of bravado to hide his nerves. Krid looked up at the pine trees as if he had already lived too long, and couldn't care less if he survived the journey.

Nils dropped another scoop of dumplings into Orrinas' metal bowl, Cheli sliced crisp peppers for him, and Hodo ground up another thimbleful of horocaine root and stirred the powder into a strong Samartanian coffee drink.

Orrinas hovered over his bowl like a scrier trying to read the future in his stew. He had a method, he had assured her. Just the right amount of vegetables for true energy, with a solid base of meat and dumplings to sustain him, and then the coffee and horocaine to keep his focus clear. "We can do this."

"All that matters is that *you* can do it. And Krid and Zalash."

"We are taking precautions. We are splitting the travel into three groups. We are taking great care in preparation. And we are all aware of the stakes."

"Are you sure we can't just go through on foot?" Leucas asked for the thousandth time.

At least I am handling it better than him.

"The Lamani will stop us, you idiot," Hodo said. "They don't let wanderers through the Gap."

"The woods will be crawling with Greycloaks," Krid said. "You ever seen a Greycloak?"

Leucas shook his head meekly. "No."

"Neither has any of the people who ever got killed by a Greycloak. Now understand me, boy?"

He nodded.

"They let the soldiers through," Nils said.

"The soldiers had passes from the Great King," Krid said. "Stop bothering Orrinas. He needs to eat his stew."

"Don't you need to eat a stew?" Hodo asked. "You are...leading one of the groups."

"Don't you worry about what I need," Krid said. "I have done this trick since your father was in swaddling. I know how to be ready to do this."

"I still don't see why we have to go through at all," Cheli said.

"Bite your tongue there, girl," Krid said.

"I am not saying I won't go," Cheli said. "But the southlander is already in Laman in pursuit."

"He has limited resources," Zalash said. "He cannot do this without us."

"And *he* has people in there also," Keluwen said. "Or have you already forgotten?"

"I have not, Kel," Cheli said. She frowned.

I'm sorry. I know you haven't. I am on edge. We are all on edge.

"How did *he* get through?" Leucas asked. "The same way as us?"

Orrinas looked up briefly. "He has a different way. One that we cannot use."

Shut up, you little shits. Orrinas needs to focus. For all our sakes. "All we know is that *he* is after something in Laman," Keluwen said. "That means he will move slowly. Carefully. It will be our best chance to catch up to him since Westgate."

"What if we can't get to him in time?" Cheli asked. "Does anyone know where he will go next?"

"Nothing definite yet," Nils said. "I would let you know if I learned something else." He leaned over her. "Do you need help with your gear?"

Cheli smiled and nodded. He set himself about helping her stow everything in good order so her pack would not be spilling out everywhere.

She smiled an eye-closing smile at him, shrugging her shoulders.

You shits are too sweet by half.

Zalash was chewing another piece of beef bark, gazing into the wind.

"Do you need any vegetables?" Cheli asked him.

"No." He did not even look at her.

"We have spare apples as well, almonds, cake bread."

"I need nothing," he said. "How many times must I tell you?"

Cheli backed away and moved on to Krid. He waved off the almonds and the cake bread, but he took her up on one of the apples and gnawed on it with what yellow teeth he had left.

Keluwen spent the next few minutes unpacking her rucksack and then packing it again from scratch. "Everything needs to be secure. Your pack cannot make a noise, your eating utensils cannot ping against your bowls. Or against each other. Each leader will need all of their concentration. All. Understand Hodo? No flatulence. And no laughing at a half-remembered joke from yesterday, Leucas. No innocent questions, Cheli. And no helpful encouragement, Nils. Understand? This is not something they can just sit back and relax for."

"She is right," Vessander said.

Of course I'm fucking right.

"No one has streams for the *duration* that we need to do this," Vessander said. "So they need to be able to focus for the changes, and to anticipate the expiration as closely as possible so that the next iteration does not begin too early. If they become distracted during the journey, we will fail. If they run out of energy because they did not time their spheres correctly, we will fail. I hope all of you understand this."

Everyone nodded.

Even Orrinas.

Even Krid looked up from his ruminating to nod. It was that important.

When Orrinas had finished eating, Cheli took the bowls and utensils and rinsed them in the creek, dried them and packed them carefully for him, with clothing in between each.

"Anyone else need help with their pack?" Nils offered.

Hodo and Vessander took him up on it. He smiled cheerfully, making sure everything was where it was supposed to be. Keluwen watched him to see if he still had Cheli's handcloth. He did. He brought it out twice to wipe his face.

We do not deserve you, Nils.

Keluwen took what she thought would be her final piss seven times in the final seven minutes. Her mouth was already dry, but no one had been permitted to drink any fluids for the last hour and a half. The travel was going to take a good long time, and there was nowhere to set down safely until they were past the Gap. And there was little Keluwen could think of that would be more distracting than everyone standing in a puddle of piss.

She had already cracked her knuckles a good fifty times. She had paced and she had practiced thought exercises. She had run out of things to distract herself with. Yet she still was not ready when Orrinas finally smiled at her and said it was time.

Each of the groups lined up: Keluwen and Leucas behind Orrinas, Hodo and Vessander behind Zalash, and Nils and Cheli behind Krid Ballar.

Orrinas looked up and down each group. At the last moment he pulled Nils out. "Nils, switch with Hodo."

Cheli became frantic, reaching after him as he moved. "It is a long travel," she said. "I can go with Zalash, too."

"No," Orrinas said. "The weight distribution must be even for each of us to have the best chance. Hodo and Vessander together are too much weight to suspend."

Keluwen shook her head. She felt it was unfair. She got to travel with Orrinas, after all. Cheli would, of course, be in a panic the whole way. But Orrinas was right.

When the time came they separated into their groups, spaced out across the clearing.

This is it. No more waiting.

Time to travel by bubble.

Orrinas rendered his sphere around his group. It had been half a lifetime since she had been inside a totally sealed blank sphere. The sound of the outside world vanished. She could hear her own heartbeat, *in her ears.* She felt dizzy in the silence. It made it worse that she could not see the sphere at all. There was no shine or reflection as if it was glass. It was a purely invisible barrier. Just like every shield she had ever rendered. The sphere closed around her and Orrinas and Leucas. It also sliced out a few inches of the little patch of earth they were standing upon, as the sphere completed itself underground.

This was important, Orrinas told her. It was less taxing for the three of them to stand as normal within the sphere than it was to tether each of them to the center and make them seem weightless. The only drawback was that they would feel the force of any acceleration and deceleration. He warned them both to brace themselves and be ready. *The last thing we need is either one of us to fall over during this.*

Keluwen glanced out of the sphere she shared with Orrinas and Leucas. She saw Krid complete his own around Cheli and Hodo. Cheli had both hands on the edge of the sphere as if it was a window. Nils smiled at her beside Vessander in Zalash's sphere.

Her heart rose until it choked her.

Seb had once told her there was nothing else like it.

The very idea of it terrified and exhilarated her.

Then the spheres began to lift off the ground.

First Zalash, then Krid, and finally Orrinas.

Keluwen felt her stomach drop. At first it did not even seem like they were going up. The trunks of the trees looked like they were dropping into holes in the earth, leaving nothing but the endless sky. And then she passed the tips of the trees and kept going and she almost laughed out loud with wonder.

The sky opened up in every direction. The treetops became a new ground, rolling like hills, bending in the breeze like blades of grass. Higher and higher. She saw the sun through the clouds, the sky so blue, more blue than her thirdbrother's eyes, the one who had taught her how to be sweet. More blue than the dress Maejlah wore the first night she taught Keluwen how to make a blank point in space, her first render. It was a pure blue, with depth, infinite, different from the way the sky looked from the ground. It transformed from a two-dimensional shell into an ocean of layer upon layer. The sun was high overhead and the light was blinding.

Belleron guide us.

She looked right and left and saw the other two groups inside their own spheres.

Orrinas nodded to Krid and Zalash, and then the travel began.

The sphere glided gently forward, gradually picking up speed as Orrinas swapped ever higher streams of velocity into the ingredient list of the render. The others were less fortunate. Krid's started forward, stopped abruptly, started again, sped up, stopped and reversed. Poor Cheli and Hodo were tossed about like toys, and Keluwen was fairly sure she saw Hodo vomit at least once. *That will be an unpleasant journey.*

Zalash at least went in the proper direction, but he had mastery of far fewer streams of velocity than Orrinas, and therefore his acceleration was not smooth. Going from five feet per second, to ten, to twenty, to twenty-five, to forty. Nils and Vessander did their best to lean forward into it to anticipate the changes, but they were so varied that they spent more time on their hands and knees than standing.

At last all three finally reached a speed to glide, and held it.

Keluwen looked down. Even the high mountains were below her. The summits, like the treetops, were now like distant grass. She watched the old grey rock, nearly purple, slide by beneath her on either side of Farguard Gap, rolling by like a picture-wheel.

She looked up at Orrinas with awe. To be able to do something like this. How could anything be better? She wondered how he ever came back down after the first time he did this. What was the world after this? How could anyone go back to walking on the ground after being in the sky, coasting on invisible wings like a golden bird with feathers of sunlight?

The world fell away.

Fear disappeared.

All that remained was wonder.

Keluwen wanted to throw her arms around Orrinas and kiss his perfect mouth out of sheer excitement, but she dared not. His concentration was what would keep them up here.

It was fifteen minutes of pure joy.

Then Zalash made his first swap. In order to avoid precedence effect, he bound streams of a very nearly identical set of attributes, so close it was almost the same. A sphere an eighth of an inch wider, with a strength one degree less, with a duration one second more, and a direction one degree to the east.

When it came time for Orrinas to do the same, the earth slab she stood upon dropped a tiny bit, just enough to keep her on her feet while also making her feel like her lunch was halfway to coming up.

It was the first reminder that this was a task, not an adventure.

One hour and four more swaps later, it transformed from a task into an ordeal. Sweat began to bead on Orrinas' brow. His legs began to wobble here and there. His eyes became bloodshot, his hands clammy. After the second hour, he asked her for more of the sweet peppers from her pack. She fed them to him, bite by bite.

By the third hour, he had to sit down within the sphere, and he asked for a bit more horocaine powder. Raw. With no more than a chaser of water to rinse his mouth of the bitter taste.

By the fourth hour, Orrinas was having difficulty keeping his eyes open. He began to slap himself awake every few minutes. Krid's sphere fell behind. He could no longer summon the strength to bring in streams of velocity so high. Orrinas and Zalash were forced to do the same, lest they become separated. That kept Orrinas going longer, but it also slowed them all down, prolonging the journey.

By the fifth hour, Orrinas clenched his teeth tightly, spittle leaking out one side of his mouth, water streaming out the corners of his eyes, his hands balled into fists, white knuckled and trembling. The peppers were all gone. And he dared not take any more horocaine, lest his heart explode. As it was, it was beating so hard she could feel it like it was inside her. Leucas looked worried.

By the sixth hour, the gap opened up below, and the trees once again spread out on either side. But they were not quite safe yet. The Greycloaks watched these woods very closely. They needed to reach the first open plain. So they kept moving, but Orrinas had his sphere dive to only a hundred feet above the ground, to once again coast as the quilt of treetops raced by beneath them.

By the seventh hour they were in trouble. They reached the first open plains of southern Laman, but it was crawling with Vuls. The first warband saw them and pointed. But the second a few minutes later fired arrows at them.

Shit.

They caused no harm, deflecting harmlessly off the invisible bubbles, but it meant they would not be able to set down anywhere near them, or within a day's walking of them. So they kept on, passing more patches of trees and more plains, until Orrinas thought it far enough and began to lower his sphere back to the ground, swapping his velocity gradually down to twenty feet per second.

Keluwen smiled.

Then just over the next patch of trees they flew over another band of Vuls.

Orrinas' eyes shot open. He ground his teeth. The sphere lifted and increased speed once more. Leaving them behind. One hundred feet back. Two hundred. But still the Vuls gave chase.

Keluwen looked back for the other bubbles. She saw Krid's keeping pace.

But she could not see Zalash's bubble anywhere. She looked right and left. "Orrinas!" She looked up. She looked down. She saw it. Zalash's sphere was racing along, jerking and sputtering, dropping altitude. One hundred feet above the ground. Ninety. Eighty. Slowing.

Orrinas turned to look.

Zalash had run out of strength. He was trying desperately to swap smaller, less taxing streams of every attribute of the sphere into his ingredient list. But they all kept failing. He had reached his limit.

Oh gods high and low.

Zalash's sphere winked out of existence. The bubble vanished. In one instant the one thing keeping them aloft disappeared.

Keluwen watched it happen. Her heart sank into a sea of tears. One moment it was there and the next it was gone.

The dirt patch they had been standing on crumbled and fell away like sprinkled dust. And Zalash and Vessander and Nils fell from the sky. Faster and faster. Still speeding forward diagonally through the air, but dropping farther and farther.

Keluwen screamed. She tried to make planes for them all. Elastic. To bounce them. But she did not have the strength to make them so far away. She was too high up and more than a hundred feet from them. The three of them were already beyond her reach.

Orrinas saw it, too, but he could do nothing. He had used everything he had to bring his own bubble this far.

Vessander hit first, his body clipping the top of a pine tree, spinning him round and round until he disappeared into the blanket of needles. Zalash smashed flat into a patch of rocks. His body seemed to burst like a split tomato. Nils was the last. He disappeared below the line of trees and was lost to sight.

Orrinas slowed his bubble, lowered it, slowed it some more, and dropped it to the earth. It blinked away just before the ground, and they all tumbled and rolled. Krid landed a hundred feet away.

Keluwen was already running back toward the patch of tall trees where she had seen them fall. Hodo was on her heels with Cheli. Leucas remained behind to care for Orrinas and Krid, pouring water into their mouths and feeding them. Both were well past exhausted, and had reached a point of danger, where if they did not replenish themselves and quickly, they might suffer more permanent consequences.

Keluwen found Vessander first. She thought he might be all right, from the way he was sitting up. But when she reached him, she realized with horror that he was dead and broken. The hit with the tree had shattered his right arm and broken his spine. She could tell from the matted and red-streaked grass he had flipped and tumbled and rolled more than a hundred feet, and the momentum of his body, by sheer chance, spent itself when his body had rolled upright, chin tucked to chest, one hand on his knee. He was gone.

She then started to backtrack. Hodo found the rocks where Zalash had obviously not survived. She carried on past him, her eyes attuned to every detail of terrain, looking for Nils.

Please be alive, Nils. Please. Please be okay.

She found him among a little field of furry voles. They scattered when they saw her. She ran as fast as she could, dropping to her knees and sliding to reach him. She cupped her hands to his cheeks as she slid to a halt in front of him. Cheli was racing up behind.

Keluwen looked deep into Nils' eyes.

And nothing looked back.

His eyes were empty as a moonless night. The spark was gone. His body was slack, and it pressed into the ground as if he were merely some object of the forest, slowly sinking, to be swallowed forever into the grass.

Forever goodbye, Nils.

Cheli saw him and screamed. She dropped to her knees, both hands over her mouth. She began to wail like a siren. Birds scattered. Her eyes cried until she went blind, and she pitched forward and slammed her head into the earth and pounded the grass with the palms of both hands, screaming into the dirt.

Keluwen had to lift her up and drag her away.

"No!" Cheli screamed. Her voice was shredded to tatters. She wrestled Keluwen, trying to break free, to run back to his body, and throw herself on him to weep for eternity.

Until never meets forever.

Keluwen heard voices hooting in the woods, they were distant but closing.

Keluwen slapped her across the face. "Vuls are coming. We have to go."

"Not without him! Please! We can't just leave him here. We can't leave him nowhere!"

Keluwen wrapped her arms about Cheli and held her close. She squeezed her tightly, and then pulled back, looked into her teary eyes. "I'm sorry, Cheli. He deserved better. We all do. But he would not want you to stay here. He would wring my neck if I *let* you stay here. Understand?"

Cheli nodded.

"We will send him off the right way," Keluwen said. "The old way. We will sing the songs. We will do it right. I promise."

Cheli nodded through the tears. She let Keluwen take her by the hand and lead her back to the others. She waved to Hodo along the way, and he turned and followed.

When they reached the others, Orrinas and Krid were back on their feet, but they were shaking. Leucas had to guide them. Hodo threw everyone's rucksack over his own shoulders, even Cheli's extra sack of heavy old tomes. He carried them all without complaint.

Seb had said there was nothing else like it. He had meant that it was pure joy. Now that joy was as dead as he was.

The first of the Vuls broke from the trees behind them.

Keluwen turned to face them.

They wore knobby old rusted armor and bowls for helmets. But their spears and hatchets were as deadly as any other.

Orrinas was near collapse. Krid was spent. Zalash and Vessander were dead.

But Keluwen was fresh as morning dew.

She rolled one glove down and slipped her fingers out. She pointed a pair of double-fingers at them.

One, two, three, four, five.

She shot a tiny blank impulse into each of them. The size of marbles.

She rendered them with streams of velocity as high as she was capable.

Each sphere struck a plate of armor.

And punched through that armor.

And shattered ribs.

And scrambled their soft tissues.

And exploded their organs.

And burst out their backs.

Some Vuls ran, but more would come.

They had to keep moving. What remained of her crew hobbled away, making for the safety of the highways of the Great King.

They had made it over the Gap.

But Keluwen was not sure if any of them would ever make it anywhere ever again after this.

16

The White City

I CANNOT BELIEVE I am here, seeing this with my own eyes.

By his reckoning, there were several things that he considered the most wondrous in all the world—the towers of Medion, the bridges of Ethios, the ocean off the capes of Rutland, and the morning mists of the Sarenwood in springtime. Cair Tiril now joined them.

He was so stunned he dropped his Jecker monocle into the grass. *Shaot.* With the many rare elements it contained, and its construction performed by a master artificer, the device was worth more than its weight in gold. He leaned down in the saddle, feeling a fool, knowing already he would not be able to reach.

But Hayles was there. The Sarenwalker drifted by and effortlessly bent down midstride to pick it up. He passed it back into Aren's hand as delicately as if balancing a cup of crystal atop a flagpole. He nodded, smiling, and never slowed down.

"Thank you," Aren said to his memory. Hayles was already gone down the column to where his horse waited.

The city was curtained by fifty-foot walls, a full circle of pristine white stone, so perfectly sculpted that he could not even see the joints. The wide open doors of the Golden Gate were thirty feet high, bronze riveted over wood, plaited in gold. It was a mouth capable of swallowing the Outer Guard even while riding eight abreast.

The Processional Way ran in a straight line from the Golden Gate to the Gala Ismori, with its forty foot statue of Great King Ismorien overlooking the Palace where the current Great King lived. Someone aggressively rang the signal bell within the tower of the famed Hammersmith to announce their arrival.

They rode past green gardens, lavishly lacquered white columns, careening colonnades, and courtyards rimmed with enormous obelisks. Every avenue was overlooked by white marble facades, two or three stories high, with a mountain range of towers and monuments and mausoleums beyond.

The streets would open abruptly to wide parks, filled with emerald grass, sturdy evergreens, still ponds, sugar flowers, and bubbling fountains carved into the shapes of mythic battles. Statues of the famed Andristi heroes marked the center of every market, every corner, every small shrine. Syn and Eren, Ban and Thurin, Sanaman and Poliniana—all the way down to the ones the Histories forgot.

The Outer Guard were on their best behavior. They feared Donnovar's wrath more than any prejudice. But they seemed pleasantly surprised that the Andristi were just...people, not cannibalistic murder-creatures. Ordinary people. A little taller on average, and a little lighter of skin on average, and their faces more slender on average. But otherwise the same. Most of the Outer Guard men could have been mistaken for Andristi had they been dressed differently.

Everyone here wore robes. Even the children. He did not see a single pair of trousers anywhere, except on the soldiers. The common folk wore pastels, but the wealthy had silks of luxurious reds, blues, and greens. They laughed and pointed at the Outer Guard on their warhorses, staring at their suits of armor, polished to a shine. The children ran along beside them, clapping and throwing flower petals.

The Palace was a white mountain. It boasted its own wide lawn, high walls, temples and towers. It looked different when viewed from each side, he had heard it said—a temple atop a grassy hill from one vantage, a flowery paradise atop a hundred steps from another, and yet another where it looked like a little door within a garden right on the side of a city street.

The Royal Guard were statues about the door in their ornamental armor. Breastplates were lined with gold, tall helmets plumed with blue horsehair, and ceremonial sashes dangled blue and green from belts and the tips of spears. The crying hawk of Santhalian's royal house had been hammered into the steel above each man's left breast, and they each were draped in cloaks of rich blue silk which rippled like water off their shoulders.

"Enter and await the Chancellor," one said.

Donnovar passed command to his lieutenant, and motioned for Aren, Terrol, and Raviel to come with him into the entrance. Margol followed.

Aren passed through an anteroom filled with statues of angels and princes wrought from marble. The ceiling was vaulted high above, covered from end to end with frescoes. Aren could not remember if they had been done by Loyol or Gaderian. He saw the depictions of Palan's revolt, and of Salas and Rogar marching together through leagues of razed forests to fight during the Great War against Kradishah.

The Chancellor emerged from the far doorway. He was tall enough to look down on Donnovar. He seemed to glide along the marble floor, as if he were perched on an unseen skiff with silent wheels. His hair was long and shined like spun silver, beneath a tall squared hat that widened at the top. His face was smooth and pale, showing no hint that a beard could ever grow upon it. The orbs of his eyes were grey within grey, and they seemed to indelibly capture all that passed before his gaze, like tiny scribes etching all that he beheld into the stone of his memory. He was appareled in the finest robes of silken brocade, hanging about him in many layers of whites, blues, and reds—all shining with traces of silver and lined with gold trim.

The Chancellor leaned toward Donnovar, his head slightly downturned. "You are now before Solathas," he told them in perfect Westrin. "Chancellor and advisor to Great Santhalian. Solathas gives you the blessing of light from the Father and firm ground beneath your feet from the Mother. May you be welcome in love to the Palace of the Great King." His voice rose and fell like a smooth song.

"We give thanks," Donnovar said. "It is our honor to be here."

"Your coming is a good omen for Laman. It will help them to keep faith. In times of strife all men seek for the deep earth. They fear for their souls, and pray to the warm embrace of the Mother within for salvation. Your coming is seen as a divine portent. Come now. You must be brought before Great Santhalian."

Donnovar glanced at Aren. Aren nodded to the Captain, and fell into file with the others behind the towering Chancellor.

Each room they passed through had great arching doorways, rising twice the height of a man, and the series of interconnected rooms seemed to meld into one long hallway, lit by dozens of windows. Each separate space was accented by a unique mixture of incense, and each was decorated with different colored tapestries. They passed statuettes of lapis lazuli and polished quartz, door frames of dark basalt, and pillars of porphyry.

On the winding stairs they passed cupolas housing tall statues in life-sized likenesses of the many Great Kings of Laman—Ismorien, Siristall, and Lithlinon. The alcove that contained the effigy of Prince Palan had a dark shroud pulled across it, represented in this way ever since his uprising.

They at last came to the fifteen-foot high double door of the throne room, called the Mournful Door. Seven Royal Guard stood before it, each as motionless as the statues of the kings. At the precise moment Solathas reached them, they parted, and allowed him to glide silently past. The doors opened wide at the touch of the Chancellor's fingertips.

The throne room was wide and deep, easily two hundred feet in length, with the throne chiseled atop a series of steps, each of a different color stone, radiating like a pale rainbow. The vaulted ceiling had the look of the heavens, with tiny stars painted in silver that seemed to wink with lights of their own. Ten-foot diameter azure columns lined the walls to either side.

Santhalian sat atop the throne, flanked by a man and a woman, both wearing garments of fine silk, the same blue color as the Great King's royal robes. The man was the most forgettable thing in the room, but the woman was something else, her hair a cascade of blond curls, eyes ocean blue. Aren kept finding himself drawn to her, his glances pulled by some subtle gravity. She somehow competed with the most stunning room Aren had ever stood inside. The sight of her made him forget that he had just seen marvels of art and architecture he had dreamed of all his life.

Behind the Great King stood four tall knights, all wearing shining silver breastplates and pure white cloaks over white tunics and polished mail hauberks. They were the Order of the White Moon, the four sacred bodyguards of the Great King. They stood as emotionless as Sarenwalkers, their eyes as distant as marble statues.

The Great King was at attention in his throne, his posture a model of perfection. He was well built, and his hair was of long, shining strands of gold. His hands held the edges of his throne like the talons of the royal hawk of his household totem. His sharpened amber eyes were ever moving over those present.

"Great Santhalian," Solathas said. "Solathas stands before you with great gladness to present Donnovar, Aren, Margol, and Raviel. Solathas has deemed them worthy to proceed before your sacred throne."

Santhalian nodded. "Solathas tells me that even after being informed of the danger of invading warbands, you made the decision to enter a realm of uncertainty without hesitation. Some men would have chosen to ride around danger to ensure their own safety, or turn back altogether. I am told that you never entertained such a thought. Your bravery is proof of the strength of your word. Fear not to speak. Solathas assures me that you are wise despite your young years." He spoke Westrin nearly as well as Solathas.

Aren leaned close to whisper to the Captain. "Great Santhalian is easily three times *your* age."

"Yes," Solathas said. "Those of the Andristi lineage live far longer than the span of your countrymen. It is a blessing and a burden."

The Great King glanced at his Chancellor. "Solathas loves to speak. Perhaps he might give others a chance."

Solathas bowed his head. "Great Santhalian is wise." He floated back a step.

"Where is the one named Raviel?" Santhalian asked.

Raviel stepped forward, and bowed before speaking. "I stand here."

Aren bit his lip. *He forgot to address Great Santhalian in his response. A poor start.*

Santhalian frowned. "You come to our aid."

"I have come," Raviel said. "I must go to Synsirok."

Santhalian frowned more deeply.

Aren bit his lip harder. *This is not beginning well.* Why Synsirok? For someone who was at this point just a glorified escort, Raviel certainly seemed intent on trying to dictate plans of travel.

"These papers state that you have given your permission to move about in these lands," Raviel said.

You were supposed to tell them you are here to cleanse their land. No matter the goal, it was customary to couch every request in a way that made it seem like it was begging to do the Lamani people a favor. No matter how you have to tie logic into knots to do so.

The Great King glanced aside, appearing bored.

Shaot. I have to do something. They could turn us out, send us back. He could ruin everything for Donnovar. For me.

Aren stepped forward uninvited. His hands shook, and his heart smacked against his ribs. "Our only wish is to help the people of Laman," he said. He glanced at the young woman beside the Great King. His mouth went dry. His knees shook. "Apologies for speaking out of turn, Great Santhalian."

"How shall you help us?"

"We come on a mission of peace," Aren said. "To strengthen the bond of our two lands. I have always wanted to come here, to see this place. But we are not here for pleasure. Any aid we can give, we will." Aren knew Donnovar would have agreed.

"We are invaded," Santhalian said. "Violent men walk our land, with violent beasts. My heart is torn that my people suffer."

Aren froze for an instant. "Yes, Great Santhalian. We have seen the beauty and the grandeur of your magnificent royal city. It would pain us all to see it tarnished."

The eyes of the Great King perked up as Aren spoke.

People in high places always enjoy praise. And he had no doubt that kings enjoyed it most of all.

"You are familiar with my people?" Santhalian seemed surprised and delighted.

"I am indeed, Great Santhalian. The Histories have much to tell of the heroism of your ancestors. I have read the story of Bandiel since I was a boy."

"Bandiel was the champion of one of my predecessors, Great Siristall."

"The Mahhennin of my home in Amagon remember him as the Black Death of Synsiros. They say he led his armies to crush the Vuls, fighting until he was covered with the blood of his enemies. The Histories say he defended the walls of Cair Tiril itself, slaying a hundred men with his own sword."

"My own family line includes Bandiel," Santhalian said. "I myself am seven generations removed from his time, but his name lies near the center of my household's lineage."

Aren smiled. "You bear a striking resemblance to his portrait in the Library of Lenagon. That is what brought him to mind in the first place."

"Yes, my mother reminded me often of that when I was a young man. She also spoke very highly of your own lands in the west. One of my great uncles took the path of the Mahhennin, following the setting sun to the shores of the west."

"Haldiem," Aren said, remembering the name. "He was the great-grandfather of one of the heroes of my homeland, Coralian the Sur-Slayer. There are many links between Laman and Amagon."

"You speak well of my people," Santhalian said. "What royal favor do you wish of my throne?"

"There is a reason we have come to Cair Tiril, Great Santhalian. We captured an assassin from Amagon, an assassin with the magick. We have reason to believe that he may have been working with others. Conspirators who may be within the city at this very moment. We wish your permission to allow Donnovar and his men to help you seek them out within your walls." *This is Santhalian's city. We are in his house here.* He did not dare say they caught the wrong man, though he felt it in his bones. He needed to secure the continuation of his investigation without overtly seeming to. It was a fine line to walk.

Santhalian held out a hand to Donnovar. "You may make your request."

Donnovar stepped forward, sweating like a firstyear in the Academa. "We have come with a delegation to discuss mutual aid, to secure your borders, and thereby our own. Our man, Margol, is here to make private arrangements on behalf of the Lord Protector of Amagon. And Raviel is leading our investigation of the conspiracy."

Aren bowed. "It brings great joy to offer our aid to your people, Great Santhalian, though we do not doubt you have the power and resources to resolve the affairs of your kingdom. Please allow us the joy of doing this one small thing for you that you could certainly do without us."

The Great King smiled. "You shall not only be given leave to perform your investigation within this city, but you shall have all the assistance that my people may provide. You have but to speak your request and it shall be fulfilled."

Aren smiled. This was his chance. "Any information your people might have of the presence of strange sorcerers in this region would be most helpful."

Raviel raised an eyebrow to that request. So did Donnovar.

"Done," Santhalian said. "And you shall be given access to our knowledge of enemy forces within our boundaries so that you may conduct your business and return home in peace."

"Thank you, Great Santhalian. Your grace is more than we deserve." *You see, Raviel? You see how worthy I am? I saved this trace. Remember that the next time you try to spit on my success.*

"Here is Erethion," the Great King said, gesturing at the man in blue silks beside the throne. "He is the Commander of my Southern Host. He shall appraise you of the dispositions of our enemies, and aid your investigation in any way you require."

Erethion gave a curt nod. He wasn't exactly hideous, but his face looked like two hawks had crashed into each other in midair.

"This beauty is Eriana." Santhalian gestured to the girl with the golden hair. "My youngest cousin, and the rose of my Royal House. She will see to it that you are treated as guests in this city." She smiled once more. She was slender, but not tall, lithe and muscular by the way her blue gown hung about her shoulders. Her eyes were blue like sapphires, set in a face pale and delicate as porcelain.

"Erethion!" the Great King said. "To the map room. Humbly offer them council."

Erethion stepped down, and led them out a side door.

As they fell in line behind Erethion, Donnovar tapped Aren on the shoulder. "How do you do that?" he whispered.

"Do what?"

"You just snap your fingers and can talk like that," he said. "Talk to a king. As if you turn yourself into one of them."

Aren could not help but smile. "Just speak as if you are reading one of the Histories and no one can tell the difference."

Donnovar laughed and clapped him on the shoulder. "Books," he said. "All that from books."

The map room was square, lit by dim golden light-bowls in the corners, shelves lining the walls. They were packed well with aged manuscripts and wide scrolls. A rectangular table of solid basalt stood alone at the center, covered with maps of Laman and Palantar—detailed sketchings of landscapes, interconnected roads, and wildernesses.

Erethion scanned the maps with distress. "The Vul raiding parties are only the beginning," he said. "They are across our borders and on the move, led by one who is called Krundaggas. My men in Talithlin, which you came through to get here, have been tracking three large warbands there. Reports have come in from Synsirok. Vuls in large groups moving through the forests of Synsiros as well."

They spent another hour combing the maps, Erethion providing the most recent numbers and positions. Erethion agreed to have his maps transcribed for Donnovar to share with his officers.

Raviel never once looked at the maps. Aren was sure because he watched him to see if he would. He yawned repeatedly, looking around at the shelves of scrolls, not caring in the slightest what might be in store. He waited until the very end to speak up.

"Tell me about the magick men," Raviel said.

Erethion squinted, but he did not argue. "We have had reports of strange men moving on the roads nearby. I have received reports noting abnormal occurrences and clouds of thick fog which shines. We do not know if any of these instances are related, but the frequency has increased dramatically. Some of my patrols have indicated similar stories of men avoiding their checkpoints, and disappearing into the woods."

"Any indication where they are going?" Raviel asked. "A pattern to the sightings?"

"No pattern," Erethion said. "But two women have reported being approached in separate instances by a foreign man, from the west like you, who asked many questions relating to the city of Synsirok, and the paths which lead to it. They both claim that the man would only converse with women, and that he behaved threateningly toward them if they attempted to dissuade his advances."

"Any sightings in this city?" Raviel asked.

"We have had an unfortunate incident which appears to involve the magick," Erethion said. "Though, as you say, it is not presently related to the reports of men on the roads."

"I would like to see the reports of this incident," Raviel said.

"I shall present you each a copy," Erethion said.

"No," Raviel said. "Only to me."

Only to you? Who do you think you are? I got us into this room. But Aren kept his mouth shut. He would not dishonor Donnovar by arguing with Raviel in front of their hosts.

Everyone dispersed from the map room. Raviel disappeared completely, moving so fast to leave that he seemed to dissolve.

Aren fumed to himself, silently yelling at his boots as if they were Raviel. He was concentrating on them so furiously that he almost stumbled into someone rounding the corner.

Eriana appeared in the hall before him, the tumbling curls of her hair like spun gold. She was suddenly right there before him, within arm's reach, standing coolly beautiful in the hall. Aren froze, stuttered the beginning of an apology, failed to put any voice to the words, and glanced uncomfortably at his boots.

When he looked up, she was still there, and what was worse, he still had nothing to say. He was hoping Donnovar would say something, to save him from further making a damn fool of himself, but he seemed a little shaken as well. Even Margol deftly reached a hand to one of the shelves of scrolls near the door to steady himself, then stuffed it quietly into the folds of his shirt as if embarrassed to be caught off guard.

Aren stood there speechless, feeling like a ridiculous mime. Eriana blinked at him, and it was the most memorable blink he had ever witnessed. *I am a fool, aren't I. Talk to the Great King, but can't manage a single word to one girl.* He felt her eyes on him, and smelled the urgent perfume that flowed from her gown.

At last she bowed, finally and blessedly turning to Donnovar. "I have come to invite you to a royal feast outside the Palace tonight," she said. "The royal dancers shall present a performance in your honor."

I shall go anywhere that you will be, Aren found himself thinking. It was not fair of her to just stand there looking at him. How could he be expected to think of something to say when her eyes were so blue?

"Our honor?" Donnovar asked uncertainly.

"Rare are travelers from the west," she said. "Great Santhalian will not allow anything to diminish the celebration. Where is your Amagon Glasseye? I am to invite him as well."

Aren was so busy looking at her that he nearly missed it. "I...well, I am Aren."

She blinked in surprise. "You...are the Glasseye?"

Aren was too bewildered to say yes.

She smiled suddenly, unexpectedly. "You both are to be accorded the honor of Guest of the Throne."

"We are honored by the thought," Donnovar said.

"Many of my kinsmen are overjoyed at your coming. It is seen as a sign from the Mother and Father," she said. "You would honor them by attending."

Aren's stomach tightened. He turned from her, trying to hide his nerves. He turned to Donnovar. Speaking to him was no problem whatsoever. "We do not want to disappoint our hosts."

Donnovar smiled. "We will go. It would bring some cheer to my men. You speak our Westrin tongue better than I think I even do, Eriana. I wish I could pay you in kind. Your Great King is very generous."

Eriana clapped her hands together. "Wonderful," she said. "It shall please Great Santhalian much that you have accepted his invitation."

She smiled and Aren felt his stomach turn upside down. She rested one hand on her hip, and his eyes glanced at it and he wanted it to be his hand, but of course it wouldn't be, and it couldn't be at all because of who she was and who he was and so he looked away from her hips altogether, but he didn't know where else to look and so he looked up at her face and that was another mistake because then he was looking directly into her eyes. He fell into them as if they were wells that just opened up beneath his feet. He shook his head to clear his thoughts, about as eloquently as a dog sneezing.

She seemed disappointed by his response. She turned to Donnovar. "Please follow me. While you wait for those that will help you, Great Santhalian wishes you to have a tour of the Lamani Chapel and the Marble Forest."

"I will give my leave now," Margol said suddenly. "I will see to the camp. I must speak with Terrol."

"We will join you there shortly," Donnovar said.

Eriana turned quickly down the hall. "What is it you search for in a trace?" she asked as she led him down the endless corridors of Santhalian's Palace.

Aren had to jump to match her sudden pace. No one had ever asked before. Most people were preoccupied with fear of who he was tracing to bother asking him how it was done. What *did* he do? How did he trace someone? He suddenly couldn't remember. Words escaped him. "Residuals," he finally managed. "The leftover traces of altered reality. Afterglow."

"The bending of light?"

"That's only a part of it," he said. "When you first step into a fresh scene, that is only what you look for at the start, to confirm the presence of recent magick. Visible cues—steam, light-bending, tunnel vision, vapor trails, and sometimes even aural afterglow that can be seen by the naked eye." He wished he hadn't chosen that precise wording, because all of his knowledge vanished again in the wake of a hazy vision of her lying naked in his arms. It was not a good start for introducing her to his profession.

"If you search for that which is invisible, how do you hope to see it?"

"Why do you ask?" Aren asked back, mostly because he could not remember the applicable words necessary to answer the question. "Only Priests and Librarians ever care about these things."

That did, however, manage to fluster her a bit. She squinted at him. "I wish to learn," she said, her golden hair bobbing as she walked.

"A Jecker monocle," Aren said. "You use a Jecker monocle to see invisible signs." He produced the lens from his tracer satchel. "If a scene is fresh enough, it can tell you nearly everything you need to begin a trace."

"What is so special about it?" Eriana asked. "It looks like poorly made glass."

Donnovar laughed again.

"It is a lens of ranum crystal," Aren said, not sure if he felt insulted or if it was merely the funniest thing he had ever heard. "It reacts to the residue of altered reality. It has four filters, each of a different element, and each one reactive to different aspects of the magick." He pointed to the colorful filter lenses attached to the swivel joint at the corner.

"Yes, but what do all the lenses do?" she asked, touching each one with a fingertip as she walked beside him. He watched her finger as she tapped each lens, his mind frantic to break the hypnotic trance induced by her every gesture.

"The primary lens allows you to see the afterglow, the clouds of multicolored particles from recent magick. There are wave patterns within the afterglow. Reading these colors and patterns can give very specific information about the user and the magick they performed. You can determine the types of renders used, and determine if his renders were active or passive."

"What is the difference between those? How can magick be passive?"

"Passive renders affect a force or aspect of nature which already exists. Sliding something over a surface..." He scraped his boot on the stone street. "...creates natural friction. Passive friction renders would alter aspects of that preexisting friction. Active friction renders, on the other hand, create friction where it normally would not be, between two objects that are not touching. Or controlling fire only after it is already lit by conventional means, instead of making your own fire out of nothing."

"What do you do once you see the colors?"

"Then you bring the Oscillatrix into play," he said, taking out the small cylinder. "The elements inside are highly reactive to residuals in close proximity. The metals inside warm and expand in a certain way based on the amplitude and frequency of the waveform of a user's renders. We call these the *primary values*. They are the most telling evidence of a user's skill and power.

The values are the same in any of the user's renders, and can help to identify them, and determine the rate of the growth of their power."

He followed her to the end of another corridor, through a heavy oak door, and down a columned portico to a placid garden surrounded by fruit trees.

"But I thought your purpose was to identify a user absolutely," Eriana said. "Would it not be possible for two users to share similar values?"

"Yes, technically. But we can also look to the *core color* of his residuals."

"I was under the impression that the colors indicate different types of magick forces."

"They do through the Jecker monocle's primary lens alone, but with the blue filter to remove the surface patterns, all other colors are filtered out, and all that remains are the core color of the waveform particular to that user, the color of their key. It is nearly impossible to come across two users who share the same primary values *and* the same core color. And even if you did, imprints with the blue filter *also* show the *exact* pattern of that key they use to unlock the source. Every one is based on an individual's interpretation of reality, and every one is unique. It is the user's fingerprint. The blue filter is the workhorse. It can even show me whether the core colors are shifting red or blue, so I can tell where a user *is* by looking at where he *used to be*."

"I see." She smiled at him, stepping deftly around a small fountain among the garden fruit. Aren himself nearly tripped over it, prompting another laugh from Donnovar.

"Next, we recreate the scene," Aren said. "First employ the green filter alone." He held it up for her to see. "It filters out the quantum peaks of altered reality. It allows you to see the *spectral lines* among the residuals. Spectral lines show size, direction of motion, and position of any effects a user renders."

She took his hand and brought it close to her face, and all he could think about was her hand touching his, and he forgot which filter he was describing and forgot what it was for, and he could only focus on the sensation of skin touching skin.

Eriana squinted her eyes through the lens. "Green," she agreed. "It would make me uncomfortable to watch anything through that."

Donnovar laughed to himself again.

That broke Aren's trance, and he gave the lens a second look to remind himself which filter he had been talking about. "The white lens filters out the time-arching, allowing you to see the warping of the afterglow. This displays the magnitude or power behind the forces used, to help determine a user's experience and mastery of each render."

"Ugh," she said, peeking through it. "It is like looking into a world of ghosts."

"The rosy lens filters out the spatial warping of afterglow to show how well the renders merge with reality. Knowing how detailed and efficient a user is comes in handy when it comes time for capture."

"I see," she said again, leading him through an ancient iron gate, and down a cobbled lane. She held his hand up to her face again. He could feel her soft breath on his skin. "I like this one much better. It is a pleasing tone."

It immediately became Aren's favorite filter. "Using the white and rose and green filters together exposes the *variants*. Variants are like interruptions in the resonance of each render. These breaks delineate individual streams within each one, so I can isolate them and target recurring ones for the Stoppers."

She looked through all three of the filters. "Everything looks like mud."

She then let go his hand for the last time, and Aren wished he had more filters to show her, dozens more, but of course there were no more and so he followed her in silence as she led him away from the Palace grounds, across a vast courtyard ringed by obelisks. She said nothing for what seemed a long time.

"I assumed it would sound boring," Aren said, disappointed.

"No," she said. "Not boring. Overwhelming. You must be very intelligent to perform these traces."

Aren hoped the shadows cast by the setting sun would hide his reddening face. Eriana's reaction was new and startling to him. It made him feel both warm and hopelessly ridiculous at the same time. Most women made the sign of the witch at him whenever he walked by. Often enough that it didn't even bother him anymore when they did. Save for the whores, of course. They were always kind to him. More like they were kind to his silver. They didn't care what he did as long as his money was good.

"What do you do with all of this knowledge you gain?" she asked. "From the *scene*?"

"And then the trace begins."

"How?"

"*Using* leaves residual afterglow, and afterglow can sensitize anything it touches. Like their hands, or clothes. That stain will follow a user as they move away from a scene. Like when you spend a long time near a fire, the smoke smell adheres to skin, hair, and clothing, and will only lessen over time or with washing. And if I can get ahold of something that has been sensitized by their afterglow, I can use spectral shift to determine which way they went. I can hunt them."

"What if the user is too far ahead? What if the residuals all die out?"

He smiled. "There is one thing I know about users—they can't stop using. They are addicted to their own magick. It's only a matter of time."

"It all sounds so exciting," she said.

Donnovar yawned. "Yes, I cannot wait to turn in my sword for a chance to wield books and papers."

Aren rolled his eyes.

Eriana flashed a smile at him as she took them to the end of the wide court, and across another, boasting a massive fountain of swirling nymphs and winged dogs. Beyond its sputtering jets of water sat the Lamani Chapel.

It was a pure white dome capped with winged statues of solid gold. Enormous buttresses ringed the walls, supporting the weight of a circular vault. There were many inlets and alcoves within the facade, giving the appearance that the Chapel had been set atop the mammoth skeleton of some long extinct animal.

"This building hosted the inauguration of Great Lithlinon," Eriana said. "It was built by his father, Great Siristall, and required fifty years to complete."

"I have heard this," Aren said, trying to appear composed, even somewhat aloof. "The final stone was laid on the morning of the *Dancing of the Moons* festival."

Eriana's eyes darted to him, flustered a bit as she went on. "It housed the... Conclave of the Elders in which...Great Salas made known his decision to aid High King Rogar of Olbaran against the hordes of Kharthist."

"It also hosted the wedding of Erelin to Great Soraman," Aren added.

Eriana's eyes were locked on his lips as he spoke.

Could she really be...? No, it's impossible.

"The marriage joined the two Great Households of Laman more than five hundred years ago," she said.

There was a long silence.

"Were we going to go inside?" Donnovar asked.

Eriana was startled when she realized she was being addressed. She said nothing, and motioned them to follow her, flashing a brief smile.

The interior was full of soft browns and mellow golds, in great contrast to the plain white marble that made its skin. Dim light-bowls glowed lazily from the ends of chains suspended high above them, and the interior pillars were also paneled in rich redwood, all trimmed in gold. The floors were checkerboards of multicolored marble, and the pillars rose into rounded arches high overhead.

They moved into the dome-capped central chamber, sixty feet across, its lofty height lit by the flickering flames of hundreds of candles and lanterns.

He leaned to Donnovar. "I've seen the sketches, but I never felt the size of this place. It's like the towers of Medion or the bridges of Ethios." Even his whispers echoed loudly.

"You have seen the towers?" Eriana's eyes went wide. "And been to Ethios?"

"Of course," Aren said.

"I wish I could see such sights as those. I pray to the Mother and the Father every day to make it so." She sighed.

Aren was surprised. "But why would you care? You have so many treasures and monuments here in Laman. You walk past works of art every day." How could anything he had ever seen account for even an ounce of her attention when she lived within the White City and all its splendor?

"If you have been to Medion, you must have seen Loyol's memorial," she said.

"Naturally," Aren said. "I noticed some of his works in the Great King's palace."

"You know his work?!" she exclaimed. "I love Loyol."

"He was a master," Aren agreed. "His frescoes were always—"

"Better than his sculptures," Eriana finished for him.

There was a long pause where he tried not to look at her and failed, and she never took her eyes off him.

"This is massive," Donnovar said, smiling at the austere walls. "I have seen other works of man in my time, but I have never seen anything so grand and so subtle all at once."

"The far end of this chamber bears the tomb of Direthan," Eriana said, jolted out of her silence. "He was considered by some to be one of the greatest wielders of the magick to have ever lived."

"Though many claim that he shouldn't be considered beside the great users of the Arradian Empire," Aren said.

She eyed him coolly. "You think Arradan is better than Laman?"

"Not better," Aren said. "Different." he paused. He very suddenly, very urgently, very aggressively wanted some malagayne smoke in his lungs. *Give it to me.* He looked around. He could not do it with either of them watching. *I need to get out of here.* "Thank you for showing us these things. We appreciate all of it, but I am also here for a reason. Magick men. Users. It may be best if we...separate."

"Separate?" She pursed her lips and squinted.

"I need to look over the trace materials."

"Why? Are you hunting someone here? In Cair Tiril?"

"No. Not exactly. Just something that has been bothering me. I can't really explain it."

"Erethion will be providing information this evening to your friend, Raviel," she said.

"No!" Aren did not realize he was shouting until the word was already out of his mouth.

She recoiled, a look of disgust on her face.

"Apologies," he said. "I did not mean to shout. *I* want to see it. Me. I did all of this, not him."

"I thought you were all working together," she said, frowning.

"Only a fool would think I would work with *that*," Aren said. He froze. He did not even realize what he was saying until it was already out.

Eriana turned to face him, grimacing. "You are not as careful how you speak to me as you should be."

Aren bit his tongue. *Shaot. Fool. Idiot. Stupid, stupid fool. You must keep your cool better than this. Malagayne is right around the corner. Hold yourself together.*

Donnovar was looking down at the ground, arms folded, shaking his head and smiling.

Eriana said not a word more to him, walking silently ahead, never turning to look his way.

He was simultaneously relieved and utterly despondent.

She stopped them at the entrance of a wide park. "Follow this path of lanterns," she advised. "Walk in the light. It will take you through the Marble Forest to where we began."

"You will not accompany us?" Donnovar asked.

"I am sure this boy can tell you all about its origins," she said curtly. "I will see that Erethion is providing whatever help you require. Good day." She turned without waiting for him to respond, and was off down the street.

Her sudden absence stung. But then again, what did it matter? Tomorrow he would be gone and she would go on being a member of a royal house, and this would all be a memory and that would be that. She would disappear into the past and be gone forever.

He led Donnovar through the Marble Forest, though it was not a forest at all. It was a green park teaming with stone statues of Andristi warriors and gods. Thousands of them. They seemed to sprout from the grass like angry but beautiful weeds. Birds darted from one to another, sitting proudly upon the heads and shoulders of heroes and princes, swordsmen and lancers, ancient spirits and mythological hunters. Each face was unique, from the lowliest herdsman to the most renowned oracle. The eyes were inset, making it appear that they were aware of all who stalked through their domain.

"I think she is fond of you," Donnovar said.

"Eriana? Did you not see the way she tore off down the street? She thinks I'm boring and pompous, a nervous fool, prattling uselessly about traces."

"That was not my impression."

"You must have seen something that I did not."

"That is the way of women. One minute hanging on every word, the next minute ignoring you at any cost. Have you no experience in the matter?"

"Of course I do. But she was so...she would just..." He gave up on whatever he had been trying to think of to say. "I've never talked to someone who I could offend that quickly."

"Not as easy when there isn't a pile of coins on the bedside table, is it?"

"That was rude."

"I always thought Sarker was doing you a disservice with that. When every interaction with a woman begins in the bedroom, you never learn what kind of words it takes to get them there."

"I have talked with Merani for hours."

"And it would not matter what you said as long as the silver was good. That is not a real audience."

"I think I know how to talk to a woman." Aren was offended.

"Clearly." Donnovar seemed skeptical. "May I provide advice?"

"Go ahead."

"You should try letting her speak without interruption. It works marvels with a woman. At least pretend to listen. They say only a well guarded tongue can make it past the gate of a woman's lips."

"If you say so." He was trying not to think of lips at all. "The idea is ridiculous. Santhalian would have my head for an ornament."

"I don't think that is the common practice among the Andristi. I believe they chain men to trees and starve them." He laughed. "Something to think about to boost your appetite for the coming feast." He excused himself to attend his officers, leaving the thought of execution hanging in the air.

Aren laughed. "I will see you there."

When Donnovar was gone, Aren looked up at the sky and took three deep breaths. *I cannot believe I am breathing the air in this place.* He looked over each shoulder. He was alone. He leaned against a statue at the edge of the Marble Forest, back to back with Ban the Thrice Blessed, and crushed a quarter leaf into the pipe and lit it. He stared at the clouds and counted the inhales. He made it to fifteen before he heard footsteps coming. He dispersed the smoke with a quick wave and rolled the pipe into its cloth.

When he stepped out from behind Ban he thought he was dreaming.

Eriana was coming toward him again.

He rubbed his eyes and blinked to be sure it was really her. It was. She was back already, and he already had nothing new to say. He felt it was liable to drive him mad. He bit his lip.

She was leading a pale Andristi man to him.

"Eriana," Aren said. "I did not expect you."

She pursed her lips. "I heard you say you asked for our reports of the evidence you seek. It was given to the other Glasseye, Raviel, instead."

"A sour thing to bring up," Aren said. "Look, I am sorry for what I said. I didn't mean it the way it came out."

She wrinkled her nose and cracked a corner smile. "So I have brought you something better. I have brought you the man who *wrote* those reports. I have brought you *our* Glasseye."

Aren was stunned. He wasn't sure if his jaw fell open wider, or his eyes.

She smiled a smile that very clearly said: *you think you are so very smart and that there is no one on this earth who can surprise you, but I can, and I did.*

Aren smiled back at her. "You win," he told her.

17

River Quarter

"IF THE PERSON WE are here to talk to is so important, then why are we hiding in the back room of a fish frier in the River Quarter?" Keluwen folded her arms and waited for a decent answer.

Krid was the one who turned to her, so she knew it would be an answer, just not the decent kind. "What would you have us do? Prance up to the Palace doors? This is Cair Tiril, not Westgate."

Keluwen looked around the room. Blobs of spilled chowder congealed on tabletops like old glue, gumming up Leucas' hands. The floor was more grease than stone, and had nearly toppled and killed Hodo ten times already. The air was suffused with the aroma of the worst parts of a fish, enough that Cheli had to disappear into the back alley for air more than once. Of ten tables, only one was occupied, and even then it was by some hunched-over crippled old man in robes, hood pulled up around his head and tucked into a whale tongue of a hat. "Sounds like the right choice to me."

"This is not some backwater like Kamedol," he said. "We are in Laman now. Do you have any idea what happens to foreignborn who pursue our kind of mission here? Without approval from their Great King? Do you?"

"Oh, well, let me see, would it be something *bad*, Krid?"

"Do not let their sweet songs and graceful strides fool you. The punishments in this place are severe, and ornate. Andristi live twice as long as you or I. That is twice as long to dream of bitter agonies. They can drown our minds in sorrow with nothing more than word and song."

"You sound scared, Krid."

"I knew it. I knew you would not take this seriously. We should never have brought you here."

"Why don't you tell me what you really mean to say?"

"Orrinas should never have brought you in at all."

"There it is."

"I have never tried to hide it," he said. "You are rash."

"I am effective."

"Quiet!" Orrinas said. "They come."

Two Lamani men with swords on their hips approached from across the street. They wore clothes that seemed unfamiliar to them. Disguises. Making themselves plain. They glanced all ways, suspicious. They stopped ten feet before the door. They waited there so long, Keluwen thought she might have to toss a tomato at them, just to see how they would react. Finally one of them stepped forward and opened the door. He looked back over his shoulder and across the street.

Another man emerged from a hidden spot there. He took three strides toward them, but then turned away and fled down an alley.

"What in the deepest hell?" Keluwen asked.

Three men in old coats across the street stood up sharply and pursued him. The two men with swords watched this all go on, and then they both turned around and left, taking a different street.

Keluwen thought she was going mad. "Was that our man? Were those his bodyguards? What did I just witness?"

"A distraction," the hunched-over old man at the corner table said.

Keluwen turned on him, her fingers twitching on the edges of her gloves. "Who are you?"

"He is the one we are here to meet," Orrinas said.

"How long?" Keluwen asked. "How long were you going to spy on us?"

"As long as you needed to be spied upon." His voice was made of sand and honey.

"You sabotage trust from the start," Keluwen said. "You have no idea what it is like."

"Fear not, fair Luminauts," the man said. "You hunt the luminous, the most dangerous ones in the world. And you will need your strength, and your speed, and your luck."

"This had better be the part where you tell us where he is and how you are going to help us kill him," Keluwen said.

"This is the part where you are disappointed," he said.

"Who are you?" she asked. "Show me your face." *And then you can tell me how the fuck you knew my god is Belleron.*

Krid Ballar stepped in between them, blocking her with his hands, he walked her back a step.

"You said you wanted to know where our directives come from," Orrinas said. "This is one such place."

"Him? This bent and sad old man? He is a part of Axis Ardent?"

"When you fall, you may be still and weep, or you may rise stronger," the hooded man said.

Fall. Keluwen felt her cheeks hot. Her head began to ache. The light seemed so bright. She closed her eyes, saw Nils falling through the air, and opened them again in a flash before she threw up again. She was keenly aware of Leucas, Hodo, and Cheli looking at her. She knew, and so she made sure to never glance their way. She thought she might curl up on the floor if she saw their faces right now.

"Forgive her," Orrinas said. "We have lost friends."

"That much is obvious," he said. "A tragedy. You are mourning."

"How do *you* know?" Keluwen demanded.

"Your eyes tell," he said. "They speak stories. They say how you do not like to be sad, so you choose to be angry instead."

"To the furthest hell with you, philosopher," Keluwen said. "Don't you dare judge me."

"There is nothing right or wrong with the way you feel," he said.

"Stop letting her speak to him," Krid said. "Orrinas, step in. This is unacceptable."

Keluwen leaned around him. "What are you going to give us then? What?"

"To warn you," he said. "To be aware of the children."

"Children," Orrinas said. "Who? Why? What are they?"

"They are an accident. A mistake. I saw them made, from the inside. It was intended for him, but an error was made. Now they are loose in the world, waiting for others to prey upon them, to use them. This must not be permitted to happen."

Orrinas nodded. "I understand. It will be done. We will follow every word of them, and protect them as our own wherever we may find them. This I swear."

Keluwen fumed. She hated that this bent old man was forcing such promises from Orrinas.

"They are for when there is nothing left," the hunched over man said. "When there is no more of you, they will bring you peace. When the river is in your path, they will be the bridge. When the world is dark, they will show the way."

"What *is* this?" Keluwen asked. "Forget these stupid children. Why aren't we talking about *him?*"

"You will have need of them," the man said. "When the time comes. And it will come."

"How will we know?" Orrinas asked.

"It will be revealed to you," he said. "It will be too obvious to deny. Just like the book."

"We know he took the Codex Lumina," Orrinas said. "We do not know where he is keeping it."

"It should never have been within his reach," the man said.

Orrinas closed his eyes and nodded. "It was our failing."

Don't take the blame, Orrinas. It was never for us to keep it.

"The book must be found," the man said. "It is important for what comes next."

"This is a waste," Keluwen said. She saw Nils, eyes open, face blank and cold, dead and broken. She felt tears coming and strained to muster enough rage to send them away before they fell. "Orrinas, you make him give us what we are owed."

"No one could ever give you what you deserve," the man said to her. "For your life is beautiful and you deserve the whole world. And how could that be given?"

"You are making fun of us," Keluwen said. "You are mocking when people are dying."

"Each one of you is a beautiful star in the sky. You glow, lonely and unique, hanging in the darkness, and you disappear in the presence of the sun."

"Orrinas!" she shouted.

Orrinas turned on her. His glare withered flowers for thousands of feet in every direction. He slowly, powerfully, glacially, raised a hand with finger extended toward the kitchen. "Out. Now."

She had never seen him like that. It shook her. She stopped talking. She turned. She stormed out through the kitchen. She slapped the handles of three pans as she walked past, flipping them and crashing them to the kitchen floor.

Three surprised Calabari cooks looked up from their work, cold stares, hardened sneers.

She kicked the back door open and stomped into the alley. The smell of frustration mingled with pools of stale fatty oils and the urine spots of half a hundred stray dogs.

There she waited for Orrinas to come for her. She knew he would. He was too kind and patient not to, and the others were too afraid of her wrath to do it themselves. Except for Krid, but he didn't care enough to bother.

She waited a long time. Long past feeling angry. By the time she finally heard the whine of the hinges, and saw his hand gently guide the door open, she felt foolish for making him come out here to handle her. *Stupid. Now I look petulant.* And maybe she was, after all.

He wore his calmest expression, not blank, but somehow an actively soothing look. Something he did with the corners of his eyes. She couldn't figure it out, how he could do that without seeming to change his face at all. Even after all these many months it was a mystery.

"That was disappointing," he said.

"Me? Or the information?"

"Both."

"I hope you are not wondering if I am embarrassed to stand up for what we are doing."

"I would never accuse you of being embarrassed. It is more a matter of not biting the hand that feeds. We rely on those above us to finance our mission, to grant access to allies all across the continent. It is not usually considered proper to offend them."

"That is not what I am here for," she said.

"Keluwen, listen to me."

"No, Orrinas. You listen to me. I have been with you all this time. I have never asked for anything."

"You were content to let me direct the path of my team."

"Yes, and do you know why? Because we hunted *them*. We hunted the luminous, the *soon-to-be* luminous anyway. To stop them from doing what *he* is doing. Years of my life, gladly given. But we are not stopping now. Not after all that has happened. First Rin, then Dromergo, then Satianya. Now Seb. And Nils. What are we doing this for?"

He sighed. "They want us to make sure these children are protected."

"Do you really believe that tripe about this child being something of value to us?"

"I do. I believe it. I believe it with my whole heart."

She leaned back from him. The surety in his voice stunned her. "We should not have two missions. We are already failing at the one we have."

"They are not two missions. They are one and the same."

She frowned, arms folded. "Please, Orrinas. No distractions now. We have one goal. That other is not our job. This is our job. We are so close to it."

"I know."

"It has been two weeks now since Farguard Gap. And I have cried every night in your arms. Do you understand what this is doing to me? There is no going back for me. Not after Nils. We have lost too much to gain nothing."

He looked upon her with that sad, concerned smile, that look he always gave her that made her feel like he felt her pain worse than she did. "I know it hurts. It hurts me as well. And I know it hurts you doubly that you feel hurt in the first place."

"You know me too well. I should never have let you bring me in out of the cold."

"We are going to find him. We are going to catch him. And we are going to finish him."

She leaned in, interested. "That is what I want to hear. Now, can you match it in deed?"

"I already have."

"Is that so?"

"We will be given support here in Cair Tiril," he said. "And escorts if we must travel further to pursue him. And gold."

"Gold?"

"A small chest of Samartanian sols and Levantine gold dolars."

"Untraceable money."

"More than Hodo can lift on his own with those strong arms of his."

"That brittle old man had a chest of gold?" She looked up at him skeptically.

Orrinas nodded. "Enough to sustain us for years."

She elbowed him. "It had better not take *years*."

"This one, no. But this is only the first luminous immortal we have needed to pursue. There will be others."

She looked at the wall. "There will never be another like him. He is something different."

"We are going now," Orrinas said. "We must get back to the hostelry. We have an ambush to plan. Hodo and Leucas will carry the chest."

"And the old man?"

"Gone. It is just us now."

She made half a smile. "Do they know where he is?"

"He is near. You know how hard it is to pinpoint a location for one of them. But as far as they are aware he will be close for a little while."

"Good." *This journey could not have been for nothing.*

They walked along the widest streets of the River Quarter. The people watched them go, but mostly left them alone. It was easy at a glance to tell they were new to the area. But so were a great many of them as well. They moved into the Foreign Quarter, and disappeared into crowds of Da'Ari, Civy Malar, Calabari, Biss, Malorese, and of course Vandolines.

Keluwen stretched and shook the kinks from her neck, hopped from one foot to the other, anticipating stretching out on the old skandrilar bedding with the greatest man she had ever known filling the best possible space beside her. She needed everything to be all right for a moment. Just for a little while.

She felt herself dance into a jog, wanting to rest more than she had anticipated. She listened to laughter in five different languages, and smelled the hot sun and the sizzling spiced lamb. She hopped along to the beat of the music, played on a bruised bass dromba and a Lamani zinge, with an army of tabla drums setting the rhythm. Whole neighborhoods would join in and play, all joining together with pure joy to be a part of creation. She heard the hiss of cymbals and the jingle of bells and the clapping of hands, and the music and the smells and heat swirled around and around her.

She pulled up before the two-story house they had rented. From the outside Keluwen would barely have called it a shack. But somehow it was two stories and cozy enough. She was already deciding which bottles of summerwine to open to drink and sing the twentieth day song for Nils, and which to save for another day, but something caught her eye.

A man. Alone. Leaning against a bench. A shortcoat, a tear at the shoulder. His hair in strings, dangling over his forehead. His arms folded, but the rear hand snaking down, fingers tickling something at his belt, just behind the fringe of the coat.

Seb always used to say: *if something feels off, that only means your subconscious is aware of something you are not, and best to heed it.*

Keluwen stopped in her tracks. "Orrinas," she said. The drums thumped. The bells jingled.

He stopped and turned to her.

The zinge whined. The bells jingled.

Leucas and Hodo stopped. Cheli ran into the chest, falling forward on top of it.

She heard the bells. They jingled in a rhythm, like footsteps.

She saw a man with a wide mustache walking toward her, twin shortswords in his hands

A Da'ari butcher came from the other side, a cleaver swaying.

What in all hells is going on?

She raised a hand and pointed. She noticed a man atop the house, bow in hand.

She saw her glove still on, yanked the hand back. Pulled furiously at it. The arrow flew.

It struck her boot, just outside her a ankle. She felt the bite of the arrowhead like a saw, rubbing her skin open. She went to one knee.

A Da'ari man came out of the crowd behind her, bent down, grabbing for her.

Hodo was there in an instant, wrapping the Da'ari up in a bear hug and dragging him to the ground.

The man with two swords rushed Cheli. Leucas headed him off.

Three more breached the edge of the crowd and reached for Orrinas.

"No!" She tore her glove free. She pointed at the first of them. She rendered a sphere that punctured through his ribs and into his heart.

The other two pulled up short, hesitated.

That was long enough for Orrinas to turn. He focused on them. Their swords turned white hot in their hands. Their fingers released, skin sizzling. But another arrow flew, barely missing him.

Keluwen had been trying to get her other glove off, but abandoned that, bared her teeth and pointed at the man atop the house. She rendered a sphere, punching through his gut. He pitched forward and dropped off the roof. His head smacked the cobbles.

One wrapped both hands around her wrist, yanking her hand upright, and holding it like a vice. She strained to get her captive fingers around the end of the other glove, but he kept yanking her arm away, twisting, throwing her onto her back.

She struggled, strained, pulled. She rolled herself, and managed to hook the end of the glove onto a buckle on his boot. She yanked her arm free, the glove sliding away. She rendered a sphere, pointed straight up at him, and let it go. It went in through his mouth, scattering teeth, and then it blasted out the back of his skull.

She rolled over and kicked herself up. Two more Da'ari were right on her. They each tried to draw their weapons, but they found their swords stuck. Keluwen glanced at Krid, as he rendered friction on their swords, locking them inside their scabbards.

Hodo grabbed one and strangled him. Leucas stabbed the other.

But Keluwen still heard the jingling bells.

She looked up. Another man was right behind her, sliding a blade up against her throat, her hands pressing it back. She panicked. She could not straighten her hands in the right direction. She tried to bend one arm behind her back, but her fingers merely shot a blank impulse harmlessly between their bodies.

She should have been able to think of a way to bend where her power would work, but she kept losing track as the sword dug into her flesh.

She looked up.

He looked down at her.

But then his head was wrapped in a bubble of heat.

Orrinas!

Keluwen felt it like an oven opening against her face.

The man screamed as his face turned red, his nose bled and his breaths turned to steam. The heat increased within. It grew and grew. He screamed and screamed. He doubled over, dropped his sword. The heat continued to build, until his eyes vaporized, his hair erupted into flame, and his eardrums burst in gouts of steam. He went silent, and then finally keeled over.

Keluwen rolled over, shook free of him. She leaned down on her elbows and knees, her nose touching the ground. She threw up until her stomach was sore.

The Da'ari filtered back into the crowd. She heard the man with the jingly boots, his steps growing fainter, and then disappearing.

Are we safe?

She looked up at Orrinas. She spit twenty times. "They knew we were here. *He* knows we are here."

"I know," he said.

"So much for our plan," she said.

"I know."

Two young Andristi sprinted into the courtyard. Keluwen raised her hands, but paused when they stopped short and bowed.

It was a man and a woman. They raised their hands. "Friends," the woman said.

"This way," the man said.

Keluwen looked back at Orrinas. "Do we trust them?"

"Turn about," Orrinas shouted. "Follow them! Go!"

Hodo and Leucas struggled with the chest, trying to hold it while running. Cheli carried her books over her shoulder, running behind them.

Keluwen backed away, just as more Da'ari stepped forward from the crowd with weapons.

Not safe.

The Da'ari were led by another Lamani man, his arms long and gangly, razor-hooked knives in his hands, his face ferocious, his eyes cold and dead. *Another one of his. He can even turn the ageless Andristi.* She felt hopeless. She turned and ran. Orrinas and Krid followed.

They raced down alleys and across streets until they reached a canal. The Andristi man and woman stepped aside and gestured at the water. "Jump," the man said.

"Jump?" Keluwen asked.

He pointed at her hands. Already they were silvered with afterglow, and her sleeves were infused with it. "They will follow you. Water washes away."

Orrinas, his hands and sleeves radiant sparkling orange, nodded to her and jumped in.

She looked over her shoulder, and then she followed.

18

Witness

AREN FORGOT FOR A moment that he was here to meet another Glasseye.

It was hard to think of much of anything whenever his eyes glanced at Eriana, which was often. Every other step she took or thereabouts. She walked the man up to Aren, and then stood slightly aloof, leaning toward them as if eavesdropping.

"I am called Malvaegin," he said. "I am Arch-Lord of Torilillion-Amath, and Master of Magick to Great Santhalian." He spoke the Westrin dialect fluidly and without a hint of accent, even better that Eriana.

"Aren of Amagon," Aren introduced himself. "Render Tracer."

"It will be my pleasure to share with you what I have," Malvaegin said. "It is my hope that some of our evidence may be of value to you in your quest." His nose was a brutal hook upon his face, beneath eyes both wide and deep. His hair was jet black, and dangled in sharp shards like blades of midnight grass. He wore a scarlet tunic fringed in gold. He walked a lord's walk, but there was a hint of the outcast about him.

"Excellent," Aren said.

"I will take you to our staging room. Eriana has asked that she be allowed to accompany us, and I have granted permission, if it is of no bother to you."

"Well...of course. I have no problem with that. Though I am afraid she may find it somewhat boring." He hoped she would and politely excuse herself, but of course she did not. Instead her eyes lit up eagerly, and she smiled that dreaded smile, and he forgot his own name.

"On the contrary," Malvaegin said, raising his index finger. "She has most eager interest in matters of...trace. Though she has never before been quite so demanding in her requests."

Eriana shot a stern gaze at him, her eyes narrow barbs. Perfect narrow barbs.

Malvaegin's face registered the slightest of smiles. "Please follow me."

Aren did so, with Eriana beside him and matching his step. He tried not to notice her, but failed miserably. He found it impossible to avoid glancing at her, to see her shifting expressions, to see what she looked at, to see if she ever looked at him. She did once at least that he could see, and of course he made certain to dart his eyes away to avoid giving the impression that he had been staring at her...which of course he had been.

The staging room was not at all what Aren expected. It was tucked between two enormous facades. A white door opened to reveal a long, unadorned hallway, a single oil lamp providing the only light. At the terminus was another door opening to a spiral stairwell of ancient stone, winding its way deep below the surface. At the base was another hallway, this one with many doors. Malvaegin produced a ring with five exquisite bronze keys, selected one, and unlocked the first door.

Beyond lay a room sparse and sterile, offering nothing but cold grey stone as its walls and table. In one wall was another door, and another had an immense rectangular window carved into its center, offering a view of a similar room, lit with reed candles.

"Where is your trace analysis?" Aren asked.

"I thought you might first wish to speak with the witness."

"Witness? What witness?"

"She was brought to me only this noontide. Found wandering in the street. They said she rambled about magick men."

"Where is she?"

"In there." He pointed down the hall. "Through that door. It is unlocked."

Aren coasted through the door, Eriana hard on his heels. At first he saw nothing but a great stone table in the center of the room. He thought he was in the wrong room until he heard faint breathing. Someone was indeed there, huddled on the floor in the corner.

She sat with her back to the wall, her knees pulled up tight to her chest, no more than twelve or thirteen years old. Her breaths were hollow, her dress wrinkled and torn, the bodice stained red. She smelled of stale fear and burnt oil.

Magick.

"Oh, by the Mother," Eriana said.

The girl had brown hair, tinged red, but it was a mess of bloody streaks and tangles. Her eyes were vacant and bloodshot. The sleeves had been torn from her golden dress, and deep indigo bruises covered her shoulders. Her knees were shredded badly, as if she had knelt upon shards of glass.

Aren put his hand to his face. He started forward. Stopped. Started again, more slowly, kneeling as he came close to her. She flinched when his boots squeaked.

"My name is Aren," he said. "What's your name?"

Her eyes twitched up, met his, but swiftly slid away.

"Do you understand my words?" he asked gently. "Westrin?"

Her eyes swiveled up to look at him again. She nodded yes, then looked away.

"Would you like some water?"

She nodded again.

Aren turned to Malvaegin. "Water," he said.

Malvaegin left the room swiftly, returning moments later with a small stoneware cup. He passed it to Aren, who then held it to the girl's lips.

She sipped at it a few times, then he drew it away from her. "What is her name?"

"Liriella," Malvaegin said.

"Liriella," Aren said. "Are you cold?"

She pulled her arms in tight, but did not speak.

"Blanket," Aren commanded.

Malvaegin did not hesitate. He soon reappeared with a thick wool coverlet, which Aren draped over her shoulders, waiting while she tucked it about herself.

He looked up at Eriana and pursed his lips. It was the same every time. The magick was always the same, ruining whatever it touched, corrupting whoever could wield it. *Why would anyone do this?*

He heard Sarker's answer in his head. *There is no why to them. They use because they can.*

He kept his tone calm and gentle. If he said the wrong word, she might just shut herself off into silence. It had happened to him before, the first time Sarker had ever let him question a victim. He had only managed five words before he had been slapped, cursed, and spit upon. It had taken Sarker days to convince the woman to talk to him after that.

"You have a lovely name," he said. "There was an Andristi princess named Liriella once upon a time. She loved to walk through the woods and gaze at the trees. She even forgot to come to her wedding, and her father had to send his captain of the guards to fetch her."

No answer. Liriella blinked at him, her eyes vacant.

"Do you like going for walks?"

After a long pause, she nodded.

"Me too. I walk in Vithos, where I come from, but it does not look as nice as Cair Tiril."

She shrugged.

"Were you taking a walk today? Going to play? Running an errand?"

She nodded.

"Did you see anyone...unfamiliar on your walk?"

She shuddered.

"A man?"

She nodded.

"Alone?"

She shook her head.

"Two? Three?"

She glanced aside when Aren said three. He took that for an affirmation. "Liriella, I need your help. I need you to help me find who did this. I stop people who do these things, but I can't do it without you. I need you to tell me what you saw. Can you do that for me? Can you tell me where you were?"

"Crispos," she whispered.

Aren looked back at Malvaegin.

"An eastern marketplace," Malvaegin said. "In the Foreign Quarter."

"Would you tell me what you saw there?" Aren asked.

"They said I had pretty eyes," she said. "They said that pretty girls should have flowers in their hair. They took me somewhere. A room. A hostel. Dark. It was cold inside."

"Can you tell me anything about what happened?"

"They held my arms. They asked me questions."

"What kind of questions?"

"About roads. About Synsirok. They said Synsirok over and over. I don't know what I did wrong. I told them everything they wanted, but they still didn't stop."

"You didn't do anything wrong," Aren said. "Nothing."

She nodded, looking at her feet. "They said I shouldn't bother telling anyone because no one would believe me."

"I believe you," Aren said. "I promise." He looked back at Eriana, but she could only offer a helpless expression. "You told my friend, Malvaegin, that they were magick men. How were they magick?"

"Magick is when things move that you cannot see. I know what it is. More so than most."

"Did they say anything else? Was there anything else that you remember? Any little thing that might help us?"

"That I was lucky to be born so pretty. They were going to change me into something better."

Aren already knew what they did. *I am going to change you. I have heard that before.* Aren hated them, whoever they were. Loathed them and wished for them nothing better than the fires. Even if they were not his to trace, he wanted to find them. He wanted to find them oh so badly.

"They said they would come back if I told. Are they coming back?"

"No. They were liars. They are not coming back."

This seemed to make her feel better. "Can I go home now?"

"Soon," Aren said. "You have been so brave, Liriella. I'm so sorry this happened to you. But you are safe now. You are not alone. Malvaegin is going to take care of you. Soon you can go home. Someone will come to bring you there, all right?"

She nodded, and almost smiled at him.

"Someone will come to help you wash and give a salve to lessen the pain." He eyed Malvaegin. "Won't they?"

"Yes, of course, Lord Aren."

Aren stood up before his face could give away his helplessness. He waited with Liriella until Malvaegin could fetch the watchwomen to care for her, and then he thanked her and said goodbye.

He motioned Eriana and Malvaegin to join him in the other room, shutting the door after him. He turned on Malvaegin immediately. "What was she doing in there all that time?"

"I do not understand the question," Malvaegin said.

"In that cold room," Aren said. "Before you came to get me."

"Keeping a witness in a bare room aids in memory recall. Your western texts recommend this."

"You left her *completely* alone in there."

"I had no one else to watch over her. I was told to speak with you immediately." He glanced at Eriana. "I was instructed to drop whatever I was doing and come to meet you."

Eriana's face froze over with guilt, and she turned aside.

"The scene," Aren said. "Has it been tested?"

"We have tested it to the best of our abilities," Malvaegin said. "Only myself and my assistant, and we do not have the tools that you do."

"Show me what you have."

Malvaegin led them into another room, boasting another stone table, and shelves lined with old tomes and parchment. The room reeked of old dust and leather. Malvaegin placed a leather-bound journal on the table. Aren leaned over it. He could not read the Silis Script letters of the Andristi Sinjan language upon its cover.

"We followed the afterglow in Liriella's wake until we located the scene. We studied it, but as I said, we do not have the same tools at our disposal. We measure waveforms on a different scale, exponential. I am unable to convert these figures into your mode of measurement quickly."

Aren flipped through the pages. "Did you take any imprints at the scene?"

"We have no such device at our disposal."

"Can I view the scene?"

"I would advise against it. It is in the Foreign Quarter. There has been some unrest there of late."

"Unrest?"

"Many Palantari live there, and Malar men, and Da'ari immigrants. They do not behave well toward westerners."

"I should view the scene with my own instruments."

"Great Santhalian would not be pleased with me if I allowed harm to come to his guest."

"Great Santhalian has given me leave to pursue my mission."

"He should be allowed to see it," Eriana agreed.

Malvaegin turned on her. "And would you be the one to offer an explanation to Great Santhalian if Aren of Amagon is harmed?"

"His safety is your concern," Eriana said.

Malvaegin chewed his lip. "Very well. My apprentice, Baslon, should be returning shortly. He will take us to the scene."

"I will come along," Eriana said.

"No, you will not," Malvaegin spat. "I am obliged to assist Aren of Amagon, but I am not required to be a party to your every whim."

"What?" Eriana stammered.

"It is not safe for a member of the royal household to travel there unless under guard."

"But..."

Malvaegin raised a hand to her. "Your lineage does not give you leave to order me about my business. You will return to the Palace."

"And if I am guarded?" she asked.

"Are bodyguards present here? Would you care to produce them?"

Eriana pursed her lips.

Aren looked at her reassuringly. "He's right. There really is no need for you to be there."

"No need?" she fumed. She turned and stamped out of the room without a word. She swung the door hard.

Shaot.

Before Aren could express his surprise at her second sudden departure, Baslon arrived, as if on cue. He pushed the door open a scant few inches, and peeked his small face into the room. His fat brown eyes shot wide when he noticed Aren, and he tried to pull back and close the door.

"Baslon!" Malvaegin shouted. "Enter!"

Baslon hopped through the doorway. Both his eyes and lips were dark. His hair was matted and brown to match. His tunic was burgundy and very plain compared to the shiny silk of Malvaegin. In one hand he held three misshapen plates of polished crystal—one clear, one white, and one blue. It was an Andristi attempt at a Jecker monocle.

"My lords," Baslon stuttered, bowing numerous times.

"This is Aren of Amagon," Malvaegin said. "You will now report to him what you have been doing."

"Yes, yes, yes, of course," Baslon said, his eyes twitching to and fro as he stepped up to the table. He placed the crystal plates haphazardly on the cold stone. "I have been plotting traces of great magick in the city in an effort to—"

"Enough!" Malvaegin said. "Where?"

Baslon's brow tightened, and one corner of his lip quivered. He turned his eyes down and stalked to the nearest of the bookcases, carefully removing a folded map from between two portly leather-bound tomes. He delicately unfolded the parchment upon the table, and Aren saw the magnificent city of Cair Tiril spread out before him in lines and angles.

Baslon pointed to the edge of one of the lines. "Here is where we stand." He traced a line across the rows of streets, beyond the Marble Forest, and through the interweaving patchwork of districts, until it came to rest in a neighborhood of narrow streets and suspicious angles. "Here. At the edge of the Foreign Quarter. I found two distinct paths of afterglow. One streaks away to the Golden Gate. The other seemed to go here, to the Silent Quarter."

"Which path was most fresh?" Aren asked.

"Both," Baslon said, then thought for a moment. "Or neither."

"We need to know where the user was most recently, to plot his path. Now which one was most recent?"

"They were both of equal quality," Baslon said. "I saw no difference."

Of course not. With the absurd tools you have to work with. "I would like to see the scene now."

Baslon flinched as if he had been hit. "But...the Foreign Quarter..."

"Is where Aren of Amagon wishes to go," Malvaegin said. "We are obliged to obey his requests."

Baslon looked back and forth between Aren and the map on the table.

"Now, if you please," Aren said.

Baslon jumped and fluttered to the door. Malvaegin pursed his lips and followed, with Aren just a step behind.

The high pediments and white porches of Cair Tiril were empty and quiet as they walked. Many were anticipating the great feast that was to begin soon after sundown, and were well busy preparing for the celebration. The walk was long, but Aren was willing to crawl on broken glass for a chance to put these men in the fires.

As the sun finally dipped below the horizon, they arrived at the Foreign Quarter.

Only narrow roads and stark alleys, it was astonishing to Aren how closely it resembled the slums of Westgate. Though separated by more than a thousand miles, the proximity of shops and homes and hostelries bore an unmistakable familiarity. The suspicious expressions of the Malar merchants, the hesitant movements of Da'ari families with their unintelligible culture, and the forlorn Palantari, displaced by famine and lost in this new place, were each identical to the Hezzam.

These people did not care about the feast of the Great King. Such things did not touch their lives or affect them in any way. Their daily labors were not altered by any of this. He somehow thought that it would be different in the White City, where the ancient Andristi had ruled with benevolence for so long.

When he came within sight of a great empty market square, Baslon stopped him at a narrow alley separating two monstrous tenements. Baslon ducked into it, stopping at a pale white door. He opened it for Aren, while Malvaegin glanced furtively about in the street outside.

Aren felt something in the air of the room, a faint prickling of his skin. He saw distortion burns on two of the walls. He sniffed. Almonds. *Pressure renders?* The last time he had smelled those had been at the *Red God* in Westgate.

I knew it. I knew it wasn't over.

He started with the Jecker monocle, and discovered traces immediately. They swirled around him and through him, brushing against the walls like paint. He noticed some familiar patterns and some unfamiliar.

"Just like Westgate. He always uses waveform compression masking. It's as if he can't even help it." He slid the green filter over the lens. He could see the translucent streak lines still hovering fourth-dimensionally among the residuals —arcs of movement frozen in time. He made out the vectors of force that had been applied to Liriella, and the directionality of the displacement. They indicated where she had been held down, and where small forces had been repeatedly applied to her as she lay helpless.

"She was attacked here," he said. "Forces were rendered to hold her on the floor. Most likely a generalized force equalized to her weight and applied to her center of gravity. A blank impulse most likely, but this user specializes in pressure renders. See here?" He pointed out some areas on the floor. "A pressure field was placed here, most likely around her neck, by the shape of the streak lines. Similar renders were applied to the wrists and ankles."

Malvaegin and Baslon both nodded to him.

Aren cleared his throat. "It appears that the magick was used to...hurt her. The spectral lines are concentrated on two sides of the area where she was held. One I presume to be representative of a force striking her face over and over. The other by the waist...a blunt force designed to be projected inward, and then extreme pressure to expand within. She was assaulted by the magick."

"Scum," Malvaegin said.

"Users," Aren agreed. *Any of them are capable of anything.*

He switched to the blue filter. *Pale orange core afterglow, fringes redshifting, but indecipherable Introduction-Of-Change patterns.* He should have at least been able to recognize the key structure, even with the masking the user applied to their renders, but he could not.

He pulled out the Oscillatrix, and held it near the peak points. The values kept jumping wildly back and forth, and refused to reflect any concrete result. He had similar results with the Finder, which he had already set to the primary values listed in the composite from Vithos. The meter leapt up at first, but then returned to a null reading.

The words of Sarker were in his head. *What else? What are you forgetting? What is the simplest solution with the tools at your disposal?*

He bit his lip. How could there be an incomplete reading on the Oscillatrix? No user can have more than one value. *More than one.* "Wait. The mixing of the residuals. There are two values represented because there were two users."

"What?" Malvaegin asked.

"Here," Aren said. He darted a hand into the tracer satchel, and withdrew his mirror, a rectangle four inches by six, and handed it to Baslon. "Hold this."

"What am I...?"

"Just hold it and move it as I tell you." He pulled Baslon by the arm and positioned him across the room. He then returned to stand by the door, so that the residuals now hovered between them. He held up the Jecker monocle and stared through it. "Walk to me slowly."

Baslon obeyed.

"Stop. There. Hold it. Now angle the mirror upwards. Good. Now slightly to your left. Up a bit more. There. Right there. Now bring it forward just an inch." There it was. Through the Jecker monocle, the mirror reflected the invisible luminescence of these residuals, and scattered it to the walls in sharp beams of light. Some of the beams shot out to the right and down, but others bounced off the mirror upward and far to the left and behind where Aren stood. "The diffraction of residuals will be at a different angle if made by different users with different oscillation frequencies. There were two men here with the magick, two men who did this and then left in opposite directions."

He had Baslon turn until Aren found a single patch of afterglow that had not cross-merged. He tested it with the Oscillatrix. The primary values were a precise match to the composite of the assassin. And the core color was orange.

He is alive. He is still out there. I don't know who we captured in Westgate, but it wasn't my trace.

Baslon started to say something, but Aren stopped him with a glance. "Show me where the trails begin."

"Yes," Baslon said. "Yes, yes, here." He led the way.

Aren stepped out into the alley. The sun had set, and the warm air smelled of burning meat. Malvaegin wrung his hands nervously as they returned to the street, and turned toward the market square, Baslon leading.

But dozens of Da'ari abruptly blocked their path, wearing thick wool vests, carrying cudgels and curved knives. They stepped excitedly from foot to foot, their short hair like weedy grass patches atop their flat heads. Their eyes showed malice.

Aren took a step back, clutching the hilt of his sword. He looked right and left for some avenue of escape. The only path was back into the alley—a dead end. He looked behind him to see more men coming that way. They closed in on him with silent menace.

Their hands clutched his clothes and his satchel. They milled around him, and pressed close as the crowd grew larger and pushed inward. He could barely move in the crush of Da'ari. He could not bend his elbows to draw his sword from the scabbard. Fingers pulled at his hair and yanked on his clothes. Someone tried to pull his sword free. He clamped one hand down on the hilt to stop them, and slapped desperately at the hands grabbing him. He could no longer see Malvaegin.

He heard the clanking of metal boots on the stone street, and he felt the hands begin to pull away from him. The press of bodies around him began to thin out, He heard the clang of steel on steel as a dozen Andristi soldiers clapped their swords and shields together.

The mob was hastily dispersed by the well-armed soldiers. The Andristi immediately made a ring about Aren, Malvaegin, and Baslon.

Aren breathed a sigh of relief.

One of the Andristi stepped up to him, bearing officer's decorations on his celadon tunic. "You do not come here," the officer said, his accent thickly Sinjan.

Aren blinked at him.

"You do not come here," he said again.

"My investigation..." Aren started to say.

"Not safe."

"And you are?"

The officer's expression soured, and he looked hastily to Malvaegin. "Pordraedos. You leave here." He grabbed Aren by the sleeve.

Aren recoiled, pulling his arm away. "No!"

"No?" Pordraedos repeated, frowning.

"I stay," Aren said.

"You stay?" Pordraedos continued frowning.

"My mission is to find a criminal."

"Not safe. Dark here. You go to light. You leave now." He gestured down the street.

Aren turned to Malvaegin. "Tell him I need to be here."

"I cannot command this man," Malvaegin said. "He answers to Erethion."

"Erethion," Pordraedos agreed. "You leave now. You go to feast."

"But—" Aren started.

"No!" Pordraedos shouted. "You leave now."

Three Andristi soldiers moved in around him.

There was nothing more Aren could do. He cursed under his breath. *So close.* He struck his satchel in frustration. *Raviel. Raviel did this. I can feel it.* He slapped a soldier's hand away from his wrist. "Fine."

Pordraedos and his soldiers escorted the three back to Malvaegin's staging room, and then took Aren on alone to the edge of the great palladium beside the palace. There they left him stunned, still not believing that his trace had been spoiled at such a critical moment. He stamped his heel into the ground.

He now knew for certain that his trace was still alive. And he knew the two users from Westgate were working *together*. And once more Synsirok came into focus.

It also confirmed something else; that these users were cruel and needlessly destructive.

I have to stop them before this happens again.

19

Feast

ALL THE FOOD I could have ever asked for and I have no appetite at all.

The feast was served about a wide outdoor palladium with an amphitheater descending in many rings to a stage below. About the palladium were set scores of wooden tables, lacquered white to match the walls of the palace.

As dancers twirled to the beating of resonant drums, servants in white satin robes brought roasted meats from nearby fires to be dipped into pots of sauce spiced with garlic and ginger. Butter was spread over salty goodcrust and thick slices of sweet bread. An entire orchard of apples was diced and cubed and spread with a cinnamon-sugar dressing.

Silver plates piled high with peppered beef and fillets of salmon from the banks of the River Tiril were served to the soldiers by women in bright dresses that fluttered like multicolored birds. Great platters of duck and pheasant were brought to each table, where soldiers of the Northern Host shared the honor of first cut with veterans of the Outer Guard, exchanging stories of life and battle, bedding and hunting, as the royal dancers spun like dervishes around them to the twang of Lamani zinges.

Great Santhalian himself sat within a small gazebo. He drank smooth brandy alongside his nobles. Aren thought he saw Eriana among the celebrants, but he wasn't sure.

To Aren, the brandy tasted as bitter as defeat. He dumped his and stood alone, ruminating. He did not have a chance to talk to Donnovar. Margol and Terrol took turns keeping him busy, Hayles the Sarenwalker and Retheld the axe-man keeping watchful eyes over their shoulders. The other Sarenwalkers were spaced throughout the feast, silent sentinels. They never took any substance with the power to dull the mind, not even the painkilling kind. Such things would only inhibit their perfection.

He glimpsed Eriana across the court standing among several lesser lords of Laman. She wore a long gown of fine white silk. It was desperately thin, and clung to every curve of her body like a second layer of skin. He watched her laughing at some jest he was too far away to hear. He had to stop his eyes from studying the shape of her body. He found himself wishing he was among those lords who were of a quality to be with her, leaning in close. He thought he heard someone call his name, and he turned his gaze aside, shamefaced at his own staring.

He wandered silently about the celebration, making his best attempts to smile at the Andristi and making his best attempt to ignore everyone else. And so of course he chanced across the one person he wanted to see the least.

Raviel.

Raviel's body leaned forward, bent like his spine was the trunk of a crooked tree. His hair was unknowably wet, and his clothes smelled like old, unopened rooms.

Aren could barely keep from recoiling in disgust.

"It is time for you and I to speak," he said. His voice sounded like skin splitting under the strikes of a switch.

No. Anything else but that tonight. "Fine."

"I have been watching you since we departed Vithos."

"Likewise."

"You admit it."

"I have nothing to hide," Aren said. "I cannot say the same about you."

Raviel hovered for a time in silence. "You went out into the streets in Westgate. Alone."

"So did you."

"You spoke with people you should not be speaking with. You let the Rover go."

"What I do is my business. You do not give me commands. I do not care what the official orders say."

"You spoke with Malvaegin without consulting me."

"I did not come all this way to sit on my hands. I don't know what you told the Lord Protector to get into his head like this. I don't know how you turned him from me, but if you think you can cut me out of this, then you are dead wrong."

"They didn't tell you why we are here, did they?"

"What are you talking about?"

"I thought you were one of *them*," Raviel said. "All this time. All this way. I thought you were here to undermine me. I thought you were one of *theirs*."

"I don't belong to anyone. I am a Render Tracer of Amagon. I serve my homeland and the Lord Protector."

Raviel looked away at the dancers and chuckled. "Of course you do."

"Did you have something to say?"

"I need you to speak with Donnovar."

"*You* need me to?"

"I need you to tell him we need to go to the city of Synsirok."

"Give me one good reason."

"Because you want to go there as well. By now you have heard the rumors. The map. The magick men on the road."

"How do you know what I want?"

"Because if you are not a part of it, then you are here hunting a murderer. That is where the murderer is going."

"Part of what?"

He chuckled, if it was possible to cackle a chuckle. He never looked back at Aren. "I have spoken with Donnovar, but he is unsure, because of the Vuls in the woods there. He trusts you above anyone else here. If you tell him we must go there, he will lead us there."

"What aren't you telling me?"

"This is going to end soon," he said.

"Traces always end."

"This will all be over. And when it is, I wonder where the pieces will fall."

"This will end with a user going to the fires," Aren said. "Rogue users burn. That is what they do. I catch them. That is what *I* do."

"I misunderstood you," Raviel said. "Now I see. You are not the one."

"What does that mean?"

He began walking away. "Talk to him. Convince him."

"That is all? You are just going to walk away?"

"I cannot keep my eyes on all of you at once."

"All of who?"

But Raviel was already gone, disappeared into the crowd.

Aren shook his head.

He dissected every table of pastries and meat pies he walked by, but nothing tickled his appetite, no matter how savory. He ran one finger along the edge of the long line of tables, as if he might careen up into the sky if some little touch wasn't reminding him he belonged here.

"What did he say to you?" a voice rasped.

The question nearly knocked Aren off his axis. He already knew who it was. Only one man sounded like he was speaking from beyond the grave. "What do you want, Terrol?"

He was dressed in his finest silks, shirt and cloak of Inner Guard blue, boots shined until they were obsidian. His eyes were already slicing Aren up, vivisecting his posture, his expression, the condition of his clothes, the precise length of the stubble on his chin. Even Terrol's breaths made accusations. "What did you tell him?"

"Nothing," Aren said. "What business is it of yours anyway?"

"The security of Amagon is my business."

"But we aren't in Amagon."

"Wherever we go, Amagon is always with us."

"You don't have to worry," Aren said. "He is chasing his own tail. You can spend your time enjoying not having any fun at the celebration."

"Watch your step, motherless," Terrol cautioned.

Aren bared his teeth, jaw barely able to keep from opening wide to scream. "Why should I? I'm sure you will be watching it close enough for the both of us." He shrugged past Terrol, brushing his shoulder aside.

Aren wandered to the edge of the celebration, passing beyond the cordon of Royal Guards, stepping out into the vacant streets. *I need to get away from all of them. I need to think.*

He slipped around a shadowy corner, and lit a pipeful of grey leaves. He smoked it greedily in the hazy golden light of the oil streetlamps. Terrol was easy enough to ignore. If he wasn't suspicious of virtually everything, Aren would have had cause to worry. But Raviel was another matter. *What was that about? Who did Raviel think I was before? Why doesn't he think so anymore? He was acting as wary of me as I have been of him.* Aren felt the distinct impression that Raviel viewed *him* as a threat.

He rubbed his eyes with thumb and forefinger. *I need to sleep. I need fresh eyes.* He dumped out the pipe, wiped it clean.

He wandered further away, the echoes of celebration soft and distant now. The laughter was shrill. He smiled for the Outer Guard, who had traveled over a thousand miles without much rest. He turned away from the sounds and began walking.

He wandered the streets alone for a time, winding his way along the curvature of the great white wall surrounding the city, and toward the Silent Quarter. This district lived up to its name. With so many attending the festivities of the Great King's feast, the wide lanes and columned porches were devoid of people. As the dusk settled into night, he found himself within a white courtyard adjacent to the high wall.

He kept his eyes open for afterglow, but he did not really expect to find anything.

But he did find something.

The pale resonance of sensitized fluorescence.

It was small and barely noticeable through the Jecker monocle. It was emanating from the far side of the courtyard, beneath a pavilion with high columns. Aren stalked toward the source. Then he saw her. A young Andristi girl sitting alone on a stone bench.

He approached her from behind. His heart raced. The afterglow shined brightly. He flipped the blue filter into place and gazed at the core color. Pale orange. His breaths stopped. His blood pumped faster and faster.

She turned to face him, and smiled sweetly. Then she noticed the Jecker monocle at his eyes and her smile slid into an expression of revulsion.

Aren reached for her. She recoiled. He stumbled over the edge of the bench, and the girl shrieked. She turned and ran.

Aren reached out a hand to the bench to keep himself upright. He caught his breath. He lowered the lens from his eye, and slapped himself in the face. The girl was no user. The malagayne had slowed his senses, turned his desire opaque.

It was sensitized fluorescence. It would adhere to anything the source user touched, even the clothes of a young girl. It could have been passed from person to person to person a dozen times before it ended up on her.

Fool, he thought. How else would she react to a madman with a demon's eye coming out of the night to grab her? He stood and stared after her. He knew he should have questioned her. Who had she been near? Who had she talked to? Who had touched her? She may have seen the user, but now she was gone into the night. He knew the chance was gone. In his embarrassment, he dipped into the malagayne, and sniffed a pinch of powder.

He closed his eyes and let it settle.

He looked across the court, and saw someone else walking alone. The shadows were dark, and the man's face was obscured, but Aren recognized him. It was the same stranger who had spoken to him in Westgate.

Aren felt his stomach drop into his gut. *It's him. Impossible.*

The stranger walked directly toward him. He stopped ten paces from him. His face was lying half in shadow, but his eyes were the same black. He was tall and slender, his hair cut short. He wore a black riding coat over blue and violet tunics. His face, cheeks, and nose were all made of hard lines, as if his face was the rough sketch of a child. "So here you are," he said. "Are you mine yet?"

"What do you want?" Aren asked.

"What do *you* want?" he asked. "Do you finally think you are *the one*?"

"I am a Render Tracer. From Amagon."

"No. Not that. That is what you *were*. You are changed. I am *luminous*. As soon as I entered your life you became something else. That is what happens when someone like you chances across an *immortal*. You became a piece of *my* story. A piece of a puzzle. One that ends with you either by my side, or dead. It is always the same. It is an endless game. You are not the first."

"I won't be by your side."

"You will be. I can strip you of everything, and then build you again as I wish. I can see the future. I can see what you will become. Come to me. I will give you what you desire most. I will help you kill rogue users."

Aren's heart stopped beating or near enough. "How do you think you know what I want?" *I do.*

"It is what you want, isn't it? Who is it in Amagon they still haven't caught? Pyat Pedrin? Charman the Riot? Koseph Mordon Gravet? Josper Frei-Del? How about *all of them*? All of Amagon's worst rogue users, murderers at large. How about you capture all of them? You alone? Is that not worth it?"

"I know you have something to do with this," Aren said. "I can feel it. Everywhere I go I see you there. I think you are a user. I don't know how you are hiding it, but I will prove it. You are a part of this somehow."

"I am part of *everything*," he said. "I see through the world. I would walk lightly if I were you. I am immortal now. And with your help I will become invincible."

"I do not help people like you. I hunt them. I catch them, and I burn them."

"Others have tried," he said. "Many have thought they were the one. Many have tried to challenge me. They always join me. Or they die."

"You think you are the man in the prophecy," Aren said. "You have heard the same story. About the Sanadi. Now I understand. You think you are special."

"I can kill you with a thought. Does that not make me special?"

"So can anyone. Some use a knife. Some use poison. Some use their bare hands. You use magick. Should I be more scared of you than I am of them?"

"You do, don't you?" he said, smiling. "You *do* think you are the chosen one. This shall be very interesting."

"There is no such thing as a chosen one. You are living in a fantasy, where you use a prophecy to try to make sense of your life. I have traced madmen before. You are no different."

"That is where you are wrong. I do not *follow* a prophecy. I *bend* prophecies. I *break* them. I turn them upside down and inside out. You were supposed to destroy me. But instead I have changed *you*, made you my servant. Now I laugh, while the ghosts of ancient prognosticators weep at their own failure."

"Those are the words of a lunatic. You know nothing about me."

"I know you better than you know yourself."

"What could you possibly know?"

"That underneath this facade, you and I are *allies*."

Aren almost laughed.

"You think it is funny. They will turn on you. They always do. All they want is control. I am here to save you from control."

"Riddles and more riddles. What do you want? Why do you think we know each other? You have imagined a history for us that does not exist."

He looked away at the stars. "The light," he said. "The light plays such intricate games. It is beautiful. So beautiful. It allows you to see. I can see *everything*. Do not end up like the others. The ones who refuse to see. Do not make *their* mistake. They are endangering the future. And some of their leaders know more than they let on. But I will change them. I can change anyone. Even you."

"You left one out," Aren said. "When you said the names of the most wanted men in Amagon. You forgot the one most sought after. The one who terrorized Amagon—Kinraigan."

He laughed. "You have already found him." He smiled with satisfaction.

"You?" Aren's blood froze. He felt himself shatter as two things collided in his mind—a name spoken in whispers to frighten children, a shadow of fear as hazy and fleeting as a golem made of smoke, and this real shape of a man, body, face, mouth, with breath and voice. When those two things became one, the world as it had been dissolved, and a new one rose in its place.

Right here before him was the most hunted man in all the world, the deadliest user in Aren's lifetime. Someone so terrifying that someone like Degammon was nothing but a pale shadow.

"Your name is a curse where I come from," Aren said.

"Only on the lips of people who do not understand. They will see. And when they do, they will worship me instead. They will love me the way you will."

"I hate you."

"Because you were taught to. But I will show you the truth. I will change you."

Change. I have heard that before. Aren's rage boiled over. "It was you. You were there. You did that to the girl. You did them all, didn't you? You will burn for that."

Kinraigan leaned forward, his eyes black and bottomless. "You should be mine by now, but you are not." He narrowed his brow. Then he looked away across the city. "Perhaps it is them. The safety they provide, the protection. It must be comfort to know you have so many men supporting you here. It must give you strength to know you have the backing of the mighty Lord Protector of Amagon. But what if those things were to change?"

"Those things will never change."

He smiled. "That is it. It must be. There could be no other explanation. Once they are gone, then you will come to me. They all do. You will have to. You will want do. Because I will give you everything."

"You make threats, but you won't do anything. If you use magick here they will know. They will track you and they will find you and they will burn you."

"You speak to me as if I do not already know everything that will happen." Kinraigan backed away so quickly that Aren thought it was a dream. He turned and walked along the wall until he came to an open gate. He exited the White City like a shuddering breeze, gone as abruptly as he arrived.

Aren drew out his monocle. But of course Kinraigan was clean. Not a hint of fluorescence on him. He must have had a very robust cleaning regimen to erase everything he would have had on him from when he attacked that child. *Barely anyone is that good.* He stood there a long time, tapping he monocle against his thigh, chewing his lip. His fingers dipped into the malagayne.

He felt a sudden shiver in his spine. Someone was behind him. He spun around, half-expecting to see Kinraigan again, coming back to kill him.

But it was only Solathas, the Chancellor, standing straight and tall as a column, mirror eyes dark like a starry sky.

Aren gave a start at seeing him. He stumbled back, brushing the powder on his fingers furiously against his trouser leg. "I'm sorry. You startled me. I didn't hear you coming."

"All is well, Aren of Amagon. Out for a little light walking this evening?"

"I had to move. I could not be near so many people tonight." He looked at the nearly empty courtyard, all stones and shadows as night fell. Then he looked back at Solathas. Alone. Unwarded. How was that safe? This was arguably the second most powerful man in the Kingdom. He carried no weapons, had no bodyguards. "Wait. What are *you* doing out here?"

"Malvaegin speaks highly of you," Solathas changed the subject. "He is notoriously difficult to impress." He paused. "You said you had to move. The inability to be still implies distress. What troubles you?"

"There was a man I saw in Westgate, a man with black eyes. He acted like I knew him. I have now seen that same man here. He just left."

"Black eyes. Pupils so wide that it seems looking at our daylight world is like looking into the pitch."

"His name is Kinraigan. He is a part of this. He has been together with the assassin I trace. That can't be coincidence."

"Nothing ever is," Solathas said.

"Do you have any idea who that was?" Aren asked. "He is...He is...He has killed more people in Amagon than every other user I have hunted combined. Maybe more than *all* other users combined."

"He is a very dangerous man."

"You know of him? Even here in Laman?"

"He is known in Laman. It is believed he is involved with the Vuls. That he is responsible for them being here."

"You are lucky you arrived when you did. You almost ended up face to face with him."

"He would have been loathe to cross paths with Solathas. He is not ready yet. He is still trying to become something. He is aware that if he uses his power against Solathas within these walls it would not be so easy as it might be against someone with no way to resist him. He did not wish to risk discovering which would be the victor in such a battle at this time."

"Battle? You mean a duel." Aren was stunned. "You are a user." *So that is why he does not need bodyguards.* But the more he thought of it, the more it made sense. *Of course Solathas is a user. Why didn't I realize it sooner?* Every Great King of Laman had kept users in their service, and they were always powerful. Aren never thought to be glad to be in the presence of one, but Solathas was somehow a comfort to him. He felt no fear of the Chancellor.

Solathas bowed. "The agents of Great Santhalian have been searching all over for this man. Fate brought him to you."

"Do you know what he could want with me?"

"Kinraigan is a faded man," Solathas said. "He has discovered a secret, a secret which has consumed him. He has learned how to make himself a luminous immortal. But in so doing, he has ruined himself."

"What does that mean? What is a luminous immortal?"

"Someone who walks in the light. One who has discovered the secret to infinite life, or near enough. But it is no blessing. Immortality is an invitation to madness. He does not love this world the way Solathas does. This world could be nothing else but hell in his eyes. If he thinks he will live forever, he cannot permit the world to exist as it does for the eternity he anticipates for himself. Life is his nightmare. People are his ghouls. They haunt his waking moments unless he can change them. Now that he believes he is immortal, he will not rest until he is also invincible, limitless. Like the Sanadi of ancient times, he wanders alone until he is prepared to create his own paradise where the rules of other men have no meaning."

"*Sanadi*," Aren said. "The ancient immortals. The godlike users of the past. He called himself by that name."

"Kinraigan is convinced that he can make himself one such person."

"That is impossible. They are mythological. And the powers ascribed to them are ludicrous."

"Of course it is impossible," Solathas agreed. "Yet such hubris is not beyond the reach of one such as Kinraigan. Magick or no, men are often lured by the promises of immortality. It has always been so. Kinraigan is no different. He believes that he is the living embodiment of a powerful Sanadi. He believes that within him is the power to save the world, and to rule it."

"Someone else has spoken of the Sanadi," Aren said, remembering the words of the elder in Westgate. "Some legend of their return."

"Ah yes," Solathas said. "There was a prophecy uttered ages ago of one such thing. A false lord coming forth to claim the title of Sanadi. A man who was destined to leave nothing but ruin in his wake. Only *he of sorrow* would have the power to stop him. A man of sorrow. The prophecy speaks of one who will come and endure such profound suffering that the false Sanadi and his plans will be brought down and laid low by it."

"It doesn't mean anything," Aren said. "How can sorrow be used as a weapon? What is a man of sorrow?"

Solathas nodded. "Prophecies are always riddled with metaphor, Aren of Amagon. Sometimes a knife is a symbol of aggression, deceit, and revolution. And sometimes a knife is just a knife. Perhaps it only means that the one who has the capacity to destroy him will be full of sorrow, or perhaps the sorrow will be necessary for him to understand his potential. Perhaps it means something else altogether that one will not understand until seven years have passed."

"Sanadi. What man alone could stand against anyone with power like that?"

"A Render Tracer might, Aren of Amagon. No binder of the streams is safe as long as there is but one Glasseye."

"He is not the one I was sent to find. But they know each other. That much is clear. But I lost my trace again. And there is no way to trace Kinraigan. He is never shedding afterglow."

"There was no way to trace the one you have been following all this way either, and yet you somehow came to the same place they were."

"I am only here because Raviel was already leading us here. It wasn't me."

"Yet you found your path. The path will always be illumined for you. If your eyes are open to see it, you will know the way."

"My path. I thought my trace was over, but it isn't. I thought I knew what was going on with Raviel, but I don't."

"It is rumored you are planning to continue on to Synsirok."

"Did Raviel tell you?"

"Solathas speaks to all. It is a beautiful place, Synsirok. Deep in the forest. Few cities are as ancient as that one. It is where the ancestors of Laman were born."

"Raviel thinks I want to go there."

"Do you not?"

"He thinks my trace is leading there. We should have been on this trace together, but even now it feels like he and I are chasing two different things."

"You believe you can do this yourself. You are fearless, and proud. You wish to take on the world alone. Fear not, Aren of Amagon. Solathas sees strength within you. Do not weep. Be strong when you have fallen. You will see the way. If you feel that your people should go to Synsirok, then you shall have all the permissions you require. If that is your path, Solathas shall see you advance upon it."

"You are saying I *should* go to Synsirok. That is what Raviel seems to think. That the assassin I am hunting will be there."

"You should do as you will, Aren of Amagon. That and only that."

"I did not want to believe it. I came all this way, and all that time I knew that he was still out there. I did not want to admit to myself that I failed."

"You *did* fail. But you are not *failing*. The failure is in the past. It is gone. *You* are now. Now you do not fail."

Aren nodded. "I think I understand."

"Do not worry over the future or the past. All that matters is now. Only always ever now."

"Only always ever now," Aren repeated. He nodded. "Do *you* believe in prophecies?"

"If one says anything vague enough, sooner or later, enough of it will come to pass to make it appear to have been prescience. And with but a pinch of knowledge beforehand, one can dress up an educated guess and parade it about as a precognitive masterpiece. Why do you ask?"

"The prophecy we were talking about before...someone said I am a part of it."

"And is the knowledge of this prophecy changing you? By making you try to live up to its plan, or by trying to reject it? Is it undoing your own nature, causing you to alter your right and true direction by *trying* to make it true or untrue?"

"I don't know. I don't know how to tell."

"No prophecy controls *you*. The past does not decide the present. You must concentrate on the *path*. Destiny is for when you look back upon your life when it is finished. You are not finished yet. But at the end, if what you have done turns out to have been a sacred prophecy...well, you simply make someone look very smart for claiming to have predicted it. Do not chase maybes. Seek ever for truth. Your truth. Be not afraid of it."

"I will try."

"Walk with Solathas."

Aren stepped awkwardly over the polished stone, while Solathas floated leisurely beside him.

"Existence is joy," Solathas said. "A radiant light where sorrows are only shadows. Always be in that light. When you are on the *path*, you will find the power of the universe stands behind you. Nature itself will align to propel you on the *way*. If your path is right, you cannot be opposed. Things which seem like setbacks are merely new steps upon the path. Every trial is a step. Every struggle is a step. But as long as you are on the *path*, you cannot be defeated."

"How do I know if it is the right path?"

"Your path is that which you were meant to do. It is already within you. It always has been. You will know when you are ready to reveal it to yourself. You *must* do what you were meant to do. But remember, every true path is always beset with peril on all sides. Your enemies only succeed when they pull you *off* your path."

"I don't know. I wish there was a way to *know* I was on the right course."

"Have no lust of result. Do not follow any path for the goal itself. It is folly. All who do so invariably end up forcing the results. Failing. The true master is not concerned with the finished product. He is absorbed by the work of getting there. If you *intentionally* reach for your goal, you will struggle and stagnate, it will always remain out of reach. Once you are focused on the *path*, the *goal* will be reached with ease, the destination arrived at by accident."

"I will try."

"You were thinking of something else that troubles you. A different thing."

"What you said, about bringing the past to *now*. I had been thinking over what happened. I wanted to ask you a favor. But you must be so busy. You are such an important man."

"Each of you are important, Aren of Amagon. You are shining stars, bright and unique. You may ask any favor that you wish."

Aren glanced down at his feet, then tilted his eyes up at Solathas. "The girl. The witness. Malvaegin brought me to her."

"Liriella," Solathas said. "That was her name."

"Yes. Liriella. Would you...make sure she has someone to look after her?"

Solathas floated back a step. "You are concerned for her."

"I...feel terrible for her. Would you, if it isn't too much trouble, at least make sure she is being looked out for?"

"Solathas shall gladly do what you ask. Solathas bears great love for all who walk this land. The goddess of *love* is the Mother in the earth, from which all things spring, and she loves unconditionally for all her children here. The god of *love* is the Father in the sky, and he too loves unconditionally for his wife, the Mother, and all of her children. He showers them with the rain of his love. The Mother stands before him in the sunlight and is not ashamed. So, too, do his children, who are united by this love. People yearn for the light. The light is the love that binds us all. The differences between man and woman are erased, and become the same, where the words for either could be both."

Aren observed the Chancellor with both awe and confusion. It was as if he was utterly beyond the mundane concerns of men, and yet it seemed that he still loved every soul of the world, as though he was the very father in the sky of which he had spoken.

Solathas smiled. "This was a good talk, Aren of Amagon. Light walking suits you."

"I'm glad that I had a chance to meet you, Solathas. Your wisdom enlightens."

"Wisdom? That is a clever way of accusing Solathas of being old."

"No, no. I mean your way of looking at things is...profound."

"Such a powerful word. All that remains for you is to find the profound in yourself."

"I will. As a favor to you."

"Be ready for everything. Accept every trial with similar resolve. Life may be sacred, but it is full of trials."

Trials. Struggles. Challenges. He thought he had at least wrapped his head around the challenge of tracing a man everyone else believed to be dead. But now the trace had changed once more. The assassin knew Kinraigan, was allied with him. Two users complicated the trace exponentially. He would have to look over his shoulder even as he looked ahead. But he could do it. He knew he could. There were sections of the Jebbel Dedder manual that provided advice on pursuing multiple users. One merely had to separate them, surprise the one being traced, and capture them before the other became aware, and then move on. *I can trace them, they can't trace me.* It was clear they were not always together. There would be a time when the assassin was alone.

Everyone has to be alone sometime.

And Aren would capture him, dose him, and shuffle him off to Amagon to burn.

But first I have to find him.

That meant he would have to go to Synsirok. "It's too bad you can't come with us. I lost my Stoppers. I would love to have one more user to back me up if something goes wrong."

Kinraigan. The murderer. The bane of Render Tracers. The never-caught. *Why does he think he knows me?* He stared off at the gate Kinraigan had disappeared through. His mouth bent into a smile. *When I catch my trace, I will convince Donnovar to come back here and I will capture you, too. I will send you to the fires just like all the others.*

"Would you be willing to work a trace with me?" he asked Solathas.

He received no answer.

He looked over his shoulder for Solathas, but the Chancellor was gone.

****

Corrin found himself to be very drunk.

The serving girls brought endless supplies of ale and smooth Andristi brandy. It was easy on the throat, and it made him feel warm. He looked around himself. The dancers were still spinning, or maybe the world was spinning for them. Corrin couldn't be certain at this point.

And the women considered Corrin at least twice as exotic and he considered them. Already one of the serving girls spread her legs for him atop a barrel of ale and let him spend his seed between her midnight lips, before she returned to her work and he returned to his table.

He sat at first beside Reidos and Inrianne, as the stools of every table were full. As the meal progressed, however, numerous soldiers lifted their plates and carried them away to standing conversations throughout the palladium. This prompted Corrin to shift one seat further away from Reidos. When a second soldier took his leave, Corrin moved over further, then again, until he at last sat beside a platter of meat four seats away from the pair.

He watched Reidos fawning over Inrianne, offering her food and drink. *Women. Nothing but trouble once they begin talking.* He turned to say something which he guessed would be callous and argumentative even before he thought of the precise words. He didn't care. He was drunk, and he would say what he wished.

But as he turned to face Reidos, there was suddenly a large curtain hanging in the way. It was many-layered silk, and full of blues and reds and whites. Corrin touched the fabric clumsily with his fingers, holding it closer to his eyes. He tapped his face as though it would help him figure out where the sheets came from. He sucked on his teeth, then he said, "Hmfhh."

The curtain began to move in his hand, and he looked up. He saw a head protruding from the top of the curtain. He shrank back, sickened, and made the sign of the witch at the curtains. "A curtain man!" Corrin cried. "Disgusting!"

The head leaned down toward him.

Corrin then experienced a sudden epiphany. There was no such thing as a curtain man. His mind had invented it. These were not curtains at all. They were robes. The man who now stared at him was the owner of the robes. He had eyes like mirrors, and his face was sharp. Corrin felt like the nose might cut him if he touched it.

The man smiled at him warmly.

"Just checking...make sure your robe's okay," Corrin said, bubbling his words and dribbling his brandy. "I'm not bothering you, Tall Man."

The man smiled at him. "Solathas is pleased that you have taken it upon yourself to watch over his robes."

"What the hell?"

"Solathas finds you to be quite amusing."

"Well you tell Solathas that Corrin-Thathas did a damn good job of it," Corrin demanded. He motioned for the man to lean down to him. "Who is Solathas, and where is he hiding?"

"Solathas stands before you."

Corrin squinted his eyes. He leaned to the side in his stool, looking around the robes. He then sat back, looked behind him, but saw nothing and no one else around. "You're trying to trick me. You are the only one here."

"You have discovered the truth very well."

"Are you Solathas?"

"That would be a truthful statement if you were to reverse the order of the first two words, and remove the interrogative intonation."

"You have some funny words," Corrin said. He drooled on himself, wiped it with his sleeve, and reached for another cup of brandy, the last in a row of seven that he had arranged for himself on his table after plundering the tray of the last serving girl. He whistled at another of the lissome ladies. "And another one for Solathasases here," he added.

The serving girl looked at Corrin, then Solathas, then back to Corrin, staring with questioning eyes.

"Get the interrogatives out of your eyes," Corrin said. "That's what good old Solathasases says."

The serving girl turned so quickly that her skirt lifted to her knees.

"Hey!" Corrin yelled. "You better bring that drink for Tall Man here."

Solathas smiled at him.

"Don't you worry," Corrin said, tapping the robes with one semi-numb index finger. "I'll make sure they don't forget about you." He then swallowed his last glass of brandy as quickly as is throat would permit him without gagging.

"Solathas marvels at your courtesy toward his parched throat."

"What can I say?" Corrin shrugged. "I'm a courteous person."

"That is a lie," Inrianne yelled from her seat.

Corrin leaned around Solathas, almost falling out of his stool in the process. "Do you mind? I am having a conversation with Apple-Sauces. You mind your own business."

Imbeciles, Corrin thought.

The girl returned with the cups of brandy. Apple-Sauces sipped delicately from the cup, holding the liquid in his mouth and swishing it before swallowing. He closed his eyes. "Ah, Solathas remembers the taste."

"Corrin remembers the taste, too," said Corrin.

"Corrin is a rare name," Solathas informed him.

"Solathasases is a rare name too," Corrin said. "You need another drink." He snapped his fingers at the serving girl.

"Solathas has not yet finished his first."

"That's the best time to request another," Corrin said. He ran a finger around the edge of his own cup. "It gives you motivation."

"Solathas sees that Corrin excels at motivation. You must do what you were meant to do, not what you wish."

"I do what I will." Corrin accidentally dribbled brandy onto his shirt.

"Precisely."

Corrin smirked. "I feel unarmed in this converstipation."

"Solathas understands that you intended to say *conversation*."

"That's what I said," Corrin said. "Anyway, that's my story right now."

"A curious choice of words. Relating interaction with Solathas as a battle."

"Everything is a battle. I don't have any weapons to help me fight this one."

"You do have a weapon."

"I have my knives," Corrin said. "But that won't do much good."

"You always have a weapon," Solathas said. "Every man and every woman is a star. Often are the times when many lives depend upon the strength of the few, and still more depend upon those in turn. By protecting the circle, that circle ensures a circle still greater outside of itself. You are the center of a circle, Corrin, with the power to preserve. You become more than yourself in this way. By securing the future of one, you shall protect ten, and then a hundred, and then a hundred hundreds."

Corrin eyed him suspiciously.

"Many men never know their own importance. Many men never know the weapons they wield. You *always* have a weapon, Corrin."

"I heard you," Corrin snorted. "I'm not deaf here."

"You do have a weapon."

"I *do* have a weapon. I got it, I got it." Corrin looked around. "Where is that girl with your drink?"

"Solathas believes that she will return after your next question."

"How do you know I'm going to ask you a question?"

The girl suddenly returned with two glasses of brandy. She placed one in Corrin's hand. He closed his fingers around the glass without looking.

Apple-Sauces received his own drink. He smiled and floated himself back a step.

"Weird," Corrin said. "Are you going to sip this one too?"

Solathas responded by throwing his head back, and taking the entire drink into his mouth in one swill. It was down his throat before Corrin could blink, and the empty glass placed softly on the table.

Corrin gave a start. Not to be outdone, he threw back his own head. Took a mouthful. Brandy dribbled down the corners of his mouth. He forced himself to swallow, tipped the glass further, and swallowed again in a massive gulp. Brandy splashed onto his shirt, and he narrowly avoided choking and vomiting. When he opened his eyes again, he was dizzy, and more importantly, he was alone.

Corrin leaned to his left, and looked around Reidos. Not there. He dipped his head low and studied the area beneath the table. Not there. He checked beneath his stool. Not there. "What the hell happened to Apple-Sauces?" he asked the stool.

He threw up a few times.

He glanced at Reidos, but Reidos was ignoring him.

Corrin groaned. He waved his hand in the air. "Another brandy, please."

20

Infinity Or A Day

"I DON'T CARE," Keluwen said. "He is here. We go now and take him."

She started for the door, but Hodo reached out and took her by the elbow.

"Let me go," she said.

"It is too late," Orrinas said. "They know we are here. Now is not the time."

"When *is* the time?" She pointed to everyone in the room, whether they wanted to be a part of it or not. "Each of us has lost something. Many things. And now here we are, a stone's throw from that little shit. I say we go and take his little head right now."

Leucas nodded, but was afraid to speak. Cheli was still crying, but Keluwen was certain she would back this move.

Kelos, their Andristi safehouse master, turned his head momentarily from the lookout position through the crack in the window shutters. "Watch your tone," he said, his Sinjan accent as thick as his lips. "This is the Foreign Quarter. The Da'ari are agitated."

"You think I am concerned about the damned Da'ari?"

He turned his smooth, unblemished Andristi face back out the window. "You should be."

"Agitated. I will show them agitated."

"We will do as Orrinas decides," Krid Ballar said. "*Axis Ardent* sends their instructions to him. He interprets them. He decides. Don't you ever forget that."

Is that a threat, you brittle old worm? "I want to see their blood." She realized she was out of breath, and closed her mouth and looked back and forth at everyone.

"With what?" Krid asked. "Are the three of you going to march over there and pound on the Great King's door? Demand they let you in? Fight your way through five hundred men? All to kill one Glasseye?"

"Yes," Keluwen said, folding her arms.

"We have not been given that instruction," Orrinas said.

"To the furthest hell with the damn instructions," she said. "The decision makers of Axis Ardent are not here. They are not *now*. They have only yesterday's news to go on. They do not understand what happened. They do not realize how close we are."

"They do," Orrinas said. "They always do."

If it had been us, Seb would have gone. He would have done everything to hit them back. But she listened to Orrinas. She always did in the end. Because he was always right. No matter how much she hated what being right meant.

"We are underpowered," Krid warned.

That was his way of tip-toeing around the fact that three of their companions were dead. *Three of our friends.* But to his practical mind it meant two of the users. And Nils had been the best stager on the continent. And the kindest. *Now we have no massman and no darknician.* But he was right. How could they set a trap now?

But Keluwen did not even care about that. She wanted the Glasseye. She wanted the Amagon-man. If he had not sabotaged the entire operation in Westgate, none of them would ever have had to go to Laman in the first place. They would not have needed to travel. *And Nils would be alive.*

That fucking scum.

"We still have a man in place," Orrinas said. "We still have a chance."

"Not if we can't leave this room," Keluwen said. "Not when we are stuck with the masses, waiting while the high and mighty eat their fill of the finest Andristi delicacies at the Palace with those murderers."

"Kelos has told us how impossible it would be to get near them," Hodo said. "He knows Cair Tiril better than anyone alive."

"You would have a better chance standing on water than sneaking into the Palace," Kelos said. "Tabiantha *is* inside though. She supervises the serving ladies. All their gossip spills into her ears. She will bring us more information tonight after the sun sets."

"Is *he* here or not?" Hodo asked. "We hear nothing but rumors."

"How could he hide?" Leucas asked. "He is luminous. He should outshine the sun."

"That is not how it works, Leucas," Orrinas said.

"How do we even know he is luminous?" Hodo asked. "What proof do we have?"

"Jharvi died to pass the knowledge to us," Krid said. "Slow and painful like. After what she went through, I believe the words that came out of her mouth that day over any other."

"We know he is luminous," Orrinas said. "We know he found a way to go there *on his own*, without the book. There are portions of the Codex Lumina that tell the secrets of how to use the light for his own designs. He now knows them. The book taught him how to be immortal. But immortal does not mean unkillable. The Andristi age slower than we, but even they still bleed, and so will he."

"Unless he finds the key he is looking for," Cheli said. "The one that will make him invincible. The one that will make him beyond luminous. A god. A god on the earth."

"Could you do it, Orrinas?" Leucas asked. "Do you know what it means to become a luminous immortal?"

"I would never open that book, even if I could understand it," Orrinas said. "The place it talks about, no man belongs there."

"I have never heard of anyone going there," Hodo said. "Have you?"

Orrinas shook his head. "I doubt anyone with the power to get there on their own would ever speak of it."

Hodo frowned. "If he already has the book, and he has already been inside that place—is already luminous—then what is he doing *here*?"

"What do you mean?" Orrinas said.

"He is immortal. Why is he slinking around Laman? What else could he want?"

"To be invincible," Keluwen said. "To never have to obey another living thing ever again. To become his own god."

"That he *cannot* do on his own," Orrinas said. "No one can."

"He would need the Crown to do that," Krid said.

Sephors. Here we go with rumor again. "If his plan hinges on uncovering artifacts lost before history was recorded, he may be doomed to disappointment," Keluwen said.

"If anyone could do it, he could," Leucas said. "I have met some of the worst men in the world, men who make brave heroes shiver. But that man horrifies me."

You and me both, Keluwen thought.

"But every scholar from Ethios to Joledo says that the Crown would be *west* of Olybria," Cheli said. "Based on everything ever written about it. It is the only thing they agree on."

"So either they are all wrong," Keluwen said. "Which is possible, likely even. Or he is in Laman for something else."

"Again, what else?" Hodo asked.

Everyone just looked around the room at each other. *What indeed?*

"He was after the Crown," Cheli said, her voice steady but oh so quiet. "But once he returned to Amagon, something made him change course."

"Cheli?" Keluwen made a sad smile at her.

Cheli sniffled and wiped her eyes. "He thinks he needs something else to become what he wants to be."

"Maybe he doesn't want to be in the light anymore," Leucas said.

"Fool," Krid said. "He would never turn his back on the light. There are none who can. Those who become luminous can no longer stand the dimness of the real world, any more than they could stand each other. Have you ever heard of two luminous immortals that could stand to be anywhere near each other? In any History? In any myth. They are always alone. They can only be alone. When you have ultimate power there is no room for *someone else* with ultimate power to butt heads with."

"He wants to be the only one," Keluwen realized. "He wants to be the only one like him. Whatever he is doing here, it must be because of that. That is the only thing that frightens him."

"He is trying to stop someone," Leucas said. "The way we are trying to stop him."

"Brings us back to the question of *how*," Hodo said. "And why Laman?"

"We will find out," Orrinas said. "Things are coming to a head soon. I can feel it."

That means we should move before he escapes once more. She cursed the day for taking so long. She wanted to know what Tabiantha had to tell of it. *Where are you, scum? Luminous scum? Immortal shit? Where?*

But when Tabiantha did arrive after dark, she had little to tell. Gossip from the soldiers, rumors of users moving on the roads, soldiers heading to Synsirok. Names of officials from Amagon. Strength. A Sister with them. All of it bored Keluwen to hell and back.

But then she caught a snippet about an investigation of an attack, right here in the Foreign Quarter, not far from here. And how the Great King's people brought one man out to look over the scene.

Aren of Amagon. The Glasseye. My prey.

Keluwen waited until everyone was enraptured by Tabiantha's words. It was not hard for the girl to do. She had a face pale and pink like pastel roses, plump lips, and eyes as wide as full moons beneath her strings of golden hair. She was the only thing that could draw Kelos away from the window. Even Orrinas watched her with a smile. *Be careful, old man.*

Keluwen took one step back. And then another. And then another. Quiet as a mouse. She inched the door open. She slipped out with none the wiser.

She took to the streets of the White City

Though it was not so white here. Dull yellow and brown, the Da'ari were dirt poor, houses huddled against one another like hunched over old women holding each other for warmth in winter. There was a fire on every corner, and a river of oil in every back alley. The stray dogs were as ubiquitous as the moon bats, and the hustlers as common as the beggars.

The White City is a lie the Andristi tell themselves.

All it really was a white half-a-city. The Silent Quarter and the Old Quarter were where the wealthy lived, where the Palace was, where the bureaucrats resided, the proprietors and officers and owners. The other half of Cair Tiril was a worn city, a rusted city, a mud-stained city. The Foreign Quarter and the River Quarter were full to overflowing with sad souls, their humanity stretched to the breaking point.

At least they don't send my kind to the fires here. That was something at least.

She followed the landmarks Tabiantha mentioned, and soon found herself drawn to it. She could feel the energy of the place. Something terrible had happened here.

Yet when she opened the door, and looked at the empty room, she felt nothing. She saw nothing. There was no evidence of anything at all. She was not even sure what happened.

She ducked back out the door and hiked up the hill and down into a basin on the border of the Silent Quarter. She watched people come and go. Middling patriarchs of the Silent Quarter slipped into the Foreign Quarter for cheap food and wares, And denizens of the Foreign Quarter brought their families to stretch out on the pristine white benches and marvel at the wide courtyards of the rich.

Here Keluwen remained, her eyes following every moving body.

It was no more than ten minutes later that she saw him.

Amagon-man.

He was wandering the courtyard, holding his glass to his eyes. He was stalking toward a young girl on a bench. She did not see him. He was so close. He reached out a hand for her.

No, you will not do this in front of me! Keluwen's feet began to run toward him without conscious thought. But she prevented herself from calling out.

He stopped at the last moment. The girl ran away. He did not follow.

Keluwen took a deep breath. Something caught her eye. She saw the man with black eyes. *Here. Right here. Right in front of me.*

She very nearly dipped into the Slipstream for a blank impulse, but she held back. *He is close enough. If I dig in he will sense the ripples. He will know I am here.* One thing she knew for certain was that he would flatten her to paste in a user's duel.

She wanted the Glasseye. To defeat the master, first you must break all his tools. Glasseyes had no powers at all. *Except the power to hunt and oppress my kind.*

But her jaw fell open when she saw the man with black eyes begin talking to the Glasseye. *Right out in the open. They do not even try to hide it.*

Whose life are you selling out today, Amagon-man?

When they parted, she waited and waited until the Amagon-man was alone. Then she dipped into the Slipstream for her fastest blank impulse. She was ready to put a sphere through his Glasseye heart, and blast his blood onto the street.

Belleron, give me strength and speed a luck all three.

She began to slide the glove over her elbow, down her arm, over her wrist, off her fingers. She pointed double fingers at him.

Then she felt two strong arms wrap around her from behind and squeeze.

She jumped and bucked and kicked for only a moment, until she felt how calm the hold was, how serene.

Orrinas.

He held her there for many minutes, more than she could count.

Someone else came. A Lamani official of some kind. The Glasseye spoke with him and then they both wandered off. The man with black eyes was gone.

She turned and looked up at him. "How did you know?"

"Because I know *you*."

"Are you mad at me?"

"Mad enough to call you wife."

"That mad?"

He spun her around, put his face right in hers. "We all have parts to play. You cannot flaunt my decisions like this. You cannot. It undermines the unity we have painfully tried to forge with everyone else."

"They understand. They know me."

"They know you think you can get away with breaking the rules because you are with me."

"Is that what they think?"

"All of them. And it must stop."

"If you had all stood up and come out here with me, you would have seen him. He was here. In this very courtyard. We had a chance."

"Now is not the right time. We do everything by design."

Her lips bent like steel into a grimace. "And look where that has brought us. Half of us dead, Orrinas."

"I am meeting with him tonight. Now."

"For another box of gold and handful of empty promises?"

"I know you are under stress."

"You know. Bah."

"The strain is enough to challenge the best of us. Even you. We must find relief where we can."

"My relief will come when I put a little hole in the middle of his skull and watch his eyes roll back. Maybe if *Axis Ardent* spent more time wanting what we should all want, they would *see*."

"They know more than we do. They are looking at everything, the whole tapestry. We are but one part."

"Do they want him gone or not?"

"We want him gone, at the right time. Barging in on him will do nothing but finish us all off. You know that it is true. Look inside yourself. In the part of your mind that you do not wish to see, the part that thinks things through."

She shook free of his hands. She began walking back toward the safehouse.

He followed her, several paces behind.

She felt so alone. She refused to turn to look at him. She cried twice along the way. She wanted to turn to him and wrap her arms around him. But she didn't. She just kept walking.

When she returned to the safehouse, Leucas and Hodo were already asleep on the frayed green sofas, blankets tossed haphazardly over them. Cheli was locked in her room alone, as she had been every night in every place they had stayed.

Keluwen slid into the tiny bedroom she and Orrinas shared, with the slender bed so narrow she had to lay partway atop him, and so short his legs stuck out off the end halfway up his shins.

She pulled her tunic over her head and threw it at the wall in a single motion. She watched it fall to the floor and thought of Nils. She closed her eyes until they hurt. She opened them again, kicked her boots off, slid out of her leggings and leaned naked against the wall, head down, eyes closed.

She had not slept in days.

She had not stopped worrying in weeks.

She heard a click.

The door opened inward.

She turned to look. Orrinas stood in the doorway, a hand on the knob, halfway leaned in. He did not smile or frown. He looked into her eyes, and she fell into him. He knew her. In his gaze she felt *known*. Finally by someone in this world. She would have been naked before him even if she wore twenty tunics and a suit of armor.

He never took his eyes off her.

Kelos and Tabiantha walked into the bedroom and stood facing her. And she them.

She looked at Orrinas. He said nothing. He made no expression. He gently pulled the door closed leaving himself outside. She knew what it meant. This was not the first time.

The two Andristi guided her to the bed. They ran their fingers up and down her body, prickling gooseflesh. They pulled her down. She sat on the edge of the bed, and Tabiantha opened her lips and kissed her while Kelos buried his head between her legs.

Keluwen closed her eyes. And for a moment all that existed was a mouth on hers and a fire between her thighs. Kelos moved with ageless speed, and she melted through her skin and turned to water and her body flowed between the two of them, like a river between two soft sandy banks.

She fell back onto the bed but it might as well have been the vault of stars in the sky, and she just kept falling and falling. Tabiantha's tongue was on her neck and in her mouth, hands running over every inch of her.

Kelos climbed atop her, his body of exquisite muscle, his skin impossibly soft, white as snow. He lowered himself onto her. She was made of dew and fire and he slid right into her and right through her and she wrapped her arms around him without thinking, eyes closed, pulling him to her, holding him close.

She fell open between them, legs wide, arms lost over her head. She unlocked a quiet door where she kept her pain, and let it all fall away for that one moment, and became weightless. She held her mouth closed, jaw clenched, keeping every sound within her, afraid she might scream.

They balanced her between waves of subtle agony, as if the two of them were of one mind. She felt a mouth on hers, parting her lips, a wandering tongue, hands running through her hair, caressing fingers sliding up and down her arms, a body falling down on hers like the pounding of a drum, a rhythmic crush, hard and steady and relentless.

Each collision drove her closer, until she stood right at the edge of the little oblivion. She hovered there for an instant, as long as a gasp, before falling in. Her arms swam in the sheets, her legs shivered, and her moans forced her mouth wide. She floated there in a place where thoughts cannot go, and pain never existed.

She let go of everything, and Kelos let go of himself, and she felt the crush of his warmth, and he fell breathless atop her, his mouth against her neck, her head cradled in Tabiantha's arms.

There she wept. And then she slept.

When she woke they were already gone. Orrinas was beside her, patiently awake, laying in the bed, his legs hanging off the edge, returned from wherever he had gone.

She rolled over and curled into a ball, pressing herself against his chest, her arms grasping for him and only him to hold for all time and forever beyond that. She smelled his skin, and felt the bristly hair of his chest coarse against her face, and his chin resting gently atop her head, like an acrobat balanced atop the apex of the world. She loved every bit of him.

He did not say a word. His breaths never wavered, or quickened, or slowed. His arms held her always not tight enough, never tight enough, but she loved it. She loved every moment of it. She closed her eyes.

She slept for infinity or a day.

21

City In The Trees

I AM COMING TO the end of this.

It is here somewhere. He is here. They have been telling me for a thousand miles that my mission is already over. It is not. The real trace will finish here.

Aren convinced Donnovar to march to Synsirok. He left the White City behind. He left Eriana and Solathas. They were already in the past. He only had time for now.

The City in the Trees lay deep in the twisted folds of Synsiros, the forest that had been the first domain of the Andristi. The Sarenwalkers were required to take them into the woods numerous times to avoid roads and bridges which had been destroyed by bands of Vul raiders. They were forced to move through perilous underbrush and between tangled thickets, sometimes single file.

Donnovar displayed the writs of Santhalian to the sentries, and the battalion streamed into the city with ease. They were shown to an unused prayer house for priests of the Mother, where they could set up a camp.

The buildings were perched between clumps of green woods, as if they had sprouted from the earth alongside the trees. Oak columns had been carved to resemble leaves and vines about every door and window, and a soft golden glow poured from every household, every house its own little glen, immersed in trees.

The stone temples were humble, lining the main avenue. Decorative arches straddled the road, each one with its own individual carvings of scenes from Andristi legends. Colored lanterns, pink and yellow, put a pale glow to the stone, matching gardens boasting roses of the same colors. It thrilled him to find the landmarks he had only seen on maps before. He recognized the fountains of Ereth Parador from paintings in Medion.

He looked over his shoulder and realized Raviel was no longer riding beside them. *Where did he go? So help me, if he is trying to run this trace without me, I will rage. But of course he had.* Aren frowned until his face hurt.

But he was not the only one. Terrol, too, made his way apart from the Outer Guard, turning down a narrow alleyway. What other business could the ghost have had in Synsirok?

Aren prepared for the hunt immediately. He cleaned the lens of the Jecker monocle and wiped dust from the Oscillatrix and Finder. He stowed his carry-bag, checked over his tracing tools, replaced them in his satchel, and made ready to move. *I will not sit. I will trace. I will.*

Before he left, he made one final preparation. He slipped into a small alcove, held the linen pouch of soft powder, and deftly snorted some malagayne. The tightness of his limbs softened, and his breathing slowed. Just enough to keep him through the trace, and a little extra for the pleasure of it.

He stepped out into the fading glow of the evening. The road branched off into a maze of walkways lined with trees, all blue in the dusk. He wandered long with the Jecker monocle, scanning the branches, the grey facades, and the chipped pavements. He stalked the streets, switching through the filters, taking random turns, and arbitrarily choosing which way to follow at forks in the road. Even at its lowest setting, the Finder registered nothing.

The streets were quiet and nearly empty. The ceremonial supper time of Lithlinon was still kept well here. Few Andristi would be seen for another hour or so, and he attempted to appear non-threatening to the few he passed.

He had not anticipated seeing anyone familiar out here, but as he turned a corner, he suddenly saw Redevir standing in his path. He felt a sudden flash of fear. *Why are you here? What are you doing? How did you find me?* But when he caught his breath, he realized it was not so odd to find the Rover out here. Redevir had come here for his own search, after all, following the past and its veiled clues on his journey to certain disappointment.

"Aren, I thought that was you."

"What do you want?"

"I didn't mean to interrupt you," Redevir said. "I was prowling the streets, same as you." He stopped and thought to himself. "I have an idea. Why don't we stroll together. Keep each other company. Who knows? I might have a use for you in case I run into any more Hezzam."

"You are more likely to run into Da'ari here."

"I don't suppose there is a giant woodland worm that they are afraid of."

"No such luck."

"Perhaps we can avoid them together. Two pairs of eyes are better than one."

A brief bolt of suspicion flashed through him, but he thought about it. The Rover's presence might keep him from blindly following his trace into danger.

"Fine. Let's walk." Aren started forward, lost his step, stumbled.

Redevir's brow narrowed, and he sharpened his eyes. "Are you all right?"

"I'm fine."

"You seem out of sorts. Are you sure?"

"It's the traveling. And the trace. Just tired. That's all." Lies. Magnificent lies to cover the malagayne in his bloodstream, but he must have said them at least halfway convincingly.

"It takes a lot out of a man."

"I've dealt with it before. I get through it."

Redevir changed the subject. "You know of Synsirok? The way you know about the Histories? What kind of things?"

"The places are as much a part of history as the people."

"Will you tell me about Synsirok?"

"If the trace permits." He wiped his nose briskly.

They entered the old city, and Aren took to its streets like a hunter, imagining his trace stepping through the avenues as he himself was. He focused, attentive to every bit of evidence around him—the rich scent of the pines, the clacking of his boots over the stone streets, the cool air washing through him, the browns and greys of wood and stone. He absorbed them all, feeling himself riding the energy of the city itself, waiting for that one thing which would appear out of place. He would make himself Synsirok, become the city, and feel out the cancerous spot that was the assassin.

He was not surprised when he finally saw it. A tiny glow of residual energy upon a lamp post. It shined an ethereal green like sunlight through aquamarine. "There," he said.

"What?" Redevir asked. "Where?"

Aren jogged over to the spot, and knelt down so that the glowing blotch of color was at eye level. He put his face right up to it, and stared through the blue filter. The core color was pale orange. "This is it," he said over his shoulder. He attempted a reading with the Oscillatrix, and flipped through the composite. The primary values were a match. The glowing of the cores were fringed with red. "It's redshifting. He's moving away from us." He turned his head and looked all around, but he did not see any other nearby signs.

"Where do we go?" Redevir asked.

"I need another sign. If I have two locations that have been sensitized with afterglow, I can compare the variance in redshift to triangulate the direction of the source user." He darted his eye up, down, left, and right, with the Jecker monocle pressed so tightly to it that he felt like it was fastened to his face.

Then he saw it. Far down the street. Between dull fence posts and the low hanging branches of trees. It winked at him through all of the objects trying to obstruct his view.

He took off at a sprint. He rounded a fenced yard, and crossed a cobbled court, Redevir matching his pace easily. Aren stopped at the source of the glow. It was a small patch upon the railing of a bridge. "The user brushed his hand against the railing."

"Where are we?" Redevir asked.

"This is the Bridge of Taris, hewn from the trunk of a single redwood. The legend says that Ismorien felled the tree with his axe alone." The bridge was fifty feet long, stretching across a small creek.

"Quite a feat. Why isn't it named for him?"

"He named it for his son, Taris. He was a child at the time."

"A bridge from father to son," Redevir said to himself.

"What?"

"Nothing. Just reminds me of an old poem."

Aren moved up to the pale stain of sensitized fluorescence, and studied it closely with the blue filter, peering into the edges of the core residuals. They were redshifting as well, but only half as much as the first, if that.

He looked back in the direction of the first sign. He guessed the distance and ran the algorithm in his head. He pointed across the bridge and down a tree-lined lane. "That way." He thought back to the maps he had spent so many nights poring over in the Library. "We must be close to the Hall of Siristall, a sacred court."

"Who was Siristall though? I assume he was a king of Laman."

Aren nodded. "He fought five wars against the Vuls."

"Too bad he is not here now."

"It was an audience hall for his entire reign," Aren said. "His successors adopted it as a summer home. It was used by one of the sacred orders of the moon after that, but I can't remember if it was the White Moon or the Blue Moon."

"I will not begrudge you a little uncertainty here and there," Redevir said.

Aren saw a sign within the patio of the Hall itself. It twinkled fervently through the Jecker monocle. He darted inside.

The Hall was long unused, and the patio was strung through with cobwebs, its interior grey with dust. It was not the pinnacle of majesty that he had expected. He found the sign, discerned the shift, and pointed out and further along the street they had just been on. "Up ahead. Near the Shrine of Sirnan."

"Shrine?" Redevir became excited. "What kind of shrine?"

"A sacred place. Three hundred years old at least."

"What does it commemorate?"

"Calm down. Why do you care so much?"

"I am just being hit with coincidence after coincidence. I am beginning to feel like something is happening here."

"Something *is* happening. I am running down a user."

"The shrine, what was it for? Tell me."

"Sirnan was the great-great-grandson of Siristall. He dedicated the shrine to the people of Thorienguard, killed by some kind of invasion from the north."

"Who killed them? How did they all die?"

"The true story was never recorded," Aren said, dropping to one knee, staring at the afterglow, running the algorithm. "I always assumed it was the Vuls. The Histories translate it as the *Nameless End*."

"The Nameless End? *From the shrine of the nameless end.*"

"What? Sounded like you were quoting something."

"Don't you see? Banwick's goddamn poem."

"What are you talking about?"

"My search. I told you I was close."

"Close to what?"

"The *Dagger*."

"Redevir, it isn't real. There is no such thing. These places have always been here, and no Sephor has ever come out of them."

"They are real. They have to be."

"The *trace* is real. *That* is what we are close to."

"Listen to the rest of the poem, and you can be the judge. If the Dagger does not sit at the end, I will burn the damn book and forsake the Sephors forever."

Aren studied the residuals in the shrine. "What does it say?" he asked, as he finished running the numbers in his head.

"Find a poet's words where there should be none, that little old man told me. Banwick placed a poem amidst his notes. *That* poem." Redevir held up his aged copy of *Mercury Woods*, and flipped through the pages. "The first line of each couplet holds a clue. *Over the bridge from father to son; from the shrine of the nameless end; on the road of the king of the hall; endless be the shining green of the twins.*"

"The king of the hall? That could only be Siristall. The hall we were just at."

"But it asks for a road."

"There is a street in the old city that bears the name of Siristall," Aren said. "It is not far from here. Around that way." He pointed. As he did so, his eyes followed in the same direction. He was not even looking through the Jecker monocle. He nearly tripped over his own boots. "I don't believe it. Aural afterglow." The particles hovered like a fine mist, stretching along the street, and coating the very air with their luminescence.

"I see it," Redevir said in amazement. "I see it, too."

"Visible afterglow indicates recent use. He used the magick. Right here."

Redevir ran toward it. Aren struggled to match his pace. He slapped the lens to his eye as he propelled himself to the cloud of radiant dust. He felt no fear now, only the thrill of the chase. The core colors matched. He did not bother to check the primary values this time. He already knew they would be the same. The smell suggested it was the afterglow of a *vectoric*, a weak blank impulse. The streak lines pointed off into the trees.

The road branched off into three narrow lanes amid the evergreens.

"What of the green?" Redevir asked. "The green of the twins."

"It must mean the twin sons of Lithlinon, Thorien and Palan," Aren said, scanning the trees with the monocle.

"The ones who made war with each other?"

"The same."

"What is their *green?*"

"Lithlinon dedicated a park to his sons at their birth."

"That must be it," Redevir decided.

Aren rose to his feet. The spectral shift suggested the user was around the corner...where the entrance of the park was.

Redevir practically flew to it.

"What now?" Aren asked.

"I don't know. That is the last clue."

"That's it? Your quest is doomed. The lawn of the park is dozens of acres. What do you intend to do, dig up the entire plot?"

"There's something wrong. The clues should have taken us right to it."

"Your clues were someone's clever joke. An ancient form of humor."

"It...It can't be."

Aren turned all around, until he saw a little trail of silvery afterglow floating down the street. "I told you, the trace is what is real. The afterglow is real." He stalked after it.

But then something stopped him. A thought floated into his mind so abruptly that he actually took his eyes off the afterglow. "Wait."

"What?"

"Endless be the *shining* green of the twins. Maybe it doesn't literally mean *twins.*"

"What do you mean? What is green and shines?"

"The two spires atop the Chapel of Ismorien are often referred to as *the twins* in the Histories. There is something green inside it."

"Where is this place?"

"Not far. Around the park. In the same direction as the vapor trail."

"Take us there."

They rounded the lawn, following the lush glowing mist, until they at last arrived at the Chapel. Marble and granite had been carved to make the walls, buttresses, and eaves. It was even crowned with a dome. On either side were two spiraling minarets, standing like twin thorns. The vapor dwindled, and seemed to fade away near the tapering arch of the entrance itself. *The user went in there.*

"What could be the green of these twins?" Redevir asked.

"The centerpiece of the Chapel is a famous necklace, three concentric strings of bright emeralds set in gold. A gift from Ismorien to his Queen, Elesora. It was placed there after her death a thousand years ago."

Aren passed up the steps and through the door. Alcoves surrounded the domed chamber, each containing silver and gold basins, each with subtle plumes of incense drifting upward from them, filling the chamber with scents of jasmine. The chapel was untended. They were alone.

The necklace sat upon an altar in one of the alcoves. It was anchored to the stone, and resisted as Redevir tugged on it.

"We shouldn't touch that," Aren said.

"There is no one here to stop us."

"That's what worries me. This place should be guarded. Besides, you're looking for a knife, not a piece of jewelry."

Redevir loosened his grip and sighed. "You're right. What now?"

Aren had a sudden thought. He put the Jecker monocle to his eye. From underneath the gemstones a gentle glow radiated. He reached out to it. The user had been here, in this very spot. He tilted it slowly, and looked underneath. He saw strange markings. "Look here. There is an inscription."

"Yes?"

"It is recent. Well, more recent than the piece itself anyway. It's awkward, like it was etched into the gold underneath after it was already anchored as it is now. See the angle of the lettering?"

"How did you know to look underneath?"

Aren turned a cold stare at him. "The user touched it. He was here before us. He is following the same clues you are. He could still be here." He squinted into every alcove and behind every shadowed bench, but saw no one, no afterglow, and no sensitized fluorescence.

"Are you sure you do not believe in destiny?" Redevir stared at the script. "I can't read these letters."

"That's strange," Aren said. "It is written in Old Ardis, the ancient language of the *Arradian* empire. Why is this here? The Andristi never spoke Old Ardis. And Arradan is more than a thousand miles from here."

"What does it say?" Redevir coaxed.

"I think I can make it out. *Two turns, door, circle.*"

"Two turns. That takes us to the rear of the Chapel. I see flickering light back there. Walk to the light."

They moved swiftly to the rear of the Chapel. Aren peered around pillars and gazed into cupolas. *Someone lit this incense. Where are all the people?* He glanced to his right and saw a pair of legs sticking out from behind a stone altar covered in green silk. "Wait a moment." He reached for Redevir's elbow.

But the Rover was already heading for the back wall. "Here it is! See!"

Aren felt himself pulled along. He knew something was wrong. But he could not stop himself.

Before them was a doorway. Aren peered through it. The room was lit by hundreds of burning candles, on ceremonial tables lining every wall. At the far end he saw an ancient wardrobe, with a stone frame. *It must weigh a thousand pounds.* It had been shoved carelessly aside. He studied the dust on the floor, and knew that it had sat in that spot for a long time.

There was a small circular hole in the wall at ankle height, and on the floor sat a piece of stone in the perfect shape to have plugged that hole.

But someone had been here first. Someone had removed it.

Aren stared into the dark circle. It yawned at him like a tiny rat hole. He stepped slowly toward it.

****

Corrin sat still on one of the benches of the old hall, surrounded by men of the Outer Guard. He smiled as he cleaned his assortment of blades.

They were his pets, each with its own personality. He finished wiping down the *Steel Whore*, admiring its deadly color. He was glad he had managed to hold onto it for so long. He had been without a sword of his own since the previous one, which he had lost in an unfortunate confrontation with a gambling horse trainer, a dwarf, and a delightful prostitute. He placed it on a wide white cloth, beside a long row of shining weaponry, eliciting a fatherly glow from him.

There was the proud decorative dagger from Cyurmer with its glittering garnet adornments; the gruff cleaver from Talorin with its wide blade and flat top; the broad knife from Pannoria, that one never shined no matter how hard he tried to polish it; and the jolly bronze-hilted dagger from Castice.

He moved his eyes on to the silver dagger from Kolac, always bright and happy; the Kokril talon, with its malicious curves; and the straight and pompous Cambrian dirk with only a point and no edge. *That one thinks too highly of itself*, he thought.

Rounding out his collection were the throwing knife from Samring, which had always looked a little fat to him, but the balance was excellent; the white steel from Albinon, so ghostly and austere; the devastating Levidian Nails from Sevonia, one of the deadliest weapons to come out of Lissaria, and he had *three* of them; and the Calabari claw, with its little hook curling back on the blade edge for locking it in a hapless opponent's body—by far his favorite.

Last, but not least was the ivory-handled blade from Miralamar. He lifted the slender knife Aren had given him as a gift years ago. He hadn't known how Aren had gotten ahold of it. Aren had never even been to Miralamar.

It was the only weapon Corrin still kept from so long ago. Its ivory hilt was well balanced and the blade shined silvery sharp. It was a perfect combat weapon, but for some reason Corrin had never once used it, not even to cut bread.

He didn't really know why, but he felt strangely partial to the blade. It was the last one he would ever use in a fight. Not that it mattered, though. He had a dozen others. He had stabbed at least one man with each of them, but this last knife was different. It was full of memories: long days of mischief with Aren and Reidos, long nights with women whose names he couldn't remember, late mornings and free meals. Using it would be like declaring an end to those days, and he just was not ready to give them up yet.

The knife had the engraving on the hilt, *Live everywhere, so to die everywhere*. Corrin had been many places, and *very nearly* died multiple times in all of them. He had gotten himself into many troubles, some of which may have seemed intentional to a casual observer.

Aren had always told him that he blundered stupidly from one bad situation to the next, and it was only by the grace of his skill with a sword, and his penchant for diving through windows, that he had managed to keep himself alive.

Corrin preferred to speak of it as bad luck, and fate, and providence, and all the other things that sounded more poetic than incompetence.

He glanced at the cook who had taken in the boy back in Westgate. He wondered what had become of that girl who had carried him. *What was her name?*

"How do you do it?" he asked the cook. "Duran, right? That's your name?"

Duran was taken off guard. "What do you mean?"

"Must be a deal of trouble to cook for so many people all the time."

"In a matter of speaking."

"Well, you are my favorite person here. When in doubt, follow the cook, I say. So, do you have an oath to the boy now?"

"For now."

"What's his name again?"

"The boy? Hallan. He still doesn't speak to anyone."

"Still?" Corrin asked. "Why don't you talk to anyone, boy?"

"Leave him alone, Corrin."

"I was only asking."

Hallan's eyes followed him.

"Just leave him alone," Duran said. "He—"

"Coren?" Hallan asked in a shallow voice.

Duran stared in amazement. "You speak."

"Maybe he just needed someone interesting to talk to," Corrin said.

"Your name is Coren?" the boy asked.

"No. Corrin, *Corrin*," Corrin corrected him.

"It sounds the same," Hallan said.

"It is slightly different," Corrin said. "There are many people named Coren. *Corrin*, on the other hand, is much more unique."

"It sounds the same to me," Hallan said.

"It may at first," Corrin said. "Try saying it a few times. You'll see the difference."

"Coren, Corin, Coryn," the boy said.

"No. You see? You're mispronouncing it already. There's a subtle inflection."

"I had a friend named Coren," Hallan said.

"That's nice," Corrin said. "But my name in Corrin."

"He is dead now," Hallan said.

Corrin froze. Duran looked at the boy sympathetically.

"At least, I think he is dead," Hallan said.

"If you're not sure, always hope for the best," Corrin said. "There have been plenty of times that I could have died, and some when I should have died, but here I am."

"I will hope for the best," Hallan agreed.

"That's the spirit," Corrin said. "Optimism."

"Amazing," Duran said.

Corrin waved at the boy. "Want to see some knives?"

22

Sephor

AREN STARED AT THE hole in the wall, black and yawning. Positioned directly opposite the doorway they stood at, a dozen strides away at most. It seemed to swell and shrink with the winking of hundreds of white wax candles in row upon row atop tables lining every wall within the room. The air stank of wet clay and brittle wood. The stillness was captivating.

Redevir stood motionless beside him. Now that he had reached the end of the line, he was frozen. His muscles flexed and released, but he did not move.

Aren leaned his head through the doorway to study the wide room that separated them from the hole. The ceiling was low, but it was as wide and deep as any prayer hall he had ever seen in Amagon, supported by three rows of slender posts, whittled to resemble vines and star charts and sea spray.

He looked right. Nothing but prayer shrouds on wall hooks, stacks of unused candles, and closed doors that looked as though they had been opened less often than the span of a lifetime. He looked left. The room went on a long way. Seventy feet at least. Something caught his eye at the far end. A black shape. A man hunched over, a black coat, back bent awkwardly.

"Raviel," Aren whispered.

Raviel was fiddling with something, hurriedly working. Aren started toward him. But then he froze, Redevir nearly bumping into him. Aren could see a pair of prone legs jutting out from behind Raviel's coat. There was a *body* there underneath him.

"What are you doing?" Aren demanded. He strode across the room, anger melting his fear.

Raviel gave a start, but quickly recovered. "Oh, it is you." He did not even turn around. He went back to his work. He considered Aren so inconsequential he was not even worth looking at.

"I asked you what you are doing," Aren said.

"I am completing a capture."

"What? Alone? No Stoppers?"

"*You* are out here alone," Raviel observed.

"I know. But I—"

"You should not be here," Raviel said.

"Who is that?"

"You need to leave," Raviel said.

"Who is that?"

"What should we do, Aren?" Redevir asked.

"Tell me what you are doing with that man," Aren said.

Raviel put a cork back in a slender oval bottle, and tucked it into his coat.

Tinwood leaf tea. He is dosing him.

"Leave it alone, boy."

"No. I need to know. I need to know what is going on." He paused. "Is that...Is that the assassin?"

Raviel snorted a laugh.

"Is that him?" Aren asked. He raised the Jecker monocle to his eyes. Blue filter engaged. The core color of the afterglow hovering around the prone man's fingertips was pale orange, like the color of peaches. It was him. A little man in the corner of a room full of candles. That was the person Aren had come a thousand miles to find. *And now here he is. Already captured. Over and done.*

"You do not need to be here. This is a done thing. Leave. Go back." He gestured with a shake of his head.

"What about the girls, Raviel?"

"What girls?"

"The ones he kidnapped."

He chuckled. "Oh yes, we must not forget about those."

"What in all hells is that supposed to mean?" Aren took a step forward.

Raviel went back to his task. "It means you still have your head in the sand."

"I will call the Lamani. I will tell them what you are doing."

"You are a fool boy. You know less than nothing. Run home."

"I will not." Aren folded his arms. "Enough riddles, Raviel. Tell me what you are doing or so help me I will bring Donnovar here to rain down hell on you."

Raviel shook his head. "This man is going to tell me where he is."

"Where *who* is?" Aren asked.

"The only one that matters." Raviel glanced over one shoulder, looking at Aren for the first time. "Who do you think we are tracing?"

"An assassin."

"No. We are tracing Kinraigan."

"Kinraigan." The name tumbled out of Aren's mouth like a stone. "I don't understand."

"Of course not. You are a tool, nothing more. The Lord Protector would not explain himself to a hammer, or a chisel. Why would you be any different?"

"Because I..."

"Because you are special? Because you are the best Glasseye? You might as well be the best saddle bag."

"So the Lord Protector sent you after Kinraigan?"

"No, I sent myself after him. You still think Lord Protector Aldarion is some trusted authority. That is why you still do not see." He worked furiously to tie the man's wrists and ankles together. "This has all been about capturing Kinraigan. Who do you think left all those dead men and women in our path? Who do you think would have the power to turn loyal men against their Captain? Who do you think has the power to bring thousands of Vul soldiers into Laman without alerting the Lamani armies? Who do you think has the power to teach them how to wrangle Ghiroergans into war animals to use in battle? Kinraigan alone. He has eluded me for ten thousand miles. But no longer. For once I know where he will be."

Aren recoiled. "Then who is that? Why am I here? Whose composite have I been tracing?"

"That is a question you may wish to ask your own Lord Protector."

"Why didn't you trust me then? Why didn't you tell me before?"

"Because I did not know who I could trust. There is so much more to this than you know."

"You thought you couldn't trust me because I work for the Lord Protector?"

"Not only that."

Aren squinted at him. "What else is there?"

"You might recognize this man," Raviel said, pointing at the unconscious man he hovered over. "Or you might not. He was a magistrate, like you. From Amagon, like you. Sent to hunt down a user, like you."

"A magistrate with magick? That doesn't exist."

"Then that must mean there are a great deal of things your Lord Protector has that do not exist."

"The Lord Protector has secret users?"

Raviel nodded. "And you will shudder to know how he obtains them."

"He has the same color as Kinraigan—orange. How is that possible?"

"This man was a mimic," Raviel said. "Chosen by Aldarion to hunt Kinraigan."

"That makes no sense. Users are the ones who employ mimics, to confuse Glasseyes on their trail, the way this one confused me. What would be the point of choosing one to send after Kinraigan? If anything, it would make *more sense* that he worked for Kinraigan."

Raviel did not bother answering. He just shook his head as he worked the man's bonds. "You have no idea."

"If this was the Lord Protector's man, then why did he try to kill him?"

"He didn't. But he is not Aldarion's man any longer."

"What is he now?"

"Now he is Kinraigan's servant."

"I don't understand."

"Did anyone ever tell you why Kinraigan is so dangerous?"

"I know all about him."

"No, you don't. You think you do. They all do. But none of you understand. Your thoughts and memorials only ever think of the destruction he causes. Kinraigan is one of the most powerful users in the world, ruthless, creative, and patient. He is able to pull thousands of streams. Perhaps tens of thousands. *The mind* to be able to do that. But it is not only the power of destruction that he has mastered, it is also the power of *persuasion*."

"You mean how he talks?"

"He seduces everyone who is sent after him. Assassins hunting him become his servants. Amagonian crossbowmen, Lenagonian cutthroats, ebon-shrouds from the southern Dark, Lamani Greycloaks, dread giants of Naphesus, Lissarian dolar-swords, watchmen, librarians, users, men, women, children. Even Glasseyes are not immune."

"No one can turn me," Aren said defiantly.

"All of those have said the same." Raviel turned to look at him over his shoulder, his sunken eyes twin gulfs of darkness. "You don't know at all. You really don't. None of you Amagon-men know the truth about the most disastrous trace in the history of your nation."

"I already know the Render Tracer Corps hunted him three years ago. He killed so many of my kind. My mentor, the man who should be here with me now, traced him. But he escaped. He was uncatchable."

Raviel snickered, little laughter like a scrape on leather. "Uncatchable. He had inside help."

Aren stopped short. He tried to breathe, but it felt like no air came in. "Help."

"He had one conversation with Lord Protector Aldarion. Just one. That was all it took."

Aren narrowed his eyes, his mouth bent with loathing. "All it took to *what?*"

"To turn the Lord Protector."

Aren felt his heart drop. "That makes no sense."

"He stood face to face with him. Spoke his words. And in a single conversation he convinced the Lord Protector to let him go. The Lord Protector warned Kinraigan in time for him to slaughter your fellow Render Tracers and escape. He convinced Aldarion that he could give him something better than his own hide as a trophy. He promised him limitless power. That is what Kinraigan does. He does not bewitch people. He threatens to give them the thing they want most in the world. The Lord Protector's greatest wish was to *be* Kinraigan."

"You lie."

"So he gave him that, gave him the promise of a way in."

"Way in to what?"

Raviel did not answer. "It was only the day you and I first met that they turned against each other, when that conversation finally wore off. Now here we are."

"You are a liar."

"You need to leave. Turn around. Go back to Donnovar. I will be back there shortly."

"I can't leave," Aren said. "I have to know."

"Look, Aren," Redevir hissed. He yanked on Aren's arm so hard he was surprised he did not pull it off. "There. On the floor. There."

Aren saw it. A sliver of light. Metal reflecting the glow from the candles. It was the shape of a dagger in its sheath.

"It is real," Redevir said.

"It is just a knife," Aren told himself. "It has to be."

"Your trace was following the same path. He was coming here for a reason. What other reason could there be?"

"What is that knife on the floor?" Aren asked.

"Nothing," Raviel said. "Why do you care?"

"Is that a Sephor?"

"There is no such thing. All that matters was that this fool believed there is. That is how I knew they would come here. His cult believes this superstition."

"Let me see it," Aren said.

"No. Leave. You do not need to be here."

Redevir started forward. "Aren. This is my dream. I need that Dagger."

"Stay back," Raviel warned. But then his eyes widened. He looked past Aren.

Aren's heart stopped. He turned to look over his shoulder. He heard footsteps echoing behind him, coming from the domed chamber.

Shaot! We have been caught. The Lamani. How will I explain this?

But the men who filed into the room were not Lamani. They were Amagonmen. And the last of them was someone Aren *recognized.*

"Terrol?"

He wore his finest Inner Guard blues, the badges of a Listener and a Questioner pinned to his breast.

Raviel turned and stood, bent back as straight as he could make it, twisted arm hanging by his side. His eyes moved from man to man.

"Terrol," Aren said. "What are *you* doing here?"

"I would tread lightly if I were you, Aren," Terrol said. "The ice is thin beneath your feet."

"Who are these people? Where did they come from?"

"I had us followed," Terrol said.

Corrin was right. "You *knew* about this?"

"I had to keep it secret, so Raviel would not suspect."

"Suspect what?" Aren asked.

"That I brought *my own* Stoppers," Terrol said.

Aren's jaw fell open. "*You* did? Why do *you* need Stoppers?"

"For him," Terrol said, gesturing at Raviel. "For the user. For the assassin."

Aren felt the blood drain out of his face.

"What is going on, Aren?" Redevir asked.

"It can't be," Aren said. "Raviel? No. It can't be him. He was—"

"With us the whole time," Terrol said. "What better place to hide than among the people sent to chase him?"

"Raviel is a user?" Aren said. *A user is a liar. A user who hides what he is from us is a rogue user. Rogue users deserve to burn.*

"He is," Terrol said.

Reality shattered. Aren's life careened off a cliff and was obliterated on the rocks below. *How could I have missed it? No one is that careful. Users can never stop using. That power is addictive. The only way to stop using is to die. And everyone makes a mistake eventually.* "I would have known," he said. "I would have seen it. No. It would have matched. I should have been able to see it."

"He tricked Donnovar," Terrol said. "He tricked you. He used us to bring him here."

For the Dagger. That must be why they came here. It was all lies. All of it. Kinraigan. The Lord Protector. Everything. He was manipulating me.

Raviel stood very still. His hands balled into fists at his side. His eyes bounced to each person in the room, one at a time, then started over. "This is a mistake," he said.

"The only mistake was trusting you," Terrol said. "One now remedied."

"I will not let you take me," Raviel said.

Terrol smiled. "Go ahead. Try."

Raviel stared hard. His teeth clenched until Aren thought he could hear them grinding.

But nothing happened.

The Stoppers have his streams. He is interdicted.

Aren imagined how it would happen. Raviel submits, drinks the tea, and the tension dissolves, and Aren could go back to the way things were.

But Raviel did not submit. He leapt toward one of the Stoppers.

Aren took a step forward.

Redevir slipped past him toward the Dagger. Aren turned to stop him, but it was too late. The Rover thrust himself into the crowded space. He collided with one of the Stoppers. Aren tripped and fell to his knees. Visions of Degammon flashed before his eyes. He wanted to leave. He wanted to get out of this room. He wanted to leave it behind and never look back at it ever again. But his legs refused to move.

Raviel smiled. He cut through the air with one hand. An invisible object of incredible mass and velocity flew from his hand. Aren could not see the blank impulse, but he could see air distorting around it.

He found streams!

It struck one of the other Stoppers in the chest. Cracked his sternum to splinters and ripped its way through his heart and out through his ribs. The shockwave and the sight of it were a one-two mule-kick to Aren's heart. He clutched at his chest involuntarily.

Aren turned to look at the first Stopper. *Take it. Take the stream!* The Stopper rose to his feet. He regained the stream. Raviel was instantly denied the render he had just used.

But Aren's relief was short lived.

Raviel had just killed *another* Stopper. That meant a *different* stream was now lost, which had been interdicting *another* set of Raviel's renders.

Shaot!

Raviel opened his palms, unrolling his fingers like flags unfurling.

Twin *shapes* appeared, each a meter wide, as thin as razors and with the force of a boulder behind them. They raced out from his hands.

They each caught one of Terrol's men, slicing them in half at the waist. Blood erupted like a volcano, pouring crimson across the floor. Torsos dropped, legs flailed. The blood was everywhere. Aren slipped in it, fell to his knees. Scrambled to get out of it, his palms turning red. Sparkling silver afterglow belched into the air above him. The shapes flew until they struck the far wall, biting into the stone, churning the air with a fog of stone chips and dust.

Redevir edged his way around until he stood directly over the Dagger.

Terrol swung his sword in tight arcs, trying to keep the point in Raviel's face.

Yes, distraction is key. Disrupt his focus.

Terrol for a moment looked like he would have the upper hand.

But then Aren felt his flesh crawl. He smelled a hideous sweet algae odor. The air rippled around Raviel, and an invisible shape radiated off of him. It was a giant rectangular wall. It floated toward Terrol, forcing him away, sweeping him and his Stoppers back. It was weak, likely all Raviel could manage to focus on with that sword wagging in his face. Once he had pushed them far enough away to concentrate on his killing renders again, he would cut them all in half.

You need to do something, Aren. But he did not know what to do. He did not know if he could remember how to walk. *If he can think straight for even a second, he will kill them all and me with them.*

Aren lunged from his hands and knees. He wrapped his arms around Raviel's leg and twisted. The motion took him by surprise. Raviel bowed, lost balance, wobbled. Tried to kick Aren off, but Aren held tight, pulling Raviel with him.

Raviel's legs buckled. He toppled.

It was enough. He was pushed beyond his break point. His next renders died before he could create them.

Terrol drew a knife from a sheath under his arm. He reached in and drove it into Raviel's ribs. Raviel hissed and shrieked and rocked back and forth.

Aren cried out, holding onto the leg for dear life as Raviel tried to roll over and over. Terrol stabbed him in the shoulder and belly. He drove the knife home again, and again, and again. He stabbed Raviel ten times. Then twenty.

Raviel stopped moving after the twenty-third.

He stopped breathing after the twenty-seventh.

Aren let go. He rolled over onto his back, coughing and wheezing. His heart was racing. He thought it might birth itself out through his ribs. He could not feel his hands or feet, and so much sweat rolled down his scalp he thought his head was underwater. He rolled onto his side and struggled to his knees. He crawled. He dipped his hands into the sacred fountain in the corner of the room. He ignored the effigy of the god whose shrine he was desecrating. He did not care. He had to get the blood off him.

"I suspected him from the beginning," Terrol said to the back of Aren's head. "I smuggled my Stoppers among the camp followers, waiting until I had unearthed enough evidence to move on him."

"What are you talking about?" Aren asked. "What evidence?"

"Raviel left his possessions alone at the way-station in Westgate. I was able to search his papers. Private letters."

"What does his private life have to do with any of this?"

"It was not what he kept to himself. It was what he shared with *others*. Namely *Sarker*."

Aren stopped swishing his hands through the water. He glanced back over his shoulder. "He was corresponding with Sarker?"

"Does that surprise you?"

"Sarker never wrote to anyone. As long as I have known him. Unless he kept it from me."

"He kept a lot of things from a lot of people," Terrol said. "Sarker and Raviel were in league with each other. Sarker had stolen one of our composites and delivered a copy to someone *outside of Amagon*."

Punishable by death, Aren thought. *Sarker was tempting fate*.

"He had dozens of letters from parties who are known to belong to a spy network. The verbiage seems very...cozy."

"What?" *Sarker, why? Working with a rogue user? How could you?*

"The documents Raviel possessed claimed him to be an official from distant *Tyrelon*. He was not from Lenagon at all. He was an impostor. It is therefore obvious he was the ringleader of the plot by users to assassinate the Lord Protector. And Sarker was helping him do it."

Aren's head was spinning. "Sarker? No. Impossible. We hunted users. He had since before I was born. I would have known. I would have seen some sign."

"Raviel was very clever," Terrol said. "No one knew where he was the night Balthoren attacked. He slipped out into the city and waited for us to step into his trap. You were there. You accused Raviel yourself. He wanted control of our men for his own purposes."

"Why did Raviel alert the Lord Protector to the plot?" Aren asked. "He warned Aldarion. Why ruin his own plan? He was standing in the room with me, with the Lord Protector. Why not kill Aldarion when he was alone with him if that was his goal?"

"It doesn't matter," Terrol said. "All that matters is that he was the one, and we stopped him."

That doesn't make sense. And Terrol does not know how to read an imprint. Something doesn't add up.

Aren held the Jecker monocle in the palm of one hand, and every time Terrol turned away, he flipped it up to his eyes to search the wealth of residuals. He studied Raviel and the air around him. He brought out the Oscillatrix.

Raviel's residuals were easy to discern, but the primary values of his afterglow were far higher than the composite of the assassin. No backward masking. Aren looked closer with the blue filter engaged. Raviel's core residuals were a lush indigo.

Something is wrong.

He looked up at Redevir. The Rover stood mutely in the corner. He had been laboriously trying to lower himself to his knees without anyone knowing he was reaching for the Dagger.

Terrol noticed him though. Terrol always noticed everything. His ghost of a face turned on Redevir with his Questioner's suspicion. "What are you doing there?"

"Me?" Redevir feigned innocence. "Nothing at all."

"You are trying to steal that object," Terrol said. "Do not move." He stalked over and picked it up.

Redevir looked like he was ready to scream.

Terrol stared at the Dagger mutely. "Tell me what this is."

"Just a knife," Redevir said. "Nothing more."

"Then why are you so keen to get your larcenous Rover hands on it?"

Redevir cursed under his breath.

"Who gave you the reports, Terrol?" Aren asked.

"A man at the highest level."

"Who gave you the composite for Raviel? Who gave you the imprints?"

"Someone who speaks for the Lord Protector."

"Who?"

"Margol."

Aren's mouth fell open. "Does everyone know about this? Did you people lie to my face this entire time? Was I told the truth about anything?"

"No more so than Terrol was," a voice said behind him.

Aren spun around. *Who in all the hells can creep so quiet?*

It was the man himself, Margol, wearing a leather vest over a red tunic.

He was not alone, accompanied by a dozen men in ash-white cloaks. They immediately spread throughout the room, moving around and behind Terrol's men. The Stoppers reacted nervously, unsure of what was happening.

"Margol," Terrol said, as if he was trying to whisper across the room. "You should not be here. We discussed this."

Margol scanned the room, eyes attending every detail. He shook his head. "I told you to move on him sooner."

"It doesn't matter. Done is done."

Margol nodded. "It is. It certainly is."

"Why are you here?" Terrol asked.

"I told you," Margol said. "You should have done it back in Westgate. Why didn't you just do it there? Why didn't you do it?"

"Who are these men with you?" Terrol asked.

"I really wish you had just done as you were told," Margol said. "You were supposed to have stopped him sooner. I told you to move weeks ago."

"Why do you keep saying that?" Terrol asked.

"He should never have made it to this place," Margol said. "Now this becomes difficult."

Aren looked back and forth between them. *What is going on?*

"Explain," Terrol said.

"Because now your people have seen it," Margol said.

"Seen what?" Terrol asked.

"Your people were not supposed to know about it," Margol said. "No one was. Now there are loose ends."

"What are you talking about, Margol?" Aren asked. "What is going on here?"

Redevir put a hand on Aren's elbow. "He knows. He knows what it is. He is going to kill us."

"You don't know anything, Redevir," Aren whispered back. "They know each other."

Margol marched across the room toward Terrol. He reached for the Dagger.

Terrol raised his sword slightly, the point hovering at thigh level, making Margol stop.

What are they doing? They are not really going to fight. They can't.

"Seen *what*, Margol?" Terrol asked.

Margol pointed at the Dagger.

"This? This little nothing object? We will take it to Donnovar."

"No," Margol said. "We will not."

"Excuse me?" Terrol raised his sword.

"No one is going to Donnovar with that," Margol said.

"You have no authority to stop me," Terrol said.

"Yet I am. I *am* stopping you."

Everyone stood still. Only their eyes seemed to flicker, like the endless banks of candles. *Something is wrong here. I have to stop this.* But Aren did not know what to do, or who to side with. *All of us serve the same master.*

"That object is the purpose of this entire expedition," Margol said. "That neither of you understand that yet is why this has to happen."

Terrol opened his mouth to speak.

Just as his lips parted, Margol lashed out so quickly that his fingers were already wrapping around Terrol's sword hand before Terrol even sounded the first syllable.

Margol snapped two of his fingers. The sword fell. He yanked on the fingers, pulled Terrol forward, drove his other elbow into Terrol's throat.

Terrol coughed blood. He staggered, clutching his neck with both hands.

Margol picked up Terrol's sword and then ran it through his belly as nonchalantly as if he was leaning a broom against a wall.

Terrol's eyes rolled back. He tipped over on his side and died, his own sword sticking up out of him.

Aren stood frozen, unable to accept what his eyes told him was true. He had seen men torn apart by invisible magick. Yet this stilled him.

Terrol's men were paralyzed with fright.

Margol turned and nodded to the men in the ash cloaks. They did not move. But Aren felt a prickling on his neck. He saw the air warping around dozens of unreal objects flying invisibly through the air. His sight narrowed to tunnel vision.

Blank impulses.

They are users! All of them!

Terrol's men were riddled with impacts, snapping their bones and punching holes in their flesh. Blood sprayed the floor in wet slaps.

Aren nearly pissed himself. *What in the name of all gods is happening?* He ducked. He did not know why. If one of those invisible shapes was aimed at him he would never be able to dodge it. He ducked anyway.

Some of them punched holes in Raviel's body. And some hit the prone mimic, tearing him to pieces.

Aren looked at Redevir. The Rover's eyes were locked on the Dagger, resting beside Terrol's body.

Don't try it, Rover. It is not worth it.

Redevir tried it anyway.

As Aren made for the wall, trying to hide himself beneath the tables of candles, Redevir lunged for the Dagger, sliding on hands and knees under Margol's swinging arm, dodging a kick, and leaning out of reach of an errant elbow.

He barely managed to get his fingers around the hilt by the time Margol caught up with him. Redevir snared it in one hand like the claw of an eagle closing around a juicy field rat. He scooped it up and tucked it into his vest, sheath and all, but Margol brought his hand down on Redevir's neck, delivering a blow that crumpled him to the floor, his hands reaching to cover his head. The Dagger thumped back out onto the ground.

Margol grabbed Redevir by the cuffs, dragged him off balance, and threw him across the room. The Rover crashed into the table Aren hid behind, shaking dust loose. Redevir swept his hand across a row of candles. The wax splashed across Margol's face. He grunted, moving his hands to scrape it from his eyes.

Redevir took the opportunity and jumped at him, drove his heel down into Margol's ankle. Margol dropped to one knee, but only for an instant. He pushed back up, tucked his shoulder into Redevir's gut, lifted him off the ground, and slammed him flat on his back.

Shaot. Aren crawled out from under the tables. "Wait! Don't hurt him." He drew his sword. *What am I going to do with this?* He couldn't remember the last time he had swung it at anything.

Margol turned to look at him. "You should not have come here. Now you have made this worse." He waved off his cadre of users with a flick of his hand. They stood still, waiting.

Aren's eyes watered. "What are you doing? Why? Terrol is dead. You *killed* him. What have you done?"

"Terrol dead, Raviel dead. None of that matters."

"Raviel was an outlander. *Terrol* was Inner Guard."

"Doesn't matter."

"I'm warning you." Aren held his sword up, pointing the blade at Margol.

Margol slapped the flat of the blade aside with his palm before Aren could even see his hand move. He punched Aren hard in the gut. Aren dropped like a rock, his sword skittering harmlessly away. He struggled to catch his breath, his eyes flooded with flashes. He hovered on his knees, leaning forward cupping his belly. He nearly choked on the sudden pain and confusion.

Margol leaned down until their faces were almost touching. He smiled. He patted Aren on the back. "There, young man. You can stay right there." He stepped back and regarded him.

Aren sucked air, pain splitting his sides. He could barely spit out a word per breath. "This...is...crazy."

"This is the part where you are going to start to wonder why I don't kill you," Margol said. "Good. That's good. The answer is that both of our lives will be better if you just go along with this."

"Go...along...with what?"

"I am taking the Dagger," Margol said. "That is why we are here."

"We are here on a trace," Aren said. "We are here for *him*." He pointed at the body.

"You think all these soldiers were sent here for one man?"

"He tried to kill the Lord Protector."

"He said you wouldn't fall for it," Margol said. "He told me you were too bright. But I knew you would. I knew that once we put a killer in front of you, you wouldn't be able to look up from the trail once to see what was really happening."

"What are you saying?"

"Five hundred men sent to the Great King as a *favor*? Hah! We are here for this Dagger. Raviel told us what it can do, and how to find it."

"*Raviel* told you?"

"Why do you think Aldarion gave him authority over Donnovar? It was worth having to deal with Raviel for a time."

"But I thought Raviel tried to kill him. Terrol said..."

"Terrol was just as bad as you. It was easy to convince him Raviel was the enemy. Terrol is suspicious of everyone."

"Then whose composite have I been carrying all this way?" *And why did it still lead me here? What are you leaving out you piece of shit?*

"It was just some user from a deal the Lord Protector was running down by the docks."

"No, that can't be. I traced from that composite all this way."

"There was no assassin. No one made it past our security that night. That *composite* we gave you was of the man who tried to make the deal. It was what we had. Just because he happened to be there."

"You falsified the Inner Guard reports," Aren said.

"Of course. Terrol wouldn't let it go. If he kept digging into the story he would have discovered the truth. We gave him something else to find in its place. Don't you see? There never was an assassin. But it put everything in motion. The Councils suspended, you and Terrol put on the path we chose, the Lamani opening their doors to us, all of it."

"Did he really massacre a whole village? Were the kidnapped girls real or just a story?"

"Who cares?"

"Why would Raviel give *you* the Dagger?" Redevir asked. "It's priceless."

"That fool. All he wanted was safe passage to Laman, away from the prying eyes of the Priests in Olbaran."

"You betrayed Raviel," Aren said.

"Raviel could have connected us to the Dagger. He should have been dead for weeks now. Terrol was supposed to be sitting complacent in the camp right now, counting in his head the accolades he would receive when we returned to Amagon. Then I would have been here to collect the object alone."

"Donnovar will not just ignore the fact that Terrol is gone."

"He will learn that he died trying to capture Raviel. He won't dig too deep for Terrol. He would for *you* though. He would put his nose in this if anything happened to you. That is why I am trying not to kill you. If you make me kill you, just know I will have to kill him next."

"I will tell him what happened."

"That is not how this is going to work. You are either going to go along with the story, or Donnovar is going to die."

Aren gritted his teeth. "You can't do that. You can do a lot of things, but you can't do that."

"Look around you. See these users? They are Palantari. Trained assassins. They obey my commands. If I give the word that is exactly what they will do. With the Lord Protector's blessing."

"Where did you find Palantari users in Laman?"

"Aldarion made a deal with the eldest Prince of Palantar before we ever left Amagon. We finance the mobilization of his armies, and he makes it certain that I walk out of here with that Dagger in my possession." He gestured at his array of Palantari users.

"You lied to the Great King. You have tarnished Donnovar forever, and all of Amagon. If the Great King finds out what you did we could all be sentenced to death. Donnovar will likely kill you himself when he finds out."

"He had best not find out. Otherwise Donnovar will not remain alive to contradict me. He will be dead at the hands of my Palantari friends, and all will be blamed on Laman. I already have documents with Aldarion's seal which will allow me to assume full command of this battalion if anything happens to Donnovar. This is what Amagon needs. This is the future. Don't stand in the way of this."

Aren was stunned. He couldn't breathe. *Could it be true?* That meant Raviel was telling the truth. *What the fuck did I do?* "Aldarion lied to me."

"Now be a good boy and go along," Margol said. "Let me have the Rover. You don't even know him. There is still a way for all of us to come out of this. We will make a triumphant return. Me, you, Donnovar. This prize will make our names for all time. The record already shows you killed the assassin back in Westgate. All you have to do is walk away from this Rover, who you know nothing about, and we can all go home. Come on. You are a Glasseye. You have no use for a blade. Kick your sword to me and we return to Amagon as heroes."

Aren looked at the blood on the floor, the pieces of what used to be men, the faint swirls of afterglow hovering above. Raviel leaking from twoscore holes. Terrol with a sword all the way through him.

A scene. One more scene for him to see and never be able to unsee.

He could go back to Amagon. He could be a hero. All he had to do was say yes. All he had to do was lie. All he had to do was quit following the trace.

But he couldn't. He couldn't make himself say it.

Redevir glanced at him nervously, understandably.

"No," Aren said.

Margol's eyes widened. He shook his head. "I am surprised. I honestly thought you would say yes."

"He's going to kill us," Redevir said.

"I know."

Redevir slipped a hand into his vest and brought out a slender throwing knife. With a flick of the wrist, he threw it at Margol. It slapped across his hand, sticking between two fingers.

Margol shook it loose.

Aren turned to look at Redevir. The Rover was backing away, eyeing Margol's users.

There was nowhere to run. Margol did not even have to lift a finger. Users could kill as quickly as a thought. And there were so many of them standing between Aren and the way out.

It's over.

But then the entire Chapel shuddered as if an earthquake had rolled over the city.

Aren felt the liquid in his eyes vibrate. The walls creaked and the ceiling groaned. His knees felt like jelly. The swirling clouds of shimmering multicolored particles shook. Aren bent over and briefly vomited. He reached out a hand to steady himself, but the wall he had expected to be there was farther away, and he tipped over.

Everyone in the room stood still, eyes everywhere, searching. Searching for what? They were only staring at blank walls and ceiling.

What was that?

Aren felt his heartbeat filling his ears. The silence pressed against his skin. He felt himself shrinking. Dust and smoke and a haze of blood misted the air. He could barely see the other side of the room.

"Someone is here," one of the Palantari users said. "I can feel—"

Before he could finish speaking, a blank impulse the size of a crabatz ball flew through the open doorway and coursed through him. It shattered his ribcage and exploded his vertebrae out in all directions. One arm was gone, and the other dangled on sinew. The head leaned over until it was touching the waist.

Aren grabbed Redevir and pulled him back against the near bay of candles. *We have to get out of here!*

A lone man walked through the only door, hood drawn, wearing a cloak that could have been green or brown. He was hunched over, like a crippled old man, incredibly tall, but Aren could see nothing of his face or even his hands within the cloak. He crossed to the center of the room and stood there.

Aren and Redevir dropped and crawled under the tables.

Margol waved a hand to his Palantari. They all dipped into the Slipstream and began to bind. They sent a hundred blank impulses at the cloaked man. They all collided with an invisible square shield he had created. Aren could hear the loud pops as each of them struck.

He responded with blank spheres of his own, with modest mass, but a speed so far beyond what Aren could comprehend. They roared across the room, quicker than a blink, louder than a scream.

The spheres peppered the Palantari users. They had their own shields, but the force of those projectiles overcame half of them, bowing them inward, ripping through them, hitting bodies, vaporizing fascia and pulverizing bone.

The shockwaves of the many impacts buffeted Aren like waves smashing against a ship. The candles were blown out. He tipped over into the wall. The tables rattled above him.

Margol fell on his back.

Aren and Redevir clung to the wall like moss, hoping to be so far under the tables that no one would notice. Crawling along, from one table, to the next one, and the next, pulling Redevir along. Four more tables and they would be at the door. He glanced to his left. They passed the cloaked man and kept going.

"Who in all hells is that?" Redevir asked.

"Shut up!" Aren hissed. He scrambled on hands and knees beneath the tables.

The remaining Palantari users counterattacked with barrages of their own blank impulses. Each impact sucked Aren's breath out of his lungs, until he thought he might suffocate before he could get away.

Three more tables. Two. One.

Aren popped out from under the last table.

Margol looked up and saw him. His mouth twisted into a snarl. He started toward them. But then another series of impacts shook the air. Margol crawled toward a sluice near the fountain and slithered away.

Aren went through the door. He flew out of the room, and crossed the Chapel so quickly he could not even remember doing it.

He was not even sure if Redevir was still behind him until he heard his voice.

"Run!" Redevir screamed.

Aren leapt free and tore out of the Chapel, Redevir following him closely. "We have to make it to Donnovar," Aren shouted. "We don't have enough protection to stop that many users."

"Who was that other one?" Redevir said. "Who was helping us?"

"I don't know. Doesn't matter. Won't be long in this world. No one can stand in a sustained user's duel against that many."

"Keep running. Margol will be hot after us when he realizes I have this." He lifted the Dagger out of his vest.

"You have it? I thought I saw it fall on the ground."

"A dummy. I switched it with one of mine."

Aren moved fast. He took blind turns. He ran through trees and under arches and finally found the Bridge of Taris and crossed it. He and Redevir reached the hall, and barreled through the doors, nearly stunning an Outer Guard sergeant off his feet.

"Donnovar!" Aren shouted.

Corrin looked up. He reached for one of the knives that sat on his lap. All the others clattered to the floor as he stood.

"What is it?" the Captain asked. "You look awful."

"We have to leave." Aren coughed out the words. His chest heaved as he fought vainly to catch his breath. The flesh over his ribs was bruised and swollen, stinging with each inhale.

"Is the city attacked?"

"It's Margol," Aren said.

"Where is he? Where is Margol? I've been looking all over."

"He betrayed us," Aren said. "He tried to kill me."

"What?!" Donnovar asked.

"Raviel is dead!" Aren said. "Terrol is dead!"

"What?" Donnovar asked.

"Margol killed him," Aren said.

"That's absurd," Donnovar said. "Why would he...?"

"Listen!" Aren screamed. "He used us. Aldarion used us to get him here. He was after some relic. Everything was a lie. We aren't supposed to get back alive. He has Palantari assassins. He has already ordered them to kill you."

Hayles had been sharpening one of his *somashalks*, but he set it down and rose to his feet, eyes as narrow and deadly as one of the fine blades. His mouth quivered in anger, trying to spread into a grimace, but his Sarenwalker training kept his lips flat, preventing any emotion from manifesting physically.

"They could be around us already," Redevir advised.

"Kill me?" Donnovar asked again. "Where is he now?"

"I don't know. He was after us. He may be coming here now."

The other Sarenwalkers stood rigid. Their eyes spoke loudly. Their love of their Captain was without limit. They were prepared to kill Margol on sight.

"I simply can't believe it," Donnovar said.

"Believe it," Redevir said. "He tried to kill me. He tried to kill Aren."

"Margol brought Palantari assassins to Synsirok," Aren said. "They are coming to kill you. Users. They slaughtered Terrol's people. They were using magick to kill just now!"

"Margol is loose in the city now," Redevir added. "There's no telling when his assassins will strike, or what he will say to the Andristi here."

"What are your orders, my Captain?" Hayles asked.

Donnovar stared at the Sarenwalker, then looked at Aren. He whistled out a breath. "Keep a guard out for Margol. Treat him like a Vul."

"We cannot stay here." Redevir said. "They will come for us."

"Erethion is not here," Aren agreed. "The Andristi in Synsirok do not know us beyond the writs of passage we carry. If we put distance between us and this place it will give them time for their own people to put a stop to Margol."

"It is still light out," Hayles observed. "I can guide us out of here."

"Vuls still wander the woods," Donnovar argued. "We will be more vulnerable without the Andristi about. It is almost night. What do I tell our hosts? We are guests here."

"Those Palantari users could be coming as we speak," Redevir repeated.

"We should move," Aren said. He was driven by his fear, and driven by the Sephor. He saw it, knew it was real. He and Redevir had it. He would not let it go. "We can regroup in Cair Tiril. Solathas is there. The Palantari users would not dare go there." All he could hear was his heartbeat thumping in his ears. *Go. Run. Never stop moving.*

Donnovar turned to Aren. "Aren, what do you advise?"

Aren took a long breath. "We are sitting ducks here. We should go."

Donnovar looked deep into his eyes. "Are you certain?"

Aren swallowed hard. His head was swimming in memories of blood and afterglow. He felt like he was upside down. "I'm certain."

Donnovar turned immediately to his sergeants. "Make haste," he said, without a tinge of doubt. "We leave now."

23

Annihilation

AREN COULD NOT HELP thinking he was wrong.

But he could not stop shuddering to think clearly. He tried so many times to reach his malagayne. Just a little. Just to clear his head. Just to hide the agony for a moment so that he could see in front of his eyes. All he could see now was the image of Raviel dying, and Terrol dying, and a dozen others with them. All he could hear were voices telling him Sarker was a mirage, and the Lord Protector was a liar. All he could feel was ringing in his ears and acid in his belly from the shockwaves.

They lied to me. They all lied to me. All his memories were ruined, tainted. Underneath every trace, every capture, was the fact that he had been standing beside someone he never really knew. And he would never have the chance to ask him why. All the smiles and congratulations the Lord Protector had ever given him had been a fraud. *He sent me to fail. He was ready to let me die for his secret.*

And that was not the worst of it. The worst part was that he had no idea. Had. No. Idea. None. *I should have seen it. How could I not have seen it?*

He slapped his fingers against his forehead as his horse guided itself along with the other riders of the Outer Guard. *Why did I tell Donnovar to flee? Why did I do this? Did I make him do this because I was afraid?*

They were packed and on their horses by sunset, riding down the arched ways to the eastern edge of the city, slipping out toward the Fields of Syn. There were no Lamani officials to see them off. Donnovar merely had to waive his passes to the city sentries and they streamed out into the woods of Synsiros.

Hayles led them effortlessly through the trees. *Sarenwalkers were made for this.* But even with such dependable guides, the men looked about themselves nervously. Dusk was upon them already, and even Aren felt like the trees were closing in around him.

They emerged from the woods into a wide plain, and the pace quickened dramatically over the unrestricted bowl of lush grass ringed with trees, like a black ocean as the sunlight died on the horizon.

These were the Fields of Syn, the most sacred place to the Andristi, where the dancing moon festival had been held since before the Andristi *were* the Andristi, when they were just tribes and loose-knit clans. This was a holy place for them, where the Father came down from the heavens and the Mother up from the earth, and bestowed sacraments upon all who came to witness it.

For all its beauty, it was eerily still. The moons were both up and the blue and silver light seemed unbearably bright. He felt conspicuous, looking over his shoulder over and over. The hooting of the evening owls faded, leaving only the breath of the wind in his ears. He felt no better than he had in the thick tangle of branches.

Please let us make it out of here. Just a quick night march and the sun would rise and they would be back on the safe route to Cair Tiril. A week of march, less even, and they would be back at the White City. If they could get back to Solathas, there would be no Palantari user that would be a threat to them.

He felt a prickling on his neck, and knew that something was wrong.

Arrows fell abruptly from above. They rose and dropped from the sky like diving birds, almost invisible, but for the shine of moonlight reflecting off the arrowheads. They plunged like sharp black raindrops through mail and hide. The Outer Guard fell from their horses in droves. Aren watched with horror as dozens of them collapsed with arrows jutting from their plated chests, necks, arms, and thighs.

The silence was blasted away by the shouts of orders from the sergeants. Horses screamed and some faltered, going to their knees or laying flat. Their riders cried out and slid from their saddles, crumpling lifeless to the ground. Men turned around on their mounts, looking for the direction of the attack.

The arrows seemed to come from every direction.

Aren heard growls from the sergeants coaxing men into lines for a charge, but the hail of arrows was thick, relentless. Men started forward, then stalled as their mounts fell screaming.

Even before the hail finally ceased, Vuls charged from the trees. Aren watched as they crashed into the deteriorating defense of the Outer Guard. The supply carts were overturned and set ablaze, the cooks slaughtered. The archers scrambled for better vantage for their own bows, but it was useless. They were thrust into the fray, surrounded, separated, massacred.

"What do we do?!" Aren shouted.

"Ride!" Corrin screamed. "We can't stay here."

"I know!" He prodded his horse forward, when suddenly it went out from under him. He fell, slamming his head into the earth. His body spasmed as his sore stomach slapped against the ground. His nose filled instantly with watery grey mud. The horse whinnied like a shrieking rabbit, thrashing his legs as arrows thumped into his hide. It kicked violently against Aren's arms as he tugged his tracer satchel from the saddle rigging and looped the strap up over his shoulder.

He clung to the ground. He heard whistling arrows and thumping hooves, and all he could smell was stagnant moisture and wet leather. He could see only the legs of horses and men about him, but above their heads he made out one of Donnovar's lieutenants, Sebel, holding the orange banner of the Outer Guard aloft to rally scores of the Guard to him. Aren watched them moving away to his right and felt a surge of hope as they gathered speed, but the charge faltered. Horses slipped in the mud. Some slowed, others took to the charge too quickly. The line rippled, and then disintegrated into a multitude of individual combats. The banner drooped below his angle of vision. The lieutenant slumped forward, his mount lurching awkwardly. The men around him, unable to hold solid lines, were separated and forced into melee.

Any still mounted fled toward the shelter of the woods, but none made it that Aren could see. The others backed toward the center, attempting valiantly to hold defensive lines. The Outer Guard killed many Vuls, but more came, and more, until the Fields of Syn were a whirling vortex of utter chaos, with shadow shapes hacking at each other in the dark.

A series of moments.

Horrible moments.

Something came out of the trees. Many things. Slippery things. Enormous things. Aren's nightmares came alive—hulking beasts, each four feet taller than a man, skin slick with glistening slime. Their slanted heads looked out from atop distended bellies, shuddering as they moved. The eyes were large and lidless, and utterly indifferent.

What in all hells am I seeing?

They lumbered into the fray, swatting Amagonian soldiers with enormous webbed fingers. They snapped bones with the lightest touch of their hands. They snatched men by the shoulders, biting through leather and mail, tearing into the necks and bellies of the horrified Outer Guard.

Ghiroergans? The Greycloaks had been right. *Gods high and low.*

Aren rose on hands and knees and vomited at the sight. He scurried away from the Vuls, but the mud clung to his palms, making it nearly impossible to retrieve his sword.

A Vul closed in on him.

Aren launched himself to his feet. His hand found the hilt, drew his sword, slashed across the unprotected neck. Somehow he hit something. The Vul clutched his shoulder and ran on past him.

Aren wheeled around to see Donnovar, unhorsed but still shouting orders to his men. The Sarenwalkers made a ring about him that refused the Vuls entry, their green cloaks turning black in the absence of the sun. Their arms flew with lightning speed and dizzying accuracy, cutting and stabbing the Vuls to pieces.

He saw nothing of Corrin or Reidos. They were gone, lost in the darkness. Tanashri had vanished, but Aren could see Redevir not ten paces distant. "Redevir," he called. "We're surrounded."

"Gather as many as you can," the Rover said. "We must break through now or we're finished."

Aren looked around, but there was no one near him to rally. The enemy were everywhere all at once, surrounding and separating the small groups of men who managed to stay together through the hail of arrows. Soldiers struck each other in the dark, mistaking their comrades for Vuls.

He saw a sudden flash of blinding fire. A dozen Vuls were drenched in flame. They flailed and screeched in agony as their skin was melted away by fire.

It was Inrianne. Aren recognized the bright white of her gown shining through dozens of soldiers. He ran toward her, dodging swinging swords and axes.

He fought through the echoes of pain in his skull, forcing his legs to take each step. His battered torso revolted at every movement he made. One Vul warrior came at him, waving an axe above his head. Aren ducked low, and the Vul passed on away from him and was gone.

He caught Inrianne by the sleeve, tearing it, but getting her attention. She turned to him, her eyes wide with fear. "Come on!" he cried. "This way!" She followed without question.

He pulled her toward where he had last seen Donnovar. He was the greatest fighter in all of Amagon. If they were to get out of here, he was their best chance. A handful of the Outer Guard joined them as they ran. None had their spears, or even helmets. They were only running wildly to escape.

Aren saw another group of the Vuls erupt into flames. Inrianne somehow had enough concentration to be leveling the fire of her magick at them as she ran. But even if the chaos did not distract her, it would not last. Whether she could throw her fire five more times or fifty, sooner or later every user reaches their core limit.

Aren saw Donnovar chopping Vuls down with every swing. He threw some to the ground with a single arm. *Braxis* was a roaring beast in his hand, severing limbs with every stroke. Aren watched hands, arms, and legs flop to the earth like the pieces of dolls.

The Sarenwalkers who surrounded him deflected dozens of blows every second. They flew about like dancers. They had killed ten times their own number already, but still more and more came at them—two for every one that went down.

Aren stood still and looked around. *There's nowhere to go.* Vuls scrambled all over, and the massive Ghiroergans struggled against their own weight, lurching awkwardly through the soldiers, hammering anything that moved with their massive fists.

Redevir strained, throwing his knives as he dodged thrusts from each new attacker. The Outer Guard began to fall around him, and the Vuls rushed over them like ants, chopping and cutting the wounded to ribbons, then trampling the bodies.

Aren felt a heavy impact across his back. He dropped to his knees. Pain. He swung his sword blindly. He cut through something, but he couldn't see anything through the pounding in his skull. He hoped it wasn't one of his own. His sight was slow to return. He could barely see Donnovar looking at him.

The Captain screamed to his Sarenwalkers. "Hayles! Fainen! Protect Aren! Guard him with your lives!"

The two Sarenwalkers looked at each other briefly, and then they sprinted to Aren's side. Hayles helped Aren to his feet, as Fainen carved a great swath through the Vuls, easily battling a dozen of them at once.

Hayles looked into Aren's eyes for a sign he was all right. Aren nodded, and the Sarenwalker was off instantly to Fainen's side, letting fly his *somashalks*.

Aren turned to see Donnovar. One of the giant creatures advanced on him.

"Donnovar!" he screamed.

The Captain looked at him.

"There!" Aren cried, pointing his sword at the Ghiroergan. "Get out of there!"

It was too late. There was no time to run. The press was too thick about him. Garis, Tamlin, and Doles, the three Sarenwalkers who remained with him, could barely hold back the tide. Vuls charged with insane fury, relentless, like deadly waves crashing in a sea storm.

The Ghiroergan took Garis by the shoulder, twisting his arm from its socket. The Sarenwalker did not scream. He cut repeatedly into its hide, even as it lifted him from the ground. The thing bit into his neck, but Garis hacked at it until the last flush of blood left his torn neck.

The creature dropped him in a heap and lurched toward Donnovar. The Captain leapt away from its swaying maw, and cleaved at its outstretched arms. The beast howled, but did not cease its advance. Tamlin and Doles behind him were being beaten down by a hail of swords and spears. Donnovar pulled away from the Ghiroergan until he stood back to back with his Sarenwalkers.

"Donnovar!" Aren screamed. He tried to run to the Captain's side, but was cut off by more Vuls. Some saw him; most did not. They just ran past him, running to attack someone or flee someone, he could not tell one expression from any other. Hayles and Fainen pulled back as he went, keeping as close as they could.

The creature heaved one of its titanic arms at Donnovar. He was too close to the Sarenwalkers behind him, and a slap of the webbed fingers caught him fully in the chest. He spun around and dropped. The leather straps of his breastplate snapped at one shoulder, leaving the armor dangling awkwardly to one side.

"No!" Aren screamed. He ran between the Vuls, hacking at them, batting them away, trying to get through. Redevir was at his heels with Inrianne. Hayles and Fainen were close behind, keeping the Vuls away from them.

Aren nearly reached him, when another Ghiroergan loomed up before him. It slobbered and drooled on itself, and stared into him with indifferent eyes. Aren slammed to a halt, but he slid in the mud, falling over backward. The creature towered over him. He grasped furiously for his sword, but it was nowhere to be found.

The Ghiroergan reached for his throat, but suddenly Fainen was there, bounding over him. The Sarenwalker seemed as though he was suspended in the air, his blade a threatening barb aimed at the chest of the hulking thing.

Fainen came down on it, and planted his feet on its thighs. His blade entered its chest with all the force of his momentum. It passed through the thick jelly skin and disappeared to the hilt in the creature's body. A flood of thick ochre blood oozed from the wound, and flowed like the sap of a tree down its abdomen. The Ghiroergan flapped its arms and released a pitiful whine from its rubbery mouth. Fainen withdrew his blade quickly, but was knocked aside by a waving arm.

Hayles flew over the other Sarenwalker, and chopped with such intensity into the knees and stomach of the thing that it shuddered backward, flopping onto its back, gurgling in the morass of mud and blood.

Fainen was on his feet in an instant, his sword at the ready, Hayles backing up to meet him, as more Vuls swarmed over the fallen beast.

Aren could barely breathe. The air came in choking gasps that seemed not even to reach his lungs. He saw Doles drop to the ground near Donnovar, with spears sticking out of him like enormous arrows.

Donnovar shot a glance at Aren. He took *Braxis* by the hilt and heaved it into the air. The blade slammed into the ground at Aren's feet and sloshed in the mud. He took it in his hand without thinking.

Donnovar was giving away his weapon.

Aren looked up into Donnovar's eyes.

"Run!" Donnovar screamed.

The words came to Aren's ears in echoes. He heard them over all the noise of the combat, as if the two of them were alone in a vacuum.

Donnovar's mouth moved.

Run.

The Ghiroergan drove its sharp fingers into Donnovar's chest, cutting through flesh and ribs like the points of spears. Donnovar gasped. His lungs emptied through punctures. The beast lifted him into the air with a single arm, its fingers locked deep in his torso.

Aren felt a sharp kick in the gut. He had no air left to scream.

Tamlin, the last Sarenwalker, turned his back on the Vuls, and lunged toward the creature. He beat it with his *somashalks*, aiming unerringly for its joints and nerves. The Ghiroergan shook under the attack, dropping to one knee.

Donnovar's body slipped off the webbed fingers into the deep mud, but the Sarenwalker never slowed, batting aside the malformed arms. He drove closer and closer to the hulk, even as the Vuls came in behind him, stabbing at his back. His final act was to drive the edge of his axe deep into the neck of the beast, killing the creature that had ended his Captain's life. The Sarenwalker then fell lightly to the ground, and his body was chopped apart by the Vuls.

Aren stood motionless. Everything sounded far away. He was staring through a tunnel with himself at one end and Donnovar's body at the other. Nothing else existed. His eyes glazed over. They shook and rattled in their sockets like hammered drums.

He blinked and he could see again. He blinked again and he saw a spark in the corner of his eye. He blinked once more and everything went white, painfully, crushingly white. Like standing inside the sun.

Redevir tugged on his arm. "Come on!" he cried.

He rubbed his eyes and the light faded to an ember, and he stumbled along, the world foggy and distant.

Redevir pulled him along. He saw Inrianne's white dress. He saw tiny Tanashri. He saw fire erupt ahead.

"Inrianne's fire!" Redevir shouted. "She is lighting the way. Go to the light!"

His head ached. His thoughts felt like poison. He did not see the combat raging. He did not see the Outer Guard dying all around him. Corrin and Reidos seemed distant memories to him. He did not understand why a grown man wearing orange sashes would sob as he desperately dragged another man by his arms, nor could he tell why the man fell to the ground and screamed when the others surrounded him. He saw it, but he did not understand.

He suddenly felt at his waist as Redevir half-carried him along. The malagayne was still there. He knew what that was. It was the only thing he knew for sure and for certain. He thought of the crushed leaves, how the sweet smoke would feel, how it would make everything just go away.

Just go away.

****

Corrin couldn't see Aren anywhere. He and Reidos were alone among the Vuls. Spears narrowly missed his head, arrows narrowly missed his torso, and swords narrowly missed everything else.

All around him, men of the Outer Guard were dead or dying.

He hacked at the necks of the Vuls. *Vul armor is weak at the neck.* He couldn't see the bodies fall. He had to turn to face the next attacker, and the next. With all the steel kisses he had handed out already the *Steel Whore* had earned her name thrice over. *Her price is a dance.* And how the Vuls wanted to dance tonight.

Reidos slipped in the mud. He scrambled across the ground like a cat, tearing at their knees with his sword, too low to the ground for them to see well in the moonlight. He never quite managed to pull himself back up, but he tore their legs to pieces before the Vuls even realized he was there, and was gone before they had a chance to swing at him in response.

Corrin held his hilt in both hands, and dashed a Vul across the face, before plunging his blade into the belly of the next. Then Duran the cook was there, suddenly slashing and harrying the Vuls. He carried a blade he must have taken from the clutches of one of the nameless fallen Outer Guard.

Hallan was standing on the ground behind him, as Duran cut his way through three of them. He then took Hallan by the hand, and pulled him along. He only made it a few strides before more Vuls appeared in his path. He killed this batch as well, and took the boy's hand again. Then he saw Corrin.

Corrin watched Duran move toward him, pulling the boy behind him. They almost reached him when something large blocked their path. It was then that Corrin saw the creature.

Hallan stood motionless before the Ghiroergan. Duran was pulled away from the boy by more Vuls. He drove them back, then reached out to the boy.

Corrin reached his hand out as well. "Come on!"

Hallan looked at Duran.

"Come on," Corrin called again. "This way."

Hallan looked at Corrin, then back to Duran. He turned and ran to Corrin.

Corrin grasped the boy's hand, but before he could take another step, the creature was upon him. The stinking thing loomed over him, reaching its bulbous arms toward him. He dodged to the side, and cut down sharply on one of the webbed hands. It was like hacking at rubber. The creature recoiled, but soon came again.

A steel kiss will not be enough for this one.

Then Reidos was there, flying across the ground, holding himself nearly horizontal, with one hand planted in the mud. The creature did not see him, and he was too low for its drooping arms to reach, but the creature felt the sting of his sword as it pierced one rubbery leg, then the other.

Corrin was there in an instant, waving the *Steel Whore* wildly. The creature was confused by his wild movements, and momentarily stood still.

That's right, you dumb farod. You are too stupid to live.

Corrin looked over his shoulder. Reidos was backing away with Hallan. He saw the horse. It may have been the last living mount from the Outer Guard. He motioned to Reidos, who saw it as well and chittered to it, clicking his teeth. The horse turned, and looked at him. Reidos chittered again. The horse came to him. Reidos pointed the animal at the creature, and swatted its backside, and it charged into the slimy giant.

The creature instantly forgot about Corrin, and began flailing its arms at its new equine foe. It wailed like a sea lion, as the horse bucked and kicked around it, pounding it with hooves. The creature toppled over onto its back, swinging helplessly at the horse, and shrieking absurdly.

Corrin grabbed Hallan by the wrist, and ran with Reidos. Duran was gone.

They ran for the tree line, but pulled up short. Corrin saw nothing but Vuls charging from all directions. He could feel his heart beating like a war drum in his chest. It felt like a cataclysm when the Vuls finally crashed into him.

24

Fields Of The Dead

BLUE AND GREEN WERE the colors of Keluwen's nightmares.

Blue sky above, green grass below. And her trapped in between, watching helpless as friends died. In the sky alone they were safe, and on the soft grass alone they were safe. But where those two places met, where the sky became earth, in the blink of an eye, the smack of an impact, the crunch of bone, good friends were gone.

Every day under an open sky reminded her of the fall. Every patch of grass looked identical to the one Nils' body sat in, where she had looked into his dead eyes, and then left him there. Every way she looked she thought she saw him, even though she knew she was more than a hundred miles away.

She held a hand above her eyes, shielding them from the sharp Lamani sunshine.

She hated being out here, in a wilderness, walking and hiking and running. It was too much time for her to be alone with herself, alone with her thoughts. She liked the city. Any city. Cities moved quick, and had endless distractions to lure her thoughts away from despair. It was an armor of noises and smells and voices and smiles. But out here she was naked. The silence of walking was no more than silk, allowing the barbed knives of her memories to slide right through.

Oddly enough, looking out across a field of corpses made her feel better. She thought a normal person should feel terrible seeing this. *I am not normal.* Hundreds of men, soldiers, horses, slumped alone or in little piles, wherever they happened to be when they took their last breaths. She liked that so many men were dead. It made the death of Nils feel smaller in the world. It did not change the size of the hole in her heart, but it made her soul grin to know there were hundreds more holes in hundreds more hearts than hers. *There should be more of you, a thousand to equal one of him.*

She worried about Cheli, but Cheli had retreated into her books and papers, absorbing herself into the pages like ink, until she was less a person and more of an old tome that spoke. But at least she had stopped crying, and stopped locking herself away alone at night. And Keluwen was the last person on earth who could fault another for growing a little harder and a little colder.

She worried about herself, too. Because today every time she thought of Seb, she felt nothing.

"Look at the size of this footprint," Leucas said, jaw askew in wonderment.

Keluwen did not look. She had seen one. They were all the same. *Focus on why we are here,* she thought bitterly.

"I mean, look at it," Leucas went on. "The size of it."

"Your mother told me the same when I spent the night last, boy," Krid said. He cackled.

He never cackles. He never tells jokes either. Something off with him today. "Stop distracting yourself with novelties," she said. "Keep your eyes peeled for what we are here to find."

"There is little *not* to be found," Hodo said, stretching his lower back, leaning to and fro, hands on his hips. "I'd say every last one of those poor men met his end here on this field."

"Not everyone," Keluwen said. *Not until I see his face.* She stood up and looked over the green grass, one hand over her eyes to block the morning sun. Twig birds and green jays hopped lazily among the bodies, oblivious.

"This place is the holiest ground of the Lamani people," Orrinas said, lifting up an arrowhead and inspecting it. "The Fields of Syn."

"Their gods must not favor trespassers," Hodo said.

"It must be nearly all of them," Cheli said, stepping daintily between the bodies, holding aloft her sack of books. "These are the markings of a lieutenant in Amagon."

"Here," Krid said. "I found their captain." He hovered over a body, torso torn open from neck to pelvis. His mouth was open as if frozen in a scream. And his eyes were left forever half-closed in death.

"One of the beasts must have taken him," Leucas said.

"He is surrounded by dead Sarenwalkers," Hodo said. "Whatever this thing was, it killed three of them. Tore them apart. These are some of the elite fighters in all the world."

"It must have been terrifying for them," Cheli said, looking over her shoulder, worried.

"I do not see the Glasseye," Keluwen said. "Would fate do this to me, Orrinas?"

He shrugged somehow without moving a muscle.

"Could that weakling scum truly be that lucky?" Keluwen asked.

"Seems so," Krid said. "No sign. Not anywhere. Not even of escape."

"We waited too long, Orrinas," Keluwen said. "We should have made our move in Cair Tiril."

"So many," Cheli said. She paused to vomit a little. "They must have been taken by surprise. This armor is good."

"Not against this many arrows," Krid said. "Hell was rained upon them."

"And then the beasts," Leucas said.

"We know," Keluwen said. "The beasts."

"What I want to know is why have no Andristi come upon this?" Hodo asked. "It must be a desecration to have all this blood on their sacred ground. It has been a day and a night."

"This is the end of three holy days," Cheli said. "Eridania Madana, they call it. For the first wife of their great hero, Syn. No one in Synsirok would even think of stepping here until the holy days are over."

"The Vuls do not share any such holidays," Keluwen said. "They have been back here at least three more times by the look of it. Stealing weapons. finishing off wounded, and dragging at least one of their large creatures away to the woods. "

"Could they still be about?" Leucas asked, glancing over his shoulder.

"Possibly," Orrinas said.

"Eyes open, the lot of you," Krid said.

Keluwen followed the battle. She could see how the bodies fell. She saw these men alive. She saw the men felled by arrows. She saw where a battle line had formed. And then collapsed. She saw a breakout attempt. She saw where it started, where it gained momentum, where it faltered, and where it failed. She saw where the last man was butchered. Fingers missing. Held his hand up to protect himself. And died.

She wound her way through the bodies. She thought of them as stones, inorganic, a part of the landscape, nothing more. As long as she did, she could feel the energy of their action, their struggles to survive, and fail. The presence of so much spent energy was like clean air in her lungs, the gift of Belleron.

She heard a rustling over a shallow rise. She walked toward it.

The others must have heard it as well. They began to converge on her from all across the battlefield. Orrinas chirped like jay bird, and Hodo scurried off into the woods, trying to sneak around the hill for a better vantage.

Keluwen crept to edge, plopping down on her belly. Orrinas slipped in beside her. And then Cheli and Leucas and Krid.

"And now we have Vuls below," Krid said.

Keluwen looked at the man she was going to kill at the bottom of the hill. A Vul from Vulgossos looting bodies on the Fields of Syn was a sacrilege so deep that even she knew how profane it was, and she knew next to fuck all about Laman.

I had never taken the life of an enemy before hunting Kinraigan. I did not think I was able to do it save for self-preservation. But I am. I am ready to kill them all. Every day I am further and further away from me.

She wondered if he had a name. Surely even Vuls had names. Something they barked to each other in their coarse language. They felt love. They had to. They were people. Savage people. But people nonetheless. Yet the hurt within her would not let it matter. They were alive. She would make them dead.

It was always harder when she thought about them. She should have just crushed them like ants and moved on, but she reminded herself that they were people every time. She wanted to. She wanted to feel the pain every time. The hurt, the guilt, *they* were real. Pain was real. It was hard to find anything else genuine in the world she lived in. Maybe it would be different if she wore someone else's skin. But she couldn't. So she made sure she felt every bit of the pain. Even when she was killing. Especially when she was killing.

"Orrinas?" she asked.

"Not yet," he said.

"I want them."

"Hodo is scouting the woods to our left first. We must be sure."

Keluwen clenched her fists. It did not help. She took three deep breaths of pine needle air. It did nothing. She kicked at the earth. Trying not to take action was like trying to hold her breath underwater. It was a finite thing. And time was running out.

"Orrinas."

"Just one more minute."

"Enough minutes," Keluwen said. She rose to her feet and exposed her position to the Vuls below.

There were five of them, and all but one were so busy bent over the prone bodies they picked at that they did not realize her to be there.

The one who did look up immediately froze. He stuttered, trying to warn the others.

"Keluwen," Orrinas reached after her, but she was already moving down the hill. *He will be cross with me for this.*

The Vul croaked to his friends. They all looked up at her. Two drew swords.

It did not matter. Keluwen did not care. She did not fear. Her focus was clear, her concentration strong. *These people, they are nothing at all to me. They are alive. They are insects. They are people. They are meaningless. They have families, loved ones who will miss them. They have no one. I hate them. I love them.*

One of them took a step toward her.

She slid one hand free from its long blue glove. She pointed double fingers at him.

She rendered a blank sphere and pushed it through air at the speed of sound. It struck him in the cheek, snapping bone, crushing gums and tongue and brain, splintering teeth and shattering skull. He seemed to float to the ground, the sunshine glinting playfully off of his old half-polished helmet

She repeated the same blank impulse. Every stream identical. She thought of Seb. She killed the next man. Another sphere.

She thought of Palad. She killed again. A sphere once more.

She thought of Nils, broken and abandoned beside a fallen tree in a forgotten glade amid a labyrinth of trees. She wondered if anyone would ever find him. Some children perhaps, scrambling through the brush, playing chase-me, running through the trees, only to stumble across old bleached bones in a sunburst orange tunic, with a rolled up handcloth in his pack, and a handwritten letter with Cheli's name written on the outside of it, undelivered, unopened, unread. She wondered if anyone would ever find it and know how much Nils loved Cheli without her ever knowing.

She killed once more.

The last man stood frozen before her, his knees wobbling, hands shaking. His eyes were leaking tears. His mouth was whispering fright.

She raised her fingers and pointed at him. Tears streamed down her cheeks.

No sphere came.

He glanced left and right.

No sphere issued from her fingertips.

He took one step toward her.

She looked at him and wept.

He reached into his belt.

She lowered her hand.

He drew a rusty knife, dull, caked with the blood of dead men.

She looked at it and thought of what it might feel like to slip beneath her skin. To slide between her ribs. To puncture her heart. What would it feel like for her heart to stop. What would it feel like to have her throat cut, to pump her lifeblood out into the grass as her eyes slowly went dark. To lay down in this beautiful green grass and never rise again.

She could only imagine it to be so peaceful.

She closed her eyes.

Suddenly Hodo was there. He wrapped her in a bear hug and dragged her over backwards. Krid stepped over her. He rendered friction onto the Vul's boots, slowing him. Orrinas flicked his fingers and the knife turned white hot in an instant. The Vul dropped it in a steam haze of melted skin and screams.

Leucas arrived last and stabbed him in the ribs with his sword. The Vul slowly lay down and ceased to be.

Hodo was shaking her. "What in all hells were you doing?!" His great big arms were half embracing her, and half crushing her in anger.

I'm sorry, Hodo. I'm sorry for being the way I am. I don't mean to make you sad.

Krid scowled. Cheli looked at the ground. Orrinas gazed at her, his eyes so wide she wanted to jump into them. But she could not. Not anymore. It was not enough. Not even all the little deaths in the arms of pale lovers could keep it at bay forever. She did not know when, but it would be soon.

She sat up in Hodo's arms.

Orrinas grimaced at her. She had never seen such an expression on him before.

"She is reckless," Krid said. "She is deficient. I told you it was a bad idea to bring her to Laman."

"What did you think you were doing?" Orrinas demanded. "Tell me."

"What we are here to do," she said. "Killing."

"That is not why we are here," he said. "And that is not what I meant."

"Right," she said. "We only kill our own."

"I cannot have you doing this any more," Orrinas said. "Charging into unpredictable situations. You cannot do this anymore."

"She is going to ruin our mission before this is over," Krid said. "Mark my words."

"You put yourself in danger," Orrinas said. "You put everyone here in danger."

She looked away. She refused to meet his gaze. She looked at the sky, at the grass, at the bodies. She did not know who she was. She did not know where. She felt like her body was a glass shell and that her mind was light passing through her skin and vanishing.

All she wanted was peace. And she knew she could never have that as long as this thread was still in the loom. She wanted to weep. She looked at Orrinas and felt like she needed to, but she couldn't. She leaned her head back expecting to have to hold tears, but none came. Why didn't they come?

Why did I let the last one live? Why did I stop? What was I going to let him do? She had no answer. Even for herself. For a moment it seemed so simple, so perfect, like that was all she wanted in the world, to let it go, and let it be done, to find freedom on the end of a knife, to have peace.

She felt empty for a moment, the light escaped. But now it was there again. The woman she was now had no idea who the woman was who had done that. She could not fathom what the Keluwen of moments ago had been thinking. She had been a different person, a deep truth escaped for but a moment and loosed upon the world to do one thing, and then bottled up and buried once more.

She looked at the dead Vuls, the Vuls she had killed. *I killed you because I wanted to.* That was the first time she had ever had that thought. Killing was forever a different thing now. Not because she *had* to, but because she *wanted* to. That was new. That kind of killing was different. She was different.

She looked at the large sacks the Vuls had been minding. One of them moved.

Leucas hopped back. "What in the world?"

The sack shifted. It rolled. And then it began to pull itself open.

She saw fingers and hands slide free, and then press the edges of the opening back. A head emerged, and then a body.

"Duran," Orrinas said. "Is that you?"

"None other," Duran said. He was somewhat the worse for wear, but in many ways he was exactly as she had last seen him. His hair had gone from brown with a whisper of white, to brown with a groan of white. His shirt and trousers gave him the look of a pauper. The only possession he still had was a leather strip stuffed halfway into one pocket.

Keluwen stared at him. *Your face.* She barely recognized it. His face was overgrown with beard. His eyes were hollow knife cuts. He seemed aged. Accelerated. "What happened?"

"Well," Duran said. "I wish I could say something more inspiring than being trapped in a burlap sack. But that was all."

"Were you in the battle?" Leucas asked. He spread his arms wide. "I mean, look at this place."

Duran nodded. "I was. It was a terrible slaughter. These men fought bravely, but they fought against inevitability."

"Nothing ever fazes you, does it?" Keluwen asked. "No matter how many times you almost die."

"Death is not the end," he said. "It did not feel like my time was now."

She glared at him. *It was time for better men than you.* She thought of Nils, and Seb. Why did it have to be them? She would have traded a thousand Durans for each of them.

"How did you come to be here though?" Hodo asked. "I do not understand."

"I was embedded with the Outer Guard," Duran admitted. "When they came to Westgate. I have been with them ever since." He shook his head. "I tried to fulfill my mission. But alas, I am afraid I have failed."

"What mission?" Keluwen narrowed her eyes. "What was so important that you left us high and dry for three months?"

"The boy," Duran said. "It was all about the boy."

"Here we have this boy again," Keluwen said. "What is so damn important about one little child?"

"Something happened to him," Duran said. "The night on the mountain. Something I cannot explain. But he is *different*. There were four of them. I do not know what happened to the others. They may be dead. When I woke, their village had been burned, the people slaughtered. This one boy was the only one that Kinraigan's people found. They brought him to Westgate. I followed. Axis Ardent contacted me there. They told me to find the boy if I could, and take him out of there, using the Outer Guard as a screen."

Keluwen fumed. "We were in Westgate, fighting for our lives. And you were across the city, babysitting a child."

"I was doing my duty," he said, eyeing her coldly. "I have been doing it since before you stole your first silver tosser."

She wanted to reach across the quiet grass and smack him. *Will none of them let me forget?* And it was only a copper bit, not a silver tosser. Her first pocket plucked.

Orrinas could read her face. He waved one hand gently between them, refocusing Duran's eyes on him. "You were set to mind this boy. What happened?"

He looked over at her, and his expression was a match to how she felt looking at him. "I had the boy," he said. "Right up until the end. Then I lost him."

"Are you all right?" Cheli asked.

"Good now," he said. "Free."

"Why do you care what happened to this boy of yours?" Keluwen asked.

"Is that not why *you* are here?" Duran asked.

"We were looking for evidence of *his* passing," Orrinas said.

"Whose passing?" Duran asked. "You mean Kinraigan?"

"The very same," Keluwen said.

"I thought there would be someone coming to take the boy."

"Take him?"

"I think many people want him. Kinraigan certainly did."

"Want him for what?"

"Maybe I am just imagining these things," Duran admitted. "But he saw what I saw. They opened a hole in our world. Something came through it before it was over. The child. Something happened to him on that mountain."

"I do not care about children," Keluwen said. "We are going to *kill* Kinraigan. That is the only reason we are here. Tell me about Kinraigan. Where is he going?"

"I heard little of that," Duran said. "These here had no knowledge. They were picking loot. I believe I was to be sold to Calabari slavers."

"Wait a moment," Cheli said. "You are saying that Kinraigan had this boy. How did he find him?"

"Kinraigan was there also," Duran said. "Atop the mountain."

"What was *he* doing there?" Cheli asked.

"Killing the Mimmions," Duran said. "He killed them. I think he wanted to stop it. He was trying to prevent what they were doing. Or steal the results."

"Prevent what exactly?" Keluwen asked.

He shook his head. "That I cannot say."

"Why would he care?" Keluwen asked. "Kinraigan. He was luminous by then. We know that."

"Why would someone who knew how to walk in the light bother with some mundane cult?" Cheli asked. "I mean, Mimmions? They are ancient but small. They hardly have any resources. Even the Ministry doesn't bother stamping them out, and the Ministry's Priests would walk barefoot across glass for the chance to strangle one little girl with the magick. Mimmions are a gnat on a cave bear's back."

"They had *something* that night," Duran said. "They opened a gateway to something."

"Gateway," Orrinas said. "To where?"

"I have never seen something like it," Duran said. "The air was alight. The light...moved. It had...agency. It had shape, dimension. It floated and wafted and beamed."

Orrinas exchanged an uneasy glance with Cheli.

Keluwen noticed. "What? What does that mean?"

"Duran may have witnessed someone opening a pathway to the Slipstream," Cheli said.

Keluwen's eyes went wide. "You mean someone *else* became luminous?"

"I cannot say with so little information, but...someone it seems was at least trying," Orrinas said.

"You were right, Kel," Cheli said. "He is not only trying to become invincible, he is also trying to stop someone else from becoming what he is."

"A competitor," Krid said. "Someone to kill next after Kinraigan."

I do not know if there will be anything left of me by the time we kill Kinraigan.

"What about the footprints?" Leucas asked. "Are they...?"

"Ghiroergans?" Duran said. "Oh yes, they were."

"Quite the coincidence," Krid said. "Savage beasts wandering into the middle of this battle?"

"They were *with* the Vuls," Duran said. "Among them."

"How can that be?" Hodo asked. "They are *creatures.*"

"I can only tell you what I saw," Duran said. "They were brought to this field by men, either men of Volgossos, or somewhere. But they were delivered here. They were brought into battle intentionally."

"What a refreshing thought," Orrinas said.

"Why did they leave?" Leucas asked suddenly. "The Outer Guard. Why did they march from the safety of the city at dusk?"

"I have been thinking of that as well," Krid said. He spat in the grass. "It just doesn't make sense."

"They are right," Hodo said. "What in seven hells were they doing out here?"

"It was Aren," Duran said.

Keluwen's skin went cold. The hair stood vigil on the back of her neck. She clenched her fists. "That name again."

"The one they called Aren of Amagon," Duran said. "He was there when the battle began. I know little else. Although he was the one who rushed in and declared that Raviel was dead. He goaded the Outer Guard to leave Synsirok."

Orrinas sat back on his heels "So Raviel is gone. Our chief ally in pursuing *him.*"

"Aren," Keluwen said. Her mouth set in stone, her heart pulsed blood like rivers of rock. *He is everywhere. He is in everything. He is under every stone we turn, behind every street corner, over every hill. Monster.*

"I did not see him among the dead," Hodo said.

She felt such a heavy hate in her heart that she had to walk away from everyone. She could not stand to be so close, her skin prickling like a terrible rash.

"He is alive somewhere, most likely," Krid said. "For good or ill."

For ill. Only ill.

Keluwen wandered across the field, looking at the trees, tall and twisted, moss covered trunks, tangled roots breaching like Isaurian whales. She looked into them, asking them to show her whatever did not belong.

"Keluwen?" Orrinas called out.

"I see nothing," she said. Nothing. "Wait," she said. She held up one hand fingers outstretched.

The others quieted their movements. She lowered herself until her buttocks sat on her ankles, peering into the trees.

There was someone in there.

Her eyes widened briefly.

She slowly slid one glove down, and then the other, pulling them both off as one and tucking them into her pocket. She rendered a handful of blank impulses. She set them at the speed of a shout. She released them and they flew, smacking into the trunks of the trees, cracking the wood.

There was a Vul there, ducked down in the thornbrush. He flew to his feet at the sudden sounds.

I see you now. She started toward him.

He turned and ran into the woods. He stumbled and fell. He rolled over another group of them, scaring them all out of their cover. Half of them ran away, the other half charged her.

She stood at the edge of the trees and raised both hands. She rendered one blank sphere for each of them, except for two that were running in line. For them only one was required.

She let them fly.

One by one, the Vuls took the punch in their ribs. It sounded like a wet smack. Ripping tissue. Cracking bone. They all dropped. Every one. They all died.

And she felt nothing.

She killed them in all the ways she wished she could kill Aren of Amagon.

It was so easy. The only hard thing to do was stop. She finally did. When there were none left. "I wish there were a hundred more of you," she told their bodies.

Or just one Glasseye.

25

Surviving

AREN OPENED HIS EYES to a headache so sharp that at first he thought someone was stabbing him in the skull.

Daylight shined brightly, making it worse. He squinted into four walls and a ceiling of pine needles. He heard the faint scraping of metal, and smelled the sweetness of meat roasting. He heard the chirping of an infinity of birds on the branches above him.

I remember these trees. This forest. I am in Laman. This is Laman.

Fainen was at the fire, roasting a horned pig. Hayles was sharpening his *somashalks*. Redevir was whispering to Inrianne and Tanashri. He did not see any other people with them. No one. Just them.

He glanced to one side. He saw *Braxis* laying casually in the dirt, its sheath lost on the Fields of Syn. He lay one hand upon it, almost expecting to feel something from the blade, some light, some of its owner's energy still trapped within, but it was only cold steel to his fingertips.

He looked at the dirt upon it and he was suddenly infuriated by its condition. Donnovar would never have left his weapon unclean. Aren took it with both hands and pulled it into his lap. He took the edge of his own cloak and began to furiously wipe down the blade, taking water from Redevir's leather bladder without even asking. The Rover raised an eyebrow, but said nothing. Aren did not stop until *Braxis* was in a state of cleanliness he knew Donnovar would approve of. Donnovar would need his sword well kept. He cradled *Braxis* as if it was some infant he had found on the ground.

Donnovar was gone. Aren saw every memory of him all at once. Years' worth of them. His strong arms would never hold the blade again. He was supposed to do so much more, and now it was all lost, his command ended, his life taken away. Cold and betrayed, alone and forgotten on a distant battlefield. He deserved a better end than that.

Aren felt emptiness, black and deep and complete.

Redevir was staring at him.

"What?" Aren asked sharply.

"What indeed," Redevir said. "You have slept through two nights and a day."

"That long?" His head throbbed. His back felt stretched and twisted. His stomach howled for food. "Where are we?" He pitched forward, clutching at his ribs.

"Calm yourself," Redevir said. "We have been moving fast, even at night. Hayles carried you. Here, move into the light. Warm yourself."

"Any sign of the others?" He knew the futility of his question before he even finished asking it.

"It is possible," Hayles said, looking up from his weapons. "But unlikely."

"I've lost friends before," Redevir said. "It's never an easy thing. It will take a lot out of you. It always does, but the best thing to do is keep busy, focus on something else, don't stop to think about it."

Aren stared at him. *Stop thinking about my friends? How? How am I supposed to do that? Show me how that is even possible.* "You don't understand, Redevir. My life is over. I have nothing to keep busy with. The one thing I know how to do is trace. It's gone now. My life, my home, my friends, my teachers, everything. I can never go back to Amagon. What am I supposed to do? Wander the world like you? I don't even know where I am."

"You are in the woods," Redevir said.

"Don't start that with me," Aren warned. He contemplated slapping Redevir, but he could not convince his legs to stand. "Do you understand? At all? In the span of one night I lost everything. I don't believe it. I...I still don't believe it. It can't be real." Donnovar was gone. Really truly gone. Corrin, Reidos, all of them.

Redevir crouched beside him, elbows on his knees. "You think I don't know where you are right now?" He raised an eyebrow. "You know what happened to my people on Signal Mountain. I lost everything once. I am still here. When someone goes to everwonder it feels like you go with them, caught up in their departure. You feel it must be some mistake that you still live and breathe. But it is not. You remain. One day you will realize that you are still here."

"I won't," Aren said. Even though in his rational mind he knew Redevir was right, he *still* could not accept it.

"You are grieving now. I know that no words of mine will mean anything to you right now. Just know that you are not alone."

"Leave me alone," Aren said. "I *want* to be alone." He wanted some malagayne.

"As you wish," Redevir stepped away.

Aren sat alone for a long time, not thinking of anything, only looking at the trees. He could not get the image of Donnovar out of his mind, the sight of him dying. No matter how hard he tried to think of something else it always crept back in. *I need some malagayne. I need it now.*

He opened the pouch, and then opened the smaller one within, brimming with powder. He waited as their eyes wandered over him, and then away. Waited and waited, one finger hovering within the lip of it, just waiting for that one moment. He waited until he was certain all eyes were aimed elsewhere, and he dipped one finger into his powder and practically shoved it up his nose, breathing deep, holding it in, screaming in silent ecstasy.

Donnovar went away. Corrin and Reidos. Terrol and Raviel. Sarker. *Mother.* They all left him alone at last.

Something reached out from his darkness, his sorrow receding like the tide to reveal it. His mind began to ruthlessly analyze his every choice, every thought, every action since leaving home. Avoiding Raviel. Going to Synsirok. Not speaking up when he was sure that he had not caught his man. "Did I do this? Am I to blame?" He didn't say it to anyone in particular. He was talking to the trees.

"Margol and his assassins were in the shadows. You heard what he said, and you saw what those users did to each other. Leaving was the best chance he had."

"We could have gone to the Lamani. They must have had users of their own. Someone there could have helped us. Why didn't we ask? Why didn't I think to ask?"

"In the moment thoughts are murky," Redevir said. "It is difficult to see every avenue before us. It was like stumbling into a blood feud between two rival clans. That situation was not something that one prepares for when the sun rises."

"I just...I just don't know what to do. I don't even know what is happening. I can't believe what is happening. I feel like my life has been turned upside down. Everything I thought I knew has been torn to shreds. My world made sense once. *This* world is madness."

"I certainly never expected to see those creatures," Redevir agreed.

"Ghiroergans. Shilillim, just like the Greycloaks told us. I saw them with my own eyes." He glanced at the Saderan again. She looked up at him, but said nothing. "I can barely think straight when I try to remember what they looked like." All the likenesses of the Ghiroergans he had ever seen came alive. Memories of the mosaics and bas-reliefs in the Library chilled his blood.

"Best not to dwell on that image. Besides, we have something much more pressing to discuss."

The Dagger. "Do you still have it?" Aren asked.

"Of course I still have it."

Aren glanced suspiciously at the two users across the camp. "How much do they know?"

"I haven't asked." Redevir pulled it from his belt, and held it up in front of Aren's eyes.

It was a nine-inch triangular blade, two inches wide where it met the crossguard. The hilt was of a hard wood, stained dark and laminated by some substance to preserve it. It rested in a silver sheath, crawling with filigree, bronze or black gold, woven in shapes of strange hexagrams and bold lettering.

He let the sight of it take over, eclipsing the faces of those forever lost to him. The Dagger could take their place for just a little while.

Redevir smiled. "A wonder, isn't it?"

"Is it real though?" Aren asked.

"Of course it is. I can touch it. That is real enough, isn't it?"

"How can you prove it though?"

"Prove?"

"That it's real. That it's truly what you say it is."

"Well, here it is," Redevir said, holding it up before his eyes and jiggling it. He drew it, looked at the blade, then re-sheathed it. He handed it to Aren. "And at least two other individuals thought it was real enough to kill for. It looks exactly as it is always described."

And in truth it did, down to the smallest detail—the silver sheath, the markings, the colors of it. They looked exactly like the tiny replica of Sangbran's infamous sculpture. But was it too much like it? "How would anyone ever believe it is not a well-made fake? How do we even know it is not a fake?"

That thought gave Redevir pause. Aren passed it back to him. The Rover flipped the Dagger over in his hands and stared carefully at it. "The clues are too old," he decided. "Some of the hints are decades, even centuries old."

"And it may be a centuries-old hoax. Just waiting for us to stumble into it."

"It can't be," Redevir said. "The clues were too numerous, and too costly to have been faked."

"Even still. I am not sure that I can even convince myself that it is real."

Redevir held it up and shook it. "It must be able to do something." He turned it over and over in his hands, squeezing its sheath, looking for whatever it was that it might be capable of. He held it up to his ear and listened to it. He shook it, tapped it against his forehead, waved it in the air, closed his eyes and *thought* at it. Nothing. "Shit. Banwick says the Dagger is a messenger. It delivers to you the news of what you are by awakening it in you. It opens the door for you to take the first step into what you will become."

"And that means...?"

"I don't know." He kept trying, waving it, miming stabs. Nothing came of any of his attempts. At last he shrugged. "I suppose we will have to find some way to prove it. By every god, I hope that will be easier than finding the damnable thing. That shall be another trouble for another day."

"Another day. We may not even make it out of Laman alive."

"We will make it," Hayles said. He did not look up as he spoke. "Inform me of where you wish to go, and I will find the best method to deliver us there." He returned to his work without another word.

"I was hoping you would help me, Aren." Redevir said.

"Help you?" Aren asked. "How?"

Redevir's eyes widened as though the answer was so obvious that he did not understand the question at all. "You know the Histories. Inside and out. I could use you. You have no idea how useful your knowledge could be."

"I'm not a treasure hunter," Aren said. *I'm not anything anymore.*

"Don't be ridiculous. You had no trouble guiding me to this." Redevir pointed at the Dagger. "You are a man of the past. Don't you want to be a part of this? Don't you want to see the Sephors? Living pieces of history?" He quickly wrapped it in a hand cloth and stuffed it back into his carry-bag.

"Never thought about it."

"Think about *this*. Your name written within the Histories you love so dearly. You could be there when they are unearthed, one by one. Do you think it was by chance that we met in Westgate? I see more than that. I see destiny."

"Destiny? You sound like that wrinkled old man. If you call me the sorrowful man I swear I will stand up and smack the madness out of you."

"You changed my path. I was there. You solved the riddles without even realizing it. Seven hells, you practically led me to the Dagger by accident. Without even trying. After years of searching, the Dagger was handed to *us*. That has to mean something. I don't believe in Sanadi and I don't believe in whatever *he of sorrow* is. But finding *this* was destiny."

"Destiny that Donnovar had to die? Destiny that my friends had to die? Destiny that we be left here alone in this wilderness? If that is my destiny, I don't want it."

"You cannot control the world," Redevir said. "But you can control how you respond to the world around you. When fate hands the starving man fruit, he eats it no matter how long he has lamented being hungry."

"I don't believe in a world where the words someone spoke a thousand years ago control me," Aren said.

"I believe we make our own destinies. I believe that a destiny is something that exists out there, but only if you step into it and take it. Like a cloak in a wardrobe. You must choose which of your destinies you are going to wear."

"The one I am wearing is failure."

"Let me offer you an alternative. A new destiny. A different destiny."

"Destiny is yours to give now?"

"Hear me out. I am offering you a chance to pursue something different."

"You are trying to trick me into hunting for the Sephors."

"I think we should help each other. What have you got to lose? You said it yourself. There is nowhere to go back to. Your own people sent you out here to die."

Aren ground his teeth. "I could kill him. The Lord Protector. That I know."

"What they did you, to all of you..." Redevir shook his head. "I have seen a lot in my time, and that was still shocking. Have you thought about what you are going to do about it?"

"Do about it? Nothing. What is there to do? I am one man. He is the Lord Protector. He has a whole nation behind him—armies, spies, secret police. He is protected by Sarenwalkers, Inner Guard, Outer Guard, the Orange. That is impossible. All I can do is run from that."

"A fair assessment of your chances."

"They made up a story, just invented it from thin air. They knew I would only see the girls in danger. They knew my tracing history. They know the first one I sent to the fires. They made up a story to manipulate me. They used it to blind me to what was going on, and everyone is gone now because I could not see it." He wanted more malagayne already. A whole leaf, rich smoke, as sweet as forgetfulness. He needed it. Faster, sooner, now.

"Look at me," Redevir said. "You have been serving someone else all this time. Do something for yourself for a change. Come with me. You want to see the Sephors as badly as I do. I can see it in your eyes. You want to know that they are real. Let someone read about you in the Histories years from now. Don't fade away like everyone else. Do this for yourself."

"How am I supposed to dedicate myself to something I didn't even believe in until today?"

"Your Lord Protector certainly believed in them enough to kill for them. And Kinraigan. That little man Raviel has trussed up on the floor was Kinraigan's man."

Aren grimaced when he said the name Kinraigan. "They were working together. They took those girls together. I was tracing one of them. But Kinraigan was behind everything." He bared his teeth at the trees.

Redevir must have noticed. "Maybe you can't touch the Lord Protector. Maybe he is out of reach. But there is someone else who isn't. You finished one trace. I think you have a *new* trace now."

"I don't know what you're talking about."

"Oh, yes you do. You are a man of many talents. Lying is not one of them. You want him. You want to catch him. Kinraigan."

"So what if I do? I am not a magistrate anymore. And he has killed dozens of men like me. Even the best Render Tracer in the world couldn't catch him."

"*I* think the best Render Tracer in the world *hasn't tried yet.*" Redevir smiled at him.

Aren rolled his eyes. "Playing to my ego now, are you? It doesn't matter anyway. The world is a big place. There is no way to find him now."

"Wrong. You know what he wants now. He wants the Sephors. And we have one. Help me find the rest. You can find the unfindable, and kill the unkillable."

"What if I want neither?" Aren asked.

Redevir laughed. "I think you want both. I think you want them so badly you can taste it."

Get out of my head, Rover.

"I am right, aren't I?" Redevir smiled. "You cannot let yourself allow him to escape. You have never lost someone you hunted before, have you?"

"No." *Shaot. He is right. He can see through me.*

"I do not think you could live your life not knowing whether or not you could have caught him. Win or lose, you have to try. Tell me I am wrong?"

"I can't," Aren said.

Redevir nodded triumphantly. "We have the Dagger. We know he wants it. I know the only way to keep our hands on this is to eliminate him from the competition. If you help me on *my* search, I will help *you.*"

"Help me?"

"Finance your capture. Hire private Stoppers. Distractors, Sweepers, hired muscle. Weapons, equipment, bootleg tracing tools. Anything you need. I have enough gold and then to spare."

"What you are describing sounds too good to be true."

"The money spent would be well worth it to have you as my partner. Do this with me. Come on. I am putting a path before you. What is holding you back? This path has the two things you want most in the world at the end of it. Don't you want to find him? The man who set us up in Westgate? The man who is, deep down, responsible for your friend's death? If it is anyone's fault that Donnovar is dead, it is Kinraigan's. No one has ever caught him before because no one has ever had anything he wanted before."

Donnovar. Aren's face soured. He hated Redevir for speaking that name. *But he is right. If Kinraigan really is the one behind all of this, then I will never see him again. Unless I have something he wants.* "You make it sound so easy," Aren said.

"You made *tracing* sound so easy. Do this with me."

"I have never let one get away. Not a single rogue user."

"Don't let him be the first. This is what your whole life was for. You have the opportunity to catch the worst of the worst."

"I..."

"Don't stop to think about consequences. Empty your mind. Decide. Right now. What do *you* choose to do?"

He felt his own sorrow like a pit in his stomach. Fate. Destiny. The words Redevir spoke were like the words of that old man in Westgate, words that might as well have meant prophecy. There was no such thing as prophecy.

He felt such rage that he could destroy a hundred fabled Sanadi. Was that what Kinraigan was? Sanadi? Was he the evil user of the legend? No. He was just another user. A terrible one. Another man who thought he was a god. Just like all the others. "I will go with you. I don't know for how long, or for how far. I will not promise."

Aren rose to his feet, his knees clicking, sharp pain in his back. Hayles appeared beside him instantly, taking *Braxis* from his hands, treating it as delicately as he had, carrying it over to the fire and placing it on a strip of cloth.

Redevir smiled. "You're doing the right thing. This is right."

"I will. For Donnovar, I will." He said the name Donnovar, but he knew it was a lie. He wanted to do it for himself. *I catch rogue users. I make them pay.* This was the ultimate rogue user.

"Aren, if you swear to help me find the Crown, I will hire an army for you." He looked at the trees and inhaled deeply. "This means we are going to take the next step on the path."

"Which is?"

"We are going to Medion."

"*The* Medion? The city in Amagon?"

"There is no other. My notebooks are kept safe by a trusted friend there. I will gather my research and we can begin. I can't wait to show you. Put the puzzle together. From where we are now, Hayles claims we can keep going south across the frontier between Laman and Palantar, then cut southwest until we reach the city of Aldria in Olbaran. We will take one of the passenger barges. They go all the way down the Alder River to the west coast. A steamer will get us there in less than a tenth of the time it would take to ride. We will have more than enough time to set a trap for him."

Aren nodded.

"We shall travel in style," Redevir said. He flashed his usual Rover smile.

Aren saw a tiny head bobbing over Redevir's shoulder, hooded with a cloak of blue and grey, small and frail, grey eyes and pointy chin.

"Tanashri," Aren said.

"She escaped on her own," Redevir said. "No one made it out with her."

"It was not easy," she said.

"It must have been harrowing," Redevir said, sarcasm oozing from his tone.

"Your friend is not happy to see me," Tanashri said. "He knows that I am aware of your discovery."

"What discovery?" Aren asked carefully.

"You insult me," Tanashri said. "You believe the Sisterhood would raise a fool to the rank of Saderan? That the presence of a Sephor would go unnoticed by me?"

"You knew we had the Dagger?"

"It was easy enough to surmise. Knowing what I know. Raviel was supposed to give it to me."

"Why would Raviel give it to you?" Aren asked.

"I am the one who introduced Raviel to the Lord Protector," she said.

"How did you know Raviel?" Aren asked. "Wait, how did you know the Lord Protector?"

"Raviel came to Templehall years ago looking for help in his hunt for Kinraigan," she said. "He told us Kinraigan was looking for the Sephors, and so he tried to find the same clues Kinraigan had, to try to find out where Kinraigan was going. We offered aid, and in return he shared with my Sisters much of what he had learned about the locations of the Sephors, including the Dagger. I was charged to take possession of it and keep it safe until it could be taken to Templehall."

"I asked how you knew the Lord Protector," Aren said, narrowing his eyes. He took a small sip of water from what was left of his leather bladder.

"Some of my Sisters had come to believe that he had already found one," Tanashri said.

Aren leaned forward and spit the water in his lap. "The Lord Protector? You thought he had a Sephor?"

Tanashri wrinkled her lip, which was the equivalent of a shrug for a Saderan. "They did. I was sent as a diplomat, to try to uncover what I could. But there was nothing. It was a fool's errand. But then Raviel came looking for help to get him to Laman. He told me about the Dagger. I decided the chances favored finding the Dagger instead after what he divulged to me. So I arranged for the mission."

"By suggesting Raviel tell the Lord Protector about the Dagger."

"I knew he would want it. I was right. I thought Raviel would be able to find it first and give it to me to hide. We could then tell Aldarion's people it was just a fable. How could he challenge us? I knew he would send someone of his own to try to find it, but I did not suspect he would run a double-blind."

"What are you then?" Inrianne asked across the cook fire. "Some kind of spy?"

Tanashri nodded. "In a manner of speaking. It is my duty to see that it does not fall into unknown hands." She held out her hand to Redevir. "You are the final obstacle to my mission. I should take hold of the Dagger now." It did not sound like it was intended to be a request.

"I will keep what is mine and I will go where I choose," Redevir grunted. "I do not bow my head before the Sisterhood. Do not seek to command me. You will not find the consequences favorable."

"Oh really?" Tanashri raised an eyebrow. "Even now?" She lifted one of her hands into the air. Her eyes narrowed in concentration. The air began to spool and bend. Redevir began to lift off the ground, as if suspended on a platform. He rose ten feet, then twenty, his eyes wide with anger and surprise, going to hands and knees to keep balance.

Aren moved toward her. "Tanashri, put him down. What are you doing?"

"He will relinquish it to me, or he will be forced to do so," Tanashri said.

"Put him down," Aren said again.

Hayles moved toward her with his *somashalks* in hand. Fainen drew his Saren-sword. They both looked to Aren for direction. He could tell they were each ready to throw themselves at the Saderan on his word, even if it meant certain death.

"No," she said. "I must take it. I must keep it safe."

"Is that so?" Inrianne said. She drew back one silken sleeve of her white gown. She released a spray of fire.

Tanashri quickly raised her other hand. The air distorted again. The fire flattened against an invisible wall, spreading out, the fringes curling and tickling their way across it. But it extinguished in a whoosh. Tanashri was untouched on the other side.

Tanashri's shield held. Inrianne pressed her hands against it, but it would not budge.

Aren looked at the Saderan. He looked at Redevir suspended high in the air. He watched Inrianne pressing against the unseen shield. He had to do something, to save Redevir, to save them all.

He dipped into his tracer satchel and slid one of the long black pins, sharp as a needle, from its loop. *Tinwood nails.* For emergencies. He unplugged the stopper from his vial of tinwood leaf resin and held just the barest tip of the needle into it, the very end kissed the resin. He took it out and palmed it, holding its sharp tip against his forearm.

He grabbed Inrianne by the elbow and whispered in her ear. "User's shorthand. Hit her again. Distract her."

Inrianne squinted at him spitefully, but she did as he said. She released a shuddering blossom of flame.

Tanashri kept one eye on her shield deflecting the fire, and another on Redevir dangling helplessly.

But Aren watched how the fire flattened, how it crawled, until he had a sense of the position of the invisible shield. He sidestepped until he was behind Tanashri, on the other side of where the shape of the two-dimensional shield appeared to exist.

He flipped the tinwood nail free and threw it. It turned end over end in the air. This time there was no shield to stop it. It struck home in her hip, just below her buttocks. She winced, turned, looked down at it, looked up at Aren. She glowered. Then she let out a tiny squeal and lay down.

Redevir dropped to the dirt. He tucked his legs and rolled to his feet.

"The Sisterhood," Aren said. "You can trust a Sister for one thing for certain. The methods of their renders are like textbook patterns. They always conserve concentration and energy if they think they can. Why make a three-dimensional shield when you get by with two?" He squatted down and plucked the pin out of her.

"She didn't think you would be resourceful enough to figure it out," Redevir said.

Tanashri glared first at Aren, then at Inrianne. "Why?"

"You think just because you brought me along that I owed you something?" Inrianne laughed.

"I see you have some luck in your favor, Rover," Tanashri said.

"It wasn't luck," Aren said. "My friends just died and you think I'm going to just roll over and let one of you waltz around? You have underestimated me from day one." He knelt down, and stared hard into her eyes. "Do you want me to read you the fucking composite again?"

She recoiled, as if he had changed into a wild animal before her eyes.

"What now?" Redevir asked. "Do we...Do we kill her?"

Aren wondered that himself. Tanashri was down for now, but it was only temporary. Would Inrianne be able to stop her minutes from now? Even if Tanashri allowed them to flee, she would be able to follow and take them unawares at any other time, and it was a *long* way back to Amagon. They certainly could not let her take the Dagger. That was out of the question, but how else could they ever get rid of her?

That's it.

Unless...they *didn't have to* get rid of her.

It was Sarker's old Lissarian Gambit. The best way to defeat an enemy is to make them an ally. All he needed was a bit of leverage, and Redevir had that in spades. Even if he didn't, Aren knew that he could at least give the appearance that he did. Make her believe they have something she needs more than a Sephor, and she would be with them until either she gets what they offer, or until she realizes there is nothing else to be had. Sarker had used it on at least four traces, to convince uncooperative witnesses not only to give him information for free, but to actively help him in the search.

But would it work on a Saderan? It had to. Sarker told him that it worked on everyone. *You just have to know what they want more than what they have.*

The only thing more enticing than *one* Sephor, was *all* the Sephors. *When you are in a position of weakness, bide your time until you are strong,* went the words of King Thalian.

"Tanashri," he said. "You were sent to look for a Sephor, but what of the others?"

She grimaced a pointy grimace.

"You said there are other Sisters out there searching," Aren said.

"There are," she said. "Saderans such as I."

"And wouldn't it be more beneficial to the Sisterhood if you found evidence of others in addition to the Dagger? Would it not be more beneficial for *you?*"

She narrowed her brow. "What is it you propose?"

"Redevir has found many hints and clues and contacts," Aren said. "As many as Raviel had. *More* than Raviel had. Maybe more than everything the Sisterhood knows about them combined." He wiped down the pin and then held it between thumb and forefinger. "If you take the Dagger, you will walk away with one thing. If you come with us, you may find as many Sephors as all the other Sisters combined. Imagine the possibilities. You could return to

Templehall with more than they ever thought possible. Even the Overseers and Sisters of Seniority would have to acknowledge that." Aren noticed a flicker of change in her eyes. He must have struck the right chord.

She looked over their heads, imagining what could be had.

"That was tinwood leaf resin I stuck you with," Aren said. "Undiluted. You are not going to be using magick for a while. You are not going to be doing much of anything for a while. But especially not the magick."

"You are a brave man," she said.

"I will dose you with it again when this wears off, and then again after that. I will do it every day if I have to or until you decide to join us, or we leave you in some way-station in the middle of nowhere. A little goes a long way, so I could do it forever if I choose. Forever not using your magick, always just out of reach, a normal, like us. Or you could join us."

"How will you know if I tell the truth?" she asked.

He put his face in front of hers and stared. "Tell me your answer. Say it out loud. Formally."

Her expression softened. "The arrangement is suitable. I will search with you. And permit you to hold the Dagger. As long as you remain always in my presence."

"Tell me again."

"I agree to your terms."

"And again." He stared into her face.

"I agree."

"Do you agree?"

"Yes."

"Are you sure?" Eyes fixed to her.

She paused. "Yes."

He smiled. "Good. This makes things so much easier."

Redevir's eyes sharpened. "Do you really expect me to believe the words of a Saderan? The only time a witch isn't scheming is when she's dead. How do you know she was telling the truth? She lied through her teeth to the Lord Protector for years it seems."

"She passed every test. Pupil dilation test, sweat response, micro-expression, gestures, tone, timing, cadence. Those cannot be faked. Even her pause was of emotional frustration, not deception. She is telling the truth. She will be a part of our crew for now."

Redevir half-smiled. "Only until she changes her mind. What is there to stop her from murdering us in our sleep?"

"Aren's argument is sound," Tanashri said.

My appeal to your ambition is sound, you mean.

"We could stop her," Redevir said. "We could end her right now."

"We are not killing her," Aren said. "We let her come with us."

"With only her promise as a Saderan to keep us safe?" Redevir threw his arms in the air.

"More than a promise," Aren said. "Her best interests would lie with us. She needs your knowledge. You have been on the hunt for decades. She would have something none of her Sisters would have; access to an expert on the Sephors. Her goal is aligned with our own."

"Are you certain you know what you are getting into with this witch?"

"I am buying us time," Aren whispered.

Tanashri looked around as if she had forgotten where she was. She slowly lay all the way down. She rested her head in the crook of one elbow. Then went to sleep.

"Well, that is done. I hope she abides her feeble promise."

"She will," Aren said. "By harming us, she would be harming herself."

"Quite so," Redevir said. "But that does not mean that I have to enjoy this arrangement." He gave Aren a sly look. "By the way, how did you know Tanashri's shield only protected her in one direction?"

"*User's shorthand*," Aren said. "It requires a great deal of concentration to bind streams together. It takes even more to commit to multiple actions at once. Two-dimensional walls are easier than three-dimensional ones. Users do it all the time."

"So they cut a few corners," Redevir laughed. "Just like everyone else."

"It was an educated guess on my part," Aren said. "Based on how superior she felt to all of us. Odds were in my favor."

Redevir clapped him on the shoulder. "You amaze, my boy. Every day you amaze."

Aren looked down at the unconscious Sister at his feet. The two Sarenwalkers were already back beside the fire, as if they had never moved at all.

The world is madness.

He looked up.

Inrianne was staring at him.

Aren forced a smile at her. "What?"

"We don't get along." She frowned, looking away at the trees. "Because of what I am, and what you are."

"What's your point?"

"We can't ever be friends. I can't be a friend to someone who does what you do to people like me."

"Not all of them are like you. I hunted a different kind."

"Yet you still detest me."

He bit his lip and scowled at her, past her, through her. "Yes. I doubt that will ever change."

"We will have to tolerate each other," she said. "Work together. Like we did just now."

Aren nodded. "I can do that. For now. But watch your step." *One wrong move and I will dose you and kill you.*

She sneered at him. There was a bitterness in her eyes. They hummed with buried anger when she looked at him. So instead she looked away. "The Sephors. What are they?"

Redevir stepped in beside him. "The Sephors are relics so old that they predate the Histories. The legends say that they belonged to someone called the Master, who made a home in a sacred temple, with walls of white beyond white."

"Or so the legend says," Aren said. "The Sephors were his magick instruments. No one knows what they were made of, or why they were so important. He possessed eleven of them—Crown, Wand, Sword, Cup, Disk, Dagger, Scourge, Chain, Lantern, Bell, and Talisman. Sangbran's sculpture in Qarsus shows each of them."

"Lost in legend," Redevir said. "Even I didn't believe they were real for the longest time."

"So what can they do?" Inrianne asked.

"No one really knows," Aren said. "Probably nothing."

"I want to see them," Inrianne said. "I want to go with you."

"You want to come along for what?" Aren asked. "Because what Redevir is talking about is not some stroll through a flowergarden."

"I want to be there. I want to be a part of it."

He tried to think of ways to dissuade her. "I don't know about that," he said. "Redevir has—"

"Redevir has given me leave to go already," she said.

"He *what?*" There went nearly all of his false reasons for sending her away. Redevir had already given her a stamp of approval. All that remained was that Aren hated her. That argument would make him look a fool.

"Why do you think I was so keen to help you deal with Tanashri?" she asked.

Aren glanced at Redevir.

Redevir shrugged. "I like having aces up my sleeve. She has fire. She has demonstrated that it is useful. I agreed because I think she could help us."

"Great," Aren said. "Fine. Bring whoever you want."

Shaot. How did I end up here? What did I do?

He turned to Hayles and Fainen. *It is time to end this.*

Both Sarenwalkers sat patiently beside the fire, Hayles sharpening his *somashalks*, Fainen fiddling with the fletching of one of his arrows. They both looked up from their work in unison. Their eyes were unblinking.

"My service to the Lord Protector is over," Aren said. "You no longer have to follow me. Redevir and I will go on our own way."

"We cannot do that," Hayles said.

"I no longer serve the Outer Guard. You are dismissed. Return to Amagon."

"That is impossible," Fainen said. "We go with you."

"But you have a responsibility to the Outer Guard."

"Our responsibility was to Donnovar," Hayles corrected him. "We are loyal to him."

"The Lord Protector betrayed our Captain," Fainen said. "We will not follow his commands."

"What does that mean?" Aren asked.

"We are Sarenwalkers," Hayles said. "We have been commanded to guard your life. It does not matter where you go. Our duty to our Captain remains."

Aren's head swam. He looked into their eyes and knew he could not dissuade them. "To ignore one's oath to the Warhost is sedition," he said. "Your punishment would be worse than even mine. You don't have to do this. You don't have to forfeit your lives this way."

"It is no longer in our hands," Fainen said.

"Only Donnovar can dismiss us from your side," Hayles said.

"But Donnovar is dead. He fell to the Vuls. You saw it yourself. He's gone."

"Then we must follow you until we meet him again," Hayles said, as calmly as if he were talking about the weather.

"I have a different mission now," Aren said.

"*You* are *our* mission now," Hayles said.

Aren stared at them in disbelief.

26

Seven Against One

WHEN THE ARROW HIT Retheld in the back, Corrin knew it was time to run again.

Three sunrises had come and gone this way. Each evening hiding in the rolling hills, and then each night scrambling through gullies and squishing through swamps, holding onto handfuls of reeds for dear life, trying not to vomit as he waded through water that smelled exactly how he imagined it would if Bol-Demar, the ancient and immense *Eater of Worlds*, had been recovering from a severe case of diarrhea there. Each night moving up to higher ground, sleeping on the upper slopes of green hills until the sky was bright enough for the Vuls to pick up their trail again.

It was tough to lose Retheld. He was strong and good with an axe. He had split a good number of heads with it the past few nights. And the others looked to him like a leader. Now there was no one. The only other man of rank was an adjutant named Mardin, who looked as though he had never once drawn his sword, and who couldn't lead his way out of a burlap sack.

The first two nights Corrin had seen them coming. Fair warning was given, and he and Reidos and Hallan had fled up and down hills and across open plains with a mixed bag of Outer Guard men. Some were soldiers, some couriers, some laborers, cooks, wagon team drivers. It reminded Corrin of the time his pursers had been a clutch of orphans, tossing him a bag of copper tossers, silver bits, Lissarian bronze betos, and a half-gold, with a quarter its weight missing from the edges being scraped off for the dust.

That had been some darkwork. The darkest he had ever done. But he judged it worth it. He was adept at passing judgment on men before he killed them. That job had featured plenty of overland running afterward, much like this.

His ankles were wobbly already, like wagon wheels halfway to coming off their axles. The people he was used to running from usually gave up after the first day or so. Some might pursue well into the second. But none ever kept coming after the third.

But the Vuls did. They crept and ran and crawled. And they kept coming. Every day a few more of the Outer Guard who escaped with them would meet their end. A few by arrows from unseen enemies, a few from knives in the dark, and some run down with spears and pole-axes.

Corrin threw himself down the hill and up the next, the Vuls racing behind. The surprise broke the Outer Guard men into two separate groups, one following Corrin and the other veering off to the left. They disappeared behind a hill and he did not see them again. They could have survived or been massacred, there was no way to tell.

As he reached the top of the next hill he was already slowing, hoping that the Vuls would be as well. And they were, at least the ones *behind* him were. He ran himself right into the middle of a scouting party trying to circle round.

"Egad," Corrin said. He flipped free his Calabari Claw with the same reflex nerve that made him speak. He drove it up under the first Vul's chin, up through his mouth and into his brain. He yanked it free before the body fell.

Farod.

Reidos stuck another with his sword, and stole a discarded bow from the first and fired off the three bent arrows that remained of its quiver into the group of them. The rest of the Outer Guard managed to cut through the others, but it slowed down the escape. The other Vuls were catching up. Reidos discarded the bow and picked Hallan up and carried him.

Some of the Outer Guard cut right and ran off. Some were too close to the oncoming Vuls and turned to fight it out. They did not last long. Oh, they fought plenty bravely, and took more than their share of Vuls with them. But they were too outnumbered to have a chance.

That left Corrin and company with only Mardin and three other Outer Guard.

The wagon driver was hit with two arrows and fell. They decided to honor him by spreading the hell out so that they would not be such splendid targets as he.

The cook tripped and broke his ankle. He was no more than a boy, but the Vuls stabbed him in the back as he crawled away.

Shaot. They are ruthless farods.

The Outer Guard horse-shoer veered farther and farther from Corrin's path and ended up amid a whole knot of them. *Poor fool.*

Corrin did not turn around. He did not go back for him. For any of them. If there was one thing that Jecks Keberan ever told him it was don't go back for anyone. Not even your own crew. Tie them off. Let them go and keep breathing. Rogues like him didn't live very long if they began to care about much of anything.

Corrin always did his best to emulate him.

It had worked out so far.

The Vuls were delayed hacking the horse-shoer to death. It allowed Corrin to reach the top of the next hill ahead. Reidos was coming up close behind. Mardin, the last surviving man of the Outer Guard, was still working his way down the last hill.

Reidos tweaked his ankle, he shuffled and hobbled. He handed Hallan off to Corrin.

"What am I supposed to do with this?" Corrin asked.

"Carry him."

"He looks heavy."

"*You* called him over to us."

"That was when one of those giant slime things was going to crush him. It was more of a favor."

"Well, now he is ours."

Corrin looked down at him. He looked over to the next hill. He saw the Vuls coming.

"Are you heroes?" Hallan asked.

"What?" Corrin began trotting down the hill with him.

"My brother always told me the men with swords were heroes, and they stopped the bad men from being bad."

"It is more complicated than that." He reached the basin.

The boy frowned. "But you have swords. You have to be a hero, don't you?"

"I am somewhere in between," Corrin said. He crossed knee-deep water, and then began to climb up the next hill.

Hallan frowned. "Oh, I thought you would be the heroes. You seemed like you were."

"That was a silly thing to think," Corrin said. "Why would you think that?"

"You said you were Corrin the Magnificent. That is a hero's name. Why else would someone call themselves that?"

"Well, hell."

"I can run fast," the boy said. "You can put me down if you want."

"You can't outrun them," Corrin said. He pointed back behind them. The Vuls were cresting the last hill. Running down. Mardin was down below, running about as fast as molasses across the water. "Mardin should buy us some time," Corrin said to Reidos.

"How?" Hallan asked. "Is he a hero?"

"No. He is more of a coward. A quintessential coward."

"Oh," the boy said. He looked down at the ground.

Corrin looked down the hill. Mardin had given up trying to climb it. He veered to the right between the two hills, threading a narrow patch of dry ground toward a wide plain. Just as Corrin predicted, all seven of the Vuls who had carried on this far diverted after him.

"Easy kill," Corrin said.

"What are we waiting for?" Reidos asked. He pointed ahead. "The hills are wooded there. We can lose them."

Corrin looked at the welcoming trees. Then he looked back at Mardin. Mardin turned back. He was trying for the hill again. He waved to Corrin.

"He thinks he is going to make it," Reidos said.

Corrin looked at the Vuls. *Seven.* Two with spears, four carrying swords, and one with a flail.

"Let's go," Reidos said.

Mardin ran toward Corrin. "Wait!" he cried. "Wait!"

"Mardin is not fast," Reidos said.

"Please wait!" Mardin cried.

Reidos was right and Corrin knew it. Mardin's legs were too slow to catch up to a tortoise. He stumbled and fell. He rolled most of the way back down the hill to where the Vuls were nearly on him.

Corrin chewed his lip. "Damn it, Mardin. You're useless."

"He's gone," Reidos said.

Corrin turned to Reidos. "He is worthless and stupid and cowardly. I'm surprised he made it this far."

"Are we going to wait for Mardin?" Hallan asked.

"He is not going to make it," Corrin said.

"Oh," Hallan said. He seemed sad.

Shaot.

Corrin looked at Mardin, then at Reidos, then back again. "Here," he said. "Hold the boy."

"What are you doing?" Reidos asked.

"Stay here, cripple," Corrin said. "I must work now."

"What are you doing?" Reidos repeated.

"I can't leave him back there," Corrin said. "I'm not *going to* leave him back there."

"Those are fully armored Vul soldiers," Reidos reminded him.

"So what?" Corrin said. "How many men have I ever fought at once?"

"Six. And they were drunk. And not soldiers. And mostly unarmed."

"Well," Corrin said. "High time I bothered to break that record."

"What the hell are you doing? Don't you like staying alive?"

"Not half as much as I like being magnificent. Do me a favor. Time me. Let me know how long it takes for me to kill them all." Corrin drew his sword, and flew down the hill.

Sorry, Jecks. Tying people off might be pragmatic, but it sure as shit isn't very magnificent.

The Vuls had already made a circle around Mardin, who conveniently stumbled and collapsed to the dirt.

Corrin slowed when he reached the bottom. He let his longsword sway from side to side. "Seven against one hardly seems fair." He gestured at Mardin. "And besides, this man is my assistant. Any complaints you may have with him, you can address them with me." He looked down at his hand and gasped as if he had just discovered his sword to be there. "Oh, me *and* my steel."

One of them grunted at him.

"My goodness you are ugly as all the hells at once." Corrin wanted to hurl a few more insults, but try as he might, he could not remember the Vulgos word for *fucking your mother up the ass.* "Come a little bit closer and we can dance."

They charged at him. Corrin stood ready with a *low guard.* He kept the point of his blade near the ground, directly ahead. He wanted them to think he did not know how to defend himself. While they charged, he studied. He noted the gaps in their armor, under the arm and below the chin. Leg plates only offered protection to the front.

The first Vul to reach him waved a flail at his head. Corrin leaned back, watching it career past his face. It seemed to come closer than he would have liked. He reached out low until the edge of his blade was touching the Vul's calf, and then he drew a cut, splitting cloth and muscle. The tendons made a sloppy sound as they split. The first Vul went down.

One.

The second Vul slowed and came in from the other side, sword in a *high guard.* Corrin jiggled the point of the *Steel Whore* in his face, taunting him. The Vul swung down at his head. Corrin cut into the cut, swinging harder than a parry, slapping the Vul's sword back, surprising him. Bought an extra half-second for a downward cut at the neck. Missed. Hit the edge of the helmet.

Shaot. He passed back, with a backhanded cut at the Vul's sword hand. He had better luck there. Shaved the thumb clean off.

The Vul switched hands.

Well shit on me.

Corrin stepped back, and let the sword slide back behind him, low to the ground. *See? You have me, Lord Thumbless. Come closer.*

The Vul moved in close, thinking Corrin to be off his balance.

Corrin was never off his balance.

The Vul raised his sword high for a heavy swing. Corrin stepped into his range, brought his blade up lightning fast, and guided a stab below the chin. All he had to do was lean forward.

Here, let me see your bloodspot real quick. It should just take a moment.

The Sabarian steel slid one inch into his throat. Before the Vul could take a step, he toppled, blood pouring from his neck. He struggled vainly to cover the wound with his hands, eyes bulging.

Two.

The rest of them moved in close together, advancing like the tight phalanx of a disciplined army. They did not spread out properly to take advantage of their numbers. Two of them held spears. The steel points darted menacingly as they came closer.

He let them come on, as if he intended to surrender. Their spears would only be useful if they could keep the points *between* themselves and Corrin. Corrin had no intention of providing them that luxury. As they neared him, he threw himself into a charge. He flew through the air, daintily knocking the tips of the weapons aside, and biting at their hands, clipping fingers. *Can't hold a spear without fingers.* But even if they could, once he was inside their range, they did not know what to do.

Too close for you now.

He drove his sword deep into the man at his right.

Red.

He pulled it free and continued the motion into a slash into the chest of the man at his left.

Blue.

Both men dropped to their knees, clutching at their bodies, as if trying to hold the blood in. The horror in their eyes was the mark of any man who realized that he was going to die and nothing would save him. Corrin was very familiar with that look.

The three who remained were suffering a sudden deficit of confidence. "All right, farods," he said. "Get ready for the magnificence."

He dashed among them. He stabbed and slashed, blocking two blows for each he delivered himself. He was not trying to kill with each swing, just maintain the initiative until an opening presented itself. They were too busy reacting to his attacks to be able to find any opportunities of their own. He found the moment he had been waiting for and hooked his blade into the belly of one.

Three.

Another came, slapping at the blade of the *Steel Whore* with a rusted broadsword. Corrin danced away from him, casually disappointed at the condition of his opponent's weapon. He feinted and stabbed. The man went down into the grass, clutching furiously at his groin.

Four.

Corrin was already engaging the final man, pressing the attack, offering him no time to think or recover or take initiative. Corrin decided to see if he could deliver three strikes for every attack the man sent his way, and made a passable go of it before managing a quick stab through the eye.

Lovely...

Corrin frowned as he realized he was one dead Vul shy of completing his favorite poem. It made him angry. He set about rifling through their armor for any salvageable weapons or equipment. There were none.

"Are you thieving?" Hallan asked. "My brother says all Amagon-men are thieves."

"No," Corrin said. "*Wrong.* Wrong, wrong, wrong. All *Lenagon*-men are thieves. All Amagon-men are adulterers. You must learn to keep your prejudices straight."

"Will we ever stop being hunted?" Mardin asked. "We are never going to make it out of here."

"Ugh," Corrin said. He threw his arms up in the air. "Let us proceed in conversation as if you were a theater performer who was delivering the role of someone brave."

They moved on until they reached the wooded hills Reidos had mentioned. There they rested. Hallan slept.

"What are you thinking?" he asked Reidos.

"You know what I'm thinking," he said. "I'm wondering what happened to Aren. I'm wondering what the hell we're going to do now. I'm wondering how we will get back to Amagon. We don't belong out here in this wilderness by ourselves."

"We have made it through tougher spots." Corrin said.

"When we had Aren with us. We need Aren's brain. He could look at these mountains, and the clouds, and the direction of the wind and tell us which way was the nearest city or river or whatever else. He would know their primary exports and the names of the last nineteen kings who lived there. Instead we are alone. We are lost in the rough of a foreign land. There are Vuls *everywhere.* Thousands of them. And what's worse, the Andristi are out in force to fight them. They may kill us for being here just as easily as anyone."

"The Andristi aren't stupid. Aren isn't the only one who can talk their way out of that kind of thing."

"You couldn't talk your way out of a saddlebag. Your only voice is your sword." He sighed. "We should not have come here."

"We had to come. It was Aren."

"I know," Reidos said. "So what are we going to do?"

"We have to get back to Amagon, clearly. If we want to live, that is where we will go."

"We're forever away from there. We don't have any horses."

"We'll find some. We'll manage. Remember the Dryden Hills?"

Reidos smiled in spite of himself. "I remember."

"We never thought we would get out of there either."

"But we did."

"But we did."

"What of the Vuls? Their warbands are all over Laman."

Hallan tugged at Corrin's sleeve. "What's a Vul?" he asked.

"Those big, ugly farods I just sent to meet their gods," Corrin said.

"I knew you would win," Hallan said.

"You know a sure thing when you see it," Corrin said. "I should take you gambling with me."

"Dice games?"

"Any kind of games. In Medion they have horse races, wrestling, everything."

"Great," Mardin said. "We're doomed to die in these hills, and you're talking about hippodromes."

"Shut up, Mardin." Corrin said.

"What are we going to do?" Mardin asked hopelessly. "Get to Amagon is not a plan. It is a thousand miles away. Laman is crawling with those barbarians!"

"And their creatures," Reidos added.

"Ugh," Corrin said. "Don't remind me. Those damned things were as slimy and bulbous as Bol-Demar's tit."

"Which tit?" Reidos asked. "Bol-Demar had seventy tits; one for each tentacle."

"And a sphincter for a mouth," Corrin said, "I know, I know."

"We will never make it back through Laman," Mardin said. "We would be better off with Bol-Demar."

"Because Ghiroergans are a hell of a lot more real than Bol-Demar," Reidos said.

"We don't have to go back through Laman," Corrin said. "We can go south through Palantar. We know where the Vuls will be. Aren told us."

"He told us where they approximately maybe could have been," Reidos said.

"We'll keep a lookout for them," Corrin said. "Once we get far enough, we can turn west back through Olbaran. The Alder River flows all the way to Medion, where we can find transportation to any corner of the world. We find a boat and stow ourselves away. Easy."

"Do you know how to get to Palantar?" Reidos asked. "I certainly don't."

"How hard can it be? We just face the sunrise and turn left."

"*Right*," Mardin said. "You face the sunrise and turn *right* to go south."

"Well that might be a little more difficult than whatever I said," Corrin said. "But I think we could do that, too."

"And what if we get lost in Provanion?" Reidos asked. "They say in Olbaran that Provanion Wood can swallow a man if he doesn't know what he's doing."

"Come on. It's *Provanion*, not the Cursed Land of Xeme. We can skirt around it if you want."

"We'll never make it past the Palantari," Mardin said.

"It'll be easy," Corrin said. "Trust me."

He heard a groan over his shoulder. It was one of the Vuls.

"What about him?" Mardin asked. "Are we just going to leave him free?"

The Vul cradled his ruined arm, holding in his pancreas with one hand. "You die," he said. "We kill you. We eat you."

Corrin stopped, turned around, and looked the Vul over one more time. "Oh, eat this," he said. He took out all three Levidian Nails and threw them into the man's neck. One glanced off his collar bone, but the other two stuck in his windpipe.

The Vul wheezed and collapsed.

"Farod," Corrin said. He trotted over to collect his Levidian Nails. They made a little popping sound when he tore them free of the trachea. He noticed Mardin staring at him. "What?" Corrin asked. "These are expensive."

****

Belaeriel moved swiftly across the shallow hills. The earth was soft, and seemed to cushion her feet. Even at her fast pace, she walked with fluid motion. She breathed the crisp morning air. It was like ice water to her lungs—refreshing, but painful if she pulled it in too deeply.

She ran a hand over one of her thighs, imagining her own skin, pale and smooth and tight beneath her silken robes. She let out a sigh. Walking alone through some wilderness for such a long time was wearing on her. She wanted to be back among the splendor of the city. She wanted to replace the pleasures that she left behind. Despite the necessity of her plans, there was always time for pleasure. She was aching for it, just as her legs ached from the strain of walking.

Belaeriel scanned the wide green horizon. She saw someone walking alone. *This must be the one he told me about.* There were no towns at any close proximity. No campers, or travelers, or wagons, or horses. She soon realized it was a little girl.

A child? Is this the source of the power I have been following? Impossible. She had assumed it had to be a grown man, from what he told her.

Belaeriel stepped up to the young girl. The child seemed to look past her. Belaeriel leaned down, and touched a gentle fingertip to the girl's face. The girl ceased all motion, and stood shaking, as though her body was not a strong enough shell to contain her energy.

She kneeled down. Rested her hand on the girl's shoulder. It was a vibration. Strong. Like nothing Belaeriel had ever felt. "What is your name, child?"

"My name is Murie," the girl said.

"What are you doing all alone out here, Murie?"

"I am going away. Far away."

"Away from where? Or who? Or what?"

"Home. Away from home."

"Why do you forsake your home?"

"It's not my home anymore. It's only a place now."

"What of your mother and father? They must worry over you."

"My mother and father are gone."

"What happened to them?"

"They died, and I want whoever killed them to die."

Belaeriel smiled. *Maybe I won't bring this child to him after all. Maybe I will keep her for myself.*

"Easy, child," Belaeriel said. She had a sudden thought. "I know who killed your mother and father. I will help you. I will show you how to hurt them."

27

Map Of The World

AREN OPENED HIS EYES to darkness. *Where am I?* It was night again. His ears twitched at the sound of harpy owls, distant, but still audible. He looked around. Hayles and Fainen both slept on the opposite side of the smoldering cookfire. Redevir was in a deep sleep with a hint of snoring. Tanashri and Inrianne were huddled in slumber.

He looked up at the night sky, the moons, and the trees.

I am on the frontier of Laman and Palantar. Heading south. South is safe.

He rolled over and looked at the side of his tracer satchel. He had carved seventeen strikes into the leather. One for each day since the Fields of Syn.

He heard a sound—the crack of a stiff twig. He traced the outline of a Vul in every shadow. He heard a sound again. The Sarenwalkers rolled in their cloaks, but did not wake. Neither of them had slept for days until now. They would not come around easily.

He felt suddenly alone. The idea of calling out to wake the others did not even occur to him. Thoughts came slowly. His eyes watered. He felt a tingling in his neck, his arms, and his scalp. He held his breath. He put a hand on his sword and listened.

He heard it again.

One step. Then another. Closer.

Right behind his head.

He tore his sword free, and jumped to his feet, kicking over the stew pot. A figure was outlined by the bright blue light of Anularia, stumbling backward, tripping over a thick root. A shriek of surprise rang out. It was a woman's voice.

The Sarenwalkers were awake and on their feet, as if they had been standing there the whole time.

"Aren of Amagon?" came a faint voice.

Aren recognized it from somewhere. "I am Aren. Name yourself."

"Eriana," she said. "Eriana. Do you not remember me?"

What the fuck is happening? Is this s dream? Aren looked at her. Her pale skin was blue in the moonlight. She was dressed in a fighter's jerkin over her blue tunic. She even had on a shirt of mail beneath her cloak, and a curved Andristi shortsword at her waist. She was dressed as a warrior, but Aren's mind leapt to the memory of her in a pale white gown at the feast of Cail Tiril. He could not reconcile that memory with the woman now standing defiant before him.

"Eriana?" Aren said. "Where...?"

"I thought I would meet you in Synsirok," she said. "It is the city where I was born. I have not been there in many years. I thought it would be a good time to go."

"There are Vul warbands everywhere," Aren said sharply, folding his arms in disapproval.

Eriana shrugged. "There are always Vuls on the frontier."

"I think you know this is different."

He could see in her expression that she did. But she merely shrugged once more. "You left Cair Tiril so abruptly. I thought I would find you there, in Synsirok, and we could continue our talk."

"What talk?"

"About magick. About anything really. I did not know you would already be gone again."

"Won't your family worry when they find out your are gone from Synsirok?"

She glanced aside. "They do not know I *went* to Synsirok."

Aren's eyes bulged out. "You mean you ran away?"

Her eyes flickered up to meet his, and narrowed. "You make it sound so juvenile. I did not sneak like a little child. I walked out of the door to my room, and then I just kept walking."

"You should have remained in Synsirok then," Aren said. "What in all hells are you doing out here?"

"I heard about what happened at the Chapel."

"That should have been warning enough to stop what you were doing. How did you know I would be here? How did you find us?"

"I saw what happened on the Fields of Syn. I worried. I followed you. Tracked you."

"You are a tracker?"

She wrinkled her lip at him. "My father commands hundreds of Greycloaks. Greycloaks love to talk about tracking. I love to listen."

"Why?" Aren asked. "Wait. Never mind. There are Vuls out there. You need to be back in Cair Tiril."

"But..."

"But nothing," Aren said. "Are you mad? You must have seen what happened to all the others. What do you think the Vuls would do if they found you?" He could have strangled an ox. The Vuls had made short work of the bravest and best warriors Aren had ever known. What did this girl think would happen to her if a handful of them were to stumble across her in the middle of the night? He thought that if she could only appreciate the danger, she might understand how wrong it was for her to come here, how mistaken she was, but she didn't. It seemed to make her grow even more bold.

She smirked at him in the moonlight. "I can take care of myself."

"That doesn't matter," Aren said. *Donnovar knew how to fight twenty men at once and it couldn't save him.*

"I think it does matter," she said.

"It doesn't. It doesn't, and all the arguments in the world won't change that. It is certain as stone." He kicked the ground for emphasis. "Where did you even get that sword? Did you steal it? Walking around with a sword doesn't make you a warrior."

She narrowed her eyes at him and pursed her lips. "This is *my* sword. The one *I* use when I train with the Knights of the White Moon. This was forged *for me* by a master from the Hammersmith. Whose sword are *you* holding? Because it looks like you have never held a sword before in your life. Your form is awful." She folded her arms.

Aren looked down at the sword in his hand. He did not know enough about how swords were used to know whether she was right or whether she was trying to trip him up. Either way, it worked. He lowered his hand and then spent a full minute trying to line up the point with the slot of the scabbard. *Shaot.* "Why did you come here? You don't even know me."

"I wanted to come with you. I wanted to see Amagon. I assumed it would be a peaceful journey. I didn't know."

"You can't come with us," Aren said. "This isn't a pleasure trip anymore. This is deadly serious. Why would you want to leave Laman anyway?"

"I want to see the home of Loyol," she said.

"No. We are not taking you out of Laman. That is out of the question."

"What am I to do then? Go back the way I came? Through the Vuls?"

That stumped Aren. She was using his own argument against him.

"That would not be recommended," Hayles said.

"I will not slow you down," Eriana promised. "I am very fast."

"I'm sure you are," Aren said. *Fast and warm and beautiful and...*

"Why can't I come?" she asked. "Do I make poor company?"

Think of a reason. Think of a reason. Get her out of here before you never let her go again. "You are a member of the royal household." *Do better. That sounded forced. Think.*

"I came here of my own free will," Eriana said. "I did not look forward with fear, and I did not look back when I left. I looked inward and saw what I wanted. To leave. To go. To fly away. I wanted *now*. Solathas always told me that all that matters is now. Only always ever now."

"Only always ever now," Aren said. *That is the same thing he said to me.* "Saying so isn't likely to pacify the Greycloaks they send to slay us and bring you back." *Better. More believable.*

The Sarenwalkers looked at each other, then at Aren, as if to say: the Greycloaks that *try* to slay us.

"Let her stay, Aren," Redevir said. "She is obviously very resourceful to have made it all this way."

Hayles sat down and began to lay out fresh branches for the fire as though he did not mind being shaken from his deep sleep at all.

Aren turned to the others.

"I have no opinion," Tanashri said. "She may help out mission or hinder it. But if she leaves now, she may be picked up by the Vuls or the Palantari. They could interrogate her. They could find our trail."

Hayles briefly snickered at that. No one else noticed, but Aren did.

Inrianne growled. "Stay. Don't stay. Just stop talking, little girl, and let me sleep in peace."

Eriana stood tall, her chin up. He looked into her eyes, pale blue and mesmerizing in the moonlight. Soft, not desperate. Calm as a placid lake. She stood close enough for him to touch her if he reached out, close enough to smell the tousled locks of her golden hair.

"I will not force myself on an unwelcoming host," she said.

No, don't go.

"You're right," he said at last. "There is no safe way to get back to Cair Tiril. You will have to come with us for now." He said it sternly, as if it was a rebuke.

Eriana just smiled, as if there were no danger at all.

Aren never did make it back to sleep after. He found he was unable to stop looking at her unless he forced himself, his eyes like twin boulders he needed to push through knee-deep mud to turn them away from her.

Even then he could still not stop *thinking* about her. He kept imagining her face and the sound of her voice, until he began to worry he was remembering them wrong, and then he would look at her all over again, and ask her a dull question just to hear her speak an answer. It did not seem as crazy in the moonlight. Once the sun rose it felt more conspicuous, criminal even.

They hiked their way through the morning. Hayles took them through tangled trees, hoping that the Vuls would be occupied with the Palantari army, allowing them to slip by unnoticed.

Hayles and Fainen never complained. Redevir did so only in grunts and throat-clearings. Inrianne complained often. Eriana did the opposite of complain; she actively pointed out how much fun she was having. She seemed to be taking the travel better even than the Sarenwalkers. Those two were indifferent. She was downright cheerful.

Aren bit his tongue to avoid groaning as they went. His head still pounded at each step. The blow he had taken on the Fields of Syn was days old, but still generated a dull throbbing pain at every turn of his neck.

Just shy of midday they crested the high ridge that gave the view of the valley around the Palantari capital city, Cair Vanarol. They crawled and climbed past a half-dozen Vul patrols, both on the way to the ridge, and while moving up it. By the skill of Hayles, they were seen by very few Vuls. By the skill of Fainen, those Vuls were all dead.

It was treeless, but covered from end to end with thick weeds and rushes. When they sat, they would be hidden from any eyes that might pass by. There Hayles stopped them, and prepared an early lunch, as they would need to wait out a heavy Vul presence in the next valley before moving on. From their vantage, they could look down on the distant Palantari army issuing out to confront a large Vul warband.

Aren excused himself, and wandered a ways over the ridge. He set himself on his knees, and pulled the crushed leaves from his pouch. The pipe was small and cool in his hand. He pressed a liberal amount of the malagayne into one end. He lit it with a tiny fire-stick.

The first inhale was always the most memorable. The smoke was sweet, and he pulled it into himself with a deep inhale. He felt it flowing through his blood, as if it rode down his nerves to the very tips of his fingers and toes. His legs slackened and he had to sit down before he fell over.

The stinging in his limbs vanished like dust wiped away by a broom—still there, but brushed away to a distant corner of the room. The sweetness of the aftertaste thrilled him. He felt desire fade to the background, not gone, but invisible. He watched the wisps of smoke drift up and away into the sky like ashen serpents. Then he rolled the pipe in its cloth.

He was free from the pain as long as he had malagayne in his body. And now he smoked twice as much as he used to. He didn't have to think about

Corrin or Reidos or Donnovar. He didn't have to think about Margol and the Lord Protector, Terrol's body and Raviel's. The dead girls. Destiny. He did not have any desire to be thwarted. Each individual moment was the only one that mattered, and when it passed, it was gone.

Only always ever now.

He returned to the edge of the ridge and plopped down beside Eriana.

She smiled to him.

"There is a profoundness to looking at something of such beauty when you know it will kill you if you stray too close," Aren said.

Eriana looked up at him, squinting, as if unsure if he meant her or the view.

He wasn't sure himself.

He looked down on the plain below as two armies met. He saw Vuls in huge block formations advancing over a shallow rise. Facing them were the brightly shining lines of the Palantari. Banners fluttered atop rigid poles in purple and orange. Their helmets shined in the sunlight and their polished mail shimmered, making their lines a long worm of rippling sparkles.

Aren watched the lines as they met, mingling in a stunning ballet of blood and death. The brown mass of Vuls joined itself to the glistening snake of the Palantari. It was so distant, he could not even hear the clash of arms, or the desperate cries of dying men. It was only a writhing, shapeless tangle of colors and textures, soft, even beautiful, to behold. *How different it is than being within.*

Thousands of soldiers ebbed forward then back as the battle raged. The tiny shapes of men could be seen falling and laying still. Boots turned grass to mud, and blood turned the mud into a swamp.

It was like a picture being painted, slowly, laboriously, as each man reluctantly released his lifeblood onto the horrible canvas of mud and pain. *So many would die for this work of art.* He was unable to look away as it changed its shape over and over and over again.

He thought of what it must have looked like to gaze down upon the Fields of Syn that night. *Would it have been this beautiful?* It probably would have. Beautiful and horrible.

"This is the very spot where Loyol stood when he had made his famous sketch of the cityscape," Eriana said.

The towers stood tall, and the walls flowed in three unbroken rings about the different sections of the city. Everything about Cair Vanarol was martial in nature, like a magnificent garden of military flowers. It had been founded by Prince Palan during his revolt, birthed from the belly of war.

Eriana never looked at the death. She didn't look at the battle. Even now, she looked away to the east at the walls and towers of Cair Vanarol, as if the battle didn't even exist.

"It's a beautiful view," she whispered. "I can't believe we stand on the same ground that Loyol once did."

"Loyol traveled all over Laman," Aren said. "You walked where he has at least hundred times." He tried to say it without sounding awkward, but didn't quite succeed. He couldn't look at her and talk at the same time without random words falling out of his head.

"It's different out here," she said.

He looked at her. Her hair was always shining. Her face always seemed so smooth. She did not look at him. He turned back to the view below. He wanted to reach out to her so badly. He didn't though. "Loyol made his sketch of Cair Vanarol during his architectural period."

"After he left Laman, he painted nothing but buildings for three years," she said.

"The last one was of Shaezrod Spur, his most famous. He considered the tower to be the ideal work of man. The Patriarchs of Arradan built it as a symbol of the joining of the gods of the sky and the gods of the earth."

"Why is Loyol's painting of it named *Sanctuary?*"

"The tower was the sanctuary for the empire during *Devron's Folly*. It protected the people from Devron. Have you heard of the Seven Saints?"

"Yes. The greatest of all the Patriarchs. I know the story."

"The tower was also a spiritual Sanctuary because of the presence of the sky-father gods in times of plenty and the earth-mother gods in times of famine. It was where the people connected with their gods."

"You know a great deal about Arradan for someone who is not from there."

"Not that it does me much good. There aren't many uses for it. Just stories to tell." He couldn't fathom why someone who had grown up in the luxury of a palace would even care.

"There was a time in Laman when storytellers were revered above the tribal chieftains," she said. "Everyone loves to hear a good story."

"I suppose so," Aren said. He caught himself half-smiling at her. For a moment he forgot that she was royalty. She was just a woman sitting beside him. He wanted to reach out and put his hand on hers, but he couldn't make his arm move.

"Let me show you something," she said. She reached into her carry-bag and rummaged through its contents until she pulled out a piece of thick canvass parchment, yellowed with age. It was folded twice over, and she held it in front of his eyes before she began to unfold it.

It was covered in sketched lines and faded colors. Aren squinted and leaned in close to it. It was a map of the world, he realized, a hand-drawn sketch of kingdoms and freeholds near and far. Each land was labeled in bold, from the wettest jungles of Chashreel to the coldest wastelands of the Shola.

"What is it?" he asked.

She gave him a look. "It is a map, silly."

"I know it's a map. Obviously it's a map. What is its meaning?"

Eriana looked down at it for a time, before turning up to face him again. "I drew this myself. When I was a little girl. With the guidance of Solathas. I was very proud of it." She looked down at it again. "I am still proud of it. Solathas labeled it for me. It shows all of the places I have always wanted to see. It reminds me of the inclination of my heart."

"Inclination towards what? Novelty? Exotic distractions?"

"No." She shook her head. "My desire for understanding. I love the feeling of understanding something, or some*one*. Not mere facts about them, but the feeling when all those facts connect together into what it means to *be them*. What better way to understand the other places or peoples than to be immersed in their cultures? I want to be surrounded by their homes, their art, their music, their food. I want to understand the world. I would have to go everywhere to do that."

Aren smiled, and then chuckled a bit. "Let me see that again." She handed it to him. He immediately took exception to at least ten of the places labeled upon it. "I would not recommend Kharthist," he said. "It is a wasteland full of cannibals. And Belegorod; they kill outsiders there. And Hylamar is not the best of climate. Sedonia, Aragol, Haradel, and Vandolin are all lands of the Olbaranian Kingdom. They are not on the best of terms with Laman at the moment. The Ministry is antagonistic toward Great Santhalian as well. That rules out Corien. The Levantine is full of mercenaries, and Calabar is full of pirates. Halsabad has been consistently at war with both Tyrelon and Hylamar for the last hundred years, and..."

She huffed a breath and sneered at him, snatching the parchment from his fingers. "Is there any place left that you would *not* suggest I avoid?"

"I'm sorry. I didn't mean to disturb your dream of seeing the world."

She smiled, and then she laughed playfully at him. "Even Solathas says that I should not go to Kharthist. I do not expect to see each and every one, only that I wish to *try* to see them all." She placed one finger on the map, pointing at Laman. Her finger meandered across the page, crossing the many lands of Olbaran, following the path of the Alder River, until her fingertip came to rest over Amagon. "This is the place that I shall see first, thanks to you."

Aren smiled in spite of himself. "That is where we go for the time being, but who knows where Redevir will take us next. Even I don't know that for certain. No one does but Redevir himself."

"It seems sometimes that even Redevir does not know where Redevir is going," Eriana said. She giggled, and Aren smiled at her.

Aren looked down at the map for a long time, as Eriana carefully folded it and returned it to her carry-bag. When she was done, he kept looking at her empty hands, where only a moment before, the entire world had been.

"Redevir acts like you are his partner. Are you a treasure hunter now?"

"It seems that way," he said.

"You sound so unhappy about it."

"It's something to do."

"The Sephors are said to be ancient. No one has seen them in thousands of years, they say."

"I did not even believe they were real."

"Why not?"

"It was easier to hate the man who raised me if they weren't."

"Hate? Your father? Why?"

"That man thought a lot of strange things about the world. None of them worked out well. Sometimes he would not come home for days, and he began to surround himself with strange men and women. I remember their faces sometimes. I used to be so angry when he was gone. But I got over it. I learned it was better when he wasn't there. Never mind. We shouldn't talk about that."

"My father was never around either."

"No?"

"He was *of the blood*, as they say."

"Of the blood?"

"Bloodlines are important to we Andristi," she said. She looked away. "Well, to many of my people. It is how we retain our long lives. They seek for the purest blood. Those like me, we are chosen from birth and told who we are to bear children to. It is arranged. It is preordained. To dilute the blood is to dilute our descendants' long lives. It is frowned upon to beget children with those further from the blood. And it is a crime to make more Mahhen."

"You mean have children with people like me?" He laughed.

"Yes. Not that I would with you anyway. You disparaged my map." She smiled. "They force us to learn all the traditions. We even had to learn the ancient Sinjan alphabet, and know it well enough to write it."

"Sinjan," Aren said. "The old alphabet of Laman that was replaced by the modern Silis script."

"It is easier on the ink and easier on the hands. So we still *speak* Sinjan, but we *write* Silis. Except for me. I had to learn both. While all my friends were out playing in the gardens, I was perched over a desk with crusty old men yelling at me."

"It was a dead alphabet hundreds of years ago."

"At least Solathas used to play word games with me to make it fun. He used the Sinjan alphabet and numerals. It helped."

Aren smiled. "The Mahhennin who moved out west used old Sinjan letters to communicate to each other without giving away their secrets to their enemies."

"Like a secret code?" she asked.

"Exactly. The great exodus of the Mahhennin from Laman before the Great War brought them to the fading Arradian Empire. They first settled around the city of Karorad. Wars nearly broke out between the emperors and the Mahhennin chieftains."

"What happened to them?"

"They were driven out of Karorad eventually. They roamed the land until they were united by Weirmaheir and settled in Amagon. That was just before Kradishah's invasion and the Great War."

"Tales of the Great War are still told in Laman. There are places where forests still won't grow because of what he did."

"It was one of the single most important events in history. The invasion united all the people of the northlands. Alliances were formed during the dark years that still bind us today. Rogar the Great unified Olbaran, and recognized the founding of Amagon and Lenagon because of his treaties with their first rulers, Weirmaheir and Atheron. It brought about the first great peace between Laman and Palantar, when Salas took a blood oath with Lanier."

"So many things came of that," she said. "You should tell me a story about the Great War some time, but not now." She glanced at the battle out of the corner of her eye.

"I will."

"My people long ago drove out the Mahhennin, as many of them as they could. That is how there came to be so many of them in your homeland. People like my father believe if they can continue long enough the Andristi people will regain some kind of immortality they claim our ancestors lost. Some say that Prince Palan thought the same way, back in his day. They say that the Kinstrife that shattered our people and watered our trees in blood and broke our kingdom in two came to pass *because* of those ideas."

"The deadliest civil war in history," Aren said, nodding in lamentation. "Of course. There would not have been a need for a great peace if your kingdom had not been sundered in the first place."

"It is the reason they teach royals like me to fight. It is tradition now. But it has dark origins. It became so because my ancestors, men and women, needed to learn to defend themselves as the warriors did."

"That is an old tradition then. The Great War was five hundred years ago, but the Kinstrife was hundreds of years even before that. History must weigh heavily on your shoulders."

"We are reminded every time we look to the east and see the border of Palantar, lands that were once united with us, a part of us, now forever separate. It is worthy of the lament of poets." She paused. Her expression darkened. "Some of those like my father think it would have been better if Prince Palan had won, and taken the throne in Cair Tiril for his own, kept Laman whole and purged it of everyone who was not pure. Their opinions weigh heavily on me as well."

"It sounds like they put a lot of pressure on you," he said. "Live a certain way, think a certain way, love a certain way."

"Oh my, yes. But it was better once I came to live in Great Santhalian's court. It is different there, better, welcoming to all. I love it so much. It is more of a home to me than where my father lives."

"Why was he never there? Your father."

"He belonged to a group that calls itself the *Bloodline Champions*. He was always pressing their rights in the court of Great Santhalian, and riding all across Laman to seek supporters. I saw very little of him."

"I am sorry to hear that," Aren said. "The last time I saw mine, I tried to burn his papers. I remember his little drawings. I didn't know what they were then. But I do now. The Sephors. I got a beating for it like you wouldn't believe."

"My father beat me the first time I ran away from home. I was small then. And again when I roughed up the boy they arranged for my marriage. His father was important blood, and he could make magick."

"Brave to fistfight a wizard."

"I knew they would not hurt me. My father was too important to them, and they were not rogues."

He paused. "Rogue users don't deserve to be alive. We have no way to know if at any moment they might unleash horrible power. Rogue users are abominations."

She widened her eyes at him. "You feel this strongly. In Laman they have a system to identify people of the magick and take them to the court for training." She paused. "I would be fearful if Solathas was not finding them and teaching them."

"Your land is one of beauty in every way. And Solathas is, well, Solathas."

"Solathas is like my father now. And I am sure he is so to many others as well."

Aren smiled. "I'm glad."

"How are things with your family now?" she asked.

"Let's talk about something else," he suggested.

She reached over and held his hand comfortingly, and together they looked at the beauty of the world for what seemed an eternity.

She leaned back, holding herself up with her hands. "When I heard that a Glasseye was coming from the west, I did not expect someone like you."

"No?"

"No. I thought Glasseyes were all old men."

"Some are," Aren admitted. "My mentor was. It doesn't matter. Most of them give it up before long."

"From what you showed me it seems like hard work."

Aren glanced at his hidden malagayne. "It is."

"But you have caught criminals before?"

"Twenty-seven of them. Thieves and murderers."

"I never asked you what happens when you catch them. I can't imagine that they would be put into a dungeon."

"Lesser criminals are handed over to the Ministry. They are given... treatments. The bad ones go to the fires. I catch them and they burn."

"It sounds exciting."

"In a way." Aren paused. "It can be...difficult."

"Everything is difficult. You are strong because you do it. The weak don't even try."

"Thinking back on it, it feels hard to describe what I did. I caught those people, but nothing ever changed. I always came home, to what was supposed to be my home, and I just waited there for the next thing to happen. It was like it wasn't even my home, wasn't even my life. It was just a space I was occupying. I didn't have any time for meeting new people. The faces I saw were the same set of faces every day. But they were not really my friends. I thought they were, but they weren't. They were my employers, or my clients, or I was theirs. I wonder if any of those conversations mattered. Or did they all forget me as soon as I left the room?"

"The past was what it was, Aren. And the future is what it will be. The only thing you have any power over is *now*. Only always ever now."

"Only always ever now," he said.

She smiled. "Does it bother you that I refer to you as a Glasseye? I will call you Render Tracer if it pleases you better."

For some reason, her asking him that was the sweetest thing he could remember anyone ever saying to him. "Either one is fine. I am used to it." *You may call me by whatever name you wish.*

"We should be moving," Hayles said, looking up from the battle.

On the field below, the Vuls were scattering in all directions and the Palantari were reorganizing, and sending companies out after them, triumphantly clearing the field of enemies.

"They will be sending war parties," Fainen advised. "We must be gone before they come this way."

Aren nodded, and that was that. They were on the move once again.

28

All The Time In The World

KELUWEN KEPT HER HEAD above the water, but just barely.

Her feet were just long enough that if she pointed her toes, she could touch the other end of the washbasin and hold herself in place such that her chin was gently resting on the water without it surging up over her mouth and nose.

She let the heat do its work, dissolving the pain, releasing muscles strained further than she had ever felt. She had not traveled by foot so far in such a short time since she had run away from *that place*. The first place she had run away from. The last place she had ever known peace.

She felt the steam softening her skin, her face radiating tranquility, like a glow she could feel. She closed her eyes and could feel the dirt and soil leaving her body, floating away on tiny ripples of water. Oil and fear leached into the tub. Pain drifted away from her like the steam. She lazily poured the last drops of a bottle of sweetwine into her mouth, and then rolled it across the floor into the corner. She let the sounds and smells and the thousand things to do in a city fill her thoughts to the brim so there would be no more room for grief for a while. For as long as she could manage.

It felt so...good. To be clean again. She had already sent her clothes to the washerwomen. They would return smelling of ambergris and myrrh, no more stains of sweat, no more stench of a myriad strange pollens. They would be clean. The girls would brush her hair and trim it. They would squeeze her feet, grind her calves, and pummel her thighs. She was already thinking of their hands on her body, stretching her neck, driving fists into her shoulders, pressing on her spine.

Orrinas walked it. He wore his pale orange robes. Also freshly cleaned. "You have lost weight," she said. He had. His chin seemed twice as long now that his cheeks had sunken in so far.

"You only just noticed this?"

"No," she said defensively. "Only that I finally see it free of the context of fear."

He smiled at her. "Are you enjoying being pampered?"

"I always do. I hate when I can smell myself more than the room I am standing in. And I prefer my hair to shine."

"I love a woman who gives such care to her hair, yet will fight to the death wherever her heart leads."

"There had better be just the one woman you love," she said. "Even when my hair is oily and full of dirt."

"Your hair *always* shines to my eyes."

"You have to say that," she said, squinting at him. "To spare yourself a good throttling."

"You have been nice to the servants, I hope."

"I always am," she said.

"Except when you aren't."

"That was one time."

"Fin Terrace?"

"Alright, two times."

"Ossamport? Ethios? Kessalmir? Twice?"

"What was the question again?"

"The servants."

"I was kind to them," she said. She planted a hand on either side of the basin and hoisted herself up until she could ground her feet. Then she stood up straight in front of him.

His eyes widened.

She liked that she could still make him do that even after all this time.

"I see they shaved your body in the *Arradian fashion.*"

She smiled. "You seem so surprised."

He shrugged without taking his eyes off her. "You have always favored the Olybrian style. For you, this is...different."

"We are back in civilization now. I have to compete with all the other cosmopolitan women once more." She allowed her wet skin to reflect the candlelight to his eyes a few moments longer. "What say you then? Midnight lips by candlelight? Play your cards right, and your fingers may find their way to Arradan tonight."

"I should be so lucky," he said.

"If you are very sweet, perhaps your lips and tongue as well."

"Have I spent my last breath and gone to everwonder early?"

She smiled. She raised her arms above her head, running her fingers through her hair. "If you take me dancing tonight the way you used to, then I may very well let you mount Arradan and ride it until the earth quakes and the towers fall."

He smiled. "We have a mission first."

She frowned. "Now? Even here? Even in Aldria?" She reached down and plucked a clean towel from its stool and set to pressing herself dry.

"*Axis Ardent* is everywhere, and so its agents are everywhere."

"How did they find out we were here so quickly?"

"Duran sent a message to them, in the hidden slot of a drop box, following the universal cypher."

"Before he even settles down to eat?"

Orrinas shrugged. "He is dedicated to the cause."

"And we are not?" She grimaced fiercely. "Have we not sacrificed?"

"He did not mention we were here. His mission was different from ours, with a different urgency regarding its updates. They found out we were here when they came to find Duran."

She rolled her eyes. "Typical."

"This information should be of great interest to us," Orrinas said. "I have been assured the information is worth looking the other way at a few transgressions."

"And we *must* go?"

"Yes."

Her face hardened. "This is real."

He nodded. "It is real this time," he assured her.

"Then I am ready." She dressed quickly, methodically, a series of actions she had performed in haste since she was a child. Everything in haste. Always. She did not move any other way. Living in a gutter long ago taught her that, how to be always ready, to go at a moment's notice, leave what she could not carry, and move on.

Stepping out into Aldria was like stepping into another world. Seb had always told her to stay away from the rich, that the wealthy did not see people the way everyone else did. They were as different from ordinary people as she was from a normal. *Never trust the rich*, he told her. *You are only a series of tasks to them, a set of functions that they can use or not. That is all. Nothing more.* It had always proven true.

But the rich were impossible to avoid in a place like Aldria. Wealthy travelers mingled with Halsabadi master-sellers, Malorese gem caravans, pleasuremongers from the Calabari coast, and Biss pain merchants. The poorest inn here was twice the size of the wealthiest in Westgate. And there were as many soldiers and armed bodyguards here as there were pickpockets back in Westgate.

It took some doing to find the filthiest, most suspicious of taverns in this city. But Orrinas managed to. A place where it seemed the air inside had not circulated out for decades. It was dim within, but it was also nearly full. Men with thick weathered fingers patted the grips of cleavers in their belts and had old bloody hammers tucked in their boots.

Orrinas sat her down on a bench beside the fire, where it smelled more of smoke and less of piss. She scanned the room briefly, her fingertips hovering at her elbows, tickling the edges of the gloves. But no one there seemed to care that either of them existed. Even the most dangerous, steel-bearing, flea-ridden, whiskey-sweating, brutal toe-cutters did not pay them so much as a glance. Everyone in this place was either a very dangerous person waiting to be hired, or was someone like her and Orrinas who were here to meet with someone equally dangerous to offer work.

To that extent, Keluwen realized that she was likely sitting in the safest spot in the entire city of Aldria. If any of these murderers tried to lay a hand on her, then they might cost someone even more deadly a well-paying job, and end up dead themselves in short order. The entire system kept peace afloat in this tavern.

"They are here," Orrinas said.

He gestured to a muscular man with as many earrings as he had missing teeth, wearing a black leather vest over a red silk shirt crusted with dried food, and black trousers tight enough that she could see his shape vividly. He looked like he had gone out to sea only half as often as his mustache.

He was accompanied by a man who needed no name, for he was a massive brute, brow as thick as his arms, and another man who was dressed as a knight of Olbaran, yellow surcoat, worn, moth-eaten, chainmail beneath splashed with piss, dried vomit obscuring whichever noble House had its sigil on it. The man leading them introduced them first. "Lilliman," he said for the brute. "Pikas Bodrum," he said of the vomitous knight.

"Do we need to know your names?" Orrinas asked.

"You are here to meet me," the first man said, shrugging. "They told me what you would look like." He dropped himself onto the bench across the table from them. "My name is Rekel Barj," he said. "Whether you want to know it or not. I do darkwork."

"Darkwork?" Keluwen asked.

"The kind you'd rather not see done in the daylight," Rekel said. "Who is this fine beauty? Average tits, I'd say. Clear skin, strong hips. I can tell from her eyes she has midnight lips as wet as an autumn storm. Is she a gift for me?"

"She is not," Orrinas said.

I feel like you should have said more than that, Orrinas, Keluwen thought.

"Hmmm," Rekel said. "Shame. I have had a hard on as big as a tower in Medion since I debarked. Came a long way to get here for just this one meeting. A long way."

"You are here to tell us something," Keluwen said. "The narrative of your life is a waste of both our time."

"I like you more now," he said. "Fire. So many of the fat rich leg-spreaders around here are sick with weakness, trying to convince themselves to remain married by fucking their boredom away on the end of a murderer's cock."

Keluwen hardened her eyes. "You are wasting our time again."

Rekel shrugged. His lewd smile flattened abruptly into a face that aimed only toward the business at hand. "You have the money?"

Orrinas nodded. "Fifteen Olbaranian gold crowns." He slid the coinpurse across the table.

Rekel lifted it, felt the weight, jingled it. "Sounds right."

"You may count it if you wish," Orrinas said.

"I trust you, friend," Rekel said. "Quintain vouches for you. Your friend in Kamedol? He has never led me wrong before. And he knows I'd gut him like a trout if this purse was even one coin short."

"The information," Orrinas prompted.

"You wanted to know about cultists and mountains and strange lights. One specific mountain. On the border of Amagon and Olbaran. They say it is in Olbaran, but the truth is no one knows for sure. We were hired by a purser more secretive than any other, and I have done darkwork on the High King's own agents. This lot leaned further into the shadows than even those."

"What did they hire you for?" Orrinas asked.

"The same thing they always wanted," Rekel said. "A girl. A pretty one. Young."

Keluwen felt her face grow hot. "What did they do with them?" *Were they for Kinraigan?*

"They were gifts for the Mimmions."

Wait. What? "The cultists?"

"Gifts. I really do not think they served any purpose. The Mimmions just liked to use them for their rituals."

Rituals. You mean sacrifices.

"Well that last night, the purser wasn't alone," Rekel said. "He was with his uppers. Men in fine capes. Blue like the night sky. Silver badges. Little crescents. Had the look of important men. I had the impression they were there to butter up the Mimmions so that they would do this ritual. Seemed like something new for them."

"Silver crescents," Orrinas said. "Authorities of Amagon."

"Why would they be there?" Keluwen asked.

"Because the gateway Duran saw was not the *Mimmion's* gateway," Orrinas said. "It was *Amagon's* gateway. The Mimmions were just being used."

"We never saw who was under the hoods," Rekel said. "Didn't care. But we saw those lights. From a good distance. They did something up there alright. No bonfire makes a light like that. And then we heard the screams and we moved on fast. Not many go there. But there is a village near. We heard strange rumors about what happened to that village."

"We keep hearing about children," Orrinas said. "Did you see any after?"

"No," Rekel said. "But that is the strange thing. The same purser hired us back the week after. Wanted us to deliver correspondence to some woman. Burlybells, or some such. The messages were meant to be secret, but I read them, of course. It was directions to where a little girl had been last seen."

"Duran said a boy," Keluwen said.

"Could it have said a boy?" Orrinas asked.

"It said *girl*. I remember clear and bright."

"More than one child, it seems," Orrinas said.

"And it seems Kinraigan and the Lord Protector are enemies," Keluwen said.

Orrinas nodded. "So Kinraigan came to ruin the Lord Protector's gateway. Does that mean the Amagon-men were sent to Laman to follow Kinraigan? Or was he following them? Does it mean the Glasseye is Kinraigan's plant, or was he actually working for the Lord Protector all along?"

"Or does it matter?" Keluwen asked. "Is the Lord Protector an ally? Or is he more of the same? Or worse?"

"We must keep our focus," Orrinas said. "Kinraigan has already become luminous. We are here to stop him before he figures out how to make himself invincible. Because if we wait, it will be too late."

"So where is he? He was looking for something in Laman, or chasing someone. But he is gone now. The Amagon-men are dead or missing. We have no path to follow any longer."

Rekel tapped the table with his knuckles.

"What?!" Keluwen shouted.

"Do you want to know the rest or not?" Rekel asked.

"The rest?" Keluwen asked.

"I have things to do. Pikas wants to have a woman while her baby cries. I do not know why but that is the way he likes to come. That means we have to walk all over this shit city just to find one to match his taste."

"We do not need to know your foul habits," Orrinas said. "If you have more to say, then say it."

"The same purser who hired us all those times was found dead," Rekel said.

"Dead? A loose end?"

"Only if the best method of a loose end was to be taken apart piece by piece," Rekel said.

Keluwen saw Pikas Bodrum licking his lips over Rekel's shoulder. She began to feel the faintest bit unsafe in this room for the first time. She slid one glove down to her wrist under the table.

"No," Rekel said to himself. He shook his head. "This was revenge if I have ever seen it."

"Was it magick?"

"That killed him? Yes."

"The only ones who knew about the purser were your people, the Lord Protector's people, and Kinraigan," Keluwen said.

Rekel nodded. "And it wasn't us. He paid better money than nearly anyone on the northern continent."

She looked at Orrinas. "It has to be him. That is just the kind of bitter, vindictive thing he would do."

"It may be true," Orrinas said. "Or it may not be. But it is all we have. Where was his body found?"

"Medion," Rekel said. "Why else would Medion be on my mind?" He thrust his hips in the air thrice.

Keluwen rolled her eyes and tried not to throw up in her mouth.

Orrinas looked at her. "He did say he had come a long way."

"Gold crowns," Rekel said, jingling the coinpurse. "Easiest coin my crew has made all year. There is a man there in Medion. Among the Glasseyes. They searched the scene of the murder. Same ones searched the scene on the mountain. For a price he makes copies. I was told that might have been of interest also."

"It is," Orrinas said. He turned to Keluwen. "Worth our time, and worth the price. Our friend, Severn, is in Medion. We must put him in touch with this spy."

"I do not aim to disappoint," Rekel said. "In my line of business, repeat customers are worth their weight in gold."

"We have our mission," Orrinas said. "The money is yours." He stood.

Keluwen did likewise.

Rekel took to his feet and leaned over the table in a caricature of a bow. His crew parted.

Orrinas led Keluwen back out of the tavern and into the streets. The sunlight relaxed her at once. And not having a nose full of the stench of piss settled her stomach. She did not bother to look back. *Darkwork*, she thought.

"We have a destination, and a goal," Orrinas said. "The money takers at the docks for the paddle barges open in the morning"

"Is there still time? He is so far ahead of us now."

"There will be time. I believe it. We will stop him."

"I know," she said.

"Now, there was a dance parlor back the way we came."

Keluwen smiled. "Are you jesting?"

He shook his head. "Rumor has it that you are in need of a little dancing"

"I am," she said.

"And I am in the mood for Arradan to ride me until she screams tonight."

Keluwen elbowed him with a smile.

They would buy passage on a ship in the morning. The Alder River flowed west from Aldria all the way to Medion. A single trip by ship could deliver them there in a matter of weeks. There was a chance to close the gap, to catch up to him, to surpass him and stop him. Time was running out, but they could do it. There was still a chance.

The ships ported at night though. There was nothing they could do until the morning.

Until then, they had all the time in the world.

29

City of Towers

"I PROMISE."

Aren said it a hundred times each day, and each time Eriana would squint at him, scrunch her lips to one side, chin up, as if she was keeping a list of each and every landmark he offered to show her. They had gone through everything in Lenagon, and half of Amagon before the Alder River passenger barge thumped to a stop against one of the many docks along the port of the city of Medion.

Medion.

It was the largest city in Amagon, dwarfing Kolchin and Palatora, and even the capital of Vithos. Its towers were cyclopean monuments that even Aren could barely bring himself to believe that people had made. He saw Darralund Tower with its crimson spires, Halladon Tower with its steep walls of polished jet black basalt, Tokrati Spur with its robust domes and glittering copper decorations, and grey Barranbor Tower, sharp and austere.

At the center of them all was the Great Tower of Medion, rising up and up, easily half again the height of the others. It had been the first of them all, its foundations laid under the supervision of Weirmaheir himself after the victory of the Northern Alliance in the Great War against the hordes of Kradishah. The towers were meant to represent the giant redwoods that Kradishah had cut down and uprooted. They could not regrow them in the salted earth, but they would build their own. And they had.

Redevir demanded they avoid any sight-seeing until he had collected his things and spoken with his informants, to which they all reluctantly agreed. Tanashri and Inrianne were already inconspicuous enough, but the Sarenwalkers had bundled their emerald cloaks in their carry-bags out of necessity. The presence of two men in green would have invited undue attention, perhaps even from other Sarenwalkers, the kind who were not keen on traitors.

Eriana was the most disappointed of all. "Are we not going up in the towers today?"

"I will take you here on our way back," Aren promised. "We can go to the top of Medion Tower, the tallest in all the world, impossible to build without magick."

"I wish you had time to take me in one of the towers right now," she said.

She leaned just a bit on the word *take*. Enough for him to do a double-take, and enough to send heat where it would be conspicuous. He tried to keep his eyes ahead. But failed. He always failed when she was near.

"I will show them to you someday soon," he said.

She squinted at him, flashed a sly smile. "You promise this?"

"I promise this."

Medion boasted as great a population as any city in the world, and the streets went on and on in all directions, some more than a hundred feet wide, curving and winding through its many districts. Statues happily stood atop enormous granite pedestals at the center of every intersection, and raised porticos could be found adjacent to every tower, sporting pleasant vine-ringed cafes.

The morning markets condensed the whole world into one place. One could find saffron and cinnamon and thyme; glass bottles of lavender, and ambergris, and myrrh from caravans coming up the Levantine; spools of many-colored silks from Halsabad, Valarna, and Tygard. Road captains brought three-pronged flutes from Mazara, tapestries from the skilled weavers of Samartania, and ancient stone statues procured in Cyrenica and Bissus. Barrels were stacked high of competing wines brought by ship from Cantabria, Pavana, and Voleto, and were surrounded by delicious calpas fruit off trees imported from the deep south, and apples fresh from the orchards in Aragol.

Beyond were the stalls of ancient figurines from Sephalon, grizzly ebony effigies from Mekrash, and dyed wool from Kessalmir that were themselves made with shades mixed in Salonica. Some carts were surrounded by ceremonial spears with gold filigree from Maratinia, and had tables crowned with Cadrian spears, Lissarian arrows, and battle-axes from Hidiom. Barges on the river unloaded oats from Pallas, wool from Gordia, and wheat from the fertile vales of Lenagon.

Eriana struggled to keep up. Her attention was constantly drawn away by the exotic wares below, or skyline above, each tower of different style and shape. She couldn't keep from gazing at every statue, demanding to know which artist had sculpted it. The western architecture was entirely new to her, and though she had seen works of Loyal before, she had never experienced the city of his birth. "Did he really live in one of these towers?"

"He spent most of his life in Cadumel Tower," Aren said. "That one there." He pointed to a distant tower of basalt, dark grey like charcoal.

She looked at him with an ambiguous smile. "What are all these inscriptions?" she asked, gesturing at numerous carvings in the stone pillars they passed.

"Dedications of the Mahhennin settlers," Aren said.

"They look so familiar. They look like the old Sinjan letters of Laman." She paused before a pillar. "Wait. I think I can read them. These *are* old Sinjan letters."

"They are," Aren said. "I told you that the Mahhennin used that language. Most settled right here in Medion."

"I have never met one," she said.

"Really?"

"Not many ever came back after the exodus."

"My friend is a Mahhen. Well, descended from them. He was with me, in Laman, when we met. He was with us. On the Fields of Syn. He's gone." He looked down and pretended to be tired so that he could rub his eyes closed for a bit.

She bit her lip and looked at him with downturned eyes. "I am sorry."

"It's okay." *It wasn't.* "It's just that I can go all morning and I will forget to think of it. And then I will remember, out of nowhere, that I will never see my friends again. I...I just didn't think I would be able to forget about that, even for a moment. But I do. And I feel terrible for it every time."

"You mustn't. The mind does this to protect itself. Solathas told me this when my mother joined the heroes. You are protecting yourself. Feeling the pain in little pieces. It would be too much all at once. So your mind chops it up and gives it to you here and there."

"I know. I mean, I should know that. But it is different to know it and to feel it. He was my best friend. He and Corrin. And the Captain."

"Now they have joined the heroes, like my mother."

"I like that," Aren said. "*Joined the heroes.*"

"Was he old?"

"Reidos? Not that old. Forty. He was in the plateau."

"Some people say Solathas is over two hundred years old," she said.

"That's impossible. They must be joking. He looks so young. Maybe at the tail of the age plateau. But even the oldest Andristi man to ever live was Lanier the Long King. And he spent the last hundred years of his two hundred and fifty in perpetual infirmity."

"I wonder sometimes what it will feel like to live in the age plateau," she said, looking up at the towers. "To stay the same for so long while everything else changes. I will be like a redwood, standing still while others change around me."

"Not if you go back to Laman. Then everyone will be that way with you."

"I wonder if my friends worry about me now that I am gone."

Aren puffed up his lip and nodded at the towers. "They are friends. Of course they miss you."

"Lania won't. But Cuthir will, and Erevian, and Prince Erenath. I wonder what they are doing right now." She flexed her fingers, knuckles white, squeezing the pommel of the sword she carried,

At least there is something to wonder. "It seems we have both said many secret goodbyes of late."

"Solathas says that when you say goodbye to a friend, that for a time they become two people. The one that lives and grows and changes, and the one that remains the same, stranded in your memory, frozen in time."

"I never thought of it like that."

"And if you never see them again, they live in your mind forever."

"At least until I die," Aren said. "Which won't be too much longer."

"I will endeavor to remember you then, Aren. You will be able to live a long time inside me."

He wished she had used a different manner of speaking, for now he became lost in his own head, urgently reminded of how much he wanted her. When she wasn't looking, he couldn't take his eyes off her, his heart racing, his chest burning, and all his thoughts dissolving into golden hair, sapphire eyes, silken skin over hard muscle, every curve savage and smooth, every proportion fixed in perfection, as if the shape of her body had been planned and sculpted by Loyol himself.

He closed his eyes, trapping her there, keeping her for that one brief moment, imagining her lips in sweet collision with his, her arms wrapped around him, breathing in her smell, feeling her warmth through her clothes and beneath them, aching to hold her in his arms.

As she looked up and away at the high towers, his eyes traced the shape of her chin and jawline up to her ears and then became lost in the subtle way her hair turned from a soft brown to a vibrant gold in such a gradual yet inevitable way.

Then she looked his way.

He averted his eyes, glanced at his boots, pretended to kick some nonexistent thing from them, and then looked up at the same towers she had just been looking at. "Magnificent, aren't they?"

She squinted her eyes at him.

"What?"

She elbowed him, grimaced, but then smiled. "We had better hurry."

"Don't worry. Redevir will never leave us behind." Though he very nearly did.

She wandered along with him, gazing at the wealthy people in billowing silk trousers and tight festive vests as they waved from the verandas of the columned cafes on every corner.

Redevir took them to the black tower of Halladon. Broad and rectangular, it tapered near the top. It was of stone as black as pitch, basalt brought hundreds of miles from the Kaman-Than, and its spires were glittering obsidian delivered by ship from Halsabad, a gift from the Emperor Chazad.

Its plaza was as wide as the tower was tall, and glowed in the morning as though the sunlight were an ornament upon the white surface of the pavements. Gracefully sculpted arcades rimmed the perimeter, two stories high. He strode into its expansive plaza, walking through the crowds with ease, avoiding collisions with the people he passed by barely a hand-width.

He brought them to a vine-ringed cafe, with trellises atop columns, strung through with ribbons of blue and red and silver. They ate spiced beef with a tart cream sauce, and asparagus, Samartanian spiced potatoes, and cinnamon apple stew, washing it down with a dozen bottles of autumnwine. Eriana was delighted, having never eaten any of the dishes before.

Even though they were all seated together, he felt like he and Eriana were sequestered alone where only their conversation existed.

He would always begin by telling her he didn't have much to say. But he did. He was amazed at what he had to say, about life and about the world, and about art and music and the past and the future. He wanted to listen to her talk about Lissarian poetry, and the difference between Tirosian and Talithline cuisine. Any subject became music as long as she was the one speaking of it.

She understood. He never thought of how good it might feel to have someone to talk to who *understood*, a person who lent their ear without expecting coin in return. She wanted to be here. She wanted to talk to him, and she knew every topic and had opinions stronger than his own sometimes. And the more embarrassingly mundane he thought a topic would be, the more interested she seemed. It thrilled him to the point of giddiness.

Even better, he was able to spend time listening to *her*. The women he knew in Vithos were not lacking for intellect, but they never seemed to have anything to say. Having a conversation with them was like having a conversation with a playful bedpost. Eriana told *him* stories and explained subjects to him that he had never known before. It was something that he had never encountered. His curiosity demanded that he know everything that there was to know about her, to learn her and study her and commit her to memory as he would one of the Histories.

She kept waving her hand at Redevir, demanding impatiently that he order different varieties of wine.

Aren could barely keep her from shouting. "Autumnwine not to your liking?" he asked.

"I want to try each of the *nine wines*," she insisted.

Aren's eyes widened. "In one sitting?"

"No," she shrugged. Then she smiled slyly. "Maybe?"

"Why the rush?"

"The brandy guildmasters in Laman do not allow imports. I have always wondered what each one tastes like. They say a traveler from each of the nine corners of the world brought back the best wine they could find. And now their gift belongs to us all."

"I have tried each of them," he said.

"Truly?"

"Outside Laman it is as easy as tossing a handful of silver bits down in a tavern."

She was delighted, her eyelids fluttering, resting one elbow on the table, her head balanced on her hand. "What are they like?"

Aren went through each of them, trying his best to describe flavor. "Spiced wine is like a hundred flavors in one, like looking into a starry sky at midnight. Sharpwine is tart and sour, like an apple before it's ripe. Sweetwine is soft and cool as a smile. Morningwine is pale and light, like an echo of a sunrise. Eveningwine is brusque and heavy and tastes like how good it feels to sit down after a long day. Winterwine is a celebration, warm and rich, laced with cinnamon and cloves. Springwine is crisp and chilled, like ice on your skin. Summerwine is savory and strong like a noontide rainstorm. And autumnwine is a sunset on your tongue, like a heartbeat in love."

She was sipping from her cup as he spoke, and some dribbled down her chin, and she laughed and tried to catch it and wipe it away with the palm of her other hand.

She did not catch it all, and his hand shot out to her, his thumb catching a drop just before it fell from her chin. His touch startled her, and her laugh vanished into a look that meant something altogether different.

He tried to make his face smile to diffuse the incendiary place he found himself sharing with her in that moment. Tried and failed. Her eyes were wide and full of wonder, looking up at him. He could not turn away. She seemed so close. Too close. Not close enough.

Both her hands enclosed the cup, shaking, cradling it tight as if afraid she might drop it. She leaned toward him. Her lips parted.

Inrianne cleared her throat noisily, like a backhanded slap back to reality. She had been drinking heavily, and it did not improve her demeanor. Aren did not even need to look at her to know she had been sneering at the both of them.

Aren noticed Redevir and the others staring at him as well. "You picked a good spot," he said quickly, trying very hard not to notice Eriana for just a moment. "Nice coastal breeze today."

Redevir nodded, but had a suspicious look on his face. He sprang for a dozen more bottles of wine after that, and then excused himself and went to Halladon Tower, where he kept a suite of rooms in perpetuity.

Eriana was nonplussed to discover the bottles were all autumnwine.

The Rover returned somewhere between the buttered squash and the frosted shortbread. Aren just happened to glance over and he was back, as if he had never left at all. He had a rucksack with him, sitting on the ground under his chair beside his carry-bag.

"What's in there?" Aren asked.

"My complete set of notebooks," Redevir said, tapping the rucksack with his boot. "And a few choice volumes I would rather not leave behind. Oh and gold. Lots of gold. And my promissory notes for the Olybrian Bank."

"Did you take a nap?" Inrianne asked. "You were gone a long time."

Redevir made a face at her. "I met with my people here. I have some paid informants spreading the word to all the backdoor criers that a Sephor has come from the east and has been seen in Medion. That should be specific enough to attract Kinraigan from a thousand miles away. And the speed with which gossip travels up the Alder, he could be on his way within a fortnight."

"What do you think we will need, Aren?" Tanashri asked. "When the time comes."

"Hit him with the magick?" Redevir asked.

Aren shook his head. "He will feel the ripples in the Slipstream if any of our users access it at that close proximity. Magick is powerful but it gives itself away to other users nearby."

"If he can react fast enough," Tanashri said.

"He can," Aren said. "I guarantee he can. Our best bet is to take him unawares. Stick him with tinwood before he even knows we are there. Something that can move very fast."

"Longbows, crossbows," Fainen suggested.

"*Somashalks*," Hayles said.

"My throwing knives," Redevir said.

"All of those," Aren said. "Every point dipped in tinwood leaf resin. We would only have one chance. The moment he hears an attack he will shield himself. Then nothing conventional will get through."

"What then?" Redevir asked.

"Then we would want to have our Stoppers," Aren said. "Dozens. We want them to take hold of all the streams he needs for all of his renders. Pulling streams does not give them away, only the act of binding them can be felt by the user, so it will be safe for them to hold them even before we strike."

"But for Stoppers to work, we must have his composite," Tanashri said.

"They should have one here in Medion," Aren said. "At the headquarters of the Render Tracer Corps."

Redevir flashed a smile. "I will bribe our way in. Arrange for copies to be made."

"If the Stoppers are successful at interdicting everything he's got, then I dose him and we are done."

"What if they aren't?" Eriana asked.

Aren sucked his teeth, and rested his hands on his knees. "Then it gets complicated. We will need our users for shielding, and to attack him. But also to distract him, disrupt his concentration. His concentration is supposed to be extraordinary. We will need a full compliment of professional Distractors, using every technique—strobing flares, foul odors, itching powders, screamer whistles, pain drums, cymbals, and anything specific to him that might generate an emotional response."

"That is a lot of people and a lot of moving parts," Redevir said. "We will have to be sure we know when he is coming."

"That will be up to you," Aren said. "Your rumors are the lure. But we will need to find some way to know when he arrives."

"I could spread the word that the information about the Dagger's location can be heard at a specific place," Redevir said. "Then have a longrunner race the news to us ahead of him."

"It would be even better if we could get ahold of some of his sensitized material," Aren said. "Induce him to use magick somewhere else earlier, and take the material. If I have enough of it, I can tell how close he is, and even where he is."

"So we would know exactly when he is coming," Redevir said.

Aren nodded. "The key will be getting ahold of that composite. We need to know his renders, all the ones that the Render Tracers recorded the last time they tried to capture him. Without it, we will have no Stoppers. No Stoppers means we have to hope a crossbow or a knife in the dark will do the trick.

Because once he knows he is under attack, he will destroy everything in sight to get away."

"So this composite," Redevir said. "What is in it? Just an archive of his streams?"

"We need a perfect understanding of how powerful Kinraigan is. We need to know his limits. Now, I have his very recent *primary values*. I took them from the *Red God* in Westgate. They will have increased since he faced off against Amagon's Render Tracers three years ago, but if I have their accurate measures from back then, I should be able to extrapolate his current power level from the new primary values."

"What are you talking about?" Redevir asked. "That means nothing to me. It's like gibberish."

"We classify users in different ways," Aren said. "We use a grading system for a user's strength. We call it the *core limit*. It is the maximum amount of power a user can release before they would need sleep and sustenance to charge up their strength. We measure it on a scale of twenty-two tiers, One is the lowest, a novice with little power. Twenty-two would be a man with power like a god. Kinraigan should be very high on that scale."

"What about their mental power?" Redevir asked.

"We have two other scales for that," Aren said. "We incorporate the number of different renders a user has under his command into another value called the *proficiency limit*. If the *core limit* measures the height of his power, the *proficiency limit* measures the breadth of his power, how many different options he has available to choose from to apply his core power to.

"And then we make our best guess at the user's ability to *concentrate* on complex thoughts, for how long a period of time, and under how much duress. We call that the *performance limit*. Measured on the Ten-Scale—how well he can focus on one thought, how well he can ignore internal distractions, how well he can ignore external distractions, and how long he can maintain that concentration. All of these scales and lists exist to simplify the process of a trace and prepare the capture."

"So you seek to measure their *minds*," Eriana said, resting her head on her palms, elbows affixed to the table.

"The *performance limit* as a measure of a given user's level of concentration is vital for the capture," Aren said. "It tells me how many Distractors I will need, and what kind of distractions might be most efficient to disrupt his attention. All renders require concentration. When a user loses their concentration, it does not matter how much strength they still have. They will not be able to bind their streams. They will hit what we call the *break point.* That is the moment a user's concentration is thrown off by distraction, even for a moment."

"The break point is crucial," Tanashri said. "If you can push a user past their break point, they will be completely vulnerable until they can regain their concentration."

"All three of the *limits* are interconnected. Most users only ever learn from one set of closely related skills. Someone with higher performance limit—greater concentration—is more likely to be able to master multiple skill sets, and therefore have a higher proficiency limit—greater mastery of multiple different skills—as well. And with more practice at concentration and training with more skill-sets, their natural strength will increase and they will be able to make more powerful renders, and *more of* them, and so up goes their core limit —their total power, their strength."

"No wonder so few ever become strong," Redevir said. "I can barely concentrate on a book when someone is talking nearby. It must be virtually impossible to focus that hard."

"It is possible," Tanashri said. "With the proper training."

"A user's power," Aren said, glancing at Tanashri, "how *dangerous* they are, is based on a dance between how strong their *body* is, how well they can *concentrate*, how *efficient* they are, and how *powerfully they resonate* with the Slipstream when they bring streams together. Experience and training can increase all of these. But every user has a limit somewhere."

"So the *limits* measure the user," Redevir said.

"Most users discover their specific power at an early age," Aren said. "And tend to become proficient in a very narrow scope of renders—a certain thing like friction or momentum or viscosity. Even with training it is rare for someone to be able to open their mind to accept the idea that they can control other forces, learn other skill-sets. It's like being born with a specific mental block."

"So someone with ability in more skill sets is stronger?" Redevir asked.

"Almost by definition," Aren said. "Someone could be incredibly strong in one skill set, but the concentration and openness required to utilize two or more proficiencies almost always signifies greater strength ability overall. But most users never have more than one type. Most users never even manage to control more than *one tiny aspect* of one type—increase temperature, change something's mass, alter velocity, decrease the friction between two objects. Most are far more weak than you would think. Powerful users, like Kinraigan, like Solathas, even like Tanashri, are very rare."

"How many types are there?" Redevir asked.

"There are some *streams* a user must learn in order to control his renders regardless of the forces they may use—height, width, depth, size, shape, toughness, direction, position, magnitude, resistance, duration, impulse. By far the most common are users who rely on vectoric magick—renders with no qualities other than the size, shape, mass, velocity, and direction. We call these forces *blank impulses*. They are the most common of all renders. The other common ones are static shapes, like shields or platforms. Glasseyes have a bad habit of lumping them all under the category of *vectorics*, whether they move or not, but you get the idea."

"But it is not all just invisible shapes and forces," Redevir said.

"Right. There are users of every variety, every specialty—heat, light, pressure, friction, and so on. In order to exert your will on reality, you have to use a frame of reference which you can *understand*. Some things are harder to understand than others. Most users tend to be mechanistic because those are the types of forces most people understand—force and friction, mass and velocity, buoyancy and acceleration. You can see those things in the world around you."

Redevir stroked his chin. "So a user has to be *born* able to do something, *and believe* they can do it, *and concentrate* well enough to do it, *and be strong enough* to do it, *and* they must *understand* what they are doing in order to do it."

"Right," Aren said. "*All* of those factors are involved. Often it is the belief that is the hardest one to master. Most of a user's life is spent learning that they *cannot* do something different than any other normal. It is difficult to be able to believe it once you find out you *can*. It seems simple, but it isn't. Concentration is tricky. If you started flapping your arms like a bird and lifted up into the sky right now it would be shocking to you. The very shock of rendering can be enough to ruin the concentration of the one doing it sometimes. Once you lose your concentration, you break the spell. Your mind turns against you. Your mind tells you that if you are in the sky, you must be falling, because that is the way the world has always been. Your mind *makes* you fall. The knowledge supports the concentration. Understanding a subject increases confidence in its application. Confidence is very important to a user's focus, and knowledge galvanizes that confidence. Tanashri would be more effective than another with the same *born* streams because the Sisters at Templehall taught her formulas and equations to make her more efficient, from books that almost no one has access to. If you know the formulas you can tailor your renders more precisely, conserve your energy better, and more easily believe you can affect something in the real world."

"That is why the Ministry is obsessed with annexing or destroying libraries," Tanashri said. "They fear that if users born with the ability to become proficient with powerful forces such as gravitation, magnetism, electric fields, molecular forces, or other properties of energy and matter, are given the knowledge necessary to understand and exploit those forces, they would be permitting the existence of fertile soil for a powerful enemy to grow strong within. By purging such knowledge from being widely spread, they prevent the vast majority of such users from ever reaching any meaningful potential."

Aren nodded. "But a rudimentary understanding of the properties of heat, light, pressure, friction, acceleration, inertia, mass, and force can be learned without the deeper understanding of the precise *reason* for their existence. The only way for the Ministry to reduce users of those types is to make it difficult to exist on their own, absorb them into their ranks, or destroy them."

"Can any user gain a proficiency in any type of render they want?" Redevir asked. "Can anyone master them all?"

"The ability must be born within the user," Tanashri said. "Only then would the knowledge be able to be applied. When I reach into the Slipstream, the streams that come naturally to me are those of common vectorics, and of momentum. Other forces such as friction and pressure and heat and other transformations of energy are beyond my reach, despite my complete understanding of them."

"Knowledge is the greatest ally of any user," Aren said. "It allows them to maximize their potential. Users can have multiple proficiencies, but they would have to have been born with them. They cannot be acquired. The knowledge of the ones you have been born with *can* be acquired."

"There are two primary types of users," Tanashri said. "*Elementals* and *Physics*."

"An Elemental user sees the world from the point of view of nature," Aren said. "Not of physical laws. It is much harder to prevent Elementals from becoming proficient with the powers they are born with, since they can be understood very easily. They get better faster, and stronger with less training, but their powers can be undone easily by Physics."

"An Elemental pulls their streams from their understanding of nature," Tanashri said. "Inrianne has streams of fire. But it could be water, or air, or wood, or stone."

"A *heater* could use the idea of heat itself to warm a bowl of soup," Aren said. "A *magnetist* could create and apply an electric current like a tiny lightning bolt. A *crusher* could use pressure. A *frictioneer* could use friction. A *lightbender* could refocus sunlight to one spot. An Elemental would have to create a flame to generate that same amount of heat. Different methods; same result."

Aren picked at what remained of his meal and waited for Redevir to finish off one more bottle of wine by himself. "What about you?"

"Me?" Redevir asked.

"Let's hear about *your* research. You said the stones Kinraigan has been stealing were shortcuts. Shortcuts for what?"

"There is a rumor, so old now it is halfway to myth. It says that the hiding places of the Sephors were preserved by scholars and wise men throughout time, and that they hid hints of their locations, so that if a time ever came that they were needed once more, they could be found by the right people. I have been trying to find and decipher these clues."

"What does that have to do with the stones?"

"I believe they have the answers to old riddles etched into them. Well, let me back up. The first hint I found was when I visited a group based in Kassanath, called the Seekers."

"I've heard of them," Aren said. "Renounced their worldly lives to devote everything to the search for knowledge. They have an enormous archive in Miralamar full of old texts and scrolls."

"I've been there. It wasn't easy to gain their trust, but my determination earned me a brief stay within their walls. That is where I found the first clue. It was buried deep within an old tome of *architecture*, in which a circular chamber was compared to the Crown itself."

"I've heard the comparison," Aren said. "In reference to the domed central chamber of the Citadel of Aberhadden."

"That's the one. The city lies on the frontier of modern Salonica."

"Was that the clue?" Eriana asked. "Do we get to go to Salonica?"

"No," Redevir said. "The clue was a reference to the *Field of the Fallen*."

"I've never heard of a place with that title," Aren said.

"There isn't one," Redevir said. "I looked. But I wrote down that line. I thought it was significant. It was out of place in the text, and it was located directly beside the *only* mention of the Crown in the entire text. It wasn't until two years later that I discovered the *importance* of that line."

"You went to Aberhadden?" Aren asked.

"Yes. It seemed a natural place to start. The Seekers have a chapter house there. I learned from one of them that the writers of their original tomes loved to include hidden secrets and veiled hints within their works. I knew I was on the right track."

"This I have heard," Aren said. "A random reference in a Seeker's book about Tabirnis of Fesser gave Kepbold the clue he used to ultimately find the lost city of Shabur."

"Exactly. This clue was no different. I discovered in Aberhadden that one of the authors of the architecture tome wrote *another* book. He wrote this one *all by himself*. It was a text with classifications of northern *flora*."

"I do not understand," Inrianne said. "You said he wrote about architecture."

"Seekers wrote on every topic," Aren said. "Whatever the subject they were charged to write about by their leaders, they fully immersed themselves in it. It was part of their discipline."

"Many of them contributed to the architecture book. This particular author was the *only one* to have another book to his credit. I thought that significant. I finally found a copy in the Library of Lenagon. I pored over it for weeks. It was horrifically dull. I almost did not finish it. But I did find a recurring phrase throughout, sometimes used out of place. It caught my eye because of what I had learned of their hidden messages. The line goes, *along the Vassian Way*."

"That's the famous road in Arradan," Aren said.

"*This flower* along the Vassian Way, *that vine* along the Vassian Way, *this mushroom*...you get the idea. It was almost comical how often it appeared. I researched for months. I looked for *any* other reference to that line, and finally found one, in an *art book* of all places."

"It's the name of a painting," Aren said. "Bordican's painting. The Lord Protector has it hanging outside his office."

"Bordican?" Eriana asked, excited. "He was one of the most renowned artists in all of Arradan."

"The Vassian Way is the key?" Tanashri asked.

"It is mentioned too many times to be coincidence," Redevir said.

"The Vassian Way leads from Arthenorad to Tallirad in the Empire of Arradan," Tanashri said.

"So we begin in Tallirad," Redevir said. "But...."

"No," Aren said. "No, we don't. In the painting the people on the road are not facing Tallirad. They are looking away from it. There is an angel above them with a sword and wand. The angel is pointing with the sword, *not* down the road to where it leads, but off to the side. They are looking at a small settlement in the upper right hand corner of the canvas. Most scholars believe that it is meant to represent the Arradian city of *Sararad*. Bordican's depiction of it is an exact duplicate of the original layout of the old city. I have seen the maps in the Library of Lenagon. The sword and wand. I never thought about it. It's a reference to the Sephors. Bordican knew something about them."

"And he hid the meaning in his painting," Redevir said.

"So should we be going to Sararad?" Eriana asked. "I have read of how beautiful the trees are in the Somnerium."

"I don't know," Redevir said. "There has to be some reference to the Field of the Fallen somewhere to let us know. I would prefer to have a path, rather than take the time and effort to blindly go all the way to Sararad."

"What could it possibly be though?" Aren asked.

"We have to narrow the choices," Inrianne said.

"Well, my first thought was that it meant a battlefield," Redevir said. "A field of fallen soldiers."

"Or perhaps a graveyard," Eriana said.

"The problem is that no battles were ever fought in the vicinity of Sararad," Aren said. "The barbarians thought the woods were haunted, and the merchant barons who lived there usually paid off invaders to stay away, even during their civil wars."

"What about the graveyard idea?" Redevir asked.

"There are dozens of them," Aren said. "But they are all named for very specific people, with no reference to a vague title like that. Would someone who dies of old age be considered *fallen?*"

"I agree with Aren," Eriana said. "In Laman it is reserved for those whose lives are cut short."

"Splendid," Redevir said. "What else could it be?"

"Field of the Fallen," Aren said. "*Field of the Fallen. Life cut short. Fallen. Cut short. Fallen. Cut.*"

"What?" Redevir asked.

"Fallen," Aren repeated.

"Field of the Fallen," Redevir said. "That is the damnable clue. What is it?"

"Eriana is right," Aren said.

Eriana's mouth fell open. "I am?"

"What do you mean she's right?" Redevir asked.

"Life cut short," Aren said. "We're thinking too metaphorically. We're looking for something fallen. Maybe it means something that *literally fell.* Think. Why *that* clue for *this* place?"

"Explain," Redevir demanded.

"What is Sararad most well known for?"

"Its towers," Redevir said. "But they haven't..."

"No," Aren said. "What else. All the cities of Arradan have towers of one sort or another. What makes Sararad different? What makes it stand out?"

"The trees!" Redevir exclaimed. "Sararad is known for its forest. The Somnerium."

"A Seeker would look at the trees," Aren said. "Especially one who was compiling a text on northern *flora*. Sararad *is* its beautiful trees. The Somnerium, the endless forest of white trees with sunset leaves. The Mahhennin refugees called it Draesevien. *Among the trees*. It was to them the Synsirok of the west, another city in the trees. The Mahhennin embraced Sararad to remind them of their old homes after they were exiled from Laman."

"So it is the trees," Inrianne said. "But the line speaks of a field."

"A field has no trees at all," Tanashri agreed.

"Not trees," Aren said.

"Felled trees," Eriana said. "Trees that were cut short."

"What do you have when you remove all the trees from a forest?" Aren asked.

"A field," Tanashri said. "The clue points to a place where the trees were cut down."

"Trees are cut down everywhere," Inrianne said. "For firewood. For lumber."

"That's where I think Redevir is half-right," Aren said. "Field of the Fallen almost sounds like a memorial, as if the trees were felled for unnatural reasons."

"Is there such a field?" Redevir asked.

"There is," Aren said. "When the Tyrant's armies drove into Arradan five hundred years ago during the Great War, they cut down some of the largest trees to make bonfires."

"Bonfires to burn innocents alive," Tanashri said. "Kradishah and his people were called tree-burners for a reason."

"Where is this place?"

"It *was* on the north side of Sararad," Aren said.

"Was?" Redevir asked.

"When the war was over, they made great efforts to plant new trees. Except for one field where they left the stumps in the ground as a reminder of the horror of the war."

"But the field was eventually dug up and paved over with stone to build the Baths of Emperor Basilis III," Tanashri said.

"You mean it is gone?" Redevir asked. "The clue is gone?"

"The History of Durnan claims that the stumps were all destroyed," Tanashri said.

"Yes," Aren said. "But Durnan was from Bolan. He never actually set foot in Arradan. His lore was all taken from secondhand sources. All the stumps were *removed*, but they were not all *destroyed*. According to Pellagien, one stump was preserved as a memorial."

"A stump?!" Redevir asked. "Where?"

"Well," Aren said. "Remember when I said this place was a good choice?"

"Yes," Redevir said.

"Well, I did not realize how right I was. The Mahennin who loved Sararad as a second home for many generations took the final stump and brought it with them."

"To where?" Redevir asked.

"To here," Aren said. "To Medion."

"You mean to tell me that the thing we are looking for may be right here in this city?"

Aren smiled. "Maybe five blocks from here."

Redevir practically flew out of the cafe, tossing a shower of coins onto the table for their meals and excessive wine.

Aren took off at a jog, moving between the white columns and worn marble facades, beneath the shadows of the towers. He ran through a small courtyard with a weed-infested fountain.

Beyond it was a wide ovular plaza, ringed perfectly by a colonnade. At the far end, overlooking the plaza, was a doubled arcade before the entrance to a temple of Zor and Tianam. The stump of a tree had been cemented in place in the center. At least four feet across, with the bronze engraving of a broad forest recessed into it, letters below it.

Good old Pellagien, Aren thought.

"Look around," Redevir said.

"We're looking," Inrianne said.

"Rip it out of the ground if you have to," Redevir said.

"Look at the inscription," Tanashri said. "Can you read those letters, Aren?"

"It says something like, *In memory of dark days*, or, *Memorial of dark times*," Aren said. "Below that it reads, *Let none forget*. It is written in Old Ardis, an early script of Arradan."

"Touching," Redevir said.

"What's this?" Eriana asked. "There are letters in the engraving, in the trees. Look close, Aren. What do you see in the shapes made by connecting the branches of the trees."

"I don't believe it," Aren said. "Those are old *Sinjan* characters."

"Sinjan?" Redevir asked. "The Lamani language?"

"The modern Andristi alphabet is derived from it," Aren said. "It has been dead for more than seven hundred years."

"That means no one can read it," Inrianne said.

"I can," Eriana said. "I know the Sinjan alphabet. Some of the engraved pictures cross over the letters," she said. "But I think it says, *Where the fast is broken.*"

"Are you certain?" Tanashri asked.

"I'm sure of it," Eriana said. "It is phrased as a statement, not a question, just like the last."

"Another clue," Redevir said. "Eriana is a genius."

"Where is a fast broken?" Inrianne asked.

"At the dinner table," Redevir said.

"This can't be an ordinary fast," Aren said. "It has to be something specific."

"A famine?" Eriana asked.

"Or a religious fast," Tanashri added.

"Are there any fasts that are ceremonially ended by someone important?" Eriana asked. "Like a king or a priest? We have such a thing in Cair Tiril. It could mean a sacred place."

"Does it mean a fast in Sararad?" Inrianne asked. "Or Laman? Or somewhere else?"

"Religious fasts were routine in every city and town," Aren said. "That is too general."

"And famines are universal," Redevir said. "They affect everyone. Something that points everywhere, points nowhere."

"What about a siege being broken?" Fainen asked. "When the starving are fed again."

"That is a good point," Redevir said. "Why not that?"

"That describes every city in Arradan at one time or another," Aren said. "It has to be something else."

"These riddles are veiled within themselves," Tanashri said. "They are cloaked in metaphor. Hints exist within the clue itself. Bordican's painting, the forests of Sararad, the book of plant life. All are related to the answer."

"What could the fast be?" Redevir asked. "Something to do with the Andristi? It's written in Sinjan. That can't be common in Arradan."

"Something people were starving for," Aren said.

"Trade?" Redevir pondered.

"Technological advancement perhaps," Tanashri added.

"Or social advancement," Eriana said. "We had a caste system from the Bloodline in Laman until Great Lithlinon ended the practice."

"What do men want more than any other thing?" Aren asked. "What can they desire that can be withheld from them? Something that has to do with the Sinjan letters."

"Freedom," Hayles finally said. "Men desire freedom above all else. They will perform great feats and make terrible errors in pursuit of it."

"And it can be withheld by the powerful," Tanashri said.

"Does it mean anything to you, Aren?" Redevir asked.

"I don't know," Aren said.

"Sinjan language in Arradan?" the Rover asked. "Tyrants? Anything?"

"That's it," Aren said. "There was one thing. During a dispute of succession, a usurper named Arkollon the Iron-Handed took control of some of the core lands of the empire, and refused to delegate any authority. He was a tyrant. He virtually enslaved the Mahhennin."

"What happened to him?" Eriana asked.

"Riots swept across the provinces," Aren said. "Led by the Mahhennin who had settled in his lands. They revolted, marching to meet him in the city he maintained as his capital."

"Did they gain their freedom?" Redevir asked.

"They did," Aren said. "They destroyed his armies and burned Arkollon at the stake, and had the members of his false house flayed alive and cut to pieces."

"That's one way to do it," Redevir said. "So where was this city?"

"A city that was once a haven for wandering refugees called the Mahhennin, who wrote their most precious messages in an ancient language called Sinjan. A city named Karorad. There is a memorial there Jordanus talked about, celebrating the end of his reign. It has an inscription in Old Ardis. *Avy Temis Volarat*. It translates loosely to: *what was broken is restored*."

"That certainly sounds like our clue stated another way," Redevir said. "Karorad is where we will go once we have caught our man."

Aren nodded to Eriana. "It looks like we are paying a visit to the Empire of Arradan."

She was so giddy at the chance to see that place she hopped in the air.

Redevir smiled. "And you doubted it."

"Doubted what?" Aren asked.

"Destiny."

Aren narrowed his eyes. "We talked about that word. Destiny. And its bastard brother Prophecy."

Redevir put his hands on his hips and tapped his foot. "How can you look at any of this and not see it as destiny? Riddles that have eluded me and other scholars for centuries before me. And we solved them in one afternoon, over meat and sharpwine."

"Redevir."

"No," Redevir said. "You knew the art, the history, the cities."

"And if you hadn't met me, you would have found some scholarly librarian who would have known the same things. You researched your clues. You could have found anyone to put them together."

"And we just happened to be in the very city that had this memorial, and you just happened to have with you the one person west of Farguard Gap who can read ancient Sinjan. I challenge you to claim that is *all* coincidence."

"It has to be," Aren said. "Because that other thing does not exist." *Or does it?*

"It is destiny that we found this. And it will be destiny that you capture Kinraigan."

"Enough, Rover," Aren said, waving him off.

He laughed. "Fine, fine. Well then, let us begin preparations for trapping the world's most dangerous man. I will put the word out to the local Stoppers and private guards here in Medion, and have my man get a copy of that composite, and then..."

The Rover's ivory shirt seemed to turn red. It began as a little dot, and then it grew, and then soaked, and then it began to drip onto the street.

"What the...?" Aren started to say.

Redevir looked down at it. Then he winced. "My back itches. Is that blood?"

"Redevir!" Eriana shouted. "You've been hit!"

"Hit?!" the Rover asked. "Hit with what? What is on me?"

"It is an arrow," Tanashri said.

Where did it come from?

Then he heard a heavy metal ping. People in the crowd began to scream and shout. He saw something towering over the them. He saw an immense double-edged battle-axe.

He saw red skin.

30

The Man With Black Eyes

A PLAN OF MANY parts is fine until the first thing goes wrong.

This plan barely lasted beyond the time it took to think of it.

Red skin.

Rashkhadhavazar. Redscar. Titan of Chashreel. He was here in Medion. He was here for them. The giant stared him down with eyes the size of citrus fruits bulging from the thick folds of his face. He let his battle-axe sway from side to side, shiny silver and gold, a grin twisting into a snarl on his face.

A small bald man stood beside him, unarmed. Aren thought he recognized him. He whispered. "Leave the Glasseye and the Rover. Kill the rest."

Redscar did not hesitate. He swept forward through the crowd, kicking and swatting his way through the people. When he struck them they flailed like children. He let his arm swing carelessly, catching one man with the flat of his axe. The blow cracked his skull and sent his body careening across the plaza.

The crowd scattered in every direction. Their paths crisscrossed in a chaotic mess like a startled swarm of bees.

Aren looked up. Atop the arcade. A man in the black coat leaned out. He let fly another arrow. It missed. Then another man appeared. And another.

Fainen was loosing his own arrows already. The Sarenwalker walked calmly beside Aren, stringing and letting an arrow fly every other step, without ever glancing away from his target atop the arcade.

Hayles flew in front of him, his *somashalks* dancing in his hands. The Sarenwalker's eyes darted from the men atop the arcade, down the colonnade, across the plaza, and back again.

Tanashri stretched out one finger and two men slid out of the crowd dead, blood leaking out of the holes her blank impulses punched through their bodies, wetting the cleavers they had dropped.

"Wait!" Aren said. "Not here!" He thought of the Medion Glasseyes that would be coming for them even before he thought of the swords and arrows.

But it was too late. She used again. And again. Then slowed. She saw the titan coming, and looked to be readying a bubble shield around herself, but then stopped. She bent over forward, fell to her knees. She shook her head, dazed. Aren saw something sticking out of her back.

They already dosed her!

She must have been hit before Redevir was, the tinwood slowly taking effect.

Inrianne shrieked and ran into the crowd. Aren lost sight of her.

Redevir reached for the arrow in his back, couldn't find it. Cursed. Gave up. Reached into his vest for a throwing knife. Fumbled it. Dropped it. Kicked it away when he reached down for it.

Something hit Eriana. She staggered, cradling the back of her head.

Aren heard a crack, and a stone fell, clacking across the ground. He reached for Eriana, pulled her in close, turned all around.

Men began filtering out of the frenzied crowd. Some were coated in black with short swords, some wore brown wool tunics with slings and truncheons, and still others fine silk, with longswords fit for dueling. He heard the sound of jingling bells.

Hayles reached Redscar. Charged the giant without a second thought. Redscar's axe darted out with lightning speed. Hayles leapt over the arc of the swing. Rolled. Slashed at his rear. The giant blocked with his axe. He kicked. Missed. Struck a fleeing man, sending him flipping into the air.

Hayles slashed with both axes across Redscar's foot, both legs, and several ribs. The giant howled. Collapsed to one knee.

Another arrow whistled past Aren's head. His eyes shot to the top of the arcade.

Fainen put an arrow into each man up there. One fell, the other two did not. So he put two more arrows into each until they did. He then returned his attention to the ground. Took aim. Loosed an arrow over Aren's shoulder. It speared through the hand of a man behind him. The man screamed. Dropped his truncheon.

Eriana wrestled herself out of Aren's grip. She drew her sword, stabbed the man in the ribs, and in one fluid motion withdrew, swung back low, up above her head, and down in a sharp cut, tearing him open from neck to hip. She backed Aren up a few steps so that the body would not trip him up when it fell.

Two men ran toward Eriana and Tanashri. Both wore fancy silks, one red, one blue. They looked like the sons of lords or merchants, but they had the eyes of cutthroats.

Aren panicked. Tried to draw his sword. Made it halfway, but it slipped from a slick palm. Dropped back into its scabbard.

But Hayles was already there, placing himself between Aren and the two. They rushed him, both attacking at once, one high, one low. Hayles looked at neither of them. His eyes locked between them, fighting each of them with his peripheral vision alone. He blocked the low cut and the high at the same time with his hand-axes, he turned his wrists, hooked the blades under the curved beards of the axe heads, and twisted.

One man's sword was wrenched away. The other held on. Tried to swing his sword up and around to strike, but Hayles chopped into him repeatedly with both *somashalks* before he could get it back around—elbow, wrist, fingers, fingers, fingers, shoulder, elbow, face. He screamed, then fell dead. The other man scrambled away on hands and knees, but Hayles stopped him with a single bite of a *somashalk* to his skull.

Fainen kept loosing arrows at everyone he saw, but Redscar lumbered back into the fray, and the arrows did not seem to slow him up at all.

Aren turned to look for an avenue of escape. Everywhere he saw men in black coats coming. He saw the giant looming. He saw...*ebon-shrouds.*

He grabbed Redevir by the cuff and pointed across the square. "There!"

The ebon-shroud seemed to drift through the crowd toward him, a sword suddenly in his hand, sliding from his sleeve like a black snake.

Hayles was already moving, placing himself between them.

Aren saw another coming from between the columns, face hidden beneath a hood.

Fainen loosed at him, but his arrows flew wide. The ebon-shroud moved like water within the cloak. Fainen loosed and loosed. Ran out of arrows. Threw his bow. He drew *Glimmer* from the scabbard, lunged. The ebon-shroud took a step back. Fainen's attacks met air. The cloaked body went between them and around them, passing through like a gust of wind.

Aren backed away, his eyes searching everywhere.

Hayles chopped at the other ebon-shroud with his *somashalks*, holding his ground. Redscar loomed above him.

Redevir threw a knife. It flew from his hand like a diving bird, stuck in the ribs of a man in a black coat.

Eriana pulled Aren back. She pointed over his shoulder.

A third ebon-shroud was coming, his sword a pendulum at his side. The weapon glistened black, like obsidian, with a curving blade and a small guard above the hilt. *Black steel.*

Eriana moved beside Aren. Her hands trembled, but her stare was constant.

The third ebon-shroud moved toward Eriana, the end of his blade pointing at her face. But she did not waver. She tipped it aside and lunged, passing forward into a deep stab. The ebon-shroud was fast, but still had to leap back from the unexpected attack.

Fainen appeared, Saren-sword held out from his body in long point, making certain the ebon-shroud knew he would not have this easy. The ebon-shroud came at him.

Fainen's steel met steel. There existed no separation between his eyes, mind, and arm. Aren stared at it, unable to look away. Fainen was faster than fast, slashing, cutting, stabbing, but the ebon-shroud never slowed and never gave ground either.

Hayles was dodging and cutting, his hands moving faster than Aren could blink. The hilt of a black sword cut him across the forehead, and he lurched backward, falling to the ground. He rolled, avoiding stabs and cuts. He flopped away, reaching blind for his *somashalks*.

Time slowed to a halt. Aren thought he was looking into a frozen painting. He saw the giant, and Fainen swinging his blade. Hayles crawled to his *somashalks*. Tanashri was down, maybe dead. He struggled to stand, but could make it no further than onto his knees.

Eriana's eyes darted all around, searching. She ducked under an incoming sling stone. She moved to block one of the ebon-shrouds, but he lunged faster than a blink and cut across her thigh. She squealed and dropped to one knee.

"No!" Aren saw her go down and his heart dropped in his chest. He was there in a single moment, as if time stood still. He had his sword in his hand. He did not remember drawing it. He cut down at the ebon-shroud. Missed by a mile. But the ebon-shroud backed away from Aren, recoiling from him as if afraid. Aren forced him to engage, swinging ruthlessly, blindly, without finesse. The ebon-shroud backed away. Aren slashed. Then cut. Blocked. Stumbled.

Flash. A knife flew.

Redevir!

The Rover howled at the air as his throwing blades sank into the back of the ebon-shroud. One, two, three, four. The ebon-shroud made no sound. He kept coming, never stopping, not even when skewered by knives.

Aren backed away, but not fast enough. Redscar lunged, and swept him aside with a swing of his open hand. The backhanded slap took Aren full in the face, and his head shook violently with the force of the blow. Pounding agony strobed into his skull before he even hit the ground. He laid there cradling his head against the splitting, aching pain.

Eriana dragged Aren away, and pulled him down. He fell to the ground with her atop him.

Fire.

Aren felt the heat on the back of his neck. He turned his head upward just in time to see Inrianne set fire to the ebon-shroud, and burn Redscar's flesh, singing his topknot. The titan roared and retreated.

The ebon-shroud was not so lucky. The flames took to him, lighting him like a torch. The ebon-shroud dropped to his knees, then he flopped forward onto the pavement. His skin bubbled with the scorching of the flames, and he shuddered into death.

Another ebon-shroud charged Redevir. The Rover cut across the knees. Hit nothing but air. The ebon-shroud took Redevir by the neck and squeezed, choking blood between his lips. Reached into Redevir's rucksack. Lifted the Dagger. Redevir clutched at the hand, knocked the Dagger loose. It clattered on the ground.

It came to rest at the feet of Inrianne. The other ebon-shroud was there, coming toward her. Inrianne scrambled away, her toes tapping the Dagger. It skittered across the ground. Inrianne reached toward it. Aren lunged for it. The ebon-shroud leapt for it.

Aren slid his fingers around the hilt, Inrianne gripped the sheath, and the ebon-shroud fumbled the pommel. Inrianne groaned. Her eyes slammed shut. She gritted her teeth so tightly Aren thought they might shatter and fall from her mouth.

Aren kicked himself back, and the Dagger slid out of its sheath into his hand. His hands accidentally touched the blade. The metal felt like cold liquid possibility. Fear evaporated and everything suddenly seemed possible. He held onto it. He stared at it. He felt it. It glittered with the light of morning, filling his eyes with an ocean of light. It began to glow. The glow became a shimmer. The shimmer became a beam. The beam became a flare. The flare became a blaze of the sun at the break of day.

Aren was knocked to the ground. Everyone was knocked to the ground. Aren couldn't hear. He couldn't see. He couldn't taste or smell anything but light. He was blind. Blinded by the light of a sun in his eyes.

He opened his eyes. He was on the ground. He tried to sit up. Something struck him in the skull. He rolled. Clutched at his head. The Dagger fell to the ground. Someone stooped over to pick it up. He saw boots with little jinglebells on the toes, ringing with fathomless echoes. A man scooped the

Dagger up with a rolled up cloak. One of the ebon-shrouds held out its sheath, and let him tip forward until the blade slid home.

The fighting instantly stopped. The men in coats, the brutes, the silk princes, the ebon-shrouds, the titan—they all stopped.

All that just for the Dagger.

Two followers who smelled of sawdust and stale cheese forced Aren to his knees, arms behind his back. He tried to look over his shoulder to see any of the others, but they were all down, stunned, some wiggling, but none able to stand yet.

Aren noticed someone striding up to him, black longcoat over his robes in contrast to the white stone, like smoldering charcoal in a world of eggshells. The way he moved looked like he was slipping in and out of the world.

Kinraigan.

Aren had never seen him in daylight before. Now that he had he could not tell which was worse. His eyes were like polished obsidian, as if his irises had long ago been subsumed by his pupils. His hair was a malignant black to match, as if a carrion bird had made its home upon his head, and his face was pale white beneath it like snowcapped mountain peaks. His nose was long and razor sharp, and made his smile look like a scowl.

I am not supposed to face you yet. This was supposed to happen later, with the Dagger as the bait for a trap. He had so fixed it in his mind that there would be a proper order to events that he was shocked to see it deviate.

Fear struggled up his spine. He knew it, he felt it. He was here, now, already waiting for this moment. What Aren had expected to happen was meaningless, he now realized. He could not understand what events had led to this moment, only that it was here, and it had been waiting for him for a long time.

Kinraigan swept over to him, kneeling to meet his eyes. "I have been waiting for you."

"You were behind us. How could you be ahead of us?"

He smiled. "I am luminous, Aren. I walk in the light. You have no idea what I am capable of."

"What does that *mean?*" Spittle flew from Aren's mouth.

"It means I have seen things you could never dream."

"You are insane."

"They tried to keep me out, but I found a way in. They could not stop me. And now it is too late. I read the book. I am immortal now." He smiled contentedly. "I have learned so many things from the book. Soon I will become a god. I am only one step away from it, from my ascension. The Power. I am becoming Sanadi, limitless, unstoppable."

"You are not getting out of here."

"*Your* people used magick, not me. I would be worried for your own if I were you. Especially if someone already told the Inner Guard that there were rogues here."

Aren spat blood. He wiped his mouth with one sleeve. "They will find you, too. People saw the fire. But they also saw your giant. You can't hide a giant."

Kinraigan smiled. "You have no idea what I can do." He looked down his nose at Aren, studying him. "Why won't you turn? They always turn by now. Why aren't you mine yet? I can satisfy your desire. I know what it is you want. This world denies it to you. I want to change it. I can make it perfect. Why won't you let me?"

"I will never ever serve you," Aren said. "I would rather die. Your name is a curse where I come from."

Kinraigan gave him a dubious look. "If you do not turn, I will not kill *you*. I will kill your people, one by one, until you are free."

Aren froze. He felt a pain in his chest. He heard shouts in the distance, the genesis of a response from the Orange. It would not be long now. *We have to get out of here.*

Kinraigan glanced at Tanashri's silent body. "I knew they would send one Sister. But now it seems there are two."

He turned to Eriana. "You have all these people. You are still not free. I will take things from you until you become what I need you to be. I will free you from the burden, free you so you can see. Free you from the worry. Free you so you can come to me."

"I am not who you think I am," Aren growled. "You do not need to do this."

Kinraigan pointed one finger at Eriana, and two of his people took fistfuls of her hair and pulled her head back, exposing her throat. Her arms were lifted above her head. Kinraigan smiled.

Aren tried to lift himself up, but strong arms held him down. He strained with his arms. He strained with his legs. "No. No, you don't do it. Don't you do it. Don't you touch her. You don't touch her. Ever."

I am going to make you burn.

Eriana struggled and squirmed. She fought furiously. If she had held her sword she would have used it.

Kinraigan studied her. "Can't you feel it? I think I can feel her wanting something just out of her reach. How she longs to give in to it."

Aren bit his lip until it bled inside his mouth. "No. Not her. You leave her alone. Stop it. You stop it."

Kinraigan smiled at him, and reached toward Eriana's body. "Do you want to change? I can make you perfect."

His smile was erased by a blast of searing flame. A raging inferno leapt around him, filling the air with bright orange light. The fire licked his cloak and singed his hair. He did not have a bubble shield ready, and now it was too late. Nothing pushed a user past their break point faster than being set on fire. He was taken so off guard that he barely recovered to protect himself from a second blast, and a third. He could only dance away from the flames. He recoiled, trotting quickly across the plaza, his coat smoking, his robes steaming.

The men holding Aren and Eriana released them and fled.

Inrianne held herself up on hands and knees, shaking. She began to glow faintly yellow, then red like the setting sun. Then she collapsed.

The sorcerer did not counterattack. He fled across the square, and around a corner, out of sight. *He just...left.*

Aren looked across the plaza but he could not see Redscar or any of the others. They all vanished, leaving their dead behind.

Eriana ran to him. She lay one hand gently on the side of his face. She frowned when he grimaced beneath the pressure. Her lips parted somewhere between a smile and a frown. "Your poor head," she whispered.

He put an arm around her.

"Inrianne?" she asked. "Is she...?"

"She exerted too much of her energy. Went past her core limit. She is young and strong. She should be fine. She needs rest and food. She may not wake up for a while. Forget her. What about you?"

Redevir appeared at Aren's side. "Hurry now." He pointed across the plaza. "The Orange are mobilizing."

The Sarenwalkers were on their feet again. Hayles scooped up Tanashri, and Fainen lifted Inrianne.

They moved as fast as they could along the colonnade, hoping the columns would mask their escape. They raced up the wide steps at the base of Halladon Tower, skirted the immense fountain and darted between the tower and an outbuilding, shaded by a cluster of trees.

There they set Tanashri down and spent what seemed hours catching their breaths.

Redevir fumed, his eyes wide, hands in perpetual fists. "Where did they come from?"

"They were after you, Redevir," Aren said. "They knew you had it."

"How could anyone have known that?" Redevir asked. "Word has not had time to spread up the street, let alone to his ears. It is impossible. How could they have found us? How could they possibly know we were here? How could they possibly know we had the Dagger? We left him behind in Laman."

"I don't know," Aren said. "But while we were planning our ambush, they were already waiting to ambush us. I know how to stop users. But how do we stop a user with his own army? That was more than just the cult of the black coats that came at us. Anyone could be one of his. That giant belongs to him. Those were *ebon-shrouds*, Redevir. That was a devil's menagerie."

"We killed one of them," Redevir said. He frowned, and looked around as though he dropped something on the floor. "After the white light..."

"The white light," Aren said. "It was the Dagger. It did something. Somehow. I don't know."

"It must be real," Redevir said. "There is our proof."

"And there it goes," Aren said. "They took it."

"We very nearly joined the heroes today," Eriana said.

"It is a miracle we survived," Aren said. "After Tanashri went down, I thought it was over."

"What happened to her anyway?" Redevir asked.

"Tinwood leaf resin," Aren said, hovering over the Saderan. He pointed to a tiny stain on her robe. "A tinwood nail. A dart, or an arrow. They did to us what we were planning to do to Kinraigan."

"Is she...?" Redevir asked.

"She should be alright," Aren said. "But resin is pure, strong. She could be out for hours, or days."

"She will have to wake on the ship, Aren," Redevir said. He pointed to Inrianne. "She used fire. Glasseyes will be coming soon. Our first priority is to get out of this city before they find us."

Aren nodded. "You are absolutely right about that. The Orange were likely converging on the plaza the moment we left. There will be Inner Guard agents there by now. Witnesses may remember a confusion of fighting, but there is one thing they will all say: someone made fire. There will be Glasseyes testing and tracing within the hour." He tried to remember the names of the Medion Tracers—Olager, Tangiv, Mora. They were all very good. *Not quite as good as me, though.*

"What do we do, Aren?" Redevir asked. "How do we escape?"

He flipped out the Jecker monocle. He studied Tanashri's prone body. He saw the silver glow, little maroon filaments of color. "Tanashri used briefly. She has sensitized fluorescence on her hands and sleeves, and on the back of her robe where she felt the thing that hit her. We were lucky she fell down when she did. Most of her afterglow floated above her so most of her robes are clear."

"What about Inrianne?" Redevir asked.

Aren turned to her. She was sitting up on her own at least but she was groggy, unaware. Aren doubted she could walk by herself. Her robes were awash in color, striking yellow and orange. It covered her hands, and splashed across her clothes and shined in her hair. "It is all over her."

He turned to the Sarenwalkers. Hayles had some radiation where Tanashri's hands had rubbed against him. Fainen's entire left side was awash with Inrianne's. "You both will need to be cleaned as well."

"How?" Redevir asked.

Aren shook his head. "I have no cleaning substances. None. Without any special ones, all we have is sand, wind, water, and time."

"Get them as far away from here as quickly as possible," Redevir said.

"Take them both the long way around the towers," Aren said to the Sarenwalkers. "Loop around, and head for the port. Get to the saltwater. Submerge them and yourselves. Rub the water on as best you can. By the time they track you, we could have a ship ready to take us out of here."

"There will be a delay, Aren," Redevir warned.

"What do you mean?"

"I have to meet my informant. I must head to the towers. I will not have time to source a ship until after I speak with him."

"Time is of the essence, Redevir."

"I will do it," Eriana volunteered. "I will hire the ship. If I am clean."

Aren nodded to her. She was. "Are you sure you are all right?"

"I am always all right," she said. She smiled.

He instantly did not want her to go. But she had to. She was clean.

Redevir looked at her skeptically. "Do you know what to do?"

She held out her hand to him. He set a small sack of gold in it. "I do the opposite of that," she said.

Redevir shrugged. "Good enough."

She smiled to Aren and then turned and darted off through the city. He watched her go until she vanished around a corner.

The two Sarenwalkers carrier the users the opposite way, setting off on their wide loops.

Aren remained with Redevir. Both of them were clean. It would be good to avoid the plaza, but they could afford to move through the towers to find Redevir's man.

They paused at the corner of a stone temple of Holy Juna, waiting for a troupe of the Orange to pass by. Aren reached for his malagayne. He set one hand on the pouch, and left it their, feeling it within, knowing it, wanting it, demanding it. He stared at the back of his hand on the pouch until it ceased to have meaning, his eyes glazed over, and he lost all sense.

"Are you all right?" Redevir asked over his shoulder.

"I'm fine."

"Are you certain you are of sound mind?"

"Why wouldn't I be?"

"Because we just faced down Kinraigan. And because you have been standing motionless here for five minutes."

"I will be fine," Aren said. "I can handle it." *Five minutes?*

Redevir looked long into his eyes. "Very well then. I cannot have my partner losing his mind now, can I? Come on. Let's get back into the light."

Aren's first hint that something was wrong was when hands grabbed his shoulders.

His legs were knocked out from under him, and his face thrust into the street. His struggles were answered with dizzying blows from wooden batons, splitting his forehead and leaving thick lumps over his scalp. Redevir groaned beside him, gnashing his teeth and shouting curses. Everywhere orange capes billowed.

A man's face hovered into view, slender and long, with a flat, crooked nose below the two slits of his eyes. His skin was pale and his cheeks had no beard. The man wore blue silk pinned with the twin blood rubies of a twice-bloodied, glittering like glass roses beside the triple nails of a Questioner. He knelt down to stare into Aren's eyes.

"What is this?" Redevir shouted. "Who are you?"

"I am Tealie," the man said. "And you already know what I am."

Inner Guard.

"We've done nothing," Redevir groaned.

"I recognize this satchel," Tealie said. "This contains priceless things. A theft of this magnitude cannot go unpunished."

"It's mine," Aren said.

"Is it now? And who might you be? I know the names of every man in Medion who is permitted to carry one of these. Quite the coincidence to find one such item spirited away the very hour that illegal magick was used in this very city."

"We're not involved," Redevir said. "We are innocent."

"We shall see," said Tealie. "You resemble in many ways one who is named Aren. A traitor to Amagon. I see your eyes twitch. Interesting. Perhaps you *are* him. I cannot prove this, but I can send away for those who can."

"There is no proof against us," Redevir said.

Tealie leaned in close to Aren. He cocked his head to the side abruptly. His eyes widened. "What's this? What's this?" He grasped the pouch at Aren's waist, pulling it open. He took a pinch of grey leaves and held them to his nose. "Malagayne," he pronounced. "It does not matter then. This alone is a crime. This is all the evidence I require to have you declared *incongruent* and have you unfingered and quartered."

Aren groaned.

"You will learn the sensation of truth and justice," Tealie said. "Harken Tower awaits you."

The dungeon tower.

Tealie mounted a horse and sat comfortably upon a cushioned saddle.

Aren was lifted to his feet and half-dragged through the cold street. He felt numb. He was not even aware of the rain when it first began to pour. He struggled through the sudden heavy downpour. Fat droplets pattered on the hood of his cloak. They felt like stones.

Small groups of onlookers gathered under the eaves, blinking through the sheets of rain. They were pressed so close together upon the street that Aren and Redevir brushed against their tunics.

Redevir stiffened. He lost his footing and slipped on the wet cobbles, falling heavily into the crowd. The people pulled away, save for one man. The face was obscured by a hood, but Redevir's hand clamped tightly about the man's ankle.

Tealie was wheeling about in his saddle. His men were leaning in to lift Redevir back onto his feet, their cloaks flapping wetly around them.

As the hooded man in the crowd tried to shake Redevir's hand away, the Rover grasped the back of the man's neck, and pulled him to his knees. Redevir then said something that only Aren managed to hear over the pounding rain. "Mallios, if you want your money, then you better get us out of this."

The man recoiled.

Tealie's men took the Rover by his shoulders and yanked him to his feet. Tealie removed a slender baton from his belt and cracked it across Redevir's head, and his body went slack, dangling loose-limbed from the arms of the soldiers.

Aren could barely see through the sheets of rain. His only hint that they had reached walls of Harken Tower was the light escaping in tiny streams from arrow slits in the walls. He saw a great iron gate swing wide, and he was ushered down a long corridor. It sloped downward, and terminated at a stairwell, leading to a tunnel.

He was pushed into a small room. Redevir was shoved in behind him. A heavy iron door slammed. The light of the torches disappeared, and they were bathed in darkness. In a tomb, buried far below the world.

31

Everything Starts Again

KELUWEN LOOKED OUT THE window of the high tower and saw herself looking back.

Far down below, scurrying between statues and columns, dodging among the clotted crowds, stealing this purse and that purse and flying away like a bird with none the wiser.

She blinked and was back in the tower once again.

"Stay clear of the windows," Severn said. He sounded anxious.

"We are ten stories up," Keluwen said. In Medion, the tenth story was the bottom of the middle stories. The wealthy floors were found there. For the wealthy required a view. Yet the amount of stairs to climb was prohibitive. So it ended up that the lower floors were the middling wealth, the middle floors were the higher wealth, and the upper stories, thirtieth through fiftieth, were populated by the poorest tenants.

"The Orange are in a frenzy," he said. "Their informants scan the windows with scopes."

"Are you worried they will see a woman in your home, Severn?" Keluwen asked.

"I have never seen them like this," he said. "And I saw them after the *incident* three years ago."

"Is it really so bad?" Leucas asked.

"None of our people can move freely right now," Severn said. "Every pedestrian is questioned if they try to leave the vicinity of their tower. They have been following even the slightest rumor about magick users. They have taken some already. One of the associates of one of our informants among them. Everyone is afraid to make a move right now. They are going to schedule burnings."

"Public ones?" Cheli asked. "In Medion? They have not done that in generations in this city. Hidden ones, yes. But not spectacle. Not the way they do it in Olbaran."

"What set them off?" Keluwen asked.

"None of them know what happened," he said. "They all keep looking for hints of magick, but come up empty handed. Everywhere they are stopping people and holding their tracing tools, even children. It is like they are scanning people. The Inner Guard were here from Vithos in a matter of days. Something lit a fire under them."

"The Lord Protector?" Orrinas asked.

"Could be," he said. "Though they came here very fast. Faster than the Priests."

Keluwen felt a pit open in her stomach. "Priests? There are Priests here?"

"Is that a problem?" Severn asked.

"She had a *hunted* experience with their Glasseyes," Orrinas said.

She had grown used to Orrinas answering this question for her. She had always been one who would rather answer questions for herself. But she let him do it. It was a small thing that made him feel he was being protective of her. She let him have this feeling. It was more than worth the rest.

"Priests hunted you?" Severn said, raising an eyebrow. "Another veteran runner. Salute."

"I hate when they call it that," she said. "Running. It makes it sound like we are cowards."

He shrugged emotionlessly. "It is just a word. There is no judgment behind it. You ran. I ran. Most of us have to run at one time or another. If any of our kind live long enough, sooner or later we have a Priest after us for a spell."

"What are they doing here?" Keluwen asked.

"Same reason as the Inner Guard it seems," he said. "There was a trace to investigate."

"What exactly?" Orrinas asked.

"Witnesses described a white light," he said. "Brighter than the sun, but soft, pleasant to look at."

Keluwen exchanged a glance with Orrinas.

"I feel like I heard words like that from the mouth of Paladan," Cheli said.

No one spoke for a long time.

"Could it have been him?" Keluwen asked.

"Witnesses claimed to see men fighting before it happened," Severn said.

"Fighting?"

"A melee," he said. "With swords. At least two factions. Some whispers say there was an ebon-shroud there."

"Flights of fancy," Keluwen said.

"If not Kinraigan, then who?" Cheli asked. "Or what?"

"No one knows," Severn said. "Hence all the investigators."

"It had to be Kinraigan," Keluwen said.

Severn shrugged. "We do know his people have been in the city. Several of his prominent followers have been searching for a little boy."

Orrinas' ears perked up. "A boy?"

Severn nodded. "Something you know about? Hmmm. Then it was more than just rumor."

"What did the informants say?" Orrinas asked.

"That they were following the boy somehow. As if he left a trail in the air. Like one of us. But something different from us. Why do you care?"

"We must find him," Orrinas said. "It is imperative we have this boy with us. He must be protected. It is too important. He has a part to play in the future."

"And it is beginning to look like finding him may bring us face to face with Kinraigan," Cheli said. "The boy may be able to help us get the Codex back from him."

"Conjecture," Krid Ballar said. "None of us know who made that bright light."

"Who else could it have been?" Cheli asked.

"There have been others on the move of late," Severn said. "Those with a special significance to us."

He means those we will likely be sent to deal with once Kinraigan's ashes are scattered in the wind, Keluwen thought.

"Belaeriel has been spotted all over Miralamar, Icaria, the free cities of the Terrangean Sea, but more recently in Palantar and Amagon."

"Amagon?" Orrinas asked. "What could she be doing here?"

"She has been in correspondence with officials in Vithos," Severn said. "The Lord Protector. We do not know why. She is not someone that I would have predicted to obtain sponsorship from a nation's government."

"The world will sleep better when she is dead," Keluwen said. *She is next.*

"What about Kinraigan?" Orrinas asked. "Where is he going from here?"

"We know one place Kinraigan will not go," Severn said. "The Shola. Something there is stirring up the Sur barbarians. War is coming to the far north once more, and soon."

"Why can he not go?" Keluwen said. "I don't understand."

"Because there is something powerful there," Severn said. "Our users have felt it in the Slipstream, but never seen it. Something he fears there could feel him coming from leagues away."

"Soon it will not matter," Cheli said. "Soon he will be invincible."

"Not if we can help it," Orrinas reminded her gently.

"We could not stop him becoming luminous," Hodo said.

"He could walk in the light far sooner than he should have been able," Cheli said. "We should have had years to hunt him before he went in. But the key he was using is unknown to us."

"So how is he getting in?" Hodo asked.

Cheli shrugged. "He found a way. Something not in any of the texts I found that talk about the Slipstream. But to do it without a pre-made key would require energy output that only a handful of users in the world have both the strength and concentration to perform at once. That is usually the only thing which opens them up to fall into the light, and then only briefly. Sustained exposure to the light is what makes him, or anyone else, *luminous.* "

"But just *being luminous* does not grant knowledge of how the light is supposed to work," Orrinas said. "He still had to learn how it works. He had to *learn* immortality."

"He has the book," Cheli said. "And he has spent far more time in the light than every other user in this world combined."

"If we know what he wants," Orrinas said. "Then all we must do is be ready to intercept him, and know where he will be going before he gets there."

"Easier said than done," Krid said.

"We only ever seem to know where he *was*," Leucas said. "And even when we do, like in Westgate, he always seems to have the upper hand."

"All we know is that he *may* already be immortal," Orrinas said. "And every moment he is still alive is one moment closer to him becoming invincible as well. Truly invincible. If he finds what I think he is after, there will be no more gods left to pray to. He really will become a god upon the earth."

"The informants said he was here," Hodo said. "Is he still?"

"No one has seen him," Severn said.

"No one ever seems to," Keluwen said.

"Only those who join him or die by his hand," Orrinas said.

"His most loyal servants are those who were once sent to kill him," Severn said.

Keluwen knew it was true, had known for a long time. But the thought still made her shudder. How quickly he had overtaken her, subsumed her, deconstructed her with a handful of words and a touch. "How many follow him? No one has ever told us."

"He has followers in many lands," Severn said. "The true number must be staggering."

"He was very charismatic," Orrinas said. "And very convincing. Even before he became luminous."

"He had a mountain redoubt on the far western coast of Tyrelon," Severn said. "He trained apprentices all over the south. Khazvhadar and Pim Pen Pert in Hylamar. Cimmeries, Demorien, and Modai in Halsabad. He crossed paths with Cethor. Raviel chased him and died. As did Paladan before him. And Selador before that. And Dhuvries before that. Countless others before *Axis Ardent* was even on his trail."

"What about the ones he turned?" Keluwen asked. "Does anyone know how?"

"It is not magick, if that is what you mean," Severn said. "We tested."

"It cannot be as bad as they say," Hodo said.

It is, Keluwen thought.

"Ebon-shrouds were sent out of the *Dark*, but he turned them. Sarcosars of Naphesus dragged Redscar out of the pits and unleashed him, and he now serves his target. Balthoren, Seekthi, Caternas—one by one he took them for his own. Some say he can take anyone, if given a chance to speak with them. "

"The Amagon-men fought him fiercely," Orrinas said. "Dozens of their Glasseyes and hundreds of others were slaughtered. Three years ago now, it was. Seems an eternity."

"They have the best Glasseyes in the world here in Amagon," Severn said. "He led them on a merry chase. Even here in Medion. He decimated their Render Tracer corps. No matter how hard they tried, how high they stacked the deck against him, it was never enough."

"We come ever closer though," Orrinas said. "Now all of our knowledge is added to theirs from back then. And soon we shall accumulate even more."

"Speaking of," Keluwen said. "Where are these new scene schematics we were told about?"

Severn closed his eyes and slowly reopened them. It was the most expressive frustration he had likely demonstrated in ages. "They are not here."

"Not here?" Orrinas asked.

"We came a long way to find them," Keluwen added, trying to fight the urge to slap him.

"Our spy has the reports," Severn said. "That much was no exaggeration."

"Why don't *we* have them?" Orrinas asked.

Severn pointed one nail of a finger out the window, out across the plaza, beyond the many moving shapes of blue capes and orange, brown leather Ministry longcoats, soldiers, Glasseyes, to a red granite tower beyond. "He is there. It would have been a simple thing to come this way. But no longer. Not when the Orange and the Listeners are standing on every stoop, peeking in every window."

"We will go to him," Keluwen said.

"Don't make promises that cannot be kept," Krid said. "We do not know how safe it is to move here."

"Which tower?" Keluwen asked.

"Darralund Tower," Severn said. "The red one."

"Do not give her this information," Krid said.

"Fuck you, Krid," Keluwen said.

"Eighteenth floor," Severn said. "Fifth room."

"She is going to do something reckless," Krid warned.

"You are right about that," she said. She made for the door leading out into the marble hallway.

"You cannot go now," Severn said.

She kept walking.

"I tried to warn you," Krid said.

"If you go out that door—" Severn said.

She was already out that door. She was halfway down the marble hall before she heard Hodo poke his head out the door behind her. He called out after her, but she was too busy listening to the sounds of her own boots clomping down the stairwell.

I am going. She had always gone where others told her not to go. She had come to believe that the act of someone trying to discourage her was proof that it needed to be done.

The stairwell was empty for floor after floor.

She remembered what Seb told her the first time they met. *Be true to yourself above all else. Your soul is a river. Let your mind be a little boat riding the current. Don't fight what you are, embrace it, accept it, go where it leads. Follow that river and it will take you where you need to go.*

This was what she did. This was who she was. *I am Keluwen. I go where everyone in the world tells me I can't. I stare the impossible in the face and I do it. That is how I live and that is how I will die.*

She rubbed her fingers together, feeling the velvet. She was alone again. Gone for the steal. Like the days of old. Like the days of free. When every tomorrow had a sunrise because no day was attached to any other. Every page turned was a new book. No need to worry about consequence. No need to plan for what is to come. Because nothing is to come. Nothing but a new day. Where everything starts again.

She felt tears welling in her eyes before she reached the ground floor.

She bumped into a servant in the lobby. His hat could have been a swan. He judged the value of the fabric her clothes were made of and deemed it safe to curse her.

She made the sign of the witch at him. "Come get me, shitstain."

Why did she say that? She hadn't said that in years. Hadn't taunted a man into chasing her so she could speed away and trip him up for a fool. Not since she was a girl. Not since so far before Orrinas that she had never thought a day like now would ever be.

He took two steps after her, but gave up. She was already too far away.

She took a deep, relieved breath. If he had come storming out the tower calling after her, the Orange were sure to come. And they would call down the Inner Guard with them, and they would bring cold chains and questions, and she would have to do something of a magick fashion to get away.

And then the Glasseyes would come.

She bit her lip.

Just as they always came. And they never stopped. Not in Amagon. They would follow to the grave. Hers or theirs. They were relentless. Like old crows.

She felt a shiver as she stepped through the glass doors, and began her descent of the wide marble steps, pale white like the steps to or from everwonder.

I am leaving.

It felt like she was climbing down from the eleventh heaven.

She let herself flow like water, sliding between wealthy patrons and elusive merchants and chattering visitors from Ethios and Samartan and Arragandis. She moved from cluster to cluster, making each deviation look like she was stepping up to rejoin her group of friends. So that the Orange would not think too much of seeing her.

When she reached the street, she glanced both ways, and for the first time noticed one of the Orange notice her. He was one of three, standing in a triangle, swords sheathed but hands resting on hilts like fingers on triggers. The one was facing her while his two fellows spoke past him to each other. But his eyes were on her, and they followed her.

She tried to put them out of her mind. But she heard the sound of their boots behind her. A hundred feet away. But a quick jog could cover that. She felt her skin turn cold and the sweat begin to bead.

She began to break into a trot. Just a few steps at first, masking it by looking like she was getting some speed to hop over a puddle in the street. She did it again when she reached the opposite side curb, trying to make it look harmless, a joyful, playful skip. She gained another twenty paces on them.

She tried not to look over her shoulder, weaving between fountains and wide circular patches of grass amid the endless concrete and polished stone of Medion. She tried the game of nearing other people again, pretending she knew them, beginning phrases of welcome, and waving smiles before breaking off at the last moment.

She was beneath the shadow of the tower across the avenue, a tall one of golden stone, like the sands of a sunset beach, sharp square features, no statues or embellishments.

Let me by, tower. Just let me by.

She tried not to look over her shoulder.

But eventually she failed. Just a little look. Just one.

She saw the same three Orange behind her, closer. She looked ahead. She saw another pair of them before the golden tower. They were not looking at her yet, but it would take only a quick signal from those behind to bring them to cut off her path.

She heard a whistle behind her.

The two Orange looked up.

Shit.

She diverted hard to the right, cut between three sets of conversations, brushed past three sets of shoulders. The two Orange were in motion. The first three were behind her like bloodhounds. She threw herself into a jog until she was among a large crowd about the wide central fountain pool of Darralund Tower. A hundred feet wide, it was crystal and shallow, with water spraying from the mouths of sirens in the center.

She heard the grunt of the Orange behind her as they shoved their way through to her. They were so close now.

She reached the edge of the fountain, amid the crush of people. They were closing.

She hopped up onto the three-foot tall rim of the fountain and ran around its curve. The five Orange were caught up in the crush of people and were left behind.

But she saw three more far across the fountain. They had not been involved before, but they certainly were now that she had made a spectacle of herself. She kept on around the circle, racing past people in the crowd. One random man reached out an arm to trip her up, out of boredom or malice, she was not sure which. She jumped over it.

The new Orange were working their way through the crowd to intercept her a bit further up along the curve.

She jumped into the fountain itself. The water sloshed up and over her boots and soaked her socks in a deluge. She ran through the water, like running in sludge. She felt so slow. But when she looked behind her, the Orange could not even see her. She was back below the bobbing heads in the crowd. By the time they reached the edge and looked out across the water, she was a hundred feet away, climbing out on the opposite side of the circle.

The Orange split up to round the fountain from both sides.

Keluwen knew this was her chance. She broke into a sprint, tearing across the courtyards, leaping between columns, jumping over benches. Each step of her boots clopped and squished. Each beat of her heart felt like a snap of thunder.

She descended a set of stairs and flew through a treegarden, using the grass of its lawn to hide her wet footprints before going up the steps of the red tower. Darralund Tower. She pulled the door open, and spun through, looking behind her without slowing her momentum.

She could see bright orange capes in the distance, milling about, but they were not coming closer.

I lost them.

She held one palm over her chest to make sure her heart was still there. She took the stairs slowly and quietly. She passed only one nervous woman coming down, who eyed her like she was the devil. But she did not speak a word.

She went to the eighteenth floor, and stopped before the fifth room. She knocked with the universal code. No one came to the door for minutes.

She tried again. And then a third time. Finally she said, "Fuck, open the fucking door, or I will scream until the Orange come."

She heard someone coming. Locks were turned. The door creaked inward. She saw a man of featheresque hair and monochromatic eyes. His face was so forgettable she could not be sure she was actually even looking at him.

"What do you want?" he asked.

"Schematics," she said.

He blinked at her.

"Schematics," she repeated. "Two sets."

"I do not know what you are talking about."

"I am with Orrinas. We are staying across the way with Severn. They are waiting for me to bring this back to them. Hand them over."

"I have not such documents."

"The Orange are circling this tower as we speak. I will call down to them right now and tell them that we are thieves who stole from the Inner Guard."

He grimaced at her. "How do I know you are not the Inner Guard trying to trick me?"

She yawned. "Because if the Inner Guard knew about Orrinas and Severn, and knew you were in this room, there would not be only one impatient woman with wet boots knocking on your door. You would be waking up in a cell with a Questioner putting needles in your gums."

He shivered. "Wait here."

Keluwen waited. Her feet felt soggy. She was not looking forward to the trip back.

He returned a moment later with two leatherbound folios. He slipped them into a leather case, and dropped it in a rucksack. "Begone now."

She gave him the Bravonian finger and turned to leave.

"You are rude!" he called after her.

She raced down the stairs. There was no old woman this time.

Keluwen waited at the front door. No one stood inside or out. The area was deserted. She crept her way along the edge of the tower. She noticed the Orange milling about the way she had come. They were far away, but were blocking the path back to her tower.

So she went the other way. Crossed from tree to tree, column to column, tower to tower, until she was half a mile up the avenue from where she had led them on her merry chase.

She joined the foot traffic and walked along, calm and cool, passing behind the Orange, content to let them think she was still over there somewhere. She walked calmly back into her tower and took the stairs until she reached Severn's suites.

She interrupted Orrinas in the process of organizing a rescue effort. Hodo was beside himself. Cheli bit her lip anxiously. Leucas paced back and forth.

"You aren't talking about me, are you?" she asked.

Every head spun to face her, like a switch had been turned.

"You are here," Orrinas said, blinking in surprise.

"I am," she said.

Hodo was furious. "You should have taken me with you. We watch each other's backs, Kel. You could have brought me."

She shrugged.

Krid Ballar hissed. "She didn't do it for us. She did it for herself. She does everything for herself."

Keluwen smirked. "The why doesn't matter. The result matters."

"What is that?" Hodo asked, pointing at what she held.

She held up the rucksack. She dipped inside and pulled out the leather case. "Someone mentioned you wanted these schematics."

Orrinas' eyes about popped from his head.

"Give that here!" Krid shouted.

Instead she handed it to Cheli. "Here."

Cheli flipped through them immediately, noting the new imprints, new renders, new streams, everything. When she reached the narrative at the end, she nearly hopped out of her boots. "This report says they followed the sensitized fluorescence trail to the docks, where it was deemed that he boarded a ship and departed the jurisdiction of Amagon law."

"By the gods high and low, we have his trail," Hodo said.

"The ship was departing north," Cheli said.

"North," Hodo said. "That narrows the ports to Volean Heights, Arragandis, Nidarorad, and Corricon."

"It was a deep draft ship," Cheli said. "Heavy cog."

"That rules out Volean Heights," Hodo said.

"We need to find a fast ship," Leucas said.

"We need a way to get to the docks unseen," Krid said. "After the ruckus you have caused, it will be days before the Orange will calm down."

I have caused. Why don't you just say you think I am a problem?

"Hodo," Orrinas said. "Find a ship. Book passage."

Hodo nodded.

"Leucas, supplies."

Leucas hopped to his feet.

"Cheli, prepare our updated composite of Kinraigan. Everything he can do. Every stream."

Cheli smiled with her mouth, but wept from her eyes.

"Krid, take Severn to the upper rooms and scout us a path to the wharves."

Krid slithered out of his chair. He spat bitterly and unnecessarily on the rug. He kicked mud from his boot heel onto the polished white marble. He left without saying a word.

"Keluwen," Orrinas said.

The sound of her name jolted her to attention. "Yes?"

"A word." He pulled her aside into one of the bedrooms of the suite.

"Are you trying to bruise?" she asked.

He released her angrily. "What were you thinking?"

"I was thinking about our mission."

"You could have gotten yourself killed. You know what the Glasseyes here are like."

"I have done worse and you know it."

He grimaced. "I keep asking what you were thinking. But that is just it. You weren't thinking."

She bit her lip and looked up into his eyes. "You want to know? I was thinking about Seb. I was thinking about Nils. I was thinking about everyone. Especially you."

"You could have compromised *both* safehouses."

She pursed her lips at him and looked up into his eyes, her brow stern. "We need to stop him from becoming a god, Orrinas. Fuck the safehouses. Fuck Krid. Fuck Severn. Fuck all carefully laid plans. We kill him or he kills the world. Are we doing this or not?"

He regarded her for a long time. He reached out both hands and cupped her face. "There were other ways of obtaining the schematics."

"This quickly?"

"No."

"Are you cross with me?"

"Yes."

"Do you still love me?"

"Yes. You could have ended our mission here."

"I know."

"But you did get the new schematics," he said.

"Yes."

"And you came out of it unscathed."

"Yes."

"Then they will get over it. I will get over it."

She smiled. She would have let him call her wife without complaint for that one moment.

"Come then," he said. "We have an immortal to catch."

32

Beneath the Ground

THE PROBLEM WITH TOWERS, in Corrin's estimation, lay solely in the number of extra steps required to get from a high room to a tavern. Any tavern. Reputable. Disreputable. Squalid. Seedy. Notorious. Partially collapsed.

After walking through a Lamani wilderness, and a Palantari wilderness, and traversing the Malorese moors, and evading bandits in the northern Malar territories, and then climbing underneath the pier near Aldria to sneak his way onto a paddle boat heading down the Alder River, he was looking forward to finally being able to stay in one place for a long time.

What has Medion for me? Perhaps the serving cups are fifty stories tall as well.

He blinked in the light of early morning as he stepped out into the wide avenues of Medion, letting the fine glass door of Cojiri Tower swing gently shut behind him. He walked to the edge of the platform, and looked down at the twenty stone steps that descended to the street.

The grey towers looked like sleeping giants all around him, casting shadows the size of mountains as the sun rose behind them. Each had a personality all its own. Some were sharp and cynical, some were broad and happy, some were angled and sad, and still others were ageless and wise. Three of the towers were black as night, all sleek and strong, and dressed in his favorite color. If the towers could have moved, he assumed that those three would have moved the fastest.

Someone brushed past him, an ass of a merchant in some kind of hurry. It was early morning still, and the wide streets between the hulking towers were only just beginning to fill with pedestrians. Endless avenues of stone blocks and pale concrete streets and walls and edifices.

The city smelled like a city should smell; it smelled tall and clean and grand. No mud on the ground. No shit in the streets. No imbeciles peddling useless wares on every corner. It was a veritable wonderland. Corrin pulled Hallan in tow. The boy trotted silently after him, looking curiously at the high towers.

"You like them, don't you? The towers."

"Tall like mountains," Hallan agreed.

"I prefer the view from the ground," Corrin said. "On the high floors I prefer not to look out the windows."

"Why not?" The boy looked at him quizzically.

"The people look like little bugs. It makes me uneasy."

"Why?"

"I don't like being so high. It's unnatural."

"What about mountains? Mountains are high up, too."

"That's different," Corrin said. He sucked in air over his teeth.

"How?"

"Do you ever stop asking questions?"

"I don't know." Hallan shrugged and looked away.

"The difference is that mountains don't come crashing down under you," Corrin said. "I was up on one of the basilicas in Kassanath once. It collapsed."

"What's a basilica?"

"Like a tower on a holy place. With a dome."

"Why did it fall down?"

"Everything falls down sooner or later. I was barely involved."

"Why were you on a basilisk?"

"Basilica," Corrin corrected. "Someone was chasing me."

"Why?"

"Because I liberated his daughter from her servitude to chastity."

"What's chastity?"

"It's horrible," Corrin said. "Like torture."

"I bet she was happy you saved her," the boy said, smiling with pride to be standing so close to such a hero.

Corrin looked up at the sky. "Oh, she was overjoyed. Let's check on Reidos." He turned to go back in, but stopped suddenly. He felt a little prickling on his neck. Something wasn't quite right. He turned back to the streets, scanning them for the source of his discomfort.

Nothing.

He saw people meandering up and down the lanes, pausing at shops behind grey columns. He saw women waving from high windows, and men glancing at the steep granite walls.

Then Corrin saw a curious man on an elevated portico of a cafe across the street, adjacent to another tower. The man's movements were stilted. He had short hair, strikingly blond. He wore the fine clothes of a wealthy man, or the servant of some wealthy man. His apparel included tight-fitting black breeches and a fine shirt of soft black wool with silver trim.

A man with hair that bright shouldn't wear black.

The man raised something to his lips. It looked like a flute or a horn of some kind. *Musicians. Practicing on the streets.* That was a common thing in Medion, but something was wrong about this man. They way he stared at Corrin. The way he stood, braced against the marble balustrade of the cafe. The way he tensed his body against the wind.

"Move!" He grabbed Hallan's arm and threw him toward the door. The man across the street put his lips to the long black cylinder. Hallan went through. Corrin kicked himself back across the landing and pressed himself against one eave of the doorway. A long black dart clicked against the steps behind him. It lay there, dripping dark liquid onto the grey stone. Luckily, the cafe wasn't directly across from the doorway. It allowed for a scant few inches of cover.

Corrin thought hard. *Through the door. Have to be real fast.* He pulled the black cloak from his shoulders, and bunched it in his hands. *Decoy.* He took a breath and held it deep. He waited. Waited. Threw the cloak toward the doorway. Another dart whistled through the air, taking it dead to center.

Corrin sprang instantly toward the door, ripping it open with one hand and squeezing his body through. A final dart imbedded itself into the fine glass, cracking a hole in it, and piercing halfway through, just inches above the spot where Corrin's heart sat within his chest on the other side.

That was too close.

He grabbed Hallan, raced to the stairwell, and began to carry the boy up the endless steps. Twenty floors to cheap suites. Or was it thirty? No, it was thirty-five. Corrin's legs were wearing more quickly than usual, and soon began to burn. He was coughing and spitting by the time he was halfway up.

Goddamn thirty-fifth floor.

After a succession of heaving and wheezing, he finally reached the correct floor, burst out of the stairwell, rushed past bewildered tenants, and tore down the hall of polished marble. He came to the room where Reidos lay, and threw the door open as if he intended to break it. He lunged through and slammed it shut behind him.

"What are you doing?" Reidos asked.

"We're in trouble," Corrin whistled.

"What happened?"

"Someone just tried to kill me. A man in black."

"I thought you were the man in black," Reidos said.

"There is at least one other one. He used a blowgun."

"Who is he?" Reidos asked. "Why not give him a steel kiss and be done with it?"

"Can't get close enough," Corrin said. "We need to displace and make a plan."

"What do we do?" Reidos asked.

"There's only one door out of the tower. He just ambushed me at it."

"There is another way out," Reidos said. "All of these towers have sub-basements with utility corridors."

"Into the sewage system. We'll be long gone while he is still watching the front door."

"I have trouble just walking. Joints still giving me hell from walking the length of Palantar"

"I'll get your gear then, but we have to go now."

Hallan was silent and still as Corrin stuffed clothes and tools into the carry-bags. The boy sat patiently while he donned the black mail shirt and leather armor, strapped on his knives, and tossed all else into the carry-bags. Finally he slung Reidos' weapon belt over one shoulder. "Ready?"

"What about Mardin?" Reidos asked.

"Shaot. I forgot about him. We better take him with us. That farod is probably after him, too."

Corrin flew through the door and sprinted down the musty corridor. Mardin's door was unlocked. Corrin went right in. Mardin sat on his mattress, looking absently at the walls. He turned slowly to face Corrin, with a blank look to match the blank walls.

"Get your things," Corrin said. "We're going."

"Where?" Mardin asked. "Now?"

"Yes, now," Corrin shouted. "Someone is trying to kill us."

Mardin groaned like a child with a stomach ache. "I knew it."

"Yes, you are very smart. Get a move on."

Mardin rose and snatched up his carry-bag. "I never even unpacked anything."

Corrin ignored him. There was no time for anything but movement. They had to go. Down thirty-five flights of stairs. Through the service corridors. Down to the basements. "Keep your eyes open. He could be coming this very minute."

Hallan began to slow, and Corrin lifted him onto his back along with both carry-bags.

A blond assassin was not seen on the stairs, nor under the wide arches of the tower lobby. Corrin slowed pace, weaving between wandering groups of silk-robed merchant lords, and wealthy patrons wearing bright sashes of blue and yellow. Corrin pressed through them, and moved toward the rear of the lobby, cutting between the high, squared columns. He stopped to look back at the crowd of people. He didn't see the blond hair anywhere. That calmed him slightly. They wouldn't be spotted now. They were almost home free.

He ducked into an unlit corridor with musty air beneath its low ceiling. The others followed closely. He checked around the corner. Empty. He took quiet steps. Reidos and Mardin did the same. Corrin turned his head back to Hallan, putting a finger to his lips. "Shhh," he said. Hallan stayed close to him, almost pressed against his leg.

The noise of the lobby dwindled into faint muddled echoes. The walkway was long like a deep tunnel, quiet and dark.

A man stepped into the hall from out of nowhere, and barred their path. He was dressed in high white stockings and a long violet tunic—an attendant of the tower. Corrin jolted to a halt as the man grabbed his shoulder. "What is this business?" He eyed them with alarm. "Sneaking into the basement! We have had enough of you street-people. Get out of here!"

"Wait," Corrin pleaded. "Let me explain." He put his hand on his arm.

"Release me," the man shouted. "I'm calling the watchman." He twisted away.

But the pommel of a sword came down on his head. The attendant stooped and crumpled to the floor like a sack of rocks. Mardin stood behind the fallen body, replacing his blade in its scabbard. He looked up at the others with a blank expression.

"What the...?" Corrin asked

"You said we had to hurry," Mardin said. "I don't want to die."

"I'll be damned," Corrin said, flashing a brief smile. "Come on then." He took off down the corridor and threw himself down dark stairs leading to the basement. He descended deep, winding stairwells. He navigated through storage rooms, and wine cellars, and rooms that seemed to have no purpose at all, until at last he came to a long, dark tunnel, leading as far away as he could see.

Corrin felt the darkness of the tunnel as if it were a physical thing. The walls were barely visible in the gloom. The lamps appeared with less and less frequency, and the walls closed in now to make the path only wide enough for one person to proceed at a time. Corrin winced as he passed the last light-bowl. He hated walking in the pitch black. He stopped the others and stood before them, his face masked in shadow.

Hallan whimpered lightly as the light dwindled to nothing in the tunnel. He stopped in his tracks like a small statue, refusing to go on.

Corrin turned to shine a wide smile at him. "Come on," he said. "No need to be afraid when I'm here."

"Yes," Reidos said as he hobbled behind the boy. "Corrin used to kill sewer monsters for a living. I'm sure we'll be quite safe."

"Besides," Corrin said. "They always eat the cripples first. Right, Reidos?"

"Of course," Reidos said, rolling his eyes.

Hallan's expression did not change, but he relented.

"This is it," Corrin said. "No more light until we reach the service ducts. We have to feel our way along from here on."

Mardin let out a wheeze. "You don't have a torch?"

Corrin grimaced at him. "Do you remember us having time to stop and think about something like that?"

"There could be debris in the tunnel," Mardin said. "Or a straight drop-off. It'll slow us to a crawl feeling along the floor for something like that."

"The only other way is to turn around and go right back up to the front door."

He felt Hallan tugging lightly on his sleeve. "What is it? Still afraid?"

"No," the boy said.

"What then?"

"Look." Hallan held up his little carry-bag, pulling it open.

Corrin peered inside, but saw nothing. He shrugged.

The boy frowned and furrowed his brow. He pulled the bag to himself, holding it against his chest with one arm. He pursed his lips as he dug around inside it. At last finding the desired item, he smiled and handed it to Corrin.

Corrin pulled it up to his eyes, and squinted through the darkness. It was a small bundle of flares. He blinked in disbelief. "I'll be damned."

He turned to Mardin. "See? Optimism."

Corrin couldn't see Mardin rolling his eyes at him in the pitch, but he knew he was. Reidos had taught him that, much to Corrin's chagrin. He lit one finger-length black stick by scraping the end against the bricks of the wall. It flared white in his hand, blazing the length of the tunnel with bright light.

They reached the aperture on the far side of the tunnel before the second flare died away. The portal was circular. Only two feet in diameter. Corrin held the flare over his head and motioned for Mardin to go first.

"You want me to go first? I can't even see what's on the other side."

"There's a platform," Corrin said. "Feel your way down."

Mardin reluctantly put one foot through. He felt around with it and finally found his footing on the platform. It was a good deal lower than the floor of the tunnel they were leaving, so Mardin's face was only knee-high to Corrin on the other side. Corrin eased Reidos through next.

Then a crash came. In the tunnel behind them. Something fell hard, like metal on stone. It blasted with echoes like trumpets. They were not alone in the tunnel. Corrin looked back, but saw nothing. The last light-bowl they had passed was now a speck of light like a faded star.

"Someone's following us," Reidos said.

"It's him," Mardin whispered. "He's coming for us."

"Impossible," Corrin whispered. "How could he know to find us here?"

"You tell me," Mardin said.

"It's just a watchman from the tower," Corrin said. "They must have found the one you knocked out."

"Whoever it is, I suggest we move now," Reidos said. "They can see your flare as plain as day."

"Can't go without it," Corrin said. "Have to outrun them."

Corrin lowered the boy through the hole. He crawled through quickly and Mardin fished him out on the other side. Corrin then leapt through the portal, landing easily. He wheeled around, handing the flare to Reidos.

"What are you doing?" Mardin asked.

"If someone follows us this far, then I want to know about it," Corrin said. He reached into his carry-bag and withdrew a roll of twine. He cut an arm-length of it with his utility knife, and tied one end to a spare flare. He then withdrew a bottle from his waist pouch. "Adhesive," he said. "Strong stuff."

"Why are you carrying a bottle of glue?" Mardin asked.

"Shut up." Corrin dabbed one end of twine into the bottle, then pressed the end against the wall on one side of the hole. He pulled the twine across the portal and did the same to the other end. He then wedged the light-stick into a fissure in the wall. "When someone trips this twine, the stick will flash when it scrapes on the brick."

Corrin lit a fresh flare, and helped Reidos to hobble along.

The sewer ducts were wider than the tunnel, stretching thirty feet across, and with high ceilings. In the flickering white light, they resembled the catacombs of a secluded tomb for some ancient god, but they smelled like that ancient god had taken a giant shit in them twice a day for ten thousand years.

It stretched on for what seemed like miles, branching off into a multitude of connecting tunnels that went on to link the lines of the entire city into one system. Thankfully there was room on either side where the various admixtures of fetid liquids did not reach.

"I won't let us get lost down here," he said. "There has to be an access point somewhere. Look for breaks in the walls."

They kept moving, but the portal never materialized. Corrin started to wonder if he had mistakenly wandered into Bol-Demar's infinite stinking bowels. *Something that eats worlds must spend most of its existence hovering over a latrine pit.*

"How much further could it be?" Mardin asked. "I don't see a thing."

"We should be able to see it by now," Corrin said.

"Are we in the wrong tunnel?" Reidos asked.

"There should only be one from the tower."

"You sure they all go the same way?" Mardin asked.

"They should all link up," Corrin insisted.

He stopped in his tracks as a white flash blinked behind him.

"They're at the hole," Reidos said.

"Go!" Corrin shouted, dragging Reidos. "Move!"

Corrin's heart raced. His breaths came at double speed. The only sounds were the echoes of scampering feet. Endless tunnel. Nowhere to hide. No hope of outrunning pursuit with Reidos in the shape he was. The walls were closing in. The flare burned low. Then he saw it. A well of stairs leading up. This was it. He passed Reidos on to Mardin, and scooped Hallan up in one arm. He raced up the stairs with the other two men hobbling up after him. Twenty steps. Thirty. Something flew past his head, clattering on the tunnel wall.

Darts! Shaot!

Corrin gained the top. He stood on a wide landing with a square steel door in the ceiling directly above it. Mardin reached his side with Reidos wheezing behind him. Corrin leapt into the air, and clutched onto a metal pipe on the ceiling. He reached up to the steel latches of the trapdoor, and flipped each one open. Mardin positioned himself beneath, holding onto his legs. Corrin pressed hard against the door. It wouldn't budge. Smells of hideous human waste filled his nose. The more he strained, the harder he breathed, and the more the shit seemed to fill his nose, until he thought his head would explode from it. *This could not possibly get worse.*

Mardin held him up, and Corrin pushed harder. With a creak and a whine, the door came open. Corrin strained to give a final thrust, sending the door swinging up and over. He pulled himself up and through. Mardin lifted Hallan over his head. Corrin yanked the boy up after him. Corrin then lowered a hand for Reidos. The Mahhen went through.

Someone was at the base of the stairs. Corrin grabbed Mardin's outstretched hand, and he was through. "The door!" Corrin shouted. He pulled on one side, and Mardin the other. Together they heaved it up and over.

A shadow of movement. Someone was at the top of the stairs. A hand came through the access hole, gripping the lip of the cavity.

"Shaot!" Corrin screamed.

The door slammed shut. The hole was sealed. Corrin slipped a silver paring knife he appropriated from the kitchens from his belt and wedged it under a metal ring on the outside of the steel frame so that the blade extended over the edge of the door, locking it shut. He fell back onto his knees, releasing a long breath. Then he looked down at the floor.

Mardin gasped. Corrin stared. Beside the door lay the tips of four severed fingers, sprawled like discarded tokens.

33

Dungeon

AREN COUNTED DOWN THE minutes it took for the numbness to crawl from his fingertips down to his hands, and then on to his wrists. His feet might as well have been sitting in a different cell entirely for all he could feel of them. His eyes burned. His skin felt like paper. His teeth rattled in his mouth until he was certain they would shatter. The air chilled each breath, freezing him from the inside out. His own exhales vibrated in his lungs like echoes in ice caves.

He could not remember the last time he had eaten, and he was almost doubled over from hunger. He balled his hands into fists and huffed his breath on them. His legs ached from standing. Sitting was impossible. The floor was beneath at least eight inches of water. It was already getting to his feet, and he gritted his teeth as his skin became soft and vulnerable, but he could only switch from leaning on one leg to leaning on the other.

He had been stripped of his cloak, and his shirts were soaked through to the skin. Drafts of air fell from above like waves of ice through ventilation shafts high above in the walls—shafts whose sole purpose was to deliver waves of frigid air from the outside to torment him. The vents were crisscrossed with heavy iron bars, making them useless to attempt an escape, even if he could somehow reach them. At least they had let him keep his boots, though so far they had only served to catch rainwater like buckets.

Redevir, too, was shifting and shuffling to keep his limbs alive. "This is an unexpected setback," he said.

Aren huffed a laugh in spite of himself. He looked around at the walls. "What gave you that idea?"

"I suppose this rules out vengeance against the Lord Protector. It is even worse than you thought, Aren. His propagandists have turned the entire populace against you."

Aren winced. "He shouldn't have done that. He didn't have to do that."

"He wants the Dagger that badly." Redevir was feeling the walls for cracks and weaknesses as he shifted. "We need to get out of here."

"They know who I am. But they don't know the whole story. Aldarion will send his people from Vithos. They will know which questions to ask, and which limbs of ours to sever. They will question us to death." He looked down at the floor. The water appeared to be rising. "If we don't drown first."

"We'll get out. Did you hear me talk to him out there?" Redevir pointed in the direction he thought *out there* was.

"That man in the street? What can he do to help us? We're deep in a dungeon, beneath a tower, surrounded by the Orange, the Inner Guard, and probably officers of the Warhost, maybe even Sarenwalkers. What do you expect one random man to do?"

"*That* was Tathred Mallios. The man who knows where the Diamond is."

"So what?"

"He'll get us out of here."

"Is he a magistrate or a general?"

Redevir shook his head.

"Then what is he going to do?"

"If he wants his money, he'll get us out. If we're in here, he gets nothing and he knows it. You'd be surprised what a man would do for a lot of money."

"This journey is over. Our path is ended. We are in a prison."

"We have suffered a setback," Redevir said. "But the plan remains intact. Our partnership continues."

Aren looked at him dubiously. "He is long gone. He didn't use here. We have no trace of him. He has the Dagger. The one thing we had as a lure is gone. We have nothing to bring him to us. It's over now."

"We do not know where he *is*. But I may know where he is *going to be*."

Aren looked up. "How?"

"We lost the Dagger." He paused. "But if you recall I told you he was looking for stones."

"And?"

"And he was willing to kill for them. That means he wants *them* very badly, too."

"So what?"

"I know why he wants them. I told you about the stones, the shortcuts. There are clues cut into the stones, about the resting place of the immortal

Crown, the *Crown of the Sephors*. There is a rumor that claims a long time ago someone found the Crown, found it but left it where it was. He was being followed by others and wanted to throw them off the trail. But he died before he could ever go back. His dying act was to scratch the answers to five riddles into the bottom of each of the five stones. He then dispersed them to his children. The stones were scattered all over. I have been looking for them. Do you see, Aren? These stones are shortcuts. If we had them we could skip any more of these riddles and they would lead us right to the Crown."

"But you don't have any of them. He does."

"Kinraigan has three of them at least, which means he *was* ahead. But in *just one day*, we have found where we need to go without them. He is using the stones alone. He is not doing the work that I have, solved the riddles the way you have. He is blind without the stones to guide him."

"He is taking them all before you can," Aren said. "He likely has the others already."

"That is where you are wrong." Redevir said. "I know something that he does not. I know a secret about one of the stones. The final stone, *the Diamond*, is missing."

"Missing? I thought they were all missing."

"Missing from where it should be. It was the first one that I sought out. It appeared among a horde of gemstones taken by an old king of Lenagon. He gave it to his second son, who traveled north. After the death of the son, it was given to a close friend of his, a noble lord of Bolan named Skirtis. It was given as a bridal gift to the family of his own son's wife. From there it was hard to follow. It changed hands a half-dozen times, but I searched through the records in Bolan. I met with the descendants of the owners themselves. I traced it to a small duchy on the Kol Plateau."

"The highlands of Bolan," Aren said to himself. "So what happened to the trail after that?"

"The lord who possessed the Diamond was killed along with his entire wagon train by Sur raiders from Belegorod. Everyone was killed. Everything was scavenged from them. There is no way to find it now. No one knows where it went."

"If no one knows, then how do you expect to find it?"

"That's the best part." Redevir smiled. "Someone *does* know where it went. One of my informants made a deal with a man from Bolan. The sole survivor. He claimed that he only ever told half the story. The Sur rode his lord down, yes. But it was *not* the Sur who scavenged. A band of Shola hunters from the north chanced upon them, and chased the Sur away. It was *they* who scavenged the lord's possessions."

"So we sail to the port of Corricon in the Kingdom of Bolan," Aren said.

"That's right. My informant who has been following these leads all over Bolan is Tathred Mallios. He knows where the final Crown stone is. I received a letter from him five days before you and I met in Westgate telling me he was waiting here in Medion. He claimed he found which band of hunters it was, and which of the Sholes they keep it in. He promised me the information if I met his price at our next meeting. The final stone is an unpolished diamond, and it has the *final* clue to the Crown etched into it. If we have it, we don't need the other stones. It will take us the final step on the path. We can leapfrog our adversary, while he is busy trying to find a non-existent monument in Karorad. He thinks he is ahead, but he is not. We are."

"All of that. All of those big plans and ideas are meaningless. We are not getting out of here."

"Tanashri will find us. She knows she needs us to find the Crown. And you have two Sarenwalkers hell-bent on keeping you alive."

"How can you be calm at a time like this?"

"You mean without malagayne?"

Aren stood there frozen. His mouth made to move, but his words were voiceless. He knew. Redevir knew. Of course he knew. He had been there. He saw Tealie take the leaves from the pouch.

"I've known for awhile now. Since the Fields of Syn."

"You knew?" *Someone knows.* He felt like he was sinking into the floor. Getting smaller. Shrinking. He heard dripping water from leaks high above. The sounds swelled until they were each a waterfall in his ears.

"I've wondered for quite some time now," Redevir said. "I've seen you act strangely, as far back as Cair Tiril."

"That long."

"Don't worry about it. You're a man of quality."

"Quality? I am the reason for our failure. I deserve this. I am surprised I didn't end up in a place like this sooner."

"We'll have plenty of time to talk about what you deserve later. We need to be on our toes."

"On our toes for what? We are helpless here."

"You are more resourceful than that. Feeling sorry for yourself isn't going to get anything done. What does it matter if I know?"

Aren said nothing. He stood sulking in the cold, wondering why it did matter that Redevir knew. What would Hayles think? Or Fainen? Or Eriana? None of them would look at him the same.

"Malagayne is widely used in the south. It has even been applied as a salve for medical afflictions. You aren't the only one who takes to the smoke."

"Should that comfort me?"

"I am merely stating the facts."

"And the fact that I can't stop using it doesn't disturb you?"

"Aren, we all do things sometimes, things that others don't understand. You stood up to the ebon-shrouds even though you are not a swordsman. You are going to help me find the greatest treasure in history *and* destroy the most dangerous man in the world *at the same time.* Literally nothing else you do matters next to those things. The others will understand."

"I am doing this. *Me.* Not them. Maybe I should send them all away."

"You know they would never go. We need them. And I think they need you, too. Hayles and Fainen aren't fools. They recognize character. They know you are brave. Honorable even."

"An honorable man doesn't ignore his own oaths. A brave mane doesn't let his captain die because he is afraid."

"You tried to *save* Donnovar," Redevir said. "I was there with you."

"He would be alive if I hadn't convinced him to leave Synsirok."

"Wrong," Redevir said. "Nothing was certain. Margol could have come, or his Palantari assassins, or Kinraigan himself. Donnovar made his own choice, Aren, and he chose to die on a battlefield. He knew the risks of entering Laman in wartime, just as he did leaving the city. He made that choice, not you."

"It's easy to say that."

"Let me put it this way," Redevir said. "I need you. I need that brain of yours. You are my partner. I need you to help me defeat Kinraigan. If a little malagayne is what you need to keep you going, then so be it."

"I know. It's just that without the malagayne all the thoughts come at me at once. They crush me." Aren looked slantwise at him. He clenched his jaw. His eyes felt like they were burning in the cold.

"What's wrong?" Redevir asked, reaching a hand to steady him.

"Withdrawal. I need some malagayne. It's been days since I had some."

"Chances aren't favoring finding any down here."

"Right." Aren's face flushed. His chin tucked to his chest. His neck began a series of brutal spasms, sending painful flutters through his head. His jaw clenched and released. His body shook.

No malagayne.

He needed it. He needed it badly.

He heard tiny echoes tapping a rhythm in his ears. *I'm hallucinating.* He knew it was a bad sign. During withdrawal, hallucinations usually preceded irregular heartbeats, seizures, and loss of consciousness. He wanted to sit down. His legs felt tight and strained. *I can't take this anymore.*

"Hear that?" Redevir whispered.

"What?"

"That sound. That tapping sound."

"You hear it, too?"

"Of course I hear it," Redevir said indignantly. "My ears aren't that old."

"What is it? I thought I was imagining things."

"If our luck holds up, then it will be Mallios."

"How could he find us so fast?"

"He can smell money. I promised him a lot of it."

"But how could he get into the fortress?"

"The walls are barely guarded. This is a place they toss smoke-slaves so they don't have to think about them anymore. They don't know who you are."

"Yet."

"All the more reason to make our escape from this place before they do."

The tapping grew louder, the echoes taking strange shapes. Whisperings of muffled curses emerged between tappings. A man's voice.

Aren looked up. Someone was in the ventilation shaft. The shaft was barely a foot tall and only two feet across. How anyone could move through it was beyond him.

Redevir backed up to the wall opposite the shaft, and called out in a low voice. "Mallios?" Several seconds went by with no answer. "Mallios?"

"Shut up," the voice answered. "I'm busy."

Redevir smiled. "Our savior."

"How the fuck did he get in here?"

"Mallios knows a lot of people in Medion, and they all owe him a favor."

Aren could hear loud chipping sounds now. He kept his eyes on the vent. He saw wisps of dust floating with the air currents. One of the bars came loose, fell from its lofty height, and plopped into the water. Another followed the first, and another, and another, until the shaft was no longer barred at all.

A small head poked through into the cell. The hair was short and soaking wet. The wide face gave a quizzical look. "That's a long way down."

"No fooling," Redevir said. "Get us out of here."

"My price has increased," the little head said angrily. "For all my trouble."

"I anticipated such greediness," Redevir said. "If we make it over the walls, I'll pay you double the promised price."

Mallios went silent in his wet perch. He said nothing, as though already counting the money in his head. His face was round and rosy, with thin eyebrows and broad, froggish lips. His eyes were wider when squinting than Aren's were fully open.

"Move it, Mallios. Time is of a necessity."

"Here." A long coil of rope snaked from the shaft down to the water. It dangled like a writhing vine from an imaginary forest.

Redevir looked at Aren. "You first."

"I...I don't know if I can climb right now. My hands feel weak."

"Climb on my shoulders then. If I hold you up, Mallios should be able to reach down to you."

"What's that?" Mallios asked. "You said something about me."

"Just pull him up when you can reach him," Redevir said. He hoisted Aren onto his shoulders.

Aren half-climbed up the Rover's body until he was standing with a foot planted on each of Redevir's shoulders. He reached high above his head, stretching his fingers to reach the outstretched arm of Mallios. Their fingers missed by over a foot.

"It's too far," Aren said. "I can't reach."

"Step onto my hands," Redevir said.

"What?"

"Just step into my hands. We have to hurry."

Aren followed the command. Redevir clasped his hands tightly on Aren's boots. The Rover gritted his teeth and pressed upward until his arms were fully extended above his head.

"Can you reach?"

Mallios strained low, and took hold of Aren's forearm. "Got him," he said.

Aren heaved to pull himself up. Mallios yanked upward, wriggling back into the shaft like a worm. Aren scraped his knees on the bricks, but managed to pull himself inside.

Redevir went instantly to the rope, almost running up the wall as he hoisted himself along. When he was safely in the confines of the vent, he called to Mallios. "Cut the rope."

Mallios did so. The rope slid away and splashed into the water below.

The shaft was barely large enough for Aren to curl his arms to his chest to crawl. He struggled through the shaft with Mallios' stubby pink face and thick eyelids backing up ahead of him.

At the terminus of the shaft they were vomited out into an empty square room, stone walls, with one barred window open to a funnel for the perpetual wind. There was a single door on one side.

Mallios gave a disappointed look at Redevir. "Who is this?" He whispered, gesturing at Aren as if he was no more than a miscellaneous object.

"He is my associate," Redevir said. "Not that it's any business of yours."

"I want to know who I'm helping," Mallios said. "Rumor has it that your friend murdered five hundred Outer Guard soldiers."

Aren choked in spite of himself.

"That's idiotic," Redevir said. "Why would you believe such stupidity?"

"Stupidity, you say?" Mallios asked. "The Inner Guard believes it. They have sent for authorities from Vithos to identify him. Someone named Margol is coming."

Aren choked. He nearly swallowed his tongue. "He is alive?" He exchanged a glance with Redevir.

"I don't like that you know that name," Mallios said.

"What have you heard, Mallios?" Redevir asked.

"They say your boy here is mind-slave to the savage Lamani, a traitor who led the Outer Guard to be slaughtered." He appraised Aren with his eyes. "They hate you in Vithos. They sing songs in the taverns hoping for your demise."

Aren's stomach rose up into his throat and he thought he might choke. *Traitor. Murderer. Hated. My own people think I am evil.* The Lord Protector had made him a pariah in the only place that had ever been close to a home.

"I have a man who is delaying their team from coming here," Mallios said. "But I find it hard to believe that an entire nation could think you a murderer when you aren't."

Redevir frowned. "I was unaware that Amagon had become a land of imbeciles. The fish rots from the head. Are you insinuating that I am lying?"

"No," Mallios said.

"That is good. Calling me a liar might lead to a reduction in your payment."

"Where's the money?" Mallios asked. "Here?"

"It is safe. Someone is holding it for me."

"Where is it?"

"When we get out of here." Redevir said.

"Fine." Mallios gave up. "Around this corner will take us to the outer edge of the prison block. After that, we follow my way out."

"Your way out?" Redevir was skeptical.

"I won't question you if you don't question me," Mallios said. "You aren't the first. Come this way." He motioned to an open passage across from the vent.

"Wait," Aren croaked. "The bags. We have to get them back."

"Hah," Mallios laughed. "Your friend is some kind of fool, Redevir."

"Why?" Redevir asked. "He's quite right, you know."

Mallios went pale. His eyes seemed like lakes that had frozen over. "Are you mad? We'd have to go through the yard. We're next to the outer wall now, and you want to go back in?"

"We have no choice, Mallios," Redevir said. "Where would they keep confiscated items?"

"You're insane. I could be tortured to death by the blue ghosts for helping you this far."

"I'm aware of the risk," Redevir said calmly. "If you want your money, then take us to the storage facility. I'm paying you *double*, Mallios."

"Damn you." Mallios bit his lip. "You're crazy."

"You said that already," Redevir said. "And it is well known. Now make your choice."

"Fine," Mallios said. "It's your money."

The door opened beside a small outbuilding in a walled off yard of dirt. Walls and moonlight surrounded them, the prison tower looming white above them. He saw silhouettes of men on some of the walls. Inner Guard private soldiers most likely. They preferred to have unaccountable men in charge of the lives of prisoners, and more so for carrying out the machinations of interrogation. But with unaccountability, came cheap, lazy guards, who were even now more involved in smoking tabac and rolling dice than even glancing down at the yard.

Aren caught glimpses of stables and short buildings clumped about the high tower, and a long curtain wall running behind. *I have never been inside this place before.* It was well past the midnight hour, and the yard was as silent as a graveyard, the guards relying on the impossibility of escape to fuel their laziness.

Mallios led them from cover to cover, hiding in the shadows, keeping as far from the moonlight as possible. They hugged the wall of the tower itself part of the way as he led them away from the moonlit courtyard. They moved in the shadows behind the tower and under the eaves of stables.

Mallios stopped them against the corner of an outbuilding. He signaled to them to look around with him. He pointed across the open yard. It was a hundred feet with no cover across ground that glowed with moonlight. From where he was, Aren counted at least three pairs of guards on the walls with a clear vantage.

Shaot.

Aren tensed his legs as much as he could, hoping he wouldn't trip over his own feet. Then, by some unknown signal, Mallios was off. Redevir tore across the courtyard after him, with Aren just behind. Each second lasted a minute, and every step sounded like thunder in Aren's ears. It seemed to take forever before they finally ducked down behind a large wagon against the storage wall. Aren thought that a dead man could have noticed them. But no one did. No shouts. No clamor of alarm. No sign that they even existed to the sentries.

"Anything they confiscated will be inside," Mallios said, tapping the wall with a finger. "Weapons, armor, equipment." He pulled open the door and they ducked inside. Within the door was a long hall, lit by an untended fireplace. Beside the glowing flames was a small door. It too was untended, but was heavily bolted with iron locks.

"How do we get in there?" Aren asked.

"I have no lock-picks," Redevir said. "They're inside."

"Don't worry," Mallios said. "Lazy shits. They hide a spare set of keys in one of these niches." He began scouring the walls for the hiding place. "Here we are," he said, as the unmistakable jingling of keys blended with the crackling of the fire. He unlocked each bolt with a separate key. It was a long, frustrating process, but the door finally opened and they were through. Mallios closed it behind them.

The walls were lined with shelves, stuffed to capacity with clothing, carry-bags, weapons, and farming implements.

Aren threw himself to the task of finding his pouch. He didn't care about the swords right now, only the malagayne.

Redevir quickly found his own blade, and Aren's soon after, then his throwing knives, and at last his own carry-bag with his notebooks safely inside.

Aren's heart rose and sank as every bag he touched was found to be the wrong one. He almost tossed his tracer satchel away in disgust, but caught himself at the last moment. He handed it to Redevir and continued digging without explanation.

Then his vision clouded over. He heard sweet song in his head. His body instantly slackened like soft putty, as though he had just dipped into a hot bath. There before him sat the familiar pouch. In it was his precious malagayne. It seemed to shine like a pocket-full of twinkling stars. His blood pulsed with excitement. He could only stare at it. It was beautiful.

"Can we get out of here now?" Mallios asked. "We've ridden luck for awhile, but it could give out at any moment." He guided them to the edge of the courtyard.

Redevir turned to Aren. "Hurry. He knows the only way out of here."

Aren's legs were burning. His body was weak, and his lungs craved sweet smoke. He was slowing despite himself. He followed Redevir behind a building and into a tunnel to a basement deep beneath the surface. He couldn't see Mallios anymore. He lost sight of Redevir around corners only to find him again as the Rover dropped through narrow portals and crawled down long storm drains into a sewer tunnel that seemed to go on for miles. He found himself struggling through jagged caves, cutting his hands and tripping over invisible stones. He could hear waves, and seawater infused the air. The rocks closed in on him. He fell to his knees in the darkness. He couldn't see.

"Head toward the light," he heard Mallios call out.

It went on for another quarter mile of constricting dampness, until they reached an opening in a sheer cliff face, where the sewage and rainwater dropped like a waterfall onto sharp, wave-carved rocks far below.

"Are we to jump?" Redevir asked.

Mallios shook his head. He directed them to handholds on the inside of the tunnel leading to a narrow well directly above. Redevir hoisted him up, and Mallios dragged him out of the well, and rolled him onto his back.

Aren found himself on a high promontory extending from a steep series of cliffs that overlooked sharp rocks and the sea a hundred feet below. To the south was Medion Harbor, and just beyond, slightly further inland, was the cluster of towers, like praying midnight monks beneath the clouds.

Silistin was still up, casting its fleeting white rays upon the world. An owl hooted a long succession of melancholy calls, then flapped away on its thick wings. Aren smelled damp mud on the cold winds. His fingers felt like ice.

He had malagayne again. He fell onto a patch of grass, still wet from the last night's torrents. He lay there with no attempt to stave off the chill. It did not matter. He unrolled the pipe from its soft linen cover, not caring if anyone saw. Redevir knew already. Mallios didn't matter. He lit the leaves right there. It did not occur to him to worry about pursuit. It did not occur to him to worry about Eriana and whether she was safe or not. Or if Hayles and Fainen or Tanashri were looking for him. None of it mattered.

The first taste came to him. He drew it in lightly, like sipping pale wine from a delicate chalice. So smooth on his breath. More natural than air. The cold vanished with the very first puff. It left him in utter relaxation. He took breath after breath, feeling his strength return. He marveled at how weak he had felt only moments before. He was so strong now. He felt like he could break rocks with his fists, tear down trees with the lightest touch. He felt no hunger or thirst. Only the smoke and the stars mattered right now. He held the empty pipe in his hand and lay still, like a part of the hillside. It seemed like forever.

He blinked his eyes and peered into the darkness. He saw only shapes. The malagayne stole his focus. He saw the shapes of Redevir and Mallios looking off into rocky clefts behind them. Figures emerged from within the rocks. Hayles and Fainen.

He saw the shape of Eriana. She gasped when she saw him. She clasped her hands together at her mouth.

"You all look none the worse for wear," Redevir said.

Tanashri sneered at him. "You expected otherwise?"

"It must have been very taxing," Redevir said. "To sit idle while the two of us were stewing in a dungeon."

"We prepared to come after you," she said. "But Hayles needed time to study the patrols."

"Don't blame it on him. You and Inrianne are both users. Between you both there was nothing you could have done?"

"I thought it unwise to burst into the prison in such a way," the Saderan said.

"I am sure you have catching up to do," Mallios said. "But if it's all the same to you, I'll take my money now."

"In the saddlebags I have gold for you," Redevir said. He trotted to where the horses rested, their harnesses tied carefully to jagged spurs of rock, and emerged from behind the crag bearing a large velvet bag. It bulged and jingled.

Mallios snatched the bag from him, as if the Rover had stolen it from him long ago.

"Tell me where the Diamond is," Redevir said.

"In the Sholes," Mallios said.

"Sholes? There are hundreds of Sholes north of here. That is a thousand mile expanse. Which Shole exactly?"

"In the mountains near Kovak Shole," Mallios said. "In a place called Vandeme Canyon. It lies near the border of Bolan and Arradan, beyond the Kotha Mountains, between Hennel Koth and Mana Ridge. They won't let you cross from the Arradian side. You will have to cross the Kol Plateau to get there. A cold journey. Within the canyon is a hole in the ground. Through the hole is an underground tunnel. The Diamond sits alone on a linen pillow in a deep chamber called the Blackwell. It is ten days' ride northwest of Kor Kollar. If you can make it to Kor Kollar, that is."

"How do we find Vandeme Canyon?" Redevir asked.

"Near Kovak Shole, I said," Mallios said.

"Landmarks, Mallios. I want landmarks. They don't make maps of the Sholes."

Mallios appeared annoyed. "If you travel with the sun from the Kol Plateau, you'll come to a river. Follow it north until you find a winding route through the Black Rocks."

"Are they mountains?" Redevir asked.

"Small ones," Mallios said. "The pass is winding, but it doesn't diverge. When you reach a high flat wall of rock, it will be on the other side."

"Where is the entrance to the tunnel?"

Mallios shrugged. He smiled halfheartedly. "There's something else," he said. "I think I've found out some more information for you."

"Let's hear it," Redevir said.

"When you meet my price."

"Your insurance policy, I presume?" Redevir asked.

"Think of it how you will. I'm not as much of a fool as you think. After we get out of here, I'm going south to Farmontaine in Corien. When you have some more money for me, I'll help you. Introduce you to some people. I need to hear more jingling gold first."

"Such greed," Redevir said. "I've given you double already."

"And I've gone well beyond our bargain for you," Mallios said. "It's only fair if you—" He stopped abruptly. His eyes spread across his face like black discs. He turned, and bolted without a word. His torch fell to the earth still burning.

Aren did not understand. They were safe here, miles from the prison, from the city and its Listeners and Questioners and Inner Guard and Orange. He turned to see what Mallios had been looking at, and he saw what Mallios had seen. The red skin shined midnight blue in the moonlight.

34

To the Death

"GO!" REDEVIR SCREAMED IN his ear. He grabbed Aren by the cuffs of his shirt, yanking him away from the titan.

Aren could barely see. The malagayne blurred his vision. He had taken too much. He knew it already. Desire had been buried alive. Control was gone. Malagayne paralysis. He wanted to stand up, but he couldn't. He couldn't run, or fight. He could only watch, horrified as it all happened around him.

Hayles and Fainen shot past him, placing themselves in front of the giant.

Tanashri whirled around right beside Aren, raising her arms to point at Redscar. Aren could tell that she was binding streams, putting each into the proper structure to render into reality, her expression relaxed as if she was adding ingredients to a stew.

But then something odd and terrifying happened.

Nothing.

Tanashri's render never become reality. Her eyes shot open. She stared in horror, frozen, her tiny mouth agape. Powerless.

Redevir saw her standing rigid in the giant's path. "What are you doing?" he shouted, as Redscar lumbered toward her. The Rover clutched her in a powerful bear-hug. He lifted her off the ground and half-dragged, half-threw her away from the range of the giant's battle-axe.

Aren saw it all, but just barely. Everyone was a shape, nothing more. Eriana was already at his side, warding him with her curved blade. Inrianne was behind him, but she wasn't using either. Aren could feel something very wrong. Something in the air.

Where is their magick?

Hayles reached the giant first. His *somashalks* swayed like pendulums. He stood his ground, waiting. Aren was on awe of him, standing alone before the titan. The giant grunted and came forward.

Hayles waited, every muscle tensed. The *somashalks* stopped their swaying. The giant charged him like a bull. Hayles twisted to the side. Let the battle-axe dig into the earth. He came in close. Leaned back. Dodged a swatting hand.

Every swing shook Aren, making his insides feel liquified. Every strike from Redscar looked like it was going to connect, and each time it did not he felt such relief.

Fainen circled the titan. Redscar whipped his massive head over one shoulder, then the other, trying to track the motion. Aren felt a surge of bright hope. Redscar was nervous. He was actually nervous.

Hayles came in again. Redscar swung the axe. Hayles dropped down on his knees, letting it pass over his head. His speed was a marvel. He reared up, one *somashalk* held high above his head. He brought it down with enough power to break through stone. It hit Redscar's forearm with a sound of metal on metal. It tore through red flesh, and stuck in the bone.

Redscar roared. Brought up one knee. Hayles caught it with his other *somashalk*. Buried the axe head into crimson flesh. But the sheer force of the titan's motion overpowered the counterblow, slamming the blunt end of the *somashalk* back into Hayles' head. His feet lifted off the ground and he dropped onto his back, splashing clumps of mud into the air.

Aren felt like someone had opened his heart and let it drain onto the rocks. *Please get up. Please.*

Fainen leapt on Redscar's back. Drove his blade down, digging into the meat of his ribs. Redscar roared. Fainen wrapped one arm about the neck. He drew *Glimmer*, but the titan knocked it out of his hand. Fainen drew a knife from his belt instead. Drove it deep into the back of one shoulder.

Aren's fists clenched involuntarily. He grit his teeth. The wound looked extraordinary. Even a titan could not shrug it off.

Redscar flailed and bucked, sending Fainen sprawling across the rocks into a crater of thick mud, his knife still sunken to the hilt in the titan's back.

Aren shook as he watched. He heard the surf pounding the rocks below. He smelled the salt of the sea. He wished that the waves would come and carry Redscar away.

Get up. Please get up. Please kill him. Please win.

Hayles was already standing again, mud caked to one half of his face like a mask, and blood rushing in a torrent down the other side, flushing one eye shut.

Aren's heart was pounding like a drum. He stared at the Sarenwalker, his face twisted in agony at seeing Hayles wounded this way.

Hayles nodded to him. "He will not reach you. He will never pass me."

He turned and heaved one *somashalk* through the air with a throw that Sarenwalkers were famous for, hitting his mark and lodging deep in the giant's ribs, and Redevir followed with his throwing knives. One, two, three, they went, thumping into his abdomen.

Aren's fingers unfurled, scooping and releasing handfuls of the sharp black rocks beneath him.

Fainen retrieved *Glimmer*. Came on again. Tried for the legs. Redscar moved too fast. Fainen couldn't hit the joints. Redscar shot out with his axe. Fainen moved, but it clipped his shoulder, spinning him around.

Hayles unlatched his quarterstaff from behind his back. His walk became a sprint in the blink of an eye, and he was suddenly cracking blows across Redscar's bones, so strong that each strike split open the skin. Fainen caught Redscar in the back, then the leg, *Glimmer* darting in his hand like a swift night bird.

Aren heard a song of hope droning into his head. They were doing it. They were beating him.

But Hayles only had one good eye. His depth perception was ruined. It was by grace of his mastery of his weapons that he had hit his marks this far.

On the next strike he misjudged. Just once.

He leaned in too close, and Redscar's arm stretched out, raised the battle-axe, clipping Hayles in the chin, cracking his jaw and skinning the flesh off one side of his mouth.

Aren gasped, then screamed through gritted teeth.

Hayles stumbled, spit blood, raising the quarterstaff over his head with both hands to block the attack he must have known would come.

Aren thought there would be some way he would be able to move out of its path. Fainen would attack, Hayles would dodge, Redscar would slip.

But none of those things happened.

Redscar brought the battle-axe down hard. It split the quarterstaff in two, and crashed its way through Hayles' body. It sheared his arm from his shoulder. Blood splashed like a waterfall. Redscar laughed at the broken Sarenwalker, raising his foot to crush him.

No!

Fainen cut him off. The battle-axe reared up, but Fainen stung the giant across the wrist with his Saren-sword, cutting cleanly to the bone. The axe flopped to the ground near the cliffside.

Redscar caught him, and wrapped his arms around Fainen as if to embrace him. *Glimmer* fell to the earth, as the air was driven out of Fainen's lungs by the crushing arms. His veins bulged as they screamed for air.

Aren's jaw fell open, his mouth dry, his lips cracked, a scream grinding itself apart in his throat. *Not them. Please. Not both.*

Redevir bellowed as he drove the torch into Redscar's flank. Sparks. Burning. A sulfurous crackling sound. Then godlike screaming. The giant spun, flailing, knocking the Rover onto his side. Fainen dropped to the rocks, gasping for breath.

Redscar left him on the ground, and moved toward his battle-axe. He gripped it in one hand and turned to Aren where he lay in his malagayne paralysis.

Aren tried to melt into the rocks with Eriana, turning her to water and letting her sink into the earth where the titan could not touch her. But he could not do that. No one could.

Eriana wrapped her arms around him, desperate to pull him away from the giant. Aren tried to grab hold of her to help, but his hands failed.

Forget me. Go! Just get out of here!

He knew the giant was coming for her, but she refused to leave him.

He strained to get just one hand to his sword. Just one. To lure the giant's rage to him, so he might let Eriana alone long enough for her to get away. He pleaded with his arms, but his efforts yielded nothing.

Something landed around the giant's neck.

Redevir's rope.

At the other end, Tanashri, Inrianne, and Redevir tried to pull Redscar off balance. It was futile. The red titan drew up his shoulders, throwing all three of them to the ground. He cut the rope with his axe, leaving one end around his neck like a broken noose, dangling to his feet.

Nothing can stop him.

Redscar cut Eriana off and lumbered toward her alone.

But he did not make it.

Someone appeared in his way.

Aren saw the faint shape of a man with only one arm. His jaw hit the ground. He couldn't believe it. It was impossible. But it was true.

Hayles stood weaponless before the giant. Blood squirted and oozed from where his arm had once rested on his body. His shoulders sagged, and his face was ghost-white under the moon.

Aren reached out to the Sarenwalker, to touch him, to help him, to thank him, to release him. But they were so far apart.

Redscar tried to sweep him aside with a swing of the axe, but Hayles went under it. His legs moved like a racing horse, and the Sarenwalker ran through the swaying arms and up Redscar's thigh.

Hayles locked his legs around Redscar's torso like clamping steel, staring him in the eyes. The giant tried to fend him off, putting the palm of his hand up to Hayles' jaw, pressing and popping the bones of his neck.

Aren's eyes leaked tears, lazy impotent streams like ice down his cheeks.

Hayles had only one hand. He reached with it. He grasped the hilt of Fainen's knife, still embedded within Redscar's ribs. He locked his grip into an iron fist around the hilt. He tore it around and around, as if he was rowing a boat and Redscar was the water. The giant screamed and stumbled back, screamed some more.

Hayles worked the knife deeper, grinding the muscle apart. The titan slipped in the rocks, still screaming. His feet stepped on the long end of the noose around his neck. His head was yanked forward by his own motion. He stumbled toward the cliff, pitched forward, and then they both went over the edge.

No sound heralded the crashing of their bodies on the rocks below. They were simply gone. Lost over the edge, swallowed by the waves.

Aren's heart dropped into oblivion. He sank into the earth so deep he thought he would suffocate. His eyes burned and flared and flashed white every other time he opened them. He tried to scream but his mouth was nowhere. His eyes could only see the bright white nothing.

Then he disappeared from consciousness.

The next thing he knew was the cool delicate touch of Eriana's hands on his forehead. He was leaning against a fat boulder, night covering him like a blanket, clouds muting the moonlight. Eriana doing her best to support his head. He felt like he was on fire. He had soaked through his clothes with sweat, even though his skin felt like ice. He heard the waves crashing below, but they sounded faded, distant. His ears were ringing. He saw the shadows of the towers in the distance, little lights winking from their windows.

"Are we safe?" he asked. "Are there any more out there?"

"Fainen scouted," Eriana said. "There is no one else. No tracks. The giant was alone."

He tilted his head away from her. It was the only movement he could make without help. He knew he couldn't move. He wanted only to hide his shame. Eriana hugged him tightly anyway. Gods it felt so good to look into her eyes. "The Orange? Glasseyes?"

She shook her head. "None."

"Yet," he said.

Tanashri came forward, the fringes of her grey robes torn and frayed by the rocks. "Are you well, Aren? You lost consciousness for a time. Fainen refused to let us move you."

"I couldn't do anything. Hayles is dead." Aren felt tears in his eyes. "I could have run. We could have run. He's dead because I couldn't stand on my own two feet." He lifted his foot and slammed it, blasting chips of rock in all directions. He wanted to shout the words. Scream them.

"It wasn't your fault," Eriana said. "You were held in the cold without food for days. It made you weak."

It made Aren feel worse. "It doesn't matter. This trace is mine. The fault is mine."

Hayles was so perfect, so pure, so selfless, and now he was gone forever.

We were overdue.

Man of sorrow. The sorrowful man. He began to fear it was more than just words, more than merely something encouraging Redevir told him so that he could muster the courage to try to stop the unstoppable. He feared it *had* to be this way.

Redevir looked at the ground. "What Hayles did was his choice."

"It wasn't," Aren said. "It was mine. I could have done something different. I could have...gone a different way, kept out of that prison, something. We should never have been there. What was I thinking?"

"Hayles was my friend," Fainen said. "His oath was given freely, as was mine. We knew the danger. Donnovar deemed you worthy. All else is inconsequential."

Aren sat in silence for a long time. "Did Hayles have anyone? Any family?"

Fainen nodded. "A brother. In Kolchin. He had a wife once, because he thought he was supposed to, but she left long ago."

"And you?"

Fainen bit his lip. He glanced aside. "There is no woman waiting for me."

Aren nodded. "I never asked before. I don't know why. I'm sorry."

Fainen looked over at the edge of the cliff. "There are words we say. We Sarenwalkers. We speak this mantra to remind ourselves always of what we are."

Aren looked up at him.

"*I am Sarenwalker. I am thought made action. I fear neither death nor pain. I possess no emotion, only perfection. I am Sarenwalker.*" Fainen smiled as he stared at the last place his friend had been alive. He walked to the edge of the cliff and knelt, his sword downturned, forehead touching the hilt. "I am Sarenwalker. I am thought made action. I am..." He repeated the mantra over and over. Fifty times at least before he stood again.

Aren grimaced and nodded. It made him feel both better and worse, but it helped to know Fainen was able to carry on. He fed off that strength when it seemed his own was gone. "We need to take stock. We almost just died, Redevir. Hayles is gone. Kinraigan told me this was going to happen. He told me he was going to kill us one by one."

Redevir stepped up to him, but a little too quickly for Eriana. Her fingers wrapped around the hilt of her sword and squeezed. Redevir eyed her up and down. "We are going. The path is set before us. We are going to walk it. I want this prize. You want to burn him off the face of the earth. This is the way to have both of those things. Your ambition is your strength. Let it be your guide."

"Revenge," Aren said. "Ambition."

The Rover puffed out his jaw. "The two reasons for every great thing ever done. We find the Crown. We lay in wait. We stop him from ever hurting anyone else ever again."

Aren thought of Hayles and Donnovar, Corrin and Reidos, Raviel and Sarker, the trail of dead girls, friends, soldiers, and Glasseyes. He thought of Eriana in *his* grasp, and him powerless to stop it.

His jaw clenched so hard he thought it would snap. *That old man seemed very certain that I am the one who will bring you down.* Aren told himself he did not believe in prophecies, any more than he believed in the gods. But this was the path. He saw it clear, just as Solathas had said.

"You know who did this, Aren," Redevir said. "He did this. There is only one question that matters. Do you want Kinraigan to pay for it or not?"

Aren gritted his teeth. "Yes."

"Are you going to catch him or aren't you?"

Aren looked up at him. "I am. I will."

Redevir smiled. "There he is. I knew you were in there somewhere."

"I capture users," Aren said. "It is what I do. It is what I have always done. I hunted the worst of them. I have never, ever lost a trace. My purpose is to break people like him. That is why I'm here. I was put on this earth to remind them that they are just men. Men can be broken. He thinks he is immortal? I break immortals."

"You have a purpose Aren," Redevir said. "Even you cannot deny that. And is the line between purpose and destiny really all that thick?"

"If it is my destiny to kill him, then I accept it gladly," Aren said.

"I do not like this look in your eyes, Aren," Eriana said. "It looks like you are not there."

But Redevir waved her off. "Aren is fine." He then turned on Tanashri and Inrianne. "Let us talk about blame, shall we? Where was the magick?"

Tanashri shrank from his accusation in a way that made Aren sharpen his eyes.

"Neither of you did anything," the Rover went on, now looking at Inrianne. "If you're going to speak of blame, Aren, then let us look there."

"You dare," Tanashri said. "You accuse us."

"Where were you, mighty Saderan?" Redevir demanded.

Aren wondered that himself.

"Your tone reeks of accusation," she said.

"Answer me," he said.

Inrianne stepped forward instead. "I don't know what it was. Something... blocked me."

"And me," Tanashri said. "This is deeply concerning."

"I'm sure we're all glad you're concerned," Redevir said. "But what concerns me is something altogether different. How did it find us again? Kinraigan was long gone, or at least he should have been. He couldn't have known we were here. Hayles said we weren't followed."

"It could have been luck," Inrianne said.

"Luck?" Redevir's eyes went wide. "Luck that he found us here? Luck that they ambushed us in Medion? That is far too much luck for a raving giant to have."

"What is your point, Rover?" Tanashri asked.

"I don't like the fact that Kinraigan always seems to know *exactly* where we are." He looked at each of them in turn, studying them.

"What do you imply?" Tanashri asked. "That one of us is helping him?"

Everyone went silent after she spoke, looking at one another with expressions half of fear and half of suspicion.

"I'm only saying that it's a mighty big stretch to believe that it's all coincidence," Redevir said. "Did he speak to any of you? The man with black eyes?"

No one spoke.

So Redevir went on, his face bent by indignant rage. "Who is Inrianne? Where does she come from?"

Was he right? What did they really know about Inrianne? He felt Eriana holding him gently, but the rocks beneath him dug into his ribs, and his thoughts made him shiver. Had Raviel been right? He had turned a loyal veteran, Balthoren. Could he really turn anyone? Everyone here was gravitating to the Sephors—Inrianne, Redevir, Tanashri. He could have planted the seed of betrayal in any one them, years ago even. Could it really have been coincidence that brought Inrianne to Amagon? Or Tanashri? Was anyone what they appeared to be? Aren narrowed his eyes in suspicion. He should have been able to trust each of them, but he could trust none of them.

"Tanashri is of the Sisterhood," the Rover said. "She knew Kinraigan before any of us. She went down quickly in Medion."

The Saderan stood silent while he spoke.

"We should move," Fainen said.

"And what about you, Inrianne?" Redevir continued. "Always quiet. Not saying much. Staying close to Tanashri. What are you up to?"

"Go to hell, Redevir!" Inrianne shouted.

"It is not safe here," Fainen said.

"What about you, Redevir?" Tanashri asked.

"Redevir the Rover is no man's pawn," Redevir said.

"Aren met you in Westgate," Inrianne said, storming forward, elbow high, finger pointed down at Redevir. "You knew the giant's name! They were your words that brought us to the Fields of Syn."

"And *you* didn't receive so much as a scratch, Redevir," Tanashri added. "Where did you go in Medion while we dined? To find your notebooks? Or to sell us out to Kinraigan?"

Redevir's eyes widened. He furrowed his brow.

Tanashri narrowed her eyes. For a Saderan that might as well have been the equivalent of smacking him across the face. "The only one of us that is known to have spoken to him is sitting right there." She pointed at Aren. "So tell me again about who might be helping him."

Aren shuddered in the cold. He stood, stepped from side to side as his legs came back to life. "We need to stop this," he said.

"Take only light steps," Eriana said. He let her cling to him, afraid he might fall if she didn't.

Redevir turned and smiled warmly at him. "I have nothing to do with Redscar."

"Explain to *us*," Inrianne demanded. "Don't commiserate with Aren. He's no better than you."

"What does that mean?" Aren asked.

"You've done nothing for us, boy. While others fight, you lay on the ground. You let Hayles and Fainen do your dirty work. You cannot even stand on your own two feet. You did nothing in Medion either. What would have happened to Eriana if I had not been there?" Inrianne folded her arms smugly.

"I tried. I would never let anything happen to her if I could help it. I don't have any power. I can't do anything against him. I can't stand against any of them, any of *you*. I can't do anything against you, and I can't stand it. I hate you so much I can't even breathe!" Spittle flew from his mouth as he shouted.

It dribbled down his chin. His body shook, his lungs burned. The ocean was in his ears. His throat felt cracked open, dried and scarred.

"Listen to you," Inrianne said. "That Rover poisoned your mind with his cowardly excuses. You can't even admit your own failure. You're not a man, you're his puppet."

Aren stiffened. "You walk around like you don't even care about what happens to my friends. You act like Hayles is just a thing to help you prove some point. Well, he's not. He was a real person, and he's gone. He was a part of my team. A Render Tracer is responsible for the whole team. Every man. Every woman. You think I don't know that it's my fault? I do. It *is* my fault. I failed him."

"Maybe you should trade places with him," she said.

"Stop!" Eriana said. "That's not fair!"

Inrianne turned a cold stare at her. "One thing that I hate is a girl who defends a boy who takes advantage of her. You think you want to be with *that*? He is the *user*. He uses people. He used Hayles, and he's using you too, the same way Redevir uses him."

Eriana recoiled, surprised by her vitriol.

"Don't act so surprised," Inrianne said. "Aren puts on a soft mask, but underneath he's no better than any of them. I know what he really is. Ha! Glasseye. He is useless, a worthless fool pretending to be a man by killing people like me. Don't waste your tender flower on that. It's disgusting."

Eriana reached out like lightning and slapped Inrianne in the face. It cracked across her cheek like thunder. Inrianne stumbled back and fell to one knee, a look of twisted surprise on her face.

"You are afraid," Eriana said. "You are afraid and so you yell at Aren because you feel safe yelling at Aren, because he is the only one here who can't raise a hand to you."

"Go to hell, little girl," Inrianne said. "Don't you ever touch me again!"

"I don't know what happened to you to make you the way you are," Eriana said. "But I am tired of listening to you pretend that you are not just a broken empty shell of a woman who only opens her mouth to complain."

Inrianne stood fuming, her hands balled into fists at her side and her face flushed as red as a beet. She shook with anger, and stared coldly at Eriana. "He has poisoned your mind," she said. "Aren has tricked you. You are being a fool. If I killed him it would be doing you a kindness."

Eriana drew her curved blade and held it up to Inrianne's face. Inrianne did not step back, but she flinched when the point came close to her eye. "Empty words. You will do no such thing. You are just being angry because you are afraid. But you will not speak to me this way ever again. You will show me the same respect you give to Tanashri. You will show me the same fear you give to your gods. Do not dare insult my ancestors by thinking I will fold before you."

"You are a fool," Inrianne said.

"My eyes are *open*." She glanced at her sword. "Yours will be forever closed. Unless you close your *mouth* first."

"You wouldn't dare," Inrianne said.

"Oh, shut up," Redevir said. "You've had your little tantrum long enough, Inrianne. You had best get used to Aren. It is because of him that we found the Dagger. And it will be because of him that we find the Crown. He's not going anywhere. And if you can't handle that then you can go your own way."

"You're a bastard, Redevir," Inrianne said.

The Rover shrugged.

"It is unwise to argue here," Fainen said.

"Ready yourselves," Redevir said. "All of you. We are going to the docks. Thanks to Eriana, we have a midnight ship waiting to take us out of here."

Inrianne smirked. "We will be lucky if they will still take us. Those who sail the Gulf of Shain do not like to do so at night."

Redevir jingled his bags of gold. "They will for me."

"We must move quickly," Fainen said. "They will discover your absence by morning. They will scour the city. They will send Sarenwalkers."

Aren nodded. "They will. You're right." He could think of nothing worse.

Eriana bared her teeth when Inrianne turned her back. "Are you all right, Aren?"

I am. I always am with you. He nodded.

"Do you promise this?" she asked.

He nodded through the pain. "I promise this."

"Only always ever now," she said, holding him steady. "That is what it means. Hayles gave us a gift. We must honor him by walking on. Every step we take will make his gift greater."

"You're right. You're right. He did. We must."

I have to go on. I have to finish this trace to capture. I will.

He snorted a small white hill of malagayne when no one was looking.

Kinraigan always knows where we are.

35

Streets

CORRIN WAS BEING CHASED by men with swords; things were finally back to normal again. He found it almost relaxing running through the streets of Medion. Sprinting past high arching facades and weaving through fenced cafes had been a game when he was a boy. Running from farmers and landlords was a simple thing. An easy thing. Guardsmen from the north countries ran harder. Merchant bodyguards from Minstilsi usually gave the greatest challenge, but even they gave up at some point.

For some reason Corrin felt that the blond man wasn't the kind who ever gave up, being that he was willing to lose his fingers and all. Every time he reached for optimism, he saw those fingertips splayed out on the floor.

He knew the Vuls couldn't have sent him. They had traveled by riverboat to Medion. Not even the crew had known. The trail should have been cold. But if not them then who?

He hid everyone behind stacks of hay in a crumpled stable while the Inner Guard and the Orange searched the street, looking for the users responsible for the chaos in Halladon Plaza. Corrin hated the sitting, hated the waiting, but he had no choice.

Once the sweep moved on past them, Corrin returned to the streets. He loped around corners, waiting numerous times for Reidos and Mardin to catch up, Hallan sitting patiently on his shoulders.

He worked his way through a maze of tall towers. They seemed like an impassable labyrinth. He began to tire, and slowed his pace, putting Hallan back on the ground. He turned corner after corner, finding himself among shorter towers with narrow streets in between. These ways were less trafficked at this hour of the morning, and the quiet made him uneasy.

He edged past a stack of old empty wine barrels, and darted around a corner without first inspecting it, and immediately cursed himself for doing so. Three Guardsmen of the Orange stood at the other end. They noticed him immediately and called for him to halt. Corrin responded by turning the other way and running. He grabbed Hallan, hoisting him onto one shoulder. He noticed Reidos looking at him.

"No problem," Corrin said, darting past him and back the way they had just come. Reidos followed with Mardin close behind, both horrified.

"Hold where you are," the spokesman of the Orange called, as the three gave chase, their bright capes fluttering like sun-streaked banners.

"Hah," Corrin laughed. "Fat chance, ass." He sprinted down a long street between two squat towers, the Orange in full pursuit, and steadily gaining.

"Where do we go?" Mardin cried.

"Shut up," Corrin said.

"Halt!" the Orange called again.

Corrin huffed his breaths. He knew he could not outrun them with Reidos in tow. He needed to throw them off his trail long enough to hide somewhere.

He arrived at the terminus of the street, where it branched off into three others. He looked down all of them, chose the path with the most windows and doors, and threw himself into a desperate run down it. He heard Reidos wincing with each pained breath behind him, but somehow he maintained the pace. Surprisingly, so did Mardin. Unfortunately, so did the Orange.

Every door looked hardy and strong. He did not have the luxury of stopping to test each lock, and he therefore searched for one with questionable integrity.

He finally found one, constructed of cheap wood with hinges rusty and old. The frame glowed in his eyes like a beacon of weakness. He drew one leg high and in to his chest, and kicked outward, making contact just above the door handle. His heel caught a bit of the latch, twisting his ankle, but not enough to sprain. The frame cracked, the bolt snapped loose, and the door crashed through into the room beyond. A great plume of dust went up, and Corrin ushered Hallan, Reidos, and the reluctant Mardin through.

He found himself in a short hallway, with a wide room beyond. It was unlit and uninhabited, but Corrin could make out the vague outlines of multitudinous low tables and chairs. He thought it was an empty cafe, and it reminded him of food. His stomach involuntarily groaned. The hunger made him angry, and he momentarily entertained the thought of fighting the Orange out of sheer frustration.

He noticed light at the other end of the rows of tables. Large windows. Thin glass. He grasped the leg of one of the chairs as he ran, reared back and hurled it at the window directly ahead of him. The glass cracked and spiderwebbed, but did not break. It was not as thin as he had assumed.

He charged the glass. He jumped at the last moment, became horizontal in the air, and crossed his arms above his head. His momentum propelled him into the window, shattering it. He flew out the other side. Landed on his hands. Tucked and rolled. Hit the back of his head. Found his footing. Leapt to his feet, dazed.

Reidos was at the window behind him, reaching out to tap loose three downturned shards of glass that had somehow survived Corrin's maneuver. They came loose easily and dropped to the floor. He lifted Hallan through, then crawled over with Mardin behind him.

Corrin broke into a sprint again, across another narrow street, toward another window. He threw himself again, and smashed into the glass like a battering ram. He broke cleanly through it, repeating his landing, though this time he hit his head *hard* on the floorboards.

He was in another room, also dark. He couldn't tell what it was, but he tore across it nonetheless, found a door, and kicked his way through it. Mardin came after him with Hallan. Reidos brought up the rear, the Orange already at the previous shattered window, swords drawn and leaping through it.

Corrin found himself in yet another street, with yet another door directly in front of him. He kicked at it. It didn't budge. *Shaot!* He tried again. Nothing. Another kick. Nothing. Not a creak. Not a groan. Not an ounce of give.

Corrin cursed as Reidos arrived behind him, noticed his predicament, and tested the doorknob. It turned easily. The door opened without complaint.

Corrin groaned. "That fucking figures."

He flew inside. No windows. One door straight ahead. No knob. Handle with a thumb latch. Corrin unbolted the lock, and flipped the latch with his thumb. The door opened inward, and he was through. He motioned furiously for the others to hurry. He looked behind them. The Orange were coming through the back door. Corrin scanned the room he just left. He noticed a line of chairs against the wall, ran back into the room, and kicked a chair apart. He picked up one of the wooden legs.

He darted back out the door, as the Orange crossed the room after him. He pulled the door shut, and jammed the chair leg through the handle, one end wedged against the frame. They pounded furiously at it, but the makeshift bolt remained in place.

"That's more like it," Corrin said. He looked right and left. The way was shorter to the left. He jogged the length, looked around the corners, saw no Orange, and motioned the others to follow. He turned right, then left, then right again. No Orange. No assassins. He smiled.

"Where are we going?" Mardin asked.

Corrin surveyed his surroundings. Up ahead, one of the major thoroughfares of Medion stretched away to either side. Karos Street. Corrin liked Karos Street already. It was choked with the morning traffic of merchants and artisans and wealthy denizens of the high towers.

Corrin scanned the storefronts behind them. Cobbler. Hat maker. Coat maker. Merchant market. The last one stood out. It was devoid of patrons, and through the windows he could see plentiful places to hide—high crate stacks of hazza ale, four-foot tall brass hookas, bronze candelabras dangling from thick chains mounted in the ceiling, draperies, and medallions swaying on overhead hooks amidst ziggurats of clay pottery.

"Right there," Corrin announced, pointing. "I've always wanted to go in there."

"You want to shop at a time like this?" Mardin asked.

"Shut up," Corrin said. "We're going to hide out for awhile. Stop being so dense." He stepped into the crowds, and meandered his way to the glass door of the shop. He pulled it open easily, and guided the others through. He closed the door swiftly, and peered out through the windows for any signs of pursuit. He saw none. "Peace and quiet at last."

He stared at the room. The rear walls were lined with silks and rare furs, waving slightly with some unseen draft. At least a score of tables were positioned all across the room, all topped off with glass cases of Talor jewelry and harlequin masks from Kassanath. Several of the tables were surrounded by stacks of cedar caskets of silver utensils, some opened to display their contents. Everywhere were hanging things—chains of copper, leather bands, feathered caps, and bronze bells which made little ringing music as they gently collided.

He turned around and was met by a small man with an impossible mustache. Short and ratlike, he blended in with the shelves of trinkets he sold.

Corrin gave a start at his sudden materialization. "I didn't see you there. Well, we are just looking around at the moment."

"May I assist you?" the man asked in a thick accent of the southern deserts. His feet pattered eerily as they propelled him past a table of wooden carvings of Mua dogs from Halzahman.

"How's the trade these days?" Corrin asked.

"Good trade. Many travelers in Medion these days. Many travelers. Acolytes of the Ministry. Many come to my shop."

"Priests? Who invited them?"

"They invited themselves. As they always do. They are most interested in the great magick which occurred this past week."

"Oh that," Corrin said. "Heard anything?"

"The Inner Guard are racing to find the culprits without the Priests. I hear they have already dragged three men from their homes and accused them of being users of magick. And that is just here on this street. It must be worse elsewhere. There will be many burnings in the days to come. They do not desire to be outdone by a Holy Marshall and his acolytes. They seem to be very interested in Halladon Plaza."

"Oh good," Corrin sighed. "That is a place we should avoid then. By the way, I seem to have lost my bearings a bit on this side of town. I have not been this far west before. Are there any landmarks nearby?"

"Of course," the man said, filling a brass basin with sweet vanilla oil. "Two streets east, follow the Causeway Road to Mondmark Square, and you with see the lighthouse by the pier."

"Causeway Road?" Corrin asked. "Another one? Is there an actual causeway anywhere?"

The man shrugged.

"Are causeways even real?" Corrin asked. "Is any of this real?"

The man shrugged. "Do you have interest in purchasing anything?"

"I never purchase trinkets this early in the morning without a proper causeway," Corrin said, scanning the crowd through the windows. "Seen any Orange up this way?" He thought he might be able to blend in with the locals until he made it to the wharves. Hard to follow anyone in that district. From there he could go north or south. He had not decided yet.

"None today," the man said. "Now I must ask you to leave."

Corrin turned on him and was about to begin a furious argument, but he heard a sound just then. Subtle. Like a door creaking closed. He turned around and looked throughout the room. He stared hard through the glass cases, and around the stacks of crates. He thought he saw movement briefly beyond a row of tall wood carvings. He looked closer, but found nothing.

Reidos noticed him searching. "What is it?"

"Shhh," Corrin said. "Something's up." He scanned over and over again, seeing nothing but trinkets, and silks, and chains, and bells, and wines, and a blond man, and censers, and silvers, and clay pots, and...

What the hell?

"Down!" He threw Hallan to the floor and dropped, pulling Reidos with him. A dart whistled over his head, and lodged itself in the window behind him. He hit the floorboards on his thigh, shooting pain down to his toes. He rolled onto his stomach, and peered under the tables. He saw legs clad in black trousers moving until they disappeared behind a stack of pottery. The shop owner was backing away, trying to disappear in the wall of coats.

Corrin snatched a breath. The bells made tinny twinkling sounds as something brushed against them. He saw a stand adorned with dark brown Mua dog carvings of various sizes. He reached out and grabbed a fat one, head-sized, and locked his fingers around one of the legs.

Have to be quick here.

Still lying flat, he threw up his hand high over his head, held it aloft for the barest moment, then yanked it back down. A black dart flew by, notching itself into a cedar casket. Corrin pushed himself up onto his knees, reared back, and hurled the Mua dog, end over end. It crashed through a stand of dangling chains, deflected off a life-sized carving of a leopard, and caromed into the shoulder of the assassin, who lost his balance behind a clay pot ziggurat.

Corrin leapt to his feet. "Out! Head for the plaza."

He watched them head for the door. Hallan had small legs, Reidos was injured, and Mardin was a weakling. He knew he needed to buy them a little time. *What would be the last thing an obsessed assassin would expect?*

Corrin opted to charge. *This.*

He tore into a run, sprinted between glass cases, and charged directly at the carefully stacked pots. He kicked off a wine barrel, launching himself into the air, and saw a brief glimpse of blond hair before he smashed through the pots, sending them crashing into the assassin. He made contact, sending the blond man to the ground beneath him.

The pots shattered to pieces all around him. The blowgun landed among the shards. Corrin saw it from the corner of his eye and kicked it away. He tried to pin the assassin, but his arm was knocked aside. He pulled free his silver dagger from Kolac, and cut down hard.

The assassin swatted his wrist, jarring the blade from his hand, and sending it clattering away. He kept his chin tucked down to protect his neck, as he received hit after hit in the side of the head. Corrin rolled his head around, trying not to give a clear shot at his temples or nose.

The assassin managed to get a hand in between their bodies, and pushed upward on Corrin's breastbone. Corrin was flipped off to one side, and landed on his back. The blond man rose to his knees. Corrin saw a table crowned with a glass case of golden medallions. He kicked out hard. His foot snapped off one leg of the table.

He heard the creaking of the wood and the assassin turned just in time to see the massive glass case smash into his body. The weight of it pressed him to the ground, and then it shattered on top of him. He writhed in the mess of glass and gold, his face and hands cut and bleeding.

Corrin snatched the lit basin of burning oil and dashed it across his face for good measure, then turned and flew out into the streets. He vanished himself into the crowds, weaving between the people.

He searched frantically for Reidos, and finally saw him across the street at the base of a wide white tower. His mouth tasted like acid by the time he arrived, and his thigh was still tingling painfully from his fall, but he managed a relieved sigh.

"We have to get out of here," Reidos said.

Corrin wiped the sweat from his eyes and tried to think of some place to go, when he abruptly felt a sharp pain in his shoulder. He arched his back. "Goddamn it!" He showed his back to Reidos. "What is on me?"

He fully expected a poison dart. He started to imagine horrible toxins entering his bloodstream and coursing through his veins. Reidos reached out and plucked the offending item out of his back.

"Ouch. What the holy hell was that?" He turned around to see Reidos holding a flat, circular object barely two inches in diameter. Its edge was razor sharp, and barbed with tiny spikes.

Reidos sniffed it, then ran a finger along the edge. Tasted it with a flick of the tongue. "No poison."

Corrin spun around searching the bobbing heads in the plaza for a short, blond head of hair. He finally saw one near the pillars of the arcade a hundred strides away. "Shaot. Let's go."

"Where?" Reidos asked.

"Anywhere," Corrin growled. He looked up the steps of the tower. Halfway up and off to one side was a cafe with a low-walled patio creeping with vines, and a dark interior beneath low eaves. "There." He pointed.

They scrambled up the stairs. At the top he turned to look back. He saw the blond assassin giving chase, taking three stairs at a time.

"Go for the stairs," he told Reidos. "Go up in the tower." Reidos pushed Hallan along. Mardin followed. Corrin backed across the patio after them.

The assassin reached the cafe, and hurtled over the vine-covered wall, knocking over a stunned patron. Those who sat eating stopped and stared. The blond man glared through them at Corrin. Blood congealed over one side of his face and around one of his eyes, and his forehead bore a knotted lump. With his functional hand, he waved a black iron baton the length of his arm.

A servant attempted to bar his path, holding out one hand to stop his advance. The blond man responded by cracking the baton over the servant's forearm, snapping the bone. The man howled, and the assassin whipped the baton into the side of his head, sending him sprawling.

Corrin slipped all three of the Levidian Nails from his belt, and let them fly with a single dramatic flash of his arm. All three found their mark, biting into shoulder, stomach, and thigh. The blond man swatted at them with his mangled hand, dislodging each of the supposedly deadly throwing knives from his body and knocking them to the ground.

Deadly my ass.

The patrons of the cafe were crying out in fear and surprise, some of them falling out of their chairs. Corrin backpedalled through them, the assassin stalking after him. Corrin grasped the armrest of one of the wicker chairs and let it fly. It was batted away. Corrin threw another. Same result. The assassin increased his pace. Corrin did the same.

Corrin tipped over a potted plant in his path. The assassin hopped over it. Corrin edged around a table and flipped it over. It crashed its contents onto the blond man's head and chest, but he managed to block most of the blow with his arm, then charged.

Corrin grabbed up a tin pitcher of steaming coffee. He unleashed its contents into the assassin's eyes. The man closed them in time, but the hot liquid still scalded the skin of his face. Corrin followed up the coffee by banging him over the head with the pitcher.

The blond man stumbled back, and Corrin made a mad dash under the eaves of the cafe, past dozens of stunned onlookers, and into the lobby of the tower. The ceiling was high, with rounded stone pillars as tall as redwoods. He went for the stairs.

He threw himself up the spiral. He thought he heard his companions moving up ahead of him, and he hurried his steps even more. He finally caught up to them at the seventh floor. He heard the sound of furious footsteps below.

"Out," he said, gesturing to the nearest door. "Move it."

They were through it and down a long hall with many of the doors closed and locked. Mardin tried several of them, but with negative results. At last Corrin saw one open ahead, with pale light issuing from the window within.

"In there," he commanded. Reidos hobbled through, with Hallan scampering behind him. Mardin went next, and then Corrin, turning to look back down the hall. As he did so, he glimpsed the door to the stairs easing itself open.

How in the hell?

Corrin slammed the door, and found himself in a wide room, well furnished with silk pillows and linen tapestries. "We're in trouble," he said.

Reidos narrowed his eyes. "How much trouble?"

Corrin gestured out into the hallway. "A lot of trouble. We can't shake him."

"What are we going to do?" Mardin asked.

Corrin surveyed the room. No other doors. No lavatory. Only the window. He pressed his face against it to look out. Below it and to the left was a high scaffold of interconnected iron bars and planks of wood. It was fifty feet wide at the base, and reached up in a tapering fashion, until it terminated just one floor below and six feet off to the side. He looked at the ground seventy feet below and winced.

Goddamn seventh floor.

He heard a sudden pounding at the door. He made his decision quickly. He searched the room with his eyes. Found a solid oak chair at the head of a mahogany table. He hoisted it over his head and launched it at the window. It smashed through the glass and continued on its way down to the street below.

Corrin ran to the window. He heard the sound of someone jerking on the doorknob behind him. He grabbed Reidos by the cuff and dragged him to the edge. "You'll have to go first."

Reidos nodded, and Corrin grasped him around the forearm. The Mahhen stepped onto the windowpane and lowered himself outside. Corrin held on tight, and began to swing him back and forth, building up the momentum. On the seventh swing he guessed that he had the necessary inertia.

"One more swing," he said. The next time back he released, and Reidos flopped awkwardly toward the scaffold. He landed on it with one leg, but the motion threw his other leg up past his waist. He tipped and fell hard on his side.

Corrin took Hallan next. "Time to pretend you're a bird." Hallan nodded, and Corrin had him out the window. Reidos was rising to his knees on the scaffold. Corrin began swinging Hallan back and forth. It only took three swings. "On the next one I'm going to let go," he told the boy. He did, and Hallan fell through the air. Reidos stretched out both arms and caught him.

By the time he was lowering Mardin, he heard someone prying at the frame of the door behind him, creaking it and forcing it inward.

"You're too big to catch. So you better make a good landing," Corrin warned. Mardin held his breath, and let go. He hit the top tier of the scaffold, but rolled and slipped off, crashing to the tier below. Reidos was already there with Hallan, making his way down.

Corrin hopped up onto the windowsill, just as the door creaked open behind him. He gauged the distance, pushed off with his legs, and leapt to the scaffold. He made a decent landing. Tucked. Rolled. Overshot his mark. Almost went over the far side. Slowed his momentum by pressing one hand against the outer wall of the tower. Finally came to rest at the edge of the uppermost tier. He looked up. The assassin was already climbing out the window.

Shaot!

Corrin yanked out the Kokril talon and let it fly, but the blond assassin ducked back in the window, and the blade deflected harmlessly off the wall and disappeared to the streets below. Corrin grasped the outer edge of the wooden plank, and swung himself down to the one below. He heard a thump on the plank above, as the assassin touched down.

Corrin looked below. Reidos was working his way down to the third tier. Mardin was on his way to the fourth. Corrin steadied himself on the fifth, planted his legs, and drew his longsword. In the center of the plank above there was a narrow gap. He heard the blond man moving over toward it. He upturned his blade and waited.

He saw the shadow above, and jammed his steel through the gap. Missed. He felt pressure on the blade, as the assassin braced his foot against the flat, holding it stuck in its place. Corrin yanked hard, withdrawing it. He heard the sound of running. The assassin was making for the far side of the plank. Corrin advanced to meet him, but before he could get there, the blond man was already swinging himself down, the iron rod tucked under his arm.

Corrin drew his white steel knife from Albinon, moved in, and cut downward with the *Steel Whore*, holding the knife back for a counterstrike. He was blocked by a swing of the black baton. Corrin sent a swing at the legs. The assassin parried, drew up one foot, and slammed it into Corrin's knee. Corrin pitched forward, his leg knocked out from under him. He dropped the white steel into oblivion in order to grab for one of the poles to steady himself. He barely maintained his balance. A swing of the baton caught him across the head, just behind the ear. He swayed in his footing and stumbled back. He parried another swing, and another, and ducked under a third, before he missed and he took a heavy shot to the ribs beneath his outstretched arm.

Goddamn it.

Corrin backed up to the very edge of the tier above. The assassin advanced after him. Corrin sheathed his sword, and took hold of the plank above with both hands. He lifted himself up and pulled both knees tight into his chest. As the blond man reached him, he was already kicking out. His heels took the assassin just below the breastbone, catching his center of gravity and sending him crashing down on his back.

Corrin lowered himself down to the fourth tier. He scurried to his right, and made it to the edge of the scaffold, just as the assassin hopped down to face him. Corrin kicked out with as much force as he could against the corner beam supporting the tier above. It cracked, and the scaffolding whined and groaned. He kicked once again and the iron pole snapped loose, tipped inward, and ceased to support the planks above it. The outer corner swung inward and down, catching the assassin in the face.

Corrin took a running start, and slammed his shoulder into the drooping planks. They cracked and dipped further, until the edge of the broken platform dangled at waist height. Corrin crawled his way up onto it, found a loosened beam, tore it free, and hurled it down, using the platinum hair as a target. The blow stunned the assassin, and he fell backwards into another beam, crashing through it and snapping it loose.

Corrin's platform dipped and drooped, cracked and loosened, and finally gave way under him. The entire fifth tier collapsed into the fourth, and he was shaken off his feet to slam chest-first into the planks. His breath blasted out of his lungs, and he sucked sharply to fill them again.

He looked up just in time to see the beams supporting the sixth tier break off and drop even more planks down on top of him. Corrin prepared to again draw his blade when he heard it. A subtle creaking at first. Then a whining groan of bending metal. He felt vibrations in the wood. The scaffolding tipped, then swayed back into the wall.

Not good. Not good.

The scaffolding shuddered. Wood planks sank in the center. Several snapped. Corrin braced himself as the entire structure heaved and screeched. Metal twisted. Beams buckled one after another. Planks snapped.

Here we go.

The scaffolding collapsed, tearing itself apart on its way down. Corrin squirmed his way onto one of the beams, and held on for dear life as the structure bore down on the ground and broke itself apart. As the far side made impact, the assassin was jolted free of his hold and thrown headlong into a row of merchant carts on the street below.

The beam Corrin held snapped loose, and Corrin rolled with it still in his arms. He dropped into a free fall. He crashed down on another beam, bending it, and hurting himself in ways he could not grasp at that instant. The beam slowed his fall before he hit the ground. Then the scaffold mashed itself into pieces around him.

Corrin was hoisting himself up by the time the dust began to settle. He threw pieces of wood and twisted iron out of his way, attempting to extricate himself quickly from the mangled mess of tangled metal and splintered wood.

He felt pain in his thigh and shoulder, and a cut somewhere above his ear was bleeding profusely. He struggled over the twisted wreckage, and climbed across broken carts that had once been used by street merchants to peddle their goods. Reidos was suddenly at his side. And Mardin. Corrin was lifted to his feet. He saw Hallan. He shook the flashes out of his eyes.

"I can't believe it," Mardin gasped.

"I can," Reidos said. "Corrin always finds a way to break everything but himself."

Corrin chuckled. It made his ribs throb. He glanced over his shoulder at the ruined scaffold. The Orange were running toward it from all directions, helping merchants to their feet. The Inner Guard were among them.

He started to ease his way from the scene when he heard a sound that made him shudder. The sound of the wreckage moving. The sound of someone sifting their way through the damage. He looked back and rolled his eyes.

Though covered from head to tow with dust and shavings of wood, the platinum hair still shined in the sunlight. The assassin was already stalking toward him, not even bothering to brush the dust from his face.

"I hate that farod," Corrin said. He began to draw the *Steel Whore* yet again, then looked around at the Inner Guard and the Orange. The capes billowed like a parade of color. Corrin suddenly had an idea. It was a good idea. Corrin liked it. It made him smile.

He turned to the nearest officer of the Inner Guard, and pointed commandingly at the assassin. He made his best attempt at sounding utterly horrified. "He has the magick! It's him! The devil is here! He used the magick!"

The officer of the Inner Guard turned instantly to the assassin. "User on scene!" he called out. "User on scene!" The Orange flew into motion, surrounding the dust-covered blond man. The Inner Guard were converging like hyenas to their kill. "Summon the Stoppers," they called out. "Halt where you are." The Inner Guard forced the assassin's arms behind his back, while he stared like an angry fire at Corrin.

Corrin smiled pleasantly in response. Satisfied, he turned on his heels and disappeared into the crowds like a phantom, working his way down to the wharves. "What do you think?" he asked Reidos. "North or south?"

"Weren't we just here?" Mardin groaned. "Are we going ship-hopping again?"

"I hadn't thought about that. That's a good idea. It's the easiest way to put some distance between us and Medion."

"I wouldn't call it easy," Reidos said. "I can barely put my arms over my head, let alone jump on a boat. It took me ten years to get down that scaffold."

"Well," Corrin said. "You should have just waited for it to collapse. It only took me two seconds."

Reidos rolled his eyes. "Sea ships aren't as easy as steamers. High sides."

"Why don't we just buy our way on?" Mardin asked.

"What?" Corrin wheeled around to face him.

"I have some silver," Mardin said.

"Silver?" Corrin thought hard. "You have some?"

"More than enough, I think," Mardin said.

"Well," Corrin said. "Let's find a boat worth buying our way onto then."

36

My Path

KELUWEN'S BOOTS TOUCHED DOWN and her heels sank three inches into mud, thick like paste.

Before she even pushed off the edge of the shoreboat, a shoreman already had his hand on her hip. She glared at him. He smiled with piss-yellow teeth. She stamped down hard with the heel of her boot onto the arch of his foot. His mouth turned into a piss grimace, and he hopped back a step. Hodo stepped off next, and his arms, thick as tree branches, discouraged any further suitors.

She would have preferred to do it herself. But Orrinas had warned her sternly before they came anywhere near the shore. They had a mission, and not a drop of magick could be wasted, no matter how right it felt.

The walk through the town felt like a funeral procession. The silence of the place groped her and embraced her unwanted. Women did not laugh. Men did not chatter. Corricon was like a tomb.

Once they began talking to people, she understood why.

"When Sarenwalkers are coming to Corricon you know you are in for a strange day," the stablemaster said.

"Sarenwalkers?" Orrinas asked.

"There was one with some travelers," he said.

"A new bodyguard for the sorcerer?" Keluwen postulated. "Someone Severn did not know about?"

Orrinas shrugged. "Yes, but where did they go?"

To that question the stablemaster tapped his chin. "Well, hmmm. Let me see." He proceeded to drone on for centuries without ever landing on a single direction.

"This will end when never meets forever," Keluwen complained.

She wandered away. Roamed the mud streets, looking at the houses on stilts, at the people kicking up mud as they walked. The sky was cold grey, a hell of fluffy ice mountains in the sky. The air stank of salt and dead fish. The streets were unpaved mud and the air stank with it. Brown slush attached to boots like a malignant growth. The avenues wound through districts of half-ruined hostelries, and dens of Samartanian immigrants.

Strands of dried grass and broken stalks of barley littered the avenues, flattened into the mud by countless boots, creating odd designs in the earth. Keluwen studied them casually as she eased over them, tracing the outline first of a cat, then a bear, and finally an octopus.

The wind bit through cloak, tunic, and shirt. She winced at each gust, and with every inhale it sharpened her breaths to cut her lungs.

The people of Corricon walked with cynical stares, grimacing behind beards and squinting their wide eyes as they wandered between clumps of curious cottages with stone walls and thatched roofs, upon which blackbirds congregated like shrouded gossipers.

Women did not wander the streets alone here. It was a long-standing custom for them to be warded by at least one male from their household. Many men moved about with their hands clamped tightly around the wrists of those they escorted, launching fiery looks at any who glanced their way.

He had been here. She could feel it. Kinraigan had been here. They had very nearly caught up to him. But here he was, gone again, and no one seemed to know where he went.

They left on foot. They went north. They went east. They went west. The only reason no one said they went south was because to the south was the sea. *Well at least they can all agree on something.*

She bounced on her knees, tensing and releasing. Glanced all around. Krid and Cheli and Leucas had spread out, asking everyone they could find. Nothing new came to light. Keluwen could tell by the defeated looks on their faces.

"No one ever sees where he goes," Keluwen said to herself, kicking a dirt clod. It skipped along the ground, bounding and changing course, ending in an icy puddle. "Just like Westgate. Just like Cair Tiril. Just Like Medion."

She wandered toward the wharf. She originally went just to have something to stand on that she would not sink down into. It comforted her to hear her boots tap on the wood. *I thought we were going to another city. Not...this.*

"Are you looking for sea passage?" a man asked the back of her head.

She turned to face him. He was old, and sad, but his eyes looked hopeful. "Why would you think that?"

He eyed her up and down. "Because you are not from here. Just like them that wanted me to bring them here. Foreigners. Odd sort. One of them was a Glasseye. I never get to shuttle them. They always ride in the Lord Protector's quickships."

Keluwen froze. Her blood turned colder than the frigid air. "What did you say?"

"A Glasseye. And a man in green cloak. He looked like a Sarenwalker."

"Did you catch their names?"

"I remember Inrianne," he said. "She was pretty and walked the deck often. And then there was another one, Aren. The others always complained that he slept all the time. They paid double to leave by stars at the quick to come here."

Aren of Amagon. I have you now. I know where you are. "The Sarenwalker is warding the Glasseye. Did you see which way they went?"

"North to Kamathar. Said they were on their way to the Kol Plateau. Who knows why? No place worse in autumn than Kol. If they don't come back, then I suppose they forfeit their fare."

"They already paid?"

"Sure did. One way by middle-draft nightship all the way to Volean Heights if necessary."

"Nightship. Expensive."

He nodded. "Their loss." He paused. "I offered my ship to some men who came after, but I could not fit so many people."

"I am sure travelers come through here all the time," Keluwen said. "Why would these stand out?"

"Their bellies were full but they looked ravenous. I have never seen folk so crazed. Their eyes danced."

It was too much to hope, I suppose. Keluwen shook her head and began to walk away.

"And then there was the one with the bells on his shoes."

Keluwen stopped in her tracks. She felt she had been struck by lightning. "He had a mustache."

"You know him?"

"Where did they go?"

"Arragandis. Have you heard of it?"

"I have," she said. *I am not an imbecile.*

"That was where they were headed."

"The gateway to Arthenorad," she said.

"Yes."

"The capital city of Arradan."

"None other. No one goes to Arragandis just to stay in Arragandis. Save for Arradian's trying to get away from Arthenorad."

She left him standing there and stalked over to Orrinas. He was still nagging the stablemaster, trying to get some tidbits of memory to come back, but he resisted.

"I know where they are going," Keluwen said.

He turned to face her. "What?"

"Arthenorad. One of the men who was there in Cair Tiril was seen here. That is where they went. They must be going because they believe he will be headed there."

"We will book a ship."

"No need. I found one for free."

He raised an eyebrow. Free?"

"Some of his people booked travel here on a nightship, they had paid to go on, but then abandoned that idea."

"Why?"

She shrugged.

He narrowed his eyes. "What do you know?"

"The Glasseye. He was here."

"The same one?"

"From Westgate. From Cair Tiril. He was here. He went inland. North."

Orrinas looked down into her eyes and his hair turned just a little bit greyer. "You are thinking something rash."

"Take the others," she said. "Take them to Arthenorad. Prepare."

"Why are you behaving as if you will not be coming also?"

"Because I will not be."

His expression curdled like old milk. "What are you saying to me right now?"

"I am going after them."

"On foot."

"Yes."

"No, you are not. That is ludicrous."

"We know he is likely going to Arthenorad," she said. "But they seem to have gone inland. I want to follow them."

"Why?"

"That Glasseye is so deep in this. I want him dead. We would have ended this in Westgate if it hadn't been for him. If I can kill him, then the next time we face him will be the last time."

"I keep waiting for you to tell me that this is some form of jest."

"It is not."

"You are going to go overland."

"Yes."

"You hate going into the wilderness. You were miserable in Laman."

"I will likely be miserable out there, too."

"You will freeze to death."

"Bearskins."

"This is not Olbaran. This is the Kamath Plateau. In autumn. Your eyes will freeze and your fingers will turn black."

"I will render a bubble to sleep in at night."

"A bubble. At this latitude there will be twelve hours or more of darkness. Can you render a duration of twelve hours?"

"It will not require any strength, nor any movement. Just an airtight barrier. Economical on the concentration."

"Impossible."

"I can do it. I know I can. I have done it before. When I needed to drown out the screams of my secondparents. I could do it for eight hours then. I can manage twelve now."

"North of Kamathar there is nothing. Do you understand? No cities. Only villages and holdfasts and fortifications. There are no sewers, no running water, no hot baths to warm your bones, and no markets to purchase food."

"Good thing we have a full compliment of supplies. I will take it all. The sweetbreads, the dried meats, the fruits, the cheeses. And give me half the jinglebells."

"This is lunacy."

"I know you think so. And I understand why."

"You understand, do you? Because I am having a very difficult time understanding you right now. I do not understand this at all."

"It is something I have to do. We failed in Westgate despite every advantage. Why? The Glasseye was there. We did not have Bonsinar when we needed him. We did not have the guidance of the elder. He knew we were coming. We cannot let that be the case next time."

"And what if Kinraigan is with him? What then? Are you going to charge in and try to do this by yourself? Please tell me that is not your intention."

"It is not. I am not a fool."

"Though I begin to wonder if you are not suicidal."

She made a wrinkled smile at him. "You worry often. You are cautious."

"I have good reason to be."

"I know you think I am rash."

"You are. I have ample evidence."

"You still love me somehow. Even thought I am young and foolish."

"I do."

"And I love you even though you are old and wise."

He raised an eyebrow at her. "I had not thought wisdom a deficit."

"The day when we were married, I didn't love you."

"I know."

"But I love you now."

"I wonder."

"I do. There was a day, back when we hunted Shadro Herrick."

"I remember him. A butcher. He went luminous one time in front of witnesses and he was so desperate to get back into the light again that he thought his godhood depended on surrounding himself with infant heads arranged in the proper geometry."

"And we ran afoul of the local magistrates and were pursued by the Horns of Haradel."

"I remember."

"And we learned they were burning the tawny estate of my secondparents, and I told you I needed to see it burn."

"I recall this."

"And you said there were too many magistrates, that we would risk running into them."

"And I let you go watch it anyway."

"Because you trusted me. That was the day I knew I loved you."

"Because I failed to keep you from being a damn fool?"

"Because you understood I needed to do it, and you let me do it. Even though you were not happy about it."

"And now you are asking the same thing."

"I need to do this. I need to take care of him. I have to do this or my heart will scream until it bursts."

"I should go with you."

"No. You must not. The others need you. Can you imagine Hodo and Leucas and Cheli stuck with no one but Krid Ballar?"

He smiled. "They would mutiny."

"They need you. And you need them. I can't pull you away from that."

"You have your kit packed for winter weather?"

She nodded. "And I will take the extra food."

"You will need more leather bladders for water. Kamathar is full of peat bogs. The water is poison."

"I will bring extra."

"And you will not go anywhere near Kinraigan."

"Of course not."

"And you will meet us in Arthenorad."

"Yes. "

"I cannot believe you have fooled me into this kind of folly again."

"I will make it up to you with kisses," she said. "And we will be in Arradan, so I will have no choice but to present myself to you in the Arradian fashion."

He smiled. "You can make it up to me by please remaining alive and in one piece."

She elbowed him. "That part is a given."

He wrapped his arms around her. "I had not thought to lose you so soon."

She held him tight, rocking back and forth with him. "We will be together again soon. I promise you."

"Now I am sure you mean it," he said.

She stretched up to kiss him. She felt his lips and warmth spread all through her. She squeezed her eyes shut and lived within his warmth for a long time, before pulling back. "For now goodbye," she said.

"For now goodbye," he said.

"When you are there, in Arthenorad, just remember every time you see one of the moons, that I am coming to find you. That in a little while I'll be there."

"I will," he said. "I always do when you are gone."

"I wanted to tell you one last thing," she said.

"No," he said. He pressed one finger to her lips. "Save it. For when next we meet. If our conversation is half done, then you will have to come back, so we can finish it."

"Fine then. We will finish this conversation when next we meet."

"When next we meet," he said.

And then he turned and went to the others while she struggled to pull the many rucksacks and carry-bags over her shoulders. She was so busy watching him walk away she forgot to put on her bearskin cloak, and had to disengage from each of the bags to don it, before starting the process all over.

By the time she finished and looked up to see him he was already gone, along with the others. She felt his absence like a kick in the gut. But she had to go this way. No matter how much it hurt, this was the path now, and she could no more turn from it than she could spin wool into gold. *My path.*

For now goodbye, Orrinas. My love. My only.

37

Things Corrin Hated

CORRIN HATED SHIPS.

Everything about them—the way the rocked on the ocean tide, the way they creaked and groaned as they crested the swells, the way the salty breeze on deck blew through his hair, the way they always seemed to smell like rotting wood, the way they always left him smelling as if he had taken a bath in fish carcasses.

He was convinced that the ship was sinking. *Merciful* had been chosen for speed of departure rather than luxury or even seaworthiness. The planks were infested with wood beetles and the beams stank of rot. Candles provided the only light below deck, and the air, thick with the odors of seawater and urine, was stifling. He was sure seawater was seeping through cracks, and would slowly bring it down below the waves before the crew even noticed.

The Captain, a man named Saibin, clicked his teeth behind a beard that dangled nearly as long as his arms, streaked white with salty residue from the splashing swells. "I was sunk with a ship once," he would say. "The ocean is a black monster at night. The winds howl and the waves are high as mountains."

Every story he told was about some kind of disaster at sea. Ships dashed to bits on rocky shores, men pulled from decks by long sea worms, or sailors killed in their sleep by poisonous, cat-sized octopi that could crawl across planks of wood as easily as they swim. It was all he could do to keep himself from constantly looking over his shoulder, searching for stealthy octopus assassins creeping across the decks to poison him and steal his blood.

The crew was frequently thrown into turbulent motion. Sailors grappled with the rigging, fiddling with the lines. They danced a chaotic ballet along the length of the deck, struggling against sharp crosswinds. Corrin preferred to remain belowdecks, grappling with salt stains, fiddling with the oil lamps in his quarters, struggling with boredom. He had already run out of knives to clean and sharpen.

Hallan would incessantly demand to be taken above to see the ocean. Corrin couldn't stand the ocean. It was blue, but a little too blue for his liking. Blue meant depth. Depth was distraction. Distraction was death to a warrior. Corrin only dealt with surfaces, most of all his own. Getting below the surface of anything required too much thinking. Anyone who stopped to think was a dead man. Jecks told him that.

So he let Reidos take the boy above. Even convinced one of the sailors to let Hallan into the crow's nest. *Wonderful*, Corrin thought. *Not afraid of assassins, not afraid of heights, not afraid of the ocean, not afraid of Danab-Dil, the Leviathan of the Deep. What kind of boy is he?*

Corrin hated heights. He wasn't exactly afraid of them. He wasn't exactly afraid of anything. A little fear here and there was a good thing. It got the blood pumping. It brought focus to the senses. Besides, you can't be brave without being afraid. Bravery implied fear, or rather overcoming fear. *If you're not afraid of anything, then you're just plain stupid. Or insane.* He wondered which was worse.

"I've changed my mind," he said to himself. "The worst thing about ships is the waiting."

Corrin hated waiting.

It was the fourth day at sea, the ship slicing a pleasant path across the Gulf of Shain. As far as Corrin was concerned, it was three and a half days too many already, and every passing second put the journey further into overtime. How far away could Arradan possibly be?

The old empire in its prime had stretched all the way through Bolan and Belegorod, and even Amagon. If he had been around back then he would have already been in a part of Arradan before he ever left Medion. Of course, there would not have been a Medion yet.

Arradan had been thrice the size of Olbaran in its heyday. He had heard about it from Aren nearly a thousand times. The cities of Arradan had been larger and wealthier than Westgate ever was on its best day. And the imperial provinces and colonies had spread as far as Tyrelon once. "Now that's an empire," he had told Aren. "I would have lived there."

Like all great eras, the golden days of the Arradian empire didn't last. Barbarians—Kargans, Belego, and Nordmagars—moved into Bolan, pushed on by the Sur. Then the Sur followed, not content to steal cheap iron and animal skins from fellow savages. They wanted shining gold, and ruby-studded crowns, and princely rings of silver. Most of all they wanted slaves. Female slaves. Arradian women were lovely creatures to the Sur. They had soft skin and smooth, shaved bodies. It made the Sur feel like gods when such loveliness was forced to service their desires.

Wars were fought for centuries. Arradan never lost, but they never really won either. The emperors staved off the decline, but never stopped it at the source. Eventually the emperors resorted to ignoring the Long Fall of their empire altogether. The lands that would become Amagon and Lenagon achieved self-rule in all but name, and the arrival of Mahhennnin only hurried the desire for secession. Bolan had kings of its own with wealth of their own, stolen from the coffers of emperors. Belegorod was forever lost to the Sur, and Kharthist was overrun by the Cron-men.

By that time its greatest cities had been sacked and re-sacked by countless invaders. Tyrelon broke off and became its own empire. Kradishah's reign of terror was the final brutal nail in the coffin. After the Great War, Amagon and Lenagon became free states, Bolan took the whole of the Kamath Plateau as its own, and the colonies were abandoned. The once unrivaled wealth was now easily rivaled.

Corrin mused over the Long Fall, and wondered if the people of Arradan ever saw it coming. People always have hope—even if it's a fool's hope—that they can turn back the tide of their own downfall.

Corrin spent five minutes trying to figure out how to spot his own downfall. Then he gave up and decided he would rather just not have one.

Corrin hated downfalls.

He heard a rapping at his door just then. It opened slowly, and Reidos entered. "Where's Hallan?" Corrin asked. "You didn't leave him alone with those madmen, did you?"

Corrin hated sailors.

"He's with Mardin," Reidos said. "And those *sailors* are letting us travel at half price."

"Call them what you will," Corrin said. "Anyone who would take to the open seas for a living has to be crazy. No sane person would bring themselves out here with Danab-Dil's hungry maw shifting about beneath the surface."

"Someone has to do it. And you're the last person who should be calling someone else crazy."

"I'm eccentric. There is a subtle difference."

"And besides, the deep sea devil is a fable. Stop pretending it is real to distract everyone from the fact that you are merely afraid of water."

"Pshhht," Corrin waved him away dismissively. "Don't let Danab-Dil hear you. He might know we are together. I would just as soon be safe down here when his angry tentacles sweep you off the deck."

"Corrin, who was that man who was chasing us?"

"For the thousandth time, I don't know." Corrin threw his arms in the air. "He must be following us from Palantar. I can't think of anything else."

"How do you know for sure?"

"Someone's jealous husband? Who just happens to be an expert with a blowgun?"

"Whoever he was, he knew we were in that tower when the Inner Guard didn't even know. He was waiting for you to step outside. How many days do you think he sat there, just waiting for you to come through that door?"

"What do you want me to say, Reidos? Someone who can see the future tried to kill me? Some telepathic assassin? And if Kinraigan could see the future, he would know that I'm not a threat. I don't want anything to do with him."

"Someone thinks you're a threat."

"Are you trying to make me depressed?"

"I'm trying to figure this out."

"Well try a little quieter. Some of us are trying to enjoy the ride."

"You hate ships."

He did.

"I hate pesky Mahhen jackasses too. But somehow I always end up getting stuck with you." He stood up and shoved him on the way to the door.

"Where are you going?" Reidos asked.

"To find Hallan. Before Mardin corrupts him with cowardice."

"You're going out on deck? You might accidentally see the ocean."

Corrin ignored him, and glided up the stairs at the end of the passenger compartment. Reidos followed him silently. Not many people were on deck at this hour. Only Mardin, Hallan, and a few sailors. When Corrin emerged, Hallan ran to him.

"Corrin, Corrin."

Corrin sighed. "What's all the fuss?"

"I saw a boat," the boy said.

"We're on it," Corrin said.

"Not this boat. Another boat. It's behind us. I saw it through the scope." He beamed a wide smile.

"What kind of boat?" Corrin asked.

"It..." Hallan stopped short, looked away, and frowned. "I don't know."

"Too far away to see clearly," one of the sailors said, a man with a crooked nose and slick yellow teeth. "Barely a speck through the scope. Heading to Arradan though. Same as us."

"How do you know that? Intuition?"

"It's been ghosting us for three days now," the sailor said. "Smaller than this tub, so it must not be running full sail."

"Why were you watching it?" Reidos asked.

"I check on it every morning," the sailor said. "Captain's paranoid about pirates. His old ship got hit once by raiders near Ethios. Now anything with a sail makes him jump out of his boots."

"If it's not pirates, why check on it?" Mardin asked.

"To keep the Captain happy," the sailor said. "But it's definitely not pirates. A ship that small could have caught up with us the second night at sea. Pirates aren't that patient. This ship just sits there, keeping pace with us. Way back on the horizon." He pointed behind them.

"Following us?" Corrin asked.

"If it were closer to us, it'd be cutting through our wake I'd say." The sailor thought for a second. "It's strange though. I never saw a ship do that before. Sea captains like to blaze their own trails, not follow in someone else's."

"Right on our trail," Reidos said. "And it's been following us for how long?"

"Three days at least," the sailor said. "Likely came out of the port in Medion. Must have been right after we set sail, too. No other decent ports up the coast from Medion until Corricon, and we haven't passed Corricon yet."

"Three days," Reidos said.

Corrin hated being followed.

****

Corrin hated being awakened in the middle of the night.

He hated it double so because he immediately remembered he was aboard a ship.

He hated them as well.

It was a thumping sound that did it, startled him from a pleasant dream about pleasant maids pleasantly pleasuring him with their pleasant mouths. His eyes shot open. He felt the texture of the sleeping cot. Rough like burlap. He squinted through the black. Reidos and Hallan were sleeping in similar bedding across the cabin. He made out their gentle breathing over the creaking of the ship. Faint echoes of the rocking ocean drifted down from the outside.

He heard another thump. Something hitting the wood.

That was a thump.

He listened for it. Two thumps this time.

That was definitely a thump.

He winced. He wasn't particularly keen on going above deck to investigate. He was sure that he would glimpse the ocean, but his distaste for open water was overridden by thoughts of the ship being boarded by pirates, or worse.

He rose quietly, took the *Steel Whore* in her scabbard without attaching it to his belt, and tiptoed across the room. He opened the cabin door, crept cautiously down the corridor, mounted the steps leading above.

The wind moaned through the rigging. At least he did not have to look at the water. Open ocean was hideous, and he was fairly certain Danab-Dil, the globulous tentacled sphincter of the deep sea hell, lived somewhere nearby.

The night was overcast, and the ship was lit only by seven oil lamps suspended by hooks in the masts. He looked over the forward positions, but did not see a soul. He knew there would only be a handful of madmen on deck at this hour of the night.

That's interesting.

Usually the sailors clustered in this area, smoking fat pipes and chugging ale by the bucket. Corrin pursed his lips. He scanned from side to side, and stepped toward the nearest mast. He heard a thump again, and a groan, and the sound of scrambling boots. It made him jump. It emanated from the aft.

He made his way to the rear of the ship. He heard jeering laughter, and he quickened his pace. He slowly peeked around the corner, and was greeted with the sight of four sailors in loose-fitting breeches and shirts. They were oblivious to the cold wind. They were also oblivious to Corrin's presence. They stood in an awkward semicircle. On the deck before them, lying face-down, was Mardin.

Terrific.

Corrin walked out into the open, whistling cheerfully.

The sailors froze in their footing. One slapped another, nervous, gesturing at his sword. They turned slowly, faces grisly and mischievous. One took a step toward Corrin, kicking Mardin in the ribs as he did so.

Corrin smirked. Kicking Mardin was one thing. Corrin imagined several instances when he himself may also have found it necessary to kick him. But there remained a subtle difference. Mardin was now on Corrin's crew. Therefore, by default, Mardin was now under Corrin's protection. This meant several things to Corrin. The first and most important was that Corrin could cause physical harm to Mardin any time he chose. The second was that Mardin was untouchable to anyone else. Jecks Keberan always said if you start letting people think they can disrespect your crew, then by morning they will disrespect you, too.

Can't have anyone disrespecting my magnificence.

The bravest of them eyed Corrin up and down, and spat. "You want to have some of this, too?"

Corrin smiled. "I would love to have *some-of-this-too*. That's my favorite thing."

The sailor offered a derisive look, and made an awkward, profane gesture before he advanced. Corrin found profane gestures amusing. He smiled as he drove his heel into the sailor's instep. Corrin found his grunt of pain even more amusing. He therefore laughed as he slapped the man across the face, whipped him over the neck with his full scabbard, grabbed the wrist, and snapped a particularly useful bone in the man's arm.

The sailor dropped merrily to the deck.

Oooh, now that is some delicious some-of-this-too.

The three remaining became suddenly hesitant, shifting in their salty shoes, eyeing one another. Corrin cleaned his fingernails while they engaged in silent committee. They now had an important decision to make. Of those that were beneficial to their long-term health they chose to forgo, opting instead to charge at him all at once.

Corrin kicked the first sailor in the shin, sending him sprawling. He grabbed the next by the cuffs, and heaved him over the railing that provided the only barrier between the deck and the open sea. He paused before engaging the final man, wanting nothing to interfere with the wonderful sound of the sailor splashing to his grave.

Danab-Dil, I give you this offering.

No one cried out that a man had gone overboard. *Some friends. Willing to let you drown so Saibin does not realize what you have been up to.*

After the splash, Corrin allowed the final man to approach him. He held his sword still in his scabbard. He allowed the sailor to throw a punch at his face. Corrin held his scabbard vertically in front of him. He drew his sword only halfway, and allowed the sailor to punch his own fist into the razor-sharp steel. He then allowed the sailor to wail in agony, before sheathing his blade, placing his foot behind the man's ankle, and pushing him flat onto his back.

"I knew it," Corrin said. "Madmen."

Corrin hated madmen.

Another man emerged out of Corrin's periphery. It was the very same sailor who had given Hallan the scope earlier in the voyage. He jumped between them, pushing the wounded sailors back.

"At last," Corrin sighed. "A man with some sense."

More sailors now appeared on the scene, revealing themselves slowly. Some made threatening gestures at Corrin. One stepped toward him.

Corrin drew the *Steel Whore* in one magnificent motion, and leveled the sharpened tip at the man's nose. "Ahh?" Corrin implied several things at once with his interrogatively enunciated vowel. This sailor was smart. He understood all of them, and retreated quickly to his comrades.

"What the hell is this, Mardin?" Corrin asked.

Mardin was still collecting himself. He had withdrawn behind the rigging to wait out the fray. "My silver. They wanted my silver."

"And they thought we wouldn't notice that you had been robbed?"

"We make landfall tomorrow," Mardin said. "They told me I would die if I said anything. They said I was lucky if they would let me live at all."

"Well, they had it backwards. They died, and you said nothing. Hmmm. Is one sailor a decent enough offering to Danab-Dil? Or should we send another?"

Mardin dusted himself off, eyeing the sailors warily.

"Hmmm," Corrin said. "Anyone else think a handful of silver is worth drowning for eternity in a leviathan's anus?"

No one spoke. The sailors tried as hard as they could to look away from him, and to not look like worthy food of the Leviathan of the Depths.

Corrin took the silence to be the correct answer. He moved very slowly, making sure that they were all watching him before removing himself below.

He then had to spend over an hour explaining to Reidos how he was not exactly a murderer, but rather a legendary hero. Reidos finally acquiesced with a quick, "Whatever you say." He then promptly returned to sleep, leaving Corrin awake and alone in the middle of the night with no pleasant dreams to keep him company.

Corrin hated being awake in the middle of the night.

38

Stories

IT SHOULD HAVE BEEN me.

I should have been the one, Aren thought.

It should be my body torn and broken on those rocks.

It should have been me going over the edge.

Aren tried to smile. But the expression burned like hateful fire on his face, which he could only extinguish with secret tears. And malagayne. Always malagayne.

Aren did whatever he could to keep the image of Hayles out of his mind. He found that he could say it in his head. *Hayles is dead.* And he would be all right, he could sustain. He could carry that concept in his mind all day long. But if he thought of even a *single* actual memory of him, he would falter, and his eyes would sting. Just like Donnovar. Just like...

So he thought of anything else.

He went over all his algorithms twice. He had been doing that every day since the ship delivered them to the mud city of Corricon, Bolan's only port. That was the last day he had smoked himself into a malagayne stupor on the aft end of the ship without the others knowing. The smoke had been sweet on his lips and in his lungs that night. It drowned his fear and desire. It kept the faces of the dead at bay.

But the journey inland offered only the most sparing moments to inhale his memories away. And so the faces closed in, whether he kept his eyes open or shut. And in moments of silence they would overtake him.

He would let himself smile to Eriana, but he could not look at her too long without seeing her face change in his mind to the way it had been in Medion, when the sorcerer's face had been inches from hers. He always had to turn away before his face turned sour. He did not want her to think he made that face because of her. It still made her sad. He could tell. But she kept smiling every time, even though she must have known by now that his reaction would be the same.

He counted out the different factors of core limitation, and went over every trace test for every stream he could think of. He turned to the mountains around him, thinking of kings and heroes. He painted the legends of Bolan onto every muddy ravine, every slope of tall grasses. He saw Swift Hale make his great run through the mountains to warn King Vergis of the invading Kargans; Bale Medlam protecting Empress Lithliana and her Andristi mother against the Kol Riders, single-handedly killing a hundred men; Adhavar leading his armies against the Sur, driving them back until meeting with Coralian in the Sarenmoor; and sheer mountain faces reminded him of the Horvath Diver, who had thrown himself from the edge of a ravine rather than be taken alive by Kradishah.

On the fifth day they met a burly man with a candid mustache named Murec in the city named Kamathar, where the castle of the King of Bolan overlooked them from a high hill. But when they had arrived, it had been more of a ghost town.

Murec had been more than happy to tell them all about it in between bites of aged mutton and gulps of mead. "Have you not heard? Sur riders have invaded. Word came in days ago."

"Barbarians," Aren told the others. "They destroyed the tribes of the Belego centuries ago, and took their place as a thorn in the side of Arradan. The modern Sur still raid across borders sometimes, just as their ancestors did before them."

"They have been at the border for weeks," Murec said. "Everyone thought it was just a show of strength, but I knew they were coming. My friends said I was crazy. Those that came before always took quick spoils and went back before the knights could muster. This time is different. They are organized now. Some say the tribes have made pacts among themselves. They don't strike and run anymore. They take and hold, or they destroy. Word says they move fast from one town to the next, moving west, heading for Kor Kollar."

"Is there no army to march against them?" Redevir asked. "Where are the King's vassals?"

"General Vols is in Kor Kollar," Murec had said. "Same as always. Got some men there, my brother says. Don't know if they'll be enough. The King is marching south to call up lords of his southern fiefs. He has taken ten thousand men and knights with him."

"Then the barbarians will reach Kor Kollar well before the King does."

Murec had frowned. "Maybe. Some say the General will hold out, but there's others that say his head's gonna be on a stake by the time the King gets there. I am taking a ship out of Corricon before the conscriptions start."

A comforting thought.

He had nothing more to say. They moved on north and Murec moved south.

On the eleventh day they entered the first of the wide valleys of the Kamath uplands, vast bowls of green grass and ancient pines. They were wildernesses, virtually devoid of people, each one an endless silence, where nothing existed that could take his mind off of the helpless anguish.

Pines sprouted from the landscape like a coarse emerald canvas, filling every breath with the sharp stench of their needles. Row upon row of savage violet mountains stood in the distance, making his legs cry out in anticipation of the agony of climbing over them. Already every step stiffened his legs a little more whether walking or riding, until he honestly feared he might not make it all way and have to humiliatingly submit to being carried on a litter. There was no snow, but the cold was bitter and biting without it, chewing on his ears and nose and fingers.

Hayles never visited him in his dreams. But that did not mean they were kind to him. He dreamed of swollen creatures within deep labyrinths. He dreamed of Kinraigan. He dreamed of Degammon.

Redevir had purchased everything for the journey—cracked cheese, breads, and thin strips of dried meat, billowing bearskin cloaks, leather bladders for water, rope, iron cups and a cook pot for Fainen. No expense was spared.

Fainen kept on in calm silence. He carried Hayles' bow strapped to his back, and the two broken halves of his quarterstaff tucked between the leather straps on his back near his quiver. He now kept *Braxis* as well, strapped among his supplies just as it had been when Hayles had carried it.

Redevir stopped them to consult his maps every few hours, and this day was no different. "There does not appear to be any way through the mountains that does not bring us close to Kor Kollar. We will have to go around."

"That could take weeks," Inrianne said.

"We must avoid Kor Kollar," Tanashri said. "That is where the Sur will be."

"And the knights of Bolan," Fainen said.

"A nice thought," Redevir said. "But I do not see any other viable points of entry to the Kol Plateau." He pointed at Aren. "We will not make it trying to blaze our own trail over those mountains. The Hennel Koth have eaten men alive who have tried."

"Durnan's Pass," Aren said. "We could look for Durnan's Pass."

Redevir stared blankly at him.

"Durnan wrote in one of the Histories of a cleft in the rock connecting to a narrow pass that leads to the plateau," Aren said. "He wrote that it was hidden by folds in the rock, but that it could accommodate horsemen. The legend says Forlon rode through it with his rangers to escape Lostrith's Sur warriors."

"So your information is based on an ancient story?" Inrianne asked. "One that is probably fabricated in its entirety? It's absurd. You can't be serious."

"Durnan swore up and down several pages that the passage was real. Many people claim to have found it."

"Who cares what your dead storytellers have to say?" Inrianne snapped. "Your tales are worthless in the present. You are a fool to cling to them."

Eriana sneered at her. "You yourself are worthless, Inrianne."

"Careful, pretty princess. You wouldn't want to trip over your skirts."

Inrianne took a step toward her, prompting Eriana to lay one hand on the golden hilt of her curved Andristi blade. "Come near either of us and you will lose a hand," she said. "I promise this."

"Enough!" Tanashri said. "You will both behave, whether of your own accord, or of mine."

Both women turned away from each other, muttering under their breaths. Eriana brushed against Aren and rested her head gently on his shoulder.

"If that's our only chance, then it's better than no chance at all," Redevir said. "We have with us a Sarenwalker. They can follow the wind. A hidden pass must be easier than the wind."

"I can find anything if it exists," Fainen said, while somehow still not sounding like he was bragging.

"Excellent," Redevir said. "Let's get on with it. The stone is waiting."

Aren stared at the high ridges of solid rock that separated them from the Kol Plateau. The white-powdered peaks of the Hennel Koth loomed above like the megalithic ruins of some long dead race of titans. *We have to find the pass. We will never make it over those mountains.*

Fainen took the lead, searching every cleft in the rocks for Durnan's fabled passage. An hour went by. Then another. Just as Redevir was starting to give up on finding it, Fainen spoke. "I see it. The pass. It is there."

"Where? Where?" Redevir swiveled his head all around.

"There," Fainen said, pointing at a flat wall of stone. Fainen moved directly up to it, and prodded his mount directly toward the wall. He looked like he was going to hit solid rock. Then he disappeared.

Eriana gasped. Redevir looked back and forth as if someone was playing a trick on him.

"It's only an illusion," Fainen said. "The stone gives the appearance that it is joined together. Come at an angle, and you will see the way through."

Redevir clapped his hands together and laughed. He smiled at Aren. "Destiny strikes again. You believe yet?"

Aren shook his head no. But he wasn't sure anymore. He had been on twenty-seven traces before this one. And each of them had proved that life was never this perfect.

Inrianne stomped her foot and sneered, but Aren could see relief behind her eyes. He knew she was not looking forward to trying to hike a mountain either.

Redevir stopped them there for supper in a small clearing beside a grove of willows just to the east of the pass to give Fainen extra time to set a dozen traps for small game. There was a large felled tree perfect for sitting. Redevir set a fire before it.

Aren stretched his legs. He pulled out his Jecker monocle.

Eriana sat beside him. She held her map of the world open in her hands, but she folded it again when she saw the concern on his face. "What's the matter, Aren?"

You are not holding me in your arms. That is all I want. "Nothing. Just tired. I'm not used to this."

"Me neither. Redevir seems to be, and Fainen, but not me."

"You are still always smiling."

"I didn't mean I wasn't enjoying myself."

"What do you want?" He did not intend for it to come out as mean as it did.

She shrank from him for an instant. She looked at him coolly. "You have been acting strange. I was worried."

"You need to worry about yourself. I'll be fine."

"Will you?"

Her voice soothed him. It always did. He looked her in the eyes. They were clear crystals of reflection. He wanted to reach out to her. He was aching to touch her. He wanted to feel her in his arms so much that it made his eyes water. His heart was in his throat, and his insides felt empty and barren. But he couldn't. He couldn't stop the pain long enough to do it. He did not want to have her in his arms while thoughts of death danced in his head. "I will. I just think about Hayles a lot."

"Hayles was a good man," she said.

"He was," Aren agreed. "I wish he was still here."

"Everyone does. He made me feel safe. Fainen does too, but Hayles was like a leader."

That made Aren feel worse for some reason that he could not understand. He wished he could slip away for some malagayne. He thought perhaps if he was riding on a wave of smoke he could float right into her arms, like he always had when Merani was in his bed. But he did not want her to know about it. He did not want her to see the truth of it, the truth of his weakness, of how much the proximity of death frightened him, how the phantoms of all those lost friends crippled him. He wanted to be the perfect person her eyes always seemed to reflect him as, a person her smile deserved. Not the sorry shape of what he actually was.

"Did I say something wrong?" She frowned.

"No." *It is me. I am wrong. Everything you do is right. Always.*

"You were thinking about what Redevir said, weren't you?"

"It's hard not to. He's right. It's like Kinraigan's people can find us no matter where we are. I don't know who to trust anymore. The two people I thought I could trust more than anyone in the world turned out to be liars."

"The Lord Protector of Amagon?"

"And Sarker, my mentor. It turned out he was lying to me from the day we first met."

"Do you trust Redevir?"

"Yes. I...I'm not sure. I'm not sure of anything anymore."

"Why do you follow him?"

"More like he and I happen to both be going the same direction."

"How sure are you Redevir didn't give up the Dagger to convince you to help him get the Crown?"

Aren thought about it. "I do trust him in one way. I trust him to be what he is. And he is the man who would literally tie me up and drag me kicking and screaming to the Kol Plateau rather than let another person even touch the Dagger."

"You know what he is. What are *you*?"

"I am the one who is going to stop Kinraigan. He is the most dangerous rogue user in the world. And the only thing I am meant to do is hunt *that*. Redevir offers the path to stop him. Everything in my life is pulling me forward. Nothing is holding me back. I have no home to run to. A part of me feels free in the world, but another part feels like I am locked out of my old life."

"I think about Laman that way, too," Eriana assured him, wiping a strand of golden hair from her eyes. "I can't be where they want to put me. I can't ever go back. But every day I remember things about it that I never thought I would miss. It's hard to lose the home you love, even if you choose to leave it. But we can only be where we are now."

"Only always ever now," he said.

"Only always ever now, Aren."

He stopped, turned the monocle over and held it up. "They say the man who invented this monocle had seen so much magick that his eyes burned with it. And he wanted to see it so badly that he had to keep looking after it faded. But the hidden story was that his wife was the one who thought of the lenses. She was a scholar who read legends of people who could see magick with their own eyes and it led her to a discovery that changed the world. It was his obsession, but her mind that made it real."

She turned her chin up and gave an adorable little corner smile. "A woman is secretly responsible for every great man."

He smiled. "I can't argue with you there."

"And you shouldn't argue with me even if you could. I will not be the secret behind you. You will be beside me, or *behind* me."

I want to be anywhere with you. To pull you close and hold you tight. I would praise every god if I could. "I would never try to hide you."

"Good," she said.

He started to speak, stopped, chewed his lip. His thoughts turned serious and sour. They always did when the malagayne waned.

"What is it?"

He shook his head and looked at the ground. "The girl."

"Girl?"

"In Cair Tiril. The one who sat in the corner of that empty room."

She nodded. "Liriella."

"You remember her name," Aren said. "I couldn't remember her name."

"She was very young. Solathas said he would take care of her."

"He did?" Aren felt a small relief at that. But the memory soured any hope of a smile. "Good to know he wasn't just humoring me. She is what I think about whenever I doubt what we are doing."

"You doubt what we are doing?"

"All the time," he said. "Whenever I think of running away, hiding, turning back, letting it go, I think about that. The first trace I ever completed, the first *real* one. After all the petty thieves and trespassers, the first *real* criminal I captured did the same. He hurt girls, children. Syman Verma was his name. I sent him to the fires. That was what opened my eyes to what people could do. That was when I knew I wanted to hunt them for the rest of my life."

"And you have hunted them ever since."

"Liriella reminded me of that first one. It stays with me."

"You hid it well at the time," she said.

"Whenever I wonder whether we should even try to do what we are doing, whenever it feels impossible, I think of that. Whenever I question whether

Kinraigan is the villain of my story, or if we are the villains of his story, I remember her and I know. I *know*."

"Redevir says you are here because you want the Sephors as bad as he does."

"Redevir thinks he knows everything."

"Funny. He says the same thing about you."

Aren moved slowly to speak, stopped, closed his mouth.

"Let's talk about something else," she said, turning away, patting her hands on her knees. "Tell me a story."

Aren blinked. "A story? I'm not very good at that kind of thing."

"Tell me the one about Devron and the Seven Saints."

"There's not much to tell. Emperor Devron thought he could do whatever he wanted with the magick. He was wrong. He tried to use more magick than his body could contain and it killed him. It almost destroyed the whole Arradian Empire."

"Except that the Seven Saints saved it," Eriana said.

"Yes. The greatest assemblage of Patriarchs the empire ever boasted. They entered Shaezrod Spur, the tower in Arthenorad. It is their most sacred place. There are always seven Patriarchs presiding over it. Devron wanted them to use their power on him, but the Patriarchs refused him. That is why he went north. To get away from them. That is why he used *autoentropic resonance*."

"What is...?" She tried to say the word, but it failed on her lips.

"It's a way that a user can amplify their own renders, but it's insane and absurdly dangerous. No one who has ever tried it has lived very long. It destroyed Devron. It sent out shockwaves that killed millions. The Seven Saints in Shaezrod Spur used their power to save the empire from destruction. That's why they call the tower *Sanctuary*. It saved everyone from Devron's Folly."

"What is that though? What exactly did Devron *do*?"

"Most scholars believe that he discovered the technique in some ancient text in the restricted archive of their great library. He learned that he could, well, he thought he could, make himself more powerful by feeding his own energy back into himself. He started to believe that he was a living god. He ignored the warnings of the Patriarchs. The Histories say he went to a hidden place north of Arthenorad, some long lost underground temple or tomb he discovered and repurposed. They always call it Devron's Altar. That is where he went to do what he did."

"What went wrong?" she asked.

"Devron wanted Arradan to be grand and glorious, safe and comfortable for all. Sounds like a decent enough person to have as an emperor. He spoke often of his desire to preserve the righteous, and save the world from what he considered its enemies. But no one can really agree on what he meant by *enemies*. Was it just invaders and criminals? Or was it the poor and the dirty and the foreigners? It is really difficult to say. Sometimes the Histories are rich with information, and sometimes they have a lot of holes."

"So what was auto...autoentering...what was it?"

"Autoentropic resonance. Do *not* feel bad about not knowing how to say it. Most of the people who *taught* me to do what I do didn't know how to say it either. Basically, Devron was binding his streams like any other user, rendering his altered reality into the world to change things. But while doing this, he was *also* using magick on *himself*."

"On himself? What for? That is the part I don't understand."

"Every user needs to tap into their own energy to perform their acts. It is incredibly strenuous on a person's body to use the magick. That is why even the most powerful and experienced users cannot sustain renders forever. Every user has their core limit, a cutoff point where their energy is used up, requiring rest and food to replenish. You either have to stop or you could hurt yourself. You could die. Just like a runner or a laborer. Do too much of what you do and you will eventually collapse. And also, just like anyone else doing any normal task, there is a maximum amount of power a user can put into each render. Like your sword. You can lift your sword hundreds of times without a break, swing it around, attack with it, defend with it. But if you tried to pick up that fifty-foot tree trunk over there, you would not be able to even budge it."

"So you mean he found a way to make himself stronger than he was?"

"He did," Aren said.

"That does not make sense at all."

"I didn't get it either. Not for a long time. I will try to keep it simple. Every user *resonates* when they bind streams together. It's a byproduct of the nature of the streams. That is where residual afterglow comes from. The user will begin to oscillate at a certain sub-aural frequency, which causes nearby particles in the air to glow with colors as they pick up altered reality. A normal resonance frequency is dictated by how strong the specific user is. Devron did something unique. He *knew* about the oscillation. Hardly any users know about how their own magick works because even they can't see that part of it. But he had access to the rarest prized texts about magick. He knew about it. And he realized he could affect his own oscillation frequency. He used his own magick *on himself* to artificially increase his oscillation frequency, making his strength increase. He used altered reality to increase his ability to use altered reality. He fed it back into himself over and over. He drew up his own power until it resonated at unbelievable levels. His aural glow would have been outside of any spectrum."

"So he was simultaneously directing the magick at the world and *at himself?*"

"And then he took the extra energy he created in himself and fed it back into himself, increasing his oscillation to draw up more energy to feed back into his own renders again. Theorists call it *zero-point-energy*, because it is something that seems to come from nothing."

"So what *happened* to him? I mean, I know *what happened*. But how did it come to pass?"

"Devron made himself more powerful than he ever imagined," Aren said. "But then he lost control."

"How?"

"He fell into the Slipstream."

"What? Isn't that just a nonsense word for the source where magick comes from?"

"They say he caused a breach in reality. A hole into the Slipstream, the place where all streams come from. You're right. That place, if it can even be considered a place, is what user's reach into to find the streams they intend to bind together. Many have written about it—a bright light that seems to be everywhere at once. No one knows what it signifies, and it is still debated as to what the Slipstream really is. Some think it is the path to everwonder, to heaven or hell, to the underworld, or to a place of gods and heroes. Some think that it is the state of energy from which all things come and all things return, and others that it is the achievement of enlightenment, and still others believe it is another world folded into our own, all around us but invisible. Pick a religion and it will have its own distinct version of what it means."

"I have never heard of this," she said. "I had many friends who study with Solathas, who could bind streams. None have ever mentioned it."

"From what I know, it seems very difficult to actually see it. All users can feel it, in a manner of speaking. They know it's there. They can feel when others are touching it, pulling streams from it. Like ripples in a pond. But only extremely strong users, performing unfathomable numbers of tasks, and handling unthinkable numbers of streams have ever claimed to *see* the Slipstream in this way. Those and the people around them. And if it is real, Devron would *definitely* have been handling the quantity of magick to be able to see it once he increased his resonance. But being in the light can cause trouble."

"What kind of trouble?"

"Rendering is a method of altering reality," Aren said. "The Slipstream is just raw possibility, infinite chaotic fragments. It can confuse a user, at least that is what is written in the Histories by those users who claim to have seen it. If they are there long enough they will begin to believe that all of those unrealities they are experiencing are reflections of actual reality. Like when you dream, some things seem the same as they are during waking, but can become strange, like when you dream of your childhood home, but there are rooms there that you never saw before, or people there who shouldn't be. You're so lost in the dream that you can't be sure if that's the way it's supposed to be or not. You can't be certain what is real. That's how it is with the Slipstream. Devron fell into a loop. As he was changing reality, his own *perception* of reality was altered. He then tried to change this *new reality* he perceived. But when he applied change to it, it was applied to nothing because the altered perception was a figment of his imagination. It did not truly exist, but he kept trying to apply energy to it, until he reached a point where his power was dispersing uncontrolled from his body. The more energy he put into changing something that never really existed anyway, the further his perception changed, until he was constantly funneling energy into nothing, growing stronger and stronger, releasing more and more energy."

"I have read that he destroyed Arradan," she said. "Caused disasters beyond measure."

Aren nodded. "He kept going until he reached what later came to be called the *final value*–when the amount of energy passing through the body catches up to the artificial strength which that energy has built into that body. After that, the body will no longer accept amplified energy buildup."

"What happens then?"

"The body is destroyed."

Eriana scrunched her lips. "So he killed himself."

"And millions of others along with him," Aren said. "Maybe more. They say people died as far away as Amagon. It must have been horrible to go through that."

"I read once that Devron was an angry person. That he hated his people."

Aren smiled. "You were reading Jordanus, weren't you?"

"How did you know?"

"Jordanus wrote a comprehensive History. The most inclusive of all. But he used old Arradian sources, written in Old Ardis. Jordanus couldn't translate Old Ardis if his life depended on it. He mistranslated the word *sorrowful* for *angry*. He should have said that Devron was a sad person. If you look at the other Histories, you will find all of his mistakes. He once wrote that the Empress Mellisandra made love to horses."

Eriana burst into a fit of giggles. "I never read that part. Is that real?"

"It's real," Aren said. "His source was describing her love of *riding* horses. But in Old Ardis there are three different words for horsemanship, and one of the words meaning *to ride* can also be used as slang for sex in a different context. Jordanus was terrible with colloquial issues. He came across texts using the slang, and he assumed that it was the common usage. He translated it wrong every time after that."

She looked away, tapping her chin. "How certain are you that he wasn't right about riding, and all the others mistook the meaning of the slang word for stud to mean horses instead of men?"

"I..." He definitely had no answer for that one. He smiled.

She shrugged playfully and averted her eyes. "She may have had more fun than the Historians gave her credit for."

"You are too clever."

"Coming from you that means a great deal. You are the most clever man I have ever met. Except for Solathas."

"Jordanus spoke fluent Coralic, and passable Vardan, the other two languages of Arradan, but Old Ardis baffled him. He argued for years that Emperor Regamun II was in a romance with a woman, when every other historian agrees that his true love was a well known male consort. Jordanus could not handle the tenses. Old Ardis uses the same word for *he, she,* and *they. Zha.* And the gender modifier is applied to the action word to let you know which *zha* it means. One entire History has been written by someone else to *decode* the History of Jordanus."

"It must be illuminating."

"He had problems with possessives, thinking that actual objects like swords and scepters were metaphors for more...provocative things. His entire chapter on the Arradians' obsession with sex was based on his own mistranslation."

"I hear they are obsessed with it anyway." She smiled, and he forgot everything he was about to say, thoughts vanishing under waves of desire.

"Well..." Aren shrugged uncomfortably.

Eriana put a hand to her lips to stifle the laughter. "It reminds me of the word riddles Solathas used to play with me. One of them was based on translating words from other languages. He used it to help teach me to speak other tongues. He would love to hear about all this."

He smiled and looked away. It was so easy to talk with her. It was so easy to get lost in stories of the past. So easy to ignore the present, not to mention the future. Her laughter lifted him up, moved him, kept his limbs going when he was sure they would give out.

That was the moment when he realized he was never going to be able to let her go. And that wherever she chose to go, he would be by her side.

If only he had taken some malagayne before he sat down here with her, he thought he might have been able to reach out and slide his arms around her, put his mouth to hers and kiss her unashamed in front of everyone. He would have. If only...

That was the moment Aren heard the sound.

A swooshing sound, high above. He looked up. He saw something in the sky hovering just over the treetops.

What in all hells?

He flipped his Jecker monocle free and looked at it. It was a woman. In the sky. He saw afterglow shedding from her bubble shield. She kept coming, floating less than ten feet above the ground. She wore blue on black and had a pair of gloves tucked into her belt. Her eyes smoldered, squinting rage.

Fainen drew his Saren-sword and charged, but he struck a flat invisible barrier, and rolled back onto the ground, his sword dropping. He reached around himself, but he was trapped in an invisible cylindrical cage, unable to move.

Aren jumped in front of Eriana.

She casually reached an arm around him and gently pushed him back behind her, holding her blade at ready to protect him.

But the user did the same thing to her. Locked her within a cylinder, cut her off from him. She could do nothing.

Shaot!

Aren pounded on the cylinder, staring horrified at her trapped within. She pushed against it and tried her sword on it, but it was too strong. Blank spheres began to pepper the ground around him, narrowly missing.

Eriana's eyes went wide. "Go hide!" she shouted. "Don't just stand there waiting to be hit!"

He looked left and right for somewhere to take cover. *Users need line of sight. They have to have it. I need to hide.*

One of Redevir's knives plunked into the woman's shield. She turned and lit into him with blank impulses. The Rover ducked behind a shallow rise. Tiny spheres at high velocity tore up the earth all around him, forcing him to flatten himself behind a hillock.

Inrianne kicked herself upright, and she raised her hands to send a spout of flame, but before she could, an invisible cylinder wrapped about her, too. Her fire was trapped inside with her. Spiraling upwards and out through the open top, very nearly setting herself alight before it flamed out.

What the hell is happening? Who is this?

Aren dropped to his knees and crawled toward his tracer satchel. Blank impulses burst all around him.

But then Tanashri appeared. The Saderan raised her arms.

Thank every god.

Aren expected for a flurry of heavy blank spheres from her to wipe the user off the face of the earth.

But something happened which Aren had never seen before.

The floating user made a temporary hole in her bubble. She tossed a carry-bag high into the air. Aren saw it through the Jecker monocle. It was shedding afterglow. *There is a blank impulse inside.* It must have been trapping an outward expanding force, set to burst in every direction.

The render exploded, shredding the bag, bursting out its contents. It scattered into the air a hail of *jinglebells.*

What in the world?

But then he realized what it was. *This is a Distractor technique.*

The explosion flung a torrent of rattling ringing jinglebells through the air, pouring all around Tanashri. The sudden unexpected noise and unpredictable motion distracted the Saderan for a few brief seconds. But that was all that mattered. By the time Tanashri recovered, the woman completed one final render.

She wrapped another blank cylinder around Aren. He felt its circumference with his palms. It was open at the top. He could still hear, but he could not get out.

Tanashri had recovered from the bells. Aren could tell she was prepared to pummel the user into oblivion with her own blank impulses.

But before she could, the cylinder around Aren began to shrink.

"Tanashri!" He felt it getting smaller and smaller, closing in until he could touch both sides at the same time, and then he could only hold one arm outstretched at one time. And then only one arm bent at the elbow. "It's getting smaller! Tanashri! It's not going to stop!"

He tried to climb up the sides but the artificial shape did not generate any friction when he touched it, like a real physical object would. It was like trying to climb greased porcelain.

"He's right," the user said, opening a tiny gap in her sphere to allow her voice to carry.

Tanashri stared hard at the woman.

Aren looked to Redevir. The Rover nodded to him, but then held his hands up helplessly. *Tell me what to do,* he seemed ot say.

"You can destroy me," the woman said to Tanashri. "I know you can. I can feel the ripples in the Slipstream when you touch your streams. You are powerful and fully rested. I am weak, hungry, and used most of what I had to get myself here past your tracker."

"Then there is no point to continuing this conversation," Tanashri said, raising her arms to strike.

"There is one," the woman said. "The cylinder around your friend there is not going to stop shrinking. It is set to continue whether I die or not. And even though you could break through my shield and destroy me, it would take time. You can't do it in time to save him. And you can't turn your back on me or I will beat you."

Tanashri stood frozen.

"Or give up and submit and I will spare you," the woman said.

Shaot. Is she right? She must be. You have to be a certain kind of right just to make a Saderan listen to you. Aren squeezed his shoulders inward. The cylinder kept shrinking, the space kept tightening. It became hard to breath.

What do I do? It kept shrinking. *What do I do? Think. Think. Think.*

Concentrate.

I need to see.

He held the monocle up to his eyes.

He could see her cylinder. It twinkled translucently all around him. He tried to look past it. The air was awash with furious afterglow, it poured out of the air and rose and sailed on the breeze.

But through it all, beyond it, he could see *her*. A young woman in blue. She stood within a spherical bubble of a shield.

But then Aren noticed something.

Every seven seconds, the woman's shield seemed to wink out and then reappear. It lasted only a fraction of a second. But it was happening.

Looping! She is looping her shield. Goddamn user's shorthand.

Aren 's mind raced trying to think of a way to exploit it. But what the hell could he do? He was trapped in a cylinder, shrinking every second. Tanashri was too far away to hear anything he said clearly. He would never be able to tell her.

He turned to Redevir. "My satchel!" he screamed at the Rover. He gestured as wildly as he could at where it sat beside the fire. Redevir was close. If he was quick he could scramble out and get it.

He did.

The woman seemed to ignore him as long as he was not coming toward her. Redevir tried to throw the satchel up into the cylinder, to see if it would drop through the open top. It struck the side and plummeted.

Shaot!

The Rover tried again. Threw higher. Same result.

On the third try he overshot the cylinder altogether.

The woman stared down Tanashri. She treated Redevir as if he was a gnat. After all, he was only foolishly trying to get *into* a cylinder.

On the fifth try, it fell through. Aren squeezed his hands up over his head, but still only partially caught it. One corner jammed into his temple.

Aren felt the cylinder shrink further. He felt it pressing in on his shoulders. He couldn't breath. He was covered in sweat.

He flipped the latches and opened the satchel. Everything was askew inside. His hand swam around inside it, fishing for his vial of tinwood leaf resin. It seemed to take forever to find it. The cylinder kept shrinking.

He looked at Redevir. "Throw me a knife!"

"What?! You can't even catch a knife in there."

"A knife! Do it! Now!"

Redevir complied. He flipped one of his throwing knives out of his vest and tossed it up into the air. It dropped down on Aren. He held his tracer satchel over his head. The point of the blade slammed into it, sticking into the side.

Aren reached up and pulled it free. He held it tight with one hand, and with the other unstopped the tinwood leaf resin and dribbled some onto the blade. A tiny amount. *Strong stuff.* Undiluted in the bloodstream it could work in seconds. But he did not have time to guess the amount.

He could no longer move his arm at all. He could only flick it with his wrist.

I will only get one chance at this.

He flipped his wrist and the knife whirled through the air. The pommel clipped the upper rim of the cylinder, and spun itself around. It dropped down onto the rim, bounced, and then tipped just outside, plopping down in the dirt at Redevir's feet.

Aren just about shit himself in relief.

The Rover looked up. *What am I supposed to do with this?* he seemed to say.

"She has a break in the shield! You have to throw it. The timing has to be right. How fast can you throw?"

Redevir shrugged.

"Practice!" Aren said.

"Now?!"

"Yes! Now!"

Redevir drew another knife and threw it. It went through the air and plinked off of the woman's shield.

Aren counted from the loop resetting, watched it hit, and then counted until the next reset.

"Again!" Aren shouted. "Time it from when you hear my voice! Now!"

Redevir threw another. Same result.

Aren calculated the timing. "Again!"

Redevir sent one more. It bounced off.

The user could not have cared less. She ignored the knives with glee, watching him with a smile as he wasted futile energy trying to break her unbreakable shield, while Tanashri did nothing.

"Ready!" Aren shouted.

Redevir picked up the tinwood knife. He held it at ready, glancing at Aren nervously.

I have to feel the timing right. He focused everything on seeing the shield. It winked. Held a long time. Winked. Held. Winked. Held.

"Now!"

Redevir threw the knife without thinking.

The shield held as it flew through the air. Then it winked out. The knife passed through its boundary. It clipped the woman in the shoulder, piercing flesh and sticking out of her like a nail.

She looked at it in a panic. She shrieked. Then she passed out more or less instantaneously. She collapsed in a heap. Her sphere winked out completely.

Tanashri did not understand, but she did not ask questions, she merely accepted that the threat had been neutralized. She immediately turned to Aren. She rendered a flat plane on the ground underneath one edge of the cylinder. She bound streams of direction and force and velocity upward. The plane lifted, tilting the cylinder higher and higher, until Aren could slide his legs out the bottom, and then wriggle his body out after, his satchel falling on his head. The cylinder kept shrinking behind him until it became just a line in the air. The cylinders around Fainen and Eriana never shrank. They simply reached the end of their predetermined duration and blinked out of existence.

Shaot. She really was going to kill me.

He rolled onto his back and looked up at the sky trying to catch his breath. Eriana ran to him, throwing her arms around him, placing her hands all over him to make sure there were no wounds from the blank impulses. Aren was too in shock to feel any of it. It seemed to take millennia before he could breathe again. When he finally rolled over, he saw Redevir standing over the unconscious woman.

"Who the hell is this?" Redevir asked.

Aren just started laughing. "I have no idea."

39

A Conversation At Durnan's Pass

SHE OPENED HER EYES and knew right away she had been drugged.

Keluwen cursed silently. Her arms sagged and her head swam. She had never been groggy a day in her life after a normal sleep. When she woke, she was always alert immediately. Something must have been wrong.

She sat on her knees, her chest bent forward over a wood beam balanced on two large rocks. Her hands were bound behind her back. Tight. She strained, stretched, folded her thumbs, tried the butterfly wings that Sadraghar had taught her. But she could not loosen them enough to squeeze free. Whoever had tied her wrists knew what they were doing.

She saw her twin gloves on the ground in front of her and had a brief spasm of hope that she could render something to free her hands. But when she reached for her streams, her mind wandered right past them. She felt the door to the Slipstream, but when she tried to step through it, she went past it.

She scrunched her cheek and blew a lock of her hair out of her face. She shook her head, but that only brought her from dizzy to dizzier. She lifted her head. *I am in the clearing. Where I killed him. Where I killed Aren.* But had she killed him? She could not remember now. She had been so sure she had when her eyes first opened, so sure that it did not even seem revelatory. It was merely something that was, and the joy and relief had felt warm all through her. But now that she thought about it, she was not certain how that memory had come to her.

She looked up and saw a menagerie around a cook fire.

A man who was obviously a Rover had been lifted out of some cosmopolitan center and dropped in his fancy clothes into the wilderness. A man in a bright green cloak sat across a cook fire, simultaneously monitoring a pot of boiling stew, sharpening one half of a broken staff, and skinning a rabbit. He had distributed the workload to either half of his body, pairing foot with hand. And he did it all perfectly. She could not believe her eyes. *What the fuck are you?* She couldn't make up her mind if she wanted to kill him, or lay on her belly, chin in her hands, and watch him work for hours.

Between them sat a Sister who Keluwen mistook for a child at first. Her face never seemed to change. It looked like she was asleep when she wasn't.

And on either side of her, like the captains of two opposing crabatz teams, sat the mutual impossibility of two women with blond hair. One mellow like goldenrod and curly to adorable distraction, and the other wavy, full, and closer to silver than to gold.

Then she heard him. Her heart sank. He was alive. She would have accepted it if the others had caught her and would soon kill her, even torture her, as long as she had killed Aren first. She would have gone to her god in peace if Glasseye blood was drying on her hands.

But it wasn't. He was alive. She knew it was him even before she saw his face. He walked to the center of the camp. She saw his boots first. He set down a rectangular honey-leather satchel, and dropped the strap over it. He kicked something off his boot and then marched over to her. He squatted down directly in front of her. He reached out and took her chin between his fingers and lifted it.

She looked into his face. He had half grown a beard but it wasn't enough to hide that smug grin. Oh, how she wished her tongue was a knife, so that she could spit it into his eye.

"You are awake," he said. "Can you hear me? Are there any echoes to my voice?"

There weren't, but she wasn't going to give him the satisfaction of letting him know.

"I know you can hear me," he said. "Your eyes are very active. Good movement. Your hearing would be back well before that becomes possible."

She lifted her chin off his fingers and sneered at him.

"Playing dumb will not really benefit you in any way," he said.

"Fuck you," she said. She had meant it to come out stronger, but the wind had cooled and the breeze blew through her clothes like they were lace, making her voice waver as her whole body convulsed in shivers.

He widened his eyes a fraction, raised an eyebrow and smiled. "That's better."

"What did you do to me?"

"Do to you?"

"I feel strange." She shook her head. Her eyes glazed over, then cleared again.

"I dosed you. Tinwood leaf. Where else did you think your magick went?"

"I have been dosed before. Once. I could not remember my own name, let alone speak aloud. How am I talking to you if you dosed me?"

He gestured over his shoulder. "I tailored your dose to you. It only took hours of calculations and days of trying."

"You can do that?" She had never heard of that. She could feel the tinwood leaf in her blood, working on her complex thoughts, unspooling them until what began as a cohesive idea dissolved into a haze of fluid memories racing to drown each other.

"Yes. Any Render Tracer can. They just don't. Because they usually don't care. Because the person they are doing it to is usually set on fire within a day or two of doing it."

"I know what you do. People like you have been hunting me my whole life. I have seen the fires. I have smelled the smoke." *He is trying to scare me with that. As if he ever could.*

"Like I said, they usually don't care."

"And you do?"

"I care what you have to tell us. You're a rogue user. I hate rogue users. Trust me when I say I would not bother with it otherwise."

"I wouldn't trust one of you to piss downhill without getting your feet wet." She looked him up and down, appraising him, declaring him loathsome.

He laughed. "Fine by me. I am not trying to be your friend."

"I would rather have a bucket of shit for a friend."

"If you had that bucket you would be luckier than you are now. As of now, you don't have anything. Or anyone. Just us. Just me."

She bit her lip, and made her eyes into those of a doe. She thought she had a shot. "If it's just us, why don't you just loosen these bonds a little and we can play?"

"If you think I would fall for that, you are crazy." He smiled. "Besides, I don't even know your name."

"Come closer and I'll tell you." *I'll chew your ear off.*

"Not a chance. But I do. I want to know. What's your name?"

"Why don't you kill me?" she asked.

"You mean because you're a rogue user? Yes, we should kill you just for that. Or do you mean because you dropped out of the sky and tried to crush me? A lot of hands were raised in favor of killing you for that, too."

"A lot? You mean six?"

"It wasn't unanimous." He sat on a low, round rock in front of her, hands clasped, elbows resting on his knees.

"Who voted to keep me? The Rover? He probably just wants me to be nice and warm when you put my head in the dirt, ass in the sky."

The Glasseye shook his head. "We don't do that. He voted to kill you before you even hit the ground. So did she. And her. And her. And him." He pointed to each of his companions.

Keluwen squinted. "*You* kept me alive?"

"It took some convincing. Of some friends who are very invested in my well-being."

She narrowed her eyes. "It was no kindness. Stop pretending it was. I am alive right now because you think you can take some secrets out of me."

"That, too."

"If you think you are going to get any information out of me, then you are mistaken." *You could burn me an inch at a time and I would never let you have Orrinas.*

"I will," he said. "I will up your dose. There is a fine line, a sweet spot, where you can concentrate well enough for memory to work, but not well enough to lie. I will take you to that point, and I will learn what I want to know."

"Why haven't you?"

"Because it takes time, and it has a bad habit of turning the mind to sap. I would rather you simply told me what I want to know. For both our benefits."

"I am dead when I'm done. If I tell you anything you are never going to let me go." *He wouldn't really let me go, would he? Could she get back to Orrinas?*

"I'm the one trying to keep everyone from killing you. The more you can give me, the better chance I will have to make a case for you."

She smiled out of the corner of her mouth. "You're good. You're a piece of stinking shit, but you're good. You almost had me there. The vote. The savior role. I almost believed that."

"You seem to think I am something that I am not."

"I don't *think*," she said. "I know what you are."

"I am a Glasseye," he said.

"That is close enough to liar."

"You attacked us. Your victimhood is questionable." He drew a small cylindrical object from his case and began wiping it down with a cloth.

"It doesn't matter. I know what you are. You hunt people like me."

"I do."

"Don't act like you don't know what they do to people like me when you hand us over."

He shrugged. "I don't stay around for that part. But I know what it is."

"You are still one of them. The only difference is your master has changed."

"It has. It was someone else. Now it's just me." He held up the object in the light and inspected it for smudges. "Make this easy on yourself. Please."

"Everyone who knows me knows I never make it easy on myself." She shrugged her shoulders and turned away from him.

"I never hunted anyone like you," he said. He returned the object to his leather case. He took out another and began to wipe it down.

"I am a user. They are all like me."

He abruptly stopped fiddling with the device. "No, they are not." He looked up at her eyes, stared at her. "They are not even close."

"Everything you say to me is going to be a lie."

"You are a rogue user, aren't you?"

"You know I am."

"Then you must know that I hate what you are more than anything in this world."

"Not as much as I hate myself for it," she said bitterly.

He looked oddly at here. "What was that?"

She shook her head. "Fuck you."

"Been hunted before?"

"Nothing I can't handle."

"The way you handled us?" A smug smirk on his face.

She turned away from him. The failure stung more than the bonds cutting into her wrists did.

"I thought so," he said. "Rogue users always think someone else is to blame for what they do."

"I know what I have done. Do you know what you have done?"

"Just tell me where he is going."

She laughed. "What did I just say? I am never going to tell you where he is." *You could torture me for days and I will never give up Orrinas. Never.*

"How much does he know?"

"More than you ever will."

"Is he here? Is he in Bolan?"

"Sure. He is right around the corner."

Aren shook his head. "I don't think I would be standing here right now if he was."

"You are right about that. He would melt your skin off your bones for me."

He squinted his eyes, glanced away over her shoulder for a moment. "You honestly believe he cares about you, don't you?"

She turned her chin all the way up, wagging her jaw at him and smiling. "I know he does. He loves me more that you will ever feel in your weak little life."

"How does it feel to know you have been abandoned then?"

"Fuck you."

"If he is not here, that means he left you all alone. He is not coming to save you. You must realize that by now."

He is good at digging the nails in, isn't he? "I made this choice," she said. "He doesn't *send* me anywhere. I am not like you."

"What *are* you like?"

"I live free. I will die free. I know both of those things are true. And neither of them can be taken away from me." She looked down. "Even if you keep me in bonds. I am free in a way you will never be."

"You don't think I'm free?"

"I think *you think* you are free. But you aren't. You're his slave."

"His?" Aren asked. "I told you I don't work for him any more. He betrayed me."

"You are a fool, or a liar, probably both. I'm sure he can't stand that he couldn't turn me." She looked around at the pack of carnival clowns around her. "But it seems he is used to having to settle."

"Tell me where he is."

"No."

"Tell me what he knows."

"More than you will ever learn in your whole life."

"You are devoted to him."

"He is the greatest man who has ever lived. He is the master." She spat at his face, but it fell to the earth before it reached him. "And fuck you."

"Do you know what he does to women?" he asked.

He sets them free. That is why I love him. "You wouldn't know what to do with a woman if she sat on your face."

His eyes widened at that.

She smiled. "Oh, does that make you uncomfortable? Good."

"You like being able to make others uncomfortable, don't you?"

She turned her head down, glanced aside. "I am who I am."

He nodded to himself. "You like it. You like to offend people. It makes you feel powerful."

"So what if it does?"

"Is that how *he* makes you feel? Does he make you feel powerful?"

"He makes me feel things that would make a little boy like you drown in your own tears."

"You are going to tell me everything. One way or another."

"How do you figure?" she asked.

"You are a user. Like all users, you rely on your magick to get what you want. I have taken that away from you. I could just hold you like this for a few days. When was the last time you went a week without using? Years, right? A decade? Users can't stop using. It feels too good."

"What do you know about what it's like?"

His eyes sharpened. "I know plenty about what it's like to need to do something every day. I know what it's like to go without it. And I know that it is hurting you and you can't stand it."

She bared her teeth at him. "I hate you."

"I figured as much when you tried to kill me."

"Don't act so surprised. I have been killing a lot of his drones. You don't need to feel special."

"I am not one of his drones," he said, doing a passable job of appearing disgusted.

"None of you think you are. You each think you are his right hand man. Well, I hate to break it to you, but he doesn't have a hundred hands."

"I mean I do not serve him. He sent me to die, but I didn't."

Keluwen laughed. "He talked to you. In Westgate. Are you surprised I know that? Why would a luminous immortal talk to you if you weren't his servant?"

"He wasn't in Westgate. He never left Vithos. Wait, do you mean Kinraigan? What in all hells is a luminous immortal?"

"He talked to you. Our people saw you."

"Your people, eh? So you *are* part of a group."

"Shit. You fucking shitsack."

"Kinraigan *did* talk to me in Westgate," Aren said. "That was the first time I ever saw him. I didn't realize who he was. I thought he was a madman. When was the first time you talked to him?"

That very same night. His mouth inches from mine. His hands on me. His mind inside me. "He can turn people in *one* conversation." *He very nearly turned me.*

"He must have been off his game that day," Aren said.

Not far enough off. "You talked to him again in Cair Tiril. And it wasn't other people who saw that time. It was me."

"You were spying on me in Cair Tiril?"

"I saw you talk to him."

"Did that make you jealous? Which hurt worse. Him talking to me instead of you? Or seeing me walk away without selling my soul to him?

"I saw you with him! I saw you with my own eyes!"

"You saw me turn him down. That is what you saw."

"You twisted fucking liar. No one can turn him down."

"I know one person who can and did."

"How did you kill Bonsinar?" she asked. "How did you know he was with us?"

"Who is Bonsinar?"

Fuck you. You don't get to not know his name. You don't get to walk away from murder like that. She pursed her lips. "You killed the elder."

"The crazy old man in Westgate? How did you know about him? He is dead, too?"

"By your hand."

"I had nothing to do with that. He just told me riddles and then we left."

"You killed Raviel."

"I didn't have anything to...oh, wait. Yes. I did have something to do with that. That one was a mistake. Me people, the other Amagon-men, were given false evidence."

"So you admit it."

"I do. It is the truth. I was involved."

"Well he was my kind. Bonsinar was my kind. Joli was my kind. Even that stinking elder was my kind. And you were there with each of them on the day they all died."

He paused. He looked away at the trees for a long time. She thought she could see wheels turning inside his head.

"Maybe you were right, Redevir," Aren said. "Maybe this was pointless."

"I warned you," the Rover said. "She is going to be a problem, Aren."

"We are not killing her," Aren said. "For the last time, we do not even know who she is."

"Is it not obvious?" the Rover asked. "Let us take a little stroll down recent history. Who tried to kill us in Medion? And Westgate? And I have my suspicions about Synsirok."

"Kinraigan," Aren said.

"Yes. Everyone's favorite sorcerer. How could any of us, at this point, think she works for anyone *but* Kinraigan."

She squinted her eyes. "You...weren't kidding about the argument. The vote."

"Cease your little innocent girl gambit," the Rover said. "We have gone through too much for more of that act. If I had my way, the vultures would be picking your bones right now."

"You said the same thing about Tanashri, Redevir," Aren said. "Aren't you glad I stopped you?"

The Rover glanced at the Sister. "Most of the time." He turned to Aren. "You think you can turn her away from him?"

Keluwen turned her chin up. "No one can turn me from him. You are fools to try." *I will be with Orrinas until never meets forever.*

Aren tilted his head to one side. "You love him, don't you?"

She bit her lip. Stop giving things away, you fool. Do better. "I will never tell you anything about him."

Aren narrowed his eyes at her.

He is thinking something over. What is he going to do?

"What color are his eyes?" Aren asked.

Keluwen's mouth fell open in confusion. She snapped it closed as soon as she realized. "I'll never tell you that. What kind of question is that anyway?"

He smiled, nodding his head. "Now I think I understand."

"Understand what?"

"Testing a theory. Tell me your name."

"No." She looked up at him. "Understand *what?*"

"Tell me your name."

"What would you care what my name is?"

"Tell me your name."

"It won't do you any good," she said.

"Tell me anyway."

"My name leads nowhere." Her name wasn't written down anywhere in the world. The only record of her existence was her name scrawled in the thief-catchers' punishment records.

He leaned in close to her, crouching, hands on his knees, his nose so close to hers. She could see the little veins in his eyes. She could taste his breath. His questions came at her fast, like fists in a brawl.

"Tell me your name," he said.

"No."

"Where do you come from?"

"Nowhere."

"Who are your people?"

"Shadows."

"What is your name?"

"No one."

"Who sent you?"

"No one."

"Where were you born?"

"In a shed behind a brothel." Her eyes widened, and she choked. *Why did I say that? How did that happen?* She had wanted to defiantly show him she came from nothing. But even that was information. But it felt good. It felt oh so good to say it proudly to someone.

"Tell me your name."

"No."

"What is your name?"

"Nothing."

"Who are your friends?"

"Fuck you."

"Where do you come from?"

"Nowhere."

"What is your mother's name?"

She coughed. Her answer caught in her throat. Her eyes glanced left and right. "What?"

"What is your name?"

"Nothing." She put her eyes into a trance, looking past him. looking through him. *I will get through this.* His voice was nothing but a foul wind. But even as she told herself that, it felt less like the wind and more like a hammer.

"What is your name?"

"Nothing."

"Where were you born?"

"Nowhere."

"What is your name?"

"Nothing!"

"Why do you hate your mother?"

She felt the question like a stab in the heart. Her eyes snapped up to his, no matter how hard she tried to keep them from doing it. "I don't."

"Where were you born?"

"Nowhere!"

"What is your name?"

"Nothing!"

"What is your name?"

"Nothing!"

"Why do you hate her?"

"I don't."

"Why do you hate her?"

"I don't!"

"Why do you hate your mother?"

"I don't! Fuck you! She was the greatest thing in the world, and I hate you."

"Your mother."

"I hate you."

"Your mother."

"I hate you!"

"What did you do?"

"I hate you." Her eyes glowered. "I hate you! I hate you! I hate you!"

"What is her name?"

"I hate you!"

"What is her name?"

"I hate you!"

"What is *your* name?"

"Keluwen!" she screamed. "My name is Keluwen! And if you don't stop talking about her, I'll kill you! I'll carve you apart and burn the bones! I will fucking destroy you!"

"Keluwen," he said. His voice was suddenly so calm, serene.

Keluwen felt her rage strangling her, but it suddenly felt so out of place. The only sound was her breaths, heaving, shaking, shivering. Her eyes watered, her nose dripped. Her cheeks ached.

Across a little cookfire, the man in the green cloak was patiently sharpening his sword. A rabbit was roasting. The Sister and one of the other women looked at her and whispered to each other. The curly blond girl stared knives at her from across the fire, arms folded.

Keluwen's heart was racing. She felt sweat everywhere, every breeze turning it to ice.

"Keluwen, Keluwen, Keluwen," Aren said. "Thank you, Keluwen." He looked at her and smiled. He actually smiled.

You little shitsack. Digging one little word out of her. And he dared to feel satisfied. Proud. She wanted to rip his eyes out and cut a hole through his heart.

The one in the green cloak came up to him and whispered in his ear. He nodded. "It looks like your little display with the bells drew more eyes than we thought. Some Bolanese outriders are crossing the valley. We are going to have to stop early to move."

"What does that mean?"

He dripped dark liquids from vials in the satchel into a little metal cup. "I'm sorry to have to do this to you again."

"No, you're not."

"You're right." He nodded. Smug did not begin to describe that smile. He forced a cup of bitter warm liquid down her throat.

"Is that more tinwood leaf?"

"No," he said. "This is sagewart."

"That is a sleeping agent."

"A sedative. To keep you quiet in the pass."

"I am going to fucking kill you."

"Better luck next time," Aren said.

The Rover and the other lifted her and set her on the back of a horse. The Rover looped a rope into a noose about her neck, pulled it taught, and then wrapped her ankles together.

Keluwen traveled Durnan's hidden passage draped belly down over the back of a horse, dung in her nose, and flies in her hair.

She fought sleep, fought the sagewart. She fought it for hours, maybe a day, refusing to close her eyes all the way. At least until they were through the pass and out onto the Kol Plateau.

But the sagewart won. And as her eyes closed for that final time, she pressed one thought into the clay of her mind, so hard it would leave a mark no matter how soft the drugs made her mind.

They will slip up. No one can be vigilant every second. They will make a mistake. Give me luck, Belleron. Strength and speed did not do for me. Give me luck instead.

40

Whispers In The Dark

WHEN THE NIGHT WAS at its darkest, it was as if the whole world had died, its people asleep in dream, its creatures slinking in quiet shadow as they searched for prey, leaving those who were awake frozen outside of time, drifting like ghosts.

Aren had never felt that more fully than he did now.

When midnight comes, we are each alone, every one of us living in our own midnight.

The midnight darkness had a power all its own.

Aren lay awake in the dark of *his* midnight, his head sunken into his rolled up cloak, his body cocooned within his sleeping sack, wearing hose, trousers, three shirts, and a tunic over them. The cold ate through it all. It gnawed at his skin. It slashed at his lips. It burned his nose like fire. He closed his eyes against it, but he could not sleep.

Eriana slept beside him, as soundly as if she was in the silken sheets of a palace. Her body was curled up next to him, her back gently leaning against his leg through her own sleeping sack. He watched the final tongues of flame shivering out of the dying cookfire. The flickers shimmered through her hair, turning her curls to all the colors of the autumn leaves.

He wished he could reach out and touch her, to pull her close. But he could not. His breath misted. His hands were cold slate, his fingers icicles. The slightest touch would have woken her with a shout, setting everyone else to alarm. If he pressed his lips to the back of her neck it would have been like pouring an ice flow down her shirt.

So he spent another night without knowing the feel of her skin on his. Another night alone right beside her.

Another night in Durnan's Pass.

His gaze wandered over the embers to the shrouded shape across the clearing.

Keluwen had been trussed up again by Fainen, her arms behind her back, wrists and ankles tied together, forced to sleep on her knees, slumped to one side against a boulder.

Tanashri had draped two cloaks over her. Aren wondered why. He mused if it might not be better if she quietly froze to death, allowing nature to end the uncomfortable question of what to do with her.

A part of him wanted her dead. Not the cold analytical part of him; the part that was hot with the fires of old rage, a furnace of pain that awoke whenever he crossed paths with a rogue user. That part of him wanted to slither out of his sleeping sack and crawl like a salamander across the cold dirt, and slowly, intentionally strangle her.

That part of him contained old memories, beautiful memories that were kept apart from him by a sheen of glass, an impenetrable boundary made from years of tears since the day that separated his life now from what his life had been when he was a child, since that one moment that he never spoke aloud.

It was his cold, uncaring mind that kept her alive. It insisted on performing calculations and comparing probabilities and refused to accept the surface appearance that she was an enemy. The last time he had surrendered to the heat of the moment, he had helped kill Raviel, the one man who would have been his true ally in all that came after. He would not make that mistake again.

If at the end of all this she had to die, then his cold mind would unleash the fire on her.

He saw her head shift. She groaned and sneezed, then cursed under her breath.

Aren sat up and scooted himself inch by inch out of the sleeping sack. He stepped around Eriana, and tiptoed toward the woman who had tried to kill him. He sat down beside her.

"I know you're there, Glasseye," Keluwen said. "I recognize your clumsy steps."

Aren froze for a moment, startled. But his surprise eased into a smirk. "You have very good ears."

"You have very loud feet."

"You have a lot of opinions for someone who is tied up."

"Are you going feed me sedatives again?" she asked.

"Not yet."

"Aren't you afraid I'll cry out?"

"Are you going to?"

"Would it do me any good?"

He glanced up at the walls of rock on either side, the walls of Durnan's Pass. "No. You could scream all night long and the most you will do is make whoever is listening at the other end of the pass believe in ghosts." He pulled back the hood until it was halfway up her forehead. A swath of her hair swayed down over her eyes. He reached out one finger and slid it aside, tucking it behind her ear.

She looked at him a long time, like she was trying to locate a secret spot on his body that could kill him if only she could find it. "Why are you here?"

He shook his head. "I don't know."

"Have you changed your mind and come to set me aflame yourself?"

"No," he said. "I don't know why I came over here."

Her jaw was sharp and square, defiant. Her eyes were obsidian lakes beneath the thin strip of starlight. "So you still lack the courage to kill me then. Your master will not be pleased." Her eyes settled on him like cold snakes spraying venom onto his face.

"You still think I am his."

The corner of her lip curled. She scoffed at him. "You are too stupid to understand how obvious it is."

He chewed his lip. "You should sleep if you can. Sagewart doesn't allow for deep sleep. Best get what you can now. I will have to dose you again by dawn. Redevir wants you quiet when we emerge onto the Kol Plateau."

"So I don't call down the Bolanese on you."

"Something like that."

"They would kill me if they knew what I was," she said. "But I would call them in a heartbeat if there was a chance they might hurt you."

"You must hate me a lot."

"Is that a question?" she snapped.

"You hate what I am."

"Are you surprised? Do you not know what you are? Do you not know what that little badge you wear actually means?"

His fingers wandered to his Render Tracer badge, the circle with the five prongs evenly spaced on one upper quadrant, like half a row of eyelashes. "It means I hunt the untouchable. It means I break gods."

She snickered angrily. "No wonder you follow him. You are a fool. Who cares what it means to *you?*"

He leaned back. "Why would I care what it means to *you?*"

"You should. You should care what it means to everyone else. To the men and women who live their whole lives hiding from you. To the children who shiver in fear every second of their lives, hoping a Glasseye isn't right around the corner. How many generations of people like me have been poisoned by fear because of the constant threat of people like you?"

Aren let his hands fall to his lap. "I never hunted children."

"You wear the badge. Even now. The ever-watchful eye. The all-seeing eye. The eye of death. That is what you do not understand. When you wear that badge, that is what everyone like me sees. Fear, pain, stress, endless sorrow, rage, burning children. And then you wonder why we hate you."

Aren looked up at the narrow strip of stars, penned by the high faces of silver rock to either side of the pass. *Is that really what I am? Is that my true face? Is that what the world sees?*

It couldn't be. She was trying to manipulate him, trying to trick him into giving away something. But it gnawed at him. All his life he hunted monsters. But he knew they were not the only ones. There were Render Tracers for petty thieves. He had heard there were some who hunted children.

But it was easy not to think about any of that when he was on the trail of someone like Degammon, or Lazal Dereus, or Syman Verma before that. He was catching monsters to save children. But at the other end of the spectrum the Glasseyes *were* the monsters, and they were catching *children* to save... something.

He thought of that moment, back before they entered the pass, when she appeared in the air. He remembered the mindless inferno of rage on her face.

"You have been quiet for longer than at any time since I first saw you," she observed. "Is it shocking for you to have thoughts of your own, you fucking scum?"

"I was thinking about that moment you attacked us."

"What of it?"

"Your gambit was going to fail."

"My gambit?"

"You knew the Sister was going to kill you no matter what happened."

"So?"

"You never planned on making it through that attack alive."

She turned her eyes from him. She looked like she wished she had something to look away at other than a wall of rock at midnight. "It would have been worth it."

"To kill me."

Her eyes snapped back to him and they stared, as if her gaze alone could grab him by the collar and shake him. "To *crush* you. As painfully as I could. I could have quick-killed you before you ever heard me coming. But I wanted you to suffer."

"I know. I know hate when I see it. It is the same way I feel in my heart when I find rogues like you."

"Like me."

"I hate rogues like you," he said matter-of-factly.

She smiled spitefully. "*You* are a rogue now. Do you hate yourself?"

That stopped Aren cold. She was right. He was. As soon as he was cut loose from his service to the Lord Protector of Amagon, he should have never picked up the tracer satchel again. It was a crime for him just to hold it. If he was not a member of the Render Tracer corps, he was little more than a thief, holding their stolen tools. "That is different." *It has to be.*

"It isn't. You Glasseyes spend so much time swallowing your own horseshit that you can make yourselves believe anything to justify what you do. Do you think this is the first time I have dealt with one of you? You Glasseyes are all alike. So smart you can't see past your own noses."

Was she right? He spent his whole life hating rogues. He had a reason. He had many reasons, but beneath them all was that *one reason*. Because it was the thing that took away his joy and left him all alone. The bitterness in her voice told him that she must have had one such thing in her own past. "You have been hunted before, haven't you?"

She averted her eyes. "Fuck you, Glasseye."

"People can't just have powers like that, carrying them around with them, the world unknowing. It can't happen. People can't live their lives worrying about what you might do next." *There. Remember what you do. You are good.*

"Is that how you consoled yourself when you burned children alive?"

"I never did that. I only trace. I don't burn."

She glanced at him, her eyes piercing him. "I have been hunted by men just like you, thinking they are just doing their job. Glasseyes are murderers. They just have someone else to light the fires for them."

"I never hunted children," he spat bitterly. "And I never would."

"It doesn't matter. You stood to be counted beside men who do. And you never questioned that. Your life before *him* was no better than the life you have now. You are just too blind to see it."

"Users can register. You can be documented. People like you don't have to live as rogues."

"They don't register people like me. Not in Amagon, not in Lenagon, not in Arradan. They don't let the poor through that door easily. Oh, they let us stand in line, but shiny coin always lets the rich cut ahead. So we never get any closer. Instead we go underground. We hide. We live our lives. We lie. We bend and scrape as hard as we can, and we survive. If we are lucky."

Aren thought to himself for a long time, thought of the pain in her voice that she tried so hard to hide beneath the anger. If he had his reason, then maybe so did she. He thought back to his interrogation. He remembered how she cracked and gave up her name on the *very first* of the common emotional pressures he had been taught to use when fishing for information—the mother. Many did on that one. Even he would have. But maybe there was something more to it than just a sore point with her. Maybe it *was* her reason.

He silently cursed himself. He felt like he was splitting in two. He felt... *sympathy* for her, he realized. He felt sympathy for a rogue user. It disgusted him. He should have felt the urge to vomit. Instead he felt the urge to explain himself to her, to reassure her, to find a way to make her forgive him. *But I don't care what she thinks. I don't. Do I?*

He rubbed his eyes and looked at the ground, littered with shards of rock. "I told you, I don't hunt your kind."

She turned to face him head on for the first time. She met his eyes with her own, unflinching, as an equal, the ropes holding her captive losing all meaning in that moment.

"Yes, you do," she said. "Because they are *all* my kind. From the little children stealing an ounce of bread to survive, to the robbers, to the Priests, to the Sisters, to the mass murderers. They are all me. I love them the way I love myself. And I hate them the way I hate myself. I feel like I am going mad every time I wake up. I want to protect people like me. I want to run and hide from people like me. I want to kill people like me. But at least they are all *like me*."

"That is just the same as it is to be anyone," he said. "You are right, I am a rogue now. I have lost myself. I'm still talking, still thinking, still moving, but I don't know where I'm going. I have a goal, but I don't know what it means, and I don't know what it will take to get there. All I know is that I have to do it. I have no other choice. It is the core of who I am. I can't turn away from it. It feels like destiny. It feels like it was meant to be. I think you feel the same way."

"You don't know anything about how I feel."

But he could see in the way her eyes turned away from him that he was right. She *did* have a *reason*, just as he did. And he knew it was so close to the same as his that it frightened him. *I see you. I see you in there.* He understood now. *I know how much pain you feel, and I know what causes it.*

"I think every time you wake up, you aren't sure whether you want to try to live or try to die," he said.

She recoiled from him, eyeing him up and down, as if he had just struck her. She looked at him in silence for a long while. He could see her lips twitch as she thought of something to say, then changed her mind over and over.

He never did hear her reply.

He heard Eriana shift behind him and he panicked. For some reason the thought of her catching him talking to this women sent shivers down his spine that could compete with the frigid air. He realized he should not be standing here. He should not be doing this. He should be with his crew, the ones who were on this journey with him, not whatever this shattered women was.

He backed away from her without another word. He wasn't sure if one more word from her mouth would convince him to strangle her or set her free. She did not call after him, she simply watched him go until he reached his sleeping sack. Then she turned away and went still. He heard the rhythm of her breaths even out. She was asleep.

Aren closed his eyes and dreamed of green grass and trees and sunlight and life for the first time in weeks.

When they broke camp at dawn, he did not tell anyone about their conversation of whispers. He watched the others go about their tasks, studying them to make sure they were still the same. He smiled at Eriana whenever she looked his way. but he did not tell her about it either.

His midnight whispers would remain between him and Keluwen.

They reached the end of Durnan's pass before the morning was half over, the high walls of silver rock suddenly falling away to reveal the knife-sharp chill of the Kol Plateau. The sun broke through a patchwork of icy clouds, its beams like a blessing of warmth.

Aren could not get his second cloak over his shoulders fast enough. And then the bearskin over them both. His fingers were already ice by the time he yanked his gloves on, and he shoved them between his thighs for warmth.

But the punishing cold aside, at least they were through. They arrived. They were one step closer to finding the Blackwell.

Aren started forward, but before he could take another step, he heard heavy steps rattling all around them. Two dozen men surrounded them, wearing tarnished breastplates over hauberks of chainmail, standing so close that the points of their spears were nearly touching his face.

Each wore a hood of mail, and each man was draped in a thick wool cloak, some black and others chestnut, pinned at their chests with tiny silver medallions in the shape of a hammer across a circular shield. One man, with shoulders as broad as a bear, held a warhammer resting over one shoulder as if it were no more than a stick.

He knew they had to be knights from the Kol Plateau. Their armor was battle worn and splotched with droplets of mud. At least half their number bore the symbol of a tower with a lance piercing a crescent moon above it, the sign of the custodians of Kor Kollar.

"Name yourselves or die," one of the knights shouted.

No one spoke.

"Name yourselves now," he repeated. His face was a shadow with the rising sun at his back. "You will die where you stand, alone and unremembered."

Aren did not know what to do.

Fainen slid his fingers over *Glimmer's* hilt, his Saren eyes jumping from man to man.

He is going to try to fight them all. He is going to die. I have to do something.

The knights advanced.

41

Knights of Bolan

THE TIP OF THE spear hovered so close to his face that Aren thought he could taste the steel. He drew his head back, his eyes fixating on tiny engravings of hammers crossing circular shields on the flat of the blade.

"Speak," a voice shouted. "Speak or be done."

Aren had no words. His tongue felt slackened in his mouth. His lips were already dry and cracked from the chill of the plateau. He didn't dare move. But if he didn't do something soon, there would be problems.

He saw Fainen slowly removing his blade from its sheath. The spears closed in.

"Stop!" Tanashri's voice was sudden and powerful, as if she were commanding a king. "How dare you threaten a man of such noble lordship?!"

The knights pulled back, their spears and swords retreating. The man who had been shouting blinked his wide eyes, glancing at his comrades. Aren watched them, barely able to stay upright. He needed some malagayne.

"The call was made," Tanashri said. "And when it is answered, you meet it with disrespect and suspicion."

"What's this you say?" the shouting knight asked.

"We have come at the behest of King Darilon," Tanashri said. "He has raised all willing vassals to fight. We are not mere messengers. You court the King's wrath with your threats. You look upon a great lord." She gestured at Aren.

The knights all stared.

"A noble lord?" one of the other knights asked, looking about nervously, first at Aren, then at his fellow knights. "We have made a mistake, Bakla."

Bakla, the shouting knight, gave his companion an angry look. "A noble lord who is only a boy? Who brings with him only two men and four women? I do not believe that."

"You look upon the retinue of my Lord's household," Tanashri said. "You look upon Lord Aren of Amberwaite."

"That is a small land," Bakla said. "I thought it had no lord at all."

"Small in land, but rich in courage," Tanashri said. "And rich in the respects of King Darilon. What is your name? It is grievous that you insult a friend of the King."

Bakla took pause. His head turned from side to side, flashing his round green eyes at the other knights as he began to wonder if he had indeed made a mistake. "Where are your banners? Your knights? Why would you come alone?" He glanced at the woman's body draped over Redevir's saddle.

"We were ambushed," Tanashri explained. "Our banners broken, our supplies taken, and our men slaughtered. No help was given by the hardy knights of the Kol Plateau." She looked deep into Bakla's eyes, accusing him personally.

Bakla recoiled at the insult. "Who are you, woman?" he demanded. "That you speak while your lord remains silent."

"Lord Aren was weakened by the fighting," she responded. "Do you think a Sister of Templehall would accompany a mere servant?"

Lances were dropped. Men backed away terrified.

Aren used the distraction to dip a finger into the malagayne powder, and lift a hefty sum to his nose. He then pretended to be scratching an imaginary itch to hide it.

"From the Sisterhood," said the knight holding the warhammer. His shaven head, round face, and large eyes gave him the look of a baby in a hulking man's body. "He must be a lord." Every lord in Bolan had a single Sister as an advisor.

"Quiet, Locke," Bakla said. "I need to think."

"There is nothing to think about," Tanashri said. "You stand before Lord Aren, and his Saderan. You will let us pass."

Aren felt dizzy. The malagayne was working too well. He took too much. His mind began to spiral down. Desire was gone, even the desire to stay alive. He began to look out over the heads of the knights to the mountains and rivers beyond, their spears like wonderful plants in a garden.

"It is not safe to move in these lands alone," another knight said through a stubble of brown beard. "They should accompany us to the keep."

"That is my decision, Rikis," Bakla said. He turned to face Aren. "Let your lord speak, if he truly is a lord."

Aren was fading. Visions flooded into him like daydreams. Lost in his own head, he began reciting a passage from Durnan's History of Bolan. "Behold," he said. "The sun shines like a jewel above the house that Tagemon built. Darkness comes, but his fortress holds."

The knights turned to each other, exchanging uncomfortable looks. Their suits of armor creaked and clinked as they shifted.

"Listen to the way he talks," Locke whispered. "He must be a lord."

"He didn't pull away from our spears," Rikis said. "Who else would have such confidence?"

Rikis prodded Bakla on the elbow, as if to remind him of his own authority. Bakla moved forward, a sheepish look coming over his face. He bowed low. "My apologies, Lord Aren. It is rare to come across one who is not an enemy."

Aren stared away over his head.

"All is forgiven," Tanashri said. "Lord Aren understands the dire affliction which has come to these lands."

"It is dire indeed," Bakla said. "Have you heard what news has come to the Plateau?"

"We have heard nothing," Tanashri said. "We have only just come to the highlands, and nearly died. We only know that Kor Kollar is threatened."

"Those who come to take this land call themselves the Sur, Noble Sister," Bakla said. "They are raising the ancient blood banners."

Fainen spat on the earth when he heard the name spoken.

"They came from the east months ago," Bakla said. "And it is not Bolan alone that they want."

"What's that?" Redevir asked. "Other than Bolan?"

"Have you not heard?" Bakla was incredulous. "We received word here on the Plateau two days ago. They have attacked Amagon."

Aren was shaken awake by that. It brought his mind back to him in a way that sharpened lances could not. The shadows of the knights became clear to him suddenly. He saw the face of Bakla, squat and round, with hair held back from his face by a leather strap and hanging to his shoulders. *Into Amagon. The Sur.* He wondered if Vithos was in danger. He wondered if the people he knew there were safe.

"I am sorry," Bakla said. "The fief of Lord Aren lies so close to Amagon that I assumed you knew already. When we received word of it, the news was seven days old. Sur riders descended from the mountain passes. There were rumors of fighting on the Sarenmoor."

"I have heard that the Sur will not go into the Sarenwood," another knight said. "That they avoid it like the plague."

"They must remember what happened the last time," Rikis said.

"I would not desire to enter a forest full of Sarenwalkers either," said Locke, fidgeting with his warhammer.

"Nor me," said Rikis.

"The messengers cannot be sure if it was one thousand or ten thousand," Bakla said. "I don't know... Locke?" He turned to the knight holding the warhammer.

Locke looked at the rocks for a moment, thinking to himself. "Two, maybe three thousand advancing on Kor Kollar, but they have not crossed the river yet."

"But they have at least two thousand more roaming the countryside burning villages," Rikis said. "They kill our women and children in the small towns."

"There are rumors," Bakla said. "Terrible rumors. They say a horde of the Sur that numbers tens of thousands is following, taking slaves."

"No one has seen it," Rikis said. "But everyone seems to have heard of it. No one returns from beyond Kor Kollar."

"This is getting better by the minute," Redevir said.

Bakla looked at Redevir. "You do not speak like a man of Bolan," he said. "Where are you from?"

"You will not ask questions of a loyal vassal," Tanashri commanded, "without first asking the permission of his lord."

Bakla bowed low. "My apologies, Lord Aren. My apologies, Noble Sister."

"Bakla!" a voice called out from below. "Bakla, we must go back now. We have been called."

"Calm yourself," Bakla said to the knight. "You are in the presence of Lord Aren, a patron of His Majesty's court."

The knight's eyes nearly popped out of his skull. He dropped instantly to one knee and bowed his head low. "Forgive me, Lord," he said. "I bring urgent commands from General Vols. All patrols are ordered to return for battle."

"With your grace we must go," Bakla said. "I bid you come with us. It is not safe here, as you well know."

"Safety in numbers," Redevir said. "I agree with him."

Aren leaned in to the Rover. "We're not supposed to go there."

"The situation has changed somewhat, *Lord* Aren." Redevir smiled. "I think I know a way to get us through. Just relax. We have an armed escort."

Aren glanced at Tanashri. "Are you sure about this?"

She nodded.

Redevir leaned in to whisper to him. "I never thought I would be happy you made me spare her. Destiny strikes again."

Aren nodded. "Maybe." He turned away from the Rover before he said another word about prophecies. He was feeling far too suggestible as it was. So he kept his mouth and his ears shut and followed the knights.

The path was steep for a short time, and Aren's mount almost teetered head over hooves at one point. But somehow the beast maintained its footing, and brought him to the flat expanse of the Kol Plateau. They quickly forded the River Tagis, and followed its meandering currents toward the keep.

They traveled all night, moving slowly along. When the eastern sky began to brighten, Aren began to hear the noise of men moving about on the far side of the river. A handful of arrows came over the water in a sudden burst, clicking against the wet stones of the riverbank. No one was hit, but Bakla pulled away from the water after that.

Kor Kollar sat on a rocky knoll like a squatting monk at the base of the lone mountain. It rose like a great cylinder with a tapering top. Before reaching it, one had to pass beyond three massive earthworks guarded by archers and pikemen.

On this side of the river a great drawbridge was down, allowing knights and footmen to move freely across the drowning waters of the moat. Bakla led them through these and up the drawbridge. He left his own score of knights with Aren, and disappeared within the walls of the keep.

"What do we do now?" Redevir asked.

"We wait," Rikis said. "Bakla must go before Gottesil, his own Lord, and bring him here to meet Lord Aren."

"Have you heard of the Beastman, Lord?" Locke asked.

Aren stared at him. "I am not familiar with such a thing."

"Quit your questions." Rikis said. "You embarrass us with your child's tales."

"Notable knights have mentioned the rumors of the Beastman," Locke said. "They say the Beastman is larger than a horse. He lives in a hole and the hunters in the Sholes are his slaves."

"Enough of this talk," Rikis said. "Lord Gottesil does not approve of such tales and superstitions."

"Forgive my impertinence, Lord," Locke said. "But I am fascinated by your battle court."

"What do you mean?" Aren asked.

"You have strange vassals about you. I am sorry that you have lost your knights."

Only one lost knight, Aren thought.

"He feels quite safe with those he still keeps," Tanashri said. "Redevir is skilled in battle, and Fainen was once a Sarenwalker."

Locke flinched. "A Sarenwalker? Here? Truly? I am honored to be near one who can make that claim. Ruling lands so far to the south must naturally bring such variety to your court."

"It does," Aren said. He tried to keep his responses succinct. The more he said, the greater the likelihood of the ruse being discovered. He wondered how long her lie would hold up. They could fool Bakla, but what about Gottesil? It was crazy to come to the citadel. It put a lump in his throat. His palms were sweating. He held his pouch of malagayne close.

"Your court concubines are of a rare sort as well," Locke went on. "Why do you keep one bound? Did she misbehave?"

Rikis couldn't keep his eyes from going wide at that. He rushed to Locke's side. "Keep your mouth shut," he said, shoving his fellow knight. "You have disrespected Lord Aren enough already. Bakla will have you cleaning the stables with your tongue when he hears what you have said."

"Wait," Inrianne said. "What did he call us?"

"Concubines," Redevir said, chortling uncontrollably.

"I will have you know that I am...."

"Silence!" Tanashri commanded. "Remember where you are."

Locke was now a statue of fright, realizing that his comment had turned into a tumult of angry shouting that he could not understand. His massive shoulders sagged, and his warhammer touched the ground. His round eyes watered as he no doubt imagined the sour flaying he would receive from Lord Aren and his Sarenwalker.

"I must humbly beg your forgiveness for this stupid knight," Rikis said, jabbing Locke with his elbow.

"That will not be necessary," Aren said. "I accept the apology." He could not believe that they were apologizing at all.

"I'm sure Locke is only excited to see a rare southern lord," Tanashri said. "We will spare the rod, if you spare us your tongue, young knight."

"Yes," Locke said. "Yes, of course, Noble Sister."

Bakla returned then. Behind him strode a tall, broad-chested man dressed in full armor, with a thick bearskin cloak chained about his neck with gold. His arms swayed as he walked, sometimes as high as his waist, and his hands were perpetually balled into fists. His eyes were narrow and sharp as if they had been cut into his gaunt face with a knife.

"Rikis," Bakla shouted. "Horses to the stable. Have them fed and watered." Rikis leapt at the command, hollering orders to a multitude of squires.

"I am pleased to introduce Lord Aren of Amberwaite," Bakla said.

"Amberwaite," Gottesil said. "I had heard that to be a lordless land."

"Lord Aren has only just taken it as his fief," Tanashri said. "I am his advisor from Templehall."

"Indeed," Gottesil said. "And how long have you been in his service, young novice?"

"Novice?" Tanashri asked. "I am a Saderan, young Lord, and have been granted the full weight of the scepter of the High Maja."

"My apologies, Noble Sister," Gottesil said. "Forgive my remark."

"It seems that the knights here are always apologizing," Redevir said.

"It is our way," Gottesil said. "When we have made a mistake. I take it that Bakla's knights have made such mistakes." He eyed Bakla angrily.

Bakla seemed to plead with Aren without speaking. He made a face that said he was praying to his gods that Aren wouldn't mention his own mistake.

"Tell us of the fighting here," Tanashri said. "What can we expect?"

"They come first with horsemen," Gottesil said. "Riders fly into the villages, throwing javelins, and setting fire to the houses. Most towns were taken without a fight. The people run at the first sight of them, leaving homes and animals behind. Those who do not escape are killed for pleasure or taken as slaves. They kill everything—oxen, feed animals, even pets. We find some of our women in burning houses. They must not have been to the liking of the raiders, or they would have been kept. What they do to the women is unspeakable. Several of my veteran knights lost their stomachs at the sight."

"How close are they?" Tanashri asked.

"They came upon Kor Kollar the day before yesterday," Gottesil said. "They are led by a man who is called Bolus. They say he cannot be killed, that he is immortal, and his men will fear nothing as long as he is with them. They harass us with hails of arrows, and have pontoons to cross the river. They have amassed nearly three thousand of their warriors on the opposite bank. We hear them moving at night, but when the day comes, they rest. General Vols expects some trickery. That is why we move against them today."

"Today?" Aren asked. "When?"

"Within the hour," Gottesil said. "Before sunrise. The General was waiting for all of the patrols to return to the keep."

"So soon," Tanashri said. "You do not await the King?"

"The General wishes to take them now," Gottesil said. "He sees plans lurking behind their strange activity. Rest here. Take of the provisions as you see fit. I will arrange for you to ride out with my company."

"Ride out?" Aren asked. He assumed they would be able to leverage his lordship into going out scouting, where they could easily disappear. This was not what he had in mind.

"How many knights will ride out today?" Tanashri asked.

Gottesil seemed a little uneasy about answering. "I lead fifty knights," he said. "Deagan has another twoscore, and Trevalin brings nearly a hundred. The General will lead the Knights of Kor Kollar, numbering a hundred and twenty. And the pikemen. There are nine hundred in the garrison here."

"That is all?" Redevir asked.

"I'm afraid so," Gottesil said sadly.

Redevir looked at Aren. "A bit outnumbered I'd say."

"We have no choice," Aren said. "You wanted to come here."

"I know, I know. Our luck is holding so far. What's one little battle?"

Gottesil gave them all a smile and said nothing as he returned within the walls of Kor Kollar. They were alone then, in the cold before morning, men scurrying around them as if they were not even there.

"Why can't we just leave?" Inrianne asked. "We're only a handful of people."

"There's no place to cross the river over here," Redevir said. "We'll have to go through Kor Kollar first."

"We can't just run away," Aren said. "Cowardice would bring heavy suspicion from these knights. Gottesil told us that General Vols is already feeling anxious. If we don't go out with them, they might dig deep enough to find out we're lying."

"And hang us as spies," Redevir added.

"So what can we do?" Inrianne asked.

Aren heard a rustling. He glanced over at Redevir. Keluwen was awake.

Shaot! He reached out to point her out, but she was already shouting.

"Help me! They are not what they say! Help!"

Knights looked up from their cookfires, some of them staring.

Redevir responded by cracking her across the back of the head. Just enough to stun her. She went quiet and hung her head.

Aren scanned around them, but most of the knights had once again turned away.

"That was too close," Redevir said.

"What are we going to do with her?" Eriana asked.

Aren shook his head. "I have no idea."

"We could always strangle her," Redevir said.

"The knights would not look kindly upon that. Killing your servants is a crime here."

"I might wager they would not look kindly upon discovering you are impersonating one of their lords."

"We must keep her," Tanashri said. "I have more questions."

"And the rest of us?" Inrianne asked.

"We will go forth with Gottesil," Tanashri said. "It would look strange if Aren did not go, and stranger still if I did not go with him."

"Gottesil will likely lead his knights on one of the flanks," Fainen said. "The General would ride in the center, so that all of his men can see him clearly."

"Once battle has begun, we can pull away," Redevir agreed. "Fight as few Sur as we have to, and ride like hell."

"And if we are all killed in the first minute of battle?" Inrianne asked.

"If anyone has a better plan, then let them share it now," the Saderan said.

"Where shall we meet after?" Aren asked.

"What do you mean?" Eriana asked.

"Eriana, you and Inrianne are not riding out with knights," Aren said.

"Why not?" Eriana asked indignantly.

"It would look strange to the knights if I brought a woman into a battle who was not a Sister," Aren said. "Even one who can fight."

"Do you expect us to simply walk through them?" Inrianne asked. "There is no cover in this whole stinking valley."

"I will show you landmarks to follow," Fainen said. "Before sunrise, there will be heavy contrast between earth and sky. South of Kollar Field the earth rolls, and the faults make excellent hiding places. You will not be seen."

Aren sighed with relief. Knowing Eriana would be spared the battle was like taking a long breath of malagayne.

"But I want to go with Aren," Eriana said. "My family did not raise me to be a coward."

"The knights will not allow it," Aren said. "And they might become angry if I even brought up the idea. Besides, there is the issue of timing. We all have to coordinate to get away from the knights at the same time. Tell her, Redevir."

"He's right. Our chances will be better with fewer heads out there."

"What about our horses?" Inrianne asked.

"I will lead the horses," Tanashri said. "It is a common practice for a lord to bring additional mounts into battle. It will not look suspicious."

"Enough of that," Eriana said. "What about you, Aren? You'll be fighting out there without armor."

"We'll likely be able to make off before we even reach the enemy," Redevir said. "Besides, Fainen will be with us."

"And I will watch every move they make," Tanashri said. "I will give you all a signal when I can mask our escape."

Aren smiled at Eriana. He could feel how badly she wanted to come with him.

"There is a rocky prominence," Fainen said. "Far to the east. I saw it from the edge of the passage yesterday. It is the tallest thing out here save for the mountains.

"Mayhan's Tower," Aren said. "A rock formation that has been there since the beginning of history. We can regroup there."

"That settles it," Redevir said. "When we ride out with the knights, the two of you will make for the landmark with our new pet."

"Quiet now," Fainen said. "The knights."

Bakla returned, flanked by Rikis and Locke. The knights smiled nervously at Aren's company. "I am overjoyed that you will ride out with us, Lord Aren," Bakla said. "General Vols has agreed to join you to Lord Gottesil's company. You will ride at our side. Lord Gottesil has given my band of knights to your disposal."

Aren's eyes swelled to the size of tomatoes. His jaw clicked as he stuttered to speak. "Why?" he finally managed. "That is half of his command."

"Gottesil believes that it would be dishonorable to allow a noble lord to ride into battle without his own band of knights, especially since yours were lost to you in coming here."

"It is unnecessary," Aren said. "I would not rob Gottesil of his command."

"It is decided, Lord Aren," Bakla said. "You may ask the General if you wish." Aren's refusals seemed to confuse the knights greatly. "Gottesil would consider it a great dishonor to himself to leave a noble of your stature unguarded in battle. Especially one who is a friend of the King himself."

Aren bit his lip. Tanashri's lie was causing a problem now. How could they ride away with twenty knights behind them? And what would it do to the battle if they did? Against so many Sur warriors, that many knights would make a great difference. Aren suddenly saw himself as the cause for the destruction of them all.

Tanashri bowed. "This gracious gift is accepted. Lord Aren, for all his wealth, is humble."

"Indeed it is so," Bakla said. "I look forward to riding beside you, Lord Aren."

"And I you," Aren said. *This isn't part of the plan.*

"Come now, Lord," Bakla said. "Rikis and Locke will feed and water your mounts."

"How soon do we ride out?" Aren asked.

"We assemble now, Lord," Bakla said, smiling.

Aren thought that even the savages across the river could have heard his jaw drop.

42

Drybridge

CORRIN NEEDED A BOTTLE of wine in his hand and a pair of midnight lips on his tongue. He already had a girl picked out. A young washerwoman, smooth, buxom, and willing. She had eyes like...well, he realized he had not spent much time looking at her eyes. Just her breasts and her ass, a little at her neck, and a lot at her mouth. He would have asked her mouth to bed alone. The rest of her body was a fortuitous surplus. But he would certainly spend every inch of that surplus on the end of his cock, and on his tongue, and as many fingers as she wished.

She had relieved him of a few ounces of his tension already with her hand behind a washerbin when her overseer wasn't looking, but he had a few thousand miles more to go before he felt right again. He forgot to ask her if she had any friends. He would have to do that when she finished her last wash.

Corrin was enjoying the city of Nidarorad. The city was superior to being over open water. When standing on dry land, one did not have to worry about Danab-Dil, the Leviathan of the Deep, trying to swallow you whole if you fell in. Just a hop and a skip from Medion. Easy.

The warm currents in the Gulf of Shain kept the climate moderate throughout the year, staving off the northern chill. He reckoned it was a bit better than even Medion. More importantly, the city was relaxed. People took their time with things, and everything was always done well as a result. No one seemed to be in a rush, and they minded their own business, and sipped cool drinks in subtle cafes amid red houses with black eaves. Corrin enjoyed cool drinks and subtle cafes. It was so...casual. He enjoyed casual.

He stopped to purchase some clean water for Hallan, and another bottle of autumnwine for himself. Corrin didn't think Arradians could make autumnwine for shit. But it was half the price of their summerwine, so there it was.

He mused at how tame the populace seemed despite being surrounded by some of the more ornate architecture of the Arradian Empire. People in Arthenorad, with all its towers and mausoleums, were pompous and arrogant. They were a little too proud of their city. Here it was different.

He gazed out at the long span bridges that stretched out across the Nidaro River, whose black waters splashed against the red bricks of the support columns. Behind them, massive granite spires stood high and straight, as abundant as the blades of grass in a field. Some bore spiraling decorations that coiled about them and climbed to their highest heights.

Public buildings were nearly all crowned with sharp steeples, domed and gabled, giving the skyline row upon row of dark teeth. Many of the structures had once had gold worked into them, but much of it had been stolen and melted down by rampaging hordes of nameless barbarian tribes hundreds of years before.

He knew Aren would have starved himself to death staring at them for days on end, as he nearly had when they had trekked south to Ethios years ago. Corrin had sworn that would be the last time he ever took Aren anywhere where there was something fascinating to look at.

He found himself wishing that Aren was with him now. Not just for company, but because every sign was written in Coralic, the modern script of Arradan. Corrin could not read Coralic. Aren could. As it was, Corrin found himself unable to tell the difference between a church and a brothel. Some of the inscriptions were still in Vardic, and Old Ardis, some were even in Hedlam, the language of the coastal immigrants. He could barely buy bread from street merchants without having to rely predominantly on hand gestures.

Mardin simply wandered around, staring at anything and everything, while Reidos continually stared at nothing through empty eyes.

Corrin shrugged to himself, and turned toward the nearest bridge. Children skipped along its length, while small two-man boats rowed beneath. Corrin loved the freshness of the air and the delicate beauty of the women walking under the tall towers. Most of all, Corrin enjoyed the fact that, for many days now, no one had tried to kill him. He was growing weary of assassins. They made it difficult to relax, to be...casual.

He glanced down at Hallan, who gorged himself on calpas fruit and cool water. Juice ran down his chin and spotted his green shirt.

He certainly did not want to see the boy come to harm. When you were as popular with killers as Corrin was, those standing near were still within the rings of a bullseye. He knew he needed to find a safe place for the boy, he just was not quite sure where that might be.

I can't leave him alone. I'm the only one he'll talk to anyway. He patted Hallan on the head. The boy smiled. Corrin smiled back. He then looked out over the spires, wishing that he had bothered to learn the Coralic word for *tap room*.

He walked with the others until he stood atop one of the many drybridges. He thought that it might help keep Hallan's mind off the dart-wielding madman on their heels. Or perhaps it was to get his own mind off of it. It didn't matter at this point. For right now he was only standing on a bridge, letting the wind ruffle his hair. Calming him. Stilling him.

The drybridge was an elevated roadway, with gentle sloping access ramps leading up to its arch-supported length. It was wide enough for two wagons to pass each other comfortably, a four-foot walkway on either side. Each drybridge was constructed identically out of concrete and raw stone blocks. They were unique to Arradan. This was the only kingdom that allowed for the use of Deepland Crawlers.

Corrin thought they looked like giant centipedes, their multi-sectioned lengths held together by rotating iron joints, and their long track cars loaded with heavy crates of every manner of wares the wide world had to offer, unloaded from Olybrian cogs and heavy merchant galleys from across the Karelian Sea.

He tried to think back to all he had ever heard of them. There must have been eight of the Crawlers, or maybe nine. They moved on wheels turned by powerful pistons, and skimmed along iron tracks from one place to another. Most were intended for the transport of cargo, and powered by steam, like the paddle boats up the Alder River, but at least two were luxurious passenger Crawlers using melenkeur to heat the water. Leave it to the rich to take something potentially useful and turn it into their personal amusement.

Several routes existed, connecting Tallirad, Coralis, Sararad, Karorad, Arthenorad, or the port of Arragandis. There may have also been spurs to Shannarad, or Volean Heights. All had one thing in common—they all passed through Nidarorad at some point along the route.

Nidarorad was the hub at the center of the wheel, and its streets had changed much with the addition of so many sets of tracks. The drybridges were one of those changes. With tracks cutting across every main thoroughfare, building the roads up over the trackways had become a necessity for a busy port city.

Corrin hated Deepland Crawlers. Created by a man named Wilkot of Deepland, the Crawlers were considered extremely dangerous, and wildly unstable by nearly anyone who had any sense, and Corrin could not agree more. Every time one took a curve in the trackway, it looked like the Crawler would tip over and grind itself to pieces. He would never *ever* ride upon one. One thing Corrin had learned in life, was that something that looked top-heavy tended to be top-heavy.

The Ministry hated them, too. Hated that knowledge of how to make them had gotten out into the world. There were many purges and assassinations, but they ultimately convinced Arradan to sign a treaty limiting the Crawlers to what existed already, and never building more or sharing the science of how they are made to work.

One of the longer Crawlers approached the drybridge, and Corrin had to run after Hallan as the boy scampered to the top to watch it come out from the other side from his high vantage. The boy began to count the Crawler cars as they went past. "One, two, three, four."

Corrin reached him just as he was climbing atop the waist-high stone barrier that was the only thing between him and a thirty-foot drop. Reidos was laughing. *Stupid Mahhen.* "Feel free to help me at any time."

"You seem to be handling the situation very well," Reidos called back.

"I wouldn't want to get in the way," Mardin said. "You always say I'll get in your way."

"What a couple of...."

Just then, Hallan lost his balance and started to flop over the barrier. Corrin lunged forward, grabbing him by the shoulders.

As he leaned over the edge, something zipped past his ear. It was a familiar whistling sound.

Corrin spun around faster than most men could, but he was still barely able to see the tight black coat before the next dart shot toward him. He ducked his head so fast that he almost snapped his own neck. He threw Hallan to the ground and clamped his hand on his sword hilt.

It was him.

This is bullshit, Corrin thought.

Reidos drew his own sword and Mardin scurried toward Corrin. The blond man tucked his jet black blowgun into a leather case looped to his belt.

"Move!" Corrin shoved Hallan into Mardin's arms, and pressed them both against the barrier.

The blond man stalked forward like one of the automatons from Old Magor's puppeteering workshop, head never turning, eyes never blinking, hair standing straight up from his head like golden spikes, his left hand missing its fingertips.

Reidos swung his blade only once. The blond man dodged, and punched him hard in the mouth, staggering him toward the railing.

Corrin charged, but it was too late. The blond man caught Reidos under the jaw with an open palm, and half-punched, half-pushed him over the barrier. Reidos fell from the bridge.

Corrin leaned over the railing and sighed with momentary relief when he saw Reidos stretched out on his back atop a mountain of crates on one of the still-passing Crawler's cars.

Suddenly, Corrin had a thought. It was a good thought. He glanced over his shoulder at Mardin and Hallan, then down at the Deepland Crawler below. He didn't have time to think about it. He ran to Mardin, and without a word proceeded to toss him over the barrier, onto the back of a Crawler car. Mardin shrieked, but that was okay. Better than death.

He grabbed Hallan by the wrist, and lifted him into the air. "When I say so, you let go. Okay?"

Hallan nodded in affirmation.

"Go with Reidos. I know where the Crawler goes. I'll find you." With that, he lowered the boy over the barrier as far as he could. He gave Hallan one last look, and the boy smiled back at him. "Now!"

Hallan let go, and fell lightly to the Crawler.

Corrin whirled about to see the blond man standing before him. Corrin drew one of his knives without even bothering to see which one it was. He threw it almost as an afterthought. The assassin dodged it.

Didn't think so. But it didn't matter much; it had only been the fruit knife he had snatched from the Calpas dealer.

Corrin drew his longsword. *Good, now you and I can finish our business. I don't know who sent you, but I must have really made them mad.*

The blond man stared at him, then glanced down to the Crawler.

Corrin raised his blade...but there was no one to use it on.

The blond man suddenly sprinted to the barrier and scaled it in one step, before jumping full force into the air.

Corrin's jaw fell open. He watched the assassin tuck and roll back to a standing position atop the Crawler, stared as the Crawler carrier him farther and farther away.

He's not after me at all, Corrin realized. *He's after Hallan.*

There was nothing else Corrin could do. He sprinted to the barrier and scaled it in one step, before jumping full force into the air.

43

War

I SHOULDN'T BE HERE.

Aren sat in the saddle amid all the great knights of the Kol Plateau—General Vols, Lord of Kol; Deagan of Tarma; Gottesil of High Latham; Par of the North; Prince Trevalin, nephew of the King and Lord of Ben Kol; Barkimer the long, standing over seven feet tall; Fry of Lake Plessar, Lord of Low Latham; and the *other* Barkimer, the Knight of Ice, who wielded a two handed sword of blue Saren-steel. Every knight held a long lance for the first charge, with swords, hammers, and axes ready for further fighting.

They had been taken aback when Aren declined to wear a suit of armor, and to appease them he accepted the gift of a shirt of mail and a conical helm with a wide nose-guard.

He looked around the courtyard of Kor Kollar. It was a wide triangular expanse, with the curving outer wall of the keep jutting outward like a pregnant giant. One wall was lined with pens for the ice dogs, another held stables for the great war-horses of the knights, and the scent of feed hay and fresh dung wafted on the wind. The triangle pointed east, with a gate near the apex. On the other side of that gate lay Kollar Field; on the other side of that gate lay thousands of Sur warriors.

The General himself was suited from head to toe in bright yellow armor which glinted like gold, and his face was hidden beneath a tall angular helmet with a thin slit for the eyes. He was a large man, and strong. He wore eighty pounds of armor as other men wore linen shirts. Upon his breastplate was a silver effigy of Kor Kollar, with a many-rayed sun in gold above it. He bore a massive triangular shield, and strapped to his waist was a two-handed greatsword. Over his armor rested a thick cloak of bold yellow wool, and draped over this was a coat fashioned from the hide of a snow white arctic bear.

Aren managed a deft snort of powder. Just one to clear his mind, to relax him a bit, and drive away the stiffness in his legs. He told himself it would be just one sniff, but it was two, and he wanted another one already.

The gate opened as the sun crested the eastern mountains. They rode four abreast onto Kollar Field, with Aren's band the last in line. Behind him, the archers and pikemen strained to keep up on foot. When all had taken to the field, they formed up in two rows, one behind the other. Aren and his band were with Gottesil on the right front.

General Vols kept his horse at front center, just as Fainen predicted. His retinue was about him, holding lances aloft in the morning, displaying banners that shined in silver and gold.

Aren looked at Tanashri. She held the reins of two horses along with her own. She nodded to him. Somewhere behind the lines, two women were sneaking away from the field pulling a third on a leash.

Tanashri would give a signal at the moment it was time to break away from the charge. Aren needed only to get away from Bakla and the other knights without leading them from the field also. If they followed him, and left the flank alone, the other knights would not stand a chance.

A whining blare of strange horns erupted from the darkness. It was answered by others, like a flock of siren birds calling to each other. Aren couldn't see them, but he heard them. A slight rustling. The clinking of mail and chains and sword-straps. Then echoes of boots crunching on the field.

I shouldn't be here.

They were coming. They were coming and Aren was waiting for them to come. That was what a knight did. Every part of his body screamed at him to run, hide, escape, survive. He did his best to ignore it all, but the sight of them made his heart rattle like a kettle drum.

General Vols waved his lance in the air like a child's baton. The twang of bowstrings could be heard, and the archers let loose a hundred arrows in their volley. Aren heard the soft sibilant sound as one and all fell short and dug into the earth.

"Too far yet," Bakla said. "The next volley will hit."

Aren heard the words, but did not reply. He looked at the Sur. They had no uniforms or armor. It was like a living patchwork quilt of dull browns and greys. They wore rough skirts and shirts of coarse leather or wool. Some were shirtless in the frigid air, with leather straps wound over their shoulders and about their waists, crisscrossing in strange patterns. Some wore amulets and bracers of raw iron. Some had shaved heads and others kept long strands of hair woven into braids, sprouting from the tops and sides of their scalps. The only color adorning them was the red paint upon their faces. Some of the Sur pulled wagons with high poles atop them. Upon these poles were bodies, some alive and others dead.

I shouldn't be here.

A second volley was loosed by the archers, and true to Bakla's word, Aren heard the familiar *thok* as arrows hit leather and flesh. Still the Sur did not charge, nor did they issue cries as they were hit. They spread out as wide as the line of knights, many rows deep.

They split apart in the center like a parting veil to reveal hundreds of horsemen on strong mounts. The leader, Bolus, rode at the head of them. He was unmistakable, and Aren could see him barking like an animal to his warriors. Upon his head was a silver helmet with a long spike at the top.

Bakla leaned over to him. "Bolus wears the helm of Mallogan, cousin of the King, slain in the town of Tamborlin by Sur. He wears it in the face of the General to dishearten him."

"They outnumber us by a hefty margin," Redevir said over Aren's shoulder. "That's disheartening enough."

"They will bleed rivers for this disrespect," Bakla said.

"Show them no mercy," Gottesil said nearby. Aren looked at the knight who had shown him such courtesy. Gottesil was strong in his saddle, his back straight and proud. Aren straightened his own posture without even thinking.

The Sur abruptly began to scream, as if not being able to spill blood was some kind of torture for them. It was the very chorus of the seventh hell, and the shrill drone set the horsemen to charge. They surged toward the knights— toward Aren. The knights were all suddenly silent. Aren felt a pulsing in his body like the beat of drums.

General Vols lowered his lance, and the knights spurred forward on their war-horses. They reached a trot, then a gallop. Aren followed Gottesil's line, with Bakla on one side of him and Redevir on the other. His hands could barely hold the reins. He was not sure how he kept himself in the saddle, let alone steered the horse true.

The sound of beating hooves surrounded him, filling his ears. The Sur seemed to stay small and distant for so long, but then suddenly were coming closer and faster and harder and then they were right in front of him. Hooves pounded, closer and closer, until he could see the rage on their faces. Aren waited for the signal, but it didn't come.

Closer. Closer. The pounding was in his head, consuming him. His heartbeats thumped in his chest, and his eyes began to water, and he thought he heard the braying of brass horns just before the lines met.

Impact. Aren's eyes closed. He heard the sound. It was like the sound of a mountain crashing down as charging horses hit each other head-on. Riders were thrown to the ground, but somehow Aren was still riding. He opened his eyes. The Sur if front of him were blasted back as if they struck an invisible wall, sweeping them away.

Tanashri!

Inertial transposition. She stole their forward momentum, and applied it back at them in the different directions, tipping them over to either side, or instantly sending them in the opposite direction. Skin split, necks snapped. None could survive that whiplash.

So that is the trick she has been holding back.

She kept waiting until the very last moment to apply it, letting the Sur horsemen come within a gallop of him before rendering. Aren expected that. Even though transposition was one of the least costly renders to perform, the expenditure of energy for a user was exponential the further away from the body they set their renders to originate, so to conserve she would have to let them in close. Very close. Too close.

Knowing it was coming did not make it any easier to see snarling warriors bearing down on him, before they were nudged aside.

Horses were cut or broken on all sides. Aren was nearly toppled from the saddle. Within seconds the horsemen were gone past him, and he found himself with Gottesil and his knights, amid the Sur foot.

Gottesil drove his lance through three men at once before it was lost to his hand, then drew his sword and chopped furiously, cutting heads from bodies.

Aren locked his legs around the saddle, swinging with his own blade at everything that came into view—every snarling face, every spear, and every outstretched arm. Everyone he passed was away and gone behind him. He wasn't sure if he ever hit a single one of them.

Fainen was behind him, deflecting spears from all directions. Aren looked left. Locke was beside him, breaking bones with his massive warhammer. The knight roared like a bear as he crushed arms and faces.

Aren saw Redevir somewhere nearby, but it was only a glimpse as he drove his horse on. Gottesil was suddenly gone. His knights were pulling away to the left, riding toward the center, toward General Vols.

Aren felt something sharp in his side. A well of pain erupted, but the malagayne kept it down.

Where's the signal?

He was lost among the Sur. He panicked. He drove to the right, trying to break out of the battle, but the Sur were massed on the flank, pushing his band of knights back toward the center. His horse refused to ride at such thick pockets of fighters. The Sur were closing up the flanks and filling in behind the knights, surrounding them.

This is the wrong way.

But he couldn't go through the massing warriors to the right. He had to go to the center. It was the only place where any knights remained.

He reached with his left hand across his stomach, and felt the slender shaft of an arrow in his side. It brought a biting pain when he touched it. He was more afraid of the idea of the arrow in him than he was of the actual pain, for the malagayne ate the pain, ate it all but let the fear remain.

Suddenly a wooden baton whipped into his arm, and the reins slipped from his sword hand. His mount started to drift, and he began to slide out of the saddle. But Bakla was there, snatching the reins and pulling his horse back toward the center.

Fainen came up behind him with Rikis and Locke. The two knights were ripping apart the Sur, swinging huge broadswords through flesh and horsehide, Locke doubling his attacks with his warhammer. Fainen himself was like poison to the Sur, killing every one that he touched.

The Sur were everywhere now. Every way Aren looked he saw them running and crawling. They thrust spears into passing horses, cutting their legs or startling them into dumping their riders. Dozens of knights were already down, being skewered through the cracks in their armor, as the Kol footmen raced to catch up to them.

Something batted Bakla in the face, and the knight went down, dropping from his horse with enough force to break his spine. Spears were driven into him. Aren turned his head back to see him, but he was already gone behind scores of fighters.

He saw Redevir, then lost sight of him again. He had to keep riding, keep moving through the masses of men. If he stopped, they would pull him down and he would be dead.

He chopped down with his blade, hitting a head. He waved it back, raking it across another warrior's ribs. Every swing seemed to hit now, but he had no idea how much damage he could do.

He drove his sword down blindly, right into the open mouth of one of the Sur, but his horse leapt wild, and the blade was yanked from his grip.

With a flash of green, Fainen was there. He clutched Aren's sword and withdrew it from the gaping mouth before the body had even fallen. The Sarenwalker slashed low with both swords as his steed propelled him forward, cutting across the faces of everyone he passed. He sent dozens of the Sur to the ground spitting teeth and spraying blood from torn faces and wrecked jaws. He caught up to Aren and passed the blade back to him without question.

Through it all, Aren could not stop moving. He heard the blasts of Locke's hammer, and the slicing sword of Rikis separating limbs from bodies. All of the knights fought desperately, but it was not enough. There were simply too many.

Where's Tanashri? Where's the goddamn signal?

The wild horns began to blow again, and Aren saw Bolus. The Sur leader whipped knights down with short sabers, razor-sharp and attached with leather straps to his wrists. His head was shaved clean beneath the silver helm, and his face was painted red—a single stripe down the middle of his forehead, and many smaller ones splaying out over his face like the rays of a star. He opened his mouth and howled. His teeth were sharpened into fangs.

Bolus pulled his horse alongside one of the knights. He grabbed the man across the chest, and began digging his sabers into the knight's flank. The man wailed as Bolus torqued his hand around, ripping apart his entrails. Blood washed like a wave across the knight's silver armor. Bolus raised his weapons above his head and screamed to his warriors.

Aren rode toward him, propelled by the need to keep moving. He had nowhere else to go. He only hoped to make it by without Bolus noticing him. He clamped his legs tight to the saddle, holding his sword with both hands over his shoulder, swinging it back and forth, hoping it would keep anyone from hitting him.

Time slowed down. Bolus abruptly looked away, his leg clipped by an arrow. He bent down, scanned the small wound, pulled the arrow out.

Aren saw the silver helm like a guiding beacon.

He swung his sword back and forth. It was going to pass just over the head of Bolus.

But at the very last moment, Bolus heard a sound, and raised his head and saw Aren coming at him.

A battle is only a series of moments.

Aren closed his eyes, his sword swinging like a lumberjack's axe. He felt it bite. The neck of Bolus was the base of a tree.

He opened his eyes. The head of Bolus rose into the air as if it had been launched by a catapult. Aren turned to see it land and skip across the ground as his horse took him past it. He saw the headless body still perched atop the horse, perfectly upright.

No one is immortal.

Everyone turned to look. The Sur were frozen, eyes trained on that one spot. They began to weep.

Rikis and Locke, General Vols and all the knights were quiet under the soft blanket of clouds. The fighting slowed, the horses came to a halt. The Sur began to flee.

Aren looked back to see Fainen behind him. The Sarenwalker almost gave a hint of a smile. Rikis and Locke were there, helmets off and mouths agape. They both looked over Aren from head to toe, unable to believe what they had seen.

"He's not immortal after all," said a familiar voice. It was Redevir.

"Lord Aren," Locke said. "Amazing."

"Bolus is dead," Rikis shouted. "Lord Aren took his head."

"Bolus is dead," Locke repeated, raising his warhammer with one hand.

All the knights began shouting. "Bolus is dead! Lord Aren took his head!"

The Sur crept away, surprised and dismayed. They had lost hundreds of their fighters without wavering, but the loss of their all-powerful leader was too much for them. They ran, many being stabbed as they went. The knights did not follow. There weren't enough left to ride them down, but the savages were going, disappearing in small groups back across the plateau.

The clouds parted. The sun shined through, blinding.

Aren felt a tapping at the base of his neck. He looked behind him, but no one was there. He heard a deep boom behind him somewhere. The air was filled with clumps of mud and sprinkling dirt. *What was that? Was that Tanashri? Is that the signal?*

Someone was leading Aren away. He let his horse carry him, unable to do anything else. He heard clinking metal and strange footsteps, but saw nothing through the light. "Go toward the light," a voice whispered.

Aren looked around. He saw no knights, and no Sur, only Fainen holding the reins of his horse along with his own. He looked back over his shoulder and saw shapes of armored men moving, so far away they looked like toys. The citadel of Kor Kollar shrank in the distance, and Mayhan's Tower grew to a looming height before him. Fainen stared only ahead as they went.

With one bloody hand, Aren took a white cloth from his pouch, and dabbed it in the powder. He took a long sniff. He took another sniff, and another, and another. Everything in the world was wonderful.

44

Deepland Crawler

CORRIN HATED PEOPLE WHO wouldn't die when they were supposed to. It tended to make him uneasy. And this assassin just did not know how to die properly. Corrin was determined to give him the bloody smile if it was the last thing he did.

He admitted to himself that the setting was not ideal. Hundred-car Deepland Crawlers looked long enough as they trundled past you, but this one seemed ten times as long now that he was actually standing on it.

It was difficult to hear any kind of ambient noise over the whining of the wheels. He had to rely on his eyes alone. The wind whipped through his hair, forcing him to wear only his black shirt and breeches despite the cold. He bundled his cloak in his carry-bag. *No sense letting a gust give me away.*

He inched along, scampering over and around ziggurats of stacked crates that rose on each of the cars. He wondered how many cars had gone by between the time Hallan landed on one and the time the blond man did. It must have been at least ten. How fast could the assassin move though?

Probably very fast.

Corrin stepped down to the lowest tier of a crate-ziggurat, massaging his sore shoulder. He was not quite as adept at tucking and rolling on a moving Deepland Crawler as he thought.

He had the *Steel Whore* strapped to his belt of course, and a further five knives looped to his belt, tucked in his boot, under his arm, and on the insides of his thighs, and another four stuffed into his carry-bag. *That should be more than enough,* he presumed. But he did have that blowgun to worry about. The knives wouldn't be of a whole lot of use if he made himself a target for a poisoned dart before he could get close enough.

So he moved slowly, scanning every possible hiding place. Unfortunately, Crawlers had plenty of hiding places. That would also have been to Hallan's benefit though. Boys were often good at finding places where they wouldn't be seen. Reidos and Mardin were also on this thing somewhere, though Reidos could have been out cold, and Mardin was only marginally better than useless.

Corrin lifted himself slowly, with his back to the crates behind him. He tilted his head back, and peered over the boxes. He saw an endless string of Crawler cars extending into the distance.

Nothing for a long time.

Then he saw it. The blond man. Maybe six cars ahead, clambering up one side of the car, and moving swiftly to the other side, where he disappeared again.

Good. That means he's not waiting for me. It unfortunately also meant that the assassin was ruthlessly preoccupied with finding Hallan.

He scampered along the car until he reached the joint that attached it to the next. It was a long iron tongue with a three-inch diameter bolt through a ring in the center. The tongue was actually two parts, one half extending from Corrin's car, and the other from the one ahead of it. The rocky ground raced by below it. Corrin looked down. He didn't like the idea of falling in between cars.

Like a goddamn cheese grater.

It was a four foot jump across the divide. Corrin made it easily. He looked for the blond man again, but saw nothing. He ran along the next fifty-foot long car without bothering for stealth. *If I can't hear, then he can't either.*

Corrin repeated this process until he reached the car where he last saw the assassin. He slowed down considerably, and checked the length of the car on both sides of its box-mountain of cargo before creeping along. No sign of his quarry.

As he scaled the next two cars, the Crawler began to take a long lazy curve, making a wide arc to the left as the track wove between hills of dead grass. It gave a full view of the left-hand side of every car. Corrin could see the power car in the distance, belching steam and smoke into the air. *Eighty cars between here and there.*

He moved along the right-hand side of the stacked crates so that he would not be visible to anyone looking down the inner edge of the curve. He had not seen the assassin for a while now, so he maintained his slow pace, checking every space between boxes, every niche within the Crawler framework. He had to fight the urge to run headlong toward where he thought Hallan would be. A dart in the back wouldn't help anyone.

He knew that he was near to the car he had dropped Hallan on. There was no sign of the boy though. Corrin climbed up to the tier of crates at the top of the pile, and caught a face-full of smoke. He choked. *Infernal machine.*

He looked over the top for signs of disturbed dirt or sooty footprints. Nothing. He looked again at the cars ahead. No Reidos either. He either moved out of sight or Mardin dragged him. Or he had fallen off. *Shaot, that would hurt.*

The curve came to an end, and the cars straightened out again. Corrin began checking both sides of the cargo beds once more. Some carried thick logs of raw lumber. Moving past them would be difficult. There was no gangway on either side. He had to try to pull himself along the logs without rolling off the edge.

He made it past the first, but there was another one immediately after. Now came the very difficult part. The logs were round, and strapped tightly together with rope and chain. He had nothing flat to push off of when he made the jump over the divide, nor did he have anything flat to land on. He looked down through the gap. The Crawler was flying down the straightaway, and sharp rocks flashed by at terrible speeds.

Cheese grater.

He lowered himself carefully onto the tongue joint, holding tightly to the bottommost log. He pushed off hard, almost tripping over the plug of the connector. He caught himself on the logs of the other side, but not before slamming his face hard into a piece of lumber. He shook off the sting, and lifted himself up the logs.

He caught a glimpse of something. Movement. It took him a moment to realize what it was. He saw the blond man two cars ahead, running full tilt over the length of the crates. One car further up was Mardin, scampering from one side to the other, trying to get out of sight.

Now's the time. He won't see a damn thing behind him.

Corrin climbed to the top log, and perched in preparation to leap. The assassin kept moving away from him. Corrin launched himself across the divide and landed on his feet. He ran like a madman over the long bed of crates, and was almost to the next car just as the blond man was leaping off of it. Corrin hurdled over the gap, and dropped down to the left side, now only one car behind.

The blond man disappeared down to the right of the crates one car ahead, following the path Mardin had taken.

But then he saw Mardin coming back up the other side of the car, racing *toward* Corrin. Trying to double back. The assassin was close at his heels.

Good thinking, Mardin. Bring that piece of shit to me.

Mardin was wide-eyed with fear, moving past the crates using his hands to steady himself.

Corrin jumped to the top of the crates on his own car. Ran full speed to the gap. Jumped it. Drew his blade in midair. Landed with a thud six or seven paces from the blond man.

The assassin stopped short, a look of surprise registering on his face.

"Pardon me," Corrin said. "You look like you need to die. Let me help you with that."

The assassin pulled a long steel chain of black rings from a bag at his waist. At either end was a solid bar six inches long. The man took one bar in his right hand, and held the chain with a fingerless hand a third of the way up its length. He began to twirl the other end in a circle.

Interesting.

The assassin took a step forward and released his hold on the chain. One black bar sailed just over Corrin's head. The blond man pulled it back, and whipped the entire length in a full circle, sending it flailing back at Corrin with twice the speed. Its arc was too low to drop beneath. Corrin jumped back, and nearly went over backwards into the gap as the bar nicked his chest.

He knew it was there without seeing it. *Cheese grater.*

He barely regained his balance.

Something caught his eye. One car ahead, beyond the blond assassin, a small shape peeped up from behind the crates.

Hallan!

Don't give him away. Don't give him away.

But it was too late. The blond man turned to see what had registered such surprise on his face. He saw Hallan and instantly forgot all about Corrin. He tore across the Crawler car, and out of the reach of Corrin's blade.

Corrin planted his feet, and drew the fat throwing knife he had bought in Samring. Threw it. It dropped low, hitting the crates before digging into the sole of the assassin's boot heel. He kicked it away.

Corrin pursued. The assassin began to whirl the chain again. Corrin looked down. Mardin was now racing past him, back the way he had come, away from Hallan.

Damn it. Help the boy. Corrin was furious. *Where the hell is Reidos?*

The chain whipped at Corrin's head. He threw himself into a dive, rolled up onto his knees, and slashed at the assassin's ankle.

But the assassin pulled back out of range, and brought the chain down on Corrin's shoulder. The *Steel Whore* was knocked from his hand and clattered down the tiers of boxes.

Shaot!

Corrin drew his old Cambrian dirk from a loop in his belt. He knew it had been a good idea to go back for it at the *Red God*. He drove it down hard into the top of the assassin's foot, pinning it to the crate like a nail in a block of wood.

Corrin tasted a faceful of knee for his trouble, but it had been worth it. He staggered backwards. The chain came around again, caught him in the side of the head. He went sprawling over the side, rolling down tier after tier of hard wooden crates.

He landed at the base of the box-mountain with his head and half his torso hanging over the edge of the gap between cars. His carry-bag splayed his belongings onto the crates nearby. He watched a decorative dagger from Cyurmer drop over the side, followed by a mahogany-handled cleaver from Talorin, and the broad blade from Pannoria, and then the Calabari Claw.

Damn it! I loved that thing.

He instinctively reached down for a flare as it rolled over the side. He just barely caught it. But it was not the knife he had been hoping for.

He then noticed something peculiar. Below him, hanging from the rigging on the underside of the Crawler car, was *Reidos*. "What the...?"

"Remember the wagon train in Delmdale," Reidos said. "Give me your rope."

Corrin thought about the words. He felt around in his carry-bag for the rope. Found it. Passed it to Reidos.

The assassin yanked the dirk out of his foot and tossed it over the side.

Asshole.

He then hopped down the tiers until he was directly beside Corrin.

Corrin pushed himself to his feet, sliding the sharp knife from Farmontaine from a sheath strapped on his inner thigh. He held the unlit flare in his other hand. He looked back over his shoulder to see Mardin perched on the tongue joint, furiously pulling at something. Reidos clung to the underside of the car near him, tying loops in the rope.

The assassin smiled as blood oozed from a black hole in his left boot. He flailed out with the chain. Corrin fell to his knees, dodging the attack, but almost falling off the side of the Crawler.

Behind him, Reidos vanished under the car again. Mardin still tugged at something.

The chain came again, smacking the knife from Farmontaine out of Corrin's hand, and sending it spinning off into the hills.

Corrin replaced it with a curving bronze-hilted dagger from Castice. The only knife he had left in reserve was the one Aren had given him. The one he had never used. The one that slept in a sheath under his arm. He thought he might have to use it today.

He saw Reidos climbing along the underside of the car.

The chain flew again. It glanced off the curving bronze-hilted dagger from Castice. It crashed into the crates, sending splinters of wood into the air. Corrin slashed the dagger across the blond man's shin. He leaned back. He swatted the knife out of Corrin's hand and over the edge.

You're off balance now, farod.

Corrin sparked the flare. It burned with white hot flame. Corrin drove it into the assassin's cheek and held it there. The assassin screamed. The skin blackened and crackled like roasting meat. The assassin took a step back.

But Reidos was suddenly under him. He slipped a loop of the rope under the raised foot. He drew it taught around the ankle.

"Now! Now! Now!" Reidos shouted at Mardin.

Mardin strained to pry out the plug of the joint, but it was wedged in tight.

"Pull!" Reidos screamed.

The Crawler slowed, ascending a hill, and the two pieces of the tongue joint were pushed together, relaxing the pressure. Mardin pulled with all his might, and yanked the pin from the joint. The Crawler cars began to separate.

The assassin looked down at his foot. It took him a tenth of a second to realize what was happening. A tenth of a second later the rope pulled taught, one end around his ankle, and the other tied tightly to the separated cars falling away behind. Confusion mixed with rage in his eyes, and then his leg was torn out from under him. His face smashed onto the crates, crushing bones. Then his body was dragged across the car, leaving a bloody smear on the wood, vanishing over the edge.

Cheese grater.

Reidos heaved himself up onto the car. It was now the last car in the chain. The other fifty-or-so cars drifted away, rolling back down the hill.

Corrin took Hallan by the shoulder. "Why are you so damn important?"

The boy shrugged. "I am not. I don't know."

Corrin wrinkled his lip. "That...*whatever he is*, sure seems to think you are important."

"I am just a boy. I come from Falsoth. It is a village."

"You must have done something."

"The only other things I have ever seen are the same things you have seen because you were with me."

"Hmpff," Corrin said. "There must be more to it than that." He sat down on one of the crates and stretched his legs. He decided that riding on a Crawler wasn't as bad as he anticipated. It was certainly easier on the legs than walking, and furthermore, he no longer needed to spend time deciding where to go. The tracks had already decided for him. They were now headed to the largest city boasted by the Empire of Arradan. A good place to get lost in—the capital city, Arthenorad.

45

Blackwell

AREN LOOKED AT THE woman who had tried to kill him. It was a new daily ritual, whether seated about a campfire, rolled tight into a sleeping sack looking past a sleeping Eriana huddled beside him, or, like today, swaying in the saddle.

Keluwen walked ahead of him, hands tied behind her back, ropes connected to a loop around her neck, and a long leash tied into the rigging of Redevir's saddle. She was lucid enough to walk and talk, but Aren kept her on a very steady diet of tinwood leaf tea. When the weather turned, they put her gloves back on her, and bound her once more, draping an ice cloak over her shoulders. Redevir and Fainen took turns watching her in the night.

Her cheeks were high and round, enormous eyes. Her hair was bobbed, hanging just above her shoulders, bangs swaying in front of her eyes, forcing her to toss her head around or blow them out of her eyes every tenth step. She was well muscled, and she wore fine clothes underneath her cloak.

Who are you? What were you doing out here all alone?

He pulled his cloak tight around his shoulders, and nodded one of his hourly affirmations to Eriana. *We are all right. We are still safe.* But he doubted she needed any encouragement from him. She seemed to be enjoying herself far more than he.

His breaths appeared as bitter clouds of steam, and every breeze bit at his hands and face. He could feel the ice cold belt buckle through his shirt when he hunched over. His fingers were each throbbing with pain, like being stabbed with needles from the inside out.

They were deep in the northlands now, and the northlands were deep in winter. The coldest day in Amagon was like the warmest day the ground would ever see here in the height of summer. He hadn't seen the sun since he left Kollar Field, and the cotton sky rarely showed even a hint of blue.

Fainen had difficulty removing the head of the arrow in Aren's belly without causing further damage. Luckily no scrap of fabric from his tunic had gone in his body with it. No sepsis.

Eriana wrapped torn cloth as a bandage about his waist, and another about his split leg. The cut of the sword had not been as deep as he thought it would be, but it pulsed with a stinging vibration. He remembered smiling at Eriana while she had wrapped his wounds, and she smiled back. He didn't really know why he remembered that.

Beyond the rushing river Mallios had spoken of, Fainen found the winding pass through the black rocks, deep in a labyrinth of ravines, all the color of charcoal. They rode through places with soft fresh snow, and then some without. Some of the rocky slopes were black and others grey. The earth was like a massive chessboard, alternating pure white with sharp black basalt.

They came across a freshly dead northern yak, frozen, covered in yellow tangles of fur and half hidden by lichenous red weeds. Fainen chased away the carrion rodents, and cut fist size chunks of meat from the carcass. The blood steamed as he worked at it. By the time he rolled the pieces in a light cloth to stow in his pack, they were already cold as ice.

The Sarenwalker located a hot spring in a high grotto. They stopped to warm themselves while Fainen boiled yak flesh and the meat of an arctic fox that had wandered within bowshot. Aren's rampaging hunger somehow managed to make it taste delicious.

The only benefit of the cold was that it kept the Sur warriors in their camps, and the tribes of Shola hunters huddled about their fires. It was a simple thing to avoid them. Fainen could smell them a mile away. Unfortunately it would also serve to make game scarce, and Aren doubted they would have enough breads, nuts, and dried meats to sustain them when the yak meat ran out.

He felt eyes on him. He looked down.

Keluwen stared at him, her eyes like hammers trying to shatter his skull.

"What?" he asked. He towered over her on the horse.

"Your nose," she said. "It's the first thing I am going to break."

"Oh, you are, are you?" He raised an eyebrow.

"Then your jaw."

"Then my neck, I presume?"

"You think you have me at a disadvantage," she said. "You are wrong."

He looked her up an down. "We have you on a *leash*."

She reddened. "And for that alone it will cost you both ankles. And that is even after you give me what I want."

"What is it you want?" Aren asked. "And no, you are not going to break anything. You're not going to do much of anything for a while."

"I am going to get out of here, you know. And when I do, nothing is going to stop me from killing you."

"You have given your whole plan away," Aren said. "Now all I have to do is never let you go."

She glared. "You think you are very clever."

"I am very clever," Aren said. "Sometimes."

"He is," Eriana said beside him, looking over his shoulder.

"Is she your pet?" Keluwen asked.

Eriana cursed at her in Sinjan. It was something Aren had never heard before.

"Maybe I will have to break her jaw after I finish with yours," Keluwen said.

"Shut your mouth," Aren said.

"She could not break anything of mine," Eriana said. She patted the hilt of her sword. "Not without her hands anyway."

"Is she your bodyguard?" Keluwen asked mockingly.

Eriana turned a cold stare at her. "I am. And you are not very funny. I think a better joke would be your head rolling on the ground at my feet."

Keluwen made a surprised face, but Aren thought he saw a slight approving nod, just for a fraction of a second. "If it comes to that, I hope you are as fast with that little sword as you think you are, princess. Because when I break free of these bonds I am going to kill your boy here, and then I am going to kill you. Faster than a thought."

"You leave her out of this," Aren said. "You will never ever touch her."

Keluwen smiled. "I already know more about you than I did before. You care for her."

"I never tried to hide it."

"You should have," she said. "Now I know how to hurt you."

"That means we are halfway to being friends."

That stumped her. She turned quiet, rolling thoughts around in her head. "You still haven't dosed me, the way you said you were. To make me tell you the truth."

He looked away ahead, breaking eye contact with her. "To be honest, I did try for the first few days. But the cold was making it difficult to saturate the water for the tea, and then I realized something that made me decide that would be unnecessary."

"What?" she asked.

He didn't answer. He smiled. He liked knowing he had something she wanted. It was a delightful little twist of the knife. "Looks like a winter storm is coming." He could feel her eyes narrowing at him without looking at them.

"Why is it unnecessary?"

"What does it matter to you? It should make you happy. Now you don't have to worry about me asking you all those questions again."

"Why not?" she asked. There was an urgency in her voice. It had not been there before.

He said nothing, just swayed atop his horse, smiling at the rocks and the sky.

"Why not?!" Her voice increased in pitch. A hint of frantic energy.

She really is worried. Good. Let her think I have an alternate source of information about her people. That ought to keep her on edge for a while.

"Where are you taking me?" she asked after a little while.

"Don't bother telling her," Redevir said over his shoulder.

"Oh, gum your own asshole, Rover," she said.

Redevir tugged twice on the leash and she stumbled, dropped to one knee. She hopped back to her feet again. "She will not believe it anyway," Redevir said.

"You will pay for that, Rover," she said.

"Not likely," Redevir said. "And if you expect me to be kind to you after you try to kill my partner there, then you have a deficiency of some sort."

"I do not intend to ask your permission when I do kill him, Rover. If I do, I will be asking your corpse."

"What was it you wanted?" Aren asked. "You said before, somewhere between breaking my wrist and my pelvis, that you wanted me to tell you something. What was it?"

"*Why* are you with him? I wanted you to tell me why. What did he promise you? What sweet words did he whisper to change you?"

"I am not with anyone. I am with my friends. We are here. What we are is what you can see."

She spat on the ground. "He does not really care about you. He is using you."

"He is not using me for anything unless his master plan is to commit suicide," Aren said. "The only favor I am interested in doing him is killing him."

Her eyes widened, and then narrowed. "You lie."

"I do not lie," Aren said. "I do not serve Kinraigan." He paused. "And neither do you."

"You thought I was one of his? Do none of you mindless jellies talk to one another?"

"I realized you were talking about someone else. The one you admire. The greatest man in the world."

Her eyes bugged out of her head and she laughed. "You thought I was talking about Kinraigan? You are a fool."

"Only as much a fool as you," Aren said. "You think the same thing about me."

"Everything about you is wrong," she said. "I am not telling you anything."

"We can trade. Answer for answer. I will tell you anything you want to know about us, if you tell me something about you."

"I have ears and eyes. I already know everything I need to know about all of you. "

"Oh really?" he asked.

"I know you smoke the grey leaf so often you don't even realize you are doing it. I know you are twice as clever as other people see you, but only half as clever as you think you are. I know you want to wrap your arms around that golden-haired girl and wear her like a coat. And I know you are navigating blind in your life, and trying very hard to hide it by always having a place to go."

He smiled, but his face tightened and it burned itself out and became a long frown. He looked away, then down at his feet, then lifted his eyes back to her. "Not bad," he said. "Anything else?"

"I know you and the Rover think you are better friends than you are. I know you and the woman in white think you are greater enemies than you are. I know the Sister admires the Rover but pretends not to, wants to crawl into bed with the woman in white but pretends not to, and thinks you are more fascinating than a glimpse of god, but pretends not to."

Everyone glanced around at everyone else, before averting their eyes and shaking their heads.

Aren widened his eyes. "Is that all?"

"I know that Saderans of the Sisterhood hiss like snakes when they are trying to hide the moment they come. I know your Rover should never be more than twenty leagues away from a prostitute, or he loses his mind and yells at foliage. I know that you have nightmares you do not tell any of the others about, Glasseye. And I know that girl with the perfect blond curls and skin like honeyed cream wants to fuck you oh so badly, yet for some reason you still haven't done it."

Eriana blushed and looked away.

Aren did, too.

Keluwen smirked smugly at him.

"You seem very observant," Aren said, leaning closer.

"I am." Her face hardened.

"So am I. I know that you knew me before you appeared that day."

"What do you mean?"

"You rendered a cylinder around me, to crush me. You didn't try to do it with any of the others. No time wasted adding the extra streams. You did not choose that for anyone else. Just me. You were there to kill me. Just me. Maybe the others, too, if you could. But most definitely me."

She sucked her teeth at him.

"That means you had been following me for a while," Aren said. "And there was no way to get to where we were except by a long, cold overland route."

"So?"

"You wear winter cloaks over your clothes. But underneath you wear fine wool and linens. You wear city boots that still shine. Your hair was recently cut. I can still smell the perfumes in your clothes. You were not prepared to be out here. It was a snap decision. That means you did not know you were coming after me until you arrived in Corricon."

"Plenty of information. None of it relevant."

"I know you are working with others. And you love one of them. I know you hate Kinraigan, and anyone who follows him."

"Well, you have said everything and made it amount to nothing. You don't know me at all."

"I know something about you that I won't say," Aren said. "Because it will make you angry if I do. But it doesn't matter because you already know what I mean."

She narrowed her eyes until they were sharp enough to cut him. "Choose carful words."

"I also know you are rash," Aren said. "You make decisions without thinking them through."

"How do you figure?"

"You attacked us on your own. I mean, you attacked our *whole party*. By yourself."

"I very nearly had you all."

"You did," Aren agreed. "But no one, and I mean no one, would ever have thought to do that. I am wondering how whatever people you have let you come out here by yourself."

"They do not control me."

"That much is clear. If Tanashri threatened to do something like that, I would have had to dose her until she came to her senses."

"I am thinking of getting back to breaking parts of you."

He laughed. "Let me ask you one thing."

"One thing? Or *one more thousand?*"

Eriana chuckled at that. Even Redevir cracked a smile.

"Why are you still alive?" Aren asked.

"Because you are stupid," she said. "Or a coward."

"What happened you your people in Westgate?"

She grimaced. "We lost."

"You told me your people died. Joli, the elder, someone else."

"Bonsinar."

"Did Kinraigan's people keep any of them around for a week to question them?"

She looked away in thought for a long time.

"I will take that as a no," Aren said. "I am willing to bet he or his people killed them all just about immediately. Does that sound right?"

She hissed an exhale. "Yes."

"The reason I know that is because he *always* kills whoever stands in his way. He doesn't wait. He doesn't play games. He doesn't question them for information, because he doesn't *care* what information you have. I have spoken to him three times now. And there is one thing I know for certain about him—he thinks he already knows everything there is to know about everyone. And if he doesn't he makes it up."

Keluwen was quiet for a long time. "I think you are right about that."

"I know I am. If he wants to turn someone to his side, he will come to them himself. The way he keeps coming back to me. If he doesn't want to turn you, it means you don't matter to him at all. And he and his people will just kill you and then go on about their day."

"That seems true to me." She was thinking it through, hopefully the direction he wanted.

"So then I will ask you once more," Aren said. "Why are you still alive?"

She paused for a long time before answering. "Because you are not Kinraigan's people."

Aren smiled. He nodded three times. "That's right."

"But in Westgate...you were *everywhere*."

"Because I was hunting one of Kinraigan's users."

"But if you don't belong to him then you belong to the Lord Protector."

"And he betrayed me, and tried to have me killed. And now here I am, on my own, trying to hunt Kinraigan myself. And I think you and your people are doing the same thing."

"Then you really are not his," she said.

"I did not realize it needed to be said," Aren said. "But yes. We are *not* his."

"They always turn," she said. "Always. They always become his. Or he kills them. I saw you talking to him. There should not be a way that you are not his."

"What are you babbling about now?" Redevir asked.

"I do not know how you did it, but you have talked to him three times and not become slave to him. How is that?"

"Simple," Aren said. "When someone talks, you do not have to listen."

She stared at him suspiciously. "It should be impossible. He knows how to manipulate everyone. He can with a single phrase open you up, deconstruct you, and make you feel like he can give you everything you ever wanted. That is how they all fall."

"Well, he did not try hard enough," Aren said. "He is not a god. Everyone keeps treating him like a god. He is just a man. Just like me. When we pierce his flesh he will bleed. When he is put into the fires he will scream."

"We are going to take possession of something he wants," Redevir said. "And then we will set a trap for him and wait for him to come to us."

Keluwen leaned back, and looked at him with disdain sprinkled with a pinch of pity. "I was wrong. You aren't evil. You are just fools."

"We are fools to you now?" Aren asked.

"Fools. Fools who have no idea what is in store for them."

"Ignore her, Aren," Redevir said. "We are on the right path. Our plan is sound."

Keluwen laughed.

Eriana leaned over to swat her across the head, but Aren stopped her. "It's fine. Let her laugh. Eventually she will come around. Whether out of boredom, or whether I have to make her do it."

Eriana smiled. She nodded and rode beside him the rest of the day. He caught her smiling three more times before lunchtime, and three more times after.

The evening brought more pale skies and more black rocks, until Aren began to feel that he was at the end of the earth, a point beyond which colors could not sustain themselves. He spent most of his time trying to guess who Keluwen was, where she came from, and what made her come after Kinraigan the way she did. He invented twenty different stories, none of which quite made any sense. He was halfway through imagining the twenty-first, when Fainen finally signaled to stop.

He pointed to a thick formation of jagged crags. "This is the high black wall. Vandeme Canyon must lay on the other side of those ridges."

"Aha!" Redevir said. "I told you. This is it. We are here. Mallios spoke truth."

Vandeme Canyon was narrow with smooth walls of basalt, white with snow. It was silent and still, and utterly devoid of life. No wind. No plants or animals. No people. No sound at all except for their footsteps.

"Where do we find the entrance?" Aren asked.

"Mallios said it was a hole in the ground," Redevir said. "There."

Aren saw a jagged aperture in the ground at the edge of the canyon wall. Redevir looked at him expectantly. Aren nodded to him, and they started to creep across the ground toward it. It was a wide hole, almost ten feet square, and as they peered over the rim, they saw steps leading down to a faint orange glow.

"Torches," Redevir said. "There are people in there."

Aren saw a fine sparkling haze about the entrance. He swallowed a lump in his throat. "Worse." He held up the Jecker monocle. Afterglow clung to the air near the entrance. "There is a user in there. Possibly more than one."

"We need to be on the lookout for Shola hunters," Fainen advised. "They roam around in winter, looking for meat."

"Aren and I will go alone," Redevir said.

"Alone?" Tanashri asked. "Are you a Rover or a madman?"

"Why not both?" Keluwen asked. "Why not add fool?"

"Keep quiet," Redevir snapped.

"You have no idea what you are doing, do you?" Keluwen asked.

"Shut up," Redevir said.

"You are in over your heads," she said.

"I am beginning to regret not insisting upon your death," Redevir said.

"How many should go in?" Eriana asked. "And who should they be?"

"The less people inside the better," Redevir said.

"You are fools," Keluwen said. "The two of you at least. Most everyone else here, probably."

"Fainen and Tanashri," Inrianne said. "Let them go in."

"Don't be a fool," Redevir said. "There is no chance that I am going to miss this moment. And Fainen needs to stay here to make sure this place remains clear as an exit."

"Since when exactly do we all follow your orders?" Inrianne asked.

"Is that not what you have been doing this entire time?" Redevir asked. "You are not going in because I don't trust you."

"You proved me wrong," Keluwen said, rolling her eyes. "You all clearly know *exactly* what you are doing."

"Enough," Aren said. "I will go. Redevir will go. Everyone else stays here."

Inrianne smirked. "The one person worse than Redevir."

Eriana glared at her. "Aren is wise. Aren knows what he is doing. He should decide."

Inrianne narrowed her eyes. "He is making you stay up here, too, girl."

"No one *makes* me do anything," Eriana said. "I judge who best to take advice from."

"Oh, yes," Keluwen said. "Apologies to you all. Everything seems to be going just swimmingly for you."

"How do you intend to find it?" Tanashri said. "How long will it take you to search?"

"Well...."

"Well nothing," Tanashri said. "You need my help."

"This is not a discussion," Redevir said. "Aren will guide me. And I will watch Aren's back. He is the only one who can see where any users have been. And my information is what brought us here. The rest of you need to keep this exit clear, or come to our aid if we run into trouble. The less people creeping around in there the better. Two have a better chance of keeping out of sight than three or five or seven. And if we need help, we have you as a reserve."

"Redevir is right," Aren said. "He and I have done this before. The best thing for you to do is stay hidden, and protect us if an alarm is given. If we all walk into a trap, there won't be anyone left to rescue us. You did the same thing in Medion."

"Aha," Redevir almost cheered. "You see? You were wise to hold back when we were taken off to prison. You know you should do the same here."

"I do not recall you being pleased with me when I restrained myself," Tanashri said. "You change your tune whenever it suits you."

"I have come to realize the wisdom of the almighty Saderan," Redevir said. "You stay here."

"Aren," Eriana said. "Are you certain you must go alone?"

He studied her for what seemed a long time. He knew somehow what she meant. It was for that very reason he did not want her to go with him. "I have to go alone with Redevir. It has to be this way. Trust my judgment."

"I do, Aren."

"Everything will turn out fine."

"I believe you," she said.

"Pleasant deaths to you both," Keluwen said.

Aren made the sign of the witch at her.

Redevir went first. Aren followed. He lost count of how many steps they took before reaching the bottom. They found themselves at one end of a long, empty corridor with no visible doorways from one end to the other. The walls and floor were all of the same rectangular stone blocks, and reed torches were fastened to the walls at intervals of twenty steps. The air was instantly warm. His fingers and toes slowly came back to life. He almost fell to his knees in rapture. He had thought the cold was going to kill him.

"No doorway?" Aren whispered. "Maybe we made a mistake."

"It must be at the other end. Follow the light."

Aren studied the footprints of sensitized fluorescence, guiding Redevir around them to prevent any of it getting picked up by his own boots. The hall seemed to stretch out, giving the impression of an unreachable end. But there was an end.

After passing a dozen torches, they came to a right-hand bend in the tunnel, around which Redevir poked his bald head. "No guards," he whispered.

"Who keeps the reed torches going then?" Aren asked. "These would have to be changed out every few hours."

"Just keep a lookout for your radiation."

At the far end it branched off in many directions, each one silent, each one glowing with orange flame. The residual footprints ceased.

"No more sensitized fluorescence," Aren said.

"Do we have a plan for that? Or do we need take our chances?"

He drew out the Finder. "I'm going to set the Finder to its lowest possible setting, with no specifications for frequency, amplitude, or variance. It might show some kind of reading in such a confined space. Tried this in an underground mausoleum once. It mostly worked. The meters should push out when we come closer to something that radiates."

"Closer to the users, you mean."

"Users tend to make themselves the most important people in any setting. I think if the Diamond really is being kept down here, then they would be the likeliest ones to be hoarding it."

"Is it picking up on anything yet?" Redevir asked.

Aren twisted the cylinder. The amplitude meter barely wavered.

"How far away could it be? I thought it would be more noticeable."

"In these tunnels, it may be closer than it seems."

"Can you tell which way to go?"

"Wait here." Aren walked to each of the branching hallways, holding the cylinder ahead of him. The first two had no effect on the meters. He stopped at the third one, the meter vibrated slightly. Then he continued to the fourth and fifth hallways, though he found no readings there. He motioned for Redevir to follow him down the third hallway.

Voices.

Aren and Redevir froze in mid-step, and slowly turned back to the doorways they had passed. From within one of the openings came the echoes of two or three men speaking some imperceptible language. Aren clung to the wall, trying to press himself into invisibility. The voices died away and silence reigned once again.

The hallway terminated in a small alcove, with a circular hole in the floor at the far end, lit by four reed torches. It might have been the most brightly lit little corner of the whole network.

Redevir lowered himself to the ground, and crawled over to it, leaned over the edge. Aren crept up behind him. The hole was three feet in diameter, a vertical shaft. He leaned over the edge. It was at least fifteen feet deep, with a dozen iron rungs forming a crude ladder. At the bottom was the glow of another torch. He held the Finder over the hole. It grew warm, and the meter extended further.

"This must be the Blackwell," Redevir whispered.

Aren nodded.

"It feels like we are going to be climbing down right through Shaab-Gulod's asshole into the underworld," Redevir said. "It had better be here."

"It's here. It has to be."

Redevir went first, feeling out each bar before placing his full weight upon it. The well opened in the ceiling of a room below. At the base of the shaft the rungs continued down a wall made of the same stone blocks.

The Rover dropped to the floor. Aren came down after. The room was twenty foot square, with perfectly worked blocks in the walls. In each of the four corners was mounted a reed torch, warming each wall with a solid glow. It smelled of old moisture, collected for centuries until it ached from the walls.

Save for the lone wall with the metal rungs built into it, every other wall bore a single wide arch, each one leading to a similar room with similar arches. Aren looked directly across from the ladder. Arch after arch, room after room, extended into the distance. He could not see where the rooms finally stopped. They stretched on into blackness. He looked through the doors on either side of them. It was the same.

Aren peered into one of the side rooms and was surprised to discover that more rooms extended back behind the well room, as if it was the center of a massive network of interconnected chambers. Each room was identical to the one before and the one after—four walls, four arches, and four torches. The air was laced with an ancient sterile stone smell, pressing in on him with a liminal immensity. The place stretched, became infinite, yet its expanse felt so close around him that he was crushed by it. It reeked of unknowable purpose, choking him with fear, demanding that he spend every moment wondering what it had been put here for.

"This place horrifies me for reasons I cannot describe," Redevir admitted.

"Like a tomb and a labyrinth at the same time."

"Let us not dwell on that, shall we? I am depressed enough already. Let us get on to the task at hand and find the stone...so we can get the hell out of here."

"Where is everyone, Redevir?"

"From the impression I got in the tunnels above, this place is enormous."

"Who keeps the *hundred thousand* torches going?" Aren asked.

"Just find it. Show the way."

The Finder extended out much farther. Aren followed it from room to room. They went straight ahead at first, keeping the ladder in sight behind them. At length the ladder became a speck in the distance. When Aren turned to look back a few rooms later, it had vanished in darkness.

They went further. The endless chambers seemed to stretch out. Elongate. Pulling Aren's eyes away to infinity. He started to lose focus. His eyes glazed over and he was struck with a sudden wave of nausea. He pulled a single grey leaf from his pouch, and placed it in his mouth. He sucked gently on it, letting it take a slow effect.

They passed through forty rooms, and then forty more. They were deep in the maze, but it was still a straight path back to the ladder. That fact gave Aren his only comfort.

"I see something," Redevir said.

"Where?"

"To the left. A shadow. We need to turn."

"Remember how many rooms we go through from this point."

It would no longer be a straight line to the ladder.

Four rooms. Five. Six. Seven. Redevir held up his hand. He went around to each of the sides. He moved into the next chamber. Every way looked the same. Four walls, four arches, and four torches. "Something here is playing with the shadows. One of these rooms is different than the rest."

Aren went into the next room, and the next. Everything was the same. Then he went one room further. Something was different. The arch to the right was dim. Aren looked through it. The chamber within had three of its arches closed off with frayed mustard yellow curtains.

At the far end, a glint of light refracted torchlight. Mallios had been wrong about the linen pillow. The stone sat naked and alone upon an altar of stone.

"Go get it," Aren said.

Redevir took one step forward, stopped, listened.

The hair on Aren's neck stood straight. Something was wrong.

A clamor of sound erupted behind them. Aren turned to look over his shoulder. He heard the sound of footsteps. Men running and shouting. Shola hunters. They were coming closer.

Then Aren heard a screaming roaring howl.

"What was that?" Redevir asked.

"I can tell you what it's *not*. It's not human."

46

You Have To Let Me Go

AREN STOOD LIKE A statue in a maze of rooms that were all different rooms, yet still the same room. All the same save for one; the one that held up its four walls around the Diamond.

Aren heard the shouting, but couldn't place the source. It echoed from every direction. Every room led to four other rooms, on an on, one arch in every wall.

Redevir tore into the chamber, grabbed up the Diamond with both hands, and ran back to Aren, shaking.

Aren heard the animal roar again. He flinched.

"We go," Redevir said.

"Where? Which way?"

"We're eleven rooms away from the center," Redevir said. "We go back to that straight path, or we can go past it. The rooms keep going beyond. We can go a long ways over, then go to the right and make a run that way. Then we cut back to the ladder room, and likely get us around them."

They sprinted back through the rooms. Aren's lungs were on fire, but he followed Redevir—keeping up, but just barely. The wound on his abdomen seemed to be splitting open with every stride. It felt like his belly was just short of rupturing to dump his organs onto the floor.

He glanced to the right in every chamber he passed. He saw the room beyond, another beyond that, and on and on down the endless maze of rooms until the end was a distant speck. He passed one, two, three rooms. He saw nothing down in the distance. Four, five, six rooms. Nothing.

"Seven," Redevir panted. "Eight. Nine. Shit!"

Aren looked to the right. Down the tenth row he saw movement, and again down the row of rooms leading to the ladder chamber. He felt the endless rows of chambers stretching out, elongating. The further he ran, the further away the ladder seemed.

Redevir kept going away from that row until they were scores of rooms away from where they found the stone. It seemed like Redevir was right. The shouting died down some, and the echoes lessened.

Redevir turned to the right, with Aren hard on his heels. They ran through room after room. As they sped through one particular chamber, Aren caught a flash of something far away to his right. He saw another flicker of motion two rooms later, only for an instant as he ran past. Still the shouting was far away.

Down one row he saw something. It was larger than a man, and shaped differently. An inhuman shrieking called alarm from the distance. The sound shot like lightning through the maze. The shouts of men grew louder again, behind them and to the right.

"Come on," Redevir said.

Aren's legs burned. Sweat dripped down his face, stinging his eyes. His breaths came like thunder-punches to the gut. His throat was dry and cracked.

"Here," Redevir said, cutting suddenly to the right. "We're behind them."

"They're...coming...back." Aren could only spit out one word per exhale. On the last one, he accidentally spit out his leaf of malagayne.

He looked to his right and saw snippets of motion. "We... should...see it... by now." The pain was starting to overtake him. He would not be able to run forever.

"We went past it. Cut back to the right."

"They're coming that way."

"I know."

They cut to the right, running directly at the hunters. Aren saw nothing of them at first, but then he made out shadows in the distance. He saw the shapes of men coming closer. He heard the roaring scream in the distance.

"Here, here," Redevir said, swinging to the left.

There it was. Iron bars leading up to the heaven of escape. Redevir jumped so hard into a sprint that he almost left his feet. But a hunter appeared in one of the corners. He was tall and lanky, with matted and tangled hair the color of dust. He wore animal skins over his arms, legs, and groin. One hand held a serrated blade.

Redevir did not even slow down. He hurled a throwing knife into the man's throat, sending him to the floor. Aren leapt over the body. Redevir was already at the ladder. He jumped up to the fourth bar and hoisted himself into the well. Aren scrambled after him, taking each bar one at a time. He looked up. At the top of the well, another man looked down at them.

Redevir drew his sword and stabbed upward, but the man blocked with a cleaver and counterattacked. Redevir parried as well as he could, but he could barely move his arm in the close confines of the shaft. He grunted as over and over again as he slammed his elbow into the wall. Aren gripped the bars for dear life while Redevir fought above him. He didn't even reach for his own sword. He could do nothing with it from his perch.

Then they were below him. Dozens clamoring at the base of the ladder. Swords rang against the bars like bells ringing, hitting just below Aren's feet. He locked his hands around the bar above him, and pulled his knees up to his waist.

One of the hunters began to climb. Aren kicked down, catching him under the chin. The hunter dropped, arms flailing. He crashed to the floor. But already a dozen others were pressing upon the bars.

Aren looked up. "Redevir!"

The Rover knocked aside the cleaver, but had no leverage to stab. He held himself up with one foot on the bar, and the other braced against the wall on the opposite side of the well. He slid around inside the well, and pushed up. He took a fistful of the animal skin shirt, and pulled the hunter headfirst into the well. The cleaver dropped below, narrowly missing Aren's head.

Redevir pulled the hunter down past him, slapping his face and neck. The man scratched and bit and grabbed at Redevir's clothes. Redevir punched again and again with the hilt of his sword, splitting open the hunter's face and cutting off his fingers. The man howled like an animal, rocking and kicking and smashing into Redevir's head with his knees.

Aren reached up and grabbed. He caught a handful of hair and yanked. The men below him were bumping into each other, all of them trying to make the ascent at once. One of them finally managed to break from the others and mounted three bars.

Aren heard the inhuman roar again. He looked down the well at the men close upon the bars of the ladder. He watched as arms that belonged on a bear swept them aside. Enormous hands, which belonged either on a wolf or an ape, grabbed the ankles of the man beneath Aren in the well, pulling the feet from their perch. The hunter's face slammed into the bars, cracking and breaking him the whole way down.

The face and half-body which came within Aren's vision was fuming like a bull, and looked like a bear or a dog or a man. It appeared different at each flicker of the torchlight behind it. One of the mammoth hands reached up into the well, held up by an arm that was longer than Aren was tall, covered in dark stinking fur. The hand brushed against his boot. It swayed again, and nearly took hold of his ankle. He pulled his legs as high as he could to stay out of reach, but it was stretching, coming closer.

He could only think of one word—*Beastman.*

"Redevir!"

Redevir drove his thumb into the hunter's eye. The hunter dropped headfirst, crashing into the dog-bear-thing, pulling it down. The arm vanished.

Aren threw himself up the well, almost climbing up Redevir in the process. He heard the roar again, and metal clanged as the hunters flooded up in the well after them. Redevir reached the top, and half-lifted Aren out after him. Aren looked around for something to throw down the well, but the chamber was empty.

"Just run!" Redevir said.

Aren ran after him. His abdomen roared in pain. He tripped twice, slamming his shoulder into the wall, but kept on his feet somehow, staggering and running at the same time.

The tunnel was empty. They reached the point of many branches in seconds. Redevir turned and threw himself down the tunnel which had brought them to this place, but he stopped in his tracks when he heard the voices. Dozens more of them were coming down the tunnel, blocking the only escape. And the rest, still behind them, were flooding up the Blackwell.

"Fight back to back," Redevir said, flipping out one of his throwing knives. His eyes twitched back and forth. "Watch the tunnels. I'll try to break through them."

Aren finally drew his sword. He looked at the Rover with resignation. "We're not going to make it."

Redevir turned his back to Aren. Hunters poured from the hallway. Pressed forward. Struggled to be the first to draw blood.

Before they could close the final distance, the first hunter lifted into the air so quickly he dropped his blade, and was jerked hard backwards into the far wall, shattering his spine.

Redevir blinked in disbelief.

The others stopped and stared. Then three more of them wailed as their feet flew out from under them. They flipped upside down, and their heads were dashed repeatedly against the stones of the floor, as if invisible giants were swinging them by their ankles. Blood and chips of bone sprayed until the floating bodies at last dropped to the ground.

Aren saw a blotch of grey. One of those hallways was not vacant at all.

Tanashri!

He looked back over his shoulder at the hunters, half of them rushing to attack, the other half scrambling to get away. A dozen of them were blasted back, as though a man had wiped his hand across a full chessboard, scattering the pieces. Then a dozen more. She transposed their own momentum back at them in different directions, tossing them about, whiplash snapping their necks. But more kept coming. Soon their users would arrive. They were in these tunnels somewhere.

Redevir turned to Aren. "Go! Head to that light!"

Again they ran. Hunters on their heels.

He reached Tanashri within moments, Redevir close behind. Tanashri's hands were shaking after her exertions. Fainen was there, holding her upright with one arm. Keluwen's bonds were intact, but no one held the ropes binding her. She walked herself here on her own. Eriana and Inrianne were both quiet.

"We followed a hunting party," Tanashri said. Her eyelids fluttered uncontrollably. "It is difficult to project from so far away. I should have come closer. There wasn't time."

"I saw you dish out twenty times that against the Sur," Redevir said.

"Distance," Aren said. "Distance takes far more energy for a user. Plus she has barely eaten. We need to get her food." Even with her experience and power, she could barely manage those few renders from such a distance. It had nearly exhausted her.

"We have to get out first," Redevir said.

Shouts came from behind them, echoing off the walls.

"Coming fast," Fainen said. "They are gaining."

Inrianne rendered fire, sending enormous plumes toward the Shola hunters in each of the tunnels. But Aren saw the flames hit invisible barriers.

"Their users are here," Aren said. "Pick a tunnel. We have to go now!"

Inrianne rendered fire again, shooting down the tunnels. The heat forced them back, forced them to hold, focusing on their shields, but it took its toll on her. Aren had no idea how much fire she had been rendering just to get them down here. But it must have been a lot. She began to waver. She half-leaned, half-fell into Fainen. The Sarenwalker took hold of her and pulled her along.

"That is a problem," Redevir said.

Aren and Eriana helped Tanashri along. Fainen dragged Inrianne. Redevir pulled Keluwen by the ropes, but there was no tension on them. She was running as fast as they were.

They wound their way through dozens of tunnels, each one looking exactly the same as the one before. Few torches lit these ways, and the going became dark, then darker still. The tunnels stretched deep into the earth, descending, then rising, only to dip again.

"I see a light ahead," Eriana said. "It looks like daylight."

A hail of arrows landed around them. Coming from ahead in the tunnel. Redevir planted his feet and skidded to a halt. Everyone flattened themselves against the walls.

"We're cut off," Aren said. "We have to turn back."

"No," Redevir said. "They are coming that way."

Arrows clicked against the walls. One lodged in Aren's boot.

"The archers block our path," Fainen said, drawing his Saren-sword. "I will charge them."

Aren turned to him, horrified. "No."

"You will be riddled with arrows," Redevir agreed.

Fainen nodded. "But it will purchase needed time for the rest of you to make it."

"I can do it," Keluwen said.

"I will not let you do this, Fainen," Aren said. "You can't."

"It is the only way," Fainen said.

"I can do it," Keluwen said.

"There may be no other way, Aren," Redevir said. "We may even have to —" Redevir paused abruptly. He turned to Keluwen. "What was that? What did you say?"

"I said, I can do it," she said.

Aren turned to her, suspicious but hopeless. "How? What can you do?"

"I know a way to get past them," Keluwen said. "I can make a way out."

"How can you make way out of here?" Redevir asked, wide-eyed, stomping toward her.

"You may not like my way out," she said.

"Arrows!" Redevir shouted. "Arrows are being shot at us. Yes, I would accept any version of a way out at this point."

Aren saw movement beneath a distant torch. They were coming from behind. "What can you do?"

"You have to let me go," Keluwen said.

"Not a chance," Redevir said.

"I can stop them," Keluwen said. "But you have to untie me."

"I would sooner untie a cave bear," Redevir said.

Keluwen pointed down the tunnel. "There is little time for debate. I have someone to get back to. I do not mean to die in this place surrounded by the most stupid people I have ever met."

"We need to find a way," Aren said. "And fast."

"I can do it," Keluwen said.

"She is lying," Redevir said.

"You are dosed," Aren said.

"It has worn off," Keluwen said. "While you fools were bumbling around down in the dark."

"Then why didn't you escape?" Aren asked. "Why didn't you use your magick up above and break free of the ropes?"

She gritted her teeth, wrinkled her nose. "I *can't*."

"You can't?"

"I can't do it when my gloves are on."

"Gloves? What?"

"The ropes are holding my gloves in place. You need to untie me so I can take them off. I can't render anything when I am wearing them. I just can't."

"This is a trick," Redevir warned.

"Say you won't kill us," Aren told her.

"I won't."

"Again." He stared into her eyes in the torchlight.

"I won't."

"Will you kill us?"

"No."

No pauses. "Will you kill us?"

"Maybe, now. Your voice is aggravating." A diversion of the eyes.

"Close enough," Aren said. He thought of Fainen charging to his death. "Either way we're dead. This way has better odds." He pulled out his knife and cut the ropes.

Keluwen shrugged her way out of the bonds, tossed the noose off her neck. She stood up straight and rolled her head around, shaking stiffness out of her arms. She slid one glove off, and then the other, tucked them into her belt. She raised both hands and pointed with two fingers down each direction of the hallway.

A pale silver glow wound around her hands and down her arms.

Afterglow? I shouldn't be able to see that yet.

She bound streams. Blank impulses. Dozens of them in rapid succession. Aren heard them plink off steel and chip against stone and punch through flesh. She kept rendering them. More and more, until anyone who had not fled or taken cover would be well past shredded.

Shaot. She is good.

She kept going until the way ahead was silent, and the arrows were stilled.

"Go now!" Redevir shouted.

Fainen was already racing ahead in the tunnel, dragging Inrianne, guiding the way to the side passage. The others followed. Arrows flew around them, sharp points clicking on stones.

Fainen wrenched the last visible reed torch from the wall, ripping it from its casement. The tunnel became black outside of the ring of light it provided.

Aren felt the stone floor become uneven, finally giving way to raw earth, with scattered chunks of rock littering the path. He ducked his head, nearly walking into a low hanging stalactite. *A cave.*

"We are deep in the earth now," Fainen said.

"No kidding," Redevir said.

"I hear them," Aren said. "Behind us. We need to move faster."

"The light ahead is getting brighter," Eriana said.

They began to descend. The tunnel seemed to go on forever.

"I feel moisture in the air," Fainen said.

"The tunnel widens ahead," Eriana said. "Listen to the echoes."

Aren took each step with both feet, barely able to see. The reed torch was close to gone. The daylight was just a speck in the distance.

"Wait...." Redevir stuttered. "There is something..."

Aren took anther step. He expected to feel the ground, but his toes kept going down, down, and down. Stretching out. Reaching for that promised next step. But there wasn't one. The floor had collapsed away into darkness. He froze, his eyes wide. He threw his arms back trying to fall backward rather then forward. His leg bent. He crashed down on his back. He felt bands of pain from the sharp edge. Hips, spine, ribs, head.

He heard someone go over. The reed torch dropped over the edge. He reached his hand out to grab hold of something, but it slipped through dust and rock chips.

He heard a scream.

And then he was falling.

47

The Boat Man

FEAR IS WHAT YOU *do not know, what you cannot see.*

At first Aren thought he was not even alive. But then he started to feel all the little things—his stomach was empty and burning, his shoulder itched, and his hand was stinging from when he had grabbed at the sharp rocks. It pulsed with each heartbeat.

He opened his eyes and saw a faint white light. He began to hear a soft trickling of water, far away and echoing. Moisture. It clung to his breaths. He felt cold rocks with his fingers. The malagayne hadn't been crushed. He felt the weight of it on his hip.

When he opened his mouth he felt a surge of bile coming up his throat. His head crashed down onto the rocks and he retched bitter acid. Pain lanced through his left arm, numbing his fingertips.

But then he heard the slow hum, growing louder, ringing in his ears, higher and higher pitch, like a swarm of cicadas. It was coming from ahead of him and behind him. Then it picked up farther away, and he began to hear echoes of it running into the distance.

He put his hand down into a patch of sticky moss, and it began to vibrate, louder and louder, until it was humming and hissing at him just like the echoes he heard.

What the hell is this?

Aren tried to roll onto one side, but a sharp pain cut those movements short. He still had stinging in his abdomen, and his thigh was swollen and inflamed. He tried rolling the opposite way, keeping his left arm straight. It took minutes, but he made it.

Aren felt around with his good arm. He felt a cloth-covered body. Soft leather vest. It had to be the Sarenwalker.

"Eriana," he said. Whispering at first. "Eriana. Eriana!" Each time louder, until he heard his voice carry across water. He had to find her. He needed to see her, to know she was all right. What if she was hurt? His heart dropped into his bowels. She could be dying right beside him and he would never know in this darkness. He felt around, expecting her to be near, but she was not. She was gone, and his thoughts turned to poison in his skull, as cold as the icy hell he had left to come into the Blackwell.

He shook Fainen's shoulder. The Sarenwalker moved slightly. He tried again. This time Fainen groaned, and his body tensed. "Aren," he said.

"I'm here."

"Strange echoes in this place," Fainen said.

They both began to move in the pitch, scraping softly with their hands.

Then they heard a sound. A pattering of small rocks. "Aren? Is that you?"

"Inrianne? Where are you?"

"By the water. There is a basin. Filled with water. It is warm."

Aren saw little rippling reflections of the distant light. "And the others? Are they with you?"

"I am fine, thank you," Redevir said.

"And I," Tanashri said.

"Eriana," Aren called. "What about Eriana?"

"I don't know where she is," Inrianne called. "Or Keluwen."

His eyes began to adjust to the light. The *cave* was no more a cave than a mountain was a pile of dirt. Titanic walls of rock extended out in all directions, stretching toward the light. Each of the walls rose hundreds of feet above them to a stalactite-covered ceiling, hovering like a drapery of rock-clouds. Dozens of Medion Towers could have been laid end to end across an immense lake of black water.

He saw Inrianne, Redevir, and Tanashri standing by the shore. Keluwen lay unconscious. Eriana was nowhere to be seen.

"Go to the light," Redevir said.

"I do not know if you noticed, but there is a lake in the way," Inrianne said.

"Can we swim it?" Redevir asked.

"I am not in any condition for that," Tanashri said.

"I don't know whether I am up for that in optimal conditions," Aren said.

Just then Aren heard the lapping of water down in the basin growing in intensity until it began to splash on the shore, bubbling and swishing.

Inrianne scrambled away. "Aren? Something is in the water."

Aren saw a shadow, growing larger.

"It is a boat," Fainen said.

There was a lone man aboard it, standing, a pole in hand, pushing himself along.

"Speak your names," the voice said in Coralic. "Speak." This time it was Vardic. "Speak." A southern tongue, possibly Adumbraic. "Speak," the voice boomed. Haradi that time, close enough to Olbaranian for Aren to understand clearly.

"I am named Aren of Amagon," Aren said in Westrin. "Can you understand me?"

"I can," the man said. He cackled a booming cackle. "I am named Vardhemar. I am the boat man. I love to talk as much as I love to breathe, and you are the better to have met me." He possessed long grey hair, draped over one shoulder. His well-shaven face was lined with age, and bore complex scars across one side. His attire was worn, mostly of tight-fitting leather and wool. He maintained an array of amulets dangling about his neck from leather straps, all large and round.

"What do you intend to do with us, Vardhemar?" Tanashri asked.

"You are very willful," Vardhemar said. "You must forgive my caution. The people who come the way you came are not often amicable."

"We are not of them," Aren said. "We were being chased by them."

"Well then," Keluwen said over his shoulder. "Is this the river we must cross to find the sixth hell?"

Aren turned to look back at her. She had a knot on her forehead and a bruise on her cheek. A rivulet of blood had dried at the corner of her lip.

"You are lucky you fell into the screeching moss," Vardhemar said. "This is my day to go down the river. Had I not heard you I might not have been home when your companion arrived."

"Companion?" Aren asked.

Vardhemar tapped his chin. "I am surprised that you had not asked of her whereabouts already."

"Eriana?" Aren said. "Do you know where she is? Is she all right? Where is she?" She was alive. She was alive and safe. His heart burst in his chest with the sheer joy of that one little piece of knowledge. The relief itself staggered him, and he almost fell over.

"Calm. She is safe and she is well. She is quite resilient, and very demanding. She came to us asking for help. She had no light. She saw ours in the distance. She came through the darkness, hand to hand along the cave wall to find us. I will reunite you with your comrade. Then we will discuss your deliverance to the overworld."

"Are we to swim?" Inrianne asked. "Your boat is small."

"I can bring three at a time, in addition to myself," Vardhemar said. He smiled as he motioned to his craft.

Aren thought he overestimated its capacity by half, but he and Redevir were able to struggle in. Fainen offered to remain with Inrianne and Tanashri while they rested themselves. So Keluwen squeezed herself between Aren's legs, her knees up to her chest, heels on Redevir's back.

Keluwen looked over her shoulder. Shaking loose the scent of her hair in his face. "It was my sincere hope I would never have to touch you again," she said. "Don't get any ideas."

"I have none," Aren assured her. But just then Vardhemar shuddered the boat away from shore, and she slid back, her rear pushing against Aren, forcing his legs as far apart as they would go. She tipped over backwards, her back crashing onto his chest, her head falling on his shoulder, her hair brushing against his face. He shivered against the pressure.

Her eyes were wide, glancing up at him. She recoiled, flinging her upper body forward to right herself. She tried to scoot forward by wiggling side to side, but that only had a further unfortunate effect, at least until she could get herself far enough away. After that she opted to not so much as look over her shoulder at him the rest of the journey.

"Would you prefer the scenic route, or the direct route?" Vardhemar asked.

"Hurry on," Keluwen said. "The less time I have to spend with these fools the better."

Aren had no arguments there.

"You do not seem to enjoy your arrangement," Vardhemar said. "Would you prefer to be facing each other instead?"

"I would rather swim," Keluwen said.

No love lost, it seems.

"Swimming is not optimal," Vardhemar said. "There are large parasites, worm spawn, darkwater eels."

The trip lasted the longest most uncomfortable silence Aren could ever remember experiencing. Vardhemar kept near to the cave wall, skimming around the outer edge of the lake, the light gradually expanding as the tunnel opened up to a wide mouth with a narrow sandy shore beneath a rocky ledge and a series of small huts beyond, a ladder of bamboo-like poles lashed with leather strips leading up to them.

A dozen very curious people peered at them from among the huts.

"We harvest the cave mites," Vardhemar said. "In the rainy season, all the tunnels above flood out into the covered lake, and delicious cave mites are washed into its waters by the thousands." He held his hands a rabbit's length apart. "Some as big as this."

Aren stifled a gag.

Vardhemar went on unperturbed. "The heat from beneath the lake keeps our village warm through perilous winter. And volcanic slugs are plentiful."

Aren opted to direct his attention to the shore instead.

Out in front stood Eriana, her golden hair flowing down her fur coat. She appeared as a golden goddess perched atop the dark rocks, gazing out over the black water. How out of place she seemed. She had a glow about her. Aren could feel it more than he could see it. She looked...warm. He wanted to wrap his arms around her, and fight the world with her, and never let her go again. She had gone alone in this place for them, and he loved her for it.

"You may move freely," Vardhemar said, waving to his people, none of whom seemed very keen on coming down to talk to them. "I shall go back for your friends. I will return soon."

Eriana hopped down from the ledge. Her smile was as wide as the sky. "I am happy that you are well."

"Of course we are," Redevir said. "Though I hear you are the hero."

Eriana blushed ever-so-slightly. "It was what I had to do." She looked at Aren again. "Solathas taught me we must always do what we aught to do first. And what we would like to do second."

Aren smiled back, and knew he could not have made himself any more obvious. He wanted to look into her eyes all day, but knew if he started to do so, he wouldn't be able to stop.

Eriana came to him, and he expected her to stop, but instead she kept walking until she was standing right in front of him, her mouth mere inches from his, head turned up, eyes as wide as oceans. "I am very happy to see you," she said. Her lips hovered apart.

"I...So am I. I mean, to see you." He wanted to press his lips against hers and tell her he missed her with his mouth, and explain how happy he was to find her safe by wrapping his arms around her. But instead he said, "You walked a long way alone. I'm sorry I wasn't there."

"You were not awake. I was." She smiled. "The moss screamed at me."

"That sounds awful."

She leaned forward, hands clasped. "It was all right. I think it would have been worse if it was silence."

"I am so happy you are okay," he said.

She looked down and frowned. "Your poor hands." She took one in both of hers and lifted it up. It was cut and bleeding from the sharp rocks. Her fingers interlocked around it, holding it up to see.

"I'll be fine," he assured her.

She looked up at him. Then she noticed Keluwen standing there.

"Not just a pretty face then," Keluwen said to her.

Eriana narrowed her eyes at her. "Why is she still free?"

"She helped us escape," Aren said.

"Only because she would have died along with us," Eriana said.

"She could have escaped without us," Aren said. "She didn't."

Eriana never removed her eyes from Keluwen. "She tried to kill you."

"If it makes you feel any better at all, I failed to do so," Keluwen said. "Failed marvelously."

"It does not make me feel better," Eriana said coolly.

Keluwen held out both blue hands, gloves like skin up to her elbows, palms out. "I will not do it again."

Eriana turned to Aren. "Why are you letting her dictate her terms?"

Aren looked at Keluwen. "Because I made the same mistake once. Only I didn't find out until it was too late."

Eriana frowned at him. She reached out and wrapped her hands around his arm, just above the elbow, a gentle squeeze. But her eyes were claws wanting to rip Keluwen to pieces.

Keluwen barked a laugh and rolled her eyes.

"I think it will be all right," Aren said.

Eriana squinted angrily at Keluwen one last time and then walked over and sat down on the shore and looked into the peaceful darkness of the cave mouth, water lapping against her boot heels.

Aren sat down on a round stone, flipped open his tracer satchel, and checked everything inside to see if anything was broken or leaking. Thankfully, nothing was.

He found himself glancing up at Keluwen more than once.

She caught him. "Your eyes bug out any further, I may have to kick them back into your skull."

He shook his head and laughed. "Just trying to figure you out."

"You still think you can learn anything about me that I don't want you to know?"

Aren flashed a smile. "I do know *one* thing that's new about you."

She laughed a condescending laugh. "You think so?"

"You don't hate me anymore," he said. "You may not like me at all, but you don't hate me."

"How do you figure that?" she asked. "Tiny gods whispering in your ear?"

"Because it has been the better part of a day and you haven't tried to kill me once."

He watched the sly smile slide off her face, and her expression of detached superiority melted away. Her eyes widened. Aren thought he saw fear there. A fear in being known, even just a little bit. A fear far deeper than being chased by hunters could make. "You are a brave man. To remind me like that. What if I had merely forgotten?"

"You don't forget hate," Aren said. "It may simmer, it may cool, but you never forget. And I think you know that."

She pressed her lips together and squinted at him, like half a sneer. But he thought he saw the corner of her mouth curl up just a tiny bit. "Yes, I know what hate feels like very well. Someone once told me hate only begets more hate but it feels so fucking good you want to do it anyway."

"Someone you looked up to?"

She looked up at the darkness hanging high above them. "Yes. Long ago."

"The two men I looked up to the most said a lot of things, but when I try to think of the wisdom they gave me, I can never think of a line like that. There are no complete thoughts, only a thousand little impressions."

"I had a friend who was like that. My thirdbrother. He was just kind. More kind than the world deserved. I don't know what ever became of him. Someday maybe I will find out."

"Both of mine died. One before I left Amagon. The other in Laman. One was like me. A loner, so good at what he did, but had no smiles left. The other was the opposite of me. He was warm and strong, a leader that people wanted to follow. And he laughed about as often as he breathed. I wonder sometimes what either of them would say if they could see me now."

She let a minute pass, looking out across the water. "What was the one other thing? You said up above that there was one more thing you knew about me, but you weren't going to say what it was."

He nodded. "I'm still not going to. Because it would hurt you to speak it aloud. And I think you know what it is. Let's just leave it at that."

She half-squinted, half-smiled at him. She paused again, thinking to herself, chewing her lip, trying to decide something. Finally she spoke. "It is because of my own mind."

"What is?"

"The gloves," she said, holding both arms out, turning her hands over and over for him to see. "I cannot bind the streams when I have my hands covered. I just can't. It's in my head. That was why I didn't escape. That is why I didn't kill you this morning when the tinwood wore off."

He widened his eyes. "A lot can change in a day, it seems." He paused. "If you can't use with them on, then why wear them at all?"

She turned her chin up, closed her eyes, pinched her lips and shook her head. "Because when I am not wearing them I have trouble *not* binding the streams."

"You mean you use *by accident?*"

"When I am focused, I have control. But I...when I am not, when I am just living, I can't be sure I am in control."

"A failsafe," Aren said. "Interesting."

"Oh, I am interesting to the Glassboy now."

"There was a user I traced back in Amagon. He could only throw his blank impulses like he was throwing a ball, high arching curves. He couldn't make his mind believe in them unless he went through the whole motion, rearing back, using his arm. It was the only way he could make himself believe what he could do."

"There is always someone worse off, you mean."

He laughed. "Take it how you will."

She let out a long breath. "When you were in Laman I almost killed you."

"Seems like you almost kill me as often as most people take a breath."

"We were after *him*. We went from one end of Laman to the other. But he vanished. It was a waste."

"Laman did not treat me kindly either," Aren said. "I lost my friends there. The two who knew me best. And the Captain."

"You called him the Captain?" She laughed.

"No. But I find it hard to say his name. I saw him go. And every time I say his name I see it all over again."

"I lost a friend in Laman, too," she said. "He fell."

"Fell?"

"Long story."

"I'm sorry. I bet they were a good friend."

She glanced at him abruptly. "Why would you think that?"

"Because they went with you to Laman, and that alone is not easy." He paused, glancing around at the others. "And you seem like the kind of person who surrounds themselves with people far better than you think you are."

She opened her mouth as if to dispute, at least until he finished, then she closed it again. "I can't argue that. I'm sorry for your friends, too. I don't know if they were good or not, but they had to be better than you are, Glassboy." She smiled.

Aren pointed to his nose and smiled back. "What were you doing in Laman?"

"Following you." She shrugged. "Well, following *him*. Some of the people with you were contacts of ours."

"Some?"

"Amicien Duran," she said.

"Never heard of him."

"No?"

He shook his head.

"The other was Raviel."

Aren's mouth was empty but he still very nearly spit everywhere. "Raviel? The Glasseye, Raviel?"

She nodded.

"He was one of your people?"

"Not mine. But he was working with us. He wanted the same thing we did. We seem to find a great many people of like mind when it comes to hating Kinraigan."

"Agreed." He turned his head up and closed his eyes. "I wish I could take that back, what happened there. I wish, I wish, all of it."

"If you don't have a head full of thoughts like that then you haven't spent a single day on this earth." Keluwen glanced up, her eyes roamed. "Do you trust your people? The ones you have now?"

Aren closed his eyes. "I don't know. I think so."

"You know how easily he can turn people. If he spoke to even one of your crew..."

"I know."

"To do what you're planning you need to be sure."

He shrugged. "When the time comes, I will be."

"You better be, Glassboy."

"Everyone seems to think I am living out some kind of destiny," he said. "Redevir, Tanashri, Solathas. Even the elder in Westgate talked about me being part of some prophecy."

"There is no such thing."

"I know. I didn't believe in those kinds of things. My whole life. But everything keeps seeming to happen the only way it possibly could to move forward with what we are doing. It's starting to play with my head. I don't know what to think sometimes. It feels...*real* sometimes."

She turned to him, suddenly deadly serious. Not even a hint of levity—and she had made jokes when she was tied to a rock. "Aren, there is no such thing. Don't ever think there is. There is only what you think, and what you say, and what you do, and that is all there is. The world doesn't care about us. The universe doesn't make things happen. We do. I do. You do. If you want to be ambitious, then fine. But don't ever believe for a minute that what you are after is guaranteed."

"I was just telling you how it feels."

"Don't do it. Don't believe it. Not ever." Each word was a knife thrust, born of immeasurable pain.

Aren glanced up at her, squinting. "That was a strong reaction. What happened to you?"

She looked away suddenly, trying to hide reddening eyes by looking back into the darkness. "Someone we knew...our friend...thought he had a destiny. He was able to make himself into something. He said he was born for it, born to become it. He sent us a letter. He said a prophecy told him it was so. He told us there would be many like him, but only one could be him. He changed himself into something else so that he could see magick with his own two eyes."

Aren fished the Jecker monocle out of his tracer satchel. "I don't need to make myself into something to see magick. I can already see it with this."

She turned her red eyes on him. "He got himself killed. He got a lot of people killed. Even my best friend, someone closer to me than my husband. So don't you say those words. Don't you believe them. My friend, he always told me this one thing, from the first time I saw him to the last. It was in his heart every day of his life. And I say it to you now. No one can see the future. There is only me and you and what we do."

Aren held his hands up in acquiescence. "I won't speak the words ever again," he promised. But he neglected to say he wouldn't think them.

"If you ever remember one thing that I say, remember this. There is no such thing as a destiny, there is no such thing as prophecy, there is no such thing as a sure thing, and no one knows how things will turn out until they do."

He nodded. He couldn't disagree. But the thought kept worming its way into his skull and taking up residence there.

Keluwen looked over at Eriana, sitting alone on the shore. "You had better go sit next to your girl, or you are going to be in trouble."

"She's not *my* girl."

"I know you are a smart man, but for a smart man you are pretty fucking stupid." She shook her head. "She's your girl. And if you say she's not I'll find your gods and tell them you're a fucking liar."

He did not argue. She was plenty right.

He walked over to Eriana and sat beside her, watching the reflections of the last light of the sparklers shimmering on the water. He sat with her for a long time. Her hand gradually reached for his and held it. He leaned over until his shoulder touched hers. Together they watched shimmering light reflected in black water.

"Did you always want to be a Glasseye?" she asked.

"That question is out of the blue."

Eriana looked ahead coldly. "I want to be sure I know more about you than she does."

"Are you jealous?"

"Are you dimwitted?"

Aren leaned back. "If it matters—"

"It does."

"You will always know more than she does. About me. Always."

That made her feel better. Tension slid out of her shoulders, and a playful little flat smile crept back onto her face. "Do you promise this?"

"I promise this."

"Then tell me something you would not tell her. Tell me how you became the Glasseye you are. The Glasseye who came to Laman."

"I remember when I was a young boy wanting to know how to unlock the mystery of those strange, powerful people. Magick users. *Users.* I wanted to know what made them, and what unmade them. I wanted to learn the secrets of tracing. It was like learning a hidden language that could turn gods into men. So I could kill them. For what they had done."

"How long ago was that?"

He shrugged. "Years ago."

"By the Mother and Father, you really were a child then. A boy in truth."

"I had seen fifteen summers by then." Aren smiled. "Crinthos was his name. My first partner. He was patient and kind. Never rebuked an honest mistake. I learned well from him how a trace should be conducted, but he was a fifth-ranked Tracer. He hunted petty rogues. My eyes were set on tracing a *true* rogue user—a real one, someone with real power, someone truly *dangerous.*"

"Too small time for such a big boy," Eriana laughed.

"You are not going to let this go, are you?"

"I keep picturing you running all around wearing clothes ten sizes too big, trying to fit in with grown men while chasing criminals through the streets."

He rolled his eyes at her. "Eventually, my superiors in the Magistracy took notice and decided to apprentice me with a veteran Render Tracer of the first grade."

"Was it everything you hoped it would be?"

"It was like night and day. You would not believe it. I barely believed it. I was instantly elevated above the others. I traced *real* users. And other people gave me respect because of it. From the very start of our first trace, Sarker grilled me for every detail of a scene. *What does this mean? And this? What else? What are you forgetting?* He asked often enough that I started asking them myself. All I am I owe to Sarker."

"It sounds like he taught you much."

"I had already memorized most of the Jebel Dedder Manual before we met. But he did not bat an eye at that. *Your books arm you with knowledge*, he said. *But Jebel Dedder will not run your trace for you. He will not diagram your scenes, or help you to notice details. You must be capable of thinking on your feet, making inferences from evidence you may never have seen an example of before, and often in situations not of your own choosing.*"

"You remember all that?" She seemed surprised.

"Every word. Sarker was a hard man, and a relentless teacher, but he was the best that had ever been, and oh how I felt such pride to work with him." His smile dried into a frown. "None of that matters anymore."

"Because you can't go back."

"The only way left is forward."

"Solathas would say that is the only direction worth moving in."

"He would say that, wouldn't he?"

Redevir abruptly snapped his fingers in front of Aren's face. Aren blinked his eyes wide, leaned back, shook his head. "What? What?" He realized he had been so absorbed in talking to Eriana, he had not even noticed Vardhemar already returned with the others.

"Time to talk." Redevir held up the Diamond between thumb and forefinger.

Aren lost track of time in it. He could not be sure if he stared at it for a second or an hour. "You held onto it."

"I would not have come very far in my profession if I was not adept at holding onto the treasures I find."

"What is that?" Keluwen asked.

Redevir snatched it away from her, closing his fingers into a protective fist around it. "Nothing much of your concern."

"My question was rhetorical, Rover," she said. "I know what that is."

Redevir stared suspiciously at her. "How do *you* know what this is?"

"That is a very good question," Aren said.

"Because my husband's people are the ones who were watching the other four."

Aren's jaw fell open. "You knew about the stones?"

"All but this one. His organization; they kept track of them. One of our people fell to Kinraigan. We think they gave away the locations."

"So that was how he found them all so quickly," Redevir said.

"What are you going to do with it?" she asked.

"We are going to find the Crown," Redevir said.

"And set a trap for Kinraigan," Aren said.

"I told you," Keluwen said. "You are both fools. You have no idea what you are up against."

"A user is a user," Aren said. "He may be stronger, but the techniques are the same. Stop his streams. Distract his mind. Dose him. Burn him. Only the quantity is different."

"You realize you are talking about Kinraigan, don't you?" Keluwen asked. "You of all people should know, Glassboy. It was your people who were destroyed trying to capture him years ago."

"We will be better prepared," Aren said. "When that time comes."

"We already tried that," Keluwen said. "In Westgate. We set a trap. He walked right into it. Then he walked right out of it."

"You tried to capture Kinraigan? In Westgate?"

"It did not go well," she said. "And then my people followed suit. We used *your* composites. Given to us by one of *your* Glasseyes. We tried to capture him ourselves, and still failed. They were not enough. You would need your own users, or an army to stop him."

"I will do whatever it takes," Aren said. "No one has ever gotten away from me."

"You are talking about the man who controls Ghiroergans," Keluwen said. "Who wants to overthrow kings. Even your own Lord Protector couldn't stand up to him."

"They were enemies," Aren said. "They were vying for the Dagger."

"Only you found it first, Aren," Tanashri aid.

"So it was you who found the Dagger in Laman," Keluwen said.

Redevir froze. "Should we be discussing this in front of her?"

"Discussing what?" Inrianne asked. "That we had the Dagger and promptly lost it again?"

"You lost it?" Keluwen widened her eyes. "Calling you fools is beginning to seem generous."

"Kinraigan's people took it from us," Tanashri said.

"So he does have it," Keluwen said.

Aren nodded. "I think he wanted the Crown, but something changed, and he decided he needed to have the Dagger first. Either for himself or to keep someone else from having it, like a Stopper with streams.

"But why would it matter?" Eriana asked. "What does it even do?"

"No one knows," Redevir said. "But some very powerful people are willing to kill for what they think it is."

Aren nodded. "The Lord Protector. That is why he sent us. Sent me."

"I heard you were being sent out," Keluwen said. "My people were aware of it, aware he was going to go to Laman. They seemed to know from the beginning that your people marching there would put Kinraigan into a frenzy."

"I am willing to bet he and his people had been searching Laman for the Dagger for a long time before we got there," Aren said.

"So what made him turn back to the west?" Redevir asked.

"You did, Rover," Keluwen said. "You were nosing around the stones. So he moved on them all at once. My people knew that, too."

"Who are these *people* you keep referring to anyway?" Redevir asked. "Who are you?"

"Back to that again?" She planted her feet and folded her arms. "I know you are a stubborn old Rover, but you must know by now that I will meet my secondparents in the seventh hell before I tell you one thing about them."

"Raviel thought he knew where the Sephor was," Aren said. "He must have solved the same riddles and followed the same clues that you did, Redevir."

"He had been trying to convince the Lord Protector to move on it for a while," Tanashri said. "Something made the Lord Protector hold back. He was very confident he would not need to waste time chasing the Dagger."

"Something changed though," Aren said. "Lit a fire under him. He sent Margol to Laman to get the Dagger before Kinraigan could, with passes Raviel secured from Laman, using the Outer Guard as cover, faking an assassination, and sending me. He put all that together in one night."

"And us taking Raviel to Laman is what made Kinraigan race back there to make sure he could find it first."

"It was the Sephors," Aren said. "The Sephors were the motive for everything. Aldarion was willing to sacrifice his best captain, his best Render Tracers, his friends, and his best men, all just to gain more power." He turned to Redevir. "The elder in Westgate was right about one thing. He said it was all a game, and it is. It is just a game between Lord Protector Aldarion and Kinraigan, with entire kingdoms their playing boards. The Lord Protector never cared about any of us. We were just pieces on a board to him, to be moved and played in whatever gambit he desired. Me, Donnovar, Margol, Sarker, Santhalian, the Palantari, Raviel, and everyone who has died since, and everyone who is yet to die in the days to come. We have all been puppets, with strings tugged this way and that by either the Lord Protector or Kinraigan."

"That means the Lord Protector knew about all of this from the beginning," Tanashri said. "He hid all of it."

"Well the Lord Protector had us all fooled," Redevir said. "And Kinraigan has been a step ahead of us ever since."

"We should have the upper hand now," Eriana said, nodding to the Diamond. "Shouldn't we?"

"Yes, Redevir," Tanashri said. "The Diamond. Is there anything etched on it?"

Redevir turned it over. He stared at it. He stared at it a long time. He kept staring at it. Then he stared some more. He frowned.

"What is it?" Aren asked.

"What's wrong?" Eriana asked.

"Redevir?" Tanashri asked.

"It...It is just numbers," Redevir said.

"Numbers?" Aren asked. "Let me see."

Redevir held it up to him. "See?"

Aren deflated. "He is right. Just numbers."

"Two lines," Redevir said. "1 7 8 9 11 12 and 2 5 3 1 6 4."

"What do they have to do with a memorial in Karorad?" Eriana asked.

"Karorad is called the black city," Keluwen said. "Basalt quarries."

"You have been there before?" Aren asked.

She nodded, her gaze distant, lost in memory. "It is where I first met Orrinas."

"Who?"

"The man who is now my husband." Her mind fell into memory. "Another time. Snow capping everything, a black and white world. Streets deserted. A handful of stolen coins in hand. Long gone was the time when the last tavern had closed its doors. A ghost city, white streets and marble figures its only inhabitants. Home of sad temples and old gods. And he stepped out into the snow and smiled at me."

"You are wed?" Redevir asked.

"I feel you are trying to say something about me with your question, Rover. Check with your gods before you say something else. Be sure which hell you want me to send you to."

Redevir held his hands up and stepped back. "We have managed to be friends for a moment or three. Let us not slip up over subtext."

"But what do the numbers mean?" Aren asked.

"It cannot be just random numbers," Redevir said.

"That is often the first thing someone says when it is," Keluwen said.

"Do we need to go to Karorad?" Redevir asked. "Visit that memorial to the Mahhennin you mentioned?"

"It won't do you much good," Keluwen said.

"Are we now going to be subjected to contrarianism at every turn?" Redevir asked.

She shook her head. "It would serve you properly, fat lot of fools that you are. But you will find nothing there. The memorial you seek was paved over to make a festival ground. Years ago."

"How do you know that?" Aren asked.

"Because I was married there," Keluwen said.

"Are we at a dead end?" Redevir asked. "We need to consult the nearest libraries immediately."

"And look for what, Rover?" Inrianne asked. "Books about shots in the dark?"

Keluwen burst into laughter. "Like I said. Fools. One and all."

Redevir began pacing. "It must be something referencing one of the other stones. It can't be nothing. It can't be nothing."

"That brings us right back where we started," Tanashri said.

"That entire journey through Bolan was for nothing," Aren said. He had to sit down. The wave of futility washed over him, turning his legs to rubber.

"The wise," Keluwen said. "The clever. How far they fall."

"Shut up," Aren said. "Just shut up."

"So much for your precious shortcut," Tanashri said.

"We just wasted so much time," Inrianne said.

"What are we going to do now?" Eriana asked.

"Start over," Redevir said. "Use the Diamond for leverage. Advertise we have it in hopes that we can set a trap for Kinraigan, while we search for something to give us the final instruction of how to find it."

"That is two dead ends in a row," Inrianne said.

The Rover's face turned red. He reared back and readied himself to throw the stone into the black water.

Keluwen nodded approval. "Now that is real emotion. To throw a fortune away for one moment of anger. That is the kind of thing that gets my blood flowing."

"Wait," Eriana said at the last possible moment. "The numbers."

"What about them?" the Rover asked.

"Show me," she said.

He held it down for her.

"Two rows of numbers," she said. "1 7 8 9 11 12 on the top, and 2 5 3 1 6 4 underneath."

"What does it matter?" Inrianne asked.

"Two wrongs," she said. "Two dead ends. A code. Solathas used to play word games, some with each letter having a corresponding number."

"A code for what?" the Rover asked.

"Isn't it obvious?" she asked. "The Karorad inscription. Aren, what was it?"

"*Avy Temis Volarat.*"

"So 1 would be A," the Rover began. "7 would be I...."

"No, S," Aren corrected. "The E sound is unwritten."

"8 is V, 9 is O, 11 is A again, and 12 is R."

"It spells *Asvoar*," Keluwen said. "It is nonsense. It doesn't mean anything."

"She's right," Aren said. "Those letter combinations don't exist in Vardic or any other language."

"Damn," the Rover said. "What about the other line?"

"2 5 3 1 6 4," Eriana said. "V M Y A I T. It spells *Vmyaith.*"

"That doesn't mean anything either," Aren said.

"Wait," Eriana said, her eyes darting between the two rows of numbers. "What's strange about these two sets?"

"One row has double-digit numbers," Keluwen said.

"That is part of it," she said. "Look at the first row. All the numbers are in increasing order, but the bottom row has numbers out of sequence."

"What does that have to do with anything?" Redevir asked.

"If you look at the top line, it has six of a possible fourteen letters, AVY TMIS VOLARAT. The bottom line is made up of numbers one through six. Six numbers. The second line unscrambles the first. Codes within codes, Solathas called it. Sometimes he would make them in a hundred steps to show that one mistake could ruin the result."

"A S V O A R," the Rover rearranged them in his head. "S A V A R O. *Savaro.* Is that a word?"

"It's Vardic," Aren said. "*Savaro* is the Vardic word for *sanctuary.*"

"Is that the clue?" Tanashri asked. "Sanctuary?"

"It has to mean something," the Rover said. "What is a *sanctuary* in Arradan?"

Aren's jaw fell open, wide as the Blackwell. "Not *a* sanctuary. *The* sanctuary of Arradan. The one safe place during the most catastrophic disaster in history. Shaezrod Spur."

Redevir smiled. "Of course you would know precisely what it means. Destiny knocks, and you answer."

Aren did not respond. He was too afraid he would agree.

"We have a place to go," Redevir said. "Arradan's Capital. We have to go to Arthenorad. What else do we need?"

"How about a way out of here?" Inrianne said.

"And a way to travel as well," Tanashri said. "Arthenorad lies in central Arradan. That is quite a distance to cover."

"We shall manage," Redevir said.

"How?" she demanded. "Hundreds of miles. Our horses remain outside the Blackwell, as do our provisions. We will not travel far without sustenance, and with nothing to prevent the cold from claiming us, we would scarcely live beyond the first sunset."

"We will find some strong horses," Redevir said.

"With what money?" The Saderan glared hard at him. "At what town?"

"We will steal the horses if we have to!" Redevir shouted. "We have to get to Arthenorad."

"Arthenorad, you say?" Vardhemar boomed behind them.

"We must go there," Redevir said. "It is a matter of some urgency."

"You are in a more cordial mood, Redevir," Vardhemar said. "That is pleasant. I can bring you to Arthenorad."

"*You* can take us there?" Redevir asked.

"Well, not take," Vardhemar laughed. "But I can arrange your passage."

"Passage on what?" Keluwen asked.

"You think you are coming with us?" Redevir asked. "The hell you are."

"You are going the same place I am," she said. "And you are alive to do it because I let you be."

"What manner of vehicle could bring us all the way to Arthenorad?" Aren asked.

"It is a long journey," Tanashri said.

"But it is a quick one," Vardhemar said.

"Quick?" Redevir laughed. "It is hundreds of miles from here."

Vardhemar smiled. "Just over these hills is the northernmost frontier of Arradan. Beyond a high ridge there is a spur of tracks. It is the furthest extension of such tracks in all Arradan, used to supply their frontier legions. They let the Shola people ride for free most days on their return."

"Tracks for *what*?" Keluwen asked.

"A Deepland Crawler," Vardhemar said.

48

A Good Tavern

CORRIN LOVED A GOOD tavern.

This particular one was exceptional. The dining room was wide and well lit by endless chandeliers dangling from bronze chains. The room was choked with tables, every last one full. The walls were of dark mahogany, lined with panels of emerald velvet.

The bar itself was as long as any three he had seen in Vithos combined. It was topped with smooth quartz, deep blue like ocean water, and fine glasses clinked against it as patrons raised and lowered their drinks.

The stools were well cushioned with soft leather stuffed with fur. He looked past the bartenders in their violet silk shirts, and watched the reflections of women wearing low cut blouses and blossoming skirts in enormous mirrors suited to the palace of a king.

Windows lined the outer wall, providing views of a long patio and the women walking upon it. Corrin especially enjoyed the women—skin of every pallor, eyes of every color, and no dress the same as any other. And beneath every skirt the *Arradian fashion* awaited.

He received his drinks from a young girl with a narrow neck and olive skin. Her slender waist was draped with a sash of green like the walls, and her eyelashes flicked like black flames when she smiled at him. He placed one of Mardin's double silvers in her delicate hand. It was a generous tip for merely an armful of beverages, but her beauty had been plenty generous to his eyes. He headed back to his table, attempting and failing to avoid staring at the shape of her body beneath her nearly transparent dress.

He stepped through clouds of smoke from every flavor of tabac that had ever tickled his imagination. He reveled in the smells, and sipped at his whiskey—a good variety, imported from Samartania. It flashed like spice in his mouth and left his throat warm.

A woman snorted loudly near him, and burst into laughter, clapping her hands together. Another man cursed and slapped someone on the shoulder, flashed an angry look, then laughed, his chest heaving like a fat barrel. Corrin smiled. These were the sights and smells of home. *They know how it's done in Arradan.*

He finally managed to squeeze his way back to the table he had selected, large and round. It already stank of spilled liquors, and Mardin whimpered as he touched a hand into the sticky residue.

Corrin rolled his eyes. He placed his load of beverages on the table with a thump, and looked past them. He took a long swig of whiskey and smiled. He turned down to Hallan. "Having fun yet?"

"Yes." Hallan smiled, pointing at the lights. "Shiny."

"Good," Corrin snorted. "It's about time we had some enjoyment." He pushed a tall glass to the boy. "Drink this."

Hallan took the cup in both hands, and sipped from it, staining his mouth red. He licked his lips and smiled wide.

"Raspberry," Corrin informed him. "Good stuff."

"At least something tastes good around here," Mardin said, wincing as he sipped from his own glass.

"What?" Corrin asked. "You don't like your drink?"

"What is it? It tastes like acid."

"It's called whitewater," Corrin said. "It's pure alcohol."

Mardin coughed and spit on the floor. "Why?"

"Why what? Why does it exist?"

"Why did you get it for me? Reidos gets ale, and...and Hallan gets raspberries. What is this for?" He held up his glass like an offensive piece of refuse.

"I'm trying to make you into more of a man."

"And this is the best you could come up with?"

"It's a good start. Quit whining. I killed some fool three times to keep our asses alive, and I'm not going to let you squander my gift. Just let me do what I do."

Mardin groaned. "Whatever you say."

Corrin tossed the final dash of whiskey down his throat. He looked around for a serving girl, saw several, but none close enough to call over to the table. He decided he would get himself three drinks next time. The only thing Corrin hated about a tavern was waiting for a drink.

He chose what was in his opinion the loveliest of the servers, and approached her quickly. He sidestepped between two large, raucous, burly men on his way, earning him a few stares, but he ignored these and kept going. Nothing was going to diminish his good time.

He was almost upon his female goal, when he noticed the rich smells of roast lamb and sautéed potato slices. It reminded him of how hungry he was.

When in doubt, follow the cook.

He looked down at the table from which the aromas issued. Five men and one woman sat there, with the remaining chairs already appropriated by larger parties nearby. One man was bearded, wearing robes of pale orange, the rest all wore tunics and trousers. The woman was slender, skin of deep olive, black hair as fine as silk, in an ivory tunic with three-quarter sleeves. The man seated next to her looked like her grumpy old grandfather. They were with two men who looked like hired hands.

As he scanned the table, the last man looked up. He had prominent cheeks, and a slender jawline. Short hair. Dark brown to match his tunic.

Corrin widened his eyes. "Duran?"

Duran looked up at him nervously, made eye contact, then looked away quickly, exchanging glances with the others.

"Duran. That is you, isn't it?" He sidled up to them. "I'll be damned. You made it after all."

The grumpy grandfather leaned over to Duran. "Get rid of him. We cannot follow the Sister out of here in stealth with this yapping dog around."

"Corrin." Corrin pointed his thumb at himself. "Corrin. Remember me? My name's Corrin. Corrin the Magnificent. Last I saw of you was on the Fields of Syn."

Duran flinched, then pushed his half full plate of food back from the edge of the table. His friends seemed uncomfortable.

"You don't recognize me?" Corrin asked. "I was the one who found that boy that you were taking care of."

Everyone at the table stopped and stared.

"The boy?" one of the men asked. "*The* boy? The one we have been looking for?"

"The same," Duran admitted.

"As long as you are not child-killing assassins, too," Corrin said, chuckling to himself. He turned around and waved through a cloud of smoke to Reidos. He gestured for him to get the others to come over and join him. Reidos gestured back that he would send Mardin with Hallan, but that his leg still hurt, and he would remain behind to hold the table. Corrin nodded approval.

The whole crowd at the table made the same disgruntled face when he mentioned assassins.

"We should get rid of him," the grumpy grandfather warned again.

The other man at the table raised his hand, signaling silence. "Has someone pursued you? Since you departed Laman?"

"Let me count the ways—the Vuls, the Palantari, disgruntled horse owners, and the assassin. He is probably the first one I should have mentioned. He is the one who was coming after Hallan."

"After the boy specifically?" Duran asked. "Can you describe him?"

"He dressed in black clothes," Corrin said. "And he had short blond hair, almost white."

"Sedmon," Duran's friend said. "It could only be Sedmon."

"Small wonder it was so urgent I try to find the boy," Duran said. "If Sedmon was sent after him it must mean the boy is very special indeed. I hope that will be of some small consolation to your wife, Orrinas."

"Who the hell is that?" Corrin asked. "You know his *name*? And how is that exactly?" His hand went to the hilt of his longsword. "You will begin providing me with some decent answers, or I may not be able to account for any wild and dangerous motions of this weapon."

"He was conditioned by the Ministry," Orrinas said. "A *sniffer*. Someone who can feel magick, and the connection to the source. He hunts people. He has served the Priests in Almar since his youth. Several years ago he went missing. Some said he went to work for the someone here in the north."

"Well, I think I found him. Or rather he found us. He came after us three times. After Hallan. It is purely due to my magnificence that we were able to get him here in one piece."

Duran did not respond, but his eyes went wide when he noticed Hallan snaking between the drinkers, with Mardin close behind. "He is with you? *You* are the one who brought Hallan here?"

"I certainly did."

Orrinas leaned back in his chair. "We must see him. He must be protected until we can determine exactly what has happened to him, and how he can help us."

Corrin flattened his lips. "Everyone thinks he is special apparently." He turned to look for the boy

As Hallan approached, he was suddenly bumped by a loud fat man, and knocked into a second man at another table, jolting him in turn. He then squeezed by.

Mardin attempted the same route after him.

The man Hallan had bumped turned and stood. His head was shaven and tanned, and he wore a sleeveless leather vest from which tattoos issued like snakes, writhing about his muscled arms. His face was round and bore a thick, black mustache. Corrin took one look at him and snorted. He didn't trust a man who wouldn't wear sleeves this late into autumn, even if it was Arradan.

The man leaned in close to Mardin's face, and stopped him with a hand to the shoulder. He began barking some drunken diatribe that Corrin could not quite understand. Mardin shrank back, leaning into a fat man behind him. Mardin was afraid. Mardin was usually afraid, but Corrin surmised that this time it might be warranted.

Mardin attempted to slide past the man accosting him, nodding his head apologetically, but the sleeveless man reached after him, hitting his shoulder hard to turn him back around.

More men at the table also stood up. They were tall and strong. Not Arradian from the look of them. Likely from Lenagon, or possibly Vandolin. Two of them wore lemon yellow surcoats. They may have been knights then, but the coats were now more dried vomit than fabric from what he could tell.

But the mustache looked like a fashion of the south, Valarna or Tobria. They obviously spoke Olbaranian common. Too gruff to be merchants, and too obnoxious to even be merchant's shipmen. Mercenaries then, or just plain brigands.

"I told you to watch your step, Juk," the sleeveless man shouted.

Mardin's face went pale. He looked around as if trying to wish himself out of this situation.

"Do you eat shaot, shaot-eater?" Sleeveless asked. He wrapped one hand around Mardin's throat, pointed in his face, and tapped his nose. "I'm gonna break you, little Juk farmer. Stomp your piss out. Put a fist in your mouth. Shaot-eaters don't need teeth."

"*What* did you just say?" Corrin demanded, stepping up to him.

The man relieved some of the pressure on Mardin's neck, and took a half step toward Corrin. "I said I'm gonna make this bitch piss himself."

"Now why in the hell would you say something like that?"

"I say what I want. Problem?"

"Problem," Corrin said.

"You gonna do something?"

"Of course."

"What you think you're gonna do?"

"I'd rather not say," Corrin admitted. "It would spoil the surprise."

"What?"

"You are as dumb as you are hideous," Corrin said. "And you fight as bad as you smell."

The man snarled at him. "I'm gonna...I'll kill you."

Corrin laughed in his face. "Oh, please do. I can't wait. Honestly."

Sleeveless released Mardin, and lunged. Corrin brought his elbow up and cracked him across the face with a twist of his torso. Before Sleeveless could recover, Corrin brought it back and smacked it into his head again, just behind the eye. Corrin kept his fist low, and then landed and uppercut that took his jaw dead to center. Corrin lifted his right foot, planted it behind his opponent's, reached across his body with both hands, and pulled the man over his leg, dropping him like a sack to the floor.

"*That,*" Corrin said. "That right there is pretty much exactly what I was going to do."

Corrin turned away from him, then thought for a moment, came back to him, and jammed a boot down hard on his abdomen. The man's bladder had been nearly full, and it emptied a bucket of urine through the trousers. "No one makes my friends piss themselves, farod."

Sleeveless' three companions were taken aback by the whole display, but not for long. They rounded the table and came at Corrin from all sides.

The first grabbed Corrin's collar with both hands and pushing him back. Corrin let the man take him back a ways. Then he locked his hands around the man's wrists. Separated them. Reared his head back. Head-butted him. Scored a direct hit on the nose. The man dropped like a crumpling doll. Blood poured like a red stream of wine down his chin.

Corrin found himself wrapped in a head lock. He struggled. Yet another man threw punches into his stomach. Corrin clenched his abdomen, resisting the blows with as much strength as he could.

He noticed that the man holding him was not pressing his head down properly. Corrin tilted his body to one side and raised an arm beneath the man's hold. The man tried to maintain his grasp, but Corrin pulled him along, leaned forward, and flipped him over his back. The man's tenacious grip actually made it *easier* for Corrin to throw him. He landed atop his companion, and then the ground.

Corrin danced back, as another man tried to shove him. He spun away and the man glanced off his hip, crashing into the fat man at the next table. The fat man stood, his chair clattering to the floor. He grabbed the man, lifted him into the air, and slammed his body down into another table, cracking it down the middle and shattering the legs. Full glasses sloshed empty and fresh plates of food broke apart, tossing their contents onto a half dozen others.

Two men from *that* table charged the fat man and drove him backward. His body leveled another table, and knocked over several occupied chairs. A young woman was thrown forward, struck a table edge, and fell with her lip split. A man whom Corrin assumed to be her beau, flew to his feet, raised a stool, and launched it at, of all people, Corrin.

Corrin ducked it easily, but heard it make contact with someone else. Within seconds the entire room erupted into a raucous brawl. Fists flew like the arrows, stools were raised like warhammers, and every dish became a discus. Corrin dipped low under a swinging arm, and grabbed Mardin by the cuffs of his shirt. "I've been to this party before. We need to go now."

He snatched up Hallan before leaping across a table. Mardin struggled to follow, slipping on plates and knives, eventually crawling over tables to make his escape. Corrin could not see Reidos anywhere, only hundreds of moving shapes. Some headed for the doors, but many others punched at anyone and everyone who came within their range.

Corrin leapt onto another table, and saw a man raising a chair over his head to swing. Corrin kicked him in the face, sent him to the floor, and ran past him. He ducked under punches and swirled away from holds until he was at the wall. He made a beeline for the door, but a man suddenly blocked his path.

It was one of Sleeveless' friends, a man in a black coat. The man's eyes went wide. "You!"

"Me," Corrin agreed, and scraped the instep of his boot down the length of the man's shin. The man howled with the quick pain, but managed to get a hand around Hallan's shoulder. But Reidos was suddenly there.

Reidos took a running start and half-pushed, half-tackled the man into one of the wide panes of glass. They both went through, with Reidos atop him. Reidos took a fistful of the man's hair, and dashed his head repeatedly against the solid wood of the patio floor until he ceased to move.

Corrin opted to avoid the door. It was crowded into a bottleneck by panic-stricken people seeking to avoid the fray. Corrin held Hallan through the window, plopped him down on the other side, and then leapt through himself. Mardin was right behind him.

Brawlers came through the window after them, taking their fights into the streets of dusk, to finish their battles under a black sky.

Corrin looked left. Empty street. Looked right. Arradian soldiers in grey shirts coming on fast. He saw Duran and his friends about to be enveloped by them. "Duran!" he called out. "This way. Come on."

Duran gestured silently to his friends, and pointed at Corrin. They made their way straight toward him, but a man ran in their way, swinging fists. The robed man raised his hands gently, and the brawler was lifted off his feet and tossed away like a rag doll.

He is a user. Corrin flinched. *Damn magick.*

Duran nearly reached him, but he was sideswiped by a drunken fighter, and jarred from his feet. Duran sprang upward, grabbed the man by the cuffs of his shirt, and rolled onto his back, pulling the man with him, and tossing him upside down to the street.

Arradian soldiers arrived and began breaking up the fights. Everyone was scrambling.

Corrin had seen enough. He pulled Hallan away toward an alley. Mardin was behind him, fear frozen on his face. Reidos followed, shaking glass from his hair.

"This way!" Duran called out to them, waving them to a dark door down an alley. "There is a tunnel under the Causeway Road."

Corrin pursed his lips. "If I ever actually find a fucking causeway, I better get to do something magnificent on it." Corrin told the wind.

Reidos nudged him.

Duran waved again. "Bring the boy. Come on."

Corrin looked at Reidos.

Reidos shrugged.

Corrin did the same. "When in doubt, follow the cook."

49

Tower

"CAN WE PLEASE DOSE her again?" the Rover asked.

He waved his finger at Keluwen as if she was a beloved neighbor's misbehaving child.

"I am not dosing her again," Aren said. "I don't use tinwood leaf resin on people just because you don't like them, Redevir."

"I should never have paid your way," Redevir grumbled to Keluwen. "Your insolence rises above that of Tathred Mallios, and I can barely stand to be near him."

Aren had listened to this bickering from the moment Vardhemar saw them off, lasting the entire ride on the Deepland Crawler, from Tallirad to Nidarorad to Arragandis to Arthenorad. He very nearly lost his temper at the Rover, but now that they were in the city, it didn't matter. He could ignore anything in this place. Even the pain from his wounds. Even the craving of malagayne. Well, maybe not *anything*.

Arthenorad was wide plazas and racetracks, stunning domes and towers, mausoleums and cathedrals. It was the crush of people moving through the markets. It was statues of saints and heroes beneath the prismatic luminescence of stained glass windows.

I am standing in the middle of history, Aren thought.

Everywhere he looked, he could have been gazing at a spot where Regamun the Great stepped, where the great conquerors Jormasir and Ladathred may have leaned against a shallow fountain while sipping morningwine before departing on their crusades, where Hadon Caida had rallied his men with one of his famous speeches for one last desperate battle to hold the city against Kradishah's hordes. The streets Aren walked upon had felt the footsteps of emperors for thousands of years.

Before it had been sacked by the Sur, it had been the wealthiest city the world had ever known, and perhaps would ever know. The main avenue had been named the Golden Way for a reason beyond the splashing of sunlight on its stones. The bronze statue of Allunevin in Talorin was a replica of the original solid gold masterpiece of Streolan, the imperial metalworker under Emperor Castagan. The quartz crystal embedded in the sword of Harowan's statue had once been a diamond. It had been stolen by the same barbarians who had melted Streolan's statue to make gold trinkets.

Unfortunately, Arthenorad was also the archaic labyrinthine bureaucracy called the Administrad. Everything that happened in Arradan had to find its way through that maze of documents, stamps, seals, and clerks.

To be granted access to the city, Redevir had been required to fill out three forms in duplicate, sending half to an architeer and half to a codicer. He then had to bribe each of them to not put his requests at the bottom of a ten-year-long pile.

Once they had taken Redevir's silver, they were sent through without delay.

Aren took to the streets, Eriana following alongside him. Even with the beauty of Arthenorad to distract him, it was difficult to keep his eyes away from her. He found himself glancing over at her when he was sure that she wasn't looking. Just to catch a glimpse of her smile, to make sure she was well. He was happy to have someone with him who would appreciate the ancient power of places like this—its energy, its rich history. None of the others understood that.

She caught him looking at her more than once, and each time her smile beamed even brighter, and she would turn her head away with a satisfied grin.

Keluwen caught him looking at Eriana at least twice as often as Eriana herself did, and every time she shook her head disapprovingly.

"Are you going to babble to us about Arradan some more, Glassboy?" Keluwen asked.

"What would you like to know?" he asked.

"They say Arradians have no hair between their legs," Eriana said out of the blue.

Aren nearly tripped over his own feet. "Perhaps a different question?"

Keluwen laughed her heart out at this. "No, let us remain with this one. They shave everything from the neck down. Even the men."

Eriana's eyes widened. "The men? How do they...?"

"They find a way," Keluwen said.

"We could talk about their culture," Aren suggested. "Their food, their history."

"Do they shave this way in Amagon?" Eriana asked.

Aren said nothing. He wondered if they had a name for the shade of red he was certain his face was turning.

Keluwen chuckled to herself. "Traveling with the same set of faces on a Deepland Crawler for days on end really brings forth the most pressing questions."

"Arradan conquered most of the western world," Aren finally said. "*Some* still follow their traditions. Of which there are many. On many *other* topics."

"In Laman they say our ancestors believed that all marriageable women had to depilate to remain scentless to the thirst of evil," Eriana said. "So the winged demons of the midnight god could not prey upon the fertile. It was a religious tradition."

Keluwen raised an eyebrow when she was sure Aren was looking at her. "So...how observant are you?"

Aren coughed. "There is a mausoleum ahead," he said. "See it there."

Eriana shrugged at Keluwen. "It is just a tradition now. Some follow it but not me. But I am curious now."

Thank every god. We can stop this conversation now. But as it was, he was now aware of something that would be difficult not to fixate on. He nodded, looking at the street, pretending to be uninterested.

Keluwen noticed and laughed. "Yes, I am enjoying this, Glassboy, if that is what you are wondering."

"I wasn't."

Keluwen laughed all the while. "There have been times when I thought I would never laugh again, Glassboy. But I cannot help the pleasure of digging a good needle in." She paused. "Why don't you tell her what the pyramid of Daath is?"

"Pyramid of Daath?" Eriana asked. "Is that a kind of temple?" She began looking all around for sign of one.

Keluwen smiled. "Oh, it is certainly something to kneel in prayer to. I am sure Aren would be able to tell you all about it."

"Daath is an upside down triangle in the geometry of Holy Sephalon," Redevir said. "That would make for perilous architecture."

"Perilous indeed," Keluwen said.

"I have to check on something," Aren abruptly said, flipping his tracer satchel open and rummaging through it for whatever it was he was supposed to be checking on until his blood cooled.

"Which way to the tower?" Redevir asked.

Keluwen rolled her eyes at him as hard as a mule kick. "It is only already visible." She pointed one gloved hand.

"Why are you here again?" Redevir asked.

"Because this is where my people were going when I saw them last," she said.

"Wouldn't you rather see *them*, not us?" Redevir asked. "Begone."

"I would rather look at the shit on the boot heel of my least favorite friend for a whole year than see your face for even a second," Keluwen assured him.

"Then by all means go," Redevir said.

"It is a big city, Rover," she said. "I will have every minute of the world to find them. I want to witness the end of your rainbow."

"How much gold, Aren?" Redevir asked. "How much will I have to bribe you to dose her with that substance again. How much?"

"I am not dosing her again," Aren said. *Unless she brings up pyramids again.*

"We are in Arradan now," the Rover said. "Everything has a price here."

Keluwen smirked at Redevir. "Even hiding a Rover's body."

Redevir made a sour face at her. "I don't like you at all. I hope to lose you soon, and never have to see you again."

Keluwen actually smiled. "That is the sweetest thing you could ever say to me."

Eriana thought every one of their interactions was the funniest thing she had ever heard. She laughed herself all the way across the city listening to them. She would take Aren's hand every time she laughed, and turn to him, making him laugh as well. Every time her head leaned in a little closer to his. Until one time where their foreheads actually touched, and she turned her face up, eyes locked on his, lips so close.

Aren felt the moment like peal of thunder, and the world stopped, and his feet may or may not have been touching the ground, and he heard no sound and felt no breeze. Her mouth was close enough he could feel her exhales on his lips. Gravity ceased to be beneath him, and became her instead, drawing him down, descending beyond the point of return.

"Aren!" Redevir called out. "Catch up. Faster."

The sound of the Rover's voice shook gravity back to its usual orientation. Aren leaned back a fraction. Eriana took a cue from him and leaned back as well, an inch at a time, each of them looking to each other whether to lean in close or pull back. Eventually they pulled back. And then they were just walking silently side by side again. But she still smiled every time she caught him glancing at her out of the corner of his eye.

"We have to move fast," Redevir said. "The tower is close, and time is not on our side."

Aren nodded. He forced himself to keep going.

He barely saw any of the people he passed. They were moving like herded animals, darting in and out of the crush. For a moment he wondered what it would be like to be one of them. To be quiet and contented. To disappear in the masses. To escape. But that little part of him would never be allowed control.

It doesn't matter. I can do this. We can. We can stop him. The old man was right. I was meant to do this.

Aren paused and leaned against the wall, pretended to adjust his belt so he could look at the pouch of malagayne, know it was still there. And once he did, he wanted to have it. Jaw clenched. Salivating. His hands tightened into fists. He was sweating in the cold. He was running low. He would have to remedy that. *Everything has its price here.*

"Come on," Redevir said over his shoulder.

Aren slid back into a stride and kept going.

Shaezrod Spur stood like a stone splinter pointing defiantly at the sky. Its wide gardens were empty. Superimposed octagonal towers rose above a heavily buttressed base. The stone was deep red, with blue marble decorations and narrow windows of colored glass running to its pinnacle. The tower lived apart from the city, approached by wide courts and gardens, away from the dwellings and dormitories, a lonely monument.

It had been called one of the wonders of the world. *Sanctuary.* Aren could almost feel the vibration, feel the resonance of the Crown within the ancient walls.

The tower was the only possible answer. When the sorcerer-emperor Devron had made his disastrous decision so long ago, Shaezrod Spur provided the only safe haven from the storm that followed. While the empire was shaken with earthquakes and floods and firestorms, the seven Patriarchs stood at the top of the tower and used their power and gave their lives to stop it. It was named Sanctuary, and those Patriarchs were the Seven Saints.

"We're here," Inrianne said. "Now what?"

"We go inside," Redevir said.

"Then what?" Inrianne pressed him.

"We'll find out," the Rover said.

"I find it marvelous how it seems like you have a plan when you very obviously have no plan," Keluwen said.

Stairs of weathered marble led up to the entrance. The doors were open wide. The central chamber was entirely hollow up to the utmost height of the tower. The ground floor was wide, with three-foot hexagonal tiles running from wall to wall. It was an enormous hollow shell, with a winding stair running up the wall in a never-ending spiral. Warm melenkeur bathed the walls with orange light. Dozens of cupolas pocked the base of the tower, with shrines and statues hidden within their recesses.

Aren immediately felt that something was wrong. No one tended the shrines within. The tower was empty.

"Is it odd that this place is unguarded?" Redevir asked.

"Very," Aren said.

"Should we be concerned?"

"Very."

"We need to work fast then," Redevir said. "Spread out. Look around."

"To the top?" Inrianne asked.

"That would be my guess," Redevir said. "The top of the sanctuary." He ran to the stairs, taking them three at a time.

Sanctuary, Aren thought. *Refuge. Shelter. Safe place.* He remembered the words of Solathas. The mother gods were of the earth. They gave shelter from within the ground. "Redevir, wait."

The Rover turned on his heels, gripping the rail of the stone bannister. "What?"

"Sanctuary," Aren said. "It's a double meaning."

"How so?" Inrianne asked.

"During times of drought and war in ancient times, the Vardans of Arradan feared that their gods were angry. They would enter sacred shrines in sacred rooms to pray to their gods for mercy and protection. It was a spiritual sanctuary for prayer. They *descended* into these holy rooms. They weren't looking up, they were looking down."

"Down?" Redevir asked. "Would their be such a room here?"

"There must be an entrance on the ground floor," Inrianne said.

"Let's find it," Redevir said.

Aren scanned the room. Every recess appeared the same. He saw no doors or portals.

"Where could it be?" Inrianne asked.

"The shrines," Redevir said. "Look in the corners."

They fanned out, each taking a different cupola. Redevir found a statue of a winged lion with four arms. Inrianne stared at the bust of an emperor. Fainen found a solemn shrine with effigies of speared angels reaching out to the sky. Aren was greeted by frescoes of tearful women praying to a man with a sun for a head.

"Nothing," Fainen said, looking at a small obelisk.

"And the floor?" Redevir asked.

"Solid," Tanashri said.

"Is this what you do every time?" Keluwen asked. "Just run around and hope you see something that somehow no one else has seen in hundreds of years?"

Redevir squinted at her. "I do not see you positing any alternatives."

She shrugged. "This is not my mission, it's yours. I would never have come here in the first place."

"Then why are you here?" Redevir fumed.

"Yes, why *are* you here?" Eriana repeated.

"To keep eyes on you," she said. "If Kinraigan is half as interested in you as little Glassboy makes it seem, then I want to know why."

"Because he is insane," Aren said. "His reason is imaginary."

"Like your reason for being in this place?" Keluwen asked. "You are like mad little tourists."

"I like her," Inrianne said.

"You shouldn't," Keluwen told her. "I don't pick favorites."

Aren shook his head. "She's right. We are fools to think we can walk into a place that has hosted thousands of people a day for centuries and see something that has not already been seen, find something not already found. Every coronation of any important dignitary is performed here. Every elite marriage, every celebration of birth. The White Penitents pray to the Arradian Firebird weekly. Even the Doomsayers of Koshie come here to be sanctified after eating the demons of the ill. The smallest crack, divot, scar, hole, recess, would have already been seen and explored a thousand times over."

"Well, now I feel like I have ruined all the fun," Keluwen said, smiling.

"Don't act like you don't like it," Eriana said.

"What do we do now?" Inrianne asked.

"We retreat," Tanashri said. "Rent rooms. Regroup. Visit the libraries. Look for some insight as to what we missed."

"I don't see how a hint could have been any clearer," Redevir said.

"My people said there was another Sister nosing around this place," Keluwen said. "Maybe you should go ask her."

Redevir glanced from her to Tanashri. His brow narrowed in anger. "*What* other Sister?"

Tanashri's expression did not change, which for a Saderan could have been the equivalent of sanctimonious rage. "My Sisters go everywhere in the world. Arradan is a place in the world."

Aren tried his best to ignore them, looking up to the top of the tower, trying to think of an answer. The words of Solathas were in his head. *Our people seek for the deep earth. They fear for their souls, and pray to the mother goddess.* "The stairs. That's it."

"What's *it?*" Inrianne asked.

"During times of joy and strength the Patriarchs ascended the stairs to the high chambers to be closer to the father gods of the sky, the ones who gave them glory and plenty. In times of suffering, they descended to be near the mother gods of protection who lived in the earth."

"You mentioned that," Redevir said. "I don't follow."

"The gods of sky and earth were *linked*," Aren said. "Joined by a funnel of energy and spirit. A shaft of power made by a spiral of limitless light. That's why the stairs of this tower were constructed as a spiral. The central shaft is the symbolic link between heaven and earth. I always thought that they were connected in the center of the tower, the midpoint between solid ground and the pinnacle."

"That is what the History of Jordanus tells us," Tanashri said. "The gods of the high sky join the gods of the solid earth."

"That's what Jordanus wrote," Aren said. "But Jordanus was notorious for mistranslating Old Ardis. I can't believe I didn't think of it before. In different context, the word *solid* actually means *deep*. The gods of the *deep* earth."

"What are you saying?" Redevir asked.

"Wisdom, Aren," Tanashri said. "The ancient Vardans built their stairs into the high sky. They must also have built them into the deep earth."

"But where?" Inrianne asked.

"They must descend as deep as the tower is tall," Aren said. "It would be the only way to achieve balance."

"So the gods would not be jealous of one another," Tanashri agreed.

"It makes sense," Redevir said. "But these stairs end at the floor."

"Not here," Aren said. "But the quarry where the stone for this tower was mined is only a quarter mile from here. It was sanctified when the tower was first built. It is considered sacred. They ceased all mining from it. It is just a wide crater now."

"There could have been a secret holy place carved in it," Tanashri urged. "The Histories. Do they say anything of the construction of this tower? Do they ever mention it?"

"No one goes there. It would be a perfect place to hide something."

"Let us be on our way," Redevir said.

They tore out of the tower. Aren flew down the steps and coasted across the wide grassy lawn and through old shacks and abandoned hostelries until he reached the edge of the quarry. It was not fenced off in any way. It was just a circular depression in the earth, with a ramp cut into the stone around the outside edge.

Redevir led the way down the ramp to the bottom. "I don't see anything. Not even footprints."

"This is not nearly deep enough to equal the height of the Spur," Inrianne said.

"This is just silly," Keluwen said. "You are little children playing in the dirt."

Redevir gazed all around. "There must be a passage somewhere. In the rock face, or in the ground." The Rover began pacing. "There must be something."

"There isn't," Keluwen said.

"What about this slab of rock?" Inrianne asked. "Near the ramp."

"What about this rock here," Keluwen said, choosing one at random. "What about that one there?"

Aren ignored her. They gathered around Inrianne. It was a slab carved out of the side of the crater, flat on one side but still unfinished rock on the other. It was more than two feet thick.

"Don't bother trying to move that by hand," Aren said. "We will need a team of laborers."

"Unless one of you can do it," Redevir said, pointing to the users. "We need some magick."

"It will be beautiful to see your face when you realize you were so wrong, Rover," Keluwen said.

"I will do it," Tanashri said. She raised her hands and focused all her thought on the stone slab. She wove a blank lever to pull the slab across the ground. She changed out the stream of force several times, trying to find one in her repertoire strong enough to do the job. Glittering silver smoke shivered out of the air around her, and around the stone.

The panel moved, caught, moved again. Little by little it came away, revealing a hole with steps leading down.

Aren glanced at Keluwen. Her mouth was open wide enough to fit a whole calpas fruit at once. Her eyes were orbs of disbelief. Aren liked the way disbelief looked on her. It was beautiful to see her realize she was so wrong.

"This is what destiny looks like," Redevir said, drooling.

"Dark down there," Aren said.

Redevir peeked his head inside. "It's deep," he said. "A few hundred feet at least. It widens the further down it goes."

"The same as the height of Shaezrod Spur," Aren said, scanning the opening with the Jecker monocle. Everything was clear.

Redevir lit an orange flare, and started down the steps, Aren and the others following.

Aren had to stoop low to enter, but found enough space to stand once inside. As he descended, the pale evening sky fell away, replaced by red reflections of the flare light. The air was musty, stale, damp clay, likely hadn't been breathed for centuries. He wondered when the last feet had stepped here.

The spiral seemed endless. Every step shook the legs more than the last. It was more like descending into a cold hell than to the warm safety of pleasant mother goddesses. He barely saw the opposite side, but its light did not touch the bottom. Over the edge was a sheer drop. Aren clung to the wall.

Three flares and two cramped calves later, he spotted the bottom. There was a single door built into the rock wall. It was ancient, metal worn, wood brittle. Redevir pulled it open and it nearly fell apart. "It was already open a crack," he said.

On the other side was a short hallway. Forty feet long. Aren saw a glowing light. "Someone has already been down here. Within hours, or minutes."

"Or maybe *still* in there," Eriana said. She slid her sword free of its sheath.

Aren set his tracer satchel on the ground and crept toward the door.

Keluwen's arms crossed, fingers twitching at her elbows.

The door opened to a room. It was more of a hollowed-out tunnel, lined with old oak shelves with disintegrating scrolls and rust-eaten metal boxes. The light flickered from within, coming from an oil lamp with tarnished brass handles sitting alone on a small wooden table.

The room around it had been torn to pieces. Shelves were overturned, and clay pots and unused candles were splayed everywhere.

"He was already here," Tanashri said.

"How could he already have been here?" Inrianne asked. "We were supposed to be ahead of him. Everything we did was to get ahead of him. You said the stone was a shortcut, Redevir. How did he beat your shortcut?"

Redevir had no answer.

Aren followed them inside. He heard a squishing sound as he walked, and he felt wetness beneath his boots. He couldn't discern color. The flare painted everything orange. He knelt down to see if it was water. He touched it with his thumb and forefinger. He rubbed his fingers together. They looked black in the light.

Blood!

He shot upright. "Redevir! Blood."

There was a woman on the ground, face down, arms crooked, a doll tossed casually on the floor. Long past dead, her throat cut. The blood pooled across a quarter of the room.

"Whoever did this is long gone by now," Keluwen said.

Tanashri stood like a statue, silent horror spreading like lichens on her skin.

"Who was this?" Redevir whispered.

"She is my Sister," Tanashri said. "She is Saderan."

"*This* is the other Saderan?" Keluwen asked.

"That rules out asking her for help," Inrianne said.

"Her name was Dalain," Tanashri said.

"Why was she here?" Redevir asked.

"She set out three years ago." Tanashri asked. "She was sent to find the Crown. She has been looking all this time, with Raviel's research to guide her."

"You knew this?!" Redevir said, turning on her, a finger in her face. "For how long?"

"The Sisters have been pursuing this directive for three years," Tanashri said, taking a tiny step back.

Redevir's shoulders heaved and fell, as if he was fighting to keep himself from reaching out and strangling her. "Years?! And you somehow thought not to mention this once to us?!"

Tanashri held out apologetic hands. "I never thought any of my Sisters would have a prayer of coming this close."

"Were you slowing us down on purpose?" Redevir accused.

Tanashri turned her chin up defiantly. "No."

"Were you. Slowing us down. On purpose?!" Redevir seethed in the orange glow.

"I did no such thing."

"Are you helping him? Are you helping Kinraigan?"

"No."

"Are you helping him?!"

"Never."

"In Medion, you gave us away to him. You left us in the Dungeon in Medion."

"Stop, Redevir," Aren said. "She isn't helping him. None of us are. The Crown is just gone."

"It...can't be gone," Redevir said. "God damn it! It can't be gone!"

"Are we too late?" Eriana asked.

"We had better not be," Redevir fumed. He turned on Keluwen. "Did you know about this? You knew about the other Sister. Did you know?"

She pulled one glove halfway down to her wrist. "Choose your next words *very* carefully, Rover. "

"No one here delayed us, Redevir," Aren said. "We just missed our chance. Keluwen is right. Whoever did this is long gone."

Then Aren heard a noise.

He turned his head.

A man stood in the doorway, his arm outstretched, holding the tip of a sword to Keluwen's neck.

"You are going to die," the man said.

Maybe *long gone* wasn't entirely accurate.

50

Ghosts

SHE DID NOT FEEL the edge of the blade on her skin, but it must have been close. Keluwen glanced down at the steel. She could see the hand on the pommel out of the corner of one eye, a part of the blade, aiming up under her chin.

She tried to look at the man in the doorway, but his face was in shadow. She could only see the barest hint of the shape of an expression. He shifted slightly, as if unsure of what to do. *Jitters. He is afraid.* It must have been another of Kinraigan's drones.

Both her gloves were all the way up. He was at an angle that the Sister did not have clear line of sight. Too far away from the others. It would only take the slightest little thrust to put her down.

"Do not move," the man said.

"Do something," Keluwen said.

"Do what?" the Rover asked.

Keluwen grimaced. "Anything is better than gawking, you worthless shitsack."

But what could they do? Not much, she wagered.

Aren stepped forward though. He stared directly at the man, squinting, like he was trying to read a book in the dark. He took a step forward.

"Do not move," the voice said.

"Fuck you," she said. "I am going to help you meet your gods."

"You are going to die," the voice said.

Aren took another step toward them. He blocked out any chance of one of the others doing something from across the room.

"What are you doing, Glassboy?" Keluwen asked.

Aren did not even draw his weapon. He did not look like he planned to either. He studied the cutthroat for a long time. Then he turned around and looked at the others.

What in all hells are you doing?

Aren turned back to the cutthroat and smiled. "Who are you?"

"Stay back," the voice said.

"What is your name?" Aren asked.

"Don't come any closer."

"Let her go," Aren demanded.

"You are going to die."

"Why not take me instead?" Aren asked.

Is he seriously offering to trade places with me? She had not expected that. She had not expected much from him at all.

The cutthroat paused, choking on a response. "Stay back."

"Can I get anything for you?" Aren asked.

Keluwen glared at him. "Have you lost your fucking mind, Glassboy?"

The Cutthroat paused again. "Come no closer."

"Are you cold in this breeze?" Aren asked.

He *must* have lost his mind.

A longer pause. "Do not come any closer."

"What do you like most about your mother?" Aren asked.

"You are going to die."

Aren took a step forward.

I hope you know what you are doing, Glassboy.

"Stay back."

Another step. "Do you like the taste of blackberries in the summertime?"

The figure stuttered. "Stay...you...are...back...don't... going...closer...."

Aren moved forward, taking step after step. All the while the shadow flickered on the floor.

He is going to stop walking. He had to. He was no fighter. There was no way Aren was going to disarm even a slow lazy cutthroat before he let her lifeblood out on the floor. ❧

"Stay back," the voice said.

"Aren, what the hell are you doing?!" Keluwen shouted.

"He won't hurt me," Aren said. He kept coming.

The sword pulled away from Keluwen, and pointed at Aren's torso. Aren walked straight toward it.

"You are...back...pass...die," the cutthroat said.

Her eyes widened. She realized he wasn't going to stop. She worked franticly to shed her gloves, but her fingers slipped.

Aren took one last confident step.

The cutthroat plunged his blade into Aren's belly, the point spearing out his back.

"No!" Keluwen shouted. "You stupid fool!"

Aren's eyes went wide. He gasped.

Eriana screamed in horror.

The Rover and the Sarenwalker both charged.

She had her glove off, and sent a blank impulse at the cutthroat. It looked like it went right past him. He stood there as if immune to her magick.

Fainen jumped at the man, trying to crush him to the ground in a bear hug, but merely flew past him, crashing to the floor alone.

Aren looked down at the blade in his belly, and then he looked up at Keluwen.

She did not have any words to tell him. *That kind of wound doesn't heal.* He was going to die.

Aren turned around to face her with the blade still in his body, only now the sword was going in his *back* and out his *belly*.

"What in all fucking hells?" Keluwen felt her mouth turn to rubber. "How?"

"Simple," Aren said. "I should have realized sooner."

"Realized what?" she asked.

"This man," Aren gestured at the cutthroat stabbing him. "Isn't real."

She narrowed her eyes. "How did you know that?"

"Shadow effect," Aren said. "This is an illusion. And it was made in a hurry. Users never include every detail. It's too much to think about, too time consuming. Illusions are *always* imperfect. And they tend to always fail in the same ways. They always drop the shadows wrong. If you look at his face it is in shadow no matter where the light source is. Because he was never given a face, just the outline of a jaw and nose, and little twinkles for the eyes."

"I don't believe it," she said. "I thought I was going to die. I fell for some trick."

"We call them *ghosts*," Aren said.

"You could tell all that just by looking at him?" she asked.

He nodded. "I had to disambiguate a much more clever ghost than this one a few years ago. That user was an illusionist-focus. He was very good. This was done in a hurry, by someone who doesn't make them often."

She tilted her head up and to the side, looking down her cheeks at him. "You are smart for a fool, Glassboy."

"I saw the shadow, so I checked his eyes. No one ever gets the eyes right either. They always swirl, and half the time they don't even have pupils. The eyes gave it away."

"Windows to the soul," the Rover said.

"So why the odd questions?" Keluwen asked.

"That was just to be sure," he said. "When a user leaves an illusion on its own, he can't directly control what it does. So he'll give it a set of responses. This particular ghost was made very quickly. Not a lot of responses programmed into him. Certain types of questions will confuse the response mechanism, or cause a certain response to repeat at inappropriate times. The ghost will speak or act erratically. I was taught how to interrogate a ghost. I knew for sure when he started to stutter, mix his responses."

"You will die," the ghost said pointlessly.

"How long will it be visible?" Keluwen asked. "It's beginning to annoy me."

"It was given a certain duration when it was created."

"Why create it at all?" the Rover asked. "It can't hurt us."

"To distract us," the Sister said.

"There is a dead body in the room," the Rover said. "That is not enough of a distraction?" He walked over to the corpse. "Would you mind explaining to me why one of your Sisters knew about this place?"

"She must have followed him," the Sister said. "He led her down here, where she thought she would have the upper hand. She miscalculated. Kinraigan took the Crown."

"How would she know what Kinraigan looked like?" Aren asked. "How would she know to follow him?"

The Sister paused. "I do not know."

"People don't follow him," Keluwen said. "He follows *them*."

"Followed *her* to the Crown," Inrianne said. "And killed her down here. Took the Crown for himself."

"That is how he beat us here," Inrianne said. "If this Sister had been studying the same clues you had, Redevir, three years would have been quite a head start. Kinraigan would not have needed to solve anything. He must have found out about her somehow. Followed her right here."

"Then why render a ghost down here?" Aren gestured at it. "If he has the Crown and made his escape, why would he bother with this?"

"You will die," the ghost said.

"It must have been to prevent pursuit," the Sister said.

"From who?" Keluwen asked. "A dead Sister? Who would have chased him from *down here*? She was already dead. If he was worried about pursuit from other Arradians he would have left the ghost up there." She pointed back up to the surface.

"She is right," the Sister said. "This was meant to delay people down here. Us. Whoever came next."

"Which brings me back to my question," Aren said. "Why would he care if he already had the Crown?"

"He wouldn't," The Rover said.

"Which means he does not have the Crown," Eriana said.

The Rover's eyes went as wide as crabatz balls. "By every god of every corner of the world, it is *still down here.*"

"How could he have missed it?" Inrianne asked. "This place has been torn apart. Nothing is left unturned."

"That is what stumps me," Aren said. "If he followed her down here, then even if she found it first, he would have taken it after he killed her. And if she had not found it, he would have been the one who ransacked the place. He still would have found it if it was here."

"Could it be somewhere else?" Eriana asked. "Could we have misinterpreted those clues?"

"I doubt it," the Rover said. "They fit so perfectly. They led us to this undiscovered place. Them, too."

"There is only one way he could have missed it," Aren said. "If the Sister found it first, and then hid it somewhere else before Kinraigan got here."

The Rover looked all around, in every corner, even at the ceiling. "But where? She clearly never left this room. And this room has been searched through and through."

"Yes," Aren said, kneeling down over the dead Sister's body. "The *room* has."

"What are you saying?" Keluwen asked.

"He killed her and searched the room," Aren said. "He probably searched her robes. But he didn't search *her.*"

The Rover smiled so wide he was liable to break his jaw.

Aren reached out and brushed the young Sister's hair. He brushed it again, raking his fingers through it. He felt a certain spot. He clutched her scalp at the top and yanked. Her thick mane of hair came off her head. He tossed it aside.

"A wig," Keluwen said.

Her real hair was tied tightly in a braid underneath, and wedged around her head was a double-band metal ring, a near circular shape, with a slight rise in front. It did not glitter and it did not shine. It did not look regal at all. The metal was nothing she had ever seen. It had the color of bronze, but it was not bronze.

Aren lifted it gently off her head. "This looks like a tool. This is it."

Well, I'll be thrice damned. "You are better than I thought, Glassboy." She looked at the Crown, then at him, nodding.

He smiled at her.

Don't you smile at me, Glassboy. We are not friends. But her face betrayed her and threw half a smile back at him before she could stop it.

The Rover clapped Aren on the shoulders. "You have done it, my boy. Hah! You see? I knew it!"

Aren looked up. He saw Eriana smiling at him. He smiled back.

"You little shits are too sweet by half," Keluwen said.

"Well," the Rover said. "We have it. Let's get the hell out of here and celebrate. We have a trap to set."

Keluwen's legs burned before the hundredth step. She felt pulsing pain in her hip. She looked out across the wide cylinder of the well, the evening sky growing wider every step.

She forced her failing legs to keep going, forced them up. Finally they gave out, and she slowed until she was almost crawling to the top, bracing herself with her hands. She felt like her lungs were on fire by the time she finally dragged herself out onto the surface.

She felt a sudden ripple in the Slipstream. At first she thought it might have been the Sister once again, but she recognized the feeling. The streams felt like heat streams.

Her eyes widened. Strength was reborn in her legs. She climbed out of the hole in time to see Orrinas and Krid Ballar standing in the quarry with their arms raised, and they were looking directly at Aren.

She raised both hands and lunged in front of Aren. She could feel the renders coming into being.

"Stop!"

****

Aren stood staring at Corrin and Reidos.

His mind did not allow them to be real. They were dead. They had to be. He thought he was hallucinating. Until Corrin picked up a pebble and threw it at him.

"Corrin?" Aren asked.

"It *is* you," Corrin said. "I knew it. I thought I sensed someone being pedantic nearby."

"What in all hells is this?" Aren asked.

"Well," Corrin said. "That is the awkward part. We were supposed to fight you, I think."

Eriana had a hand on the hilt of her sword already. When Corrin said that, it made her fingers flex around it.

Aren held his hand up to her. "These are my friends. The ones who were dead."

Corrin recoiled, offended. "You thought one small army of Vuls would be enough to kill me? Rude. Indecent. For shame."

"What are you doing with them?" Aren asked.

"And who are they?" Redevir added, turning to Keluwen. "You *know* these people?"

Keluwen's face softened. "They *are* my people. That is my Orrinas." She had a peculiar look in her eyes, very much like she wanted to say or do something urgently, but held back.

"They are rogues, you mean," Aren said. "Rogue users, all of them."

She nodded. "Only two of them left now. And me."

"You know how I feel about rogues," Aren said. He angled his eyes to her.

She barely glanced his way. "And you know the way I feel about my people. So choose your words carefully."

He chewed his lip, glaring at Orrinas and the other user. He gave his head a little shake and bared his teeth involuntarily as he thought about them. "I have never worked with a rogue."

"Until me," Keluwen said.

"Until you," he nodded grudgingly.

"You talked me out of killing you," she said. "You talked me into trusting you."

"I have not forgotten."

"And I talked you into trusting me," she said.

"I know. I was there."

"Then trust me just a little farther." She turned to face him.

He bit down hard on his lip. Stared into her eyes, wide and honest, vulnerable and dangerous. *Never trust them. There is no why to them. They hurt because they can.* He shook his head. Closed his eyes. Opened them. She was still looking at him. "These are your people?"

"Orrinas," she said. "And Krid."

"The greatest man in the world?"

She nodded. "And Krid. I don't give two shits about Krid. You can dose his ugly ass to whatever fires you want." She cracked a smile.

He couldn't help but smile back.

"Do you trust me then?" she asked, daring him to say he didn't.

He nodded. "I do. I trust you."

"Good," she said. "Then I suppose it is time you all met." She smiled warmly at Orrinas. It was unlike her to be warm at all.

Orrinas smiled to her. "Are you safe?" His eyes wandered over Aren and the others.

She nodded. "I am."

"That is the Glasseye," the old man in the olive coat grumbled. *Krid.*

"He is not what we thought," Keluwen said. "They are like us. They are hunting him."

They seemed unconvinced. "Do you truly believe this?" Orrinas asked.

"They are his," Krid said. "So is she. She has turned. We kill them all."

Orrinas held up his hand. "No, she is still the Keluwen I know."

"How can you be certain?" the old man asked. "He can turn anyone."

"Because it has happened to someone I know before," Orrinas said. "And I could tell the difference. This is her." He smiled at her as if his whole body was diving into her eyes. "I would know her anywhere."

Krid Ballar grumbled to himself, but he deferred to Orrinas.

He is as suspicious as Redevir, Aren thought.

"And who are you?" Tanashri demanded.

"We work for *Axis Ardent*," Orrinas said. He introduced Cheli, Hodo Grubb, Krid Ballar, Leucas Brej, and Amicien Duran.

"What is *Axis Ardent*?" Inrianne asked. "I have never heard of them."

"A secret group," Redevir said. "They play behind the scenes, like the Ministry."

"Not like them," Orrinas corrected. "The Ministry is ever seeking more power to fuel the gross ambition of its Priests. We seek only to redress the balance of the world."

"In Olbaran they say every lord obeys the whispers of his Priest," Redevir said. "And that every whisper is heard by Axis Ardent. They are the great listeners."

"Some of us are doers," the one named Cheli said. "We here are a special group. We hunted those who sought to become luminous. We stopped them before they could ascend." She looked at her feet, a tear hovering in her eye. "At least we did. Kinraigan was not supposed to be ready yet. We were supposed to have more time. He found a way in. Something we missed. Now he is luminous. And we hunt *him*."

"Now perhaps someone will tell us who exactly *you* are," Krid said.

"They are allies," Keluwen said. "This crew is no more one of Kinraigan's than we are."

"Wait," Aren said. "How did *your people* get to Arthenorad?"

"I sent them here," Keluwen said. "Before I started following you."

"Why?"

"Because I discovered that Kinraigan's cultists were coming here," Keluwen said.

"And they do not go anywhere unless he tells them to," Cheli said.

"But if he left empty handed, where did he go?" Aren asked.

"He could be anywhere," Orrinas said. "Arradan is not new to him. He has been here many times."

"The question is," Tanashri said. "Does he believe the hints and clues led him wrong? Or does he believe someone else found it first?"

"To be fair," Aren said. "However long it has been down there, it is surprising that it was not discovered sooner, by someone else."

"So," Redevir said. "What happens now?"

No one spoke.

Keluwen stomped across the quarry until she stood before Orrinas. "I am ready to finish that conversation now," she said. She leaned in and embraced Orrinas, and the others collapsed around her. Smiles and teary eyes abounded.

Aren smiled at that. *They really love each other, the whole crew.*

Then he turned to his own crew.

Corrin opened his arms wide and made kissing lips at him. "I'm ready for you, sir. Come on."

Aren rolled his eyes.

Corrin folded his arms in mock disappointment. "Three thousand miles, users, duels, battles, danger, magick items, and still we do not embrace, eh?"

"I'm not pleased that you let me go on thinking you were dead all this time," Aren said.

"I would have found you sooner had I known all I needed to do was follow the trail of women," Corrin said. "Four of them, and all as lovely as a flower."

"It is hard to believe," Aren said. "To see you here like this."

"Oh, it is quite believable, good sir," Corrin said. "Or have you so soon forgotten that I am a sword fighter of ineffable talent?" He paused. "Or was it effable talent? Which is it Reidos? Ineffable? I feel like that sounds right."

"I can't believe this," Aren said. "This can't be real. I mean it is just... impossible."

"Why not?" Corrin laughed. "Am I too good looking to be believed? I must be. I mean, I am, clearly."

Aren couldn't stop laughing. "What are the odds that we would all be here? Right now? At this moment?"

THOMAS HOWARD RILEY

"Hmmm," Corrin held his chin between thumb and forefinger and squinted up at the sky. "Must be at least three to one." He tapped his foot impatiently. "I think you should cease trying to do mathematics and just be overjoyed to see me."

"I *am* overjoyed." Aren wrapped him in a bear hug. "I can't believe you're here, you farod."

"Get used to it. I can't be gotten rid of. I am a goddamn Amagonian icon." He turned to Eriana. "And who might this golden lovely be?"

"This is Eriana," Aren said. "She is from Laman. I met her in Cair Tiril."

"I thought she looked Andristi," Corrin said. "How did you find her? I don't recall you having any such person with you when we parted ways."

"Actually, I found Aren," Eriana said. "I had to make sure he left my homeland in one piece. He is too pretty for me to allow anything bad to happen to him."

"That must have been difficult work," Corrin agreed. "And thankless as well."

"It certainly was," Eriana said. She jabbed Aren with an elbow.

Corrin smiled. "I like you," he decided. "You will do Aren some good. His worthless hide needs all the help it can get, pretty though it may be."

"I agree," Eriana said.

"I am Corrin the Magnificent," Corrin said.

"Actually it is just Corrin," Aren said.

"Rude," Corrin said. "You get to make up titles for yourself all the time, *Lord* Aren."

"It is a pleasure," Eriana said.

"It's good to have you back," Aren said, putting an arm around Eriana. He found no small joy in the fact that she let him. "What the hell are you all doing here?"

"We're on the run," Corrin said. "Another fool tried to kill us."

Aren squinted. "Where did you run into this lot?"

"You didn't hear what happened the other night?"

"We just arrived," Aren said. "We've heard nothing."

"There was a bit of a brawl in the street, which I was *barely* involved in starting."

Aren rolled his eyes. "Shaot, Corrin. We are trying not to attract attention to ourselves."

Corrin shrugged.

"We escaped unseen," Duran said.

"That's if we can trust you lot," Redevir said.

"We are friends," Orrinas said.

"Friends," Redevir scoffed. "Really." He shook his head.

"We must not fixate on the past," Orrinas said. "Kinraigan is all that matters. We need to focus on him."

"We," Redevir said. "There *is* no we. *We* is *us*." He gesticulated at the companions. "You are not a part of *we*."

"What can we do?" Orrinas asked.

"I want to know what you know," Redevir said. "Right now. That is how to be *friends*."

"Tell them nothing," Krid said.

"Look here," Redevir said. "For this to work, you need to tell us everything."

"Duran was sent to witness a ceremony conducted by the Mimmions of Amagon," Orrinas said.

"That insane cult?" Aren scoffed. "They light candles and sing sour songs in the woods. No one even bats an eye at them back where I come from. Why would anyone care about them?"

Duran frowned. "They get up to quite a bit more than you realize. I saw what they did. They opened a rift to somewhere else. A place where power falls like rain and omnipotence is the same as breathing. I saw children there. Something happened to them. Something came from that rift and affected them. I only found one path away from the mountain. Kinraigan's people were bringing girls from Amagon, but among them was one of the boys who I saw atop that mountain. They obsessed over him. I knew it was important. I followed them all the way to Westgate. When I sent a message to my superiors, they told me to infiltrate the Outer Guard and then seek the boy in the city. Once I found him. I was to free him, and bring him with the Outer Guard as protection."

"Only we found him first," Corrin said. " So that is why you spoke up so quickly when we brought Hallan in. I always thought there was something odd about that."

"Those above us do not tell us how," Orrinas said.

"Why is Kinraigan so interested in this boy?" Tanashri asked. "Explain."

"There is an energy," Orrinas said. "It cannot be explained."

Corrin threw his hands in the air. "You people. He is important, but no one can say why." He turned to Hallan. "Why are you important?"

Hallan shrugged.

"So the Mimmions were working for Kinraigan," Aren said.

"Wrong," Duran said. "They were there at the behest of the Lord Protector of Amagon."

"Wait," Aren said. "What?"

"The men directing things were from Amagon," Duran said. "They wore the silver moon. The Lord Protector's people arranged for the Mimmions to conduct a certain operation. One that did something with the Slipstream. Kinraigan disrupted it. Something went wrong. Whatever happened resulted in Hallan becoming a receptacle for something incredible."

"We believe the Lord Protector of Amagon was trying to become luminous himself," Cheli said.

"Don't you have to be a user to do things with the light?" Aren asked.

"The light is different, separate, yet still the same," Cheli said.

"Whatever happened, the Lord Protector was furious," Orrinas said. "He even sent an assassin trained by the Ministry to have the children be killed rather than fall into another's hands."

"Raviel was supposed to report to us on the journey to Laman," Cheli said. "We were ready to work together. We have been following Kinraigan for a reason. He cannot be allowed to ascend to become Sanadi. His murderous madness will turn our world into a nightmare. He has a long history. A long trail of dead girls. Sometimes he lets them go, and sometimes he keeps them. He has been chased out of so many nations. In Hylamar he was branded Unclean by the Royal Praetors, his compound burned. The Miramaddi of Shezail Valley named him Deathwater, claiming he was born of black sand. They purged his cult and had his proteges executed. The Black Watch of Halsabad drove his cultists underground. The Render Tracer Corps of Amagon sent their best at him again and again until he fled south once more. In Tyrelon his name was cursed, and he was sentenced to Erasure for his crimes. They dispersed his followers and sent their best hunter after him— Raviel."

Orrinas nodded. "We know the Lord Protector found one of the Crown stones, and he was willing to trade it to Kinraigan. Kinraigan sent someone to barter with him, but he was betrayed, and assassins were set upon him, but he escaped. You were set on his trail the following night."

"Why does this sound so familiar?" Corrin asked.

"But I don't understand what is so important about the Dagger," Aren said. "How could it be so vital that he would race to stop Raviel, but not bother to get it for himself before then?"

Cheli shrugged. "We do not know,"

"Raviel long ago went to many of the great libraries of the Ministry to research Kinraigan's Sephor quest," Orrinas said. "And we followed him all the while. That is where Raviel discovered the secret of the Dagger, just as Kinraigan had. Kinraigan had always been one step ahead of Raviel, just out of reach, but now Raviel *knew* that Kinraigan would not allow him to get there first. He knew he could force Kinraigan to go to exactly the place in Laman where he could lay a trap for him. It was his one chance."

"Except we killed him," Aren said. "We killed Raviel before he could do it. Killed him based on the lies the Lord Protector told us."

"Kinraigan will never stop," Orrinas said. "He is compelled to make the world in the image of his own choosing. He is obsessed with the power he can achieve, and he will stop at nothing to destroy his rivals who seek to usurp that power for themselves. Raviel was a pawn in a cat and mouse game between the Ministry and Kinraigan, and the Lord Protector was merely a pawn in a game played by Kinraigan and Raviel. Raviel might have succeeded, except that he became a pawn in turn in the game between Kinraigan and the Lord Protector. Now all their great plans have come to naught, except for Kinraigan. He is stronger than ever."

"Kinraigan is his own god," Cheli said. "I know him well. He will only follow himself. He is a slave to his own desire. He thinks he is blessing all these girls. He believes he is changing them into perfection, literally perfecting them to death. He believes that what is happening is the *Advent Lumina*, the coming of the *Days of Light*. He believes he is saving the world, and that everyone else is trying to prevent him from doing so. He knows his time is running out, that others have come who threaten his own power, other who can see behind the world. That is the reason he strikes out early—to demonstrate his influence to his new adversaries. He needs the Crown for his plans to be complete. Kinraigan believes he can make himself Sanadi—ancient, immortal, with limitless power—and he believes it so strongly that all his will is bent to this one goal. He will never stop no matter how many he hurts."

"What is Advent Lumina?" Aren asked.

Orrinas frowned. "No one knows for certain."

"Kinraigan has become luminous," Cheli said. "He has figured out how to walk in the light. He stole a book. The language and title of the original have been long forgotten. But translations of it are called the Codex Lumina."

"I have never seen a copy," Aren said.

"Stop everything," Corrin said. "A book that Aren hasn't read. Find me paper and quill. I must mark this day down."

"It is instruction for the light," Cheli said. "Its words may seem like nonsense to all of us. It is said that only those who walk in the light could ever understand what its passages mean."

Orrinas grimaced. "And now we believe he has become immortal, using the light to somehow stop aging, to remain as he is forever. There is only one step further for him to make himself a god. And for that he needs the Crown. "

"Well, it certainly sounds like we are at a disadvantage," Redevir said.

"We do have one crucial thing in our favor," Cheli said. She held up a fat leather folio. "We have his composite. Every imprint of every render from every scene. With additions from every scene we have faced him. Everything is in here."

Aren's eyes lit up. "Redevir, that is his composite. If we can pull enough of his critical streams, we could render him powerless. Where did you get that?"

"From a sympathetic ally," Cheli said. "Named Sarker."

Aren's jaw hit the floor. "Sarker? Toran Sarker?"

She nodded.

"He was my mentor," Aren said. "He was...That is where he was. He left me in the middle of a trace. It was *you* he was meeting."

"We needed this copy," Cheli said.

"He was trying to stop Kinraigan," Aren said. "Render Tracer to the end." *And to think I doubted him. What a fool I was.*

"Kinraigan must be stopped now," Orrinas announced. "We have five users between us. We have the Crown and one of the children."

"We cannot go after him," Redevir said. "Aren, we talked about this."

"He will come back," Orrinas said. "He will come for you again and again, until you are destroyed and the Crown is his."

"I am well aware that as long as he exists he will try to take these from me," Redevir said. "I am not a fool. I do not believe hiding is the answer. But we must set a trap for him. Kinraigan must be forced into the open. Set the time and place and make him come to us."

"We have tried that," Orrinas said.

"Tried and failed," Keluwen said.

"Aren," Redevir said. "Think this through."

"These are the things we needed," Aren said. "Now we have imprints of thousands of his renders. Everything we hoped for in Medion, now we have them."

"But he is already gone," Redevir said. "He has made his escape. We missed our chance."

"No one knows where he hides himself," Cheli agreed. "His secret refuge has never been found."

"He leaves no footprints," Keluwen said. "He cleans himself of stains so well there is no way to know where he is. He cannot be traced."

"There *is* a way to trace him," Aren said. His one moment to escape the destiny that the elder had placed before him was gone. He knew he wouldn't be able to stop on his own now.

"How?" Orrinas asked.

"He made a mistake," Aren said.

"I do not understand," Orrinas said.

"He rendered a ghost down below us," Aren said. "In close quarters and very recent. There will be sensitized material everywhere from all that afterglow. With sensitized fluorescence, I can tell which way he is going and how close we are to him. But it only lasts a short time before it fades."

"I thought we decided we shouldn't do that," Redevir said.

"Sensitized fluorescence fades," Aren said. "We won't have time to set a trap days or weeks from now. We will have to go after him at dawn. If we do, I can track him down. If we do not go soon, we lose him, for the gods only know how long."

"Are you certain?" Orrinas asked.

"He looks certain to me," Keluwen said. "And I have been ready every moment since we labored beneath that strong tree. Finally someone who gives me what I want."

Orrinas glanced over his shoulder at her, eyes narrow, mouth flat. He turned back to Aren. "Are you certain?" he asked again.

"I know I can," Aren said. "I am a Glasseye. And no one will ever get away from me."

51

Afterglow

IT WAS A SIMPLE task as far as Aren was concerned. Afterglow was everywhere in the hallway. No almond smell. Light renders tended not to leave any distinctive scent, and that was fine with him. He was growing to hate that smell.

It required a lengthy search with the Jecker monocle and the Oscillatrix, but he managed to locate the peak points. The ratings on the glow curve indicated how the streams were combined to create various renders within the illusion process. They were unfamiliar, but his key would still be within them. The core color stood out. Pale orange through the blue filter.

Kinraigan had been in a hurry, leaving at least two wave pockets hanging in the air, but he still imparted a stream of compression masking on every bind. Automatic. Reflex. Beneath it was Kinraigan's *Introduction-of-Change*. It vibrated fourth-dimensionally through the Jecker monocle. To an inexperienced Render Tracer it would have looked like random chaotic nonsense, but Aren saw the pattern. He always found a pattern. This is what he was born to see.

There it was. Kinraigan's fingerprint. Aren was the hunter again. He was ready for the chase. Alone in the deep chamber he felt strong. No sorcerer could escape him. There were no sorcerers, wizards, or conjurers—only users. They were all only users.

Aren could see it again. He could see the path before him. He felt as if everything in his life had been leading inexorably toward this place, this moment. His training, the Sephors, meeting Redevir, Aldarion's betrayal, Sarker's disappearance. He felt as if the accumulation of experiences of his entire life had been crafted solely for this one goal. He was meant to be here, to study Kinraigan's renders.

Aren measured Kinraigan's primary values. He discovered the extent of the masking and adjusted his results accordingly. He isolated the loops of the dialogue programming, and removed them as well.

He accumulated dozens of imprints, indicating Kinraigan's recurring streams, and added them to what he already had from the *Red God*, and added it all to the composite Cheli had, comprising every single stream of every single render Kinraigan had ever made at any of the scenes when he terrorized Amagon, with still more from when he attacked the Mimmions, when he escaped Keluwen in Westgate. It contained his core limit, his proficiency limit, and his performance limit. It documented his primary values at dozens of scenes over many years. And with those Aren discovered today, he could tell not only how strong Kinraigan was, but his rate of growth, how strong he would be in the days to come. He had recommendations of the number of Distractors, a basis for how many streams would need to be held for the interdiction, and even what sounds, sights, and odors caused him the most distraction. Everything.

He drilled Tanashri, Keluwen, Inrianne, Krid, and Orrinas on the shapes. They would each have to hold a group of his streams as if they were Stoppers. Twenty to thirty apiece. It was a tall order. But those streams were integral to nearly ten thousand variations of his renders. Everything he could do. Or very nearly at least.

He made sure to collect two sources of sensitized fluorescence in his vials, from flakes of the wall near where the ghost had been. With them he would be able to not only judge the redshift or blueshift of the particle core colors to see whether Kinraigan was moving closer to them or further away, he would be able to triangulate his precise location.

This was Kinraigan's mistake. A perfect mistake. It was the final puzzle piece, rendering happenstance into destiny.

I am the one. He was sure of it now. More certain than he had ever been of anything in his life. He was the one who was meant to stop Kinraigan, the sorcerer, the madman, the Sanadi. Aren felt it within his bones, a vibration, a tiny humming deep down inside every sinew, every organ, every pulse of his blood. He did have a destiny after all, just as Redevir suggested, but it was something much greater than what Redevir ever thought.

Every time they were in a bind, something came along to set the path straight. When they found hidden clues, Eriana could decipher them, and Aren could understand them. Redevir was right. His knowledge of the Histories had been destined to solve them. And now Kinraigan's foolish choice to leave a *ghost* was his undoing, making his path known, able to be followed, able to be taken by surprise. The man who could never be tracked down, now would be. The pieces fit. Aren knew it, believed it. He was supposed to be here. He would set the world right. He did not need to rely on a trap. The path was illuminated before him. He would hunt, as he was meant to.

He celebrated with a thick pipeful of malagayne. This was his destiny and he was ready to celebrate it. It was nightfall by the time he came up.

When he returned, everyone wanted to begin the search immediately, but the users needed rest, full bellies, water. They each needed their full strength.

And of course Corrin wanted to come, and Reidos could not say no to the both of them. And then Corrin beat, threatened, and cajoled Mardin until he relented and agreed to go as well.

Redevir purchased rooms at the *Last Horn*, a wealthy inn on the bank of the Areth River. He even paid for the newcomers. The Rover definitely took charge. He made an arrangement with Orrinas by which Redevir would keep the Crown, but only if they agreed to bring Hallan with them on the hunt.

Orrinas was convinced the boy was special, a near religious conviction, based on something his superiors had promised him. Keluwen thought it was a foolish distraction, but he won out. Aren wasn't sure how long the arrangement would last, but for the time being they were all united under a common cause. *The Lissarian Gambit*.

Aren remained with the users late into the evening, going over and over Kinraigan's renders with them, his magnitudes and patterns. It would be critical for each of the five to understand the roles they would play.

Keluwen was a puncher, with blank impulses of many sizes and speeds, always the size range of marbles, and her direction streams kept her spheres on target with incredible precision. She was not capable of sustaining outstanding power, but she was experienced and knew how to pace her renders. And she was capable with two dimensional shields, and cylinders.

None were as skilled with pattern recognition as Tanashri, and so it was left to her to attempt the bulk of precedence effect to hold as many of Kinraigan's streams as possible prior to the confrontation. The blank impulses Tanashri was able to create were of larger size, like crabatz balls or watermelons. She was quick with strong shields, two-dimensional or three, cube or sphere. And she could execute inertial transposition and momentum dumps with ease as long as they were close to her, both of which could rob him of the effectiveness of any blank impulses that they were unable to interdict.

Krid Ballar, the frictioneer, brought experience to compensate for low natural strength. His renders were passive so he would have to play the situation by ear. But everyone had to touch the ground, or their clothes, or their possessions. He would be flexible to harass Kinraigan wherever possible. Krid could also mitigate the strength of Kinraigan's blank impulses by rendering friction against them as they moved through the air, though he admitted he was not strong with that kind of thing. Every little bit of extra life he could buy for the shields would be critical.

Inrianne would be able to hold much of Kinraigan's attention focused on shielding himself from her fire. The fire could wrap around two-dimensional shapes, so he would be forced to maintain fully enclosed three-dimensional shields. Even if he had the streams to make the shields to deflect her sheets of flame, the concentration drain would be high, pushing him closer to his break point. Spreading out his concentration was vital.

Keluwen and Tanashri would be responsible for blank shields for anyone else who needed them, though it would be difficult for them to keep track of the timing, for they would need to loop the shields so that they would drop often enough for the others to make their attacks. You could render effects through *your own* three-dimensional shield, but not someone else's. Aren forced them to practice repeatedly with both Inrianne and Orrinas before he was satisfied they would be able to manage them properly.

Orrinas was a thermalist, a *heater*, his renders of choice relating primarily to increase of temperature rather than decrease. And his range of temperature streams was extraordinary. He was familiar with both active and passive renders, being able to create his own forces of heat and apply them to any medium, as well as affect natural heat sources already in existence. He created heat and controlled it. He could apply his changes to individual objects, or create wide spatial fields of temperature variance. He was both powerful and capable of incredible endurance.

He would be the centerpiece of Aren's plan for the capture. He not only could access streams of heat, he had also studied texts to gain a depth of understanding of the principles governing that form of energy. He could increase and reduce temperature with exceptional speed. This would be useful against Kinraigan's most potent weapons—his pressure renders. They were quick to turn deadly and not as easily warded as a blank impulse.

The composite showed that he could attack with moving pressure waves, static pressure fields, and create crush bubbles sealed around objects or even people, and drastically reduce or increase pressure within at his whim. He was capable of a wide range of different magnitudes, from the minute to the drastic. Aren's analysis had shown, though, that the range of magnitude Kinraigan had displayed proficiency in thus far was dwarfed by the range of Orrinas. And with Orrinas able to feel the ripples in the Slipstream whenever Kinraigan selected a new magnitude, he would be able to swap in an opposite temperature change to his ingredient list to counterbalance it. Kinraigan would not be able to apply his most potent weapon with any effect.

Orrinas would simply maintain a blank shield around any target Kinraigan chose in order to protect them from the temperature changes, and then render a shell of altering temperature around it to neutralize Kinraigan's pressure bubbles. Orrinas' blank impulses alone could not withstand the pressure, but they would not need to—the pressure would never be able to make it through the heat shields. Against Kinraigan's pressure waves, Orrinas would simply apply a general temperature effect across the width of the wave and reduce it to a harmless breeze.

After hours of practice, Aren was satisfied that their preparations were complete. They had five powerful users, a proper defense, a plan of distraction, most of Kinraigan's own streams logged in the composite, and counterstrikes against all his major powers. They had a workable plan of attack that was well thought out, and well prepared. Each of them had their roles defined and knew what they would need to do. If they all simply performed their parts, this would bring it to an end.

He left them to eat and rest, confident that their move would take Kinraigan unsuspecting, and quickly defeat him. It was academic. The actual capture was reduced to merely an afterthought at this point. The real work had already been done. The successful Render Tracer did not need to do anything on the day of capture; he had already done it. He won because the results of the capture were inevitable.

His confidence remained high, and late into the night, after the others had all drifted off to sleep in their rooms, Aren sat with Eriana on a shallow knoll of emerald grass outside of the *Last Horn*. Together they traded sips of a bottle of sweetwine, and looked out over the Areth River, staring at the winking lantern lights of the city.

Eriana stretched out over the cool grass, using Aren's cloak as a blanket. The air seemed warm for winter. Arthenorad was just close enough to the coast to reap the benefits of the warm undercurrents in the Gulf of Shain.

Aren stared out at the winking lights of the ancient towers with their dome caps and tapering tops in the distance. He looked at Eriana. He could make out her slender shape underneath the long-sleeved blue tunic. Her hair rolled off her shoulders like glittering gold rivulets, and her eyes were wide and wandering. Her freshly washed hair smelled of sweet flowers.

He wanted to reach out to her. He wanted to feel her, touch her face, run a finger across those thin rosy lips. His hand moved toward her. He felt the fear wash away like sweet smoke in the breeze.

Eriana turned to look at him. He stopped his hand, pulled it back, made it look like he was doing something else, and looked out across the water. "I've never seen the tower in person," he said. "I mean, we were standing inside the Spur, and I don't even remember what it looked like."

"I know. Me neither."

"I feel like I have been waiting my whole life to see these places and I am not actually seeing them. I...I could have walked in the Marble Forest in Cair Tiril for days, looking at every statue. I could have spent a whole summer in Synsirok, reading beneath the trees. I should be sitting in the tower right now, just feeling it."

"Sometimes you just have to stop," she said.

"I can't stop. How do you stop?"

"Not forever. Not even for a day, or an hour. Solathas told me that it is hard to see *now*. It is hard to be with *now*, because it happens so fast and is gone to the next *now*. He told me that all you have to do is take a moment, a few minutes, an hour, here and there, and just stop, and look around. Smell the air. Feel sunlight on your skin, or a cool breeze through your hair. Watch the shadows move on an old building. Or, like we are doing right now. Sitting in the cool grass beside a river under a starry sky, looking at old towers and pretty lights."

He smiled. "I can do that. I can take a moment."

"I take them all the time. I remember looking into the setting sun and feeling the riverspray on the Alder. I remember you helping Inrianne step through some old tangled roots in Provanion Wood, even though I could tell you didn't like her."

"I still don't like her." He laughed.

So did she. "I remember when you thought it was going to snow over the Hennel Koth, and Redevir scrambled about because he forgot to bring moccasins. But then it didn't snow, and we all laughed, and Redevir was so angry that he yelled at a tree."

"I had forgotten that. He certainly has a temper."

"He is harmless."

"Unless you are the tree."

"I remember you pointing up at each of the towers in Medion," she said. "Your smile was so wide. I remember thinking how happy you were being able to tell me all about them."

"That I do remember. But it feels like such a blur in my head."

"I remember when I first saw in you in Great Santhalian's throne room."

"Oh, you do, do you?"

She smiled, cheeks reddening, hands clasped together, shoulders shrugging. "I do."

"Do you remember what you thought when you saw me?"

"I do."

"What was it?"

"I thought: *I could break that boy over my knee.*"

"You did not!"

She laughed. "I did. But I also thought, *he is very handsome though, so...*"

He laughed, too. "You want to know what I thought?"

"What?"

"Please don't mess up your speech to the Great King of Laman in front of this pretty girl."

She blushed again, smiled, leaned her head on his shoulder. "I like that one."

"I feel like I missed so many moments."

"I am glad we are able to have this one right now together."

"Me too," he said.

"I always wanted to do something like this. From the time I was a little girl. I don't want you to feel like I left my home for you, because I didn't. But I am glad that I get to do what I always dreamed with you beside me."

"It was not easy to get here, not the way it is for most people."

"Everyone has struggles. Everyone has trials. Everyone suffers loss. Just because they aren't the same ones that you have, doesn't make them less real."

"Life is full of trials. That is what Solathas said."

"He says a lot of things. And all of them are wise."

"I wish I could be like him. Always in control of himself. Always in control of everything around him. Never afraid of anything."

"You don't think Solathas is ever afraid?"

"I can't imagine him being any emotion. Just perfection. Like Fainen. He seemed superhuman to me. I'm just a man. And not a very good one. I have to make compromises just to get through each day. I'm not a hero or a poet, and I never will be. I'm a long way from perfect."

"That is the very thing that makes you a hero, silly." She leaned her head back, letting her hair cascade down her shoulders. "Heroes are never perfect. Everyone thinks they are, except for themselves. It is only that no one wants to remember them for their vices and their mistakes. Do you think Rogar the Great was perfect? Or Weirmaheir? Or even Solathas? They all made mistakes, mistakes that affected thousands. They made them and moved on. If a person thinks he is a hero, it is the surest evidence that he is not."

"I suppose you're right." He couldn't help looking at her neck, her eyes, her hair. He didn't want to stare. That would make him look crazy. He forced his eyes elsewhere.

"You don't have to be the one to do this," she said. "You have given the others everything you could, prepared them every way you can. You don't have to go with them tomorrow. You can stay here. We can stay here. If you want. You don't have to go. I won't think any less of you. No one will."

"I have to go. A real Render Tracer always goes in with his team."

She smiled. "You have nothing to prove to me, or to anyone."

"I have to prove it to myself. I have to stand behind my work. I have to live or die by how well prepared I am. I have prepared. Now I have to go. I have to. I need to. It is what I was meant to do."

"Then I am coming with you," she said. "I want to be by your side no matter what comes."

"It is dangerous work. Why are you so willing to be a part of it?"

She looked into his eyes. "Because I know that no matter what happens, it will be all right if you are there. I know you will make everything okay."

"Even after everything that happened?"

"If I ever change my mind I'll let you know," she said.

He looked at her a long time. She was so beautiful. He felt like he could live forever beside her.

"I feel safe with you," she said. "No matter what danger is outside, I am safe inside. All that matters to me is how I feel when I'm with you."

Aren looked at her in profile, her brow, her nose, her lips, her chin, every curve, every angle seemed perfect, even though he could not say why. He did not know what made it that way, it just was. "What do you want out of all this?"

"I just want to *be*," she said. "Everyone has plans, ideas about the future. Sometimes you have to let it all go, and the world will take you where you need to be. "

"Maybe you should let the world take you away from here."

"But this is where the world brought me," she insisted. "This is where I am supposed to be. All that matters is this moment. Only always ever now."

Aren could only shake his head. "You shouldn't have to see things this way."

"I want to see the world as it is. If I only wanted to *know* something I could have just read a book about it in Great Santhalian's library. I want to feel it, the way an ordinary person would."

"This is hardly ordinary."

"But it's real," she said. "It's *now*."

She moved close to him, leaning her head further up against his neck.

He froze. He didn't know what to do. He knew what he wanted to do, but he was not sure if he should. The shimmering strands of her hair brushed against his neck, and he felt something within him crying out for his arms to wrap around her. Her body was warm beneath her linens. He felt the soft weight of her, and took in the scent of her skin.

He was afraid she would pull away from him but she didn't. She put one hand on his chest. She turned her head up to look at him. Her eyes were watery and deep, dark wishing-wells reflecting desire and moonlight. He let his arms do whatever they wished, wrapping around her without any conscious thought, animated by something as irresistible as the ocean tides.

"She was right," Eriana said. "That awful woman you wouldn't let me kill."

Aren laughed. "Keluwen."

She nodded, her eyes never leaving his. "She was right. About me. About what I want. About everything. I am your girl. I choose to be. And I would fight you if you ever said I wasn't."

He didn't believe it, couldn't believe it. "Are you sure?"

"If I ever change my mind I'll let you know."

"Good."

"In the storybooks this is the part where you tell me you are mine as well. Unless you aren't." She squinted at him angrily, and it was the most adorable thing he had ever seen.

"You already know I am."

"Say it anyway."

"I am yours."

"Good."

He looked down at her. Tried to speak. Gave up. He felt like his lips were miles from hers, yet close enough to feel her breath. He looked into her eyes, paused, moved a little closer. So did she. Again.

Her hand drifted up his neck, pulling him closer. Her lips were tender and hungry. It surprised him. He made to draw away, but she held him close. Her skin felt like fire to his fingertips, and every kiss was a sunburst of color in his head. Within each one he saw opalescent swirls of reds, yellows, and deep violets. With each new collision, he felt the ache of desire grow and strengthen, coursing outward until he felt that his whole body was full of flames, aching desperately to be released.

He possessed the power of a hundred kings when she whispered in his ear. She took him by the hand and led him through the door to the linen sheets. A single candle lit the room, flickering light on the walls like a watercolor brush. She smiled wide when he brought her to the bed. She gave a little laugh when he bounced her down on the cushions.

He watched her as she pulled her tunic and shirt up over her head. She covered her breasts with one arm, teasing him playfully. He stared at her hands, her breasts, her lustrous skin. He stood beside her for a moment, gazing at her until he couldn't stand it any longer, until he couldn't bear to keep his lips from hers, and his arms from wrapping around her, feeling her skin, feeling her body pressed against him, enclosing her, devouring her.

She made the world disappear. Nothing was outside of this room. He was only aware of her, and how much he wanted all of it, everything—the way her flat smile made it appear she was pouting when she wasn't, the way her fingers trailed across her skin as though she had just discovered it, the way she lifted both arms at once to pull her hair over her shoulders, the way the lights seemed to dance in her eyes as though they had tiny fires of their own. He was fascinated by all the little things that combined to make her the way she was. He knew then that he had been hers from the very moment he first laid eyes on her, and she was his.

And how he wanted her. He wanted to drown in the golden curls of her hair. His heart rattled like frenzied drums, and shook him with each pulse of blood. His mind surged ahead, leaping to her, as if his body was lagging behind him, desperately trying to keep up. He wondered why he had been fearing this moment, because it was right, it was now, it was everything.

She pulled him down on top of her, hands wandering everywhere, her lips demanding that his own open for her tongue, inhaling his breath, peeling him out of his clothes as if he was a present she was unwrapping after having long been denied.

His hands fumbled their way between her legs, sliding over and back, over and back, until she was wet as rain, fingers slipping inside until she gasped. He wanted to play with her, to tease her, to take it slow and make it last forever, but she had other ideas.

She drove her hand down and wrapped her fingers around him and squeezed him to stone, until he couldn't imagine a world where he could say no to anything she asked. She used him to brush his own hands out of the way, rubbing and sliding and pushing until she was soft water all around him.

He forgot about the world. Future and past ceased to exist. There was nothing outside of her warmth, the movement of her body, the sweet scent of her skin. Her arms wrapping around him were the boundaries of his universe, her groping kisses were his sustenance, and her wandering hands traced the avenues of the world across his back. When her eyes closed it was night in the world, and when they opened it was again day. He felt like a god here in her arms; powerful and delirious, owning and ravaging this little world that existed in the space between them.

Her lips sought his frantically, like waves seeking the shore, splashing and colliding urgently against him, her mouth rising to meet him at every thrust. With every inhale he felt the scent of her body enter him, consuming him. With every moan she renamed the world, shuddering and groaning and screaming and sighing, louder and louder, higher and higher, until every thought, every sensation, every motion of his body brought him to her, spilling out, a surging wave, unstoppable, overflowing him, shattering him.

She cried out beneath him, louder than ever, ecstatic, delirious, exhausted, relieved. She held him tight against her until he was done, not allowing him to pull away for even a moment, holding him as he kissed at her neck, head balanced in the crook of her shoulder.

It all rushed away into an unexpected and necessary calm. It took him a moment to even realize it. The raging storm was still, and he lay beside her, taking breath after reluctant breath, her legs quaking, his heart thumping, her chest rising and falling, his mouth open, her eyelids closed.

She kissed softly at his neck, resting one arm lazily across his chest. He felt her hold him so gently, and yet somehow he knew that her grip would withstand even the most violent hurricane.

He pulled her onto him and kissed her again. He had done it so many times, he realized, but it was not enough. He wanted more. He wanted the world to end itself before he ever ceased to feel those beautiful lips against his own.

He didn't remember stopping, but he opened his eyes to find her snuggled beside him underneath the smooth sheets. It comforted him to feel her subtle breaths on his skin. It calmed him and soothed him just to know she was there, to know she was with him, to know he was not alone. Just knowing that made everything else in the world into no more than dust, swept away by a casual exhale.

He held her curled beside him until she was deep in a smiling sleep. Only then did he rise and slip out of the room. The sky was black and moonless, but the malagayne was still sweet regardless.

52

We Break Immortals

"I FEEL IT," Keluwen said. "Something is different."

"We are different," Orrinas said, sitting on the edge of the bed beside her. "From each moment to the next we begin again."

"He scares me, Orrinas." She reached across the bed and curled her fingers around his forearm, covering his scar.

"Kinraigan?"

"No, Aren."

"The Glasseye scares you?"

"I do not mean that he reminds me of when I was hunted. I mean that he reminds me of Paladan."

Orrinas had been nursing a smile, but it died on his lips. "The boy was in over his head. We all knew it. Seb knew it. The others, Bann, Syman, they should have known it, too."

"And now we have found ourselves an even younger boy."

"Aren is different."

"How?"

"He is a Glasseye. Palad, poor Palad, was pretending he knew what to do. Glasseyes know this work. And the best Glasseyes always come from Amagon."

"I did not tell you before," she said. "He had been talking about destiny."

"He thinks he has a purpose. All dedicated people do. Is it not our purpose to be here with him, to finish this, to end Kinraigan's quest of madness once and for all?"

"When you say destiny and he says destiny it seems like you are each talking about a different thing."

"Aren is diligent, thorough. He swears the Sister can keep Kinraigan from using his unstoppable crush bubbles. He says with the composite that *we* obtained, and the known rate of his increased power, that we will be able to interdict him. Aren says we may be able to take him without a fight. He has never lost a trace, or so the Sister tells me. He is good."

"I hope you are right."

"Has he given you any reason to believe that he does not know what he is doing?"

She shook her head. "No."

"And knowing you, I am sure you tried very hard to find something wrong with him."

"You know me." She smiled, but then she looked away, gazing out the glass window at the moonlit trees. "But what we are up against...Kinraigan is like no other. He has found some way into the light. On his own. That is what you said. You said you saw him do it."

"It was only for a moment, and I was so close I nearly fell into the light with him. Years ago now. You have seen his eyes. There is no telling how much time he has spent in there since, what manner of things he has discovered about that place."

"Place. Funny thing to call it."

"It both is and isn't." He noticed her staring out the window. "What thought troubles you?"

"Who gave him the book? Who gave Palad the Codex?"

"That is not for us to worry about. They are surely looking into it. The list of those who had access to it is small."

"He has it now. The book."

"The Codex Lumina contains powerful knowledge, but one must *understand* it in order to use it. Reading the words on the page and truly understanding them in context requires experience."

"He has the experience. He is the worst of them."

"It will be all right. We have found one of the children. That will bring us through."

"How do you know that? How can you possibly know that?"

He forced a smile to return. "Because I believe."

"Palad believed."

"Paladan believed in his own imagined plan. I believe in this because they told us. I believe it because the mouth that spoke those words long ago proved itself to me. I believe. Let us just leave it at that."

"Do you really believe Kinraigan is a luminous immortal?"

"I believe it. I believe he found out how to make himself live forever. But an ageless life does not mean he cannot die. That much I know for certain."

"You always say that. You always say you know the luminous can still die. How do you know?"

"Because he is not the first luminous immortal I have hunted."

Her mouth fell open. "You never told me. Not once. In all our time."

"I never told any of the others either."

"Why not? We thought we had only ever been after users who were *trying* to make themselves luminous. It could have been such a boon to their confidence, to *my* confidence, knowing that this has been done before. Not just people trying to *become* luminous, but actual immortals."

"I did not tell because it would have led to questions. And those questions would eventually have come around to what it *cost* to stop the last one."

"How much did it cost you?"

"Everything." He smiled but his eyes were glass, so full of unfallen tears they glowed.

"You know I didn't love you when I married you," she said.

"I know."

"But I love you now."

"I know."

She took his face in her hands and pressed her lips to his, feeling them, intentionally knowing them, remembering them, their softness, their particular texture, how they hardened and softened and parted for her tongue.

Her hands slid inside his robes and wandered. *Put your hands on me.* But he wouldn't. He always waited. He knew how much she hated but loved it when he did that. She leaned toward him, her body humming, heat spreading. She ran a hand over the scar on his chest, the one he had received the night of their wedding, the night he saved her from the lonely death of the hunted, the day when they first met.

She touched that scar, memorizing it by touch, her mouth opening, the hum becoming a drone. She slid her hands down to the little bulb where his arrow wound had healed over, the one he received the day she first realized she loved him. She touched it with her fingers and her mouth widened like the sea, and her legs parted.

She shed her clothes, everything but the gloves, never the gloves.

She climbed atop him and lowered herself down. She was made of dew and fire, same as the first time they met. And he was iron within her, rigid, defiant, enduring, patient. She opened her mouth for his soft lips, feeling his breaths, her fingers losing their way in his hair, her body locked in the slender crucial grip of his arms.

He set his hands on her hips, but he let her be the waves, crashing against his body, a rhythmic pulse making heat rise in her chest and between her thighs. She rocked atop him faster and faster, breaths steaming, sweat beading, teeth biting tender and sharp, skin sliding on skin, her desire owning him. She wrapped arms around him, strong as iron chains, light as flower petals, and for that one moment in time, he was hers and she was his, completely, open in heart, open in body, he had her inside and out.

She threw her head back and closed her eyes, and the drone became a song, and its melody writhed and groaned and gripped her in its climax and bathed her in its fragile pleasure and surged inside her until she could no longer tell if he was overflowing her or she was overflowing him. And for that one moment there was no fear. In that little death she was free and he was free and nothing else mattered and the two of them together were all that was left in the world.

She held onto him so tight for so long her arms began to cramp, but she did not care. She wanted to feel every second of him. She wanted to feel every minute, and every mile.

Then she let him lay down. She knew he needed sleep, so much sleep, to be prepared, for what was to come. In the morning they would hunt. And everything would change again. He needed every bit of strength. And she would give it to him.

When never meets forever, my love.

She rose, pulled a linen tunic over her head, and slipped out onto the balcony to look at the moonlit city until she could not keep her eyes open any longer.

She looked at rippling waters and leaves dancing in the breeze beneath the silver light of Silistin alone in the night sky. The breeze chilled her bare legs but she did not mind. She watched friends and lovers laugh and run and embrace on the water's edge, so far away, yet so obvious. She felt herself smile. When this was at an end that is what she would have.

She looked to her left.

She saw him standing there. Grey smoke floating from his mouth, his lips sharp and silver and cold in the moonlight. The clouds drifting high above, becoming shipwrecks in the sky. She watched them sink higher and higher.

"Aren," she said.

He turned to her and gave a start. "Keluwen."

She smiled. "That must have been the Andristi girl in the sheets with you. Loud and proud she is."

"Her name is Eriana."

"She loves you."

"More than I deserve."

She laughed. "Somehow we are all always with someone better than ourselves."

"How are you?" he asked. "You and Orrinas are well, I hope."

"We are. We really truly are."

"Good. I am glad to hear it."

"I was going to kill you, you know."

His eyes momentarily widened, but then he slid into a soft smile. "I remember. I was there."

"I'm glad I didn't, if that's any consolation."

"Some. I don't blame you for it, believe it or not. Thinking I was one of his...I would have tried to kill me, too."

"We have been chasing him a long time. It starts to take over all you are. Sometimes you have to remind yourself what it means to be yourself."

He nodded. He blew a ring of grey smoke. "Sometimes to remember, sometimes to forget."

"This is going to be over soon."

"That it will." He paused. "Something is eating at you."

"I saw him, you know. Eye to eye. Closer to me than you are now. Right beside me."

"That close?"

"I felt like I was losing control."

"What do you mean?"

"There is something always about him. I do not know what it is. I felt like I belonged to him, like I wanted to belong to him. I felt like I couldn't trust myself."

Aren blew a silver smoke cathedral beneath the moon. "I have talked to him three times." He paused and looked at the moon. "Or was it four?"

She squinted suspiciously at him. "That many times? Did you ever feel... that way?"

"No. Well, maybe a little. But I remember mostly hating him, hating what he is and what he does, and wanting to make him burn. If he tried to make me into something it didn't work. I can't think of anything I have wanted more than to kill him."

"Did Cheli tell you about the book he has?"

"The Codex Lumina? Yes. Now that is one book I would like to get my hands on. It is said there are only eleven copies of it remaining in all the world."

"Orrinas says the book can teach things to people who have walked in the light."

"I don't know what I believe."

"He is not just some user. He is luminous. He is *immortal*. Do you understand that?"

He took a long sip of malagayne and held it in. "Do you know what I tell the people in my team before a capture? I tell them that users are not gods, they are people, like me, like you. They have to follow certain rules to do what they do. Breaking men like him is what I do." He looked at her and smiled. "It is what you do, too."

"I want to end this, Aren. I want to finish it. I am tired of always not quite making it. We need to stop him."

"He thinks he is immortal," Aren said. "Fine. Let him think he is immortal. We *break* immortals. He wants to be a god? You and I, we break gods. Do you understand?"

She smiled. "We break immortals."

"We are going to do this. Together. We have a purpose. It is right here. He is in our grasp."

"I am ready," she said.

"Me too," he said.

"Better find time to sleep."

"Sleep well and good. We all need to be at our best."

"We will be." She turned and walked to the door, she pulled it open a crack and peeked inside. Orrinas slept soundly. *Thank every god. He needs all the sleep in the world.* "Goodnight, Aren," she said.

"Goodnight, Keluwen," Aren said. He took a step, but paused and turned back to look at her. "And Keluwen?"

"Yes?"

"I'm glad you didn't kill me either," he said.

She smiled. She slipped into the room. She pulled to door silently closed. She crept into bed beside the greatest man she had ever known. She slept beside him wishing she did not have to miss a single moment of it.

53

No One Gets Away

AREN STALKED THE CITY streets, once again the hunter.

This was what he was meant to do. His whole life had led to this moment, to make him perfect for it. All of the things that had happened had led him here. The pieces all fit so perfectly. He was going to stop the Sanadi.

There was no going back now. He was in it to the end. He was on the hunt. Kinraigan was not a great mastermind, an untouchable power, a luminous immortal. He was a rogue user, nothing more. Just another rogue user to go to the fires.

There were scant traces anywhere Aren could find, but it didn't matter. As long as he had the samples of sensitized material, he could follow Kinraigan anywhere until those samples aged out and faded away. It did not matter how well he cleaned himself, or how careful he was. He must have thought himself safe, outside their reach.

No user is safe.

Aren guided them through choked markets, and wide empty streets, hemmed in by towering tenements, following the directions indicated by the spectral shift. He passed through centuries as they crossed Arthenorad, seeing architecture from every one of the past thousand years. But no matter how quick the steps Aren took, Keluwen was always out front, always ahead of him, daring the danger to come at her.

Everywhere they went they found evidence that the black coats had been there first. Black bloody splashes on walls, pools of slow crimson on the ground, fallen weapons, but never any bodies. There were little vignettes of the aftermath of violence all along the path Aren pointed out for them—before the seven everflames at the mausoleum of Basilis I, and outside the bone doors that sealed off the horse stalls at the Hippodrome Excelsior, and even on the six sacred steps before the Golden Gate of Regamun I, guarding the ruins of the ancient Shanna Temple tower, where the first emperor of Arradan had been crowned. They passed through the gate and then the tower beyond, navigating a maze of dried up fountains and crumbling stone prayer boxes.

But they never came across any footsoldiers of Kinraigan's cult. And the spectral shift indicated the man himself was miles and miles away.

The path led north out of the city, beyond the winter farms and the villas of the merchant barons. It diverted through a secluded glen beyond the last shepherd, and into patch of shallow hills, overlooking muddy basins. By midday the sky was drowned in grey clouds. The cold turned to only a hairsbreadth away from frigid.

Eriana walked beside him, brushing her shoulder against him as if by accident, and leaning in to kiss him when no one else could see. He left the world for an instant each time he felt her touch, or looked down into her eyes —crystal blue, like mountain lakes. Nothing could wipe the smile from her face. He wanted to stare into it forever, to lose himself in it, but he knew he could not allow himself that luxury. Not now. He had to shut it away. He needed to focus every thought on the trace.

"You should be careful," Reidos said. "They said he is immortal."

"The Sur on the Kol Plateau thought that Bolus was immortal," Aren said. "I proved them wrong. Now it is Kinraigan's turn. Users are overconfident. That is what brings about their downfall. No one gets away from me, Reidos. No one." He reached into his pocket and rolled around the three long pins, each one's tip slick with tinwood leaf residue. The ends were corked, but he wanted to be ready. "Once a Render Tracer prepares the capture, there is nothing else for him to do until the final moment. I will be ready for it."

"We are safe right now though, aren't we?" Eriana asked.

"Every time I run the triangulation algorithm it shows him miles away. If he turned around now and sprinted faster and longer than anyone alive, it would still take him an hour to get here. And I am checking every five minutes."

The core residuals had been redshifting in the blue filter of the Jecker monocle. *Spectral shift, the Tracer's best friend.* The core residual redness began to diminish. That meant Kinraigan was slowing down, and that they were catching up.

Tanashri kept close to Inrianne while trying to make it look like she wasn't. Redevir was trying to keep his distance from Tanashri and felt it unnecessary to try to hide the fact. Reidos walked beside Hallan much of the way, trying to keep Orrinas from spending too much time trying to decipher what was so special about the boy.

Orrinas and Keluwen remained close together, checking in routinely with Cheli, the girl with the books. Hodo Grubb and Leucas Brej were both men of few words, and those they did speak were almost always to each other. Krid Ballar, on the other hand, spoke often and sourly. Duran walked alone, his only weapon a long leather strip.

Fainen walked ahead, making certain the path did not have unforeseen pitfalls. The Sarenwalker held *Braxis* for him, strapped across his back with the two broken halves of Hayles' staff, *Glimmer* sheathed at his side. Watching Fainen at work brought calm to his mind, allowed him to focus on the trace, and for that he could not have been more thankful.

"Aren," Corrin broke the silence.

"What is it?"

"What exactly are we to *do* when we find this person?"

"We put our users as close as possible to him, so that precedence effect will be in play. If they can hold as many of his streams as we have logged in practice they should be able to render him as close to powerless as possible."

"I see," Corrin said. "And us? What about us? Of the non-weird sort?"

"Our job is to protect our users," Hodo Grubb said. "Keep them safe from distractions. Support them in any way we can."

"We must not allow them to lose concentration," Aren said. "And we can't have them expending their energies battling with Kinraigan's followers. It is vitally important that they are fully rested to face him."

"How do you know this is going to work?" Corrin asked.

"I wouldn't be here if I wasn't sure," Aren said. "That is why I go in with the team for the capture. To show that everything is accounted for. To show that everything is ready. To show that all the hard work is done, and all we have left to do is keep our cool for five minutes and I will prove that this great and terrible user is just a man."

"How do you know when you have prepared well enough?" Corrin asked.

"How does a sword fighter know when they are better than the one who challenges them?" Orrinas asked. "He does not. He must make an educated guess, and then hope his particular combination of knowledge, speed, strength, experience, preparation, and endurance will win out over that of his opponent."

"That is not very reassuring," Corrin said. "What if Kinraigan is the *me* of users? No one has been able to stop me."

"Look, Corrin," Aren said. "This is the most prepared I have ever been before a capture. I have imprints of thousands of his streams. I have experienced users. I have sampled sensitized fluorescence to track his exact position through the variance in redshifting. I am going to take us through this. I am going to break him."

"I have never seen you this certain about anything," Corrin said.

"I've done this before," Aren assured him. "This is what I *do*."

"This is what we all do," Keluwen said.

"I feel it is an odd place to bring a small child," Corrin said.

"Orrinas insisted on it," Aren said. "But it does not matter. He will be safer with us than on most street corners in Arthenorad."

Aren turned back to the trail ahead, descending into one of the wide mud basins—flat, desolate, and hideous. Writhing mosses abounded in icy puddles. Some were more like small ponds than puddles. Even the earth in between was loaded with moisture, with water swelling up in every footprint.

In the center, near the next hill, a rocky crag jutted up from the sponge-mud. It was the size of a house. Kinraigan's path led directly to it, then away beyond.

Aren had checked the Jecker monocle every minute when they were in the city, then every five minutes, then every ten. He checked it while Corrin was asking, and triangulated his position, still miles away. The results were always the same. Redshifting, Kinraigan running away.

He pulled it out once more and gazed at the little vials. The blue filter shrouded everything but the core color and the *Introduction-Of-Change* structure. There they were. Kinraigan's core color. Pale orange.

With a distinct shift to the *blue*.

Aren pulled the monocle away from his face. He shook his head and wiped his eyes. He looked again. The residuals were blueshifting. He shook the monocle and wiped it with his static cloth. Same result. Kinragan's residuals were blueshifting hard. Double hard.

Something was wrong. The particles glowed like sapphires. "It shouldn't do that unless the residual particles are being *approached* by the source user," he said to himself. But Kinraigan should have been well away over the next hill. Why would it be blueshifting here? It made no sense.

He held the vials out in two directions, glanced at each, and raced through the triangulation. His stomach dropped.

"What's wrong, Aren?" Eriana asked.

"I must have mixed my numbers." He ran the calculations again. And again. And again. Each time a part of his mind screamed a little louder. The numbers were correct. "It says Kinraigan is less than a hundred strides from here. It's impossible. He was too far away. It's...not...possible."

Aren's heart dropped into the pit of his stomach. He did not understand how, but he realized *what* was happening.

He is here.

The air swirled and spun. The clouds seemed like they were falling in, like a solid ceiling to crush him. Almonds. Something screamed in his head to run.

"Back!" Aren screamed. "Get back!"

"What?" Redevir asked.

They all turned to look at him.

"He knows we're here!" Aren said. "He doubled back on us. He knows!"

Kinraigan strutted his way to the top of the crag, blue and violet robes wrapped around him. A painful, agonizing smile spread across his ghost-white face. His eyes were black as night.

Aren stepped back. Corrin and Fainen drew swords immediately. Reidos placed himself in front of Hallan. Hodo, Leucas, and Cheli looked at each other in horror. Duran was the only one who remembered to place himself in front of the users.

Tanashri, Inrianne, Krid, Orrinas, and Keluwen shut themselves off from distraction. They reached for Kinraigan's streams, and began to bind their own.

Aren watched them move their arms in the ways that were most comfortable for them. He watched all of them become flustered, confused, and finally afraid. Orrinas and Keluwen traded terror-stricken looks.

It was just like Tanashri and Inrianne in Medion. Their magick was gone.

Kinraigan could stop their renders. They were helpless.

"You followed my trail well, my friend," he said to Aren.

Aren shuddered. Kinraigan had laid a trap for them, and he had walked right into it. *This can't be happening. Users want to get away from Glasseyes. They don't come to them.*

"I find your helplessness amusing," Kinraigan said, looking at Orrinas. "How frail our kind become when bereft of our sweet powers. How like addicts we are. Look at yourself, Orrinas."

Orrinas only stared.

"You thought I wouldn't be expecting you," Kinraigan said. He laughed. "I knew you would come. I knew they would send Sisters. Eventually they send everyone."

"It's not possible," Aren said to himself.

Kinraigan smiled. "Anything is possible when you are luminous, Aren. That is what I have been trying to tell you."

"How did you know we were here?" Orrinas asked. "How?"

"You thought you were following me, but I was following *you*. I have been all this time."

"How?" Redevir demanded. "No one tracked us."

"No one needed to. You gave yourselves away. In Olbaran, in Laman, in Aldria, in Medion, in Kamathar, *everywhere*. I knew. I knew where you were." He looked at Aren and smiled. "How do you think I found you on the Fields of Syn?"

He sent the Vuls to ambush us. It has been him all along.

A short bald man joined Kinraigan on the crag. He was so average, so forgettable. But Aren knew him instantly. It was the very man who had stood beside Redscar in the streets of Medion, the one who gave him commands.

"How?" Orrinas demanded.

"The same way I am blocking your magick now," Kinraigan said. "Is it not obvious? I am interdicting you. All of you. I have pulled every stream you need to make your feeble powers work."

Orrinas looked horrified. "Impossible."

"Poor fools," Kinraigan said. "Did you think you had a monopoly on Glasseyes?"

Oh god, Aren thought. *No, no, no.* That was what Raviel meant when he warned about Kinraigan. *He wasn't talking about me being corrupted.* He was talking about a Glasseye Kinraigan had *already* corrupted. Aren realized at that moment that they were no match for Kinraigan.

"Talvin is *my* Glasseye. He imprinted all of your streams in Westgate, or in Laman," Kinraigan said. "I could only interdict you if I knew the streams and renders of each and every one of you. But Talvin has *composites* of each and every one of you, painstakingly put together. Just like the one you have of me. I can turn you all on and off as I choose."

Aren nearly threw up.

Kinraigan smiled even wider. "He recorded each of your *Introduction-of-Change* key patterns. After that I was able to follow you everywhere. He collected fresh samples of three of you after you left Shaezrod Spur. He has been monitoring your position by way of Spectral Shift." He looked at Aren. "I hear they call it the Render Tracer's best friend."

Aren's eyes watered. *I was using sensitized tracking on him, but he was using it on us. He knew exactly where we were.*

"I was aware of your every step, Orrinas. I knew what you ate, what you drank, where you slept."

"You were redshifting," Aren said. "You were too far away. You should not be able to be here. It is not possible."

"You seem so certain about the way things work for someone who has never been in the light," Kinraigan said. "The Codex taught me many things." He smiled, legs apart, arms at his sides, calm, confident, impervious.

Behind him, people appeared, climbing to join him atop the rock, and spilling around its sides. Aren saw people in mid-sleeved tunics of every color. Men and women. They were just people. But now they were his. Among them he noticed men in long black coats, old tarnished swords in their hands. He saw a wealthy noble in green silks, greying hair, with a fine dueling sword. He saw half-shaved, gap-toothed road-men and alley-kings from three different countries. And one man carried two swords and wore jinglebells on his shoes.

Another man emerged atop the crag, large crossbows in each hand, and still more strapped to his back. Aren recognized him. The face hit his mind like a flash from another life. He had all but forgotten about Balthoren.

"And the rest of you met my ebon-shrouds, Gonrag and Baileras, in Medion."

Aren stared at the them. He stiffened against the desire to run. *If you cross the path of an ebon-shroud, you must change your path.* There was no way to escape, no choice to avoid them, no place to hide or even seek for cover. He was staring at his own end.

One final man joined Kinraigan atop the crag. He had arms and legs like muscled reeds, taller than the tallest man Aren head ever seen. Kinraigan clasped his hands together. "This is Tarykthies. Andristi. They sent him after me, you know. The Lamani. Years ago. To kill me. But he became mine. I showed him the truth. I let him be who he has always wanted to be. He is devoted to me. He is going to kill you for me, Orrinas."

"The hell he is," Keluwen said.

Kinraigan ignored her. He laughed. His voice like bells lined with sandpaper. "Aren, I am glad you are here on our day of celebration. You have been my most powerful ally."

"Do not believe him," Orrinas warned. "He speaks lies invented by his own madness."

Kinraigan smiled proudly. "I guided you to perform a miracle. It has all worked out for the best, hasn't it? You saved me so much time by bringing it to me."

He knows we have the Crown.

"You see now," Kinraigan said calmly. "You understand that I am Sanadi. I make the world as I will. Aldarion and all the others who are coming to challenge me, they will know how sadly they are outmatched. All of them will know the truth—that Kinraigan alone is Sanadi."

"You are not Sanadi," Aren said. "You are just a user pretending to be."

"I *am* Sanadi," Kinraigan snarled, suddenly glaring with a ferocity Aren had never seen. "I am a luminous immortal. I have spent so long in the light. None of you could ever understand. I cannot wait to show the world the things that

I have seen. I will show you. I will show you all. I have deciphered the Codex Lumina. I am not the herald of what is coming. I *am* what is coming. We are one and the same. I *am* the Advent. I am here to usher in the new era of light. I will become what no man has been for millennia, and I will make the world my own around me. And you will be remembered as nothing more than a puddle I stepped in along the way."

"You mock us," Orrinas said. "You speak to us as though we are mere children."

"I do. I do mock you. Do you not understand why I am standing here? Why I am speaking with you? Why I am telling you all of these things? It is to *humiliate* you. To show you that I can stand here, unarmed, unprotected, and have a gentle conversation with the team that has come to kill me, and there is nothing any of them can do about it."

"We will stop you."

"You will not!" Kinraigan shouted, twisting into a rage. "You can no longer hinder me at all. I told you everything because you cannot stop it now. I wanted you all to *feel* how utterly you have failed before you die. I will stand here, blocking your magick, watching my people kill you, and smiling."

Kinraigan's followers began moving. Balthoren, the ebon-shrouds, the users, the cutthroats, the swordsmen, the murderers. They were coming to conduct the slaughter that Kinraigan had willed.

Think! Aren screamed into his own mind. *Think. There has to be a way. There has to be something.* Some stream. Some thread that he could pull to unravel him. A trick. A shortcut. A hidden weakness. Something. But there was none. He had them all on their knees. As long as he could cancel their connection to the place where all magick was born, he could do anything to them he wanted. It was over. Kinraigan had won.

****

Keluwen kept sneaking glances out of the corner of her eye to see if Orrinas was looking at her. He never was. His eyes were fixed on Kinraigan. Of course they were. She knew they would be before each time she tried. But she did anyway.

She needed him to look at her. She needed to see his eyes, his smile, to know no matter what happened, everything would be all right, always.

But the only one who looked at her was the man with black eyes. The man who had been so close to her and nearly stolen her. His eyes were rats gnawing at her confidence.

She was supposed to be strong. She was supposed to stare into the abyss of fear and feel nothing but her own naked power. She had come all this way knowing that she could stand before this man, this enemy, and never wither.

But her beliefs turned to dust. Her courage wilted. She felt fear, uncanny fear, like a mouth was growing inside her, opening wide, chewing her to pieces until she was nothing but skin.

She could not touch the Slipstream. She could not access the source. She could not touch her streams, or pull Kinraigan's like a Stopper. She was powerless. And the others were powerless beside her.

Kinraigan would never release his hold on them. He would block their magick and watch his followers do the darkwork of killing. No one could stop him. No one could undo what he had done.

Except him.

He could undo it.

But he never would.

Orrinas never looked over at her. She checked once more just to be sure. But she could not wait for him. She had to step forward alone. Her boots squished in the mud, and she nearly slipped more than once, but she stepped out in front of everyone.

"You are a coward," she said to the most powerful man she had ever seen. She was sure Orrinas was looking at her now. But it was too late. If she so much as glanced away from Kinraigan now, her courage would wash away.

Kinraigan tilted his head to one side. "I do not believe that I am."

"You are afraid," Keluwen said. "I can see it in your eyes."

"You see nothing. You are insects. I could crush you beneath my feet!"

"Then why don't you?"

He sneered at her. He opened his mouth to speak, but closed it again.

"You won't because you can't," she said. "You expect everyone to just believe you when you tell your story, the clever one about you being a god. But the truth is, you need regular people to do your work because you are too weak on your own."

"When I have the Crown—"

"When you have this, when you have that. It is always the same. You are never strong right now. Only in the future, somewhere else, some other time. You will be this great and powerful man. Tomorrow. But then every tomorrow becomes today, and still you wait for another. I think you can't defeat us because you just can't."

"I can make anyone into anything I wish," he said. "I can turn water into wine and dirt into gold. I can turn a faithful man into a traitor. I can make any woman betray."

"Any one but me."

His eyes narrowed. They sliced through her skin and dissected her. "I have seen your face before."

"The only thing I have seen is how you turn yourself into a tiny crying baby," Keluwen said.

His eye twitched. His mouth twisted. His lips opened and closed three times in rapid succession.

That touched a nerve. She remembered how Aren had set off her rage. She pushed Kinraigan the same way. "Is that what it is? You are a little baby, screaming for its mother, but the mother will not ever come home? Never stop the bullies from hurting you?"

"I am more than anything," he said. "I am more than any of you."

"Those are the words of someone who most certainly isn't," Keluwen said.

"You have no idea what I am capable of."

"Go on then. Show me."

"I could show you."

"But you won't. You can't. You are too frightened. You are too weak."

"I am not. I am strong."

"Is that why you ran away from the Glasseyes in Amagon? Because you were so strong? Is that why you always move from place to place? Always hiding? That is not what a supreme being does. That is what a scared little rabbit does when they are afraid of being caught."

"I do not run away. You...you...Do you know who I am? Do you know what I can do?"

"You play pretend that you are a little king, playing with little dolls in your lap."

"I am fixing the world. I am saving it. I am changing it. Everyone will see. Everyone will know."

"You can't even change Aren into what you want. Your power is a fraud. If you let us use our power everyone will see that you are frightened little weakling."

Kinraigan seethed. His neck bent forward. His eyes became open pits. His hands balled into fists. She could see him straining. She could see him wanting to. "You have no idea what I have overcome."

Come on. Do it. Do it.

"You think you are special because you were a sad little boy. You scream and cry because you want to make everyone else feel as small as you do."

Kinraigan's eyes turned into empty holes where light could not go. "You want me to show you what it is? You want to feel what trauma the world brings?"

Do it.

She raised her chin at him. "I want you to fight me. I want you to fight me, you piece of shit. I want you to show me how you hit someone like me. I want to feel it. I want you to show me. So show me!"

"You want to see what I can do with my power? You want to see how sadly you will fail?"

Keluwen shook her head. "You won't do it. You can't. You are afraid everyone will see what you really are. You are pathetic."

Do it. Fight me. Do it.

His face wrinkled into a snarl. He bared his teeth. His mouth hung open like a vast underworld ready to vomit its contents out onto the earth. "You are going to wish you had never said that."

"I wish I had never seen how sad and sorry you really are."

"No one has ever talked to me like that."

"After today, no one will ever talk about you any other way."

Do it.

A wheel turned. Something changed. His face went blank. Then he slowly smiled. "Fine. You want your power back? You want to touch the source? You want to know what I can really do? You want to see it? You want to feel it? You want to know what I can do you and all of you and everyone? Let! Me! Show! You!"

Keluwen felt something in the air. It was like an expanding bubble pushing against her skin, a thin membrane standing between her and the realm of endless possibility.

Then the bubble burst.

54

Users

AREN COULD FEEL THE precise moment when people would begin to die.

He could see it on the faces of each of the users. He almost fell out of himself with surprise. "The streams! Get his streams!"

They each raced to pull as many of them as they could, but Kinraigan was pulling dozens at once, locking them into their structures but not rendering them. Storing them so that they couldn't be interdicted. But even if he only managed to pull a tenth of what he was capable of, it would be devastating.

Aren knew he had to find a way to hold this together. He had to make this right. There would never be another chance. He didn't know how, but he had missed something, something about where Kinraigan was, or how fast he could move. Something. There was no way to go back and try again. He had to make it work.

He watched Corrin charge, then lost sight of him. He watched Duran grappling with someone, using only a leather strip, but he deflected sword swings, bending and twisting and wrapping wrists to disarm them.

Kinraigan's followers surged forward. Young and old, rich and poor, men and women. All with knives, swords, or batons.

Fainen stared at the broad line of them coming, watched their movements. He determined which of them was running the fastest and headed to meet them. Fainen cut him down without breaking stride. He skidded to a halt in the mud and then turned back, running laterally across their charge, running through them and in front of them and behind them and in between them. He cut a swath through the mass of them, sprinting an oblique route across their charge, taking down five, and then ten, slowing them, holding them back.

The followers who made it through ran into Reidos and Hodo.

We have to protect the users. My users. My team.

Aren waited beside Tanashri, ready to put himself between her and anyone who came too close.

The air rippled with the flight of blank spheres, smashing into hastily rendered shields. The succession of concussive blasts threw Aren to the ground. Kept him there. Knocked him down all over again when he tried to stand. Each collision was a thundercrack. The shockwaves slapped him, rushing wind through his hair and his clothes. Some of the spheres deflected and hit the ground, digging trenches and blasting craters in the mud. The users only had eyes for each other, battling above everyone else, in their own world, uninterested in the desperate fighting of the normals beneath them.

A smell like burning ash hung thick in the air, expanding, spreading out in all directions. That was Tanashri. Even without the Jecker monocle, Aren could see the air distorting around a series of invisible forces. Blank impulses. At least a dozen. All of them spheres. *Always simple shapes.*

Aren felt as if his eyes were being squeezed from his skull. Time froze. His hair stood on end, and his blood flowed like thick sap. He thought his heart was going to stop. It was the magick. So much of it. More than he had ever felt. The air filled with glittering silver clouds of afterglow. The smell of almonds. Intense pressure renders, dozens of them. Tanashri had interdicted most of his pressure renders, slowing his moves, but he had many more than they had ever known about.

Orrinas projected heat fields, applying them to Kinraigan's pressure bubbles, forcing them to burst prematurely.

Keluwen rendered blank spheres and aimed them for a single spot on Kinraigan's shield. Aren saw the air warping in the same space over and over again, as she chose the same stream of trajectory again and again, trying to weaken the shield at that one point.

Wave pockets slid into being, floating and dangling around each of the users, shoving the afterglow out of the their paths, drifting like balloons. Each of the users were binding streams so fast they were bleeding excess energy into dozens of wave pockets. So many he was worried one of them might be hit by an errant blank impulse and explode, killing them all.

He realized he had been staring at the voids they made in the air instead of watching the ground. He looked ahead. Two men made it past Reidos. Aren found his sword already in his hand somehow. But when the first man swung at him, he could barely bat it aside in time. He held the point of his blade out, shaking it at one, then the other.

Eriana stepped in front of him. She held her curved Andristi sword at waist height, the point slightly up, staring down both men.

The first man cut down and in with his sword.

Eriana barely moved her own sword at all. The strike hit her blade and slid right up it and past her. She leaned in and stabbed gently. Her blade sliced through him. She withdrew it, and slid through three different stances, the sword always at the ready.

The second man lived twice as long as the first. Two seconds instead of one. He swung harder, and missed harder, but grabbed her tunic with his free hand, pulled her forward with his weight. But she brought her blade up under his breastbone and out through his neck.

Aren felt another blast, someone's blank impulse exploding into the mud, showering them like rain.

A bolt flashed between their heads.

Shaot, Balthoren.

Tanashri made sharp motions with her hands. The rock Kinraigan stood upon began to chip and shatter as she blasted it apart with blank impulses, tiny ones, with a trapped outward expanding force, set to explode on contact. She rendered more and more of them. They slammed all over the rock. Invisible, infinitesimal, they exploded, starting cracks, rupturing, turning Kinraigan's rock into shrapnel and then blasting it at him.

Balthoren scrambled down the side, jumping, tucking, and rolling in the black mud, pulling the trigger of a crossbow every other second, discarding it, then firing another.

Kinraigan lifted himself in the air, hovering like a hummingbird as the rock broke apart beneath him. He twisted and pointed as he levitated, riding a massive pressure render, holding himself aloft. He laced the air with equally minuscule pressure bubbles, smaller than any Tanashri would have bothered to Stop. So many, thousands of them—gods, but the concentration to do that!—many of them hitting nothing, but just as many catching pieces of shattered rock and hurling them at blinding speeds toward Tanashri.

The air began to swirl, and sharp shards of the shattered rock flew like knives at her. The Saderan pulled her arms to her chest. The shards diverged, as an invisible wedge formed about her. *Blank impulse. V-shaped panel. Quick thinking.*

Keluwen pointed at Kinraigan's shield again, hitting it over and over. Inrianne followed with a blast of her fire.

That's it. Disrupt his concentration. Work together. His shield may be strong, but a wall of flame coming right at you will throw anyone's concentration off.

Tanashri looked up just in time to see Tarykthies racing toward her. She raised one tiny hand. He froze in midstride and tipped over like a toy soldier.

The earth behind the ebon-shrouds exploded away, sending them sprawling, as Tarykthies' inertia was applied into the mud instead.

Aren's hands were frozen to the bone, the mud on his palms like ice. He could barely keep a grip on his sword. He worried that he might drop it if the wind gusted. He turned, took Eriana by the wrist, keeping her close. He backed toward Tanashri. His eyes darted everywhere.

The ground beneath his feet erupted. He was catapulted skyward. He landed face first in a pool of frigid water. The cold was like knives in his skin. He pressed himself up with both hands. Moss clung to his arms and face. He wiped stinging cold from his eyes and pawed furiously at his sword in the mud.

Everywhere the earth was shattering and breaking, as the users sent tremendous energy towards each other, countered each other, attacked again. He couldn't see Eriana. He couldn't find Fainen. His back stiffened, his vision blurred. Someone ran past him. People were moving everywhere, no matter which way he turned. Pressure bubbles exploded all around him, and sharp blank impulses careened in all directions. Ten rainbows' worth of sparkling afterglow swirled in the air, clinging to the rocks and the mud and to everyone who stepped through the colored clouds.

An invisible pressure bubble shot from Kinraigan's hand and tore across the ground like a supersonic plow, throwing dirt and people into the air. Tanashri toppled over. Mardin went sprawling. An ebon-shroud was thrown on his back. Only Hallan stood still.

****

Corrin watched Kinraigan's followers charge.

Either twenty men or a hundred were running toward him. *No, not toward me. Toward Aren. Toward the users.*

I am the one standing in the way.

He was determined to send them a message, to split them like a deck of Tarenian cards, give them a warm, welcoming steel kiss from the prettiest lady he had ever laid eyes on. He did not need to draw his sword as he ran because he had been holding it in a *middle guard* from the very moment Aren said: *I must have mixed up my numbers.*

Aren doesn't mix up his numbers. That was how Corrin knew the work was about to get dark. He would believe the universe turned inside out before he would believe Aren would foul up a math equation.

He felt his heart speed up. *Come on now, dear. There you go. Time to make the blood flow. We have dancing to do.* He had only the plan Aren had given him.

Keep them away from the users.

The specifics of how he fulfilled that directive he would leave up to his whim.

The most detail he had worked out so far was to run toward his enemies.

What else? What else?

He smiled and raised his blade into a *high guard*.

Ah, yes. Cut them with this.

The first to reach him was the first to fall. A quick downward cut put him away. He tried to block but missed badly. The *Steel Whore* turned six of his ribs into twelve, and gave his lung a new hole to deflate through.

The second to reach him was the third to die. He ran too fast and careened past Corrin, his sword never coming close.

The third to reach him tried upward swings from both sides. Corrin passed back one step. Then another. Then another. On the fourth swing Corrin hopped two steps forward. Got inside. He clamped his left hand around the man's wrist, keeping his sword to one side while he daintily slid his Sabarian steel blade into the man's neck. An inch was all it would have taken, but Corrin gave him ten. He wanted to see the look on his face when it came out the other side.

He withdrew it, twisting the man's arm, swinging his dying body around and using it as a shield while he leaked the wine of life out his neck. Corrin bought enough time to parry twice and then draw a cut over the belly of the second man, opening him up with a hiss of steam.

Corrin's human shield began to teeter, and slumped to his knees. Corrin kicked him forward, tipping him over into the legs of the fourth, knocking him down, presenting a nice unprotected back for Corrin to drive his blade down into.

By the time he looked up, most of the other followers had diverted around him.

"What is the matter with you all? Don't you like dancing?"

But behind the first rush came something else. He locked eyes on some fine fellows who would not mind the dance.

Ebon-shrouds.

Everyone had always told him to walk the other way when he saw one of them. Even Jecks Keberan said so, and Jecks was crazy enough to play goldcards with his back to the door.

Corrin was delighted to realize there was still one piece of advice in the world he had not ignored. But the time was nigh.

All right, farods. Get ready for the magnificence.

Corrin threw himself into a sprint, kicking up flecks of mud as he ran. Crossbow bolts ripped past his head, slapping into the ground like hail. His mind raced, but he didn't feel the fear. All he felt was the action. He slammed into one of the ebon-shrouds, pressing his sword forward like a shield and entangling his arms. A black blade deflected him, and a black gauntlet shot into his ribs, sending him to his knees.

Well, shaot. That didn't work.

Gonrag or Baileras or whoever-they-were turned and moved toward the users.

No you don't.

Corrin reached out and took a fistful of cloak. He yanked back on it, hard. A black sword spun like a whirlwind, and Corrin barely took his hand back in time.

"I like your sword," Corrin said. "I'm going to make you give it to me."

The ebon-shroud hissed like a lizard and lunged at him.

Did you just hiss at me?

Corrin threw the *Steel Whore* into action, dashing aside attacks and cutting in short arcs across torso and head. The ebon-shroud sent a hard stab. Corrin sidestepped. Let him in close. Locked a fist onto the cloak, and made to drive his blade into whatever was under those black folds, but a gauntlet latched around his wrist and spun him.

Oh right, there are two of you.

Corrin twisted free, but had to let go the other one's cloak.

Let's try that again.

Corrin held his longsword at the ready. He knew he was going to kill these two. He just knew it.

But then the earth exploded around him, and he was thrown high into the air, tumbling and whirling. White light blinded him. His ears hummed, and the world went silent.

He wasn't sure if he hit the ground or the ground reached up and hit him.

****

Keluwen held her shields in place. They were not her strong suit. But Tanashri and Orrinas held between them enough of Kinraigan's streams to prevent his crush bubbles and even the worst of his offensive blank impulses. But that did not make it any easier to feel the impact of sphere after sphere. *How had he pulled so many streams at once?* His mind was beyond anything she had ever imagined.

She shot her blank impulses at his shield but did not break through. So she sent her blank impulses at incredible speed at the sharp rocks behind him. They cracked into it, bouncing shrapnel back at him from behind.

Kinraigan snarled. He dropped his square shield and rendered a spherical one in its place.

She took aim with her own marble-sized spheres again. She sent them one at a time, each one smacking into his new bubble. They did nothing but pit and groove it. It was too strong for any blank impulse she could manage.

But maybe not for all blank impulses. I can do precision punching. I may not have the strongest, but I can do that.

She focused her aim to one spot on his shield, and she hammered it over and over again. Punching it, digging in a little more each time, pushing a dent into it. The dent became a crater. It began to rip at the edges.

Keluwen kept punching that one spot until she broke through. The next sphere she sent would pass right through. She smiled, took aim with double-fingers, and let it go.

The sphere passed through the hole, it clipped one edge, spinning it at it entered his shield. It smacked his shoulder, ripping muscle open and spraying blood, spinning him, tipping him over backward inside his bubble shield. He slid down to the bottom.

He glared at her. He rose to his feet. He rendered another shield inside the first. She could feel the ripple of that one much more strongly. *I will not be able to punch through that.* But every bit of energy he used would make him more tired. They only had to wear him down.

Krid tried to keep up with Kinraigan's blank impulses. He rendered fields of friction in the air the blank impulses passed through. He slowed Kinraigan's down, lessening their power at impact. But he was not strong with air, nor perfect with the timing, and sometimes slowed her own blank impulses along with them.

Tanashri did the grunt work, battering his shield with high mass blank impulses. One after another, sphere after sphere. *She is good. She can wear him down with those.*

And Orrinas, the master, nullified nearly every pressure render Kinraigan could come up with before he even finished rendering it.

A man with a knife ran toward her. She dropped to her knees. The knife sailed over her head. Hodo was there in a flash. He snatched the man up by the neck and shoved him away.

Leucas and Duran worked like mad to keep Kinraigan's people away from her, but there were so many. Both of them kept being drawn into individual fights.

We need to clear this distraction.

She shouted at Krid. He turned to look at her. She gestured to him. "Can't think straight when they run by."

He nodded. He looked at the people racing toward him. The mud was the perfect depth, even better than the sand in Westgate. He laced the mud with friction. A dozen of Kinraigan's servants were locked in place at once. Some were caught mid-sprint, screaming, their ankles snapping, their bodies falling forward and smacking into the mud. Those who kept on their feet Keluwen kissed with a little high-velocity sphere between the eyes.

The pressure eased on Hodo, Leucas, and Duran. They were able to head off the rest, keep them at bay, dance between them, work them down.

Keluwen sucked her lips back, baring her teeth. She punched a hole through another of Kinraigan's followers. He slapped down and slid in the mud.

She spun around looking for the ebon-shrouds, looking for Cheli, looking for Orrinas. He had moved. Walking closer to Kinraigan, staring him down. *Get him*, she urged Orrinas on. *You are going to get him. Do it.*

She kept tracking her people. Hodo shoved a man to the ground, and Leucas ran another through. *We are doing it*, she thought. *We are going to win.*

Stay focused.

She readied more blank impulses and released them toward Kinraigan. *Distraction. Eat his concentration. Make him slow.* His shield was battered and smashed and burned. He rendered a third, but it was much too small for him. *Orrinas must be holding the ones Kinraigan wishes he could use.*

She nodded to Krid.

Let's finish this.

She readied her attacks, and Krid prepared to render something Keluwen had never seen before. Krid *reversed* friction, releasing Kinraigan's shield from its interaction with the air and the ground. Suddenly, every impact from a blank impulse and every shockwave from every exploding sphere shoved his bubble shield this way and that.

Kinraigan peered out from within, face red, hands twisted. He saw Keluwen smiling at him and he screamed. She heard nothing. It was all stuck within the sphere. It might as well have been inside his own head.

Keluwen was so preoccupied watching him, that she lost track of his followers. She heard a click and a grunt. She turned around. Hodo had taken a shot to the belly from a crossbow.

Keluwen's eyes widened. Her mouth twisted into a scream. "No!"

She turned away from Krid and began looking everywhere for the man with the crossbow. She saw him before long, already reloading.

You.

She began sending blank spheres at him, on after another. He was fast at the sprint, and she was not leading him well. She cut across the basin, looking for a better position to line up her shots.

You are not going to take anyone from me.

She pointed her fingers. A sphere slapped the ground, flinging mud uselessly into the air behind him.

Fuck you.

She tried again, tracking his movement with her fingers. Missed again. Another one. Missed. Again. Again. Again.

Hold still, you piece of shit.

She kept turning and kept shooting her blank impulses. Missed. Missed. Missed. Grazed. Missed.

She kept following him. She forgot about the others. She forgot about Krid. She forgot about Kinraigan. She forgot about all his many murderers.

She fell into a tunnel where all that existed was this one slinking little shitsnake.

She kept turning.

He kept sprinting.

She shot another sphere.

She missed him.

But she hit Krid instead.

Her mouth fell open.

Oh shit, no. Oh no! Oh my sweet fucking god Belleron no!

Krid turned and looked at her. His lips peeled back to show his teeth. He hissed out a gasp, looked down at his coat. The faded olive grey was soaking with blood. It bubbled out of him like syrup.

His eyes asked her why.

I'm sorry. It was a mistake. Just a mistake.

Keluwen fell to her knees.

****

Aren couldn't see Eriana. *Where did she go?* He saw Redevir lifting Inrianne to her feet. She threw a desperate wave of fire from her hands. It was rushed, little power behind it. It missed Kinraigan altogether, but lit one of his followers like a torch.

Tarykthies appeared behind Orrinas, but so did Duran—diving, becoming fully horizontal in the air, his body a battering ram. He hit Tarykthies in the back, tackling him to the ground.

Tanashri shuddered as she unleashed fearsome power at Kinraigan. She had been holding back until now, Aren realized. The sorcerer lurched and fell as his head was knocked from side to side by the invisible swings of giant fists, blank impulses the size of boulders hitting his shield. Tanashri knew what she was doing—ruining his concentration, but she couldn't hold it. Initiating renders that far away caught him better by surprise, but she had drained herself to unconsciousness doing that for mere seconds in the Blackwell.

Balthoren was still firing at her. He was down to his final crossbow, but it must have been a Cartrosian quick-loader, because he was still able to send a bolt every five seconds. The quaking earth threw off his aim, but his arrows came close enough to distract her, stealing her concentration, pushing her close to her break point.

We're not doing enough, Aren thought. *They can't focus on Kinraigan. Damn it.*

Aren whistled a warning.

Reidos heard. He was the closest to Balthoren. He charged. The crossbow aimed at his chest, but one of Redevir's throwing knives cut across the top of his hand. Balthoren dropped it, cursed, scrambled to retrieve it.

A massive crater opened beneath him, as errant energy from Kinraigan split the earth. Reidos drove his heels into the ground, and stopped just short of the edge, then backpedaled away from it. Another one opened behind him and he toppled into it. Another opened and another, until the earth was pocked with deep depressions.

Aren turned to his left. One man in a black coat was on Redevir, trying to rip into the Rover with his sword. Two laughing women with knives were trying to stab Duran.

Where the hell is Fainen?

Eriana backed away from a duelist in green silk. He sent a flurry of high attacks. She parried them, and gave ground. Then he quietly advanced and tried again. She met each of his attacks again, but instead of stepping back, she stepped forward. The duelist slipped, stumbled, recovered, but she was already pressing the point of her blade under his arm, and into his ribs.

Aren saw Balthoren again, raising his crossbow, aiming for Eriana, waiting while people crisscrossed between them.

Aren ran to her, but his feet felt like lead. The old arrow wound was like a fire beneath his flesh. It seemed like an eternity before he reached her. He wrapped an arm around her, and pulled her down. They both fell to the ground, the bolt passing over them.

He tried to stand. He heard someone scream far away. He saw Tarykthies standing over him. He flattened himself, pushing Eriana away. He rolled onto his back as a brilliant burst of Inrianne's fire shot over him, whipping the tatters of Tarykthies' cloak into flames. He spun his way out of the cloak and ran.

****

Keluwen forced herself to stand back up. Forced herself to look away from what she had done. Forced herself to ignore her mistake.

I will give my tears for this tomorrow and all the days to come.

But not right now.

Right now I must be something else.

She turned back to Kinraigan. She saw him raise his arms and she flinched. But he was not looking at her. He was looking at the Sister.

Kinraigan brought both hands down with enough force to split a block of stone. A massive blank impulse raced toward Tanashri. It was enormous, coursing along the ground, the bottom of it digging a trench in the mud.

Keluwen could only turn and watch it go by, her eyes pulled along by its hypnotic destruction.

Tanashri braced. It broke through her shield, slowing, but not stopping. Tanashri barely put her hands up to cover her face with another shield when the invisible force struck her with the mass and velocity of a battering ram. Her body lifted off the ground, her new shield bending and shattering, her arms and legs trailing after her like streamers. Blood sprayed from her nose.

No!

Keluwen spun around, rendering blank spheres, firing them at a sprinting ebon-shroud with her left hand, and with her right she reached out behind her and did what she had always done when she fell from a high place—she rendered an elastic horizontal plane. She placed it perfectly. The Sister landed on it and rebounded, bouncing again two more times until she was safely down.

Kinraigan launched his fury at the prone Sister. The air surged and bent visibly. She saw another blank impulse take shape and move, an enormous pressure bubble. But it backfired. It rebounded from Keluwen's invisible elastic barrier, and slammed right back into Kinraigan, laying him out on the mud. He was slow to rise.

He is down!

She smiled.

But then her smile died.

She realized that when Tanashri fell, so did all her streams. And so did all of *Kinraigan's* she had been interdicting. So many that Keluwen could feel the ripples in the Slipstream as they all rushed back into the world of possibility, to make themselves available once again to the man they belonged to.

Shit.

She turned to look at Orrinas.

The look he returned to her was one she had never once seen on his face.

It was fear.

****

Eriana helped Aren to his feet.

Baileras sprang forward at him, flailing the black sword. Aren blocked and attacked, but he was too slow. Baileras' blade darted toward Aren's neck. Aren raised his sword, but he knew it would not be in time. He could almost feel it tearing its way into his throat, but the sword stopped before it hit. A curved blade deflected the swing.

Eriana stared down the ebon-shroud. She pulled back and slashed low. Baileras blocked. Eriana sent another blow up high, but changed trajectory in mid-swing. Her blade scraped beneath the black sword and disappeared in the folds of the cloak.

Baileras howled and lurched backward, found new footing, hissed. But the ebon-shroud clutched her wrist, locking her sword in place, ready to run her through.

Aren reached for her, to pull her out of the way.

Baileras lunged at them both. But he did not reach them.

Fainen!

The Sarenwalker smashed into the ebon-shroud, steamrolling him into the mud. Fainen rose without effort, and began kicking Baileras in the head and face. The ebon-shroud rolled back and flew to his feet. His black blade lay in the mud, but a knife flashed in his left hand. He drove it at Fainen. The Sarenwalker dodged, grabbed the outstretched wrist and snapped it. Baileras growled. Fainen clutched him by shoulder and thigh, lifted him, and flipped him over into the mud.

Aren looked ahead again. Duran and Hodo and Leucas were doing their best to keep any of Kinraigan's followers away, but they were running out of time. Tanashri and Orrinas would not last forever.

We need to break through his defenses now.

Keluwen was wrapping a wall around herself to deflect Kinraigan's spheres, but was taken off her guard when the ground swelled and bucked, rupturing beneath her as another tremendous pressure field came at her from underneath the ground.

She's not thinking three-dimensionally, Aren thought. *The cylinder. She's not protecting herself underneath.*

Keluwen rolled over, pushed up on her hands and knees and turned a cold stare. She wrapped three cultists in cylinders and shrank them, as she had once tried to do to Aren. Their arms pressed in against themselves until they snapped.

He turned away from her. There were still too many. He couldn't track all of Kinraigan's people.

Orrinas stood before Kinraigan. The frigid pools began to steam and boil. Mud rose and danced in the air as the two users stared each other down. *Updrafts.* It was a sign of monumental conflicting energies being accumulated. Aren could tell that Kinraigan was working with his pressure renders, but Orrinas was making each one inert with increases or decreases in heat, using more and more potent temperature changes as Kinraigan sought to make pressure waves in ever greater magnitude.

Waves of resonant power flashed and flared. Kinraigan was pouring sweat as the air around him sweltered and began to bake. The air rippled, and Orrinas leaned back as if a strong gust of wind blew into him. They both somehow stayed firm in their footing, each making tiny adjustments to their offensive and defensive renders like two men grappling with their minds. Each new stream added by Kinraigan to his ingredient list was corrected for by Orrinas and vice versa, making it appear that nothing was happening at all. Only the consternation on their faces told the story of their struggle.

Aren had to pop his ears as the side-effects of pressure bubbles accosted him, and the frost on his skin and clothes began to melt as waves of heat radiated from the two users.

Then Kinraigan did something that Orrinas was not prepared for. The magnitude of Kinraigan's pressure renders suddenly jumped so unexpectedly high that even Orrinas was unprepared for it.

Aren could actually see the pressure field on him rippling in the air. Kinraigan should not have been able to access streams of such high magnitudes. No one should have been able to. It had to have been immense pressure for it to have eclipsed the strongest countermeasure Orrinas was capable of generating.

Orrinas was caught within a pressure bubble, a sphere, wrapped around his own bubble shield. The magnitude was too high for even the most intense cold he was capable of summoning.

The blank sphere Orrinas kept around himself was the only thing preventing his eyes and ears from rupturing under the pressure.

Aren looked franticly around. Tanashri lay flat. Inrianne was nowhere to be seen. "Keluwen!" Aren shouted, pulling Eriana alongside him. Fainen followed.

She was the only one left. She was the only one who could stop it.

****

Keluwen rose to her feet.

She looked at Orrinas. He was locked inside a crush bubble. A *shrinking* crush bubble.

He couldn't get out.

She turned to Duran. "Duran, go."

Duran understood immediately. He broke away from Tarykthies and charged at Kinraigan, waving his arms and screaming desperately to disrupt Kinraigan's concentration.

Keluwen focused all of her power into a point, sharper than the sharpest spear. She felt in the Slipstream, and perceived the pressure field as a bubble, felt its shape. She sent her sharp point at her highest velocity.

It punctured the pressure field. Orrinas was thrown to the ground as a crack of light burst across the mud plain. The power Keluwen unleashed brought everyone to the ground, as the force of the pressure Kinraigan had encapsulated within his bubble was released and sought to equalize with the air pressure on the plain. The sky went dark. Then it was too bright to see. The shockwave rolled over her, flattening her to the mud. She could only hear breaths and her heartbeat, echoing in her bones. The world outside was quiet.

She sat up.

She opened her eyes.

She saw one thing.

Kinraigan. Looking directly at her.

He raised his hands.

Keluwen growled at him.

Do it. Do it!

He was going to, but something stopped him.

"Kinraigan!" Orrinas screamed in fury. The sorcerer's robes began to steam and smoke, then erupted in flames, but he stood still, ignoring the itching, burning fire.

He smiled.

She felt him pull streams of incredible magnitude, ones the Sister had let go. But they felt like magnitude streams for something static, the *strength* of a bubble shield. She did not understand. How was Kinraigan putting an unbreakable shield around himself going to harm anyone?

But then she felt the stream of *position* Kinraigan chose. One half a second before he rendered it.

Her blood turned to stone in her veins.

She screamed at the top of her lungs. "Orrinas!"

But he did not hear her. He was in a tunnel. All he saw was Kinraigan. *Orrinas.*

****

Aren rolled onto his side and coughed blood.

He saw Kinraigan staring at Orrinas. The crush bubble had failed.

Aren thought he was about to witness Orrinas deliver the killing blow to the immortal.

But then Kinraigan did something else.

He rendered a spherical shield around Orrinas' own shield. It wrapped Orrinas' bubble perfectly, holding it like a glove.

Why would...?

Then Kinraigan's sphere began to decrease in size, shrinking slowly, inevitably. Just like Keluwen's cylinder.

Orrinas' bubble was not powerful enough to maintain *its own size* as the shell of Kinraigan's empty bubble shrank, and so it shrank right along with it, compressed within Kinraigan's stronger sphere.

Tanashri had been holding the streams Kinraigan used to expand and contract his spheres. But she was down. That meant Kinraigan was now unlimited in magnitude. Orrinas' sphere could hold against the external pressure of Kinraigan's crush bubbles, but not against Kinraigan forcibly shrinking the size of the sphere protecting him from those crush bubbles.

The air trapped within Orrinas' bubble was trapped with him, and it began to press ever harder on his body as the space shrank.

Kinraigan found a way to render pressure *inside* Orrinas' own bubble shield without breaking it. By *compressing* it instead. A trick. A loophole. A move they had no way to counter.

Aren's heart sank into oblivion.

Orrinas screamed. His skin flattened against his frame as the air began to press in against him. He couldn't breath. He stooped and crumpled.

The sphere became smaller and smaller. Orrinas began to falter. His bubble became too small for his body. His knees bent up to his head, his chin forced down into his chest. His joints began to pop in his left arm and shoulder. His arms and face were blotted with deep black bruises as the blood vessels in his skin ruptured by the hundreds. His body began to press in on itself. His bones cracked and splintered. His eyes burst, and he unleashed a silent shriek, his mouth open, but the sound it made held captive within the spheres. His mouth opened so wide the skin of his face began to split.

Aren stood staring, unable to make himself do anything else. He was turned to stone by the sight of it. Leucas and Cheli were missing. He thought he saw Duran. Hallan stood behind Keluwen. Redevir was on the ground. Hodo was bleeding. Reidos was wounded. Corrin was nowhere. Krid Ballar was dead. Fainen had been knocked out. Tanashri was down. He couldn't tell if she was still breathing. Eriana rested a hand lightly on his shoulder.

And Orrinas was gone.

Aren fell to his knees.

We were supposed to win.

****

Keluwen could only watch as Orrinas was slowly crushed.

Her tears poured in a silent deluge down her face. She had nothing strong enough to puncture a sphere of that magnitude. She was helpless to stop what was happening before her eyes.

Kinraigan never stopped smiling.

She fell onto her hands and knees. She threw up. She screamed. She beat the ground with her fists. She sucked in a breath. Another, deeper. Again. Deeper still. One more, filling her lungs until they felt like they might burst.

She raised both her hands and pointed them at Kinraigan.

She rendered every sphere in her mind, focused. More focused in rage than she had ever, ever been in calm. She made a dozen of them. And she made them strong. She looked at Kinraigan and sneered.

I kill you with hate and I don't care.

She released them all.

She knew he could feel them coming.

She saw him let them come, until the very last instant, when he rendered a pressure field in front of himself, using the very streams that Orrinas and Tanashri had been Stopping. The pressure within must have been extraordinary. It caused gusts of wind this way and that, blasting through her hair and tunic.

Her blank impulses surged into the pressure field. And then they all stopped. Every single one. All her spheres, the fastest, the strongest, the heaviest—and Kinraigan stopped them all without even trying.

Keluwen began to cry. Her stomach felt like a vacuum, screaming for food. Her mouth was a desert. Her lungs, fire. Her hands shook. Her knees wobbled. Her eyes lost focus, closed, opened, closed again. Her body felt empty. She managed to lay down on her side before she collapsed. She tried to reach inside the source, but she could not. She felt so weak. She could barely lift her arms.

She had run out. Her energy was all used up. It was all gone.

She was only a shell.

She was empty.

She was alone.

****

Aren watched Orrinas die. He was so full of horror that time seemed to stop. He thought he was going crazy. He heard little bells jingling. It reminded him of Keluwen. He felt Eriana's hand on his shoulder, her touch steadying him.

He heard the jinglebells.

He turned. He leaned back, tipped over, pulling Eriana down with him. Saw twin swords. He raised his hand in reflex, fingers numbed, thinking his own sword was still held by them. But it wasn't. He was lifting nothing, too numb to realize.

The blade passed through air. Aren tried to roll. The second blade stabbed.

Suddenly Eriana was in front of him, parrying the strike, and lashing the stranger across his face, cleaving his lip and half of his mustache away.

"Eriana," he called to her, but she was already away from him, defending him, pushing the man back one jingling step at a time.

Aren climbed to his feet. He found his sword half-buried in the mud. He tried to pick it up, but his frozen fingers refused to close around the hilt. He pushed himself up and ran to her unarmed.

He watched her send a lunging stab, just as she had used on the duelist. The man fell away from her strike like he was falling down. Eriana stepped forward to position herself to stab him prone. But he did *not* fall down. He slid to one side in the icy mud. It was intentional, a move a tumbler might make.

Eriana stabbed down at where she thought his body would fall, but he slid just to the side of the blade, one leg tucked under the other like an acrobat. Her blade plunged into the mud.

The man rolled his body into her blade, knocking it flat, ripping it from her hands, yanking her forward as she reached after it. She fell to her hands and knees.

Her eyes went wide. She knew what was about to happen.

The man drove deep with his sword. The blue linen of Eriana's shirt cratered inward beneath her soft grey coat. Then the mail gave way underneath. The sword speared through her with liquid ease, a tiny point lifting her tunic away from her back as it split through.

Aren screamed. A lump rose in his throat, like a boulder to choke him. His face swelled red. He couldn't breathe. He ran.

The man scooted out from under her, and rose to one knee.

Eriana tipped over. The blade slid out of her, and she lay on her back.

Aren made his fingers close around the hilt of Eriana's sword. He found himself behind the man, barely able to hold the hilt with both hands clamped together. He brought the sword down with all of his rage. He knew no pain in that instant. He felt nothing. He knew nothing. He thought nothing. He wanted only to crush the man. Crush him into dust. He focused all his energy, all his concentration, and placed his entire life into this single action, behind this one swing.

The man raised one of his shortswords, made a simple parry, and dropped Aren to the ground with one punch.

Aren rolled in the mud, blood roaring out his nose.

Eriana fell like a feather beside him, her eyes looking into his eyes.

The man with jinglebells on his boots walked away.

Redevir was the last one on his feet. He backed away from Kinraigan, but was suddenly hit by an invisible plane that pushed him toward the sorcerer.

The ebon-shrouds forced the Rover to his knees. The man with bells on his shoes slapped him across the face. The little bald Glasseye, Talvin, overturned Redevir's carry-bag, dumping its contents into the mud.

Kinraigan held out his hand, a soft cloth unfurled, and the Crown quietly levitated to it. He wrapped it with care, like swaddling a delicate infant, trying not to touch it. "Thank you," he said. "You have been my most valuable servant of all."

He walked over to Hallan. He held out his hand. The boy took it, looking over his shoulder for someone, anyone, to make him not have to. But no one was left standing to do anything about it. "Thank you for keeping the boy safe from the Lord Protector for me. I thought I would have to face what comes next without him."

Aren's eyes glazed over.

Kinraigan led the boy up the hill. When he reached the top, he turned back to Aren. "Maybe you are ready now, Aren. I hope that you are finally free. I have a place set aside for you in the new world."

With that, he turned and stalked away. Balthoren followed after him, and Talvin, and Tarykthies, and the two ebon-shrouds, and the man with bells on his boots, and any of his others who yet lived.

They disappeared over the hill with their master.

55

Only Always Ever Now

HIS BODY WAS BURNING despite the cold black mud.

Aren felt a stabbing sickness in his chest. It rose up his arms and down his legs. He wanted to rip his hair out when he saw the tears on her face.

He pressed himself up with strength he barely had. He rolled to Eriana. Her face was whiter than white, with a black smear of mud upon one cheek. Her lips were pale flower petals. Her skin was ice.

Eriana gently touched his sleeve with a slackened arm, but when he put his own hand to her face, she felt colder than the icy water.

"Why?" he asked.

"It was for you," she whispered, her voice a breeze.

"Why did you jump in front of him?" he demanded.

"I couldn't let him take you from me," she whispered, as though it was the most obvious reason in the world.

"This wasn't supposed to happen. I was supposed to stop this. It was supposed to be over."

"It's all right, Aren. I am going to join the heroes. Like my mother."

"I should have sent you back. I should never have brought you here. Why did I let you come?"

"Because if you hadn't then you would not have been *you*." She smiled.

He tried to hold her head up, but the mud matted through her hair was too slick, and it kept slipping down. "Please be all right. Please. I have seen people recover from things like this before. They...they can recover. They can heal. They can be all right again. Please."

"Aren," she said. "Aren."

"What?" He kept crying. He could not stop.

"I am not going to be one of those. I am not going to heal."

"Don't give up now. Don't do that. Don't."

"Aren, it's all right. It's going to be all right."

"Why aren't you scared?"

"Because you are with me."

His head dipped, his face pressing against her shoulder. She was so cold. Her hand in his could barely squeeze.

"I'm so sorry, Eriana. I...I didn't know. Eriana, please. I didn't know this was going to happen."

"You can't plan for life," she said. "It will happen whether you are expecting it or not. When I woke up in my bed the morning you came to Cair Tiril, I thought I would be dancing in the harvest festival this day, but here I am."

He half-laughed, half-sobbed. "How can you do that?"

"Do what?" Her eyes turned away. She forgot his question. She was fading.

"No, Eriana!" He shouted at her. Shook her. Squeezed her arms. "Stay here. Stay with me!"

Her eyes snapped back to him. "It's not your fault, Aren. I chose to come. You didn't make me. It's not your fault."

"Please don't leave," he said.

"I don't want to leave," she said. A cough. A drop of blood hovered at the corner of her lips. "But I think I have to."

"Don't leave," he pleaded.

"I always liked the way you pretended not to look at me," she said.

He smiled through tears. "I want to take this day back."

"Don't take it back," she said. "Don't take back any day where I was with you."

"That's not what I mean."

She smiled. "I know." Her eyes lost focus. Her jaw slackened. Her head rolled to a stop in his lap.

"No, Eriana. Don't." He cradled her in his arms, rocking her back and forth. He looked down at her eyes, her beautiful blue within blue eyes. "Don't die," he whispered. "It's too soon."

But she was gone. He knew it. She was gone and he could feel it and it was his fault and he couldn't save her and he should have saved her and he failed her just like he failed everyone else. She would never see all the places she wanted to see. She would never have the chance to try all of the nine wines. She was gone.

It was unreal. It was false. It was impossible for there to be a world without her. He never even had the chance to tell her...everything that he wanted to tell her.

But the worst part, the worst part of all of it, was that he was still alive. It was so cruel for death to leave him behind when the best of him had gone away. That sharp steel was meant for him. He should have perished alongside her. Instead of her.

His team had been devastated, but he remained. He should have known. Deep down—in a place he feared to let his thoughts stray—he *did* know. He had always known. One of them was always going to die. Just as he had known before he led the capture of Degammon. And he came through that untouched, too. *Damaged*, but untouched.

Pain clawed through him. His eyes felt like oceans. He was shaking, shivering, breaking apart. He felt hot and cold. He felt dead. He felt gone. He didn't see Redevir standing over him. He didn't know what was happening when the Rover lifted him to his feet. He saw Fainen holding his head. He saw Reidos beside Inrianne, Keluwen laying on the ground and shuddering as Duran leaned over her. He saw Corrin in the distance. He saw them, but he saw nothing at all.

He thought he had known what grief was. The pain of losing Donnovar, and Hayles; the torment of his betrayal; the horror he saw when he was a child. He knew now that these little sorrows had never been enough. Not even close. None of them could touch the emptiness, the loneliness, the pure undiluted agony of being without her.

Thinking of her name made him cry, his breaths shuddering out of him, his heartbeat cold and useless. Without her, the light was taken out of the world. It left only dull grey pain, cold and meaningless.

His own ambition had brought him here, his obsession. He had been telling himself and everyone else that he was doing this because Kinraigan needed to be stopped. And that was true. But that was not why Aren came all this way. Aren came here because he had to be the one to stop him. Him. Not some other Render Tracer, not some motley band of users. Him. Aren of Amagon. His need to rise above the shadow of Sarker, of his father, of Aldarion. His foolish desire to prove his importance to the world by killing Kinraigan. His foolish hope that everything would be right in his life by completing that one ridiculous goal. By pursuing this dream of a new beginning, he had brought about the end of everything that mattered.

He spent his whole life denying superstitions and spitting on prophesies. *I always hated when people tried to tell me what I was. They told me I would never become a Render Tracer. They told me I would never be any good. They told me I would never have the respect I was due. I proved what I was. I proved every one of their prophesies about me wrong.*

I thought I owned my choices. I thought I could change my path. Maybe every step I have ever taken was that path. I thought I was one thing. Maybe I was wrong about everything. Now I am what the elder said I would be. Maybe I always was and never knew it.

I had a choice. I could have turned back. I could have sailed across the sea. Gone south to find a new place to live humbly with her by my side. I could have done that. I had more than enough chances to turn back. But I kept going. I did this. I alone. I made this happen.

The man of sorrow does not exist. He never existed.

Only me.

I am empty. I am broken.

There is nothing left of me.

I do not exist.

I am the man of sorrow.

****

Keluwen stood over the body of the greatest man she had ever known.

He was so broken that she could not recognize the parts of him she knew so well. And she could not bring herself to look at the parts that she did recognize.

It was so unlike him. To be cold. To be motionless. To be empty. He had been so full of patience and love. The world did not deserve him. *I did not deserve him.* And he did not deserve this. After all the people he had saved in his life, all the horrors he had prevented, to walk into the hills one day and never come back...

She hovered over him, unable to bring herself to reach down and touch him. She knew if she did that it would all become real. Once her fingertips felt the shape of him, she could not take it back. She would know it. And she would always know it.

Orrinas was dead.

So she looked at him, tears stinging her eyes, her cheeks tightening. She slammed her eyes shut, trying to crush the pain. Trying to flatten the tears to nothing. But when she opened them again, it all remained.

It was still there. Exactly as she left it. She had come on this journey, pushed them all on this journey, because at the end of it she was supposed to have peace. Instead she lost everything. And peace was a faraway star, like the ones she had seen the night before, now invisible in the daylight.

Hodo and Leucas were quiet, but she could hear Cheli sobbing. *They all loved him. They all knew him longer than me.*

A life was finite. It was made up of moments. Seconds, minutes, hours. One only had so many. *And he had chosen to give so many of them to me.* She remembered the night before. How happy he had been in her arms, waking beside her. Holding her. She thought of how he had been finally so happy, and for his joy to go to waste this way...it wasn't fair. *It's not fair! It's not fair!* Right when he was so happy. How was that fair?

She smiled and cried. She gave Orrinas all her tears. Just as she had from the first day they met. *I don't know what I am going to do without you.*

"Forever goodbye, Orrinas," she said

She dropped to her knees. She reached out one hand. It floated above him for so long, unable to drift the final few inches to touch him. His face was so dark, almost black, turned away from her. One eye swollen out of its socket, and the red coming out his mouth like paste, piled atop the cold mud.

She set her hand on his bruised and blackened arm. The shock of it made her wince. His head rolled and she almost screamed, thinking him still alive through such agony, suddenly wondering if she would have to end his misery on her own.

But it was just him settling under her touch. He was gone. There was no life in his eyes.

She put her other hand on him and just held his arm for a long time. She wanted so badly to wrap her arms around him. But his body was not him any more. It did not have his warm chest to lay her head upon. It did not have his slender arms, that could wrap themselves around her like a blanket and always shut out the world for just a little while.

It was not him anymore.

It was just a thing in the mud.

She wiped tears away, but more came to replace them.

She stood after ten thousand years had passed.

She looked down at him one last time.

"I will see you when never meets forever."

****

Corrin could tell Inrianne was not doing well before he made it within a dozen paces of Reidos. When he reached them, he saw blood soaking through her white robe, staining it cherry-red. Tanashri was working at it with torn fabric.

Reidos was strangely silent. He didn't fret or fuss.

Mardin, on the other hand, was frantic, pacing back and forth and wearing a trench into the ground as he did so.

Corrin then trotted over to Reidos, and stood next to him with arms folded. "Well," he said.

Reidos half-turned his head to him, but kept his eyes affixed on Inrianne. "Well what?"

"That went less magnificently than I thought," Corrin said.

"I think Mardin did more fighting than you did," Reidos said.

Corrin frowned. "They took the boy."

"They did."

"What are we going to do about it?"

"We?"

"As in, you and me. And maybe Mardin. Definitely Aren."

"What in all hells could we possibly ever have a hope of doing?"

"We are adept at not-being-seen."

"I don't think Aren will be able to help us this time."

"Why not?"

"Eriana is dead."

"The Andristi girl? Shame. She was a pretty thing."

"She was with Aren," Reidos said. "They spent the night together in Arthenorad."

Corrin's eyebrow shot up. "You mean *together*? Really. But...Oh shaot."

"Now you get it," Reidos said.

"So it will be just us then," Corrin said.

"You are acting as if it is a done deal that I am going anywhere."

"Goddamn it, Reidos. We lost the boy."

"Because you let them bring him here. Now you want to keep going after Kinraigan."

"He has his little tiara that makes him a god. So what? If you ask me, that means he will be too busy gloating to look over his shoulder."

"No one's asking you."

"You should be game for this."

"Why? So we can try to beat him with half of what we couldn't beat him with before? I like those odds."

Corrin jabbed a thumb over his shoulder at Tanashri and Keluwen. "I have a sword, sir. A delightful sword. A deadly sword. A sword no man would want to be on the other end of. And those ladies have power. What have we always done when there is a user about?"

"We run. Fast. The other way."

"Why?"

"Because there is nothing more dangerous."

"We have them on our side. We have come back from worse odds, with a worse crew, and after losing twice as many of them before the steal was done. Remember Ethios? That crew was a pack of foul shits, well, most of them anyway."

Reidos nodded.

"Look around. We are alive. We lived through the worst that users can do."

"Everyone is alive just fine until they die," Reidos reminded him.

"You think I can't defeat my enemies? The correct answer is *of course you can, you are the world renowned Corrin*. It is usually said in a celebratory tone of voice, you may recall."

"This is over our heads," Reidos said. "This is more than stealing pigs or bags of gold."

"Exactly," Corrin said. "We were willing to get lynched for a handful of silver tossers, we should be more than willing to do the same for a good cause."

"Good cause? You don't fight for causes. What is your cause?"

"To help Aren. To look my enemies in the eyes and show them my magnificence. If they think that they can hurt my friends and not pay for it, then they are sadly mistaken."

"You really want to do this, don't you?"

"I do. And so should you."

"It's not our business," Reidos said.

"Aren is our business. He is still our friend. Tell you what, if *he* goes then *we* go."

"If you say so."

"I do say so. Aren is my friend." He kicked mud at Reidos. "Your sorry self is my friend, too."

"Don't remind me."

"And what do we do for our friends, Reidos?" Corrin tapped his foot in the cold mud.

"Call them names and kick shit in their eyes?"

Corrin smiled. "And then?"

"We walk through fire for them," Reidos said.

"We brave the storm for them. We walk the wind for them. We cross the world and shake the heavens for them. We meet their enemies as if they were our own, steel in our hands. We love them to hell and back."

Reidos glanced across the basin at Aren. "I don't think he is going much of anywhere."

"We'll see, won't we?" Corrin asked.

"I don't have a sword anymore," Reidos said. "It's lost in the mud somewhere."

"I won't accept excuses. You're coming. Trust me. It will be legendary."

"I'll go," Reidos said. "I never said I wouldn't go. I'm ready to die if I have to."

"Good to know," Corrin said. "Now let us see if we can find something for you to hit people with."

****

Keluwen walked through the mud. She swatted Leucas away. She shrugged out of Hodo's embrace. She drifted past Cheli.

She walked up to Aren of Amagon. He sat alone in the mud beside the body of his Andristi girl. He puffed like a chimney on his silver pipe, suffusing the air with the sweet smell of malagayne. He had smoked enough to sedate an ox, yet he kept going. He did not look up at her.

Keluwen kicked him in the knee.

He winced. He stared daggers at her.

"Get up," she said.

"Go away. Leave me alone." He fumbled the pipe. It fell into the mud. He reached after it but it lay out of reach of his fingertips. He dropped his fire-stick into his lap. His hands drooped uselessly to his sides.

She kicked him again. "I am not asking."

"I failed," he said.

"*We* failed."

"But I wasn't supposed to fail. I was supposed to stop him. Everything always seemed to point this way. And then it didn't come true. They all say I was *he of sorrow*. But I wasn't."

"Words are just words. There is no such thing as prophecy. There is only me and you and what we do."

"I don't know what to do," he said. "I want to be alone. But if I am alone, all that I will hear is my own thoughts. I can't listen to them. I can't take it."

"There are only two things that can take pain away," she said. "Time and action. I learned that a long time ago. That is why I go. Because if I don't, I will be lost here. Like you."

"What do you want?" he asked.

"I want you to make imprints."

"Imprints?"

"You are a Glasseye. You make imprints. Make them. Every stream that scum used. I want to know them all. I want to see them. Get up and get them for me."

"What is the point?" Redevir asked.

"I am going to find him," Keluwen said. "I am going to fight him. And I am going to kill him."

"We can't win," Redevir said. "There are only three of you, and you are all worn. You could stuff your face with food and not recover half the energy you lost here. What is it you hope to do?"

"There are seven hells," she said. "I want to show him which one he is going to."

"You are serious."

"He took everything from me. Everything. I am going to make him feel how badly he hurt me." She turned to Aren. "You are going to help me. Get up and make them. Then you can drown yourself for all I care. But Orrinas trusted you. And I trusted you. So give this to me, and then you can go on hating yourself until you stand looking into the abyss at the end of time. I will see you there when I am done. And we can be *they of sorrow* for all eternity. But I am going."

She looked into his eyes, streaked with tears, bloodshot and sour. She saw all the tears she wished she could cry. But she would not. Her tears were for Orrinas alone. And he was gone now.

She saw herself in Aren. Herself from long ago, the night that ended everything that had been, and forever changed who she was. She had almost walked off the edge that night. But someone named Seb, who she had never met before that night, sat on the ground beside her and told her not to. He gave her half a cake-bread when she had been running empty. And she kept going every night since. And now she was here.

She knelt in front of Aren, her knees sinking into the mud. She reached down and gently picked up his silver pipe. She wiped it clean on her tunic. It still had a ring of crushed leaves inside. She plucked the fire-stick from his lap and flicked it alight.

He looked up at her, his expression stone, but his eyes yearning to be released from the poison prison of his thoughts.

This is not good for you, but it is what you need now to keep you going, to keep you trying. Someday maybe we can all try to be good again. But not today.

She held the pipe up to his lips. His neck stretched out until his mouth touched it. She lit it and held it there as he inhaled the grey smoke of forgetfulness.

She watched him until it was empty. Then she stood and reached out a hand to him.

He glanced up at her, surprised. His hand found hers. She helped him to his feet.

He did not look at her.

But he made the imprints.

He worked in silence. He dropped his tools in the mud here and there, little accidents. Each time it made him cry. She knew the reason. She said nothing. She let him work. And when he was done, she took what he had made and left him alone.

"Why did he take the boy?" Leucas asked. Poor, sweet Leucas.

Cheli shrugged. "As a prize. One more thing that the Lord Protector could make that he could take away."

"Orrinas said the boy was important," Hodo said.

"How?" Leucas asked.

"It doesn't matter," Keluwen said. "Orrinas thought he was. That means he is."

"Keluwen," Duran said. "I am still whole. If you are going, then I will go, too."

"Don't," she said. "I don't know where it is I am going, but it's not a place you come back from."

He nodded. "I know."

"We each choose our fate," she said.

"We go, too," Cheli said.

"Don't be stupid," Keluwen said. "Walk away now, Cheli. Go live your life. Find a safe place and live."

"I can't live if I walk away," Cheli said. "You will need someone to guide you through his streams. I have been studying him my whole life."

"I thought you were a smart girl," Keluwen said. "Now I am beginning to think you are more like me."

"Hodo and Leucas are coming, too," Cheli said.

"We will not abandon you," Hodo said. "Not ever."

"Orrinas was life," Leucas said. "My gods say that I cannot live while he remains unavenged."

"We are with you, Keluwen," Cheli said. "Let us be."

Keluwen nodded. "Fine. This will be what it is. One last hunt."

****

"He had us the whole time," Redevir said to himself, as Aren dug with his hands into the mud. The Rover's optimism was gone. He gazed all around as if he could not believe he actually lost his game. He didn't say a word. It made Aren feel even worse somehow. The sulfurous air closed around him, soaking his breaths with the horrible stink of magick.

Aren watched him out of the corner of his eye as he settled Eriana onto the driest patch of the endless plain of mud. He refused all who offered to aid him. He never uttered a word.

Once her body lay safely away from the cold water, he began to gather her things, placing them back into her carry-bag. He set it beside her. He scrubbed the chunks of mud from her curved blade in a puddle of icy water that numbed his hands. When he was finished, he returned it to its scabbard, and gently lay it upon her chest. He would come back with a litter and carry her out of here, take her to a place that was beautiful, like the grass beside the river where they were the night before. He had never seen her more happy than that.

He stood, and looked down at the mud. He saw a folded piece of parchment, yellowed with age, sitting upon a pale lichen growing at the fringes of an icy puddle. He bent down to it, took it carefully in his hands, and wiped the mud away with his cloak. He opened it and stared at Eriana's world. His eyes followed every coast and every river, stared into every forest and mountain range. It was the only thing in the world that he knew had come from her own hand, that she had created herself. He folded it and placed Eriana's map of the world into his tracer satchel, beside the pouch containing his Jecker monocle. He clasped it shut, and then stood beside Redevir.

"He played us," the Rover said to the sky.

Aren looked past him. "There is no such thing as destiny. I knew that all along, I think. I wasn't fulfilling some ancient prophecy. I was just letting you tell me I was. It was easier that way. Then I could pretend it wasn't just my own pride that brought us here. It was my own ambition the whole time. What brought me here was the hunt. The trace. The thrill. The need. To never let one get away. I needed it. It's nobody's fault but mine."

Aren wanted to cry out, do something, but there was nothing to do. It was the end, and Kinraigan was the winner. He managed to take everything Aren held dear. Everything worthwhile was dead and gone, ruined and destroyed.

Eriana was gone. She was his final dramatic failure. He thought of what Solathas had told him. *Do not weep. Be strong when you have fallen.* He wept anyway.

Suddenly Duran was there. "Aren of Amagon," he said. "Keluwen and I must go. Kinraigan is not finished. We must find where he has hidden himself. We will find him. We have to."

"I wish I could say the same," Redevir said. "I think that this is the end of the line for us." He gestured at himself and then Aren.

Aren watched him, but it meant nothing to him. He didn't answer. He leaned over, and began to scoop what remained of his malagayne back into the pouch, saving as much as he could. Some of it was still safe and dry.

"That is your decision to make," Duran said. "As I said, we must go. Whether we win or become lost in oblivion, we must at least make the attempt."

Aren blinked. The air was suffused with afterglow. Even with a stiff breeze it was everywhere. It bobbed in the wind like sparkling particles of dust, alternately appearing as individual points and as colored waves of cloud. The air shone with a rainbow of perilous color. Drifting clouds of silver and white and crimson and blue came together, passed through one another, merged together.

So many patterns converged that it was difficult to denote any pattern at all, the residuals vibrating to an incredible degree. *Extreme stepwise excitation. So much power. Incredible magnitude.* The warping was like twisted time, where space had overlapped onto itself by the sheer power of altered reality.

Aren saw the silvery shine of vectorics, each ribboned with the tinge of red that indicated mass, the olive green of velocity, red-orange of friction, black and orange of heat, the colors stronger and brighter the greater the magnitude was. But by far the majority of his residuals bore the deep dark purple and sharp yellow that signified pressure renders.

He could see the streak lines all around, hundreds of them, frozen like bright white claw marks in the air. Every force that had come from Kinraigan, from Keluwen, from Orrinas, from Tanashri and Inrianne, left a white arc in its path—every vector plotted out in the sky.

Even without performing the calculations, he could tell at a glance that the magnitude of the pressure waves Kinraigan had used had been overflowing with power, terrifying quantities of power.

Aren noted a cover on the pattern, an iridescent, interlocking network of obscurative streams. *The compression masking.* Even in the middle of a user's duel he could not render anything without adding a mask.

He blinked and focused on the attributes of the multicolored clouds. He thought something must have been wrong with the monocle. The streak lines should not have been visible from the primary lens alone. He could see it all, the dispersion, the variants, all of it, all through the same lens.

Then he realized how clear the world looked. The cloudscape of the lens should have turned everything a dull grey haze.

This was clear as day.

Except he could see the afterglow.

He looked down at his hands.

They were empty.

He looked at his tracer satchel in the mud beside him, still buckled, the Jecker monocle still tucked securely within.

Aren looked off at the ridge. He saw the residual colors roiling and glowing. They glittered with an alien phosphorescence, twinkling and rippling like a mirage. It was mesmerizing.

It should have been invisible by now. It should have faded. He should have needed the monocle to see it.

"I can see it," he said.

"What?" Redevir asked.

"I can see the afterglow," Aren said.

"But I thought you needed that glass thing," Redevir said. "The monocle."

"I do."

"But you're not using it."

"I know."

"Aren," Redevir said. "Eriana was...."

"I know where Kinraigan is going," Aren said, ignoring him.

Redevir stared at him skeptically. But he nodded. "If you are going, then so am I. I want my Dagger and I want my Crown."

Duran leaned over him. "We will do this together," he said, touching Aren's shoulder. "It was meant to be this way."

"Are we really dong this?" Redevir asked the sky.

"We are," Tanashri said, her pale grey Sisterhood indifference a match for the cold wind. "This is the one moment that all of us have been given to save the world."

Redevir looked at Duran, then back to Aren. "I suppose it is destiny after all."

Aren stared at the ridge. "I don't believe in destiny. I never have."

The air swelled with deep-hued violet and indigo, like the swirling of the sorcerer's robes. Within them he saw glittering clouds of pale orange, like the color of peaches. He felt the colors in his eyes, in his brain. It was like touching a sunset. He began walking toward it without even waiting for the others.

"I can see what no one else can see. It doesn't matter why. It doesn't matter how it came to be. It doesn't matter all the thousands of years that led up to this moment. All that matters is now. Only always ever now."

56

Nemesis

I CAN SEE IT.

Kinraigan's residual trail was enormous. Aren saw an exploding kaleidoscope of colors all around him. Vapor trails. Sensitized fluorescence. It was like a multicolored elephant had run amok, painting every rock, every patch of air it touched. Aren saw them even though the Jecker monocle remained unused at his side. He didn't stop to think of the reason why he could see them. It did not matter.

When you stop to ask why, you cannot move forward.

Aren followed the trail. He didn't know how he saw what he saw. He didn't care. His only thought was of finding Kinraigan. Finding him and killing him. There was no need to think of anything else.

Fainen followed effortlessly behind him. He had given Hayles' bow to Reidos along with all his arrows. Reidos needed something to fight with. Aren knew the bow would suit his friend well. Reidos hadn't used one in a long time, but he had been such a good marksman once. It seemed so long ago now.

Tanashri hobbled along, helped by Mardin. And Corrin walked side by side with Duran, each of them keeping Inrianne from teetering while she ate and drank what little she could keep down.

Hodo, Leucas, and Cheli followed Keluwen. They each looked like they wanted to help her, carry her, give her a shoulder to lean on, but they were each afraid to touch her. Hodo only ever came close enough to hand her the next bite of fruit, or handful of nuts, or sweetbread, or provide the next gulp of water from the leather bladders, or cold bitter tea to keep her on her feet.

Beyond the green hills and muddy basins Aren found a high ridge, with a narrow pass through. The walls were of blue-grey rock that rose to incredible heights on either side. The ravine widened the further he went, expanding like an amphitheater of smooth weathered granite.

The ground was covered in dust and abandoned ore from a hundred dead gold mines, the canyon floor strewn with jagged, haphazardly scattered rocks ranging in size from pebbles to boulders. Every few hundred strides they would pass another open shaft, yawning into the promise of fathomless depth. Liminal space. Vacuums of life. Places where men had toiled and died and been abandoned and forgotten.

"Something lies ahead," Fainen said.

Aren saw crumbling walls, the ruins of ancient dwellings. His eyes traced patterns over the rocks, until he could make out the foundation lines of dozens of eroded stone houses. Few of the remaining walls were higher than ten inches, but several pillars of solid rock still remained at some of the corners. It stretched nearly to the terminus of the canyon.

"There was a village here once," Redevir said.

"Older than the mines," Tanashri said.

Dried and rotten tree limbs lay all over, mingling with discarded planks of wood. Off to his right stood hundreds of tall wooden stakes jutting out of the ground like a dead forest, with tangles of wire wound through them. Among them hung countless torn sheets, cloth and canvas, waving in the wind like laundry hung out to dry. When the icy wind blew through them they fluttered like ghosts.

"Tents," Fainen said. "Or what remains of them. There was an encampment here, recently. I see tools scattered about that could have been made yesterday."

Kinraigan's trail led on past it. Just beyond the maze of billowing cloth was a flat expanse of earth and dust, a hundred feet across. On either side were piles of immense stones.

The terminus of the ravine rose just beyond them, a shallow slope covered in cracked stones and scrub and dried out thornbrush. A thick outcropping of rock stood out from the slope, with nearly vertical sides. In the center was a passageway leading into the solid stone, a black corridor. It was outlined by two slabs of foot-thick basalt, twelve feet high, and a third, shorter slab across the top.

"This must be what they were excavating," Cheli said. "Another mine."

"No," Aren said. "Not a mine." He suddenly knew where he was. He knew this place, though there were no depictions of it in artwork, and no descriptions in old tomes. He felt it with a certainty that surprised himself. Of course Kinraigan would want this to be the place where he became a god. "Devron's Altar."

"I cannot imagine a worse idol," Tanashri said. "Nor a more perfect one."

Redevir looked at them, then looked out at the rectangular hole, and then back again. "I suppose it's fitting then."

The entrance was not blocked or guarded. Beyond it, the hallway of smooth stone blocks stretched into impenetrable blackness.

It was mere happenstance that Aren looked up when he did. He saw what looked like the shape of a cross next to a patch of colorless weeds high up on the slope beyond the doorway. He watched it lay itself flat.

Balthoren!

Aren grabbed Keluwen and dragged her to the ground. The bolt flashed between Aren's fingers, tearing a gash across the back of his hand. There was an immediate flash of pain. He cupped one hand around it.

Everyone dropped to hands and knees. Dust billowed.

"Inside!" Redevir shouted.

Duran hauled Keluwen into to cover of the tunnel. Fainen pulled Tanashri in behind Aren. Mardin and Hodo carried Inrianne through. Corrin was right behind them with Cheli and Leucas.

Reidos remained out in the open.

Corrin shouted over his shoulder. "Reidos, move!"

"He'll only follow us," Reidos said. He raised the bow Fainen had given him, and nocked an arrow. He let the arrow fly as another bolt slammed into the earth at his feet. His own arrow strayed away to the side. He sprinted back the other way, ducking behind the cover afforded by the stone ruins.

Aren looked back to see him leap over a knee-high string of bricks and vanish into the grey. "Reidos!" No answer. There was no time to stop.

Redevir struck a flare. Duran followed suit. They illuminated the tunnel with flickering orange light, showing an endless stretch lined with heavy wood beams as supporting pillars.

Fainen took the lead. Aren followed to the end of the tunnel. A hundred feet further along it turned sharply left. The second tunnel took Aren another hundred feet, before descending a wide staircase cut into the very stone itself. The ceiling sloped downward, following the angle of the steps. The deeper he went, the more spacious the echoes became, until at the base of the hundredth stair, he found himself in a cubic vestibule opening wide to the right. Yet it was merely an anteroom for the chamber beyond.

Lit by its own reed torches, the chamber possessed dimensions hundreds of feet across and hundreds more from side to side. The ceiling vaulted high above his head nearly fifty feet up, like the great hall of some cyclopean temple. Within the far wall enormous arches rose up almost halfway to the ceiling itself. Each portal was fifteen feet wide, as if these tunnels were populated by titans. Five total hallways were in the far wall, and two more such arches in the walls to the right and the left. Each tunnel trailed away before turning off in some other direction.

His steps were only faint taps upon the chamber floor. The silence was deafening. It unnerved him more than hearing a cacophony of giants coming through the tunnels would. But there was nothing. Not a sound.

"Which way?" Duran asked. "Do you still see his path, Aren?"

"Yes. To the far wall. The last tunnel in the left corner."

"What a maze this place must be," Mardin said. He shook so much his voice rattled.

Duran stopped abruptly in the center of the chamber. Aren froze behind him. They all stood as quiet as the mountain itself.

"What is it, Duran?" Cheli asked. "What do you feel?"

"I feel a vibration in the floor," Duran said. "It is subtle. Something is not right."

Then Aren felt it. A fluttering in his boots. It grew stronger as if the stone itself was rattling. Aren saw Duran spin to the right, and he did so as well. A circular stone in the center of the great hall began to give way and sink down. It left a large opening, like an empty well.

Duran took two steps toward it, froze, and then turned around. "Run!"

"What in the...?" Corrin's words died in his mouth.

Out of the hole rose a slick, slippery, scraping sound, like a mass of giant frogs flopping on one another. Then, like ants erupting from an anthill, Ghiroergans poured out of the hole, dozens, pressing against and climbing over each other.

"Keluwen!" Duran shouted.

Hodo grabbed her up and carried her as fast as he could toward the passage in the corner.

Tanashri threw her hands up. Blood dripped down her forehead. She began to walk toward them.

"What are you doing?" Duran asked.

But Aren knew the purpose. She had to get as close as she could. To render as near to them as she dared, to preserve her energy. To an untrained eye it appeared like suicide.

Many of the Ghiroergans were drawn to her, the nearest motion. Aren could not imagine the confidence it must have taken to walk unarmed, unshielded toward a wall of writhing rubbery flesh and razor teeth, trusting her exhausted body to manage what she willed to happen.

She rendered inertial transposition on each of them, one by one, setting a simple duration on them, tethering each render to the body of the creature it was meant to affect, so that it would continue to affect them long after she walked away. They were slow enough and consistent enough to not throw off her concentration.

It was ingenious. She set the renders so that whenever one of the Ghiroergans tried to walk forward, its body would instead move backward. Every step they took, their feet would slide backwards along the floor with the identical momentum they would otherwise have generated. The hideous blubbering creatures shrieked and groaned and became confused, their bulbous, lidless eyes growing distracted, until they all began to wander themselves backwards into the darkness.

When Aren turned forward again, he saw a massive battle-axe swinging at his head. He barely fell away in time, flopping onto his backside. It whisked over him like a diving hawk. Inrianne screamed. Everyone was scrambling and tripping. Aren looked up at what stood in his path.

Redscar. Alive.

The giant tensed. Blood and yellow ooze leaked from unhealed wounds all over his body. Half his face was flattened and broken, causing one eye to droop.

Aren turned and ran. He saw Mardin and Leucas backing away from a lone Ghiroergan that had escaped Tanashri's renders. The two of them ran in a panic, cut off from everyone. Redevir was gone.

He saw the two ebon-shrouds. They were walking Hallan between them out of the mouth of one immense hallway, and down another, away from the one Kinraigan had taken.

"Corrin!" Aren called out. He pointed. "The boy!"

Corrin leapt into motion. "I have business," he said. He drew his sword raced to intercept them.

Duran did not question them. He turned on his heels, sprinted away, dived, and rolled between Redscar's mammoth legs. He hopped to his feet and darted away from the backswing of the battle-axe. He grabbed Tanashri and pulled her into a run down the last tunnel in the corner.

Corrin followed the ebon-shrouds down a different passage. He was gone.

Aren waited until Inrianne and Tanashri and Cheli were all gone down the passageway, holding Redscar's attention.

Redscar moved toward Aren, his feet pounding on the ground like a beating drum. Beside him stood Talvin, his small bald head bobbing beside the giant. The traitor Glasseye laughed. "I have been looking forward to this for a long time, Aren. You really think I will let you replace me by his side?"

Redscar backed him into the corner. Redscar was too big, too strong, too fast. Aren knew he didn't have a chance against the giant.

But someone else did.

Aren heard the sound of metal skidding on the stone floor. Looked down. At his feet lay *Braxis*, Donnovar's battle sword, in the scabbard Hayles had fashioned for it. He looked up.

Fainen walked with the impenetrable calm and ferocious ease of a Sarenwalker. He stopped thirty feet from the giant, and drew both *Glimmer* and a slender knife. The Saren-steel of the blade winked in icy blue. Redscar and Talvin both heard him, and they grinned simultaneously, turning in his direction.

Aren's jaw dropped. He knew that *Braxis* was being returned to him for a reason. *Fainen must not believe he will have another chance.* Aren reached down and clutched the hilt. He lifted Donnovar's sword to his chest and backed away, watching helplessly.

Talvin stepped toward Fainen with no pretense of defending himself, but Redscar followed behind him. The giant would be his weapon.

"You killed my friend," Fainen said.

"I enjoyed watching him die," Talvin taunted. "Maybe you can—"

Without a word, Fainen launched his knife through the air. His arm moved so fast Aren did not even realize it happened until the knife struck. It drove itself like a spike into Talvin's forehead, splitting his brain, and dropping him like a discarded marionette. His body twitched as he lay dead, a stupid grin frozen on his lips.

"There will be no laughter permitted," Fainen said to his corpse.

Redscar roared and charged Fainen, completely ignoring Aren. Aren jumped away, and tore down the tunnel. He didn't want to leave the Sarenwalker—*his* Sarenwalker—alone, but he knew he had no choice. As he looked back, he saw Fainen backing away into another tunnel, the giant lumbering after him. They both vanished from sight.

He was alone. He ran hard. He could barely make out the faint glow of Duran's flare ahead and around the corner, but he didn't need it to see. Kinraigan's glowing trail illuminated the walls like paint.

He rounded one corner, then another. The ceiling was lower now, and the walls closer together. He was deep beneath the mountain, running through darkness. The halls smelled stagnant and stale. The musty air coated every breath. His feet began to ache at every step. After another turn, the flat walls gave way to raw unfinished rock, like a mine shaft, descending gradually and turning to the left. As it curved away, it terminated at a hollow chamber filled with stalagmites. He felt the air crushing against him. The walls seemed to come closer.

At the deep end of the tunnel was a small circular opening. The astral light of Kinraigan's afterglow was gradually replaced by natural light, and Aren saw Duran's guiding flare lying discarded at the hole.

The chamber beyond glowed bright with flames, shooting up from a dozen wide fire pits cut into the rock of the floor. The pits were spaced out on either side of a central causeway which descended from Aren's position, down to the middle of the chamber, before rising again to a wide platform of interlocking stone blocks, like a puzzle made by gods.

The chamber spread to either side like an ancient amphitheater with a stone stage, and upon this stage sat a mighty stone altar, as long as a man and rising waist-high. It exuded at once burning sulfur and rose petals. Dozens more of Kinraigan's followers gathered on the platform, silent, still, awed by their master.

Kinraigan stood upon a causeway, his robes cascading from his shoulders in waves of indigo and violet. Aren saw a shimmering square shield in front of him. *I can see it.* It should have been invisible. Not even a Jecker monocle would have been able to make the actual shapes of magick visible.

I can see what no one else can see.

At the low point of the causeway, Keluwen faced him. Duran was behind her with Hodo and Cheli. On the platform behind Kinraigan stood the man with bells on his shoes.

You. You took her from me.

Aren's legs went numb. Blood trickled down from the wound on his hand and pattered on the flat stones beneath him. His eyes felt like they were sinking back into his skull. His hands were claws around the hilt of *Braxis*. He knew his whole life had all been leading to this moment...and he had no idea what to do.

He had arrived just in time to watch them all die.

57

What No One Else Can See

REIDOS LAY ON HIS back, flattening himself against what remained of a crumbled stone wall. Listening. Hearing nothing. Had Balthoren moved? Then a bolt came down. It nicked the inner edge of the wall, ripped a gash across Reidos' tunic, and tangled in his cloak.

Reidos pulled himself against the wall and flopped onto his stomach. He flattened himself and crawled like a gecko, pushing his bow ahead of him. Another bolt flashed over the wall, grazing his knee. He straightened his legs, and pulled himself along with his arms alone. He reached a column, broken off at the top, leaving the base standing half the height of a man. It wasn't much, but it was better than what he had now.

He painstakingly rolled over and lifted himself into a sitting position, his torso upright behind the column, and his legs straight behind the wall. He had to keep a straight back. Beyond the column was a six-foot gap, an old dried tree trunk beyond that.

Balthoren always seemed to fire at the first sign of motion. He was a shooter, a marksman, and so he would expect everyone else to behave like one, too. He would likely train his sights on the inch or two on the fringes of cover. He would expect another shooter to pop out from behind safety for but an instant to get off a shot then pop back.

Reidos assumed that if he leaned back just a little, he'd likely take an arrow in the chest. Balthoren would not expect a wild movement though. Reidos strung one arrow with his left hand, and pulled the string taught across his body, being careful to keep his bent elbow behind the column. He tried to envision the spot where Balthoren was perched on the slope. The bolts had come at an angle. That meant he was still fairly high up. Reidos inhaled and held the breath in.

He threw his back flat, slamming his shoulders down into the ground. A bolt streaked over him, just a little high. His eyes searched. Searched. Scanned the cover. Scanned the slopes. Saw movement. Just a speck. Held the bow already raised. Arrow loosed. It all took him less than a second.

Reidos heard the crack as the arrow struck stone. He was already kicking himself backward, his elbows flailing like flippers. It was barely two strides of ground to cover to make it to the tree trunk, but it felt like two hundred. As he dragged his feet after him, a bolt slammed into the heel of his boot, and he scraped it against the trunk until it flopped loose.

The trunk was a few inches taller than the wall had been, and its roundness allowed him to wedge himself part of the way under it. He listened. He heard the rustling of a bush. Two minutes later he heard pebbles disturbed and sent cascading down the slope. Nothing for a long while. He strained his ears. Then he heard a snap. Far behind his head, and low to the ground. *He's trying to circle me.*

Reidos flipped onto his stomach, snatched a piece of loose wood from behind him, and held it out and away from his body, an inch at a time, in the direction he wanted to go. No bolts came, so he judged the path safe. He crawled. His chest burned as the rocks scraped beneath him. His hands were caked with dust, and his fingers started slipping.

He heard the thump of boots behind him. The footsteps rang out like thunder through the silence. He pulled furiously. He heard a thudding sound. Balthoren was at the trunk. Reidos felt a target painted on his back. His eyes shot around and around. Rocks. Clumps of dirt. Shredded fabric.

Something. Something. Come on!

He saw the plank of wood. Three feet long and six inches wide, and it was fairly thick. He let go of the bow, and took the board in both hands. He rolled onto his back, and raised the board over him.

A bolt pierced it right through the middle, lodging itself above his heart. The tip nearly reached his skin before the wood stopped it. He threw the plank aside, and reached for a stone the size of his fist with one hand. Balthoren was reloading his crossbow.

Balthoren saw him, ceased loading, and dropped the crossbow to the ground. He unclasped a handbow from his belt, already loaded. Reidos threw the rock. It crashed into Balthoren's hand. The bolt shot into the ground. The handbow dropped. Balthoren growled, reflexively cupped one hand over his fingers.

Reidos lunged at him, swatting him across the face with his bow. Balthoren's head snapped back with the impact, but reached out a hand and snatched the end of the bow as he swung through. Reidos yanked back on it, but Balthoren held fast, and drove his fist repeatedly into Reidos' ribs.

Reidos drew an arrow from the quiver and locked a fist around the shaft. He drove it down into Balthoren's hand, spearing it through. Balthoren's hand released the bow even before he screamed. He backed away to where his crossbows lay in the dirt.

Reidos spun around and dashed to the shallow trench. He dove onto his stomach. Pain flared across his chest like an elephant kick. His body convulsed. He missed the trench, landing just to the left. He rolled, letting himself tumble into it. He saw Balthoren working on the loading mechanism of the handbow, then sliding a finger behind the trigger.

Reidos nocked an arrow, and fired it off while lying on his back in the ditch. It flew wide of its mark, but threw off Balthoren's aim as well, rushing him, making him fire before he was ready. Missed by inches.

Reidos flipped over and scrambled away through the trench, rounding the pile of loose dirt and rocks and wood, and between more standing columns. He stopped there and lifted his head to peek out over the rubble. Balthoren was gone.

****

Corrin stepped around the corner.

The two ebon-shrouds sat on stone blocks in the middle of a titan's hallway, sharpening their black swords. Hallan leaned up against the wall behind them, knees tucked up to his chest.

Corrin cycled through his forms as he walked, battling invisible enemies. He nodded to Hallan. The boy rose to his feet.

The ebon-shrouds both rose at the same time. They turned to look at the boy.

Corrin leaned down and clutched a small chunk of stone from the shattered floor. It was jagged and sharp, the size of a calpas fruit. He hopped and skipped and sidearmed the stone. It clipped one of the ebon-shrouds in the skull, knocking him over a few steps, hand bracing on the wall to keep from tipping over.

Hah!

Hallan made to slip by them, but the other one stepped in his way.

The first ebon-shroud raised an arm as if to hit the boy, but Corrin stepped into his path, arm extended in long point, jiggling the tip of his blade in its face. "No, thank you," he said.

There was no response. He assumed there would be no response. He had never heard of one of them speaking in any of the stories. He doubted they had tongues at all. Aren always said they *needed* to die for their god to be happy.

I love making gods happy.

Hallan crouched beside the wall behind them.

"You all right?" Corrin asked.

"I hurt my thumb," Hallan said.

"Oh, is that all?"

"Yes."

"Is it going to be all right?" Corrin asked.

The boy shrugged.

The ebon-shrouds separated, trying to circle him. Corrin gave ground to keep them both ahead.

"What about you?" Hallan asked.

"Be quiet. I have to do something magnificent."

Corrin lunged at one ebon-shroud, and then the other, pinging their blades to keep their attention.

"I have need of both of you right here," Corrin said.

Gonrag and Baileras. He didn't know which one was which. He didn't care. The faces were shadows, the cloaks billowing clouds of smoke. The jet black blades were the curved claws of a mythical dragon. They stood in front of him like silent, mouthless demons, faces obscured by the sheen of shadow masks, legs stood poised to move only forward, as if the edge of the world was at their backs.

And the edge of my blade at their fronts. Finally a challenge worthy of my legendary sword.

He decided that the limp-wristed one should be Baileras, and he would call the other one Gonrag. "There is a lesson I need to teach you," he said. "We were interrupted last time."

He studied their weapons. *Small guards.* They would not be able to bind his sword easily, and their fingers were vulnerable. *Too much clothing.* Their flowing cloaks would distract his aim, but at the same time would give him more to grab with his free hand to pull them off balance.

"You're already dressed for death," Corrin said. "That's good. When I kill you, you can just roll right into your graves." He smiled at them and cocked his head to the side. "Come closer, and we can dance."

Both shadows obliged him.

****

Keluwen stared at the heart of the place the Histories called Devron's Altar.

She was surprised to see an actual altar there, in the center of a wide dais atop a platform carved out of solid rock on the far side of the immense cavern, so distant that neither Kinraigan nor any of his people even noticed her yet.

Only one path led across, a flattened mound of earth and stone descending from the hole at the entrance, like a causeway over a dead lake. The path bowed down, hitting a low point in the center, and then gently rising until it reached the dais, Devron's dais. There were deep basins to the left and right of the path, each side pocked with firepits, roaring inextinguishable flame. The ceiling of the cave was thirty feet above, and echoes of every tiny motion Kinraigan made were delivered to her in perfect clarity.

"There it is," Cheli whispered. "The Codex."

Kinraigan kept it atop the altar, protected by his pet Andristi, Tarykthies. The cave wall behind him glowed golden, reflections of light off brass. Light-bowls full of stolen melenkeur stones. But his face was in shadow.

She saw the man with bells on his boots beside them. A gap-toothed woman held the Dagger. But the Crown, Kinraigan held the Crown. The same hand that had carried it away from their battle, as if he had never let it go even for a moment.

Behind him stood an array of his followers, men and women, mad grins, dirty, tangled hair, awestruck eyes. Dozens of them, standing silent like statues up against the far wall. She wondered how many people he had done this to, all across the world. How many secret cults met to worship him in the dark.

Everyone he talks to. Except for me. Except for Aren.

"We need to get it back," Cheli said. "The Codex"

"If you don't take the Crown from him then the book won't matter," Hodo said.

"No one knows what it can do," the Sister agreed. "He will destroy himself. He will destroy the world."

"What are *we* going to do?" Cheli asked.

"I don't care," Keluwen said. "As long as he dies at the end."

"He hasn't seen us yet," Hodo said.

"What is the plan, Kel?" Cheli asked.

"I'm going to walk right up to him and punch holes through him," Keluwen said.

"He is shielded," the Sister said.

"And we are weak," Inrianne said.

"We take him head on," Keluwen said.

"We need to take him by surprise," Tanashri said. "I have little left in me. I could transpose inertia, but there is nothing moving. To make a sphere I will need to be close to him. And he is upon that dais protected by a hundred of his cultists."

"We will take him by surprise *by* taking him head on," Keluwen countered. "Like in Westgate, Cheli. I will be the distraction, the bait." She pointed to Inrianne and Tanashri. "The two of you can work your way down to either side of the causeway." The area was bathed in shadow, save for the wide circles of fire. "I will keep his eyes fixed on me. And I will make him leave the protection of his followers."

"It is dark enough to either side," Cheli said. "I think."

"I don't want to hang my life on *think*," Inrianne said.

Keluwen stared her down. "You are already hanging your life on it. And it is dark enough. I will make sure he is only looking at me."

They both nodded to her. Tanashri was determined, but she had never been stretched this far in her life, never met her true self in a place of fear the way Keluwen had. Inrianne had seen pain before, she could tell. But she was inexperienced, and anxious.

Hodo prepared a little pile of horocaine powder for each of them, mixed with meal for Tanashri, eaten bitter and raw by Inrianne, and snorted up the nose by Keluwen. She had rarely touched the root, bad as it was for the heart. She had made a point for as long as she could to never allow herself to be put in a position to *have* to use it.

It hit her fast. She felt a surge of blood move down her limbs, slow enough that she thought she could see her veins slowly bulging inch by inch down to her fingertips. Her eyes snapped open, as wide as they could go. She felt each individual hair on her head distinct from any other. She felt hot. She felt strong. She felt clear.

She gave the others time to work their way down off the sides of the ramp. Once they were out of sight, she hardened her face. She gave a reassuring nod to Hodo and Cheli. They remained by the entrance, but Duran came with her.

Keluwen swept across the ramp. She stopped halfway to the Kinraigan's platform.

She screamed. So loud it stung her own ears. Her voice echoed until it sang like a chorus.

The man with black eyes looked up at her.

Kinraigan.

He smiled.

Then he looked down and continued moving things about on the altar.

Keluwen glanced over each shoulder, making sure both of the others made it down safely.

She threw her highest velocity blank impulse at him. It crashed into a flat shield. It barely shook. "Kinraigan!"

He ignored her. He whispered directions to himself.

"I am standing in your refuge," she said. "Don't you care?"

"No," he said. "Why should I?"

"You think you can face me?!" Keluwen shouted. "You think you are good enough?!"

He kept on ignoring her. It wasn't working. He already knew he was.

She ran her fingers through her hair. "Do you remember me? Don't you want to come down here?" She ran her hands over her hips. "Don't you want to finish what you started?"

He never looked up at her.

"God of every god, come down here! Come down here you piece of shit! You scum! You worthless..."

He didn't come down. He didn't leave his safe haven to come fight her. He didn't even look up. He didn't care.

I need to do something else.

"Kill me," she said.

That did make him look up.

"Kill me. I want to die. Come kill me."

"You do?" he asked. "How very interesting."

He believes me this time. Because a part of it was true.

He stepped around the altar.

Yes, come closer.

He came so close to putting the Crown down. But at the last moment he stopped. He walked calmly across the dais, and then walked down the ramp toward her. He kept his square shield in front of him, tethered to his body so that it moved when he did, turned when he turned. She could see the haze from the burning pitch flowing in currents around it as he walked.

He stopped in front of her on the ramp, looked both ways. "I do remember you. You were the one in that room. You were the girl."

"I *am* the *woman*."

"Do you remember your racing pulse under my hand? Because I do. I felt it from inside you."

"I remember you failing to turn me," she said. "And your people dying."

"I remember you failing to capture me. And your people dying. And dying. And dying."

Keluwen bit her lip and it bled in her mouth. Her brow was stone. She could not hide the rage and misery behind her face. Her mouth and eyes betrayed her. "Are you ready to kill me?"

He squinted at her.

She stared hard into his eyes. *Look at me, look at me. Don't turn away.* Just like the last time. Only this time instead of a naked body she was offering him life. Her life entire.

He was one step away from being caught between Tanashri and Inrianne, with his square shield angled poorly to block.

Just one more step.

But he stopped. He stared at her and he smiled.

He knows.

He growled. He stepped back.

The chance was lost.

He was worn and tired, but the three of them were more so. Their attacks could not penetrate his strong shields. And he knew it.

He was going to do the one thing Orrinas had spent his whole life trying to stop. He was going to make himself a god. He was going to do it right in front of her, spit on the life of the man she loved right in front of her. He would not even allow her the dignity of dying. He was going to let her live. He was going to make her watch.

****

Aren thought he was about to watch Kinraigan obliterate Keluwen.

But he didn't. He backed away until he was on the dais once more. He stood tall, and placed the Crown upon the altar. It seemed so light, so small, like a child's toy.

Tanashri was in the chamber somewhere, which meant she was holding the key streams interdicting his pressure renders, same as before. Took no energy to do that, just focus. But he didn't need them. He could master a thousand different vectorics to cut everyone here to ribbons if he chose. The only reason he didn't was because he considered the cave slugs more of a threat to him than her.

Keluwen screamed something at him.

Kinraigan ignored her. He walked in a circle about the altar, staring at the Crown as if preparing himself for an ordeal. He placed his fingers on it, touching the metal, caressing it. His mind was away from her distraction.

The light in the chamber seemed to flutter and bend. The air began to glow. The glow held no colors, or maybe it held all colors. Aren felt it like bright silver light. Tanashri, Keluwen, and Inrianne were black shapes before the light, Kinraigan's light.

A part of Aren wanted to flee, to turn and run and never look back, or to give up and surrender to the inevitability of Kinraigan's ascension. How was he going to fight a user so powerful? How were any of them? What choice was there but to surrender to Kinraigan and join him in his madness?

Kinraigan focused, eyes closed. The glow became a beam of white light, a vertical pillar from the Crown to the ceiling, and maybe out through the ceiling, maybe as high as the sky. The light strobed and swirled and radiated.

Fire suddenly erupted in the center of the chamber. It arched and crashed into the swirling light, pulled into it, caught within its spiral, flames swirling upward and inward. Inrianne was sending her fire in a great rush of orange flame. The light began to turn from the purest white to a mellow gold. The swirling slowed down, became hazy and dull.

A worried expression came across Kinraigan's face. He glanced over his shoulder. His brow furrowed. Tarykthies felt some silent communication, and descended the ramp, the hooks in his hands like animal claws.

Duran touched Keluwen on the shoulder, and spoke something into her ear. Then he advanced to meet him.

Inrianne stopped. She bent forward, catching her breath.

Aren realized none of them could see the beam of light.

She is just attacking Kinraigan. She thinks he is just blocking her somehow.

They couldn't see what Aren could.

Kinraigan was focusing on the Crown again, eyes closed, whispering concentration mantras to himself. The beam began to grow and expand again, white as snow.

Inrianne remained still. She thought it wasn't working.

Aren bit his lip. *I won't let Kinraigan win. Not now. Not after all of this. I have to try.*

"The fire!" he shouted. They all turned to look at him. "Inrianne, the fire is working!"

Inrianne smirked at him, showing teeth. "There is nothing we can do."

"The fire!" he said. "Goddamn it, just trust me!"

Inrianne turned back to the altar. She raised her arms and unleashed a river of fire at Kinraigan. It crashed into the living tornado of light, shaking and singing it. The fire was absorbed by the light, sucked up into the shimmering vortex. The light became warm and impure once more.

"It's not doing anything!" Inrianne shouted.

"It *is*," Aren said. "Trust me. I can see it. Just keep burning it."

"Burning what?" Tanashri asked.

"Just do it!" Aren sprinted down the causeway. He flew between Hodo and Cheli, and they rushed to follow him.

Inrianne's body shook. Her hands trembled as they pointed at the altar. Her eyes closed. She strained in her concentration. She sent fire in a continual stream.

The light screamed in Aren's head. He felt it.

Kinraigan felt it, too. His head shot up. A look of consternation twisted its way onto his face. He backed away from the altar. He stepped through the swirling light. His robes smoked and steamed, glowing with a flameless fire. He emerged looking pale and shaken, but he still stood tall. He looked down at Inrianne.

Aren saw a blank impulse forming in the air before him. A sphere, translucent silver, glowing the way a hum would glow if sound became light. A glowing cloud of sparkling steam laced the air around him. *I can see afterglow with my own eyes. I can see it before it happens.*

Inrianne froze.

Tanashri reached out one hand. A bubble blinked into existence around Inrianne. It was rushed, weak, untethered. Kinraigan's sphere shot toward Inrianne. It smashed into the bubble shield, knocking it over, rolling it backwards, shredding through it, until the energy obliterated itself in a splash of light. Inrianne tumbled over the stones, rolling down the causeway, sliding to a stop, her clothes tearing on the stones.

Aren could actually see the bubble. He could see its shape. It should have been impossible. *I can see it. I can see all of it.* Not just afterglow, but the magick itself. He rubbed at his eyes. Looked again. He could still see it all so perfectly. It shocked him so much he dropped *Braxis* onto the causeway. It rang like a bell when it touched down.

Aren looked at Tanashri. He saw the light bending like a sphere of glass around her hands. The sphere shot away from her, and hit Kinraigan's shield, spinning it and him with it, dropping him to one knee.

Inrianne climbed to her feet, her clothes torn. Blood dripped from a wound in her hip, soaking the fabric.

Duran was still holding Tarykthies at bay. Tarykthies leapt forward, whirling the hooks like a double-edged windmill, trying to get past him to Keluwen. Duran held his ground, blocking strikes with his bare hands and trying to wrap up a wrist with his strap.

We don't have much time.

He was nearly to Keluwen when she began to render. She moved her hands. Aren could see her resonant waveforms with his eyes, the very streams themselves. He could see each render as a construct of its component streams. He was looking at a living, moving ingredient list, so close that he thought he could reach out and touch it.

He saw Tanashri bending benign reality into a dangerous force. Vectoric. He saw each stream—trajectory, velocity, size and magnitude, duration, with the impulse of force to set it in motion. He knew what she was going to do before it even happened. He could see it like he was reading her mind. *The way users feel what each other are about to do just before they do it.* He looked to the right. He read Keluwen's streams—height, width, strength, resistance, shape.

She's weaving a wall.

He looked at Kinraigan. He saw the sorcerer with a wall of his own—height, width, strength, resistance, *elasticity*.

Aren squinted. *Just like the one Keluwen made before.*

He is learning.

Aren knew what was going to happen even as Tanashri was releasing her sphere and hurling it at him.

"Tanashri," he shouted. "Get down!" He reached her just as her force hit Kinraigan's wall. It bowed inward, and then Tanashri's force rebounded from it, and flew back at her with terrible speed.

Aren dragged her to the ground. Her sphere flew back over her head and crashed into the cave wall, spraying shards of stone into the air.

Tanashri stared at him. "How did you...?"

"There's no time," Aren said. "I can see it all." He turned to Inrianne. "Kinraigan's shield extends in only two dimensions." A force of Kinraigan's own smashed into Keluwen's protective wall as Aren spoke. "User's shorthand. In the heat of the moment no one thinks three-dimensionally."

Inrianne knew instantly what he meant. She threw her hands up like spears, and sent curling flames flooding around the shield at the last moment and turning in on him from both sides.

Kinraigan had been rendering something, but it vanished when the flames erupted around him. The sorcerer pulled his arms in to his chest, curling his upper body into a ball. His shield evaporated, and a smaller, spherical shape enveloped him. Inrianne's fire surrounded it, glanced off it, and winked out in a colossal haze of steam and smoke.

Tanashri lashed out with another blank impulse, this time designed to explode with an outward expanding force on contact. *No more elastic loopholes.* It crashed into Kinraigan's shield, but glanced off it and exploded to one side.

Then Aren saw something. He could not believe he was seeing it. Kinraigan's shield flickered for an instant, then was still.

A loop! He's looping the shield.

No one else could see it, because no one else could see the shield at all.

"Keluwen!" Aren reached out and touched her arm.

She turned to him, her eyes full of rage and despair. "He's too strong," she said.

"He's looping," Aren said.

"How can you know?"

"You have to trust me. Do you trust me?"

She bit her lip. She nodded.

"His shield. He's looping. I can see it. I know when it will break. Be ready." He looked into her eyes. She nodded. She was not the strongest, but she was the fastest, most precise puncher he had ever seen.

Aren could feel her blank impulse taking shape. She was tired, balancing on the edge of her core limit. He hoped she was still strong enough. She raised double fingers, aimed at Kinraigan.

Kinraigan smiled as the light bent before him.

The shield flickered in Aren's eyes. He counted down to the next break. "Now!"

Keluwen released her sphere. It flew lightning quick. The shield flickered again. Aren watched her sphere pass right through the shield. It smashed into Kinraigan's shoulder. The sorcerer's smile vanished. His renders vanished. His shield blinked out of sight, and his body spun, sliding him back and dropping him to one knee. She had drawn his blood again.

Kinraigan began to bind streams again before he even stood up, a look of rage on his face, crafting something of enormous magnitude.

He thinks she punched through his shield. He thinks she still has the strength. He didn't know Keluwen was already failing, that Tanashri had nearly exhausted her powers.

He was working on immense numbers of renders, each of godlike magnitudes, and all of them too quickly to keep all the power inside himself. Aren felt the vibrations of the sorcerer's oscillating energy. He felt the color of the resonance. It glowed around Kinraigan and within him, spilling reverberating bubbles of colored particles into the air. They coagulated in loose sacks full of invisible untapped energy.

Wave pockets. I can see them.

Kinraigan rendered a shield. Stronger. No looping this time. Aren could feel a hundred more deadly renders distinctly coming together in a matter of moments. He was creating each and every one of them before releasing them. He wanted them all to fly at once.

Keluwen was readying to fire at him again, but her energy was weak. Her attacks would bounce off the new shield like drops of water. She couldn't pierce it.

But she could pierce the wave pockets.

They required next to nothing to break. The bubbles of cloud drifted harmlessly in the air around Kinraigan's shield, and within his shield, only reactive to altered reality.

Harmless, Aren thought. *Unless they burst.*

He grabbed Keluwen's elbow. "Not the shield."

"I have to hit the shield," she said. "*He* is in the shield."

"I have something better."

She looked at him. "What else is there to do, Aren? Tell me!"

"Wave pockets," Aren said. "Dozens. I'll point them out. You only need a pinprick of force. The lightest touch. Barely any strength."

She shook her head once and grimaced. "Be right," she said.

He leaned in close to her, matching his line of sight to hers as close as he could, his cheek touching hers, her hair against his face, her skin hot to the touch, the sweat sliding behind her ears wetting his neck. He stretched out his arm. He heard her breath in his ear, felt her body lean into him, shoulders overlapping, joined from ankle to brow. He pointed above and to the right of Kinraigan. "There."

She sent a sharp needle of energy racing toward the wave pocket, a sphere so small that Aren couldn't see it, only the streak line showing its path. To Keluwen, it was launched at nothing, but Aren saw it heading straight for its mark.

When her tiny sphere hit, the edge of the cloud seemed to bow inward for an instant. Then it ruptured, spilling violent exploding energy in all directions, a multicolored explosion that even Keluwen's eyes could see. It tore into Kinraigan's shield, pitting it, melting it, bending it inward.

The sorcerer looked at them in silent fear. Kinraigan was actually afraid.

"There!" Aren said, his face so close to hers he could have whispered the words.

Keluwen sent another needle.

Kinraigan did not understand what was happening. He did not bother trying to deflect her tiny spheres. He could not even fathom how such a thing could hurt him.

Tanashri took her cue, and began slamming blank impulses into Kinraigan's shield, hammering dents into it, weakening it, throwing everything she had left at him.

The next wave pocket burst. Then another and another. Then two at once. It was a rainbow flare of blazing colors. Kinraigan's shield bowed and sagged, and finally collapsed, leaving him unprotected as the final wave pocket annihilated itself on him.

The exploding energy knocked Aren and Keluwen to their knees. Hodo, Duran, and Tarykthies were thrown off the ramp. All of Kinraigan's followers were tossed on their backs. Cheli only held on because she had flattened herself on the causeway before the first one burst.

Kinraigan pulled himself along the floor, his clothes smoking, his skin burned and bleeding, his face red, crawling away, drooling, trying to regain his feet. He rendered a shield. It lasted three seconds then died. He rendered another for one second. Then one that lasted ten, before finally keeping one going. He remained on hands and knees even in the shield, shaking his head. He vomited.

Tanashri dropped to her knees, slumped onto her side, drained of all energy, drained of hope. She used the last of what she had to hold on to Kinraigan's streams. It should have taken almost nothing for her to do it. But she had barely more than nothing left. When her eyes closed, her hold on his streams would be gone. Hodo ran to her, pulling out peppers and kelp and stimulant weeds and feeding them to her, trying to get her just a little something back to keep going long enough to keep Stopping those streams.

"What now?" Aren asked. "We are out of wave pockets."

"I can't break that shield," Keluwen said. "Your Sister can punch with enough mass to break it. We need to hold him until she can get enough energy for one good shot."

Aren saw Cheli staring at the platform, her eyes wide. She licked her lips. She tensed her legs.

"What is it?" Aren asked.

Keluwen noticed, too. "Cheli girl, what are you doing?"

Cheli never looked at her. "I can get it," she said. "I can get the book."

"Cheli, no!" Keluwen tried to grab her, but she was already running.

She darted past Kinraigan, and raced up to the platform. She threw her hands onto the Codex and lifted it so fast Aren was surprised she didn't fling it up into the air.

She reached for the Crown. But the man with bells on his shoes was back on his feet and he lunged at her. He slapped her hands away, spinning her, knocking the Dagger off the altar, and sending it clattering across the platform.

Cheli recoiled, spun, skipped into a run, and cruised back down the ramp. She kicked the Dagger as she ran, and it spun down the ramp, but when she reached for it her fingers missed. She danced past Kinraigan and returned to Keluwen, holding the book in her arms, smiling.

Keluwen threw her arms around her. "Cheli girl, you stupid beautiful thing."

Cheli looked down at the book and smiled, hugging it in her arms, her one true mission completed.

Kinraigan rose to his feet again. His shield held. He was wounded, and the pain of it was taxing his concentration. *Pain is distraction.* But a weak, wounded Kinraigan was more dangerous than any other at full strength.

Keluwen threw up a valiant shield, a cylinder. It was big enough for all three of them to fit in. But it bought them little time. His shield was too strong for her to break. And Aren did not think they could make it to cover before he could break through hers.

He saw Kinraigan pull streams into a blank impulse, incredible magnitude, position, velocity. He bound within it an outward expanding force locked inside it, ready to explode the instant the sphere made contact. Then he bound *trajectory* into it.

Trajectory!

Aren felt the stream as though he was looking at an imprint. It shined like an arrow pointing to its destination—the causeway beneath their feet. The explosion would turn the ramp to shrapnel and blast it up through Keluwen's cylinder from underneath, ripping them apart.

Aren moved as fast as he could think, shoving both of them away from where Kinraigan aimed. "Run!" He pulled Keluwen by the shoulders to get her moving further from where the sphere would hit. It was going to explode any moment.

Only it didn't.

The explosion never came.

Kinraigan never completed the render.

Aren looked up.

Kinraigan was smiling, his eyes shining.

He knows I can see it. He fooled me.

Aren turned to face Keluwen. Her expression was exhausted pain, resigned terror. Her eyes glazed over. He realized with horror that dragging her away had pushed her beyond her break point. Her concentration was gone. Her shield had vanished.

They were defenseless.

Aren tried to lift Keluwen. Tanashri was not ready. Inrianne was on her back shaking. None of them were ready.

He looked up at Kinraigan. His glow was shimmering with raw power. He was strong. Aren watched him keep the other streams already bound in the ingredient list of his explosive render, but swap in new ones.

Aren thought it would be a new stream of *trajectory*, to send the sphere toward them. But it wasn't. It was a new stream of *velocity* set to zero, and new stream of *duration* for the outer shell resisting the explosion set to twenty seconds. But the exploding outward force was left the same.

It was tiny, the size of a marble, but Aren could feel so much energy screaming to be released from it, pressing outward from the center.

What is he doing?

Kinraigan set a stream to *tether* the render to something. But Aren could not understand what he tethered it to. What was the point of tethering anything to yourself other than a bubble shield?

There was one final new stream bound to the render, a stream of *position*.

Aren's mouth fell open and his heart dropped. He stared in horror when he realized what Kinraigan was going to do.

58

The Luminous Immortal

REIDOS LISTENED.

Nothing.

He pulled himself forward. Listened again. Still nothing.

He crawled to the end of the trench one foot at a time, listening before each movement. At the end of the depression he propped himself up behind the mound of dirt and wooden planks. He tilted his head back, and peeked one eye back to the spot where he had last seen Balthoren. Nothing.

He was somewhere in the field of debris, hidden in a maze of crumbling walls, broken columns, piles of rock and wood, and the forest of poles with torn cloth whipping like wraiths in the breeze.

Reidos nocked an arrow and waited. He needed to be the hunter here. He tried to think back to the time when he was a shooter in the Warhost, tested in the thick of the Sarenwood. A worthy marksman. He doubted that was still true. *Patience. Watch and wait. Fire and displace. Work the way to the best positions.*

He scanned the terrain over and over, looking for the slightest movement. Nothing for seconds. Minutes. No sound save for the subtle flapping of shredded cloth in the wind.

Then a sound! A rock clicked. To his right. Behind one of the low walls. Reidos turned. Looked. Loosed. His arrow clicked against the wall. Balthoren was there. Popped up. Took aim. Fired. The bolt slammed into the wood pile, spraying Reidos with dust.

Reidos flipped, rolled out of the trench, and scrambled along the ground to the right, trying to circle Balthoren. He threw his back against one of the broken walls. He looked over the wall. Silence. Stillness. He knew Balthoren had already moved.

Reidos pulled his legs in, and rolled up into a sitting position. He leaned around the corner. Quiet low walls and blowing cloth were all that he saw.

He drew two arrows from the quiver. He set one across his lap, and nocked the other. He waited, counting his own thumping heartbeats. Minutes passed under the clouds. Tiny raindrops began to sprinkle down like mist.

He raised his bow and set it flat across the top of the stone wall. He didn't want it to be seen. He pulled the string halfway. He waited. His shoulder went sore. The string pressed into his fingers as one minute passed, then another, and another.

His eyes scanned left-right, left-right. Something caught his attention. A tiny movement in his periphery. He raised the bow, and pointed the arrow in line with his eyes.

Flash. He released. Nocked the other arrow without looking down. Saw the head pop up. Heard the twang of the crossbow. He saw the bolt coming. He dropped behind the wall. Waited. Heard the click when the missile scraped over the stones of the wall.

He threw himself up. Took aim. But he saw Balthoren there waiting for him, holding a *second* ready-loaded crossbow, aiming it back at him. Waiting for him. Reidos realized that he had made a mistake.

He tried to move. But the bolt was already coming. He felt a smack on his chest, then stinging and tearing. His arrow released on its own. His bow dropped over the other side of the wall. His head cracked sharp on the ground. He struggled against unconsciousness, but unconsciousness won.

****

Corrin cut and slashed with lightning speed, high and low, forehand, underhand, backhand. He met both blades with his own. He dodged chops, and hacks, and stabs. He maneuvered around them, letting some of their slashes pass over his head, and knocking others aside with his steel.

He tried to attack in a pattern, to lull them into complacency, but they did not fall for it. They blocked what he thought were his most surprising strikes as if they were his most mundane.

He clenched his teeth together. *Not as easy as I thought.*

What was worse, he found it impossible to adapt to *them.* They mixed forms, combined styles, and switched from one rhythm of attack to another without lagging. He adjusted himself to every new technique they used against him, mixing his offense and defense, but he was slowing as they were only getting faster.

Corrin felt, for the first time, that he was in trouble.

And while he was failing to learn them, they were making instant adjustments to every strike he made, testing his defense, probing it for weaknesses, finding the patterns of his attacks. They began altering the angles of their swings, lunging where he was least able to counter, and making attacks in concert with one another.

As he dodged one shot, another came at him. He barely parried it. As he blocked a stab, another was already aiming in at his neck. He was nearly unable to pull his head back in time.

One blade cut across his head, the other swept low at his legs. He deflected the low attack, and let his upper body fall away from the other, twisting as he did so. He landed on the ground on his chest, holding his sword out past his head. Gonrag and Baileras moved in, stabbing down at him.

Back, back, back.

He rolled away from them, kicking himself along. One shot from a black sword cut into the floor just inches above his head.

Shaot!

Corrin swept a kick at their ankles. Missed. Jumped onto his hands and knees, backing away. Created some distance. Flipped himself upright.

Gonrag stood still. Baileras, with his broken wrist, began to circle him. Corrin watched from the corner of his eye, until Baileras stood fully behind him. Corrin turned his head back and forth, looking from one to the other. He started backing off to one side, trying to put them both back in his periphery. The two shadows sidestepped along with him, not allowing him out from in between them.

So this is the game, Corrin thought. *Let's change the rules.* Corrin spun around to face Baileras, and without warning, threw himself into a charge. It was instantaneous. One moment he was still, and the next he was almost airborne. He gripped his hilt tightly with both hands this time, using the pommel for leverage to speed his attacks.

He heard Gonrag coming fast behind him.

Need to be quick here.

Baileras staggered back. Corrin grabbed at the hood of his cloak. Fingers missed. Tried again. Wrapped his fingers in it. Yanked down, swinging the ebon-shroud around behind him, running him into Gonrag like a sack on a rope.

Gonrag caught himself on one knee and waited. Baileras wasn't so lucky. He tried to catch himself on his broken arm. Failed. Careened face-first into the ground, his cloak flopping on top of him.

Corrin smiled. He held his blade at ready.

Gonrag was on his feet already.

Don't worry. I'll make you look like a fool, too.

Gonrag brought a whirlwind of steel with him, slashing and cutting furiously. Corrin parried. Raised his sword. Angled it. Lunged. Stabbed. Gonrag dodged, whipping his arm back again, cutting a cleft over Corrin's ribs.

Corrin heard the sound of tearing leather as the black sword pierced his vest, shirt, and flesh. It left a stinging pain across his side. He grabbed at the wound. *That hurt. Not deep enough to split me open though. That's good.*

Gonrag never slowed. Cut to the neck. Stab at the shoulder. Pull across the forearm. Low swing at the knee. Corrin blocked the swings, but had to give ground. Gonrag pressed him, driving him back. The tip of the blade caught Corrin on the elbow.

Baileras was on his feet again, cutting in tight arcs. He hissed at Corrin. Corrin hissed back. Baileras cut high. Corrin parried, protecting his head. But while he was focused high, Baileras raised a leg, and leveled Corrin with a swift kick to the face.

Corrin landed hard, slamming his head into the stones. Blood dripped from his nose. His eyes were filled with sparking flashes of light. *Didn't see that coming.*

He heaved himself up. He saw black shapes behind the lights in his eyes. He waved his sword blindly. It was deflected. He backed away, almost losing his balance. The footsteps were like dry echoes, but rang in his head like thunderclaps.

Baileras cut high again. This time Corrin slid his own blade up the length, past the ineffectual protection of the small guard, and took two fingers off Baileras for good measure. That gave him an extra moment to regroup, as Baileras struggled to switch to his already injured wrist.

Corrin felt wetness on his forehead. Too much to be sweat. He wiped a hand across his face. Blood. The sword had given him a little slice to go with his luck.

He backed up. The flashes were gone, but he found that he could only see black and white. The images of the ebon-shrouds were melding with the walls and the stones of the floor, like they were vanishing and reappearing every few seconds.

He made what should have been an easy block, but the blade of his enemy slid off his swing, and skimmed over his forearm, peeling away the skin like parchment. He felt his grip loosen momentarily. He clasped his other hand around the hilt. Blood poured down his face, and blotted the vision from one eye.

Not good! Not good!

His depth perception was now woefully ruined. He tried to wipe it away with his sleeve, but more flowed to shut his eye up again. He couldn't tell if Baileras was twenty feet away, or right next to him. He saw the swing of a sword. He brought up his own to block. He hit nothing but air. His blade went wide, throwing him off balance.

Damn it. I'm never off balance.

He blinked through his good eye, and realized that Baileras was a full five feet away from the reach of his sword.

He tricked me. Oh shaot.

Something hit his head. He toppled. One leg went numb. The air blasted from his lungs when he hit the ground flat. His blade skittered away, leaving his empty hand reaching, finding nothing.

He looked for Hallan, but his vision blurred to absurdity. His hand felt about wildly. He had no weapon in reach, his own or otherwise.

The ebon-shrouds loomed over him.

****

Fainen had no thoughts. Only action. He led Redscar away from Aren. His most immediate task was complete. Remaining alive was secondary, but now he was free to focus his full attention on this goal.

He darted down the tunnel and around a corner. Stone walls, ceiling twenty feet above, lit by half-burned reed candles and loose chunks of melenkeur carelessly scattered on the ground.

He knew where Redscar was without looking. He heard the giant's steps, felt the giant's breaths. There was no need to see. Halfway down the hallway he wheeled about. He looked up at the looming giant without fear. His eyes were soft and curious like a child's. He saw the giant coming. Blood and puss congealed in Redscar's unhealed wounds.

Fainen did not give ground. He kept his eyes fixed on the giant's chest, waiting for it to give Redscar's intentions away.

Fainen raised his Saren-sword. The giant brought the battle-axe down, all his force in one swing. Fainen leapt forward. The axe chipped the floor. Fainen lashed Redscar across the forearm. Blood slid from the wound like sap.

Redscar tore the axe free, spraying Fainen with bits of stone. The axe shot out. Missed. Came again from the other side. Fainen dodged. Redscar slapped him with a swing of his open hand. Fainen flew back. Slid ten feet across the floor.

Fainen sprang to his feet before Redscar took a single step. Charged. Redscar reared up, and swept with his free hand, the axe swinging right behind it. Fainen ducked the giant's arm, and jumped over the axe. He spun in midair, and brought *Glimmer* down, but the giant moved aside. Fainen's foot slipped on a loose stone. His blade swung away from its mark, and he flopped down against Redscar's leg.

Fainen scrambled to his feet. The giant cornered him against the wall. Smashed a fist into Fainen's chest. His shoulder slammed into the wall, and his sword dropped away. He hit the ground hard on his stomach, knocking the wind out of him.

He pressed himself up quickly, ignoring the spears of pain through his body. He backpedalled. Found his sword. He ducked under the swinging axe, and brought *Glimmer* up, cutting a cleft over the giant's torso.

Redscar lifted one leg. Fainen saw the kick coming. He arched his back to one side, but the edge of Redscar's foot caught him in the jaw, spinning him around and dropping him. He felt his neck throb. Bile rose in his throat. He was not certain he would be able to stand.

The world tilted. He found himself on his back, cold stone against his cheek. *Glimmer* on the ground, unreachable. A red titan in a black hallway, so close, the flickering light so fragile and faint, so intimate and deadly.

Redscar loomed above him. A smile spread over the titan's lips. The eyes shined like rubies. The mouth drooled in anticipation.

Fainen felt his final moment upon him. He blanked his mind of everything. He summoned every ounce of strength. He looked up and saw the giant's foot coming down to crush him.

****

Aren watched Kinraigan's sphere render into reality.

Cheli looked at him and then at Keluwen, eyes wide, face melting with horror. She could feel it. She knew it was there. She began to cry, hugging the Codex Lumina to her chest with both arms.

The sphere rendered directly beneath her chin. And it was tethered to *her*.

She shook her head, it shook with her. She stepped back, it moved with her. She stepped side to side. The sphere moved with her, always exactly the same position relative to her body. Like it was a part of her.

Aren and Keluwen turned to look at Kinraigan.

"You took my book," he said. He was smiling back at them. He was not even trying to kill them. He wanted to watch them go through this first.

"No!" Cheli screamed. "No, no, no, no, no. Please no. I don't want to die, Kel. Please don't let me die."

"A shield," Aren said. He turned to Keluwen. "Can you render a shield? Between it and her chin?"

Keluwen tried. But her concentration was shot. And her strength was nearly gone. She could not get the shape right to protect Cheli from under the chin and the body at once. So she tried to render two square shields, but her high magnitude strength streams lay just out of reach. All she could do was render a slightly larger sphere around his to contain some of the blast. She wrapped another around that, and another. But they were weak, eggshells when she needed steel. They would not stop what was coming.

"I'm so sorry, Cheli. I..." Keluwen reached out to her, but Cheli took a step back. She shook her head, crying, trying to make distance, trying to protect them. She kept backing away and away and away. Tears in her eyes. Hopeless.

Kinraigan started laughing.

Cheli's face squeezed in sour anguish. She closed her eyes and then opened them, tears leaking. She lifted her chin up defiantly. She looked directly at Kinraigan, meeting his eyes, her jaw set strong. Then she held the Codex Lumina up to the sphere, pressing it against her chin.

Kinraigan's smile vanished. His mouth fell open.

Aren grabbed Keluwen and half-pulled half-dragged her back down the ramp. She let him pull her along, but her arms still reached out for Cheli, hands grasping the air. He couldn't get her to move fast enough. She was too close. He opened his mouth to scream something.

Then the sphere's *duration* expired.

Cheli closed her eyes.

The sphere burst. The shockwave shattered her and then tore her apart. The heat release incinerated her. Jets of blood sprayed, then turned to steam. Bits of flesh and chips of bone blasted in every direction like shrapnel. The Codex was obliterated, raining down on them like flaming confetti.

Keluwen took the brunt of the explosion. She was lifted off her feet, her tunic set aflame from the heat release. She flew over the edge of the causeway and dropped into one of the eternal peat-fire pits.

Aren was blown back, tumbling and skidding and scraping along the rocks. His knees and palms were torn bloody. His head cracked on the stone and he felt liquid flowing through his hair. He slid over the edge, just barely hanging on to the lip of the causeway, tearing his fingers to shreds trying to maintain a grip.

Kinraigan had needed to shield himself from the explosive results of his own render. But he did. Easily.

Aren pulled himself up. His lungs felt like they had been crisped to ash. His eyes would not stop watering. He wiped at them desperately, trying to see what was ahead of him. He coughed and spit up foam into his hands.

Hodo reached out a hand and helped him to his feet. He had been feeding Tanashri powder and peppers, helping her to sit upright on her own. But he dropped it all now and leapt down to search for Keluwen in the black emptiness of the basin where she fell.

The air swam with dust, making Aren feel like he was underwater. He couldn't see anyone but Kinraigan on the causeway. And it took a moment for his hearing to return. Keluwen was gone. Duran and Tarykthies had disappeared. Inrianne was unconscious. Hodo was down in the dark, rooting around.

Kinraigan walked away contentedly. There was no one to stop him now. No *way* to stop him. They had done everything. Tried everything. It was over.

Aren looked sadly at the glowing immaculate clouds of twinkling silver and purple and yellow afterglow. It was like he was still holding a Jecker monocle to his eyes. The compression masking Kinraigan layered into every render only made it harder to see through.

He laughed hopelessly. "Even now."

"What?" Tanashri asked.

"Even at the closest moment when he thought he was going to die, Kinraigan *still* bothered with putting a stream of compression masking on every render. Just like at the *Red God*, and in Cair Tiril, and in the valley outside. Just like every scene in his composite the Render Tracers made. Just like he made his mimic use masking in Vithos, and Westgate. As if *even now* he is worried about anyone finding his afterglow down here." He laughed again.

"It must be a reflex," she said.

"Reflex." Aren nodded.

Reflex. He used masking on *every* render. Every single one Aren had ever seen himself, and every one in each of the imprints from the composite folio made by the dozens of other Render Tracers he had eluded in Amagon, going back years.

The realization struck Aren like a diamond arrow through his skull.

"The compression mask is a *stream*," Aren said.

"What was that?" Tanashri asked.

"I never thought of it. I never...No one ever uses it. Maybe once or twice. I never even thought about it. I looked right past it."

"What are you thinking?" Tanashri asked.

"You saw the imprint of his masking stream. From the composite. I showed you. Pull it."

"What?"

"Pull the stream. Interdict his compression masking stream."

"He doesn't need the masking to make any of his renders though. All he would have to do is abandon his render and begin an identical one *without* the masking stream."

"But it will take him a few seconds to realize it. Three seconds? Five? Ten? He has been saving his concentration, guarding his break point closely. That means he is only rendering a new shield when the old one fails. One stream can block an entire render. That means if you can break through this current shield, and use the masking stream to interdict the next shield *before* he tries to raise it in its place, he will be completely undefended."

He could see her thinking it over. "But he has rendered multiple forces before with that same masking stream. Does precedence effect even work on it?"

"Because the masking stream is applied to the *other streams* themselves. It only lasts a millisecond in the real world. While the other streams of his renders last longer, the masking dies instantly. But if you Stop it, you are Stopping the *whole render* before it can start. He can render so fast the masking stream will free itself up a hundred times in a second. But it has to *be there for him to take*. If it isn't none of them will ever render in the first place."

Her eyes widened. "And he *won't know why*."

"If you interdict the masking stream, he won't be able to pull in a new shield, or a new blank impulse. Everything he does has that stream in it. He won't be able to attack. He won't be able to do anything. No blank impulses, no pressure fields, no crush bubbles, no shields, nothing. You will have free reign to do anything you want until he figures it out. Five seconds. How hard can you punch his shield in that time?"

Tanashri smiled, horocaine making her eyes wide. "I can *crush* his shield in that time."

"Do it."

She pulled the stream.

Then she began pounding his bubble shield with blank impulses, not her strongest, just enough to get his attention.

He looked over at her. "Have you not had enough?" He began to bind. A look of horror slowly spread across his face. He looked down at his hands. His eyes roamed everywhere. He could not understand. He could not figure it out.

"Now!" Aren shouted.

Tanashri unleashed the strongest blank impulses her body could still create. She sent them over and over and over. Three at once. Five at once.

Inrianne was back on her feet. She took her cue from the Saderan and sprayed a tide of fire, putting everything she had left in them, wearing the shield down.

Kinraigan began to panic. He moved his hands faster and faster. The spheres crashed around him. The shockwave of one collision spun him, making him stumble. He slipped in the dust and fell.

Aren felt the shockwaves of the impacts. They whipped his hair, rumbled in his ears. He heard a rattle on the ground. He looked down. The Dagger was on the ramp beside him. He reached down and picked it up. He was not sure why.

Kinraigan was desperate to bind his streams, to render a new shield. He worked franticly. But he still could not understand why his magick was not working. His shield finally collapsed.

He dropped to the ground. Tanashri's next blank impulses flew over his head.

A lucky break. She adjusted.

But before she could finish him, he began doing something that Aren did not understand. He pulled all the streams that he could find, and instead of binding them into a render, he pooled them, turned them in on themselves. He began to vibrate, as if the cells of his skin were bees swarming. The vibrations spread to the air around him.

What is he doing?

Tanashri released her blank impulse but it seemed to pass in a strange orbit around him, thrown off by his vibrations.

Kinraigan's body began to glow. He lifted off the ground and floated. His body became just a black shape against crashing waves of light.

Tanashri sent another sphere toward him, but the light diverted it, as if it was its own force field.

Kinraigan's body shuddered. His visage became a host of particles, detached, held near by his gravitation alone. His body welled up with brightness, and streaks of white light shot out from him. He was getting stronger. Aren could feel the power swelling and seething. More power than any man could have.

Aren looked up in horror.

No. He can't be doing this.

It was autoentropic resonance.

Kinraigan had no idea that he could simply reach out and crush Tanashri with his magick. She had no more power left to stop him, but Kinraigan must have thought he needed more, must have thought she was still powerful. He stood at the very spot where Devron had ruined the world a thousand years ago, attempting to do the same.

The white light was Slipstream, joining together and spreading over everything in a lustrous intoxicating light. When he touched the light, he could feel it. It was pressing itself against the air, expanding.

"I am luminous! I am immortal! I am invincible!" Kinraigan's voice roared like a mountain come to life. "Come all you who worship me! See my awesome power! Know I am your one true god and give your lives to me eternally!"

His ragged followers fell to their knees on the platform behind him, clasping their hands together and weeping with joy.

"Kill all who stand before you!" Kinraigan called out to his army of cultists.

Then he disappeared in the light.

Aren looked at Tanashri.

"That is how he was able to enter the light," she said. "This is the loophole that allowed him to become luminous."

The light closed up, balling up into itself until it was just a point.

Aren could hear the raw power being released. Rumbles from above, outside in the air, and deep below the earth. Incredible energy, more powerful each iteration, as he made himself stronger, and made his perception stranger.

Kinraigan was in the light. He was outside of time. His zero-point-energy was going to keep releasing until everyone and everything was destroyed. And with him safely walking in the light there was absolutely no way to stop him.

No! You can't get away like that. No. I won't let you.

Aren swung the Dagger through the air, leaving its sheath upon the ground. He swung it back and forth over the spot where Kinraigan had been, trying to kill the memory of him.

But it was too late. He was gone. Fled. Leaving his followers to finish the work of killing. His power expanding to obliterate the world.

Kinraigan's people stirred, surging across the platform, heading for the ramp, coming to murder them all while Kinraigan lounged in the unknowable light.

Aren's arms drooped. His head hung. He looked down at the Dagger. It was charcoal blue, something he had never seen. He touched the cool metal of its blade, running his finger along it. He felt tiny sparks, minuscule static snaps on his skin. It tingled. It rushed. It warmed but never burned. It cooled but never froze.

He opened his eyes wide and he tipped forward and fell through the world. Light erupted around him, as if every single point in the universe became a separate source of light all at once. A million things and one thing.

Inrianne was frozen, her arms suspended in midair. Tanashri was still. The Slipstream was bending time, curving it and stretching it. Slowing it for everyone.

Except for Aren.

He looked around in disbelief. He was seeing it. It was real. He stood outside of time. Removed from the confines of space. He reached out and touched the expanding light. His hand passed into it easily.

How?

How am I doing this?

I am no user. I have no power.

How is the light opening for me?

The light was warm and thick, and cold and smooth. It welcomed him.

The Dagger is a messenger. It delivers to you the news of what you are by awakening it in you. It opens the door for you to take the first step into what you will become.

He looked upon the light and thought of Eriana at that moment. He wasn't sure why, but he saw her face.

It made him remember the words of Solathas.

Light walking suits you.

He moved forward, and entered the Slipstream.

59

Slipstream

CORRIN'S WORLD WAS ENDING in a black and white haze. No sword. No balance. No position. *You can't win a sword fight without a sword.*

He lay flat on his back, as vulnerable as a sacrificial lamb. *Optimism,* he thought, laughing in his head. He knew he was finished.

Jecks Keberan always told him to never fight fair. It was the surest way to an early grave. But you had to have a weapon to fight. *I don't have a weapon, Jecks.*

Then something curious happened. A thought came into his head. He remembered something. Something someone said to him once. He couldn't place the source, but it was strong. It shot through his consciousness like a diamond-studded arrow. An image of a gift given to him long ago. He saw Aren's smiling face, as he handed over a magnificently engraved ivory-hilted knife from Miralamar. The long lost memory flooded into his brain in a rushing current.

The knife. It was his most prized weapon. The last one he would turn to in a fight. The one he had never used. The only one he hadn't lost fighting Sedmon. The only one that still rested in its brown leather sheath under his arm.

I do have a weapon.

Gonrag and Baileras were standing over him, black blades ready to strike. Corrin flipped the knife free, and locked it in his fist. He could only see black shapes, but black was all he needed to see. He reached out. Saw a leg standing like a black pillar beneath a shadow cloak. He lanced into the heel with the precision of a surgeon. He pulled out and away, severing tendons like cords of string.

Lay down. You look tired.

Baileras screamed and dropped onto his back. He tried to roll sideways.

No. Don't get up. You need your rest.

Corrin rolled away from Gonrag's stab, and thumped against Baileras. He clamped one hand around the ebon-shroud's good wrist, and cut with the knife. Elbow, shoulder, and neck—one, two, three. The tendons snapped like cheap rope, and blood issued like a pitcher of wine overturned.

Corrin jumped to his feet. He stumbled on the landing, pitched forward, tipped back, then caught a firm footing, and somehow remained on his feet. He felt bile rise in his throat as the room spun with vertigo. *I hate vertigo.* He vomited onto his shoulder, but it made the world spin one degree less.

He looked at Gonrag. "Alone at last."

The shadow stepped toward him, the black sword held in a ready posture.

Corrin smiled through the drying blood on his face. *I am going to beat you.*

Overconfidence. It was an enemy to everyone, even an ebon-shroud. *You think you are so much better than me. Well, let me help you think that even harder.* "You have been looking everywhere for a savior to help you die. Maybe it's me." He held his arms out at either side.

Meanwhile, Corrin's head was swimming. He could barely stand. It was a godlike effort to keep from stumbling like a drunkard. But Gonrag didn't know that.

Gonrag attacked. The sword screamed at Corrin's unprotected neck. Corrin waited until he was committed to the motion, then leaned back out of reach. The tip of the blade scratched across the bridge of his nose.

That was too close.

Instead of backing away, Corrin stepped into his attacker, parrying and knocking away the black sword with nothing more than the downturned eight-inch knife. Every time Gonrag passed a foot back to gain the advantage of his blade's length, Corrin stepped into him, refusing him the distance required to use the black sword to its maximum effect. He waited for a frustrated swing to come at him, leaned back, and backhanded a parry, exposing Gonrag's entire arm.

Corrin locked a hand around the wrist, and pinned the sword arm out of his way. Corrin raised his knife over his head. He brought it down like he was slamming a mug of ale onto a bartop. The knife planted itself to the hilt behind Gonrag's collar bone.

With a satisfied grin, Corrin twisted the blade in its new home, exploring the ebon-shroud's tender tissues. Gonrag's arm went limp, and Corrin snapped it, broke the elbow, and popped the shoulder from its socket.

Gonrag reached for him with his only useful hand, but Corrin swatted it away. He planted a foot behind one of the ebon-shroud's legs and pushed him over. Gonrag slammed to the ground.

Corrin watched him twitch for awhile and then lie still.

Ebon-shroud god, I give you this offering.

He forgot to tell him to get ready for the magnificence. Now it was too late.

Corrin reached in to check beneath the thick hood, not quite certain whether ebon-shrouds died the way other men did. He made to draw the hood down from the still face to see for sure, but thought better of it, stopped, and pulled his hand away.

He picked up Gonrag's curved black blade. He drove the sword four times into the corpse, then hacked apart Gonrag's neck until the head flopped away.

Farod.

He wiped down his new black steel blade, his last knife, and his longsword.

Well, that's that then.

"Well, boy, did you see that? That is what...I..."

Hallan was gone.

"Where in the hell?"

He turned to look over his shoulder. He saw the boy scampering around the corner, back the way he had come. Corrin followed.

The boy made for the massive room with all the hallways. But then he took a turn toward the passageway in the far corner, the tunnel he had seen Aren take.

That is not the way out.

The floor began to vibrate. It bucked and heaved like a ship in a storm. Corrin shook his head from side to side.

If it's not one thing, it's another.

****

Keluwen opened her eyes.

She tried to lift her head. Pain streaked down her spine, her nerves ringing out like the peals of a hundred bells. She gasped. And the gasp hurt worse than moving. She grit her teeth and sipped air. She coughed and hacked a bloodball the size of a plum onto the rocks. Her nose was wet. She wiped her face. Saw red on her hands.

She moved her left side. Her arm and shoulder could rotate freely.

She tried to move the other, but nothing happened.

She looked down at her side. Half her tunic was burned away to nothing. Her right arm was more purple than a blueberry bath. Her skin was a cooling lava field, blackened and cracked open like a dried out mud lake, rivulets of blood and muscle exposed. Flesh charred, peeling, breaking apart.

She tried to shrug her burned arm ahead of her. It scraped along the ground. Fire shot through her head, ripping another scream from her.

Every inch she moved was grinding her burned and torn flesh on the stones, turning her body brown with dust. Pain scraped inside her head. She pushed herself up on hands and knees. She hovered there, vomiting.

Suddenly Hodo was there beside her. He leaned over her, trying to help, but afraid to touch her. "Seven hells, Kel."

She tried to speak, but it set off another bout of vomiting. She closed her eyes and her belly spasmed. "Hodo," she said.

"I am here," he said. "Right beside you."

"Where is Cheli?"

"Do you not remember? She is gone, Kel."

"Where is he, Hodo?"

"He went into the light."

Keluwen spat blood. Pink foam dribbled out her mouth in a long stream. She laughed in agony. "Gone. Gone...again."

"Not exactly. The other man, the Glasseye. He went into the light after him."

"What do you mean?" She pulled up and lay on her left side, holding herself up with one hand.

She saw Kinraigan's minions overflowing the dais. They walked over the platform, coming toward her. Coming toward the Sister, and the bitter girl. There was no one left to stand in their way. The users were spent. The fighters exhausted.

Keluwen sucked in a breath, filling her lungs until it burned. "Help me up."

"They are coming."

"Help me up."

"I have to get you out of here. We have to go now."

"There is no getting out of here, Hodo. Win or die. That has always been the game we have been playing. Since Seb. Since before him even. We spent all this time pretending it was something else, but deep down we knew it would be this way."

He looked down at the ground, tears in his eyes. "I don't know what to do."

She had never seen him cry. This big burly man, so loyal and patient, so strong and kind. It hurt her more than the peeling of her skin to see him weep.

"Look at me, Hodo."

He turned up his chin to her. "Tell me what to do. I don't know what to do."

"We fight, Hodo." She spat blood. "That is what we are going to do."

"Alright."

"Look at me, Hodo. Look at me. Before this I was just a thief. I stole little shiny coins and thought I was queen for a day. I thought that was all I would ever be. But I found something more. We chose this. This is who we are. We are fighters now. When others give up, we keep going. We are here to save the world. And when *we* go down, we go down fighting."

He nodded along with her, steeling himself. His face hardened. "We go down fighting."

"Give me the horocaine powder."

"What? How much?"

"All of it, Hodo. Give me all of it."

"Your strength is already scraping the bottom."

"Well I am going to scrape it a little harder."

He opened the little box in his leather pocket. He held it out to her.

She took it and drove her nose into it. She inhaled deeply. She shoveled it into her mouth with two fingers. She felt the blood surge in her body. It stung her nerves, and opened her eyes. She felt her heart beat as fast as light. She felt like she could break mountains.

"Pull me up, Hodo."

He took her by the left arm and lifted. Her left leg was intact, and she found that she could put the slightest bit of weight on the right, enough to hobble like an old woman.

She heard footsteps coming from the entrance. She and Hodo looked back.

"Is it more of them, Hodo?"

"It's the boy," he said.

"The boy?"

"The one Orrinas told us we had to keep safe."

Keluwen felt her heart grinding apart at the sound of his name.

Hodo gasped. "I am sorry, Kel. I am so sorry."

She held up her hand when the boy was fifty feet back down the causeway.

He stopped and looked at her curiously. He seemed so innocent, so pure. She had not seen that in a person in forever many years.

A child.

She had never bothered to learn his name. But his name didn't matter. He was *any* boy. Any child. Anyone who should have been living a life of joy, free from worry, free from pain, surrounded by love, and parents who would do anything, give anything, be anything for them.

For when there is nothing left. When there is no more of you, they will bring you peace. When the river is in your path, they will be the bridge. When the world is dark, they will show the way.

The boy was special.

Orrinas told her so, and even if she did not believe it, she believed *him*. It didn't matter what the boy was. She was going to protect him because Orrinas thought he was important. She did not care why. Orrinas said it was so, and she would do what he would have done. She would not let them take that away from her.

She shook her head. "Stay back with him, Hodo. If they get past me, you take him and run, understand?"

Hodo nodded.

"You are so brave, Hodo."

"So are you, Kel."

She smiled. "Get back there."

She looked into the boy's eyes. She nodded her head to him.

I will not leave you all alone, they way everyone all my life has left me.

Keluwen looked up the causeway.

She recognized the man with the mustache on the platform. She heard the bells on his boots jingling as he came closer. He drew his twin shortswords, shaking his shoulders loose. "We're going to skin you," he said. "We'll make dolls of your bones. Unless you give us that boy."

"Well," Keluwen said. She spat blood and foam. "I'm not going to give you shit, except for a new hole in your head."

"If you make this hard, we'll make this hard."

"I always make everything harder than it has to be," she said. "But this time, I think I'll like it."

"You have no idea what is in store for you," he said.

"Want me to show you which hell you are going to?" she asked him.

He raised his swords and pointed at her. Dozens of the others rushed down the causeway toward her at his command.

Keluwen raised her left hand and pointed. She selected the first ten of his followers. She sent off ten blank spheres, one after another. They punched through skin and muscle and bone. They cracked skulls and burst organs. All ten fell.

The rest charged, crowding the ramp, fighting to be the first to die for their master.

How about all of you?

Keluwen hobbled forward. The horocaine powder moved her body for her, keeping her upright, keeping the pathway to the Slipstream open. She grimaced so hard it made her face hurt, but she didn't care. Every day was a new day. Today was pain and tears.

The Crown was still upon the altar. It was still radiating power, a swirling beam of light rising from it, holding open a gap in reality. She raised her hand and aimed a sphere at the Crown. She released it and it flew over their heads, over the altar. It spun off, thrown by the resistance of the energy around the Crown. Magick could not touch it.

I have to get through them. I have to stop it.

She killed the nearest follower.

A woman came next. She screamed. She wailed. She groaned. "My master will rip the skin off of you!" she said.

The followers surged forward, propelled by her voice.

Keluwen looked at them. "Fuck your master."

She summoned twenty-five blank spheres. Every single one she had ever learned, mastered, and controlled. One for every year of life. She sent them all.

The barrage tore the followers apart. Blasting through arms, legs, ribs, joints, skulls, and bellies. Men, women, young, old, everyone who followed Kinraigan she ripped to pieces in a frenzy. Blood sprayed like fountains, and ribbons of skin fluttered in the air like streamers, festooning the collapsing bodies like garlands.

Keluwen dropped to one knee. Her heart leapt then slowed, nearly stopped, staggered, started again. Pain lanced down her arm. Her body constricted, squeezing her lungs. She stumbled, clutching her chest. She threw up white paste.

Nine of Kinraigan's followers remained. They came toward her. She plinked a sphere off one of their skulls. She was running out of energy. She did not have enough strength to render something that could break through bone any longer, but it cracked it good enough to kill.

She took aim at a second one, but then something struck her in the head. Her vision blurred, cleared, burred again. She shook her head. She opened her eyes. One of them stood over her with a frog's eyes and a rusty knife.

She kicked out with her bad leg, sweeping his feet out from under him. He toppled. She rolled her torso onto him, pinning his arm to his side. Another rose above her, swinging a heavy club. She leaned back. The swing missed. The man on the ground rolled and slid the knife an inch into her thigh. Keluwen bit her lip.

Another two stood over her with downturned swords. But Hodo stepped past her. He grabbed one by the hands, turned them out and broke them. He kicked the other between the legs. He took the sword from the first and split his head open with it. But two more tackled him, carrying him off the ramp.

He managed to get a fistful of cloak, enough to take a third with him over the edge.

Keluwen rolled over the prone man's arm, kicked out at one knee of the man above her. Two more reached down hands to hold her.

She looked up at the man above her. She recognized him. He was the man with bells on his shoes. She heard them jingle as he struggled. He pinned her good arm back.

But she had one other.

She rolled hard onto her right side. Pain roared into her head. Her entire body burned. But she freed her charred and broken left hand. He did not bother to restrain it, thinking it bent and useless. But Keluwen did not need the bones and muscles to work to render magick. She only needed to point two fingers.

Time seemed to slow down.

She looked up into his eyes.

You're the one who killed Aren's girl.

She was sweet. Not like me.

You shouldn't have done that to a sweet girl, you piece of shit.

She raised her arm, held burned and broken double fingers up to his chin.

His eyes went wide.

The sphere shot from her fingertips up through the inside of his face. It crashed around within his skull. It mashed his brain to pulp, and cracked the bones of his face outward one by one as it bounced inside, before finally blasting out through his eye. He tipped forward into the path of a downturned sword. The stab meant for her went through his body instead.

She cupped her fingers together. Cylinders wrapped around the two men above her, shrinking and squeezing until every part of them was broken and mashed.

Keluwen at last held her fingers to the eye of the man beneath her. She felt the streams of the sphere. She felt them binding. She rendered the sphere into reality. She let it fly.

Blood erupted from his head and spilled across her hand, but she didn't care.

She rolled over, pushed herself up on her knees. Looked down the causeway. The boy was still there, alone. He looked so terrified. But he smiled at her. He actually smiled.

The horocaine was still burning bright, but even that could barely keep her going now. Her arms did not want to move. Her legs were stone. It was a day's worth of effort just to hold her head up every second.

She heard voices and footsteps.

She watched as dozens more people flowed into the chamber, coming through unseen passageways behind the dais. More of Kinraigan's followers. So many more. As if they had been waiting in darkness for all their master's other servants to die so that they would have their moment to shine in his eyes.

She had not killed all of Kinraigan's people. Not by a long shot. She had used everything she had, and it still wasn't enough.

She rolled onto her side and saw the Crown still there on the altar. The hole in reality remained open. And something was stirring on the other side.

All her effort, all her pain, all of it had still not been enough.

She put one hand over the other and crawled down the ramp, heading to the boy.

She bared her teeth. There were tears streaming down her face.

She kept going.

I haven't had my last breath yet.

****

Aren was in a world of white. His body was light. His hands were pale outlines. The light flowed around him like veils of silk. His footing was firm, but he did not stand on any ground. He saw Kinraigan move, then disappear behind a white wall of light.

This is the Slipstream. I am inside the source. He was floating in a sea of infinite possibility. *I never knew it was like this.*

Aren moved forward. His knees ached, his wounded belly throbbed, and his torn hands raged with pain, dripping blood into an infinity of light.

Kinraigan became visible again. The sorcerer stood adorned in multicolored robes. Even his pale skin seemed dark against the brightness of the light.

Aren moved closer. He began to see things. Things that Kinraigan felt. What he saw. What he heard. He saw them in color at the ends of the white corridors, and through holes beneath him. He saw images of children murdering their parents, and people feasting beside decaying beasts. He saw animals dressed as men and living in their cities, and men and women engaged in sexual acts while others cut open their bodies and destroyed their organs. He saw boys suffocating one another, and village children crushing their pets with stones. Mothers dying and babies crying. Especially the last one. Recurring infinitely.

He looked at Kinraigan. The sorcerer saw these things as well, his eyes flaring with madness as he stared. His hands twitched. His veins bulged ice blue on his arms and neck, and his lips pulled back, baring clenched teeth.

Aren thought of Eriana, and Hayles, and Donnovar. He thought of his mother.

A rage filled him. It tugged on his breaths. The hatred burned in his lungs, and his heart climbed into his throat to choke him. He moved out from behind the veil.

Let him see me. Let him kill me. I don't care.

Kinraigan looked up. He saw Aren. His face was alive with worry and surprise. "Ordinary people cannot come here." He glanced down at the Dagger and smiled. His mouth opened, and he laughed, as if it was the greatest joke the world had ever heard. The sound of laughter echoed off of the light—echoed and repeated like an insane chorus. "Of course you are here," he finally said. "I knew you were special, Aren."

Aren looked down at the Dagger in his hands. "Now I know why you wanted to stop the Lord Protector from getting his hands on this. The Dagger is a key. It takes the body into the light, the way an *Introduction-Of-Change* is a key for the mind to reach into it."

As soon as he realized what it was for, he understood everything. All the trouble going to Laman, the conspiracy and double-cross, all of it, was because Kinraigan feared someone else being here. He did not want anyone else in the light with him. There must have been something in here that could hurt him. Aren needed to find out what it was. *But how can I know anything about a place I have never been?*

Aren floated a step closer. "You were afraid he would be able to find you here. Why?"

"I am Kinraigan. I fear nothing."

"You were worried when you first saw that I was here." *You think you are vulnerable here. There must be some way to hurt him in here. But how? How can I stand against him?* Aren's mind raced, trying to think of what he could exploit here. But he knew nothing of the light. *He likes to brag. I need to make him do it.* If he could keep the sorcerer talking, he might slip and reveal the thing he feared.

Kinraigan kept working, glancing lazily over his shoulder at Aren. "You are so misguided. Even now you are still thinking of ways to stop me, instead of becoming what you were meant to be."

"You have invented a path for me to walk out of whole cloth. The man you think I am is imaginary."

"Are you? Imaginary? I know you can see it. You think that went unnoticed? You could see. Like the others who came before. You have brightborn eyes. Like I did."

Aren felt a chill down his spine. His teeth scraped against each other. "You are lying. I am nothing like you."

"You think you are so very smart. I think you are exactly like me." White light swirled all around him as he spoke. "You have been in the light now. You see it for yourself. Do you really want to leave? Do you really want to go back to the way things were? Don't you want to know everything about it? I could show you. Stay here, with me. I can feel how much you want the light for yourself."

Aren tried to open his mouth to say no. But he could not. Something stopped him, like a block of wood in his mouth mashing his tongue into a futile lump. The light was intoxicating. It swam over his skin, bathing him in luscious waves of luminescence, patiently caressing him. He could feel it reaching out to him, and surrounding him, and embracing him, and protecting him, and holding him forever in its gentle grip.

Kinraigan smiled over his shoulder. "Look around you. I see the truth this world has been hiding from you. See the death, the pain, the sorrow. How many of my kind do the Priests burn? How many of your kind do lords and kings slaughter?"

"What are you talking about?" Aren growled.

"Have you ever asked yourself why your Lord Protector and I are enemies? Too long has the world been left in the hands of the kings of men. What have they done with their power? They use the people as slaves to fight their bitter wars. They murder and enslave the innocent. They slaughter children. They preside over atrocity. They are demons. They are monsters. They deserve to be destroyed. You must understand the truth of this. This is what the Advent is all about. The coming of the light will reset our world." He gave Aren a stricken look. "Do you not *want* this?"

His words left Aren speechless. How similar they were to the way he had described rogue users—the way he had described his own hatred of Degammon. *Degammon was a monster. He deserved to burn in the fires for what he had done.* The atrocities he had committed were as repugnant as they were terrifying. But how many children had died at the orders of King Rogar, or Great Santhalian. Were they any less guilty simply because it had not been their hands tying the noose or wielding the sword? If Great Santhalian executed only one man each day, it would take less than a month for him to be responsible for more lives than Degammon ever was. Did he not also deserve to be put in the fires? Did everyone who called themselves a king deserve it? Or a Priest? Or a Sister?

Kinraigan watched him closely, a smile broadening. "Yes," he said. "Now you realize the truth. Kings and emperors sit upon thrones built from the skulls of children. They construct their palaces out of the suffering of the people beneath them. They hide behind the mask of religion to obscure their profanity."

Aren thought about the numbers of men and women who had been slaughtered since the beginning of mankind—all the pointless wars, the executions, the genocides. It had to have been a staggering figure. Millions. Hundreds of millions. In the name of Arradan, and of Palantar; and of Olbaran, Amagon, and Halsabad; and of ancient Abumbar and Abbad. It was a never-ending parade of slaughter. It was one long string of massacres, captured on the pages of the Histories he held so dear.

"You must join me, Aren," Kinraigan said. "This is the crucial moment. This is why I struggle as I do. This is the reason I fight—to protect hope. I fight to preserve our future. How rabidly does a man defend his family? How hard would a man fight to save his children? Would he not kill anything that threatened them? A wolf? A bear? Another man? A king? Would he not fight *anything* for them? If there was an obstacle between him and the safety of his family, would he not do all in his power to destroy that obstacle?"

Aren nodded in agreement. He would have done anything to change what happened to Eriana, even if it was his own death. Even if it was to trade her for someone else. Light cascaded around him in thick silence. He had come here to kill Kinraigan. He had been so sure that it was what he wanted to do, but now he was confused. The light distorted his emotions, stretched his memories. What if he was right? Would Aren become the man who allowed his own selfish emotions to destroy the hope of the entire world? The choice left him frozen. Either way, whatever he chose, the consequences were irrevocable. But he no longer understood which choice would be the right one.

"Do you not *want this?*" Kinraigan asked again, passionately.

Aren looked down at his hands, so dark against the pale beauty of the light. "I thought you were a madman."

"And what do you think now?" Kinraigan asked. "Now that you understand?"

"What is the Advent?"

"You mean what am I starting?"

"Tell me what it is."

"People all over the world want to know what it is. I could show you. Here in the light. Take my hand. Stand beside me."

"No. I will never do that."

"Then Advent Lumina will be forever beyond your reach."

"What is it?"

Kinraigan smiled. "There is only one way you will ever know."

"What were you doing out there? That pillar of light, what is it?"

"It is the road to infinity. It is limitless."

"What does the Crown do? How did it make that pillar of light?"

Kinraigan smiled. "Join me and I will tell you everything. Or reject me and lose it all."

Aren gritted his teeth. His hands wanted to reach out and strangle the sorcerer. "You must know that I never will."

"You sound so certain. What if I showed you the secrets of this place?"

"It is a blank place. A place where magick comes from."

"You are only scratching the surface of what the light can do." Kinraigan stared him hard in the eyes, studying him. His hands began to move. His eyes twitched suddenly. "What if I could bring her back to you?"

That stopped Aren cold.

He thought of Eriana. He saw her smile, and her eyes sparkling so beautifully. How she would have loved to see the wonder of the Slipstream. How he wished she was with him, alive and full of joy and curiosity. How he longed to hold her in his arms one more time. His mouth twisted bitterly when he remembered that he could not. "I promised I would kill you if anything happened to her."

"*You* happened to her. You brought her after me. You let her come. That was your choice. *You* killed her. I am the one offering to return her to you. What would you give to hold her again? Join me. That is all you have to do."

Aren's eyes began to fill with tears. He wanted it. He wanted it desperately. The thought of her looking deep into his eyes once more was more seductive than the smoke of malagayne.

"Wouldn't you like me to do this thing for you?" Kinraigan asked. "I would do it gladly for such an ally."

Aren wanted to believe him. He wanted to believe his words so much so that he felt himself *trying* to believe them. To have her again, to have a second chance to be free. It was all he desired in the world. "You can't. It's not possible." But he wanted it to be so much.

"We do not have time for the explanation," Kinraigan said. "Be assured, I *can* do it. I will do it. I swear it. I am Sanadi and I will do this for you if you join with me now." He reached out one hand to Aren.

Aren watched him. He looked down at the open hand. He imagined himself taking it. He imagined becoming Kinraigan's friend, his partner. He imagined Eriana returning to life. He imagined her smiling at him, and holding on to him as she had once done. He lived so many moments in that one fleeting second of time. He saw their life, their home, their children, their struggles and joys.

Aren was ready to let millions die just to see her one more time.

But then he saw something which pulled him out of his trance. He saw shapes of streams joining together, binding, the patterns, the structures. He saw them from *inside* the Slipstream, saw what the little pieces of magick really looked like, as if he was staring out from inside a carnival mirror. *Someone is using. This is what someone in the real world is binding together.* He felt like he could understand what they were, these little shapes. Like reading a sign.

They felt like small blank spheres. And *cylinders!*

Keluwen!

She was still alive. She must have been. No one else would have made those.

By the gods high and low she is still there. She is still fighting.

What am I doing?

His face hardened.

Eriana would never forgive me for choosing her life over what was right. She would hate me. She would look at me with the same expression of horror she had when she saw what Kinraigan had done to that little girl in Cair Tiril.

Kinraigan noticed his grimace. "What is your answer?"

"I just realized how good you are at convincing people to do what you want them to. But I remember what you did. Everything you say is a lie. I remember a little girl from Laman who you *changed.* I remember her because she did *nothing* to you. She did not stand in your way. She was not an obstacle. You did that to her because deep down that is who you are. That is what you do. You hurt people. You assault them and torture them and murder them because you *like* doing it, because beneath all your fancy magick that is all you really are. *I* stop people like you. That is what *I* do. I have done that since I was a child. And do you know what else? I have *always* caught the one that I hunted."

I came here to fight. It is time to fight.

Kinraigan pulled his hand back. "I was hoping that this would turn out differently. There would have been so much we could have accomplished together. I thought you were the one. When we first met and fought side by side against untold armies, you seemed so true. You are a shadow of what you were."

Aren squinted at him. "Who do you think I am?"

Kinraigan stared off into the light. "You were so different then."

He has lost himself to madness. He is gone. There is nothing left of him to reason with. There will be no way to talk him out of using autoentropic resonance. I have to find a way to stop him with force. But how? "There is a reason the Sanadi disappeared," Aren said.

"You should have been the one."

"I am not the one. There is no such thing as the one. The only one I am is the one who is going to kill you. I am a Render Tracer. Where I come from there are three rules about people like you. You are not a god. No one is immortal. And no one *ever* gets away."

Kinraigan's eyes snapped back into focus. He seethed. "No one has ever said no to me the way you have."

He stared with cold rage at Kinraigan. "You are not Sanadi. You are just a man, a man who has to follow certain rules to do what he does. You are just a rogue user."

"I will show you. I am so much more than that."

"I will show you the fires. That is where you belong."

Kinraigan laughed. He threw his head back. He went back into autoentropic resonance. He began to glow. The glow grew brighter. Red hot. White hot. The glow became a shimmer. The shimmer became a beam. The beam became a flare. The flare became the blaze of the sun at the break of day.

Aren staggered. The energy felt like brutal fire, driving nails of pain into his every nerve. He doubled over. The particles of air started to glow. Aren felt heat, cold, light, dark. His skin felt like it was melting and freezing.

He looked down at the Dagger in his hand. He remembered something. Understood something. Suddenly his rage drained away. *The Dagger. The Slipstream.* The Dagger was a tool of the Slipstream. *This is how I opened the door to this place. What can I do now that I am here?* The silver and gold reflected beams of light in all directions, flashing across Kinraigan in whites and yellows. The air grew hot. Steam erupted from the corners.

Kinraigan began to bind streams. Aren watched them come together. They were like strands of string, but also little spinning tetrahedrons, coming close, touching, entwining about one another, combining, bonding into incredible shapes.

Aren stood ten paces from them, but space had no meaning in this place. He reached out. His fingers touched the streams. He plucked one like the string of a harp. It vibrated in colorful drone.

Kinraigan looked up with eyes like spears.

Aren took hold of one of the sorcerer's renders, grasping it in one hand like the branch of a tree. It felt solid and fluid at the same time, a twisted helix. He held it for several moments, ignoring Kinraigan's expressions of fear and anger. Then he pulled it to him as if it was a physical object. He looked at the render in his hand. It shrank away and died. He looked up at Kinraigan.

The sorcerer blinked.

"That was going to be a sphere with an outward force for an explosion in Medion," Aren said tonelessly, as if instructing a child. "You are rendering in the real world."

Kinraigan looked away. He began furiously binding streams, but just as he completed them, Aren reached out again. This time he pulled a lone stream to himself, sliding it out of Kinraigan's render.

"This one is the toughness of a bubble shield." He looked up at Kinraigan. "For you."

Kinraigan's eyes blazed. He grew brighter as he summoned more zero-point-energy into himself. He wove his streams at double-time now, moving his hands frantically to aid his concentration.

Aren reached out again and again. "This one was to be the duration of a pressure field covering the entire city of Arthenorad. This one was meant to accelerate an impulse force to destroy a castle in Olbaran. This one was a velocity. This one was the magnitude of a pressure bubble. This one was the mass of a house. This one was the pressure of a massive crush bubble around an ancient temple in Halsabad. You are trying to destroy the world."

Kinraigan growled like a wolf. He funneled more and more energy into himself, giving him power a thousandfold more that he already possessed. He raced desperately to duplicate the lost streams, his glow hotter than a hundred suns. Aren watched Kinraigan melding the streams into a single, united fabric of will. Aren gazed with wonder at it. It resonated with beautiful music. He heard it, saw it, felt it. His eyes were curious. His expression calm. He gripped the Dagger tightly in his hand.

"You aren't different. You aren't a god."

"You sniveling shit! I am luminous! I am immortal!"

Aren thought of Keluwen, fighting alone, giving everything she had against impossible odds. He looked into Kinraigan's eyes, teeth clenched in hatred. "We break immortals."

Aren reached out with the Dagger. He brought it down over all the render structures. The blade cut through them, splitting them apart, rending the streams from their bonds. Kinraigan stared with a horror he had never known as his magick all came apart before his eyes. Aren felt it splitting. Ripping. Tearing. The Dagger passed through it like water, and came to rest at his side.

Then came an explosion that whipped his face like a hurricane. A catastrophic sound erupted in his ears, like a hundred clashing swords, a hundred splitting stones, and a hundred peals of thunder all at once. Boiling fire lapped against his skin, but he did not burn. Rays of unleashed light pounded his eyes, but he was not blinded.

Aren blinked. The white light was gone. The veils were gone. He stood upon the platform in the middle of Devron's Altar. Kinraigan was flying away from him and spinning in the air, as if thrown by a catapult. The sorcerer landed on his stomach upon the platform, sliding to a stop.

The sorcerer pulled himself to his hands and knees. His eyes were sunken in their sockets, his face charred and blackened. His mouth foamed with rabid fury. "Fool!" he screamed. "You cannot stop this! You are already dead. You are all dead. I will destroy it all. Everything! Everyone! All dead. All gone. You will not change. You would not begin. And so you will end instead."

He dipped into the Slipstream. He was vibrating with radiance, full to the brim with zero-point-energy.

Aren tried to wave the Dagger, tried to make it do something. It did nothing. He might as well have been waving a bit of straw.

Aren could see the sphere Kinraigan was now rendering. It was a crush bubble, located around Aren, with as much pressure as the weight of a city pressing down on every inch of his body. There would be no surviving it. There would be no controlling it. Pressure of that magnitude would cause artificial depressurization near it. It would implode the caves. It would flatten him to nothing, and then collapse the tunnels, burying them all.

Maybe this is how it was supposed to be. Maybe this is how we beat you.

Yes. Do it. Kill me and yourself with me.

Go ahead. Take it. You have already taken everything else from me.

Take the last thing.

Take life.

60

When Never Meets Forever

REIDOS LOOKED UP AT the sky. Clouds dangled heavy above him, matted grey on white, beautiful. He saw the ruins in his periphery. He felt the bricks with his hand. They were rough, and the wetness made them feel like clay.

He inhaled. No pain. He tried to move his right arm. Pain.

He pulled his other arm away from the wall, and put it to his shoulder. He felt the shaft of a crossbow bolt protruding from his skin. It passed underneath the joint, but he knew it had torn the muscle. He tried to pull it out, but the slightest tugging sent slivers of pain striking out in all directions, making him gasp. His eyes swam in his head when he sat up. He felt the wetness of blood on his fingers when he touched the base of his skull. He looked around for his bow. Gone.

He knew he lost it over the edge of the wall he was using for cover. He was only inches away from it, and yet impossibly far. He would have to lean over the wall, snatch up the bow, and retreat back over, all before being struck by another bolt. Balthoren was surely sitting out there, waiting for him to move. He guessed that his adversary had already displaced to a new location. That is what Reidos would have done.

He knew he would be a sitting duck if he went for the bow, but without it, Balthoren could walk right up to him and kill him from five feet away. That made his decision.

It was going to be awkward. Reidos couldn't use his right arm to push off with once he held the bow in his left. That would add a precious second to the time it would take—more than enough for Balthoren to exploit. If he tried to grab it and pull back over the wall, he would earn a bolt in the neck.

He scanned the terrain for likely hiding places. They were everywhere. Balthoren always fired at the first sign of motion, but an unexpected movement *could* make him fire early. It had worked once already.

Reidos decided to do something unexpected. He leaned up over the wall. Saw movement in the corner of his eye. He pitched forward over the wall toward Balthoren, kicking hard with both legs. Locked one hand around the bow. Landed on his shoulder. Rolled. A bolt smacked the stones behind him just above his face.

It worked. He had the bow. Now though, he had another problem. He was lying flat on his back. Out in the open. An easy target. Balthoren was moving to the left, toward the flapping sheets of cloth, reloading as he ran.

Reidos rolled onto his knees. Moved left. The bolt in his shoulder felt like it was reacting inside him to every step he took. He scampered back to the mound of rubble, and dropped down behind it. Balthoren saw him. Stopped moving. Fired. Reidos ducked. The shot missed, but Balthoren knew where he was.

Reidos kept moving. He stayed low to the ground. The pain in his shoulder made him grind his teeth. He looked over the mound. He caught a flash of motion. Saw Balthoren vanish within the forest of billowing cloth.

Reidos stood straight. He moved around the mound, stopping to listen after each step. He heard nothing but the breeze carrying raindrops to the ground. He needed to think.

What does Balthoren expect me to do? He must know he hit me. He thinks I'll hole up behind the cover and wait for him. Why would he move away into the cloths? He must be counting on me staying put. Otherwise he would have charged me. Forced me to take lesser cover. He thinks I can hurt him. Balthoren would expect him to advance around to get a better position to view the area, while he was masked by the cloth. *He's trying to circle me again.*

Reidos decided to do the last thing Balthoren would expect—walk directly into the forest of billowing canvass.

He stalked forward until he was enveloped by it. He took step after step, stopping and scanning at each instance, moving closer and closer to where he last saw Balthoren.

He heard something. Thought it might be a footstep. He froze. He looked to the right. He noticed a flash of dark color as the wind whipped up the sheets. His head turn back to the left, but it was gone.

He pulled a single arrow from the quiver with his bow hand. He held it in position against the bow with that same hand. He stepped forward once more. He listened to the wind. He took a step. Scanned the cloths. Took a step. Listened. Stepped. Listened. Stepped. Listened.

He found himself directly in the center of the billowing sheets. The wind whipped them like banners. He was out in the open. No good cover to hide behind. He felt vulnerable from all directions.

He glanced to his right.

What? By the gods high and low.

Before him, a dozen strides away, was Balthoren. He was stalking in another direction, taking a path perfectly perpendicular to Reidos', Balthoren had his back to him, stepping, listening, stepping, listening—just as he was.

Reidos raised the bow and arrow together in his left hand. He bent his right elbow with ease, but when he tried to move his hand across his chest to take hold of the string, the pain from the bolt lanced down the length of his arm.

He forced himself through the motion. His teeth clamped shut. He held his breath. He willed his fingers to clench about the bowstring. Then he pulled back on it.

He drew one inch at a time, but every pull shook him ten times worse than the last. He felt the bolt moving around and within his muscles as he flexed, and it was agony. He wanted to scream, to roar the air back out of his lungs, to release his arm from the torture. He pulled the final distance. The string squeaked as it stretched.

Balthoren froze.

Reidos was still, like the constellation of the hunter.

Balthoren turned.

Reidos released the arrow.

Balthoren's eyes came around.

Reidos dropped the bow.

His right arm fell to his side. The slackness was rapture. He felt the pain wash away. He stared dreamily as his arrow exploded into Balthoren's neck. He sighed as blood sprayed across the rocks. He nearly grinned as bones were shaken from their homes in Balthoren's spine.

Balthoren's eyes bulged. His crossbow fired into the rocks at his feet. His finger continued to depress the trigger several times as his body fell and hit the ground. All Reidos could think about was the sweet release from the pain.

****

Fainen's mind was blank. A black windless room. No distraction. He watched casually as Redscar's enormous foot came down at him. He reached out to his sides as if he could see with his fingertips. Stretched. Found *Glimmer*. Whipped it up, and let the giant step through it like a nail in a board. He took no satisfaction in the giant's roar of suffering. He felt no joy as the blade passed up and out the top of the crimson foot. His mind was blank.

Redscar stumbled away and tipped over into the wall. The ground shook when he dropped. Fainen's stare was constant, his eyes searching the giant for weak points.

Fainen darted left and right until he reached the kneeling titan. Redscar swung with a fist. Fainen dodged. Speared with his sword. Redscar caught his forearm in a titan grip. Lifted. Flipped Fainen into the air. He flailed and slammed into the ground like a rag doll. His sword fell away again.

Through it all, his mind was clear like glass.

Redscar left him lying there, and lumbered over to retrieve his own weapon.

Fainen rolled onto his stomach, and heaved himself up despite his battered hip and shoulder. He wobbled on a half-numb leg. Redscar was already turning to face him, holding the battle-axe locked in a fist.

Fainen had no blade. *Glimmer* was away from him, lying on the floor, too close to the advancing titan, and so Fainen reached over his shoulders, and slid the two slender halves of Hayles' quarterstaff out of the straps. Each was three feet in length, each sharpened at one end into spears. The look in Redscar's eyes told Fainen that he remembered them—the weapon of the man who had taken him over the cliff in Medion.

Redscar charged. Fainen flew at him with his arms outstretched like a hawk's wings. The giant could not bring his weapon to bear in time, and Fainen hit him across the face with both halves, ducked down, put his foot on Redscar's thigh for balance, and stabbed one of the sharpened ends into the giant's ribs. But as he stabbed, his foot slipped from its perch, and shot away from him. He fell face-first onto the giant's thigh, and then flopped onto his back on the floor.

He somehow maintained his grip on the broken pieces of the staff, and rolled away from the falling axe. It slammed down behind his back, digging a trench into the floor.

Fainen kicked at Redscar's elbow. The giant left the axe sticking in the ground, and grabbed Fainen's shirt and cloak, lifted him, and rocked him against the wall.

Fainen felt a rib snap in his side. Pain roared into his black windless room. He felt his sight draining away. The pain set fire to his silent concentration.

With his last available thought, he stabbed through Redscar's forearm with the sharp point of one half of the split staff. Redscar released him, and he crumpled to the ground.

Fainen forced himself to stand. He nearly toppled over. *Down* seemed to be seven different directions at once. He staggered to the right. Looked up. Saw the battle-axe coming. Half-dodged, half-fell out of the way.

Redscar's fist shot out. Fainen moved. Misjudged. Took half the blow on his left shoulder. His feet left the ground, and he was catapulted back. He came to rest face down on the stone floor. There was so much pain.

He stood again. Saw the axe swing. Dodged. Stumbled. Fell.

Redscar attempted to step on him. Fainen rolled left. Redscar slammed a hand down on him. Fainen leapt forward. Tucked. Rolled. Misjudged again. Knocked his shoulder on the ground. He flopped awkwardly to one side. Stood. Moved against the wall. Saw a kick coming. Slid out of the way. Redscar brought the axe down with both hands. It split into the wall, caught, frozen in stone.

Fainen slammed shut the door of his black windless room.

I am Sarenwalker.

He left the pain outside that door.

Redscar yanked with both arms, and ripped the axe out of the wall.

Fainen was already lunging underneath Redscar's arms.

I am thought made action.

As the titan raised the battle-axe over his head, Fainen was already climbing up his body.

I fear neither death nor pain.

Fainen kicked off one crimson thigh, then the other, planted his feet, and looked in the giant's eyes.

I possess no emotion, only perfection.

He drove both sharpened halves of the quarterstaff deep into Redscar's neck. Pushing. Hitting arteries.

I am Sarenwalker.

Redscar's eyes bulged. He dropped the axe. His massive hands grabbed ineffectually at his face, as the blood pumped out of his neck, spraying across Fainen's cloak and onto the two severed halves of Hayles' broken staff.

Redscar's eyes rolled back in their sockets. He slumped to the floor and was still, Fainen straddling his body until the last flush of blood ran out of him.

Only then did Fainen allow himself a single thought of his own.

It is fitting that I kill you with these.

****

Keluwen crawled away from the altar.

Kinraigan's people were coming behind her. She could hear their steps. She could hear one of them had a limp, scraping the edge of one foot along the ground. They were there. They were everywhere.

They did not react with urgency. She could barely crawl. They had all the time in the world to kill her.

But then a blinding white light flashed in her eyes. The ground shivered. Keluwen looked over her shoulder. She saw two men emerge from the light, on the platform beside the dais, Aren and Kinraigan.

They stared at each other the way a madman stares in the mirror.

Where did you go? she wondered. *What happened to you in the light?*

She looked at Aren. His face was drawn, his shoulders sagging. *He is defenseless.* All he had was a little knife in his hand. That was useless against a normal user. Against Kinraigan it was ludicrous.

She tried to spit blood but it was like her mouth was full of dust. She raised her hand and pointed two fingers at Kinraigan. *You don't get to kill him.* She summoned the streams of direction and size and shape, but the velocity and mass she wished to bind to them sat out of reach.

She was too weak. When she looked into the Slipstream her core limit was staring uselessly back at her. She reached for a velocity three degrees slower, and a mass half of the first try. Tears squeezed out of her eyes. She couldn't do it. She couldn't do anything. For the third time he was making her watch it.

I hate you. I hate you and curse you and hope to kill and burn you.

She reached for the lowest velocity stream she had ever learned, and the lowest mass. She almost just barely convinced them to bind together, but they fell apart. She felt the streams tugging, bending, wanting to come to her, but she did not have the strength. She knew it now. She had nothing left. Nothing but despair. Pain and tears. Alone.

She turned away, and sank to her belly, her head in her hands. She could not watch it. Not another one. A flash of memory burned through the backs of her eyelids. *Orrinas.* She could not bring herself to see it again.

Her eyes passed over the causeway behind her. She saw the little boy still there. On his knees. Not afraid.

Her eyes met the boy's.

He had seemed so scared before. But now he smiled. His face looked so serene. His eyes were like pages in a book. She read kindness, generosity, courage, and strength on the pages.

He stood and ran toward her.

She dragged herself down the causeway, away from Kinraigan, toward the boy. She reached her one good arm out to him. Kinraigan's people ran past her. They lunged for him, hands reaching. She swung her arm to trip them up.

One fell off the causeway and screamed. More hands grabbed her from behind, pulling her by her clothes and by her ankles, back toward the platform.

Hands tripped the boy up and he fell. One of the followers lunged on their belly after him. Another tried to grab him, but slipped, fell. The boy squirmed between them, crawling on his hands and knees toward Keluwen, reaching out.

They fought so hard to keep her away from him. *Why?*

She reached for the boy. Just one touch. Just because they wanted to keep them apart.

The men grabbed her, squeezed her, tore at her burned flesh, pulling on her ankles, trying to drag her away. Their fingernails were knives against her skin. She bucked and kicked and twisted. Her body screamed with pain. She wept. She cried out. She shivered and shook. Thoughts vanished, her mind subsumed by delirium.

She looked at the little boy, but it was Orrinas she saw in his eyes, and she wept rivers down the blood on her face, and she reached.

You don't keep us apart.

You can't keep us apart.

This is the last thing I'll do.

I will reach my love one last time. I will touch his skin. I will see his eyes and feel his heart.

After that you can kill me and I won't care.

Keluwen stretched out her arm, reaching with her fingers, straining.

The boy reached. A man and a woman in old coats fell atop him, grabbing him with their hands, trying to pull him away.

A woman dropped her knee onto the boy's back, pinning him down. She had a knife in her teeth. She dropped it into her hands and smiled gap-toothed. Another man kneeled beside her, cleaver raised over his head. A third stood beside him, tall, in a rich man's coat, with a rich man's sword turned down. All three made to drive their sharp blades into the boy's back.

No! You don't take him! You don't take my Orrinas!

Their arms began to move.

But Keluwen saw something behind them. A fast moving shape. Black as night. She thought it was an ebon-shroud at first, but it wasn't. Ebon-shrouds did not smile. It was Aren's friend. The one they called Corrin.

He flew along the causeway so fast the three cultists hovering over the boy only barely began to turn their heads to look. By then, Corrin dropped to his knees, sliding the final distance to them. He held a black sword in his hands, shimmering like liquid obsidian.

The three blades stabbed toward the boy.

There would not be time for Corrin to make more than one strike.

Corrin's sword slipped into the woman's belly, and out her back, pushed to the hilt. Her eyes bulged, her knife dropped. His sword continued in one fluid motion, a single stab sliding through her, puncturing the next man in the ribs and popping out his back in turn, before sliding into the last man.

Keluwen didn't think the stab was going to take all three.

But the tip of the blade just barely slid to a stop at exactly the proper angle, piercing one inch into the artery in the rich man's throat. He dropped his rich man's sword beside the cleaver and the knife, and for one brief moment all three remained upright, frozen on the blade in Corrin's hand. The light of the fires burned them into silhouettes in Keluwen's eyes.

She turned to face Corrin.

He looked directly into her eyes, mere inches apart, breaths heaving, holding the three skewered people like meat on a stick. "I finally found the fucking causeway," he said. Then the bodies fell, yanking the sword out of his hands as they went.

One of the cultists pulling on Keluwen's ankles released her and lunged over her at the boy, hands scrambling on stone, fingers reaching for one of the fallen blades.

Keluwen tried to roll over to face him, but the pain made her shudder.

She looked up at Corrin. He seemed startled, kneeling where he came to rest after his slide. But then he glanced down, saw something, and picked it up.

"Oh," he said. "This is very convenient for me." A green steel greatsword materialized in his hands.

Where in all hells did that come from?

Corrin swung it awkwardly with a twist of the waist, its size far too large for him. He cleaved the cultist open from belly to shoulder anyway, spilling his insides out.

"Don't worry," Corrin told her. "I always have a weapon."

Keluwen nearly laughed out loud. But the pain was too much for her body to release a sound.

She shuddered and groaned. But she did not give up. Would never give up. She knew what was happening behind her. She could feel it without looking at it. She could feel it in the ripples of the Slipstream and she *knew*.

Kinraigan began to render behind her. Not a blank impulse. No, not that. He was playing his favorite card. After all his hiding, employing his cultists to do his darkwork, or using tiny blank impulses to obscure his profile from Render Tracers all across the continent, here he was finally free to use his favorites. These were pressure streams. These were what he had used to kill Rin, and Satianya, and Dromergo. This was the same thing he had done to Paladan. Crushed him. Tortured him until he died. He no longer had to hide them. He was no longer interdicted. He could do as he wished.

He was rendering a crush bubble around Aren.

Keluwen looked down.

The boy was right there. His smile grew even brighter now that Corrin was beside him. He reached out one little hand. From that hand he stretched out one little finger.

Keluwen reached. She did not even know why.

I always have a weapon.

The boy touched her fingertip.

Keluwen felt a jolt, like a fist punching her from the inside out. And suddenly she was full. Energy poured into her, spilling into every cavity, infusing every tissue, permeating her bones, entering and filling the spaces between every cell of her body.

She rose to her feet. She felt no pain. She moved her arms and the world tilted. She reached into the light of the Slipstream and found streams of mass and velocity she had never dreamed of ever being able to touch. With so much power inside her, the streams were fighting with each other to get to her.

That is why you are special.

Kinraigan began turning to look at her.

There were hands touching her. She rendered spheres without even looking. The hands disappeared. She pointed at every single one of his insane, murderous cultists and killed them. Her spheres flew so fast she did not even see the work they did.

She killed them all in an instant.

By the time Kinraigan's face completed its turn, all of his people were dead. He dropped the streams he had been binding to kill Aren. He focused all his attention on her.

"Now you have to look at me," she said.

He glared at her, then at Aren, then at Corrin, and back again. "Pride, wrath, sorrow—the children of desire. It can't be. You?" His mouth opened and closed. It looked like he was screaming at her but there was no sound. He stared into her eyes, trying to crush her with his gaze. To dominate her. To make her afraid. To make her small.

"You will not make me shiver," she said. "You will not make me weep. My tears are all gone. My soul is dry. You have taken everything. Now I take it back."

Kinraigan raised spherical shields the instant he felt her touch the Slipstream, fifty layers thick, all of them stronger than steel.

Keluwen pointed at him. Power blossomed from her body. She rendered spheres. More powerful than she ever dreamed she could make.

They flew through the air faster than sound. They struck his shields. They pushed in. They broke through, shattering holes through layer after layer.

She watched his face. She watched his expression turn to fear and she smiled.

Her spheres penetrated each of his shields, barely slowing. They punched through the innermost ones. He summoned more, but Keluwen's spheres tore through them as well.

The first one passed just over his shoulder.

The second clipped his arm, gnawing a chunk of flesh away, leaving his elbow attached by bone and fibers.

The third struck his leg, just above the knee. It exploded in a rattle of shredded muscle and chips of bone.

The fourth struck his arm at the shoulder. It blasted its way through the joint, obliterating every tendon, every fiber, every nerve. His arm fell away from him, leaving nothing there, not even a sleeve to show what once had been.

His shields vanished. He screamed and screamed. He shuddered and groaned. He begged invisible gods. He cried.

Keluwen began to smile.

I have finally killed you.

He toppled to the floor, his body landing within the vortex of white light around the altar. He crawled across the platform with one arm, kicking with one foot, dragging his ruined leg behind him like an ox pulling a wagon, a trail of blood behind. He reached the altar and slowly pulled himself up until he sat leaning against it, steadying himself with his good hand.

Keluwen peppered him with blank impulses, but the spinning vortex of light above the Crown diverted everything she sent, altering their paths. Even with the incredible power aching to escape from her, she could not get to him.

Kinraigan reached one hand up and took the Crown. He then slumped forward, blood spilling everywhere, holding the Crown with his only hand, hugging it to his body, tapping into its power. "Insect. Weak. Greedy. Foolish. Parasite." He spoke in a whisper, his voice already spent on screams.

The ground began to vibrate.

"You shouldn't have done that," Kinraigan said. "You have ruined it all. You have ruined the future. You have ruined everything." He raised the Crown above his head, looking up through it at the ceiling. Power began channeling through it like a magnifying lens. The altar grew hot beneath him. The ceiling turned molten above him, glowing orange like warm coals.

"All we have done is show you what you really are," Aren said.

Kinraigan's eyes darted to meet his, confused. "You have met him? You know about *Janos?*"

"I don't know what you're talking about." Aren said. "Who the fuck is Janos?"

"No, of course you don't. How could you? He would not have shown it to someone like you." His eyes softened. He smiled.

The blood drained from Keluwen's face. *He is lost in madness. He still thinks he can win.*

Kinraigan looked away and cackled. "Let me show you something," he said. "I will show you the kind of things I have seen. I will show you your future." The spiral of light cracked open, as if the light itself was linen tearing. Space seemed to split open, and bright energy poured through the gaping wound. "There is more than just light in there," he said. "So much more." Something began to emerge, as if crawling out from behind reality, clawing its way into the world. "Don't you want to see what I have to show you?"

"He's going to do it again," Aren said. "He thinks he's the hero. He's going to use autoentropic resonance to kill us all. And the world with us. And this time he has the Crown in his hand."

Kinraigan smiled. He began to funnel energy into himself once more.

Keluwen wept.

She sent a thousand blank impulses at him. None of them touched him. The light protected him from everything.

You can't get away with it again.

But he had.

****

Aren watched the universe rip open around the pillar of light. He watched the tear split wide. Something was pushing against it, forcing it apart, trying to birth itself through the opening.

Then he saw Keluwen. She seemed to glow, like she had swallowed a golden sunset. She stepped between them. She raised her arms and released an unrelenting wave of spheres, more than Aren had ever seen at once, even more than Kinraigan himself. She launched hypercharged blank impulses at Kinraigan, but they only spun out and rotated in strange orbits around the pillar of light. Nothing made it through.

Kinraigan noticed and smiled. "You can't stop me," he said. He lifted the Crown with both hands. "Magick cannot break through this. I am going to make myself Sanadi now. While you watch. I am Caldannon. And I am going to save the world from *you*. I won. I am victorious. I am infinite. You are extinguished. I am going to live. And you are going to die. I am going to watch. I am going to smile."

Aren knew he may have only been a few moments away from watching the whole universe be rewritten to the designs of a madman.

Kinraigan was weak. He likely couldn't put a two-dimensional shield together. But he was right. There was no way to get a blank impulse in him with the vortex deflecting every bit of magick. No render was ever getting through that. *I need something powerful enough to break through that pillar of light.*

Keluwen was running on borrowed time. Already she was slowing, power overwhelming her body. She dropped to one knee.

Aren looked down at the Dagger in his hand. *Still there.* He tried to make its magick work, but nothing happened. He focused his mind and will on the power of the Sephor, but nothing happened. No white light. No secret answer.

What could he do? Even now, broken and ruined, bleeding, maybe dying, Kinraigan could still wipe Aren off the face of the earth in an instant with his magick.

The words of Sarker were in his head. *What else? What are you forgetting? What is the simplest solution with the tools at your disposal?*

Aren fought back fear, pushed away the hate, waded through sorrow. He emptied his mind.

The simplest solution.

If Keluwen's magick couldn't work in the pillar of light. Then neither could his.

Aren's eyes went wide.

Kinraigan wants us to think he is safe. No magick can touch him. Nothing could pass into the pillar of light. But *he* did.

And so can I.

He is impervious to magick in there.

I have no magick. I need no magick.

Against me he is defenseless.

Sometimes a knife is just a knife.

Aren lunged at Kinraigan. He passed through the pillar of light. He felt his skin steam and his eyes burn. He wielded the Dagger through air, then robes, then flesh. He pressed it home to the hilt in Kinraigan's body, piercing his heart, flooding the stones at his feet with blood.

Kinraigan's eyes widened. He dropped the Crown and it bounced off the altar and rolled across the floor. He placed his hands on Aren's chest as if greeting a long lost friend. His face bent from confusion to nothingness. His eyes rolled back in his head, and he fell.

No one is immortal.

There was a flash like a bursting bubble of light, expanding outward from Kinraigan's body like an echo of lightning.

Kinraigan was dead. The pillar of light vanished.

The Crown rolled to a stop at his feet. Aren bent down and picked it up with the end of the Dagger.

Silence reigned beneath many-layered clouds of glittering color.

Aren looked at Tanashri. The Saderan sat on the ramp, holding herself up gracefully with one arm. Her lips gave a barely perceptible smile.

Beside her sat Inrianne, her white robes stained brown and red, frayed like windblown cloth amid a field of razor blades. Her golden mane was clumped and knotted. Her body shivered. Her expression was blank.

Duran stood tall and unafraid beside Redevir the Rover.

Hodo sat cross-legged on the ramp, arranging and rearranging the supplies in his rucksack. He moved things back and forth and all around, never quite able to get it the way he wanted it to be, unwilling to look up from his task.

Tarykthies was gone.

Mardin crawled through the hole and walked down the causeway, eyes wide, knuckles shaking, tunic matted and torn. He seemed both relieved and horrified. Aren did not know what happened to him after the Ghiroergan chased him away, but Leucas was no longer with him.

He saw Corrin standing beside Hallan, appearing simultaneously relieved and disappointed to see that the fighting was over. He smiled. "I see you are well, *Lord* Aren."

Aren looked out over the chamber. He saw the afterglow shining and dancing in a polychromatic effulgence. He did not understand how he could see it with his own eyes. He did not understand what was happening to him, but he smiled. The hunt was over. The trace was complete. The user was destroyed. He would never hurt anyone ever again.

No one ever gets away.

He fell to his knees, overcome by joy and sorrow, grief and relief. He held the Crown in one hand like a child's toy, the Dagger in the other like a mere utensil. The bittersweet victory was like no victory at all. It tasted worse that the ash and dirt in his mouth. It smelled worse the sulfur and oil saturating the air.

He looked at Keluwen, slumped over beside the altar, dirt on her cheeks, blood on her chin. She was broken and bleeding, half-burned, ghost white, and still.

But she smiled. She looked him in the eyes and she smiled.

He smiled, too. He nodded to her.

She nodded back. "We break immortals," she whispered.

****

Aren leaned over Keluwen. He held her up in his lap so she could lean over to spit blood as she needed to, which was frequently. Her face was turning white. Her body shook. She had dust matted in her hair, and blood and mud streaked through her clothes.

"Your gloves," Aren said. "They aren't on."

"I don't need them anymore. I'm not going to make it. I know it. You know it, too."

"You can't know that. You're not bleeding."

"I am inside. My heart is beating wrong. I am dying and the sun sets in the west, Aren. Neither of these things you can change."

"Why are you so calm?"

"We came to fight," she said. "We fought."

"I wish it could have been different."

"It could only ever have been this way." She leaned over to spit. "I feel like a part of me always knew that this is the only way I would ever have peace."

"We stopped him though," he said.

"Yes, we did."

"How many lives do you think we saved? A hundred thousand? A million? Ten million?"

"More."

"I'm still not sure whether I would trade all of them for her," he said, looking at the ground.

"I know I *would* trade them," she said. "But Orrinas wouldn't let me." She laughed, groaned.

"I feel like I don't even know how much I miss her yet. Every moment with her made me better. When I think about her, I feel like she will be right outside waiting for me. Smiling and ready for whatever comes. But I know she isn't. It doesn't seem real. But I know it will soon."

"I know," Keluwen said.

"I'm afraid."

"I know." She paused. "When I saw you with her, when she went, I thought it was so unfair that you got to say your endwords when I didn't. But now I know I wouldn't have been able to stand up ever again after if I had."

He nodded. "She gave me a gift. That's what she would say. That every step I take will make her gift greater. But I don't know if I can. I'm afraid of tomorrow. Tomorrow it will be real. If I ever sleep again, I don't know what the sunrise will bring."

"Pain. It will bring pain. Better to know that now. Better to face it. There is no way to hide from it. I am sorry for what you lost."

"And I you."

"I would say to you that it will get better, but it won't. Not until you die. Like me."

"I know."

"You have to promise me, Aren. You have to promise me you won't let anyone else do this. Don't let anyone else find these tools, learn these powers. Don't let anyone else end up like us. Find them before they do. Stop them before they ascend."

"I will."

"Promise me."

"I promise you."

She looked away and laughed. Winced. Laughed again.

"What is it?"

"No one will ever know," she said. "No one will ever know any of this about me. About what we did here. I never thought of it before. The only place in the whole world where my name is written down is in the lists of the punishment record of the thief catchers. If my firstfather ever went looking for my name that is all he would ever find. That is all I will ever be."

"I will tell your story," Aren said. "I will see that you are in the Histories. Somehow."

"I would thank you even if all you do is try. I never had a chance to tell him I was sorry. All these years."

"I will tell your firstfather."

She paused. "I always told my husband that I didn't love him when I married him, but that I love him now." She winced, fighting back the pain. "Well, I was not your friend when we first met, Aren. But I am your friend now."

"I'm yours," he said. "I probably was sooner than you thought."

"No, I knew when." She smiled. "You are *my kind*, Aren. I will talk to Belleron for you."

"Belleron?"

"He is my god. I will ask him to give you strength and speed and luck all three." Her skin grew three shades paler in the blink of an eye. "I think I'm going. I never thought I would see it coming."

Aren's eyes welled up. "I didn't want to lose everyone."

"For every one you lose will be one you find. Every tomorrow has a sunrise. Tomorrow is nothing but a new day, where everything starts again."

Aren nodded, looking at the ground, tears in the corners of his eyes.

Keluwen glanced up at Hodo. "You did such a good job, Hodo. You always did. Orrinas did not tell you enough. You did a good job."

Hodo was crying too hard to reply. All he could do was smile and nod through the tears.

"Forever goodbye, Hodo."

Hodo rocked gently back and forth. He did not speak, but the way she smiled at him said she heard him anyway.

She coughed. Cleared her throat. Closed her eyes a long time. Then opened them. Looked up above Aren. Then back to him. "Forever goodbye, Aren."

"Forever goodbye, Keluwen."

"I'll see you again when never meets forever," she said.

Aren held her hand for eleven minutes, as she closed her eyes and opened them, shivered and was still, groaned and was silent, was alive and then finally not.

She slipped gently and quietly into the last sleep.

Keluwen was gone.

Epilogue

AREN LOOKED OUT OVER the snow-covered vistas of Coralis. Arradan looked so different here. So new. So normal. He stood on the balcony with his wool coat pulled tight. The wind was not biting at least. A cotton cap provided enough warmth for his head, and a brand new pair of leather gloves graced his hands.

He gazed at the endless snow over the ground and the rooftops. He looked past the faces that tried to climb into his periphery. Faces of lost friends, loves and pains, and unknown enemies. As long as he kept his eyes open, he could prevent them from manifesting clearly. His breath misted and helped to cover them.

He heard ponderous steps behind him. Redevir was awake. The Rover walked casually beside him, and placed one hand on the balustrade.

Aren did not turn to face him. He looked on a long while before speaking. "What now, Redevir?"

"For us?" Redevir shrugged. "We go south. That is where Tathred Mallios will be, where we begin our search for the next Sephor."

"Where were you, Redevir? Where did you go in Devron's Altar? I didn't see you."

"The time is right. We have to stay ahead of everyone else. They will know it is real. Better not to lounge around. Put some distance between us and this place. "

He knew Redevir was changing the subject, and Aren let him. He released a sigh. "It will be good to move on. Too many memories. I need to get away from them."

"Hmmm," Redevir mulled it over. "We're halfway into winter. Down south it will be warm. Fresh. Better weather makes better memories."

Aren shivered, but not because of the cold. He didn't care about new memories, as long as the old ones left him alone. He saw Eriana's face when he closed his eyes, and Keluwen's face when he opened them. He feared he would never be able to get over the one, and would never be able to live up to the other.

The quest was solitary in his mind now. It was all he had left. The Sephors were strong medicine. He could forget for just a while if only he could turn his attention to a mission—finding them, stopping everyone else from doing what the madman had done. He needed something to pursue. He needed something to trace.

He glanced at Redevir. He could see the pale resonance on Redevir's shoulder, where Tanashri had touched him after using magick. It flickered like a dull blue haze. He had yet to tell him about what he could see. He wondered if he could ever tell anyone that he could see what should have been invisible.

I can see what no one else can see.

It was impossible. It was absurd. It was true.

"They will be coming for us," Aren said. "Won't they? People like us. People worse than us. People like him."

"Yes. What we have, what we are looking for. There will be more of them."

Aren nodded. He scanned back across the winter city. The snow made everything beautiful. It hid the darkness and the shadows and the dirt and the rust. It was a powdery white veil to mask the ugly truth. It looked just like powdered malagayne.

He tapped the pouch at his waist, nearly empty. He smiled. South. That would be good. He knew he could convince Redevir to stop in Palatora. He knew a dealer in Palatora. It would be the easiest way to find more malagayne.

****

Corrin swallowed a great gulp of ale, and slammed his mug on the table. Reidos gave a start from his prone position. Corrin wiped his lips with his sleeve, and glanced at the slender, black blade leaning against his chair. It was a fitting prize with which he could begin a new collection. He wanted to buy more knives already. He felt an itching sensation, goading him to bring more raw steel into his possession. He rolled his head around on his neck, counting the cracks and pops.

"One or two more than last year," Reidos said.

"I don't remember you being there to count," Corrin said. "But you're right." He waved drunkenly.

"I have a question for you," Reidos said. "What are we going to do now?"

Corrin leaned back in his chair, enjoying the soft cushions. He swiveled his head to face Reidos. "We can get out of here. Go back to Amagon."

Reidos looked at him as though he expected more of a response. "That's it? No plan?"

Corrin thought for a moment. "What else should we do? What should we plan for?"

Reidos pointed at the sleeping lump on the sofa that was Hallan.

"He's coming with us," Corrin said. "And that other fellow."

"Mardin?" Reidos was surprised. "I thought his whining annoyed you."

"I've grown to like it," Corrin said. He became suddenly stern. "Don't tell him that though." He waved his finger at Reidos as if warning a child.

"And what if someone else comes for Hallan?"

"To kill him?" Corrin opened his eyes wide. Doing so hurt badly. He didn't think so much pain could come from focusing. "They'll be looking in the north. They won't think he'll be safe down in good old Amagon."

"It doesn't seem to matter where he is," Reidos pointed out. "Or where we are. What do we do about that?"

"We can keep moving if you want. Enjoy another little adventure."

"We don't have a plan. We don't have a weapon to fight what's coming."

"I am Corrin," Corrin said. "Corrin always has a weapon. You can ask Apple-Sauces if you want."

Reidos rolled his eyes, but he couldn't stifle a laugh. "To Amagon then." He raised his cup.

"To Amagon," Corrin repeated. He clinked the cups together. "To Amagon."

****

You stinking shits cost me everything, Margol thought.

The Andristi had been more than happy to speed Margol's return to Amagon after what had happened to the others upon the Fields of Syn. They brought him to Sedonia on their fastest horses. They gave him gold to find passage with caravan masters back to Vithos to face the Lord Protector.

I had to face Aldarion with such a failure at my feet. You know that, don't you, Aren? Don't you Redevir? You know that. You know.

Margol could hardly wait to wrap his hands around Redevir's throat. How good it would feel to snap the bones of his spine, one by one. He held onto the feeling, held onto his hatred for the filthy Rover who had blundered in at the last moment to steal the goal from his very hands.

The Dagger gone. Months on the path, and all for nothing. Ruined in the last critical moments. *Ruined by the Rover.* The one thing that could have redeemed Margol for the catastrophe atop Mas Morrin had slipped from his fingers. And now instead of setting things right, he had now presided over two failures.

He would not survive a third. He had this one last chance, and he would lead one last hunt for the men who had destroyed him. And this time he would not be alone.

You will all pay for trying to ruin me.

The anger sat in his stomach, building up through his nerves to the top of his head. He put a hand to the hilt of his sword and squeezed.

You think running will save you? You think distance will keep me from reaching you?

I am strong.

I can keep up with you easily.

I will see you soon.

****

It was midnight, and Belaeriel was with a man. She felt his weight on top of her. A crushing weight, pressing her into the bed. He kissed drunkenly at her neck, and groped clumsily at her breasts. His body radiated heat into her, but he moved stiffly, joltingly, mechanically. Belaeriel slid fluidly beneath him, received his energy, became slippery with sweat. The man's body heaved and shook, and he surged into her. Belaeriel took it into herself like ecstatic fire.

The man shuddered, and then was still. Belaeriel rolled him off of her. She rose and stood naked, examining herself in the mirror. The glistening of her own pale skin brought a smile to her face. She raised her arms over her head, offering herself to her own reflection. She ran her fingertips down her sides all the way to her hips. She moaned lightly, and shook her black curls.

She felt powerful, elastic, and energized. Her bed partner lay still on the silken sheets. She took what monies she could find among his belongings. He had been a wealthy man, and his coinpurse was heavy and bulging with gold.

Belaeriel glanced to the corner of the room. Murie stood there silently, eyes gleaming. Belaeriel gave a start, but quickly regained her poise. "I told you to wait in the other room, child." Her tone was chastising.

Murie said nothing, only glared at her.

Belaeriel dressed quickly. "Come, child. We have much to do."

****

The farmer watched the two boys for a long time as they approached. He knew instantly that something was odd about them. They seemed to waver like a mirage on a hot summer day. But it was the depth of winter.

As they came closer, he became alarmed. Their skin shimmered like a smoldering fire, eyes glazed red and shining, footsteps soft hissing squishes, sending up pluming clouds of steam into the air. They radiated as if full of fire.

The farmer turned away to run, to find his family and flee, but he stumbled, his face stretched in terror. He felt sudden, searing heat as one of the boys touched him. Then he felt nothing. He was dead before his skin began to melt under the flames. He did not feel his own organs bursting. His eyes were destroyed before he could see the wind carry the flames of his body to his house, his barn, and his granary. He could not hear his home burn to the ground along with everything he owned, and everyone he loved. He was dead before he could even scream.

The boys looked upon the incineration with expressionless eyes. Then they continued silently on their way.

****

He understood the merchant's revulsion even before he approached. He was aware of his own soapy skin—how frog-like it was. So glutinous and nauseating were the folds of his own face that he would have reacted in the same way, had he approached his own reflection. The merchant feared him, and so he stared at the merchant before speaking. He wished to exacerbate the fear. It pleased him. Finally, he spoke. "Aren," he said. "Benham."

"I do not understand." The merchant said, confused.

"Aren. Benham." A sloppy whisper.

"Is it a name?" the merchant asked nervously. "I don't know any Arens, but there is a Benham." He pointed to the armory on Cellar Street. "He is a Magistrate. He works there."

The man turned to look where the merchant indicated.

"What was your name?" the merchant asked cautiously.

"Emmory," he lied. "My name is Emmory." He did not give his true name. Too many knew of that name. Too many people feared that name. His true name would travel on the lips of messengers as fast as a horse at the gallop. Even though the Lord Protector had freed him, he would not be able to stop them from hunting him again.

He said his name within his own head, to remind himself of his own delicious malignance.

Degammon.

Appendix: Magick

MAGICK - the creation of any unnatural result in reality by drawing out (pulling) streams of altered reality (also referred to as streams of possibility) from the source of infinite possibility (the Slipstream). It is given an alternate spelling throughout the Jebel Dedder Manual as well as all serious texts on the subject in order to differentiate it from common and harmless sleight-of-hand.

General Terminology:

AFTERGLOW - the residual patterns of colored particles that occur when any streams have been brought together into reality. The quantity, color, and brightness of the afterglow is determined by the types of renders created, their magnitude, and how much time has elapsed since the render was created. They are most often invisible to the naked eye, but can sometimes be visible when very fresh. All afterglow decays over time (both true visible afterglow, and that which can only be seen through a Jecker monocle) and eventually disappears completely.

AURAL AFTERGLOW - any residual aftereffects of magick that are visible to the naked eye until they are dispersed, including: light bending, vapor trails, visible afterglow, and residual tunnel vision.

AUTOENTROPIC RESONANCE - a theoretical application of magick to amplify itself in a loop of constantly increasing power.

BLANK IMPULSE - the most common form of render, composed of a specific two- or three-dimensional shape with a certain mass and velocity placed inside it, set to start at a specific location, and either remain still or travel in a certain direction for a certain duration, and then set in motion by an impulse force of generic non-specific energy.

BLUESHIFT - a tinge of blueness to the core color particles specific to any individual user. Indicates the user is moving closer to the location of the residuals.

BREAK POINT - the point at which a user's concentration is broken and their ability to render will be lost until they either remove themselves from distraction, or strengthen their will.

CAPTURE - the act of neutralizing and apprehending a rogue user, the culmination of any Trace.

COMPOSITE - a file record of the skills and attributes of a particular user that is being traced.

COMPRESSION MASKING - techniques employed by users to avoid detection or positive identification. Different methods of layering extraneous streams over the practical streams in order to obscure the true patterns from a Render Tracer.

CORE COLOR - the color of the residual particles given off by the vibration of the *Introduction-of-Change* key pattern. This color never changes even if the user's Primary Values (hence overall strength) increase. They are the equivalent of eye color or hair color, and cannot by themselves positively identify a specific user, but are commonly used to rule out afterglow with obviously incorrect core colors.

CORE LIMIT - the maximum potential energy a user is capable of projecting through the application of streams before they will require water, food and rest to replenish.

DECAY TIME - the time required for different forms and magnitudes of afterglow to become completely dispersed. The decay time can be affected by how confined a space they reside in, the altitude, the temperature, the presence of wind or water, or the presence of certain forms of smoke.

DISTRACTORS - men assigned to use certain strategies to disrupt the concentration that is critical to a user being able to focus to pull the streams of magick together.

ELEMENTAL - a user who creates renders from a nature-based view of the world. Based on common-sense knowledge of the environment an Elemental user inhabits, with much less technical knowledge required than for a Physical user.

IMPRINTER - a device that reacts to the shining of bright light through the lens of a Jecker monocle and then through the residual afterglow of magick. When parchment is placed upon the Imprinter, a bright light shined in such a way will render the patterns onto the parchment.

INGREDIENT LIST - the recipe of individual streams a given user utilizes to create a desired result. It is the list of streams that comprise each separate render a user creates.

INTERDICTION - the act of using Stoppers in close proximity to a user in order to take advantage of precedence effect, so that the user would be cut off from access to the streams of magick he employs to render into magick.

INTRODUCTION-OF-CHANGE - the introductory wave shape pattern that is unique to every user, and is used as a key to bridge the gap between reality and the Slipstream. It is the only pattern that can, with absolute certainty, confirm the presence of a particular user. Although the Primary Values of a given user's introductory pattern vibration may increase over time with experience and consistent use, the pattern itself does not ever alter in shape.

JEBEL DEDDER MANUAL - the text that is still used as the primary source for the understanding of techniques and applications of magick, and how to recognize it. It is the textbook of all Render Tracers.

JECKER MONOCLE - an oval lens of ranum crystal, a mineral that is highly reactive to residual afterglow of magick. Attached to the primary lens are four filters: white, rose, green, and blue. Each filter is made of a different mineral, and can be slid into place over the primary lens. Each filter can be used individually, and the white, rose, and green can also be used in combination to expose different aspects of the afterglow.

Use of the Jecker monocle:

PRIMARY LENS - The primary lens of the Jecker monocle displays any ambient afterglow or sensitized fluorescence that has not decayed completely. However, the nature of the transposition of streams from the Slipstream into reality will also result in spatial warping, time arching, and quantum peaks, all of which can obscure subtle details of the afterglow.

BLUE FILTER - used only individually, and filters out most of the layers of afterglow caused by specific forces and specific renders, and thereby exposes the *Introduction-of-Change* pattern, as well as the core color of the introductory wave pattern particles. By studying the core color through the blue filter, it can be determined if the residuals are redshifting or blueshifting.

GREEN FILTER - filters out the quantum peaks caused by the altered reality and displays the Spectral Lines - the temporary scars left in reality after a render has existed, whether stationary or in motion. Any stationary force would leave faint lines in the air where the force was located, indicating its shape. Any force in motion would leave a haze of lines indicating the shape of the force and the direction of its motion through the air. The greater the strength of the force, the thicker and brighter the lines would be. This indicates the vectors of force, which can aid in determining the size, strength, direction, and position of forces used at a given scene. Streak lines decay at a slower rate than the colors of other afterglow, and can allow a Render Tracer to make some inferences about what occurred at a scene that is otherwise cold.

ROSE FILTER - filters out spatial warping caused by the altered reality and displays the Glow Curve - the bleeding of different afterglow colors into one another. This is an indicator of merging residuals, showing how the streams were used in combination to create each effect and how well they merged with reality. Knowing how a user combines streams allows a Render Tracer to identify common streams for Stoppers to look for during a capture.

WHITE FILTER - filters out time-arching caused by the altered reality and allows a Render Tracer to see how the residuals react to the warping of the afterglow alone, displaying the Prismatic Dispersion - the magnitude or power behind the forces used. This aids in determining a user's strength and mastery of each render.

ROSE AND WHITE AND GREEN FILTER IN COMBINATION - filters out all side-effects of the altered reality and displays the Variants - these are the interruptions in the Resonance Spectrum. The breaks in the pattern show the separations that delineate each individual stream so that their patterns can be analyzed one at a time.

LIMITERS - Stoppers who are not yet aware of the streams that a user employs to make his forces (because a Render Tracer was not yet able to discern those streams for them), but do have knowledge of the general streams he uses to control those forces, such as direction, magnitude and speed. Most users only ever learn a few varieties of these vectoric (control) streams, and holding some or all of them would prevent a user from being able to employ his magick accurately.

LOOPING - a specific strategy employed by users to create an action and then set the action to repeat and tie it off, in order to spare more concentration for other actions.

MORTEN'S DEW - a fine crystalline powder that is reactive to certain specific results of magick. It glows red in the presence of renders that altered the properties of space, and it glows green in the presence of renders that altered the properties of time. Although it does not render any further specific knowledge of what actions a user performed, it narrows the range of inquiry and thereby saves time for a Render Tracer by ruling out certain possibilities.

OSCILLATRIX - a tool that is composed around a core of rithrin, a mineral which is highly reactive to the residual afterglow of magick. It is used to measure the amplitude and frequency of a user's *Introduction-of-*

Change render pattern to quickly rule out any unrelated afterglow during an investigation.

PEAK POINTS - locations of highest concentrations of residual afterglow, usually the place where the user was at the time that they created a given render.

PERFORMANCE LIMIT - a method of quantifying the degree to which a user is able to concentrate whether under calm conditions or under duress. It is measured with a system called the Ten Scale.

PHYSIC - a user who creates renders from their understanding of the laws of nature and the underlying forces of the universe. Requires natural ability and also the knowledge of how a process works in order to gain proficiency.

PRECEDENCE EFFECT - a phenomena of the Slipstream in which a specific stream specific to a particular user cannot be used by more than one user or Stopper within a certain proximity (or even used twice by the same user at the same time).

PRIMARY VALUES - the amplitude and frequency of a user's introductory wave shape, generated by the fourth-dimensional vibration of a user's *Introduction-of-Change* pattern. It indicates the overall strength of a given user, and can increase over time with practice.

PROFICIENCY LIMIT - a measurement of the quantity of different forces a given user is capable of understanding and creating renders for. Measured on a scale of 22 tiers.

REDSHIFT - a tinge of redness to the core color particles specific to any individual user. Indicates the user is moving farther away from the location of the residuals.

RENDER - a separate a distinct magick result generated by the combination and binding of multiple streams. A unified fabric of possibility translated into reality.

RENDER TRACER- anyone trained in the arts of detecting, tracing, and apprehending rogue users. Often armed with tools that are reactive to the presence of the afterglow of magick. Commonly and derisively referred to as Glasseyes.

SCHEMATIC - a method of diagramming the actions of a user at any given scene where they employed magick, and can be later used to determine which streams were used to create which results at that scene.

SENSITIZED FLUORESCENCE - the attaching of afterglow to people, clothes, or other physical objects that it comes into contact with, resulting in stains that can be seen through a Jecker monocle. These decay over time just as the afterglow itself. The decay time of sensitized fluorescence can be affected by washing with water, the use of certain herbs, and the smoke of certain plants.

SLIPSTREAM - the source of all streams, the realm of pure possibility that any user must reach into with their minds in order to create magick.

STEPWISE EXCITATION - the increasing energy created when a given cloud of afterglow interacts with other afterglow from another user or different renders of the same user.

STOPPERS - men trained to reach their minds into the Slipstream and hold the streams of a particular user in order to prevent that user from employing them to create magick.

STREAMS - the building blocks of magick that a user must match together and combine in a specific fashion in order to achieve a coherent result. A different stream is required for each aspect of the desired result.

TINWOOD LEAF - a plant with sedative properties that make concentration extremely difficult, and as concentration is critical to the pulling and binding of streams, it can render users inert for as long as it lasts, and can be administered indefinitely. It is the most common method of sedating users.

THE FIRES - the general term used to refer to the most common method of ensuring a user is destroyed.

TRACE - the act of tracking or pursuing a rogue user.

TRACE TESTS - the use of prisms, plates, reflection, submersion, or the application of acid, vinegar, sulfide, saltwater, sugar-water, lemon-water, or quicksilver upon various forms of sensitized afterglow in order to determine the precise type of force that a user employed to create a certain result and rule out other possibilities. It is applied primarily when the afterglow has become too faded to accurately view through a Jecker monocle.

USER - anyone with the ability to both pull streams and combine them into renders.

USER'S SHORTHAND - a strategy employed by users to make their actions as simple as possible in order to conserve their concentration for additional actions.

USER-TYPE - names given to categorize different user skill-sets in order to generalize the nature of their common renders. For example:

CRUSHER - manipulates pressure

DARKNICIAN - manipulates darkness

FRICTIONEER - manipulates friction

HEATER/COOLER - manipulates heat

INERTIAST - manipulates inertia

LIGHTBENDER - manipulates shapes that can affect light/vision

PUNCHER - employs vector-based magick, called vectorics

VECTORIC MAGICK - streams that are applied to any force to give it properties that allow it to interact with reality, and common to all users. Examples: streams of direction, location, size, shape, velocity, etc.

WAVE POCKETS - invisible clouds of energy that leak through from the Slipstream when streams are bound together at a speed or skill level that is beyond the effective ability of a given user. An unintentional side-effect of rapid and inefficient use of magick. The potency of the energy contained within a Wave Pocket is proportional to the total amount of energy created by the user. Wave pockets cannot be punctured under normal circumstances as they do not react to physical objects, however they can interact with altered reality when it is specifically targeted at them.

ZERO POINT ENERGY - the theoretical energy generated by autoentropic resonance, that seems to come from nothing, as it does not draw power from reality of from the Slipstream.

Greetings from the Wasteland Metropolis.

My name is frequently Thomas Howard Riley.

I sincerely hope you enjoyed your time in Luminaworld.

Luminaworld always enjoys those who tumble down the rabbit hole.

But whether you did or not, please consider leaving an honest review of your experience. It is the best way to help others know whether this journey is right (or wrong) for them.

Your actions could help someone who needs to find this story.

Or spare someone time to find a different one entirely.

Please help your fellow reader.

Change someone's life.

Leave a review.

Thomas Howard Riley currently resides in a secluded
grotto in the wasteland metropolis, where he reads ancient
books, plays ancient games, watches ancient movies, jams
on ancient guitars, and writes furiously day and night.
He sometimes appears on clear nights when the moon is
gibbous, and he has often been seen in the presence of cats.

He can be found digitally at
THOMASHOWARDRILEY.COM
where you may subscribe to his
luminous newsletter,
or as **@ornithopteryx** on Twitter.

CPSIA information can be obtained
at www.ICGtesting.com
Printed in the USA
BVHW072325151221
624026BV00007B/118